CROSS OF IRON

Stalingrad has fallen; the German troops know that they are beaten; and Corporal Steiner's platoon is cut off far behind the Russian lines. Resourceful and cynical, he coaxes, goads, bullies his men; but somehow or other he keeps them going through the bitter hand-to-hand fighting in forests, trenches and city streets. A dramatic encounter with a unit of Russian women troops leads to the horrible death of one of the platoon in recompense for a brutal rape; but eventually, through Steiner's courage and leadership, they regain the German lines. Then follows the tension of waiting for the last overwhelming Russian advance; the futile counter-attacks and murderous house-to-house encounters, and finally the decimation of Steiner's platoon.

CROSS OF IRON

THE GREAT NOVEL OF COMBAT ON THE
EASTERN FRONT IN WORLD WAR II

WILLI HEINRICH

CASSELL&CO

Cassell Military Paperbacks

Cassell & Co
Wellington House, 125 Strand
London WC2R 0BB

First published in Great Britain as *The Willing Flesh*
by Weidenfeld & Nicolson 1956
This Cassell Military Paperbacks edition published 1999
Reprinted 2000, 2001

Translated from the German *Das Geduldige Fleisch*
by Richard and Clare Winston

British Library Cataloguing-in-Publication Data
A catalogue record for this book is available from the British Library

ISBN 0-304-35241-1

Printed by Guernsey Press, Guernsey, C.I.

I

WITH THE RUSSIAN artillery savagely blasting away, the sun went down behind the enormous woods. It had been the same yesterday and the day before yesterday, and it would be the same tomorrow and for ever. The men sat around in the bunker. Schnurrbart pried at the tar in the bowl of his pipe. Corporal Steiner felt for a cigarette in his pocket. The shrilling of the field telephone cut the silence. Steiner attended to it. He listened at length, then slammed the receiver down with a curse. Startled, the other men looked up, their peaked, unshaven faces all anxiety.

'What did he say?' Krüger called from the table. Steiner did not answer. His haggard face was glum; when he set his lips, the deep creases at the corners of his mouth brought out the hardness of that face.

The silence persisted. The two candles burning on the table cast huge shadows of the men on the wooden walls. Outside, a German machine-gun hammered out a short burst. Krüger cleared his throat and repeated his question: 'What did he say?'

'He said the whole war was senseless.'

The others stared at him. 'Lieutenant Meyer said that?'

Steiner nodded. 'Why not? After all, a company commander, too, is entitled to a private opinion about the war.'

'Why yes.' Dorn, whom they called the Professor, rubbed his slender hand over his bristly chin. 'But I think——'

'Don't think so much,' Steiner said.

'Ah, let him think.' Schnurrbart put his feet on the table and grinned. 'You can't order him not to think. Once he has that Russian bullet in his brain he'll stop of his own accord.'

The men chuckled, their shadows jerked on the walls.

'The regiment is withdrawing,' Steiner remarked indifferently.

Krüger was the first to react. 'Why don't you say so right off?' he cried, springing to his feet. With one swift movement he pulled the blanket off his cot and began to bundle it up. One after the other the men of the platoon followed his example. The lethargy in

5

the bunker gave way to the furious bustle that comes before sudden departure.

Steiner had remained in his seat, his cigarette drooping from the corner of his mouth. He turned his head and looked at Schnurrbart, who was still sitting, pipe in mouth and feet on table, making no move to join in the packing. Steiner grinned. Schnurrbart was the only man who saw through him. Actually Schnurrbart's name was Karl Reisenauer; the heavy black stubble on his face, a vigorous growth that withstood even the strongest razor-blade, had earned him the nickname of 'Moustache'—*Schnurrbart*.

Steiner looked at the men. They were deeply absorbed in their work. Kneeling on the floor, Dorn was neatly rolling up his blanket while the others were already hoisting their packs.

'Idiots!' Steiner muttered.

'Why?' Schnurrbart grinned. 'If I didn't know you so well, I'd be packing, too.'

'They're idiots all the same,' Steiner replied moodily.

The men, their gear packed, became aware that Schnurrbart and Steiner had not moved. Dorn looked at each of them in turn, an uncomprehending expression upon his thin face, to which glasses gave an air of insignificance.

'He's thinking again,' Schnurrbart commented. Now the other men became attentive. They stared uneasily at Steiner. An uncanny silence fell. From somewhere came the blasts of another heavy battery and the staccato chattering of a machine-gun. At last Krüger stirred. He approached Steiner slowly.

'What sort of a game is this?' he asked through his teeth.

Steiner regarded him with amusement. 'It's your own game,' he said. 'I didn't tell you to pack your stuff.'

'You said the companies were withdrawing,' Dorn said reproachfully.

'No I didn't,' Steiner said.

'You did,' Krüger shouted. 'We have ears!'

'Pig's ears,' Steiner said. 'I said the *other* companies were withdrawing.'

'Drivel!' Krüger said heatedly. Suddenly he wrenched the pack from his back, smashed it to the ground, and strode off to the bunks along the wall of the dugout. With a crash he let himself drop on the lowest and stretched out, clasping his hands under his head. Steiner grinned and turned to the others.

'Battalion is withdrawing in twenty minutes. We, that is our platoon, are to stay here as a rear-guard.'

All the colour drained out of the men's faces. Unsteadily Kern dropped into a chair, mumbling, 'What a mess.' Dietz clasped his hand to his throat. 'The idiots are mad!' he said in a trembling voice.

'Idiots are always mad,' Steiner stated. He rose, took a map from his pocket, and spread it out on the table. The men crowded around him.

'Here is the situation,' he explained. 'Tonight the division is moving into new positions east of Krymskaya. Tomorrow night it will move on into permanent positions west of the city. Every battalion has left one platoon behind as a rear-guard. The plan was for us to stay here until five o'clock tomorrow morning. Now they've found out that the Russians have smelled a rat and have at some point advanced beyond the evacuated positions——'

'You mean they'll get to Krymskaya ahead of us?' Krüger asked.

Steiner shrugged. 'Very likely. But orders are orders.'

'You don't mean to stay here until tomorrow morning, do you?' Dorn asked in a shocked voice.

'Not till morning, no. But for two hours we have to hold this position. Maybe three.' Steiner grinned. 'Otherwise we might get to Krymskaya before the battalion.'

The faces of the men turned pale. Maag forced a hoarse laugh. 'That wouldn't do, would it?' he said. His white face twitched under the mane of red hair.

Zoll brought his fist down on the table with a crash. 'It is sheer idiocy,' he said violently. 'I'm for clearing out now, right this minute! This is so unreasonable——'

He fell silent under Steiner's cool, steady gaze and tugged nervously at the flashy yellow silk scarf he wore around his neck.

'What you are for interests nobody,' Steiner said coldly. 'If I wanted your advice, I'd ask for it. You ought to know by now that a conscript talking about reason is like a Jew shouting Heil Hitler.' Krüger slapped his thigh in appreciation and the others grinned vindictively. None of them liked Zoll. He was the eternal trouble-maker in the platoon. Steiner watched him clenching his fists in helpless rage. The scene disgusted him. He straightened up, buckled his belt, and turned to Schnurrbart.

'You better hit your bunks till we're ready. Who knows when

we'll next have a chance to get some sleep. Put a sentry out—take Maag, Dietz, and then the Professor. By then it will be time to go.'

They watched gravely as he picked up his cap, slung the tommy-gun over his shoulder and turned toward the door.

Schnurrbart involuntarily took a step forward. 'Where are you going?' he asked tightly.

'Recce,' Steiner said. The door slammed shut behind him.

There were eleven men in the platoon. Too few by far to keep watch on the tricky wooded terrain. By morning the Russians would be on to the enemy's weakness. Anselm could not bring himself to think of what would happen then. An hour's delay in pulling out would not have been so bad. Perhaps even two. But to stay until the morning! A regular suicide job, he told himself.

One of the men sat down beside him. He looked up and recognized Kern. 'What do you say about this?' he asked. Kern shrugged. 'What's there to say? A stinking deal if there ever was one. The bastards won't be satisfied till we're all dead.'

Anselm regarded him with disgust. Kern's vulgar manner jarred on him. From the first he had never liked the fellow. He drew in his lip in contempt, and his voice sounded hostile as he said: 'If that's all you have to say, you can keep it to yourself.' Kern returned his glance with malice. 'If you don't like what I say, don't ask me,' he growled. His thumb darted under his collar at the back of his neck. He had huge, hairy hands. Anselm studied his flat, ugly nose, his low forehead and mane of shaggy hair. I'm glad I don't look like him, he thought. He ran his hand over his own boyish face.

He did not know much about Kern who had joined them only two weeks ago, transferred from a bakers' unit. No one knew the reasons for his transfer. No one cared particularly. Perhaps it was a punishment. All they actually knew about him was that he had owned an inn at home; he brought this up on every possible occasion. When he talked about the bottles of wine he had stowed away in a corner of his cellar, the men listened raptly. He implied that the inn brought in a tidy income, and Anselm felt resentment whenever he thought about this. Moodily he watched Kern as the baker rolled a cigarette with unpracticed fingers; half the tobacco dropped to the floor. The man's clumsiness filled Anselm with fresh contempt.

The others were sitting around the table. Krüger took a pack of cards out of his pocket, saying: 'There's no sense trying to get any sleep now.' He rubbed his nose and frowned. He looked bad-tempered but then he usually did. Anselm, watching him, remembered that he was an East Prussian from Königsberg. Rumour had it that his father had been a Russian, for he spoke the language. Krüger himself had never accounted for this.

The Professor was sitting beside him. He was easy to get along with. Anselm liked his quiet way of talking. He had often wondered why Dorn had not become an officer. Krüger said the Professor did not want to. That didn't make sense, as far as Anselm was concerned.

The last man at the table was Dietz, a Sudeten German and the youngest of the group. Steiner's name for him was Baby; Krüger said he was a dreamer. Anselm looked them over as though their individualities might somehow cheer him up. The thought of having to leave this bunker depressed him. He sighed heavily and said: 'Too bad.'

'What's too bad?' Krüger asked.

'That we have to up and leave this place.'

'I should think you'd have got used to moving by now.'

'I'll never get used to it,' Anselm retorted vehemently. 'We worked a whole week fixing this place up—the devil take the army.'

'Amen,' Krüger said, slamming a trump down on the table so hard that the candle went out.

'Watch what you're doing, you idiot!' Kern snapped. 'Idiot yourself,' Krüger answered. His eyes narrowed. For a few seconds the two stared at one another like fighting cocks, until Kern threw his cards down on the table. 'I'm sick of the whole thing,' he growled in extenuation. Krüger grinned. 'You're scared stiff.' Kern folded his arms across his chest, obviously wondering whether to let this pass. He contented himself with a mocking smile. 'If you think I'm scared you don't know me, that's all.'

'No reason why I should,' Krüger baited him. 'You've only been with us for two weeks.'

Kern flushed. 'You've got nothing to boast about,' he said angrily. 'Two weeks at the front is as good as two years. Once you've learned the ropes, all you need is luck.'

Krüger turned to the others. 'Did you hear that?'

'We're not deaf,' Anselm said. 'He can't tell a Russian from a German and thinks he's an old swet.'

Kern looked up at the door again. 'I wonder what's keeping Steiner.'

Schnurrbart yawned with great deliberation. Then he turned to Krüger. 'You might take a look around for him,' he said. 'The rest of the company must have left long ago.'

'Why me?'

'You're the most reliable man here.'

Krüger stood up and reached out for his tommy-gun. He detected something in Schnurrbart's face that he did not like. He quickly dropped back into his chair again. 'I'm not a nursemaid,' he said sullenly. 'Steiner can look after himself.'

'I'm sure of it,' Schnurrbart said, getting up in turn. 'If he had to depend on you, I'd be sorry for him.' Before Krüger could reply, he had left the bunker.

In front of the door he paused. The position ran through a dense forest, but it was too dark to see even the nearest trees. Schnurrbart groped his way to the trench. He found Maag who wanted to know when his relief was coming. 'In ten minutes,' Schnurrbart said. 'Was Steiner here?'

'He went over there.'

Schnurrbart peered at the dim white blur which was all he could see of the man's face. 'Over where?'

'To the Russians, of course,' Maag answered. 'To see what's happening.'

'Alone?'

'Naturally—he always does. What about it?'

'That idiot!' Schnurrbart exclaimed. He ought to have looked for Steiner earlier.

The forest smelled cold, spicy with old leaves, sodden with snow recently melted into the spongy ground. The trees were full of noises. Tiny insects fell from above and rustled through the layers of dead vegetation on the forest floor. Schnurrbart stared into the darkness. 'Did he say how long he'd stay out there?' he asked.

'How could he? That depends on the Russians.'

Schnurrbart nodded. If only I knew what to do, he thought.

For a while they remained silent. When one stood still any length of time, the forest dampness pierced one like a frost.

Schnurrbart took a few steps down the trench. His uneasiness continued to mount. He returned to Maag. 'Go back to the others and tell them to get ready,' he said. 'We'll wait another ten minutes. If Steiner isn't back by then, we'll look for him.'

While Schnurrbart settled down behind the heavy machine-gun, Maag climbed out of the trench and sped off. For a while Schnurrbart looked thoughtfully over the rim of the trench. His thoughts again reverted to Steiner. Probably he was a fool to be concerned. He grinned to himself as he pictured Steiner sitting somewhere in an abandoned Russian bunker reading the book he always carried with him. Just the sort of thing Steiner would do. Ever since Schnurrbart had known him he had carried Eichendorff's *Collected Works* in his pocket, and he would start turning through it in the oddest situations. He must have read the thing a hundred times over. Odd, because otherwise reading didn't seem much in his line.

Schnurrbart remembered how offhand Steiner had been toward him at the beginning, until one day their casual and almost hostile relationship had changed to friendship. The change had come about a year and a half ago. The battalion had held positions south of Kramatorskya, on an endless plain of Russian snow. . . .

For days the snow had been coming down, a veritable blizzard. They were sitting in their bunker warming themselves by the small drum stove. It was late evening. The other men were already asleep on their cots. Steiner was reading, Schnurrbart toasting some slices of bread on the red-hot top of the stove. Suddenly Steiner laid his book aside and asked: 'You play chess?'

'So-so,' Schnurrbart replied. He watched Steiner take a travelling chess set out of his pack and arrange the pieces on the board. They started. After the first few moves Schnurrbart realized that Steiner was several classes above him. The game was over in half an hour. He had no better luck in the second game. When by an oversight he lost his queen, he angrily swept the pieces from the board. Steiner expressionlessly rolled a cigarette. 'Bad, losing her,' he said.

They sat in silence while the storm raged with unremitting violence, driving powdery snow through the cracks in the door. Schnurrbart took out his pipe and began filling it. After lighting it he looked up at Steiner and said: 'I'm not inquisitive, but——' He hesitated, considering how best to put his question. It was harder than he had thought. Finally he gave himself a mental push and went on 'But I'd be interested to know whether you have a girl.'

Steiner's features hardened. His eyes narrowed, and Schnurrbart hastened to apologize. 'I don't mean to step on your toes,' he said hastily, already regretting having brought up the subject. Steiner had indicated on former occasions that this was something he did not want to talk about. But after all, they had been together for more than three years now. What harm was there in asking? Annoyed, Schnurrbart knocked out his pipe against the leg of the table and crammed it into his pocket. If he doesn't want to talk, that's all there is to it, he thought, yawning ostentatiously. 'Think I'll turn in,' he murmured. 'I'm dead tired.'

But this time Steiner relented. 'Wait.' He glanced quickly over at the sleeping men; then he laid his arms on the table and leaned forward. 'I had a girl, but she's dead,' he said.

In the silence that followed the roaring wind shouldered the door as though it would knock it down. So that's it, Schnurrbart thought, trying to keep his expression blankly polite. He leaned back in the chair, crossed his legs and met Steiner's eyes squarely. 'I can imagine how it must feel,' he said carefully.

He fell silent again. Somewhere nearby a heavy shell burst. The bunker rocked, and one of the sleeping men groaned and mumbled something. Schnurrbart looked at the door. A thin ribbon of snow lay on the floor just below the threshold. 'This will go on for ever,' he murmured. Steiner said nothing, and at last Schnurrbart turned to face him again and asked: 'What was her name?'

'Anne.'

Schnurrbart nodded. 'Nice name,' he said noncommitally. 'What happened to her?'

'She died in an accident,' Steiner replied curtly, and Schnurrbart had the feeling that this was the most he was going to learn. He scratched his head, searching his mind for some way to turn the conversation toward some other subject. But again Steiner anticipated him. Gesturing toward the door, he said: 'It was weather just like this. The two of us used to do a lot of mountain climbing. Just below the peak the storm caught us by surprise. She slipped and——' He fell silent, staring into the flickering candle flame. Again there was a long pause. Schnurrbart hunched his shoulders uncomfortably as he spoke. 'Terrible. When did it happen?'

'In 'thirty-eight. Shortly before the war started.'

'Five years ago. Seems like a long time to me.'

'Seems long to you, does it,' Steiner said tightly. He shook his head slowly. 'It was yesterday, I tell you. Yesterday and today and tomorrow and always.' A strand of dark hair fell across his forehead; he brushed it aside with an impatient movement of his hand. 'You see,' he said, 'you see, it was all my fault, mine alone. I let go of her—these hands you see here let go of her. If you had been through it you would never forget it, any more than I can.'

His face suddenly seemed corroded as though acid had flowed across his skin. If only I had not started it, Schnurrbart thought. In an agony of discomfiture he reached for his pipe again and began filling it once more. The wood in the stove crackled and popped. After a while he began to feel the silence like a physical pain. He propped his elbows on the table, cleared his throat several times, and said at last: 'I know what you mean; it's hellish for you. But you can't go on feeling the same way for ever.'

Slowly, Steiner lifted his hands from his face and stared at his friend. 'For ever?' He moved his head as if listening for something. Then he gave a strained laugh. 'No, it will not go on for ever. It will stop when I meet her again,' he said.

'Meet her?' Schnurrbart asked blankly.

'Of course. You may think I'm off my head, but I tell you I will meet her again. If I'm still here, she must be too. Somewhere, when this war is over, she will cross my path.'

'That's going pretty far,' Schnurrbart said.

Steiner shook his head. 'Everyone goes as far as he can.'

For a while there was silence between them, until Schnurrbart ventured again: 'Suppose you don't meet her?' he asked.

Steiner slowly turned his face toward him. 'What's that?'

'I mean, what will you do if you don't meet her?'

Steiner waved that away with a light motion of his hand. 'If I live through this war,' he said quietly, 'I will meet her. And if I don't come out of it——' He stood up, stepped up quickly to the tiny window by the door, and peered out.

Schnurrbart drew the pipe from his mouth and sat looking meditatively at the toes of his boots. When he glanced up he saw that Steiner was watching him with an expression of mockery. 'What are you thinking?' he asked.

Schnurrbart sensed that he was seeking a quarrel. 'This and that,' he said, shrugging pacifically.

'Give it up,' Steiner said with scorn. 'You can't understand it anyway.'

'Why not?'

'You can't,' Steiner repeated with sudden anger. 'None of you can understand it; you're a crude lot.'

'Look here——' Schnurrbart began, but Steiner cut him off.

'A crude lot; you cannot imagine what a woman can mean. For all of you a woman is nothing but something to sleep with, and it doesn't matter who she is as long as she lies down.' His voice had risen, and some of the men on the cots woke up. They stared sleepily over at the two, and one of them grumbled: 'Be quiet, damn it, let a man get some sleep!'

With a thrust of his hands Steiner forced himself from the wall and took four big strides over to the man's side. 'You shut up!' he snarled. 'Shut up, you damned idiot! Sleeping and eating and——' He fell silent abruptly. Disgusted, he gazed for a moment at the cowed faces of the men, and whirled around.

As he went to the door, Schnurrbart gripped his arm firmly. 'If you want to believe that kind of thing, go ahead,' he said quietly. 'But you aren't fair to the fellows there.'

Steiner stared into his eyes. Then suddenly he leaned forward and asked: 'What about you? Aren't I unfair to you too?' He turned and left the bunker.

Every time he remembered that incident, Schnurrbart had felt a mingling of uneasiness and satisfaction. He was surer than ever that a wrong word at the time was all that was needed to make any future relationship with Steiner unendurable. As it was, they had become quite close. Not as close as he had hoped, for even afterwards Steiner never quite dropped his reserve. There was no one at all in the platoon who could boast of sharing his undivided confidence. Every so often, in small matters, he would make it clear that he wanted to remain aloof and that he felt obligations toward none of them. He kept his thoughts to himself even at such times as this, when he was undertaking a dangerous reconnaissance which might well turn out badly.

The thought brought Schnurrbart to the present. Sighing, he peered over the top of the trench. Darkness hung among the trees like powdered soot. He glanced at the luminous dial of his wrist-watch; in letting his mind wander, he had wasted more than twenty minutes. In a hurry now, he scrambled out of the trench, listened again for a few seconds and then turned toward the bunker.

A figure appeared out of the darkness and came toward him rapidly, He recognized Hollerbach.

'You haven't heard from Steiner, have you?' he asked.

'No, the devil only knows where he is.'

'It's sickening,' Schnurrbart grumbled. 'Always this hide and seek business. He might have taken one of us with him.'

Hollerbach shrugged. 'You know how he is.' Although Schnurrbart was good-sized, Hollerbach towered over him. His head was uncovered, and his pale blond, almost white hair gleamed like a helmet in the night. He, with Krüger, was one of the few 'old boys' in the platoon. A steady, easy-going fellow, he was noteworthy for receiving a letter from his girl in almost every mail. For the past week, however, no mail had reached the battalion, and Schnurrbart recalled the rumours of a huge encirclement in which the entire Caucasus army was trapped. Although he took little stock in these tales, he was aware of the possibility that a good many unpleasant surprises might be in store for them all. If only Steiner were here, he thought. Aloud he said: 'He's stubborn as a mule.'

'Since he came back from leave he's been in a bad mood,' Hollerbach said. 'Wish I knew what happened back there.'

'So do I.' Schnurrbart had given the matter much thought these past several months.

'At any rate,' Hollerbach lingered on the subject, 'he must have kicked up his heels quite a bit to get himself demoted from sergeant to private and four months in a punishment battalion besides.'

Schnurrbart scratched his belly thoughtfully. He didn't particularly want to go into this matter. The platoon had heard one thing and another, but the reasons for Steiner's demotion remained obscure. 'There's less to it than you think,' he replied in a standoffish tone. 'All a man has to do is to jabber and they get him for it.'

'True enough.' While the conversation lapsed, Schnurrbart reckoned out the time on his fingers. It was just half a year ago that Steiner had rejoined the company. He had been wounded at Izyum and invalided back home. There something must have happened that he refused to talk about. At any rate he had been transferred to Disciplinary Battalion 500. After doing his spell in that unit, he had been promoted to corporal, and six months ago had turned up in the company again—a bit more close-mouthed and grim than he had been before. Schnurrbart recalled how he had responded to all questions with an indifferent shrug, until at last they gave up asking him. In any case, the hectic pace of recent weeks had kept them concentrating on the present. The retreat from Tuapse to this position could no longer be termed 'an elastic defence'. It really looked like the beginning of the end. Thinking of that, and of Steiner, Schnurrbart sighed.

'I suppose we'll have to look for him,' he said impatiently.

'I've been thinking about that. Where can you look for him in this darkness? For all we know there are still Russians over there.'

Schnurrbart was inclined to agree. He hitched up his cartridge-belt, settled back and said: 'Why don't you go back to where it's warm. I'll stay here and keep my ears open, just in case. If anything comes up, you know where I am.'

Hollerbach nodded and started wearily back toward the bunker.

By now most of the men had dozed off. Dorn alone continued to sit at the table. Since he had to relieve Dietz in an hour, there was little point to lying down now. Besides he had been bothered for days by painful cramps, probably from the skimpy rations, which did not let him sleep.

He glanced about at the furnishings of the bunker, and sighed. For two weeks they had worked like dogs, had brought stuff from the nearest villages, had dug, carpentered, made window frames, fixed straw mattresses—done everything possible to make the bunker comfortable, and now all that work was for nothing. How hard we cling to a place, he thought, if we have done things to it that make for a bit of pleasantness. Of course it was only a hole in the ground. But for all of them, leading the soldier's nomad life, it was much more. In this land of boundless expanses and unnerving strangeness, this land with which none of their memories were linked, the bunker was a semblance of home. And like home, they attached all kinds of emotions to it.

Now again they were pulling up stakes, forging out into the unknown, with all the apprehension such moves carried with them. Steiner's report had not sounded encouraging. Who could say where they would spend tomorrow night?

He sighed and looked at his watch. Time for him to take over. Heavily, he stood up, clapped the steel helmet on his head, took his rifle and went out. As he raised his face, he felt rain falling. Cautiously he climbed the slippery steps. His glasses misted over. He removed them and tried to accommodate his eyes to the darkness. A few steps away from the door he came upon Dietz, who was leaning against a tree.

'You here already?' Dietz asked.

'It's time,' Dorn replied. Dietz took a step closer to him. His teeth chattered lightly as he said: 'Dirty weather.' He eased the rifle from his shoulder and shook himself. 'Nice time we're going to have tonight,' he said. 'A regular funeral march. Just imagine it —twenty miles in this kind of weather through a swampy forest.'

'It will be ghastly,' Dorn agreed.

'If only the rain would stop,' Dietz said, peering in an effort to see Dorn's face. They both fell silent and stared gloomily into the night.

The rain drizzled down steadily; the trees let fall big drops which slapped into the dry leaves on the ground. Dorn draped his groundsheet over his steel helmet and leaned against a tree. 'Well, take it easy,' Dietz said. He gave Dorn a helpful pat on the shoulder and disappeared into the bunker. Minutes passed. The darkness seemed to grow thicker. From somewhere sounded the wailing cry of an owl. A gust of wind shook the trees, producing a pattering like hailstones on the roof of a tent. Dorn pushed the steel helmet back from his forehead and strained to see into the blackness of the woods. His glasses were in his pocket; in weather like this they were useless.

What could be keeping Steiner so long, he wondered. His stomach cramps were getting worse. He pressed his fist into his belly and held his breath. For a few seconds the pain diminished. But when he removed his fist, it returned with redoubled intensity. He bent over, and when that brought no relief squatted on his heels. It was more bearable that way. He propped his chin in his hand and became aware of his unshaven face. His skin was damp and sticky. Filth, he thought in disgust; everything is filthy, body, underclothes, everything. After a while he propped both arms on his thighs and let his head droop; his rifle he held clamped between his legs. Again and again he heard strange noises, but he was too apathetic to pay attention to them. It was as though his basic fear, which had been with him for so long that it felt like part of himself, was overlaid by dull indifference.

His head drooped lower and lower. His lips were parted and he could feel the spittle trickling from his mouth. In his present state it gave him a spiteful, silly satisfaction to let himself go completely. This is what I am really like, he thought, this is me. If Maria could see me now. The thought of his wife revived him momentarily. He raised his head and closed his mouth. Maria, he thought, Maria, Betty, Jürgen. Jürgen would be going to school this year. He shook his head at the swift passage of time. Then he tried to picture his wife taking Jürgen to school every morning. He smiled happily, and the smile lingered when his thoughts had already taken a graver turn. There was Betty, two years younger than Jürgen, a quiet, serious child like her mother. Always rather sickly, and not like other girls the same age. The doctor had said Betty ought to be sent to a rest-home in the country for a few months. If only there were no war. Certainly it couldn't go on much longer, but how would it end?

He was still thinking about this when a hand gripped his shoulder brutally and pulled him to his feet. Paralysed by fright, he stared into the face of Steiner. 'Existential philosophy, Professor,' Steiner said coldly, 'presupposes existence. You won't exist much longer if you go to sleep at your post. Pick up your gun.' Released from his grip, Dorn stooped for the rifle on the ground. When he had straightened up he saw that Steiner was listening to the sounds from the woods. He turned to Dorn: 'You can do sentry duty sitting, for all I care, but don't fall asleep.' Then he climbed down into the bunker. A few minutes later he was back, carrying blankets and ground-sheets. He spread the blanket out on the ground, hung the canvas over his shoulders and sat down at the foot of a tree. 'Sit beside me,' he ordered Dorn. 'By night you see better from lower down.'

Dorn obeyed in silence. He had recovered from his slump and now felt guilty. Ought he to mention his cramps to Steiner, he wondered. But oddly enough, he no longer felt any pain. For a few minutes they sat without talking. Then Dorn asked: 'Did you go to the highway?'

'Yes.'

'And—how does it look?'

'Lovely,' Steiner said with a humourless laugh.

Anxiously, Dorn peered into his face. 'What does that mean? Did you see any Russians?'

'I certainly did. Infantry, trucks, tanks—the whole damn Russian army.'

Dorn stared at him aghast. 'On the highway?'

'Not in the air, I assure you.'

Dorn took a deep breath. 'My God,' he murmured. He could feel his legs growing leaden; the wet uniform seemed to weigh him down like a suit of armour.

Steiner drew his knees up closer to his body and thrust his tommy-gun between them. 'Why the surprise,' he said scornfully. 'That was predictable. I warned you, didn't I?'

'So you did.' Dorn pushed the steel helmet back from his forehead. 'Then we cannot use the highway?'

'I doubt whether the Russians will let us have a concession for it. But we must cross it in any case.'

'But you said yourself that the Russians——'

'We'll just have to wait until the traffic slackens off. It ought to be quieter by tomorrow morning.'

'But that's hopeless,' Dorn said, hoarse with agitation. 'Can't we avoid the highway altogether?'

'That would mean covering twice the distance. We haven't the time. If the Russians reach Krymskaya before us, we're sunk.' Steiner's very matter-of-factness made Dorn feel panic. He rubbed his wet face with the back of his hand and stammered: 'Then what are we going to do?'

Steiner snorted angrily. 'You heard what I said. We're crossing the highway.'

'And suppose the Russians see us?'

'Then we'll clap our hands and say good morning.'

Dorn closed his eyes before the wave of fear that swept him. He saw Russian columns marching toward him, a thousand tommy-guns pointed at him. It might be better if we left right away, he thought. It's so dark now that the Russians could not see us. The thought bucked him up a little. 'Why do you want to wait until morning?' he asked Steiner. 'Our chances would be better under cover of darkness.'

'I've considered that. But don't forget we're setting out into unknown terrain. Besides, if we should come upon Russians unexpectedly in the darkness, we could easily lose touch with one another. I've thought it all over carefully. We'll cross the road shortly before dawn; I want to be able to see what we are going into.'

Dorn gave a tired shrug. 'Whatever you think,' he said.

By the time Hollerbach had gone to fetch Schnurrbart, the men inside the bunker were sitting at the table, Steiner among them. Even without looking at him, Schnurrbart sensed his mocking expression. He went over to a cot and sat down.

'I hear you have been worried on my account,' Steiner said. The sarcasm in his voice sent the blood rushing to Schnurrbart's forehead. The bastard, he thought, trembling with rage, the bastard! He felt painfully humiliated. To hell with him in the future, he resolved and began fumbling with his pipe. Steiner watched him, his grey eyes glistening with amusement. Then he turned to the table, smoothed down the map, and motioned the men to crowd around him.

'How far is it to Krymskaya,' Maag inquired anxiously, craning his neck to get a look.

'About twenty miles—if we used the road it would be nearly forty-five.'

'Then we certainly won't be using the road,' Krüger said.

Steiner stared at the map. 'The stuff between is regular wilderness. At least, that's how it looks to me from the map. And a stream running through. The whole region is marshy. The big question is whether we can get through.'

'Then let's take the road,' Krüger said.

'Certainly,' Kern nodded. 'It's a lot better walking on the road. We can do forty-five miles by tomorrow night easy. The battalion must have marched along the road too.'

'In the first place,' Steiner explained, 'the battalion didn't march; it went by truck. In the second place, I doubt that we'll be able to stay on the road without interference.'

Kern looked blankly at the map. 'Why?' he asked.

For a moment Steiner sat still looking into their anxious faces. Then he rose: 'The Russians are on the highway. That means we have to go through the woods. Before we reach them we have that highway to cross.' He slung his tommy-gun over his shoulder and went to the door, opening it. 'Come on! Stay close together and keep your traps shut.'

One after the other the men squeezed past him. The last to leave the bunker, Steiner kicked the stove so that it fell over, spilling its glowing embers on the floor.

He went out, closing the door behind him. The men were waiting for him a few yards away. He took the lead and the platoon set off into the woods. They spoke scarcely a word as they marched. After some twenty minutes the forest began thinning out, and in another five minutes they reached the edge of it. As they stepped out upon the open ploughland, a cold wind lashed the rain into their faces. By the time they had gone a few yards great lumps of muddy soil clung to their boots. They panted under the burden of their machine-guns and boxes of ammunition, and with every step cursed under their breath. Krüger kept close behind Hollerbach. He was carrying the heavy machine-gun over his right shoulder like a shovel. Once he slipped and fell into a furrow. Tired, he scrambled up and wiped the mud from his hands. This stinking war, he thought bitterly. Schnurrbart came over to him. 'Come on,' he said. They moved forward side by side until they bumped into Hollerbach. 'That's what you get for falling asleep on your feet,' Hollerbach whispered, shifting his rifle to his other shoulder. Krüger jabbed his fist into Hollerbach's back. 'Shut up. What I'd like to know is how far we still have to go. This damned field is never going to end.'

'No more than another thirty miles,' Hollerbach replied. He suddenly stood still.

Krüger pushed forward toward the group in front. 'What the devil's the matter now?'

The men did not answer. Out of the darkness before them rose the low drone of big motors, the creaking of heavily laden trucks. Occasional shouts, windblown and stirring, reached their ears.

'Russians,' Hollerbach whispered.

'A whole army,' Kern stammered. With quivering fingers he unthinkingly reached for his cigarettes and thrust one between his lips. As he struck a match, Steiner suddenly appeared in front of him, his hand sweeping back. There was a sharp clapping sound, followed by a rain of sparks from the crushed cigarette. Kern uttered a whimpering noise and pressed both hands against his mouth. The whole incident had taken place so swiftly that the others only began to realize what it was about when Steiner took a step backward and raised his tommy-gun. 'You idiot!' His voice sounded thick with rage. The men stared at him in alarm, while Kern still stood among them, his hands at his face. 'You ought to be shot!' Steiner whispered harshly. He whirled around and started forward again. They followed him without a word. For another hundred yards they continued in the same direction. The ground sloped upward somewhat. The noises ahead became increasingly distinct. They could already hear the crisp tread of nailed boots. But it was still so dark that they could not see ten paces ahead. They must have been about fifty yards from the highway when Steiner ordered a halt. He called to Hollerbach and Schnurrbart to join him. 'You fellows come with me. The rest will wait here.' Bent low, they disappeared into the darkness.

The men squatted on the wet ground, listening to the noises from the highway. They were all wide awake now. Krüger looked at his watch. It was already four. The rain had stopped. I wish it would pour now, Krüger thought. He turned to Dietz beside him and said: 'We'll never get across there.'

Dietz shrugged. He looked at Kern, who had buried his face in his hands and was sitting in a posture of resentment. 'He shouldn't have hit him,' Dietz whispered.

Krüger spat, 'Ah, shit!'

'What do you mean, shit?' Dietz protested. 'He shouldn't have done it.' He began to stammer indignantly. 'Where'd we be if every corporal could slap us in the face?'

Krüger rubbed his sleeve over his wet face. 'What are you making such a fuss for?' he grumbled. 'Forget it, for God's sake, there are more important things to think about at the moment.'

Intimidated, Dietz fell silent. He sat regarding his dirty hands unhappily. It just wasn't right, he thought. A reprimand—all right, punishment exercises—that was all right, too. But smashing a lighted cigarette into a man's face—that was going too far, much too far. The more he thought about it, the more indignant he became. Steiner had always been decent to him personally, but that, too, might change, some day. It was a matter of principle. What had just happened to Kern might easily happen to any of them tomorrow. Although, of course, he himself would hardly be caught making a mistake like that. After all, he was a soldier, a front-liner. At this point in his train of thought, Dietz saw the thing clearly. 'If a thing's wrong on the lowest level, it's wrong all through,' he said. 'That's why it's a serious matter. Do you think——' he hesitated. 'Don't you think that if they started hitting each other in the face at the Fuehrer's headquarters, we wouldn't be feeling the effects of it quick enough. I tell you, we've got to have order. Order and discipline from the bottom to the top, but also from the bottom to the top.' He spoke these last words with the utmost conviction.

Krüger grinned. 'It's the same thing.'

'What is?'

'Well, you said we've got to have order from the bottom to the top, but also from the bottom to the top. It's the same thing.'

It took a moment for Dietz to grasp this. 'That was just a slip of the tongue,' he said irritably. 'You know what I meant: from the bottom to the top and from the top to the bottom. In the Fuehrer's headquarters——'

'Don't strain your guts, my boy,' Krüger said. 'In the Fuehrer's headquarters they gargle with champagne. If we were up there we'd be gargling piss.' He wiped his hand over his mouth. 'Yes, we'd feel the effects if they started hitting one another.' The thought amused him and he chuckled. 'Maybe they will, at that; but not until all of us right here are in the soup. You know what the issue is at the moment?' He brought his face close to Dietz's. 'The issue is that we have to get out of here. And you know why? I'll tell you.' He poked his finger into Dietz's chest; affronted, Dietz moved back. 'I'll tell you,' he repeated. 'We have to get out so that we'll be on time to get into the next mess. Out of one mess into the next. That's been going on for three years and it'll go on until we get into one mess good and deep and don't come out of it.' He came to an end of words, having worked himself into a rage.

Dietz gazed at him dumbfounded. Then he turned to Dorn, who had been genially listening to the conversation. 'What do you say to that, Professor?'

Dorn forced a grave expression. 'It is difficult,' he said. 'I shall have to consult my books.'

The men grinned and turned their attention back to the highway. It was slowly beginning to grow light. The terrain was now fairly visible. In front of them the field sloped steeply up to an embankment and beyond rose the black silhouettes of mountains against the greying sky.

'Where the devil is the highway?' Zoll whispered.

Krüger shrugged. 'It must be in a dip. Once we get our carcasses over it, we're clear.'

They lifted their heads. The sounds on the highway had stopped.

They all jumped to their feet and stared up the sloping field. 'Here comes somebody,' Dietz whispered hoarsely. A figure emerged out of the dim foreground, came running toward them with great leaps. 'Hollerbach,' Zoll whispered. At this moment Hollerbach stopped and waved his fist in the air. 'Let's go,' Krüger said. They snatched their guns and ran up the slope. Hollerbach waited a moment for them, then turned. Panting, they followed him. When they reached the crown of the hill they saw the highway beneath them in the grey dawn light, deserted. They slipped down the steep declivity and raced across the trampled, rutted width of the road toward the edge of the woods which rose like a dark wall against the further mountains. Schnurrbart and Steiner were waiting for them. Seconds later they were trampling through the dense undergrowth and were several hundred yards within the woods. Gasping, they stopped to catch their breath. It had by now grown so light that they could see clearly. When they looked at Steiner they saw a wild gleam of triumph in his eyes.

Krüger raised his hand. They turned in unison to face the road, from which the rumble of vehicles could again be heard. But now that they had made the crossing, they did not care. The fearful nervous tension of the past few hours dropped away. They grinned, slapped one another exuberantly on the back. 'We've got the stuff,' one said boastfully.

'Precision work,' commented Hollerbach. To celebrate he lit a cigarette.

Schnurrbart looked around. 'What mountains are those?' he asked.

'Just hills,' Steiner explained. 'We have to cross them. The marsh begins on the other side of them.' He turned to the men. 'Get ready,' he ordered.

They picked up their gear. Kern hung back; now and again he would rub the burned spot on his face and give Steiner a dirty look. 'Don't take it so hard,' Dietz said to him. Kern did not condescend to answer.

They started off once more. For a while their way led over springy, moss-covered forest floor. The slope grew steeper, and they began toiling uphill, gasping for breath. The climb seemed everlasting. Tight-lipped with determination, they gained ground slowly; every yard uphill represented a scramble. They kept their eyes fixed in the direction of the invisible crest of the hill which must lie somewhere up above these trees. Their good humour ebbed away and they began cursing.

'They ought to stop for a bit up front there,' Dietz panted. He stood still and wiped the sweat from his forehead. Krüger, who was behind him, also stopped. 'What's the matter, Child? Fuel running low?'

'They ought to make a break,' Dietz repeated plaintively. He was done in. Krüger regarded him with a frown. 'If you start giving out now, how is it going to be later on?' He shifted the machine-gun to his left shoulder. 'Let me have your boxes.'

Dietz sighed gratefully. While Krüger picked up his boxes of ammunition, he loosened his belt. 'I have a stitch in the side,' he said apologetically.

'You'll get over that in a little while,' Krüger lied reassuringly. 'Come on, or we'll be holding this position alone.'

The others had meanwhile gone a considerable distance ahead. But after several more of the men protested, Steiner allowed a rest. It was full daylight by now. The woods were filled with the hearty song of birds. The men sprawled on the ground and looked up the steep slope. 'Damned tough going,' Zoll said. 'We ought to be on top soon.'

'We will be,' Steiner replied. 'You all could have done those few yards more.'

Maag yawned. He turned on his side so that he could look up at Steiner and asked: 'Where's the rush? We'll get where we're going soon enough.'

'It depends on where you're going,' Steiner growled.

Maag refused to back down. 'Same place you're going.'

'If that's so you have no time to lose.'

'We'll make those twenty miles by tonight easy,' Maag retorted, confidently. He was enjoying the rest and had made up his mind not to stand up for another ten minutes at least.

Steiner regarded him contemptuously. 'If it's only twenty miles. But if the battalion doesn't succeed in holding the position where we're to meet them until tomorrow, we'll have another fifteen to go.'

Krüger pinched his nose between his thumb and forefinger. 'Where will they move to in that case?' he asked.

'I told you yesterday,' Steiner replied curtly.

Schnurrbart rolled over on his belly and explained: 'West of

Krymskaya.' He turned to Steiner. 'Do you know what positions they're supposed to take there?'

'Yes.'

'Then everything's under control,' Krüger said contentedly.

Steiner glanced irritably at him. None of them seemed to realize what they were facing. But it was better that way, he reflected. What worried him most was the stream marked on the map as cutting at an angle across the forest. There was no reason to assume a bridge in this uninhabited area. If necessary, he thought, we'll have to fell trees. Without the proper tools that would be exhausting and time-consuming work. The sooner they reached the river the better. 'Let's go,' he ordered loudly.

They stared up at him in dismay. 'Already,' Zoll said. 'You can wait a few minutes more.'

Steiner stood up. He walked over to where Zoll sat. 'Listen to me,' he said, his voice quivering with rage, 'you're beginning to get on my nerves. Maybe you better not call attention to yourself for a while.'

Zoll propped himself up on his elbow and became aware that the muzzle of Steiner's tommy-gun was dancing right before his eyes. 'Take that thing away!' he squawked in alarm.

'I plan to,' Steiner stated. He turned, and they saw him taking long strides up the slope. Hastily, they stood up, brushed the wet leaves from their uniforms and followed. In ten minutes they had reached the brow of the hill. The ceiling of leaves was less dense up here. With surprise they saw that the sky was cloudless. The tree-tops were glistening in the rosy light of the rising sun, which was itself still out of sight beyond the woods. Steiner turned to the right and kept to the ridge, which ran north and south. He had quickened his pace; the men trailed behind, strung out at longer and longer intervals.

Zoll lingered behind to wait for Kern, who came trudging up to him with a sour expression. Last in line, they walked along silently, side by side. They were bowed over by the weight of the heavy boxes of ammunition. Sweat drew grey streaks across their filthy faces. There were burn-spots around the innkeeper's mouth; Zoll observed his tongue lick out occasionally and moisten the reddened skin. Each time Kern did this, his face twisted in a grimace of pain and resentment.

'I wouldn't have stood for that,' Zoll said.

Kern cursed. 'You're the one to talk!'

However, gradually his rage was losing force and conviction. It had been idiotic of him to light that cigarette. It was the act of a green recruit. This thought had been gnawing away at him more than the blow in the face. But this toilsome climb was beginning to wear the edge off his anger. They had really been lucky. A Russian might really have seen the flare of light from his match. He shuddered. What luck, he thought, what a break. His relief made him feel almost light-hearted. If it were not for the burns around his mouth, he would be able to put the episode out of his mind. Again he ran his tongue over his lips. 'Haven't you any salve?' he asked Zoll.

'Think I'm a beauty shop?' Zoll replied sulkily.

Kern grinned. 'Not a chance,' he said. He liked Zoll no more than the others did. Zoll's appearance was as unpleasant as his manners. There was something shifty about his face, and his eyes seemed to goggle behind his horn-rimmed glasses.

They walked in silence for a while. 'I wonder where the devil he's taking us,' Zoll said after a while.

Kern tried to see beyond the man in front of them. But the line was now stretched out over a good distance. Steiner was out of sight.

'There's something up ahead there,' Kern said.

'Where?'

'There, above the trees.'

Zoll stretched his neck forward. 'What the hell is it?' he asked.

'Must be the pylon of a powerline.'

They quickened their step. Before them, the girders of a huge tower rose out of the trees, and a few yards farther on they came to a cleared ride through the woods. The men had gathered around Steiner, all looking in one direction. Zoll and Kern, when they came up to them, opened their eyes wide with astonishment. Below them was one long downhill slope. At regular intervals the steel pylons rose above the ride. To the west, as far as the eye could reach, all the way to the purple-tinged mountains on the horizon, lay a tremendous forest. The bright, even green of the trees flowed on wholly unbroken; nowhere was there a sign of a clearing, of human habitation. The scene took their breath away. Kern looked in awe at the great forest. 'Like a sea. A green sea,' he murmured reverently.

They all were deeply moved and solemn. 'Anybody got a camera?' Krüger asked.

Suddenly Anselm cried out: 'There's a city over there. See, just to the left of that mountain with the sharp peak.'

'Yes, yes,' Krüger said enthusiastically. He turned to Steiner. 'Do you see it?'

'I can see it,' Steiner said quietly. 'That's Krymskaya. Where we're headed for.'

With mixed feelings they eyed the fine cluster of towers and roofs set at the foot of the distant hills as clear, as still, as incisive as a pen sketch. Krüger seemed utterly lost in the sight. After a while he sighed. 'If only we were there already,' he said.

'We'll make it,' Dietz said, looking at Steiner with trust.

Steiner nodded briefly. 'By evening we'll be there with the others.'

'The others,' Krüger murmured. He had a queer feeling in his chest. 'Funny. I mean,' he went on in answer to their questioning looks, 'it's a funny feeling to know that the rest of the battalion is somewhere out there.'

'Yes,' Schnurrbart agreed. Lost in thought, he took his pipe out of his pocket and began packing it. When Steiner sat down and folded his arms over his knees, Schnurrbart looked at him in surprise. 'What's up—aren't we going on?'

'We can spare a few more minutes,' Steiner said. His impatience had suddenly vanished. It would be best to stay right here until the war was over, he thought. Nobody would look for them in this isolated region. But then he remembered that they had no rations with them. He bit his lips. There's no getting away from it, he thought bitterly, and only then realized how familiar this pattern of emotions was to him. Whenever, after hours of climbing, he came to the top of a mountain and saw the land lying at his feet, his feelings had always been similar. Always in the past the knowledge that he would have to return to ordinary life had spoiled the pleasure of the mountainous solitudes. The tension which had driven him to climb steadily to the summit would snap; nothing would remain but the dull perception that the trivial burdens of existence were inescapable. Wearily, he lit a cigarette and looked at the men, who had all sat down on the ground and were smoking.

Schnurrbart's eyes were fixed upon the oceanic forest below, whose western half was already bathed in the rays of an as yet invisible sun. The mist above the trees shivered with motion and dispelled itself even as he watched. The purple of the distant hills was slowly lightening to blue; the contours of the hills merged imperceptibly with the horizon. The mood he was in alarmed him somehow. This mood was dangerous, he thought; it entered the blood and then there was no getting rid of it. It only made everything harder, the whole damned war, everything. Trying to distract himself, he concentrated on the rifle which lay at his feet. Finally he cleared his throat noisily and turned to Krüger. 'Weird, isn't it?' he said to Krüger.

The East Prussian picked at his nose. 'If I sit here much longer,' he said harshly, 'I shall never get up again, believe me.' He looked at Dietz, who was sitting open-mouthed, staring up at the sky. 'What's the matter with you?' he asked. 'Seeing angels?'

Dietz raised his hand. 'Sh——' he said, closing his eyes.

'He's out of his mind,' Krüger declared.

Dietz shook his head violently. 'Be still,' he whispered. 'Don't you hear them?'

Krüger gave him a suspicious look. 'Hear what? The angels?'

'Don't be silly, you can't help hearing them. The bells.' He turned to the other men. 'Do you hear them? There! Now—it's perfectly clear.'

They all stared at him. 'What do you hear?' Kern asked.

'Bells,' Schnurrbart said. 'The Child hears bells, bells in the middle of the wilderness.'

'Be quiet a minute, will you,' Krüger said, straightening up and cupping his hands behind his ears. After a while he shrugged. 'I don't hear a thing. He's just trying to make fun of us.'

'I don't hear anything either,' Kern said.

They were all indignant and glowered at Dietz. 'You're just hearing things,' Zoll growled.

Dietz lifted his shoulders helplessly. 'I swear I heard them,' he said uncertainly. 'I couldn't be that mistaken.'

'It's easy to diddle yourself,' Krüger said, feeling sorry for the little fellow. He turned to Dorn who was standing behind him. 'Isn't that true, Professor?'

Dorn took his time about answering. He adjusted his glasses and regarded Dietz, who was looking anxiously up at him. His face was serious as he said: 'Hallucinations.'

'My God, what is that?' Krüger asked aghast.

'When your senses deceive you,' Dorn said briefly.

There was a silence. Krüger shook his head. 'Never heard of it. Strange business.'

Dietz turned to Steiner. 'Didn't you hear them?'

Steiner, eyes half closed, took a drag on his cigarette. 'The bells?' he asked. 'I did.'

'There!' Dietz fairly puffed with relief, while the others stared indignantly at Steiner.

'Typical,' Krüger whispered, turning to Schnurrbart.

Schnurrbart did not answer. He had noticed long ago that Steiner had a weakness for little Dietz, who always seemed a little lost among the others. Not that Steiner showed favouritism toward him in matters like standing guard or carrying gear. His feelings came out in the almost paternal tone he sometimes adopted toward the Sudeten German. It had happened before that he took the side of Dietz in quarrels among the men; Schnurrbart recalled incidents he had observed with just the smallest touch of jealousy. Once more Steiner's incomprehensible attitude angered him more than he would admit to himself. Naturally there had been no bells, he told himself. Bells in the middle of a forest in Russia! It was ridiculous. Irritably, he drew on his pipe, wondering whether or not to let the subject drop. But Dietz spoke first. Perhaps he *had* been hearing things. If Steiner hadn't backed him up about the bells, he would have been willing to grant that it was a mistake. Perhaps Steiner had been mistaken also. He turned to him. 'Did you really hear them?'

Steiner frowned. 'Of course. I said so clearly enough, didn't I?'

'Yes,' Dietz murmured, intimidated. He glanced again at Anselm who was staring tight-lipped into space. The others, too, all seemed ill-humoured; a wall of hostile faces surrounded him with silent menace. He felt that he could placate them, but could not decide how to do it, especially since he did not want to offend Steiner. Finally a diplomatic solution occurred to him. With a weak smile he turned to Krüger and said: 'It's odd, all the same.'

'There's nothing odd about it,' Steiner said sharply. 'What's odd about bells ringing on Sunday morning?'

They stared at him in surprise. Abruptly, Krüger slapped his powerful thigh with a report like the crack of a gun. 'Why of course,' he exclaimed loudly, 'today's Sunday. I never even thought of it.'

'There you have it,' Schnurrbart said with relief. 'Why shouldn't bells be ringing on Sunday?'

Their mood had changed instantly. They nodded and threw one another meaning looks. 'Sunday!' Maag sighed. 'Back home, at this hour, I'd still be snoozing.'

'And then getting up for coffee and cake,' Pasternack said nostalgically.

Krüger cursed. 'Cut it out,' he protested. 'What's the use of water in my mouth when there's more room for it in my bladder.'

'Pretty good,' Schnurrbart chuckled. He had removed his steel helmet and was busy scratching his tangled hair. But Pasternack was still lost in pleasant recollections. He twisted his thin, hungry face into a grimace and said: 'I think a man has a right to talk about cake.' He sounded challenging, and Krüger turned his face toward him. 'You can talk about shit too,' he declared irritably. Pasternack shook his head. 'Do you have to be so foul-mouthed all the time?'

'Foul-mouthed?' Krüger stared at him in astonishment.

'Yes, foul-mouthed,' Pasternack repeated emphatically. His usual melancholic expression returned to his tired face. A strand of blond hair dangled over his pimpled forehead.

'Look. Who's talking filth all of a sudden,' Krüger sneered.

Dietz intervened. 'Cut out the bickering for once, since it is Sunday.'

'You can stick your Sunday,' Krüger said violently. 'What the hell does the army care about Sundays? Here!' He ran his hand over his unshaven face. 'Is that what you call Sunday?' In sudden fury he opened the top buttons of his tunic and pulled out a patch of filthy shirt. 'We look like pigs!' he snapped. 'This is the way they let us go around, the bastards.'

Schnurrbart grinned at his flushed face. For him, there had always been something likeable about the East Prussian's crude candour. And he's right, he thought; no clean clothes for a month. The thought aroused a twitching feeling in his skin that travelled up his back all the way to his head. The damned lice, he thought. For a moment he tried to imagine what it would feel like to be standing under a hot shower and scrubbing his back with a stiff-bristled brush. It was maddening to imagine it. He sighed and

with his thumb scratched his neck where the itching was worst.
Krüger had meanwhile shoved his shirt back under his tunic. He
looked over at Steiner who had watched with expressionless face,
while listening with half an ear to a conversation between Dorn
and two of the others.

'We have about twenty miles to go,' Steiner reminded them
roughly. 'According to the map, the woods are all marsh. Besides
which there must be a stream somewhere in the middle of it. I hope
you realize what we're facing. Anyone who passes out is going to
be left behind.' He turned and started down the mountain. They
watched him for a moment in consternation, then stood up,
shouldered their gear and followed. They kept to the middle of the
clearing and took care not to slip on the smooth grass. Dorn came
last. His diarrhœa had improved somewhat since last night, and he
felt glad about that. He was still thinking about Dietz's peculiar
hallucination. After all, bells must be ringing somewhere at this
hour. But a thousand miles away at least. Perhaps the bells they
heard had come all the way from the ruins of Germany, carried
on waves of longing to wherever the German armies were fighting
a desperate struggle. A lost struggle, he thought. And the worst
part of it was knowing this.

They had reached the plain meanwhile. The lane came to an
end here, and when they went forward among the trees, the sky
vanished as the foliage closed in overhead. A cool breeze from the
dim depths of the woods blew over their hot, flushed faces and
made them shiver. One after the other they walked into the green
dusk.

II

THE REGIMENT'S NEW positions ran west of Krymskaya through hilly terrain bare of vegetation. The dominant feature of this sector was Hill 121.4, which was crowned by a wooden tower. The 1st Battalion was holding the positions on the southern slope of it. From here there was a good view deep into the enemy hinterland, and the artillery observers could see as far as Krymskaya, which the last companies of the division had evacuated only a few hours ago. There was great activity everywhere. Bunkers were being dug out, machine-gun emplacements being sunk deep into the ground, wood for construction being brought up. The staff officers were well aware of the importance of the next few hours. The terrain was so open that the enemy would not be able to advance until after dark. But then the Russians would come, and from tomorrow morning on their snipers would be at work. The men did not need the admonitions of the company commanders to realize the urgency of digging in. Although they had done without sleep the night before, they set to work with a will and kept going with hardly a pause.

The battalion commander was standing in one of the 2nd Company's advanced dugouts. He had been scanning a patch of woodland some way away through a stereo-telescope. This he considered the weak spot of his sector. Along its northern edge ran the Krymskaya-Anapa highway which was sure to be the target of the enemy's next attack. Those woods, about a square mile in area, offered an ideal deployment area for the preparation of an enemy offensive.

The longer the commander studied the terrain, the grimmer his expression became. Finally he straightened up angrily and turned to the commander of the 2nd Company, who was standing directly behind him. 'Incredible—an irreparable oversight,' he snapped. 'Those woods should have been cut down or destroyed by fire.'

Lieutenant Meyer's good-natured, somewhat flushed face took on the hint of a grimace. 'We came sooner than expected.'

33

'Sooner, what does sooner mean here?' the commander replied irritably. 'By God, they had ample time to establish the lines for the bridgehead. I should like to know what raw beginner is responsible for this.' He stooped over the telescope again.

Meyer regarded him coolly. That longish face with high forehead and light blue eyes gave an impression of extreme forcefulness. An impression underlined by the thin-lipped mouth and the angular chin. The man's thick hair was white at the temples, emphasizing by contrast the healthy tan of his face. His uniform was the work of a first-class tailor and effectively showed off his broad shoulders and narrow waist. He was certainly a superior specimen of officer, but in spite of that Meyer could not stand him. He watched with disgust as Stransky moved the knobs on the telescope with long, thin fingers. On his left hand he wore a heavy signet-ring. No doubt with the family crest on it, Meyer thought, recalling that the regimental adjutant had told him Stransky owned big estates in East Prussia. Not that estates impressed him. We're all the same here, he told himself; a handful of life trying to preserve itself like the candlelight in the bunkers; a bundle of duties in uniform, feeling and thinking like human beings, but trained to act like automatons.

Stransky straightened up again. 'I shall send a report to that effect to Regiment,' he said. 'Unfortunately it is too late to do anything about it.'

Meyer agreed. 'Perhaps the Russians are already in those woods,' he said. 'I shouldn't want to ask anyone to try to cross to them in broad daylight.' He glanced uncomfortably across the flat terrain, which was wholly without cover. Its rust-brown colour was scarcely distinguishable from the dark strip of asphalt highway.

'I doubt that,' Stransky replied. 'It was already daylight when we got here. The Russians couldn't possibly have followed at our heels.'

'So we thought last night,' Meyer said gloomily, 'and still we were unable to hold the planned positions.'

'That is something else again,' Stransky said with annoyance although he was aware that the company commander was right.

According to the original plans, the battalion was still supposed to be holding the positions east of Krymskaya. Toward midnight, after an easy ride on the trucks, they had reached the reception line. But an hour later the order had come from division to move into the final positions.

Stransky suddenly remembered the 2nd Company platoon which had been left behind for a rear-guard. Thoughtfully, he reached for his cigarette-case. 'I suppose we will have to write off your 2nd Platoon,' he said.

'I think not, sir. I gave the platoon leader appropriate instructions in case we might have to withdraw sooner than anticipated. And then Steiner is in command of the platoon.'

'Who is Steiner?' Stransky asked with a frown.

Meyer stared at him for a moment, then nodded. 'I forgot you were new to the battalion, sir. Corporal Steiner is a soldier, let me tell you. As you may know, I joined the battalion at Tuapse. A few weeks later the Russians rolled up the battalion on our left and suddenly appeared in front of my combat H.Q. If it hadn't been for Steiner turning up with his platoon at the last minute, we would all have been done for. He's a reconnaissance specialist, incidentally. One of your predecessors, our present regimental commander, thinks the world of him.'

'So,' Stransky said without interest.

'Yes,' Meyer said. 'He was battalion commander when the regiment was stationed in Pribram. They got into a bad spot—that was at the beginning of the Russian campaign—and Steiner saved his life.'

Bored, Stransky took a drag on his cigarette and glanced across at the woods again. These stories about a corporal somehow jarred him. The man sounded like a typical Wild West hero, he thought, one of these young kids who were quick on the trigger and had a run of luck. He knew the type—crude and arrogant. 'Sounds like a universal genius,' he said with sarcasm.

'I wouldn't know about that,' Meyer said. 'At any rate, he is a fine soldier.'

'I tend to be cautious in my estimate of men,' Stransky replied coolly. 'There are human as well as soldierly traits that determine worth. It surprises me, incidently that this—ah, what did you say his name was?'

'You mean Steiner?'

'Yes, that's it, Steiner. As I was saying, it surprises me to hear that this man Steiner in spite of his remarkable talents and services is only a corporal.'

Meyer was startled. The argument was sound. To judge by all he had heard of Steiner, the man must have been in the army at least five years. There must be some explication of that. He would find out some day.

Stransky's voice cut into his private thoughts. The commander had folded his arms over his chest, and a mocking smile was playing about the corners of his mouth as he asked: 'Well?'

Meyer glanced away from his face. Pompous ass, he thought. Aloud, he said: 'I have not yet had occasion to look into the matter. Steiner was evacuated to hospital for some time, as I understand it, and returned to the company about six months ago, shortly after I joined the battalion.'

'Has he been in command of the platoon since then?' Stransky asked.

'No. In that case I would have promoted him to sergeant long ago. Up to two weeks ago he was the group leader. I handed the platoon over to him after Sergeant Graf was wounded during an artillery barrage. Ever since there has been so much doing that I haven't had a chance to promote him.'

Stransky dropped his cigarette butt and stepped on it. 'If your Steiner succeeds in bringing the platoon back here, I'll promote him to full sergeant.'

'Then he has his promotion,' Meyer declared.

'You certainly are sure of yourself,' Stransky jeered.

They looked at one another, their mutual dislike plainly written in their faces. Why am I letting him depress me? Meyer thought. He sits so high in his saddle he will never stoop low enough to see the grass his horse is eating. A corporal hardly exists for him, any more than I do. The thought angered him, and his voice sounded sharper than he meant it to be as he said: 'I know Steiner long enough to vouch for him.'

Stransky raised his eyebrows. Anger did not come quickly; it rose slowly into his throat and thickened his voice. 'I did not ask your opinion, Herr Meyer,' he said tightly. 'Moreover, I am accustomed to a somewhat different tone from my subordinates.'

Meyer saw the white patches under the captain's cheekbones. For a moment he regretted his insistence. With a mixture of anxiety and curiosity, he waited to see what would happen next. But Stransky seemed to have regained his self-control. The spots in his face began to colour, and in a moment they had disappeared.

Without a word he turned toward the trench, and Meyer followed him. When they came to a machine-gun emplacement, Stransky stopped. The trench had been widened out into a square room at this point, and covered over with a few planks. The man behind the gun turned his head and looked uncertainly at them. Meyer gave him a friendly nod. 'Anything new, Ott?'

The man snapped to attention. 'Second M.G., nothing to report,' he said tensely.

Stransky studied him attentively. In addition to the Iron Cross the man wore a silver infantry assault medal. 'What is your line of work?' he asked.

The man's face flushed. He opened his mouth, then appealed to Meyer with a look. 'He lives in Birgsau in the Bavarian Alps,' Meyer said. 'Until he was called up he was the community cattleherd.'

'I see,' Stransky said. He dropped his official tone as he asked: 'I imagine that was a very monotonous occupation, wasn't it?'

Ott grinned in embarrassment and swallowed several times. 'No,' he said at last. His eyes were fixed upon Meyer, who gave him an encouraging wink.

'Then it was not so dull?' Stransky asked.

'No,' Ott replied, shaking his head violently.

Stransky smiled fleetingly. 'Take these men away from their mountains and they behave like fish out of water,' he said to Meyer. 'Still'—he looked at the man's medals—'they can still bite, it would seem.'

They went on. Stransky had assumed a greater curtness and answered the men's salutes with brief nods. They ran into Lieutenant Gausser, the commander of 1st Company. His youthful face was pale and sleep-starved. Because of the heat he had taken off his tunic. His green shirt was sopping, and Stransky regarded him with disapproval. 'What a way to go about, Herr Gausser,' he said sternly.

The lieutenant shrugged indifferently. 'I have been working on my bunker, sir,' he said. 'This is what they call a prepared position in these parts—they haven't even provided a company combat post.' He turned to Meyer. 'How are conditions over your way?'

'Not quite as bad as here. There was at least a bunker for the combat post.'

'Happy man,' Gausser sighed. 'They certainly had enough time to prepare a decent position. As things are now we would have a hard time repelling an attack.'

Stransky studied his well-manicured fingernails. 'Good positions Herr Gausser,' he said reprovingly, 'do help in keeping losses at a minimum. But you must not overlook the fact that a successful repulse of enemy assaults depends primarily on the morale of the troops. And the attitude of the officers is of the utmost importance.'

Gausser exchanged glances with Meyer. To the commander he said coolly: 'Perhaps you will permit me to remark that the morale of troops presupposes some sort of physical substance which, in our experience, reacts with extreme sensitivity to superior enemy fire power.'

'What do you mean by that?' Stransky asked haughtily. Once more Gausser exchanged glances with Meyer. The little lines of irony at the corners of his mouth vanished as he said, in dead earnest now: 'If none of the fighting men survive the enemy barrage, all your morale will do is add a nice touch to the communiqué.'

Stransky threw a look at Meyer. Seeing the naked spite in Meyer's face, he stiffened. Icily, he retorted: 'The probability that at least one of the four machine-guns in your company will survive even the most intensive barrage is far greater than you think. But perhaps you lack the experience to judge this matter.' He paused. 'You will have opportunity to prove your morale with this one remaining machine-gun.'

Gausser, who had meanwhile slipped into his tunic, replied calmly: 'If my physical substance survives the barrages, my morale will meet your standards, too.'

'You have effrontery, if nothing else,' Stransky snapped. Meyer hastily covered his mouth with his hand to conceal the twitch of his facial muscles. Gausser finished buttoning his tunic before he said politely to the commander: 'Effrontery can be a good point for a soldier. It keeps him from overestimating his enemy.'

Neatly parried, Meyer thought. Stransky's frown darkened and his voice sounded a shade colder as he said: 'Effrontery can also lead to an irresponsible underestimation of the enemy. To call it a good point involves a degree of naïve optimism which ill suits a company commander.'

The conversation had reached a critical point, and Gausser seemed to sense this. There was no point in forcing the issue.

Equably, he said: 'That calls for some thinking. To be frank, after being awake all night and keeping going on the bunkers this morning, I am too tired to concentrate.'

Stransky eyed him for a moment. Then he turned to Meyer. 'I do not need you any longer. Return to your company.' He dismissed both officers with a nod and strode rapidly away. The two men watched him until Meyer cleared his throat. 'I must say, I've taken quite a liking to you in the past few minutes,' he said.

'That's a bloody thing to tell a man,' Gausser replied, unbuttoning his tunic again. 'With my effrontery, I thought you'd liked me all along.' He ran his thumb between his collar and back. 'Damned heat,' he sighed. 'And here it is only ten o'clock.'

'Take your coat off again,' Meyer recommended.

'So I will. I don't see how my sweat can promote the morale of the troops.'

While Gausser removed his coat, Meyer fell to thinking about his 2nd Platoon again. Although he had vouched for its coming through in talking to the captain, he had no illusion about the situation of Steiner and his men. He had spent over an hour studying the map early this morning and the picture he had formed of the terrain was scarcely reassuring. That damnable forest, he thought; I should have taken the platoon along with me. In all that confusion nobody would have noticed.

He turned abruptly to Gausser. 'I must make a call. Will you come with me?'

'Glad to.' As they made their way to 2nd Company's combat post, Meyer spoke of his fears for his platoon. 'I'm going to call Kiesel,' he said. 'The 2nd and 3rd also left platoons behind. Perhaps Regiment has had some report from them.'

The field telephone stood on a low table in the centre of the bunker. Gausser sat down on a corner of the table and let his feet dangle while Meyer made his call. The conversation was brief. When Meyer hung up he was frowning blackly. 'I can't believe it. The other battalions took their platoons right with them.'

'What?' Gausser stared at him. 'How could they have?'

'The order came from Division. As soon as 3rd Battalion left, the Russians pushed up with strong forces. Well, you know Major Vogel. He said to hell with Division's order and took his platoon along. Same thing happened in 2nd Battalion, or must have happened. Kiesel wouldn't commit himself over the telephone. Apparently he's worried about complications.'

'God! What call is there for complications? That's two platoons saved from certain destruction. Does Division think two dozen men would have held up the Russians?'

Meyer smiled feebly. 'Kiesel will find a way to make it right with the general—if he ever finds out about it.'

'And what does the Lieutenant-Colonel Brandt have to say about it?' Gausser wanted to know.

'I don't know. I assume——' He fell silent and abruptly stood up.

'What's the matter?' Gausser asked uneasily.

Meyer clapped his hand to his forehead. 'Why didn't I think of that sooner,' he said slowly. It had occurred to him that the regimental commander could not know who was leading the platoon that had been left behind. He would be highly interested, Meyer thought. Quickly, he picked up the telephone. Hand over the mouthpiece, he said to Gausser: 'If Stransky knew I was telephoning Kiesel over his head——'

'That has already occurred to me,' Gausser said. 'Aren't you afraid he will find out?'

'Who'd tell him? Besides, as you know, I'm on pretty good terms with Kiesel.' At that moment the regimental adjutant's crisp voice answered. With a wink at Gausser, Meyer clamped the telephone under his chin. 'Meyer again. I forgot to report something which I am sure will interest the lieutenant-colonel. The platoon I had to leave behind is commanded by Corporal Steiner.'

For a few seconds there was silence on the other end of the wire. Gausser brought his ear close to the telephone, holding his breath. 'Steiner?' the voice questioned. 'Yes, Steiner.' Again a brief pause. Then: 'I shall inform Colonel Brandt.'

As Meyer hung up, the two men looked at one another. 'I take it Brandt thinks a good deal of Steiner,' Gausser said.

'Rightly so,' said Meyer. He drew on his cigarette and blew smoke at the ceiling.

'What kind of a man is he?' Gausser asked.

Meyer frowned. 'A problem,' he said. 'First-rate soldier; often impossible as a subordinate. He doesn't seem to know the meaning of respect. But, you know, in cases like this one looks the other way.'

'Why hasn't he been promoted?' Gausser asked.

Mayer scratched his chin uncomfortably. It's like a conspiracy, he thought. He wished he had some plausible explanation to give Gausser, even though he knew the lieutenant was asking only out of idle curiosity.

Stransky had reached Battalion Combat H.Q. The bunkers were set in the midst of a small orchard whose gnarled trees offered excellent cover against air reconnaissance. At the door of his dugout Stransky paused and studied the terrain carefully. The chain of hills running from west to east dipped into a tapering, trough-shaped hollow here. At its lowest point, some distance from the orchard, the hollow merged into a steep gorge. Sunlight blazed upon the naked soil, which stood out reddish-brown against the cloudless sky. A mousetrap, Stransky thought, and tried to calculate the possibilities for escaping if the Russians should suddenly penetrate into the trough. We would have to retreat through the gorge, he told himself. According to the map, the gorge ran due west for about a mile to the village of Kanskoye, where the battalion's transport was parked.

The noise of someone clearing his throat behind him startled Stransky. He turned. A soldier stood some yards away. Recognizing him, Stransky gave a gracious nod and asked: 'Well, Dudek, what is it?'

The man came to attention. 'Your bunker is ready, sir.'

'Good. Where is everybody? The place looks deserted.'

Dudek glanced over toward the trees, beneath which half a dozen other bunkers were concealed. 'The signalmen are all out laying lines, I think, and the runners also. They are finding out the positions of their companies.'

'And Lieutenant Triebig?'

'He must be in his bunker.'

'Tell him that a sentry is to be posted here at once.'

'Yes, sir, sentry posted.' Dudek clicked his heels again. Stransky went into his bunker. Inside everything was extremely neat and clean. Along the wall stood a narrow army cot already made up with blankets. Stransky glanced into the mirror and nervously rearranged some of the toilet articles on a shelf. Then he took off his belt, laid his cap beside the telephone and dropped down on the bed. He found himself unable to stop thinking about his conversations with the two company commanders. The blood rushed to his face at the recollection. He closed his eyes, brooding angrily over Gausser's impudence. Then his thoughts turned to Steiner. A man he would have to know more about. What had Meyer said—that Brandt thought the world of him? Probably that had gone to the corporal's head.

The shrill ringing of the telephone startled him. He reached for the receiver and gave his name. With some uneasiness he recognized the regimental commander's incisive voice: 'You left a platoon behind, I hear?'

'Of course. I received a clear order to do so.'

'The other battalion commanders also received this order. Are you aware of that?'

'So Captain Kiesel informed me.'

'Indeed.' There was another pause. Stransky pressed the receiver to his ear and heard the rushing of his own blood, excessively loud. Then the commander's voice spoke again: 'Are you also aware that the other commanders took it upon themselves to countermand the order?'

'No,' Stransky murmured. 'I cannot understand such conduct, sir. I, at any rate, have strictly obeyed the orders I received.'

'So you have, so you have, Captain Stransky. I suppose you have not yet had enough front-line experience to realize when some adjustments are in order. Unfortunately, there was no time to send revised instructions. Vogel and Körner used their judgment in taking their platoons back with them. I have commended the good sense of these officers in my report to Division.'

Stransky bit his lips. All this is only because of this man Steiner who had saved Brandt's life, he thought bitterly. He must know that Steiner is in command of the platoon. I wonder who——

'Are you still there, Captain Stransky?'

'Certainly, sir. You must understand that I—I mean, that this situation is most unpleasant for me. If I had only guessed! But we had not the slightest difficulty in evacuating our positions. I, therefore, saw no reason for taking the platoon along. I——'

'Very well, Captain Stransky,' the commander cut him off. 'You certainly cannot be blamed for obeying an order. It is simply unfortunate. How strong is the platoon?'

'I am sorry, I have not yet inquired,' Stransky replied uncomfortably. 'Ten or fifteen men, I believe. I can check immediately with Lieutenant Meyer.'

'You might have done so earlier. I want to be kept informed on how this matter turns out.'

The hum in the receiver faded. Stransky slowly replaced the telephone on the hook. He stood up, cursing softly. He went over to the little window beside the door and stared wrathfully out upon the sunlit landscape. Why in the world did he have to suffer all this? After all, he himself had asked to be transferred here from France. I must have been mad, he thought, stark raving mad. He turned back to the table, took a map out of the briefcase hanging over the chair and spread it out. His eyes travelled over the vast area of forest stretching eastward from Krymskaya to the positions the battalion had occupied yesterday. The green surface was crossed in many places by fine blue lines. Undoubtedly a marsh. The observation gave him a peculiar sense of triumph. The commander's protégé would have a tough time getting through there, he thought. First the woods, then the city and finally the Russian front line. Slowly, he straightened up. The trouble men could make for you without your even knowing them. Meditatively, he folded up the map. First of all he had to establish himself solidly; the next task was to teach his subordinates their place. Once he had achieved a strong position in the battalion, not even Brandt would be able to undercut him. In France he had succeeded in doing that within the first week. Here conditions were somewhat more complicated. But he would manage. Although there were certain limits to the jurisdiction of a battalion commander, his opportunities for operating in depth were greater than those of a general. The smaller the pebble in the shoe, the more it could hurt. The comparison amused him.

There was a knock on the door. Stransky turned his head impatiently. 'What is it?'

The door opened, and Stransky recognized his adjutant. 'I just heard that you were back, sir. Am I intruding?'

'Did you need me?' Stransky asked in an unfriendly tone.

Lieutenant Triebig returned a gentle smile. 'Major Vogel telephoned about twenty minutes ago. He asks that you drop in on him some evening soon.'

'Thank you. Anything else?'

'No, sir. Do you have any orders?'

Stransky regarded with distaste the lieutenant's soft womanish features. What kind of man was this? he thought. His voice had no soldierly timbre to it, and his wavy hair was combed back far too carefully for Stransky's taste.

'Yes, something has just occurred to me,' he said in the same unfriendly tone. 'Inform the company commanders that they are to report tomorrow morning for a conference. Here, at nine o'clock.'

'Yes, sir. Any other orders, sir?'

'No, you may go.'

Triebig saluted. When the door closed behind him, Stransky dropped back on his cot. Major Vogel, he thought. Why the sudden burst of friendship? he wondered. Last week, when they had met for the first time at regimental HQ, the elderly major had treated him with condescension. But he was commander of the 3rd Battalion and one never knew when it would prove useful to be on good terms with one's neighbours. Nevertheless, Stransky felt no great urge to accept the invitation. Their conversation last week had been very brief, but Stransky had taken away an impression of the major's opinionated bluntness.

Stransky became aware of how heavy his eyelids felt. Last night's lack of sleep was overtaking him. He stretched out full length and turned on his side. Nothing but vexations, he thought.

After his interview with Stransky, Lieutenant Triebig returned to his bunker and put through a number of telephone calls to the company commanders. Then he sat down at the table and languidly turned through some old picture magazines. The air in the bunker was stale, and the fierce outside heat could be felt even here in this half-underground room. He came to a stop at a picture of a scantily dressed girl lying on her stomach and kicking her feet into the air. Under the low-cut blouse her pointed breasts showed clearly. Triebig studied the picture for some time. Finally he tore the page out, crumpled it into a ball and tossed it into a corner. He glanced at his watch. It was after twelve. Time to eat, he thought. He went over to the tin basin and washed his hands. Then he reached out for the loaf of bread standing on the table and cut off a number of thin slices. Conscientiously, he spread the tiny portion of butter over each of the slices. From his canteen he poured cold coffee into a tin cup. Nostalgically, he recalled the aromatic coffee that had been served hot by the field kitchens in France.

His meal completed, he remained sitting at the table. There was a knock at the door. His orderly opened it and stood hesitantly at the threshold. 'Is there anything you wish, sir?'

'Not at the moment,' Triebig replied. Thoughtfully, he regarded the shy, boyish face. Then he beckoned the man into the bunker. 'You can keep me company for a bit,' he said. 'I really hardly know you. Sit down somewhere.'

The man looked around the bunker, indecisive. Triebig was sitting on the one chair. 'Sit down on the bed,' Triebig suggested. 'Are you always so timid?'

The orderly risked a shaky smile as he obeyed. 'No,' he murmured under his breath. He perched on the extreme edge of the narrow army cot.

Triebig lit a cigarette and studied him with interest. Keppler had been sent to the battalion from a replacement unit only a few weeks ago. Triebig had taken him for an orderly because his own orderly had just been wounded. Keppler was also a runner for 1st Company. No older than nineteen, Triebig guessed. His soft, unformed features bore a helpless expression which was further accentuated by the way he kept his mouth slightly open.

'Where do you come from?' Triebig opened the conversation.

Keppler clasped his hands over his knees. 'Frankfurt, sir.'

'Is that so? I know Frankfurt quite well,' Triebig commented. 'I used to run over that way frequently in my car.'

With satisfaction he noted the look of respect that came into Keppler's face. 'You have a car of your own, sir?'

Triebig nodded casually. 'Had one for years. Though it's been taken over by the army now, like everybody else's. But we must all do our share for victory.' Raising his eyebrows, he put on a lofty expression. No need for the boy to know that the car had belonged to his firm. It was always wise to impress these fellows right at the start. Made everything easier. He puffed reflectively on his cigarette for a moment, then leaned forward. 'Do you live with your parents?' he asked.

Keppler shook his head sadly. 'No, they're dead. My father's been dead for ten years, and my mother died seven years ago.'

'Oh!' Triebig pretended sympathy. In a kindly tone he said: 'That must have been very hard for you. Where did you live?'

'In an orphanage, sir. Later I went to work for a baker. I learned the trade there, and lived in the baker's house.'

'Didn't you have any relatives?' Triebig asked. 'I mean, anybody who could take you in?'

'No, sir. You see, we used to live in Munich. Then we moved to Frankfurt and my parents died there.'

'Well, well,' Triebig said. I couldn't have made a better choice, he thought with gratification. He felt excitement spreading from his thighs throughout his body. He moistened his lips, while his eyes rested upon the boy's narrow waist. Keppler's face slowly reddened as if he guessed the lieutenant's thoughts.

'You've had a tough time,' Triebig declared. He sat down on the bed beside Keppler. 'But time heals all wounds. If you get along with me, you'll have a good life here. You may go now. Come back this evening and arrange my gear.'

Keppler jumped to his feet with repressed excitement. 'Yes, sir! When shall I come, sir?'

Triebig considered. It was clear that he would have little trouble with the boy. A naïve young fellow, and just the type to while away the boredom of long, dull spells with little to do. 'Don't come too early,' he replied. 'Around ten. We'll have a chance to talk.'

Keppler's face flushed with pleasure. He clicked his heels sharply. 'Yes, sir,' he began briskly. 'I——' Abruptly he paused and lowered his eyes.

'Well?' Triebig smiled. He stood up and chucked the boy under the chin. 'What did you want to say?'

His jovial tone restored Keppler's confidence. He raised his head, looked into Triebig's eyes, and said: 'I want to make good on this job, sir.'

'That's the spirit,' Triebig said patronizingly. He barely touched Keppler's cheek. 'Do your best and I'm sure I shall be satisfied with you.'

I hit it just right, he thought, as he watched the boy go out. He felt perspiration starting all over his body. 'Damnable heat,' he murmured, dropping on to the cot. For a while he stared blankly at the ceiling. What the hell, he told himself. Who knows whether we'll be alive tomorrow. You had to grab your chances. But all the same he would have to be careful. For a moment he tried to imagine what would happen if Stransky found out, or one of the other officers. You could not trust anybody. His thoughts drifted back to Keppler. Closing his eyes, he allowed his imagination free rein.

The bunkers of the Regimental Combat HQ were situated on the western slope of a chain of hills that ran from south-east to north-west, shielding the headquarters from the enemy. In the commander's bunker Lieutenant-Colonel Brandt and Captain Kiesel sat at the table opposite one another. The commander's gaunt face was angry. 'I have to attend to every damn triviality,' Brandt complained violently. 'Ought to have every corporal in the regiment reporting directly to me every day.'

Kiesel shrugged equably. 'That would be a good deal of trouble,' he remarked. 'Besides, you can hardly blame Stransky. He's a conscientious officer and was strictly obeying orders.'

'Don't tell me that again,' Brandt replied irritably. 'To me the word conscientious stinks of pedantry. I need officers able to act on their own initiative when the situation demands. Look at Vogel—by God, I wish I had more like him.'

Kiesel shook his head in mild disagreement. 'Not everyone can be expected to take on the burden of independent decisions when there is a chance to shift responsibility to superiors. However, if I know Steiner, he will find some way out. I count on his turning up tonight.'

'It's not only Steiner,' Brandt said with sharp reproof. 'It's a whole platoon.'

Kiesel smiled fleetingly. 'Of course, I was thinking of the platoon too. But without Steiner the others would never get through.'

'Hm, do you think so,' Brandt murmured, regarding Kiesel with suspicion. Brandt was tall and thin, with sparse hair covering an elongated knobby head. Under a high forehead were eyes that seemed to express a permanent bitterness. When he compressed his narrow lips, the tautening skin of his face deepened the hollows beneath his cheekbones.

The commander gave an impatient shake of his head. 'I know what you are thinking. You can't put anything over on me, Kiesel, remember that. But you are right to think so. People can think what they like of me, and have done so. But nobody can say I don't know the meaning of gratitude.'

'Certainly not,' Kiesel quietly agreed. He had been adjutant of this regiment for eight months now, and had served under three commanders. With neither of the others had he reached so good an understanding as he now had with Brandt. I must look this fellow Steiner over some day, he decided. So far he knew a great deal about him from reports, but had never met the man. A few months ago Brandt had spoken to him about a black mark on Steiner's record and had asked him to investigate. He had done so, but with inconclusive results. There was no question about the charge, but there was something suspect about the evidence, an unexplained contradiction somewhere. Brandt had had the same impression. Later, they had let the matter ride.

Kiesel stood up and began pacing back and forth in the bunker. For a while Brandt ignored him. Then he turned upon him. 'For heaven's sake stop the marathon. You bother me more than the Russians. Tell me your private opinion of Stransky.'

Kiesel stopped by a chair, pulled it between his legs and sat down backwards on it. 'My private opinion?' he said, drawling. 'To tell the truth, I have not yet taken the trouble to form an opinion. Herr Stransky seems to think very well of himself. But that may be because he comes from a fine old family. Or maybe he is just too rich to be human.'

Brandt dismissed these suppositions with a gesture. 'Stop beating around the bush. You're a judge of people. What do you think of him?'

'I have so far met Stransky only once,' Kiesel answered non-committally. He lit a cigarette, holding the burning match in his fingers until it went out. 'The few words I've exchanged with him were instructive in one sense. On the other hand, they were hardly enough to justify an objective opinion. My personal impression is that Herr Stransky considers himself an unusual personality who is above criticism. If I understood him rightly, he believes he has a great mission to perform, namely to achieve spiritual domination of the battalion.'

'What's that?' Brandt asked in utter incomprehension.

Kiesel smiled. 'It does sound odd, but I have an inkling of what he wants. To put the matter more clearly: Herr Stransky wants his orders obeyed not because of his rank, but because of the sheer impression his personality makes upon the men.'

'If that's so, his chances are pretty poor. I've had my own experiences with the obstinacy of the 1st Battalion.' He laughed harshly. 'You've dreamed all this up, Kiesel. I've been wearing this uniform a long time and I've never yet met such a case.'

Kiesel nodded. 'I grant it is unusual for a commander to want to rule his men's emotions as well as their actions.'

'And how, may I ask, does Stransky intend to achieve this, ah, spiritual domination?'

'I didn't sound him out on this. But I gather he intends to use his company commanders as his tools since, in his own words, the influence of a commanding officer diminishes in intensity the lower you go in the ranks. He considers personal contact with the other ranks a dangerous experiment.'

'Beautiful!' Brandt brought his palm down against the table top in exuberant amusement. 'You know, Kiesel,' he said, with a confidential wink, 'I am rather impressed by this man Stransky, even if he is a visionary.'

'Not all visionaries are as unpopular as Stransky,' Kiesel commented.

'Do you think so?' Brandt suddenly wore a look of studied indifference.

For a second there was silence between them. Then Kiesel said casually, 'Oh, well.' He regarded the tip of his cigarette and resolved to say no more on this dangerous topic.

Brandt drummed his fingers nervously on the table. At last he raised his head with an impatient gesture. 'At any rate, in the First, Stransky will find few officers or men who will go along with his little game. Less than ever now. To tell the truth, the morale of the men is troubling me. No pep to them. They're like a set of chess pieces; they'll let themselves be moved around, but they won't move of their own accord.'

'Chess pieces?' Kiesel frowned reflectively. 'Haven't they always been that?'

'Not a bit of it.' Brandt shook his head vehemently. 'I tell you, up to a year ago we had the best troops a commander could wish for. The men knew just what they were doing and why they were doing it. They were capable of winning a battle even when it was being run by an amateur up on top. But today! I never feel easy unless I'm right up there in the trenches myself. It's impossible to have any confidence in them.'

'The feeling is mutual,' Kiesel remarked.

'What's that?' Brandt gave him a look of astonishment that

quickly became reproach. 'What do you mean by that?' he asked sharply.

'What I said,' Kiesel replied easily. 'The men no longer have any confidence.'

'Confidence in whom?'

'In us, of course. We misunderstand their psychology if we think that they put the blame primarily on the top leadership. If I hop into a cab which gets in an accident because the brakes fail, I blame the driver, not the company he works for. I'll say that he should have refused to drive a cab with defective brakes.'

'Just what are they blaming the leadership for?'

Kiesel crossed his legs. 'The morale of troops wears out after a time. The division has been on active duty for twenty-one months without a break. The men are fed up. You know yourself how often they've been promised they'd be taken out of line.'

'Is that our fault?'

'I'm no general,' Kiesel replied evasively. 'But the way things are now, the men consider every new commander a candidate for the *Ritterkreuz* who wants to earn his medal with their blood. Once he gets that Cross pinned on his chest, a new commander comes along. Within these twenty-one months they have changed their commanders, from general to company leader, as often as a man changes his shirt in peacetime.'

'Yes, yes, I know.' Brandt's fingers drummed impatiently on the table. 'We burn up replacements as fast as they arrive. On the other hand, the general staff know the situation better than we do, and what they say counts.'

'I don't agree. I think they make some big mistakes and that this is one of their biggest.'

Brandt smiled briefly. 'I wish you could come forward as advocate of the other ranks' interests. Unfortunately there doesn't happen to be any such post in the Tables of Organization.' He slumped back in his chair. 'I agree with you that our men absolutely must have a change of air. I'm beginning to feel the same way myself. This damned country! The men have been lured into these steppes and endless forests. At first it was all new and exciting for the troops, but the excitement didn't last long. These frightful spaces, monotonous, repetitive; you can't help feeling that one of these days they'll swallow you up. You end up with a complex about it. We're getting that now. Still, we're here and here we have to stay. The men must be made to realize how hard it is to relieve them. Where would we get the transport? You know how much it takes to move a division from France to Russia, and vice versa. Then again, you talk of twenty-one months of uninterrupted duty. Let's be honest, Kiesel—how many of the original personnel are left?' He laughed mirthlessly. 'In my former battalion I could count the survivors on my fingers. The regiment today consists 90 per cent. of replacements who have served no more than a few months in Russia. The general is right when he insists that relief of the division would not be justified for the sake of the few old hands. Don't you see that?'

'No.'

'Why not, in the devil's name?'

Kiesel crushed out the remainder of his cigarette. Brandt's words had impressed him, less by their logic than by their psychological penetration. He would not have expected such insight from the commander. Abstractedly, he gazed at the small window near the door. Tiny particles of dust danced in the band of sunlight that fell through the single pane.

'It isn't easy to explain,' he began hesitantly. 'You have to put yourself in the soldier's place. Consider what the situation was just a few months ago. That was when the first defeats began. But the defeats were not enough to shake the men's confidence.'

'Why not?'

'For various reasons. The most important probably is that our men have a certain sense of justice; after all those grand victories they're willing to grant our top leadership the right to make a few mistakes.'

'In other words they want to be fair.'

'I think that's about it. The soldier is far away from the direct influence of the demagogues, but because of his sense of fairness he has managed to retain a good measure of patriotism.'

Brandt rubbed the knuckles of his left hand. 'Those are harsh words,' he said.

'Perhaps. If it weren't for the presence of a superior officer, I might express myself even more clearly. But I don't intend to discuss politics.'

'If you did I would ask you not to. Go on.'

'If you wish,' Kiesel puffed misshapen smoke-rings at the ceiling. 'It is the few men who were here from the start that I am concerned about. They have been steady as steel all along, and they are the ones who have been keeping the replacements in line. To them we owe——' Abruptly he fell silent as he caught the faint smile on the commander's face.

'Why are you stopping?' Brandt said. 'What you say interests me enormously. I'd like to hear it to the end.'

'It isn't worth saying,' Kiesel murmured.

The commander studied him coolly for a moment. 'It is always worth saying when I am your audience, remember that. But I can guess what you were going to say. You take the same view of the replacements that I do. They're no longer any good; they're infected by a spirit of tired resignation. They have experienced nothing but retreats here at the front, and have every reason to believe the myth of Russian invincibility. I started at the bottom, remember, and anything you can say about the old hands interests me now just as much as it did then.'

'All right, let's talk about the old hands. To them the recent set-backs have been nothing more than the shifting fortunes of war. During the years we were on the offensive, they saw the retreating back of the enemy too often to be frightened by his face now. The replacements, on the other hand, think every Russian is an infallible fighting machine.'

'Good, we're getting to the heart of the matter. Go on.'

Kiesel propped his chin in his fists. 'I could spend hours praising them. And what is happening now? The *élite* of the division, the men who wear their medals as though they were a natural part of their uniforms, are becoming just as unreliable as the replacements. Why?'

Brandt nodded thoughtfully. 'I suppose you are going to say that the men feel mistreated. Their sense of duty has been shame-fully exploited; they've been disappointed in us, and distrust and bitterness are the result.'

'Precisely,' Kiesel said. 'What do you think is going to be the end of it? If we can no longer rely on our experienced men, if we can no longer——'

Brandt interrupted him. 'Enough,' he said wearily. 'With the situation as it is, we can't blame them. Perhaps it is best not to talk about all this. It seems to me such conversations only make things harder for us.' He sighed and stood up. 'You can accompany me this afternoon. I intend to see for myself how the positions look.'

'I'll be here,' Kiesel said. As he went out, he saw Brandt sit down at the table again and rest his head on his hands. The issue of the war had already been decided, Kiesel thought. They both knew it; there was no sense pretending any longer.

Late that evening the men were still working on the positions. Meyer had left his bunker a few minutes before; he was nervous and wanted to inspect the trenches and foxholes. He noted that the work was progressing well, and turned back toward his headquarters. Lost in thought, he trudged slowly along the head-high trench. Steiner would certainly be coming in tonight. Once the Russians built up a solid front line, there would hardly be any chance for the platoon to get through. Even as it was, the platoon would have to detour around the city and that would take time. Meyer looked at his watch. It was shortly before ten. He stopped walking and stood for a moment, indecisive. Then, since he felt not the slightest inclination to sleep, he swung himself up out of the trench, climbed a few yards up the slope, and sat down on the ground. There was a deep stillness all about, broken only by the clank of shovels as the men dug deeper here and there. The star-studded sky arched high above the hills, casting soft light over the landscape. For a long while Meyer sat staring into the night. Longing thoughts of home filled his mind. He lay back, clasped his hands behind his neck and closed his eyes. If only it were over soon. Since November the hopelessness of it all had been obvious. At that time Tuapse had been almost within their grasp, the Turkish frontier only a few days' march away, and no one doubted that the war would soon be won. While now! The collapse of the front at Stalingrad and the resultant danger of encirclement for the divisions fighting in the Caucasian forests had reversed the picture. It was true that their division and a few others had escaped envelopment by withdrawing from the Caucasus into the present bridgehead. But what had been gained? At their backs was the sea, in front of them were the superior forces of a fanatical enemy who had seized and was holding the initiative. Here were a few undermanned German divisions clinging desperately to the Circassian hills and the Kuban swamps, exhausted from endless fighting, without hope, with nothing but endurance. Meyer sighed. He craned his neck to see beyond the positions. The moon was rising and it was growing lighter. The highway, a pale band, ran eastward along the edge of the forest, and Meyer suddenly became aware of how intensely he hated this country with its murderous distances and its miserable roads.

A noise in the trench roused him. There was a murmur of voices nearby. He sat up, listening, alert to danger. But it was only a sentry being relieved. He lay back again and watched with half-shut eyes as the head of a man appeared over the rim of the trench. As Meyer watched him, he felt his bitterness slowly dissolving. Perhaps I am seeing things too blackly, he told himself; perhaps we will still make it. The sentry in front of him stood motionless. He was probably watching that patch of woods where—possibly at this very moment—the advance scouts of a Russian assault division would be groping their way forward.

Somewhere beyond the hill a flare rose against the sky, flooding the ground with light for a few seconds. The man in the trench turned his head to the right. Meyer got up and went to his bunker. He opened the door, lit a candle, and sat down at the table. Later he pillowed his head on his arms. He waited for the platoon to arrive until the first dawn light trickled into the bunker.

'Gentlemen,' Stransky began, his voice cool and business-like, 'I believe there is no need of my going into the general tactical picture. The daily army communiqué should be keeping you up-to-date on that.'

Meyer gave a slight cough and received a stern look from the commander. Merkel clasped his hands patiently over his knees. Gausser and Schwerdtfeger stared at the floor with ill-concealed expressions of boredom.

'The map, please,' Stransky said. Triebig hurried to the table, took a map out of a portfolio, and pinned it to the wall. Stransky went up to it. 'Very well,' he said, and paused until Triebig had returned to his place. Then he continued: 'A few words are, however, in order concerning our own particular situation. Parts of the army, withdrawing through Rostov, have been fitted into the new main line of resistance in the north, which runs'—his finger pointed to a spot on the map—'east of Taganrog northward in the direction of Voronesh. The front seems to have become stabilized again. The Supreme Command regards the maintenance of the Kuban bridgehead as indispensable since, as you will recognize, its tactical importance for future offensives will be of the greatest importance.' Stransky paused briefly. Meyer thought, bitterly: Where were they to get the material and the men for future offensives? The other officers were also looking sceptical. Apparently Stransky sensed their doubts, for his voice grew louder. 'A new offensive starting from the bridgehead and moving north will shake the entire Russian southern front. Striking as it would against the rear of the Russian army, it might well decide the outcome of the war.'

'For God's sake!' Merkel whispered. Schwerdtfeger nodded derisively; Gausser passed his hand over his face as if to wipe away a grin.

'It may be assumed,' Stransky went on, 'that the enemy is aware of this danger and will spare no efforts to eliminate the threat to his rear. Our division's sector runs from here north-westward as far as the inlets near Temryuk. As you see, the bridgehead resembles a bow with the Black Sea forming the bowstring. To the south, touching our right wing, are two rifle divisions; to the north an infantry division. I am afraid that a Russian attack would be directed primarily against our sector since, as you see, the marshes to the north form a natural obstacle. Moreover, do not overlook the importance of the highway which leads through our sector. Given the limited extent of the bridgehead, every square yard of ground yielded would represent a serious loss. Our present line, the Siegfried position, must be held in all circumstances.' Stransky turned away from the map. Emphatically, he continued: 'See to it that the positions are sound. Put maximum pressure on your men to get the work done. Every shovelful of dirt, every dugout and foxhole, offsets the danger of a break-through. Do not forget that we have only water at our backs.'

He fell silent, letting his eyes rove over the faces of the officers. They were attentive in earnest now. Meyer cleared his throat and asked: 'Where is the ferry landing?'

Stransky turned to the map again. 'We have two landing places. The first is near Tamanskaya, the second west of the salt marsh. Up to the present six ferries have been employed. They require about an hour for crossing the strait. So far, mines and low-flying planes have sunk two of our ferries. Moreover, it is to be expected that the Russians will be sending in submarines to stop the ferries.'

'Nice prospect,' Merkel exclaimed. 'What are we going to do about that?'

'The proper measures will be taken when the time comes,' Stransky said stiffly.

Gausser, who had been listening with obvious uneasiness, spoke up. 'What reserves have been provided?'

Stransky went over to the map again. 'An assault regiment stationed west of Kanskoye is at the disposal of the division. Furthermore, in order to assure swift and smooth communications, the construction of two asphalt roads is planned. Engineering companies have already started work. Incidentally, I must not forget to mention that the construction of a large airfield north of Novorosisk was decided on today. Have you any other questions?'

The officers crowded around the map. They began vehemently discussing the chances for the bridgehead. Meyer turned to Stransky, who had stepped somewhat to one side. 'If the Russians should succeed in making a break-through beyond Taganrog and occupying the Perekop peninsula——' Meyer did not continue. The company commanders exchanged significant looks, while Stransky frowned darkly. He pointed to the map again. 'As you can see, Herr Meyer, Taganrog is some 200 miles east of Perekop. The development you suggest would take a good deal of time, which would enable the Supreme Command to make the necessary precautions.'

'As at Stalingrad,' Merkel put in.

Stransky whirled to face the speaker. 'I believe, Lieutenant Merkel, that superior authorities are more competent than you to form a proper estimate of Stalingrad. A company commander's horizon is too limited for a view of the larger problems of the struggle. In any case, in the event of such a thing, the situation would be just the same for you whether you were in the Crimea or here in the Kuban bridgehead.' He took a step away from the group. 'I shall expect your reports by telephone on the progress of construction work at 1700 hours. That will be all.' He made a gesture of dismissal. The officers saluted stiffly and were shown to the door by Triebig. Outside the bunker, they separated. Meyer, accompanied by Gausser, slowly climbed up the slope. They did not speak until they reached Meyer's headquarters. Then Gausser asked: 'What do you think of all that?'

'No comment needed,' Meyer said.

Gausser grinned. They stood for a moment on the top of the

steps leading down into the bunker. The sun burned fiercely. 'I don't like this quiet,' Gausser said. He glanced toward the woods.

'Neither do I,' Meyer murmured. 'The Russians ought to have got here long ago. And the hill makes a beautiful target for them.'

'It sure does.'

They looked at one another, and Meyer said: 'Let's hope for the best.'

Gausser nodded. 'We can use a little hope.' He hesitated. Then he held out his hand to Meyer. 'I'll be off. Good-bye!' A few steps away he turned and called back: 'Steiner will certainly be along soon.'

Meyer smiled gratefully. When Gausser disappeared around the next bend in the trench, he sighed heavily. Where could the platoon be at this moment?

III

THE PLATOON HAD been slogging for more than four hours
through the pathless woods. The thorny undergrowth ripped the
men's uniforms and scratched their hands and faces. They moved
through a sultry hothouse atmosphere which made them sweat
from every pore, while the repulsive odour rising from the marshy
ground sickened them. To make matters worse, a cloud of almost
invisible stinging mites had descended upon them. There was no
defence against these. In places the ground was so mucky that they
had to take big detours, losing precious time.

Krüger marched behind Schnurrbart. His face was streaming
sweat; his eyes were burning as though pepper had been thrown
into them. The machine-gun felt like a ton on his right shoulder.
Following the example of the others, he had long ago thrown away
his gas mask and steel helmet. When he stopped for a moment, as
he did frequently, he could feel his legs quivering and threatening
to collapse. His throat felt like a dry sponge which would not let
the air pass through and which sucked every drop of fluid out of
his body.

The other men were no better off. Dietz was suffering the worst.
He kept his mouth wide open and reeled forward from one step
to the next. The heavy boxes of ammunition hung from his arms
like lead weights, dragging his feeble body down. Steiner had carried
the boxes for him for a while. But Dietz was already so done in
that this temporary relief did not help. He stared dully at the
ground as he trudged. His mind had almost ceased functioning,
and he was so exhausted that he felt little pain. Worst of all was
the thirst. There was a steady roaring in his ears as though a clear
mountain stream were pouring down over nearby rocks. But
whenever he raised his inflamed eyes expectantly, he saw nothing
but the endless tangle of underbrush and the labyrinth of trees.

He forced himself to go on for a while; then his knees suddenly
gave way and he fell forward on his face, moaning. Dorn, who was
close behind him, stopped in alarm. Then he tried to shout to
make the others aware of what had happened. But his voice

sounded like the hoarse cawing of a crow; he had to call several times before the men up front paused. When Steiner came running back, the men dropped where they were and did not stir.

'What's the trouble?' Steiner asked.

Dorn shrugged helplessly. 'He's collapsed.'

Steiner cursed. He stooped and shook Dietz vigorously by the shoulders. 'Get up,' he said. 'Let's have no nonsense. We've got to keep going.'

Dietz did not stir. Steiner glanced quickly around at the men. They were lying on the ground, gasping, and he realized that it would be some time before he could get them to their feet again. His face darkened. He took his canteen from his belt and poured some of the lukewarm water over the unconscious man's temples and forehead. With his other hand he unbuttoned Dietz's tunic. But it was some minutes before Dietz opened his eyes and looked around in bewilderment.

'Well now,' Steiner said, pleased. 'You musn't give out on us, Baby. We still have a long way to go.'

'I'm done in,' Dietz sighed, struggling to sit up. Steiner bit his lip. This was all they needed. They had not yet covered even half the distance, and the fellows were breaking down already.

'You'll have to call a rest,' Schnurrbart said, getting up and coming over to Steiner.

'It's two o'clock,' Steiner said tersely.

Schnurrbart shrugged. 'I know, but what can't be done can't be.'

Reluctantly, Steiner growled, 'All right.' He noticed Zoll, who was lying on his stomach off to one side, his head pillowed in his arms. Steiner went over to him and asked, 'Where are your ammunition boxes?' The others became attentive. When Zoll still did not stir, Steiner dug the toe of his boot into his side. 'Didn't you hear me?'

'Lemme alone,' Zoll grunted.

'He had 'em ten minutes ago,' Krüger said. 'The shirker must have dumped them.'

Steiner shifted his tommy-gun to his left hand. 'Then he'll go back for them.' When Zoll still did not move, Steiner stooped down quickly, gripped him by his cartridge belt and pulled him to his feet. His face twisted with fury, Zoll whirled round. Before Steiner could stop him, he snatched up his rifle and raised the barrel threateningly. 'Keep your dirty paws off me,' he whispered hoarsely. 'If you touch me again, bang!'

Steiner looked into the man's maddened face with a sort of curiosity. 'You're too yellow,' he declared quietly. 'Watch?' He dropped his tommy-gun. When Schnurrbart and Krüger started toward them, he gestured them back. They stood still and watched as Steiner stepped so close to Zoll that the barrel of the rifle was directly in front of his stomach. 'They'll hang you if you shoot,' Steiner said. Quietly he reached out, grasped the rifle by the barrel and took it from Zoll's hands. It was done so matter-of-factly that no one was surprised. A sigh arose from the men; their tense bodies sagged like a taut rope that has been slashed in two. 'The bastard,' Krüger muttered. They stared at Zoll, who still stood motionless, his face reflecting fear and rage and shame. Steiner picked up his tommy-gun. In the same matter-of-fact way he said: 'We're going on in fifteen minutes. Fetch those boxes.' Zoll hesitated for just a second. Then he turned and went off into the brush. Krüger cursed. 'Next chance I have I'll let the bastard have it.'

'I'll take care of him,' Steiner said. He went over to Dietz. 'How are you feeling?'

'Coming along,' Dietz said valiantly, forcing a weary smile. Steiner gave him a heartening nod. The others had stretched out again, and Anselm asked, 'How far do we still have to go?'

Steiner shrugged. 'More than half the way.'

'We won't make that today,' Pasternack said.

Maag disagreed violently. 'The hell we won't; man, we've got to.'

'Not through these lousy woods,' Hollerbach said gravely.

Krüger cursed again. 'I wish we knew where we are,' he raged. 'God damn this bloody forest; we should have tried the road. The devil take these things!' He slapped at a gnat that had settled on his forehead. 'They're driving me crazy.'

'Crazier,' Schnurrbart murmured while he filled his pipe.

Kern, watching him, said: 'Smoke it up. Perhaps it'll drive the bugs away.'

Steiner came over to them. 'How you doing, Professor?' he asked Dorn.

His amiable tone made Dorn look up in astonishment. He smiled. 'I'll manage, if it doesn't get any worse.'

Steiner stuck a cigarette between his lips. Thumb on the match-head he said: 'It's bound to get worse.'

He showed no signs of tiredness. Tough as nails, Dorn thought. He asked: 'Why don't you sit down?'

'Because when the time for getting up comes round, you're more tired than you were,' Steiner replied.

Schnurrbart nodded emphatically. 'That's true.'

'Then why have you sat down?' Dorn asked.

Schnurrbart puffed fiercely at his pipe and blew smoke into the centre of a huge swarm of insects. 'I can answer that,' he said grimly. 'I sat down because I'm so tired now that I couldn't be any more tired.'

Dorn smiled. 'That coming from you!' He knew that Schnurrbart was if anything tougher than Steiner, and recalled the forty-mile marches they had put in daily on their way to the Caucasus. In the evening, the men had often been so exhausted that they were unable to eat, although those rations were the first which had been distributed all day. Not so Schnurrbart and Krüger. As soon as they reached their quarters for the night, the two had scouted through all the houses and barns, requisitioning everything they could lay hands on. Long after the others were asleep, they would be sitting up in the kitchen, the smell of roasted chicken wafting through the peasant hut. The memory reminded Dorn of how hungry he was. He swallowed and pressed his hands against his stomach. If only I had a slice of bread he thought. But like the others, he had finished off his last chunk of bread early that morning. A fragrant slice of fresh bread such as he used to have for breakfast every morning at home. He closed his eyes, a voluptuous shiver running down his spine as he pictured the bakery on his corner, the windows heaped with piled-up loaves. Maddening.

He looked up when Schnurrbart spoke to him. 'We're going on Professor.' He forced his eyes to stay open. The other men were already on their feet. Zoll stood to one side, his face inflamed and sweaty, but a box of ammunition in either hand. As Dorn stood up, he felt how shaky he was. Schnurrbart asked: 'Were you asleep, Professor?' Dorn shook his head.

'Ready?' Steiner called out.

Schnurrbart pulled his belt higher and grinned. 'Ready and willin'.'

'You take the rear,' Steiner said to him. 'See that nobody drops any more ballast. Come on!' They followed him wordlessly. The ground where they had rested had been firm, but it soon turned to swamp again. Water welled up under their footsteps and seeped into their boots. Fortunately the underbrush was less dense and thinned out even more as they went on. Maag shook his head. 'I think we're heading straight into a lake.'

'So do I,' Anselm said. 'What's that up ahead there? Reeds or something.'

Maag stretched his neck forward. 'Sure is,' he said, distressed. 'What's the sense of going on? He ought to stop.'

They were already sinking in up to their ankles when Steiner came to a stop. About thirty yards ahead of them an enormous expense of reeds cut a swath across the woods. Brown water shimmered among the thick stems. Beyond the reeds the woods were thinner; they could catch glimpses of blue sky.

One by one the men came up to Steiner, who was staring at the reeds with a set expression.

'We can't cross that,' Krüger said.

Schnurrbart nodded. 'Not a chance. What do we do next?'

Steiner unstrapped his pack, dropped it on the ground and looked about. Finally he went up to a tree with low-hanging branches. He swung up to the first bow and climbed from limb to limb until he was lost among the leaves.

The men looked expectantly at him when he came down.

Steiner dropped from the last branch of the tree. In a few words he described what he had seen: a hundred-foot stretch of reeds, open water, more reeds, and forest beyond. 'It's 300 feet across at least. Worse than I ever thought it would be.'

'There must be some way to get over,' Krüger said.

For reply Steiner dug in his pocket, took out the map and spread it out on the ground. The men looked over his shoulders. He showed them the delicate blue line cutting across the woods.

'The devil,' Maag said. 'Are you sure this is the creek?'

'No doubt about it.'

Dietz swallowed hard. 'Couldn't it be a lake?'

'No, it's the creek.'

'Then we're done,' Krüger declared.

Steiner folded up the map, reached out for his tommy-gun, and

turned in the direction from which they had come. They followed
him about 300 yards back into the woods, until they reached a
comparatively dry spot. Here Steiner stopped. The men dropped
to the ground and lay brooding dully. Schnurrbart went up to
Steiner. 'Are we staying the night here?'

Steiner nodded. He looked like a man who had made a weari-
some climb up a mountain only to recognize just below the peak
that the last hundred feet were unscalable. Schnurrbart watched
him out of the corners of his eyes, sensing his discouragement.
He realized that it was up to him to restore Steiner's confidence.
If the other men guessed how Steiner felt, they would lose heart
completely. There was just one thing they could do. They would
have to follow the creek toward the north until they reached the
road, cross the bridge there, and then turn south-west again and
go back through the woods toward Krymskaya. He tried to
calculate the number of miles they would have to cover. Since they
had been marching steadily south-west, it would be a good thirty
to the highway. Then another forty or so to Krymskaya. Seventy
miles at least.

Seventy miles without rations through this swampy forest was a
sheer impossibility. Steiner was right to be discouraged; they were
done for. Best make an end of it before they just collapsed somewhere and croaked of hunger and exhaustion. He glanced at the
tommy-gun which he had placed between his legs. Devil take it,
that was one hell of a death. And Erika? What would she do
without him? He suddenly recalled the last time they had been
together. That was more than a year ago now. This filthy war.
Leave came rarely enough anyhow, and when your turn did
come, there was sure to be a general ban on leave. Twelve
months, he thought; my God, twelve months.

He heard Steiner clearing his throat and looked up quickly.
Their eyes met.

'That damned creek,' Schnurrbart said.

Steiner nodded. 'The map doesn't do it justice, does it. Listen,
you,' he said to the others. 'We're going to spend the night here.
Tomorrow morning we'll start before dawn.'

'Straight into the creek?' Krüger asked querulously.

Steiner frowned. 'We'll march to the road,' he said.

'How far is that?' Maag asked.

'About thirty miles.'

'Thirty miles!' Krüger laughed crazily. 'Before I march thirty miles I need something to eat.'

'You mean to march those thirty miles tomorrow?' Anselm inquired.

Steiner shrugged impatiently. 'If we don't get there tomorrow, we will the day after.'

Dorn wagged his head soberly. 'Even fifteen miles a day is too much without food.'

Their carpings infuriated Steiner. The harshness returned to his voice. 'When you're marching for your life, fifteen miles on an empty stomach is nothing. I'll tell you something.' He straightened up and stared down the row of dispirited faces. 'We'll reach that road by the day after tomorrow at the latest. If you've got to have something to eat, try tree bark. Cooked in water till soft, it's supposed to be edible. You've got your mess-kits, you've got wood, you've got water and matches—damn it all, don't behave like a lot of children.'

They looked shamefaced, but Krüger growled: 'If we can drink the muck. Didn't you see what it looks like? As if a hundred cows have been shitting in it.'

'Then boil it and skim it. You won't mind the filth—you've got a pig's stomach anyway.'

The men grinned; they were gradually becoming infected by Steiner's confidence. Schnurrbart stared at him, wondering at the sudden change of mood. But now that Steiner was himself again, they'd make it, damn it all. He grinned cheerfully. 'Of course,' he said, 'we'll eat tree bark like the ancient Teutons.'

'The ancient Teutons ate bear steak by the ton,' Anselm said, rubbing his belly.

'Yes,' Kern added, 'and drank mead by the barrel.'

'If you still had your iron rations, it wouldn't be half as bad. Any of you have them left?' asked Steiner.

There was a shamefaced silence. Steiner reached into his pack, took out a small bag and dropped it on the ground. 'We'll make a soup,' he said. 'Put the meat and the bread right in it. Two men fetch water. If you can't get to the creek, dig a hole in the ground. But don't anybody try drinking the muck before it's boiled. The rest can gather wood.'

The men got up. For a few minutes they bustled about. It was already growing dark beneath the trees. Steiner appointed sentries, and the fire was lit only after these had reached their assigned places. The wood was wet and smoked heavily, but this proved to be a boon, for it drove away the swarms of insects. Kern and Anselm had meanwhile gone to the creek for water, each carrying half a dozen mess-tins. They went as far as the soft ground permitted, then dug a square hole which immediately filled with water. The water was black and stinking. Kern made a face. 'Ugh, when I think of what I could be drinking back home,' he said. He stared mournfully into the gathering gloom among the trees.

Anselm looked at him from the side. He suddenly felt that Kern was not such a bad fellow after all; all the quarrels they had had now seemed foolish and needless. He watched Kern filling the mess-tins and felt a great gladness that he was not alone in the woods here. All along the edge of the creek numberless frogs had begun a concert which was rapidly rising to an unbearable fortissimo. Kern raised his head. 'Listen to that!' he said grimly. He finished filling the mess-tins and straightened his back, groaning. 'Shall we go?' he asked. Anselm nodded. Holding the vessels carefully so as not to spill the water, they started back.

In the last few minutes night had descended fully. A feeble glimmer of light directed them toward the camp. When they reached it, they saw the men sitting around the fire, which they kept burning low. A flat hole had been dug, and the burning branches rested on the bottom. Kern and Anselm sat down with the others. Steiner was sitting with his back against a tree. Beside him lay Schnurrbart, Krüger and Maag. Dietz was chatting with Hollerbach. Dorn, off to one side, had his arms clasped over his knees and was staring vacantly into the fire. Zoll and Pasternak were doing sentry duty. The confidence Steiner had injected into them all a few moments ago had already ebbed away. The uncertainty over what faced them was as depressing as the tiredness in their bodies.

Kern turned to Anselm. 'You know what I wish I had? I wish I had a barrel of vodka.' He squirmed restlessly. 'How I would drink!'

'No more than you can hold,' Steiner said; he had been sitting with closed eyes, listening to the conversation.

Kern was wary of getting involved in a conversation with Steiner. But he felt misunderstood, and so he said more than he wanted to. 'You don't know how much I can hold. After ten bottles I sick it up; then I'm ready for the next ten and the next.'

The others pricked up their ears. The boasting irritated them. Krüger said: 'Listen to his boasting before he touches a drop. I'd like to see him after one bottle. I'll bet he's done most of his drinking from a bottle with a rubber nipple.'

The others laughed. Kern spat on the ground. 'Don't you wish you had half what I've drunk in my life. Why, I can handle vodka even better than I can women, and that's saying a lot.'

'Really?' Krüger leaned forward. 'And how many women can you handle at one time, may I ask?'

'Don't you wish you knew!' Kern grinned significantly. Now that the conversation had taken its usual turn, several of the men yawned. Maag, however, spurred him on. 'Come on, let's have it.'

Kern pretended reticence. The presence of Dorn inhibited him.

'Why, you can see by his nose that he hasn't lost his sex yet,' Schnurrbart drawled. 'He just boasts. He's so bad at it he lives from hand to p———.'

'Hell to you!' Kern snapped, enraged. 'If you'd had all the sex I've had, you wouldn't have to.'

Maag looked enviously at him, recalling his one and only experience. He'd had a few drinks for courage, then gone to a whorehouse. He'd paid his money and the blonde girl had taken him to a small red-carpeted room. But something funny had happened to him there; when she pulled him down on her, all his excitement had evaporated and nothing she could do helped. He had lain with his head on her breasts, tears streaming down his face. Finally she had sent him home, keeping the money. Ever since he had been scared stiff it would happen again; he was always worrying about it. If the same thing ever happened to him with Monika, she'd be sure to find somebody else. Perhaps she had already done so. The idea made him sweat. He tried to distract himself, and looked at Kern who was just relating his latest adventure with a twenty-five-year-old war widow. The men listened with mingled fascination and scepticism. Dorn had turned away indifferently. Now he stood up brusquely and walked a few steps away, sitting down by a tree.

Schnurrbart had meanwhile begun distributing the soup among the mess-tins, measuring conscientiously and handing each man his portion as it was doled out. He looked around and asked: 'Where is Steiner?' Krüger shrugged. 'I don't know. The Professor isn't here either.' Maag jerked a thumb over his shoulder in the direction of the trees. 'They must be somewhere back there.' Hollerbach stood up and walked in the direction Maag had indicated. 'Extras for us,' Kern growled irritably. He had placed the mess-tin on his knee. He sniffed several times at the dark concoction and began carefully spooning it out. The soup was hot. He burned his mouth and cursed. 'Tastes like prussic acid,' he observed. Krüger grinned. 'Spill the muck off the top first,' he said.

'What muck?' Kern asked, examining the mess-kit suspiciously. Krüger shook his head. 'Can't he tell muck when he sees it. I wonder what kind of stuff he serves his guests back home.'

His professional pride slighted, Kern threw his head back and snarled: 'Shut your mouth!'

For a second Krüger looked at him in surprise. Then his face hardened. 'You want to make something of this?' he said calmly.

Kern stared into his icy eyes and suddenly felt frightened. He mumbled something indistinct and looked down at his mess-tin again. This time he discovered the layer of filth floating on the surface. Sickened, he dumped half the soup on the ground. 'Looks like spunk,' he mumbled.

'You should have skimmed it,' Maag advised. He was eating rapidly. But Kern had lost his appetite. Disgruntled, he placed the mess tin on the ground.

Hollerbach returned to the fire. 'What's up?' Kern asked him uneasily. The others lowered their mess tins. Hollerbach shrugged. 'I don't know. Steiner's gone off somewhere. Pasternack says Steiner walked off by him without saying a word.'

'Where to?' Krüger asked in perplexity.

Hollerbach sat down. 'The devil only knows.'

There was a moment's silence. The wet wood crackled in the fire and sent a rain of sparks spurting from the hole. Schnurrbart turned to Hollerbach. 'Where's the Professor?'

'He's asleep. Though he doesn't seem to be really asleep, Pasternack says.'

'Sick?' Schnurrbart asked with concern.

They fell silent. Schnurrbart scratched his neck, wondering. Probably another of Steiner's mad notions, he thought. Poking around now in the darkness, as usual.

'What'll we do?' Kern asked. He looked around helplessly at the men's gloomy faces. The thought that Steiner might not return terrified him. His glance fell upon Anselm's pale face; Anselm was staring over the fire at the trees beyond. They're all scared, Kern thought. When Steiner isn't here they're all scared. The realization intensified his own fear. 'Should we go looking for him?' he asked Schnurrbart.

Schnurrbart tossed a branch into the fire, sending up a shower of sparks. 'Where would you look for him!' he answered roughly. 'He'll be back. Anyway, you can relieve Pasternack,' he ordered Kern. 'And you,' he turned to Anselm, 'can relieve Zoll.'

'Why me?' Anselm asked rebelliously. He stared at each of them in turn. When his eyes met Krüger's, he saw the East Prussian suddenly lean to one side, pick up a dry stick of wood and toss it across the fire at him. Anselm avoided it only by throwing himself backward. With the stick clattering against a tree behind him, he jumped to his feet with a cry of rage. Krüger rose slowly. Something in his expression warned Anselm. His aggression died within him; Krüger was twice as strong as he. He contented himself with a glare of hatred and said to Kern: 'They feel important already.' Kern stood up without a word.

The men watched them walk off side by side into the encompassing darkness. Dietz turned reproachfully to Krüger, who was sitting down with a grin of complacency on his face. 'Why do you make trouble all the time?' he said gravely.

'Yes,' Hollerbach chimed in. 'Dietz is right; all this wrangling is disgusting. I should think we had other things to worry about——'

'Oh, shut up,' Krüger interrupted wrathfully. He was on edge and ready to fight even with Hollerbach.

Schnurrbart interfered. He put his hand on Krüger's shoulder. 'Cut it out now. It is sickening; as soon as Steiner is gone for ten minutes we go to pieces. Let's get some sleep now; there's a tough day ahead of us.'

Kern and Anselm stood some twenty yards away from the camp, talking in undertones. 'You don't know how fed up I am with all this nonsense,' Anselm muttered bitterly. 'I'd like to walk right out on them. But you wait, I'll get that boaster one of these days.'

Kern laughed spitefully. 'In the first place Krüger's too tough for you, and in the second place where would you go? To the Russians?'

'I'd like them a damn sight better than these damned boy-scouts,' Anselm replied.

Kern leaned against a tree and sighed. At regular intervals his stomach made protesting noises. I should have eaten that soup anyway, he thought. He was irked with himself now for not having overcome his disgust, and he began to feel sorry for himself. He took out his handkerchief and blew his nose loudly and lengthily. Anselm snapped at him: 'Don't make such a noise—we're on guard, you know.'

Clumsily Kern thrust the handkerchief back into his pocket. 'On guard against what?' he grumbled. 'Against the mosquitoes maybe?' His eyes probed the dark woods. 'Who's supposed to relieve us, anyway?'

'I'll wake Krüger,' Anselm offered maliciously.

Kern grinned. 'Won't he be pleased?' He paused. 'Is . . . he going to make corporal soon?'

'Of course, he and Schnurrbart; their turn comes up at the next promotions. Listen, when they get to be N.C.Os. we can pull in our tails. They're all alike. Rank goes right to their heads; that's the way it is from bottom to top. It stinks. The whole damned army stinks.' Anselm fell silent and shifted his carbine to the other shoulder. He felt very strongly about the whole matter, but found it hard to think of the right words to express his feelings. For a while he listened to the fading concert of the frogs. It was a sad music. You just aren't treated like a human being, he thought. That was it; 'They' didn't think you were human. You were just cannon-fodder for them to order around, and you couldn't do anything about it. Not a thing. His despondency deepened.

Meanwhile Kern stood gazing moodily between the trees. A light breeze had sprung up. It shook the branches, and Kern hunched his shoulders anxiously. He envied the other men who were lying by the fire and sleeping. When you were asleep you didn't know you were afraid, he thought. You could close your eyes and draw the blanket up over your head as he used to do at home during thunderstorms. His teeth suddenly chattered so loudly that Anselm exclaimed: 'What's the matter with you?'

Kern hurriedly clasped his chin. 'Nothing, nothing at all,' he murmured. 'I'm just cold from standing around.' He wagged his head from side to side. 'It's weird, you know. When you start to think about it: here we are in the middle of the woods, right in the middle of the Russian army.'

His fear provoked a giggle from Anselm. With an immense feeling of superiority he recalled that Kern had come to the front only two weeks ago. 'It's not so bad,' he declared superciliously, 'I've been through this kind of thing for ten months now—why, it'll be a year soon. We've been in spots ten times worse than this,' he boasted. When Kern remained silent and depressed, Anselm slapped him on the back. 'By the day after tomorrow we'll be all right,' he said reassuringly.

His confident tone did nothing to convince Kern. The innkeeper continued to peer fearfully into the unrelieved darkness. 'One way or another we're for trouble anyway, I tell you,' he said.

His plaintive tone increased Anselm's sense of superiority. 'Now look here,' he said patronizingly, 'you and I haven't got along so well until now, but I tell you, if we want to we can be pretty good friends. We'll come out of this all right.' His voice took on a confidential note. 'Let me tell you, the friendships you make at the front last a lifetime. I'll come to see you some time after the war, with my girl, I mean. We can spend our vacation at your place.' He grew enthusiastic at the idea. 'We'll take a room at your place. A double room. Boy, it's a shame I didn't know you before the war. A fellow gets too old for going to the park. And no chance for anything at home; you know the old lady keeps her eyes open. The old man, too. They watch one like a hawk.' He went on talking zestfully, and Kern listened patiently to his fantasies. . . . An hour later, when they went to wake Krüger, Steiner was not yet back.

Dietz and Hollerbach were the last to stand sentry. During the night Schnurrbart had given orders that if Steiner were not back by four o'clock all the men should be awakened. It was twenty minutes to four when Steiner appeared among the trees. Hollerbach spotted him first. He lowered his rifle and stared in mingled anger and relief into Steiner's exhausted face. 'Where did you go to?' he asked reproachfully. Steiner ignored the question. He nodded to Dietz and walked past the sentries. His incisive voice roused the men. They scrambled up, rubbing their faces sleepily. When they realized it was Steiner, they thronged around him, hurling questions. Quietly, he lit a cigarette. Schnurrbart studied his face; in spite of the darkness he could make out Steiner's expression, and his fear instantly took flight. The questioning gradually subsided as Steiner continued to say nothing, until at last there was silence. Schnurrbart cleared his throat. 'Are we going?' he asked.

Steiner nodded. Schnurrbart knew him too well to ask anything more. He turned without a word and began assembling his pack. Krüger followed his example, while the rest stood around indecisively. 'Hurry up,' Steiner said. They looked at him blankly until Schnurrbart, who was already buckling the straps on his pack, called out: 'Get ready.' Hesitantly, the men began to move, angrily rolling up their blankets, tramping about heavy-footed.

They gathered in a group, shivering in the morning chill. Grey light trickled through the dense foliage above them, giving their faces a hollow, ghostly appearance. 'Now for a cup of warm coffee,' Anselm said, his teeth chattering.

'I'd like a warm belly better,' Zoll remarked.

Maag turned toward him inquisitively. 'A woman's.'

'Think I'm a pansy?' Zoll growled.

Krüger chuckled. 'Everything in its proper time and place,' he said. 'When we get back to the company, they'll send you to a whorehouse for a two-weeks rest cure.'

'Rest-cure in a whorehouse!' Anselm grinned scornfully. 'Just as likely as you going ski-ing on the North Sea.'

'You got anything against it?' Krüger demanded belligerently. 'If I decide to go ski-ing on the North Sea, it's none of your bloody business.'

'Kiss your arse,' Anselm retorted.

The East Prussian took a step closer to him. 'What did you say?'

Steiner took two big strides and came between them. 'Cut that out!' he said sharply. 'If you have any extra energy, you'll have plenty of chances to use it up today.' He looked around. 'Where's the Professor?'

The men looked crestfallen. They had not noticed that Dorn was missing. 'He didn't seem to be feeling well last night,' Hollerbach said. 'I'll go and see.'

'Where is he?' Steiner asked.

Hollerbach turned toward the trees. Steiner followed him. The Professor was still lying where Hollerbach had last seen him. He had drawn the blanket over his head and seemed to be asleep. 'Get up!' Hollerbach said, shaking him vigorously by the shoulder.

The blanket was thrown back and Dorn's sleepy face emerged. 'What's up?' he asked.

'We're going on,' Hollerbach said. 'Feeling better?'

Dorn sat up, brushing his hair back from his forehead. 'I think my cramps are gone—I didn't sleep most of the night,' he said in extenuation.

The others had drawn near. Before anyone could ask Dorn how he felt, Steiner spoke. 'There's a dirt road about five miles from here. The road leads to a bridge; by the bridge are three houses; and there are Russians in the houses. That's all.'

The men stared at him, too surprised to speak. Schnurrbart recovered first, for he had been expecting some sort of surprise. Swallowing hard, he asked: 'How many Russians?'

Steiner tapped the barrel of his tommy-gun impatiently against the tip of his boot. 'Since we've got to cross that bridge, it doesn't matter how many there are.'

'What do you mean?' Krüger interposed. 'If there's a regiment posted there, it would be mad to start anything with them.'

'It would be madder to imagine that a regiment of Russians have been quartered in three houses—actually they're little more than log huts. They must be either a guard for the bridge or a column passing through. At any rate their maps are better than ours or the road would be marked on my map. Let's go. And hang on to your ammunition boxes. We're going to need them.'

It had grown considerably lighter during the past few minutes. Slender shafts of light came through the leaves of the trees like jets of so many invisible fountains. Above the tree-tops birds broke into a wild morning concert. Pasternack, walking last in the line, thought of the fairy-tales his father used to tell. Most of them were set in forests, and these, as he had imagined them, were much like this one. After his father's death in the mine, the family had had a hard time of it. He was the oldest of seven, three boys and four girls. His mother was away all day, working as a cleaning woman. A quiet woman who seldom smiled and who bore her misfortune as if it were a distinction. On Sundays she would wash the children with special care, dress them in the best of their patched clothes, and take them to the cathedral. There she often cried. Once, when he had asked her why she cried in church, she had said: 'Other people leave an offering in the box; I have nothing to leave but tears.' And she had begun to cry again. The memory saddened him. He forgot where he was, no longer felt the painful tug of the ammunition boxes, the scraping of his belt against his hip, the pressure of the rifle slung over his shoulder. Staring down at the ground, he put one foot ahead of the other as he had already done for thousands of miles, and he moved along between the melancholy memories of the past and the gloomy prospects of the future without being fully aware of his grief.

At the head of the line, a few yards behind Steiner, Schnurrbart and Krüger were talking. They spoke in low voices, occasionally glancing suspiciously in all directions, although there was little to see; the brush became thicker as they advanced.

'Shit!' Krüger spat on the forest floor and peered up at the leaves, trying to see through to the sky. 'Think it will rain today?' Schnurrbart shrugged. 'I doubt it. It'll probably be the same as yesterday.'

'Shit, anyhow!' Krüger stated. 'It doesn't matter one way or the other.' His stubborn pessimism made Schnurrbart smile. 'Old grumbler,' he said. He hitched up his belt and glanced at Krüger's unshaven face. 'You look like a hog,' he said affectionately. Krüger ran his hand over his chin and grinned. 'Take a look at yourself. You're in a fine position to talk.' He turned his eyes ahead and shouted: 'Slow down there, think I'm an express train?' Steiner stopped and waited for them. 'Don't yell around here,' he snapped. 'You might scare the Russians away.'

Krüger swore under his breath. They walked on together. 'How far is it now?' Schnurrbart asked, wiping the sweat from his face.

Steiner glanced at his watch. 'About thirty minutes.'

'To the road?'

'Yes.'

'And then?'

'Then we cross the bridge.'

Dully, they marched on. Steiner held to a slower pace and stopped occasionally to listen. Each time he did so the men looked up uneasily. They spoke little. The silence of the woods seemed to radiate menace; they felt the danger like a pain that transformed their senses into supersensitive instruments. Anselm walked behind Schnurrbart. Although it was still cool here beneath the trees, he felt his shirt sticking wetly to his back. His thoughts hovered on the edge of a dark chasm; every moment he expected to hear the sudden crackle of a Russian tommy-gun.

Once he glanced back and saw behind him Dorn's pale face. The awareness that Dorn was frightened too only intensified his own fear. This damned forest, he thought, this damned forest. The noise Steiner made as he broke a path through a clump of bushes sounded like an infernal din. If the Russians don't hear that, they're deaf, he thought. For a while he tried to imagine what it would feel like to be wounded. Only not in the belly, he thought, anything but that. He pictured himself lying on the ground, writhing, while the others ran away. 'Jesus, Mary and Joseph,' he whispered. Perhaps he should have prayed before going to sleep last night. Once upon a time he had prayed consistently. His parents were deeply religious and went to church every Sunday in spite of the Party's opposition. His parents had insisted on his attending mass and taking communion as they did. He'd been a good boy until he was seventeen, until he met Gertrude. She was three years older than he, a tall girl with long legs. It wasn't that he had wanted to. It had just come over him all at once. He could still remember her gesture, the way she had pulled her skirt up over her knees, saying she wanted to get a tan. And then she had just reached out, and pulled him toward her so suddenly that it took his breath away. And then . . . he swallowed hard as he remembered.

The first time he had confessed, of course. But then confession had become harder and harder, and finally he no longer bothered. After a while he gave up praying, too. For the first time in years this struck him as a sin. Gertrude had not been the only girl. There were Hildegard and Gisela and Christa. Though it hadn't worked out with Christa. She came from a good family, with a religious background. When he had tried, she had simply run away. . . .

Despite his present, repentant state of mind he grew angry even now as he thought of it and for a moment he even forgot his fear. The silly goose, he thought indignantly, why did she follow him into the woods at all? Did she think he wanted to catch glow-worms with her? 'After the wedding,' she had said. When could they have married? After the war, perhaps, in the mass-grave? Oh, all that nonsense! If two people wanted to, they should go ahead, church or no church. In fact, it was all their fault. If 'they' had not been so stubborn, he would have continued praying and going to confession and everything would have been all right. Oh, well, he thought, when I am home again I shall go back to confession and just leave out the part about the women. Perhaps he would start praying again, too. All one had to do was to survive this mess. The thought relieved him. Until now he had not missed anything he could not catch up on afterwards. And why should something happen to him, of all the many men. He had been in Russia for a long while, and he had survived worse situations.

There was a halt at the head of the line. Steiner had stopped. The forest floor here was covered with tall fern. Steiner looked at his watch. Krüger asked: 'What's up?'

'We're at the road,' Steiner said. Seeing the bewilderment on their faces, he jerked his thumb toward a fringe of brush ahead. 'It's just behind that. Sit down; you'll want to know how we're going to do this thing.'

'Hope nobody can hear us here,' Schnurrbart said. He sat down beside Steiner. The other sprawled in a semi-circle around them.

'It's another hundred yards over to the road,' Steiner said. 'If you talk as low as I am doing now, nobody can hear.' He sounded mellow.

'All right, let's have it,' Schnurrbart said.

'It's fairly easy,' Steiner began, puffing at his cigarette. 'The main thing is to make certain none of the Russians gets away. The houses are on this side of the bridge. If we can take the other side at once, we'll have them between us. Half of us will wait on the edge of the woods. No prisoners are to be taken. Clear?'

'Hmm——' Schnurrbart nodded speculatively. 'Might work. With a little luck we ought to make it.'

'Good,' Steiner said. Now that the critical moment was upon them, his impatience had vanished. If there were no complications, they would have the bridge in their hands within twenty minutes. He turned to Dorn. 'How's your stomach, Professor?'

His voice sounded almost friendly, and Dorn looked at him in astonishment. Harder and harder to know what to make of him. 'Thanks, the pain is gone.' Steiner reached into his pack, took out a flat bottle and handed it across Schnurrbart's legs to Dorn. 'Have a drink—it's vodka.' Mechanically, Dorn drank off the bottle. He coughed and made a face. 'Strong medicine,' he said gratefully.

Steiner grinned as the bottle was handed back to him. 'But it helps. If you'd mentioned the matter yesterday, you could have spared yourself a sleepless night.' He returned the bottle to his pack.

Krüger had been watching jealously. Suddenly, he thrust both hands under his belt and put on a pitiable expression of pain. 'Oh,' he moaned. 'My stomach's gone to hell too.' The men laughed softly. Steiner did not even grin. 'Go and have a shit,' he said brutally.

Anselm giggled spitefully. 'He's got his breeches full already,' he said, grinning at Krüger's angry face.

Krüger turned toward him swiftly. 'I'll shut your big mouth for you, my boy.'

'You'll need another hundred men for that?' Anselm said. He was surprised at his own bravado, but he knew that Steiner would not permit a fight.

Sure enough, Steiner intervened. 'Wait till we're out of here. I don't give a damn what you do to each other once we're back with the battalion.'

Krüger grinned at Anselm. 'All right,' he said.

Steiner stood up quickly. 'Let's go. Don't forget that anyone who is wounded is going to lie where he falls. We can't drag anyone along with us.' He chose the words deliberately, and he could see that they took effect.

When they reached the road a few minutes later, Steiner stopped and waited until the last man had come up. Schnurrbart looked around him, shaking his head. The road was about six feet wide and ran straight east and west. At this point it was lined on both sides by high bushes. 'Why couldn't we have found it yesterday?'

Dietz uttered a low cry. 'Look,' he said, 'tracks.'

Schnurrbart stooped. 'Wheel tracks, and still fresh. How many are there?'

The wheels of the vehicles had sunk deep into the soft ground. Exposed tree roots had been scoured clean by sharp rims and there were innumerable impressions of unshod horses' hoofs in the mossy ground. Schnurrbart straightened up. 'Three wagons, horse-drawn. There are some footprints too, but it's hard to make out how many. In any case, it can't have been too large a force.'

'Enough to give us a hero's death,' Kern growled.

Schnurrbart grinned. He turned to Krüger, who enterprisingly tapped the butt of the machine-gun against the ground. There was a metallic click as Steiner took out the magazine of his tommy-gun.

They watched him check the magazine and then replace it. Silently, they inspected their own weapons. Krüger put a cartridge-belt into the machine-gun; Zoll helped him and then slung several belts of ammunition around his neck where they would be handy. They began moving cautiously toward the invisible bridge. The bushes on either side of the road grew denser. The ground steamed; birds twittered in the trees, and the sun cast diagonal beams of light through the leaves.

Zoll had removed his glasses. As he walked, he tried to avoid stepping on any of the withered leaves strewn all over the ground. He kept telling himself that he was not afraid, but he could not overcome a queasiness in his stomach. It hampered his walking. From his clothes a repulsive stench rose to his nostrils. As he moved along, eyes fixed on his feet, he noticed the small patches of sunlight on the ground; they changed shape, expanded and contracted each time the leaves stirred over head. Sometimes a shaft of light would dart like a silver arrow across the road. He recalled a game he had played with other boys years ago. On a hike through the woods they had arranged a race in which none of the runners was allowed to step on the spots of sunlight. Strange that he should be thinking of this game right now. If I don't step on a spot of sunlight before we halt again, I'll come through all right, he thought. He became so obsessed with this idea that for a while he forgot the impending attack on the bridge. He found a pretext for standing still until the last man had passed him. Then he followed, his attention concentrated on the ground. In the next five minutes he crossed the road a dozen times, now taking mincing little steps, now jumping or skipping to avoid a band of sunlight. The ammunition boxes weighed him down. He began sweating, but did not notice. He was so absorbed in his game that he ignored everything else.

Steiner, happening to glance back, noticed Zoll's strange progress. He left Schnurrbart in the lead and stood still. Zoll was on the point of jumping over a broad strip of light when their eyes met. His intended jump became a halting step that carried him right into the middle of the sunlit band. Zoll's glance shifted rapidly from Steiner's immobile face to his foot, which still trod the same spot. I'm done for, he thought. He felt paralysed with terror. A few seconds passed while both men stood motionless. Finally Steiner asked: 'What's the idea?' His cool voice brought Zoll to his senses. He raised his head slowly and stared into those unfriendly eyes. Steiner repeated his question: 'What's the idea?' For the space of a few heartbeats Zoll fought the temptation to drop his ammunition boxes and fall upon Steiner with flailing fists. But Steiner had the tommy-gun crooked in his arm; only a motion and the barrel would be pointing at him. Slowly, with bowed head, Zoll walked by him, gradually increasing his pace.

When he had come level with Dorn, Steiner trotted past him and took the lead again. Zoll was still quivering with rage and disappointment. That skunk, he thought, that rotten skunk. He could hardly restrain his tears. While he automatically trudged ahead, he tried to adjust to the idea that he would be killed in the attack on the bridge. It gave him a certain amount of pleasure to imagine himself the centre of a dramatic event. Marching along behind Dorn in a haze of muddled thoughts, he began ransacking his mind for the memorable happenings of his twenty-five years. He felt like a man who is being compelled by financial reverses to part with precious belongings, and who examines each article in turn with love and pain. Suddenly Dorn stopped.

'What's the matter?' Zoll asked, startled out of his sombre meditations. Then he saw the men clumped together on the right side of the road, watching Steiner cautiously negotiate what seemed to be a turn in the road. Steiner vanished for a moment, then reappeared and beckoned to them.

'How does it look?' Krüger asked.

'We're there,' Steiner whispered. 'It's about a hundred yards to the bridge—and it's guarded.' The men exchanged anxious glances. 'We'll stick to the plan. Krüger sets up the machine-gun on the edge of the woods. Dorn, Dietz, Zoll and'—he hesitated for a moment, studying their faces—'and Pasternack stay with Krüger and see that no one gets out of the windows. The doors are on the other side. The rest will come with me. Don't fire until I start. Keep your heads behind the trees. If I see that we can't silence them all, I'll send up a flare. That's the sign for everyone to dash across the bridge as far as he can run. If the worst comes to the worst, we'll set fire to the houses over their heads. Let's go.' He crossed the road and started into the bushes. They moved forward very slowly, crawling most of the way. After a while the underbrush thinned out, but it still offered some cover.

When they topped a small rise in the ground, they saw the buildings in front of them: three one-storey houses made of massive logs, all on the right side of the road. Above the slate roofs rose two chimneys from which dark smoke mounted into the cloudless sky. The creek flowed parallel to the row of houses; here, too, its banks were overgrown with shoulder-high reeds which swayed gently in the wind. The bridge was close by the first house, a primitive but wide wooden bridge with rails on both sides. In the centre, leaning against the narrow slats of the railing, stood the guard—an elderly man with a yellow, wrinkled face. His cap was pushed back on his head and he was staring dully at the dirty surface of the water. His tommy-gun was slung diagonally across his back.

For a while the men lay motionless. Then Schnurrbart crawled over to Steiner and whispered: 'Funny business. I don't like this silence.' He glanced at the three wagons which stood near the long side of the middle house, their contents concealed under dark-brown canvas. 'Funny business,' he repeated suspiciously.

Steiner glanced irritably at him. 'What's funny about it? The rest of them are still snoozing. We'll wake them up soon enough.'

'I don't know,' Schnurrbart murmured. 'There's something in the air.' He paused a moment. 'The house on the right seems empty; the chimney isn't smoking and the shutters are closed.'

What mattered now was to determine where the horses were. The horses could not be inside the buildings, nor behind them. If they had been stabled elsewhere, there must be a guard with them. He had not thought of that before. If the man guarding the horses succeeded in escaping, there would be the devil to pay. As long as their presence behind the Russian lines was unknown, it was not half as bad. Once the Russians found out, there'd be hundreds of men beating the bushes for them. But how could he track down the horses. Searching at random through the woods would be dangerous and time-consuming. They would just have to take the risk.

He looked again at the Russian guard, who had not changed his position. Then he turned his head slightly and whispered: 'Get ready!' A suppressed moan arose from the men. They stared fixedly at the bridge.

A few yards behind Steiner lay Dorn, his chin propped on his left forearm and his eyes narrowed to slits. For the past few minutes he had been afflicted with a torpor that smothered all feeling. He saw Steiner lifting the tommy-gun and then he threw a rapid glance at Dietz, who lay beside him and suddenly began to shake violently. The boy's teeth chattered audibly. Dorn felt tempted to close his eyes, press his face into the damp moss and just lie still, ignoring whatever happened. But instead he touched Dietz's arm reassuringly. As if through a curtain he saw Steiner sighting upon the man on the bridge. He tried to think of his wife. But each time he had almost summoned up her face, the outlines of it grew vague, like smoke rings dissolving in a sudden draught. He gave up trying. Then he suddenly recalled what Professor Stahl had said to him in parting: 'You have been an excellent teacher; I hope you will be just as good a soldier. But you must go into it without illusions.'

Dorn smiled bitterly. With a curious sense of remoteness he saw the barrel of Steiner's tommy-gun jerk a little higher. The whipping round of shots reached his ear without arousing in him the usual sense of horror. The man on the bridge started to move as though he were standing upon a whirling disc. Then his hands gripped the wooden railing for support, his legs sagged as though the sinews had been slashed, and he slid, knees first, underneath the railing and into the dirty water, which reached up to the stringers of the bridge. At the same moment the machine-gun began to chatter. Steiner leaped to his feet and raced with giant strides toward the bridge. Close behind him ran Schnurrbart and the others. When they reached the bridge, they threw themselves on the ground and immediately began firing at the doors of the huts, until Steiner changed his magazine and cried out: 'Stop!' There was a sudden stillness. Krüger, too, had stopped firing. The men looked around questioningly. Several minutes passed. Nothing stirred inside the houses. Steiner muttered: 'What do you make of that?' Schnurrbart shook his head in bewilderment.

Cursing under his breath, Steiner straightened up somewhat and stared blackly at the silent houses. 'I thought there was something fishy from the start,' Schnurrbart declared. Suspiciously, he regarded the silent woods across the bridge. Then he turned to Steiner again: 'What are we going to do?'

Steiner did not answer for a moment. Had a single shot been fired from the houses, his next steps would have followed automatically. But this uncanny silence put him in a cold sweat. He glanced down at his hands and saw that they were shaking. 'We have to break in,' he said. 'If there's so much as a mouse inside there, we've got to make it squeak.'

The others were still lying on the ground, white-faced. 'Get up!' he roared at them. They rose cautiously to their feet. Steiner gripped Anselm's arm. 'You go over there to Krüger. Tell him to post a guard at once about a hundred yards back along the road. Then hurry back here, cross the bridge and stand guard on the other side another hundred yards back in the woods. If a single Russian comes along, kill him; if there are more, run for it and report to me. Got it?'

Anselm nodded and began running back. Steiner turned to Maag. 'You and Kern run past the houses now. Duck your heads; we'll fire to cover you. Run as far as the last house and see whether there are any doors or windows on the north sides. If there are, see to it that nobody comes out. Get going.'

'On this side?' Kern asked.

'Of course. If you run on the other side, I won't be able to see what's happening.' He turned to Schnurrbart. 'Fire high—I'll take the first house, you the second and Hollerbach the third. Get ready!'

Kern and Maag started toward the houses. They moved leadenly. Steiner shouted: 'Speed!' They began running. When the three behind them started firing above their heads at the windows, they dropped to the ground. Steiner cursed. 'Those idiots!' he raged, and shouted: 'Get up. That's us, you idiots; we're covering you.' He waved his hand reassuringly toward Kern, who was glancing back anxiously. Behind his back, Schnurrbart and Hollerbach suppressed a giggle. Hollerbach said: 'Those tin soldiers.' They watched as Maag, too, raised his head and looked back. Seeing Steiner point the tommy-gun menacingly at him, he stood up quickly and began running on. Kern stayed on the ground a few seconds more; then he, too, rose and stumbled behind Maag. 'Do we fire?' Schnurrbart asked.

Steiner shook his head impatiently. 'Those idiots will think it's the Russians again. Anyway, they're all right now.' The two had already reached the last of the buildings. As they disappeared around the corner, Steiner wiped the sweat from his forehead. Although they had had no trouble at all up to now, he was filled with forebodings. Schnurrbart was right; there was something fishy here. The Russians couldn't be giving up without a fight. Minutes passed. He stared again at the houses standing green-shuttered, quiet and peaceful in the morning sunlight. At that moment a volley of shots rang out from the north side of the house, where Kern and Maag must be.

When they reached the end of the third house, Kern and Maag had looked around them quickly. The building had no doors or windows on this side. Kern sighed with relief. He leaned his back against the stout logs and said: 'Nothing here. What'll we do now?'

Maag suspiciously eyed the woods, which began about fifty feet away. 'I don't know,' he said hesitantly. 'We'd better wait here. If Steiner wants us to do something, he'll tell us.' He crouched down on the ground, groped forth a pack of cigarettes from his pocket and handed it to Kern. They said nothing until both cigarettes were lit. Then Kern pushed his cap back on his head. Sighing, he said: 'I wonder what's going to happen next?'

'We'll find out soon enough,' Maag replied gloomily. His freckled face twisted into a grimace. 'I tell you, this thing stinks like limburger cheese.'

Maag again eyed the edge of the woods. How many times he had gone into the edge of dense woods just like these, on Sundays, with his girl, of course. He could see her now. She had a red dress she wore often. He recalled how he would tremble when they sat down anywhere, she with her long tanned legs folded beneath her. He would lie on his stomach and talk to distract his attention from her legs, while Monika regarded him with a faint smile. Still, she said she liked his self-control. Once she had given him a long kiss and remarked that he was the first boy she knew who didn't lose his head right away. He had swallowed the compliment like a soldier receiving an undeserved medal. What would Monika have said, he wondered, if she knew the real reason for his restraint. He had to do something about that. When the war was over, he'd go to a doctor, to a specialist in mental things. He didn't want to lose Monika. Though it would be a long time before they'd be in a position to get married. Maybe he would own his own garage some day. If it weren't for this damned war, he'd be on his way now. He sighed again. The time a man lost, all on account of those bastards, those stinkers with their goddamned war.

Thinking of all these things, he stared into space. When Kern suddenly gripped his arm, he looked up angrily. 'What's the matter, what the devil do you want——' The outburst faded.

Kern's face was chalky white. The innkeeper was staring in terror at the woods. 'Do you see him?' he stammered. His fear was contagious; Maag was frightened too. 'What?' he whispered, peering at the trees but seeing nothing unusual. 'Russians,' Kern whispered. Maag threw himself forward on his stomach and raised his rifle. 'Where, where the devil do you see them?' But Kern was so worked up he could not say another word. He pointed silently at a spot on the edge of the woods where the underbrush was particularly dense. Maag stared intently at it. He could feel his heart beating in short, hard thrusts, and tried to master his excitement. Once or twice he thought he detected movement among the branches, but each time he fixed his eyes upon a particular spot, he became unsure. Finally he turned to Kern, who lay beside him, 'You're imagining things.'

But Kern shook his head violently. 'I saw it, I tell you—a head with a cap, a Russian cap.'

'Where, damn it?'

'Right in front of us. Over there by the crooked tree, where the branches are hanging low.'

'Near the reeds?'

'No, further to the right, over—there he is again—do you see him?' Kern's voice broke with excitement. Maag raised himself a little and immediately dropped back flat on the ground. Kern was not mistaken. Above the bushes, close to the trunk of a twisted alder, he could distinctly make out the face of a man staring steadily in his direction. It was impossible to tell whether the man had sighted them, but Maag had the feeling that the Russian was looking straight into his eyes. For a few seconds he lay paralysed, torn between the desire to jump up and run and the feeling that this would be bad for the whole platoon. Kern's fear intensified his own uncertainty.

As he slowly raised his rifle, he was acting against his will. Seen through the gunsight, the Russian's face looked like a white spot in the greenness of the wood. Maag lowered the barrel slightly. His finger tightened on the trigger. Then he fired. The shot screamed in the unnatural silence. As he shot again, he saw out of the corners of his eyes Kern raising his rifle and beginning to fire. Wildly, heedlessly, they both fired their magazines empty, turned on their sides, opening their ammunition pouches, reloaded with trembling fingers, and again fired like mad. The Russian's face had long since disappeared. Before they could load again, Steiner appeared. He came rushing around, threw himself on the ground beside them and raised his tommy-gun. 'What's up?' he shouted. Maag lowered his rifle and stammered: 'R-R-Russians.'

'Where?'

'Over there.'

'How many?'

'I saw one.'

'And?'

'I don't know,' Maag murmured uncertainly. 'He's gone now.'

Steiner turned to Kern, who had meanwhile reloaded and was raising his rifle again. 'What are you banging away at?'

'Russians,' Kern responded eagerly. Dimly inside him his fear still resounded like an echo. But now that Steiner was here, he felt more confident. Grinning, he said, 'We gave it to him.'

'Did you?' Steiner said. He stood up slowly and looked scornfully down at the innkeeper. But Kern did not notice. He had suddenly become aware of how courageously he had fired into the woods. The others couldn't have done any better, he told himself. The thought filled him with pride. After all, this war business wasn't half bad. Keep on your toes, and you were all right. You just had to show the Russians you weren't afraid of them. His fear gave way to almost hysterical high spirits. He looked up at Steiner, who was now regarding him with absolute malignance.

'You're the biggest fool I ever came across. Get up.'

Offended, Kern stood up and looked at Maag, who was fussing with his rifle and glancing uncertainly at the edge of the woods. 'Come along,' Steiner ordered. He started moving carefully toward the trees. They followed him at a considerable distance.

After some searching, Steiner found the Russian. He lay among the undergrowth, holding both hands pressed against his waist, bulging eyes resting on Steiner, who paused a few steps away from him and studied him thoughtfully. Kern and Maag came up to him. When they saw the Russian, they stopped in alarm. Maag regained poise first. 'We got him,' he said with satisfaction. 'I thought so. I aimed carefully.' Kern glowered at Maag and was about to say something, but Steiner did not give him the chance. He stepped closer to the Russian, who watched each of his movements in fear. This one, too, was an elderly man. Their last reserves, Steiner thought. He looked around for the Russian's gun until he noticed it lying half-concealed among the branches of a bush. Then he turned to Maag. 'You did enough shooting to kill a regiment. But it's good you got the man. Go and bring Krüger back here with you. The others are to stay at their posts.'

Maag hurried off, while Kern stood staring uncomfortably down at the Russian. He suddenly felt sorry for the old man, who lay helplessly on the ground, his face clenching with pain now and then. His eyes were still fixed upon Steiner who was indifferently studying the Russian tommy-gun. I wonder what he's going to do with him? Kern thought. Lousy business sending old men like this up to the front. Maag must have hit him; I was just firing into the air. The thought relieved him. It was rotten to feel you'd killed someone, especially when it was a sorry-looking old bird like this. He turned his head and saw Maag and Krüger approaching.

'What's up?' Krüger asked.

Steiner indicated the Russian. 'Ask him where he was.'

Krüger went up to the wounded man and spoke to him. He had to repeat his question twice before the man moved his lips. The Russian's voice was so faint and shaky that Krüger had to stoop down to him. When the man stopped talking, Krüger turned to Steiner. 'He says he was watching the horses.'

Steiner nodded, pleased. 'So I thought. That was the weak point in this deal. He must have heard the firing. Ask him if there are any more men with the horses.'

To Steiner's relief, the Russian shook his head. Steiner thrust a thumb into his belt. 'How many men are there in the houses?'

But this time the Russian did not reply. When Krüger translated the question, he closed his eyes and turned his head aside. Steiner frowned. He was acutely conscious of how much time was passing, and he decided to act quickly. In an icy voice he said: 'If he doesn't open his mouth, we'll hang him to a tree. Tell him that.'

Krüger spoke in an urgent, imploring voice to the old man. Finally he shrugged hopelessly. 'He won't say.'

Steiner took one long step up to the wounded man and held the muzzle of the tommy-gun against his forehead. 'He has to,' he said sternly. 'Ask him again.'

Krüger glanced at the other men's faces. The whole business sickened him, but he felt that there was no other way. He began expostulating with the Russian, illustrating his words with unmistakable gestures. The Russian slowly opened his eyes and turned his face toward Steiner, who was regarding him expressionlessly. As he spoke a few words, a brief smile passed over his wrinkled, parchment-like face.

'What is he saying?' Steiner asked.

Krüger jerked his shoulders irritably. 'He says he is an old man.'

'We can see that,' Steiner said calmly. 'Nothing more?'

'No.'

'Did you tell him we'll shoot him?'

Krüger nodded.

For the space of a few heartbeats Steiner was conscious of admiration for the old man. He felt how dry his mouth was. His finger was resting on the trigger guard of the tommy-gun, but he hesitated. When he closed his eyes and pulled the trigger, he did so with the sensation of a person who is tearing a scrap of skin from a bruise, skin that hangs only by a thread. The shot sounded low, as though he had thrust the barrel of the gun into the ground. The Russian's body heaved up. The whites of his eyes bulged out, his feet beat a tattoo on the ground, and then he abruptly lay still. Steiner looked at the white faces of the men and turned around without a word. When they reached the house, he said to Krüger: 'Go back to your gun. Don't let anyone out of the windows, remember. We're going to see these places from the inside.'

As they moved around the corner, they pressed close to the wall of the house. At the bridge, Hollerbach and Schnurrbart were waiting for them, peering anxiously. When Steiner raised his hand and beckoned, they came rushing, doubled up, past the houses. 'What was it?' Schnurrbart asked.

Steiner explained.

'And now?'

'Now we're going in.' Steiner turned to Hollerbach. 'You stay out here. With your tommy-gun you can command all the doors and windows from the side. Make sure nobody gets away.' He gave Hollerbach the Russian tommy-gun he had picked up. 'Take this one; it's better than ours.' He turned to the others, who were pressed close against the wall of the house, and seemed content to stay right there. 'Don't fire unless you see something, and don't run unless I give the order.'

Kern rubbed his cheek excitedly. 'And if you fa——' He corrected himself quickly—'I mean, if something should happen to you?'

Steiner stared him down. 'In that case Schnurrbart will carry on; but don't worry, I won't give you the pleasure.' As Schnurrbart started to protest, Steiner cut him off with a wave of his hand.

'Aren't we awful few for the job?' Maag asked hollowly.

'No. In the houses we'd only get in each other's way. A few hand grenades will do it.' As he spoke he drew a stick grenade from his belt. Turning, he ducked under the first window. Most of the glass had been smashed by their firing earlier. Crouching under the window, he pulled the pin on the grenade, rose quickly and threw it into the house. The others were still taking cover around the corner. Steiner heard the grenade thud to the floor; then he leaped to safety. There was a low, booming noise as though a heavy object had been dropped in a large, empty room. The men's tense poses relaxed. They watched Steiner run to the window, hesitate for a moment, and then slowly bring his face level with the empty window frame. For a few seconds he stared into the house; then he straightened up. 'Empty,' he said quietly, stepping back. Cautiously the others approached and peered through the splintered frame. Although the interior was in semi-darkness because of the closed shutters on the other windows, they could see at once that the big, rectangular room was vacant. It was utterly bare and the floor was covered with a thick layer of dust.

'I thought so,' Schnurrbart said. 'The chimney wasn't smoking.'

'But it was smoking in the other two,' Maag said.

Steiner turned to Hollerbach. 'Listen, you can come with me around the next corner. The range is shorter there. But there are only two houses left to worry about; that makes it easier.'

He started forward slowly. Suddenly he stopped. His tense expression was replaced by a look of utter incredulity. The men froze in their tracks. Steiner stood with head cocked, listening. Then he beckoned to the others, and they approached on tiptoe. They were only a few steps away from him when he raised his finger to his lips. From the house came low moans and sobs that were unmistakably the voices of women. Their faces went blank with astonishment. Schnurrbart opened his mouth, pinched his own arm and began rolling his head back and forth. 'I've gone crazy,' Maag stammered. Kern shook with silent laughter. He turned to Maag and gasped: 'Women!' Maag took a deep breath, his fear vanishing. He ran his tongue over his lips, half expectantly, half fearfully. 'Maybe it's a brothel,' he whispered. Kern grinned. Why not, he thought. Maybe the Russians have set up mobile brothels. In his enthusiasm he tugged at his pants and shifted his weight from one foot to the other.

Hollerbach shook his head in vexation. 'You're both nuts. Is that the first thing you think of?'

'Maybe it's a maternity hospital,' suggested Schnurrbart, who was the first to realize the humour of the situation. 'Boys, we've stormed a maternity hospital.'

'We'll get a maternity medal,' Kern gurgled joyously. He slapped Maag wildly on the back. Steiner threw him an angry look. 'Cut out the noise,' he said sharply. 'We don't know anything for sure yet.' He glared at all of them. 'You're acting like children. Wait and see where we stand first.'

He was far from charmed by the turn of events. The action he had been conducting in deadly earnest was turning out ridiculously. He felt that he had been made a fool of. As he approached the house, his face was set and mean. He took one leap up to the top step and shook the door latch. The sounds inside stopped. 'It might be a trap,' Schnurrbart whispered, raising his tommy-gun suspiciously.

Steiner continued to try the latch. 'Locked,' he said. 'Two hand grenades.'

Schnurrbart took two stick grenades from his belt, unscrewed the locking cap, and passed the grenades on to Steiner. 'Watch it,' Kern said anxiously, retreating a step. Steiner put a short loop of string through the rings and fastened them to the latch. Then he gestured with his head toward the corner of the house. They hastily took themselves off in that direction. When the last man had vanished, Steiner gave a powerful tug, pulling the two wooden sticks down. Then he let go of them.

The grenades dangled under the doorknob and began hissing like a tea kettle filled with boiling water. The men began to count: 'Twenty-two, twenty-three, twenty-four——' Steiner came rushing around the corner; the explosion followed immediately. The thunderous noise echoed and re-echoed from the woods, and was still ringing in their ears as they followed Steiner back to the steps, which were now littered with splinters of wood. The shattered door hung askew from one of the upper hinges. Schnurrbart kicked it in. Tensely, they peered into the room. It seemed to be a kind of entrance hall, at the back of which a miscellany of things were heaped. As their eyes became accustomed to the dim light, they saw two doors, one on either side of the hall. Steiner raised his gun. Slowly he moved across the threshold, followed closely by the men. Under their nailed boots the floorboards creaked. From outside, where the reeds rose high in the warm sunlight, a bird's cry sounded strangely loud and penetrating in the dusk of the room.

But suddenly there was another noise. Steiner halted and listened. At first it seemed to be coming from the back of the hall. It sounded like the hollow moan in a stove on a dark, rainy night, when the wind howls over roofs and chimney-tops. The moaning swelled in volume, then faded into soft sighs. Then again it seemed to be coming from above, to be trickling through the walls and filling the entire room. There was something horrible about it.

Steiner's eyes were narrowed to tiny slits. Vainly he tried to escape the hypnotic effect of those uncanny moans. While his mind persistently sent orders racing through his body, he was curiously outside of himself, aware of his own ego in all its helplessness. He seemed to be standing off from himself, just a few yards away, and observing his own weakness with the eyes of an outsider who had no way to interfere. Sweat ran down his face and dripped from his chin. He could feel himself oscillating wildly, painfully, between rage and shame. From some misty distance he heard Kern's voice stammering incomprehensible words. Then there was a thudding crash which abruptly brought the moaning and whimpering to a stop. Steiner reacted like a turbine revolving at high speed that is suddenly relieved of its load. He whirled around, caught a glimpse of Kern's rifle lying on the floor—that must have been the thud—and saw Kern spring to the door and rush out into the broad day-light. Schnurrbart and Maag were staring agape after him. The episode struck Steiner as so funny that he lost all control of himself. He suddenly began to laugh in a frightful manner. He doubled over, his body jerking in unnatural, ugly movements. And each time he raised his head, gasping for air, and saw the horrified faces of Schnurrbart and Maag, the abnormal laughter burst from him again. Schnurrbart tensed; he felt his nerves going to pieces. He glanced quickly at the door, where Hollerbach's alarmed face appeared. Hollerbach stood staring in bewilderment at the scene, gradually lowering his tommy-gun, which he had been holding ready to fire. 'Have you gone off your heads?' he bellowed. 'What the devil's the matter?'

The loudness of his voice rather than his words brought Steiner to his senses. He slung the gun over his shoulder and rubbed his face with his hands. Then he turned swiftly to the door on the left and opened it. It gave on a narrow room, one half of which was filled with a huge stove built of clay. From an iron rod above the flickering fire hung a soot-blackened kettle; the water was boiling over and falling hissing and steaming into the flames. There was a long table, on which cooking utensils stood, along the opposite wall. A few chairs and a bench completed the furniture. Steiner glanced over the room and turned around. He bumped into Schnurrbart, who was staring past him at the Russian pots and pans. The others also tried to see into the room. But Steiner pushed them ahead of him back into the hall and approached the opposite door. Just before he reached it he turned to Hollerbach. 'Where is Kern?' he asked.

Hollerbach grinned. 'I don't know. He raced past me toward the bridge.'

'Did he!' Steiner regarded him malignantly. His voice became a shade sharper. 'And where are you?'

Stunned, Hollerbach gaped at him. At first he thought it was a joke. But there was nothing but anger in Steiner's expression. Uncertainly, he answered: 'Right here—where do you think?'

'Right,' Steiner said fiercely. 'And where are you supposed to be?'

Hollerbach started. He suddenly realized that he was supposed to be standing outside, guarding the windows. He rushed out the doorway. Schnurrbart turned to Steiner and asked: 'What's the matter with you?'

'What do you mean?'

Schnurrbart hesitated. It was obvious that Steiner was behaving like a madman. The question was, should he tell him so. Perhaps it would be better not to at the moment. He shrugged: 'I only mean——' he began tentatively. Again he shrugged: 'Anyway, this business is beginning to get on my nerves. Did you see those pots?'

'I'm not blind,' Steiner answered curtly.

Maag had been witnessing the scene uneasily. He would have liked to have followed Kern out, but the favourable moment was gone now. With a worried look at the closed door, he said: 'I wish I knew what that queer howling was.'

Steiner said nothing. He was gnawed by the feeling that he had behaved like a woman. Twist and turn the thing whatever way you liked, the fact remained that his nerves had simply given out. It was the first time anything of the sort had ever happened to him. As he glared indecisively at the door, behind which the owners of those cooking utensils must be, he became aware that he was afraid. A few hours ago that would have seemed an impossibility. Now he was constrained to accept the fact and wonder why. Strangely, his recent conversations with Dorn came to mind. But before he could put it all together, Schnurrbart took the initiative. He had been watching Steiner in silence. But when minute after minute passed while Steiner stood utterly motionless, his patience gave out. He brushed Steiner aside, planted himself in front of the door, raised his tommy-gun, and fired the entire contents of the magazine at chest height through the planks. At the first shot Steiner had started. Now he stood watching almost indifferently as Schnurrbart pressed down the latch and shook it. The door was locked. Quickly Schnurrbart reloaded, took a step back, and fired at the lock. With the first few shots the door sprang open. Steiner slowly raised his gun, while Maag crouched against the wall. They stared at Schnurrbart who stood at the door slowly letting the barrel of his gun sink. He said a few words. Steiner slapped his left ear. The hammering of the tommy-gun in the narrow hall had left a droning in his head so that he could not hear. Schnurrbart had to repeat loudly, 'Come over here,' before he understood. They stepped up behind him. 'Take a look at that,' Schnurrbart said.

Steiner looked and swallowed hard. The entire long wall of the room was taken up by a heap of straw covered with blankets. In the corner opposite the door stood an old wardrobe chest. Crowded together in the rear half of the room, faces half-defiant, half-terrified, were a dozen women in Russian uniform. They carried no weapons. They stared fixedly at the men. When Steiner slowly entered the room, they moved closer together and their faces paled. At their feet, bedded down on the straw, lay a younger woman, the clothing stripped away from the upper part of her body and a blood-soaked bandage covering her right breast. Her eyes were closed, and as Steiner stepped forward she began to moan again. It was the same weird sound that had unnerved the men when they were outside in the hall. Steiner stopped in the middle of the room, as he looked down at the woman in amazement. So that was it, he thought; that had made him lose his nerve—a groaning woman, a. . . . Rage sent his thoughts scattering in all directions; he burned with shame. Schnurrbart, sensing his feelings, laid a hand on his arm. 'Keep your head, Rolf,' he said. 'It can happen to anybody. We're all of us on edge. Better let it be something like this than anything else. Now what do we do with them?'

His calmness was itself an affront. Steiner turned toward him and stared absently at him. Then he looked back at the women. Hoarsely, he said: 'What do you do with armed guerillas, male or female?'

'These are not guerillas,' Schnurrbart replied quietly. 'They're regular uniformed troops. Besides'—he grinned—'they have no arms.'

Steiner had recovered. 'If they belong to regular troops, we'll treat them as we must treat all prisoners in our situation.'

'You mean shoot them?' Schnurrbart gasped.

'Do you see any other way? If one of them escapes and gets to the Russian front before us, we're done for.'

Maag had recovered from his astonishment and spoke up. 'Steiner is right. The women must be killed.'

They stood in the middle of the room not knowing what to do. Schnurrbart irritably gnawed his lips. The idea of shooting women shocked him, and he tried to think of a better solution. Finally he turned to Steiner and suggested: 'We can tie them up. I mean, we could tie them and lock them in here.'

Steiner glowered scornfully at him. 'You've read too many cowboy and Indian stories. This is Russia, not the Wild West.' His voice took on a hysterical note. 'What are you going to tie them with? With their panties? Or their bras? And where are you going to lock them in? This place here has more holes than all the women put together. Cut the cackle. I'm going to——' He fell silent abruptly. His glance fell upon the woman lying on the straw. She had opened her eyes and these were fastened upon him now. Perhaps his loud words had roused her to consciousness. Her winsome oval face bore an expression of such wild horror that Steiner's rage evaporated. Quickly, he raised his eyes and looked

at the other women. They all looked about the same to him, with
Slav cheekbones and smooth black hair combed straight back.
A few of them had more delicate features, which gave their faces
a certain attractiveness. They wore the usual Russian uniform.
Their full blouses, reaching down over their hips, were gathered at
the waist by broad belts. They were big-breasted, stocky women
and the blouses made them look the more so. Their breeches were
tucked into high leather boots such as Russian officers wore.

Schnurrbart said: 'We better do something; the others will be
going crazy out there.'

Steiner nodded. He hung the tommy-gun from his shoulder.
'They'll go crazier when they see the women,' he said. 'Send
Krüger in to me. Add a man each to the guards on the road. Take
the rest into the next house and bring everybody who's in there
over here. Watch your step; there must be another man among
them.'

'How come?'

'Obvious. The two Russians we killed must have been the
drivers of the wagons, and there were three wagons.'

'Don't you want to go along?' Schnurrbart asked in surprise.

Steiner shook his head. He looked around. As Schnurrbart
went to the door, Steiner beckoned to Maag. 'You stay here,' he
ordered. 'We'll see what's the matter with the woman.' He went
up to the wounded woman. As he bent over her, he met her
frightened eyes. She tried to roll back against the wall. Steiner
held her firmly. 'Take it easy,' he said quietly. 'What do you think
I want to do?'

Carefully, he lifted the bandage. The wound was a big one and
looked bad. From nipple to waist there was a dark-brown rent in
the flesh almost an inch wide. When Steiner removed the bandage,
it began bleeding heavily. Thoughtfully, he looked down at her.
Then he ordered Maag to bring hot water. The other women had
not changed their position. They still stood close together against
the wall, fearfully watching each of his movements. As he stared
down at the woman's bleeding breast, he became aware of the
absurdity of his behaviour. He looked at her face; she had closed
her eyes again. Above her right eyebrow was a small scar. His
gaze moved down along the fine nose to the full mouth and
lingered finally on the uninjured half of her breast. It quivered
from the beating of her heart, and for seconds he felt tempted to

close both hands around that soft flesh. With each heartbeat the blood ran down along her narrow hips. An ugly stain on the woollen blanket was steadily spreading. When she opened her eyes again, he stooped down and asked: 'Are you in pain?' When she nodded, he knew she understood. 'The pain will be all over soon,' he said. Her face fell. She moved her lips without uttering a sound.

Maag returned and placed a bowl of hot water on the floor. 'That ought to do,' he said.

Steiner nodded. While he was busy cleaning the wound, Maag stood so that he could look on, but from a sense of shame he made sure the other women in the room could not see his face. Since the wound ran as far down as the waist, Steiner unbuttoned the woman's trousers and pushed them down a little. Maag suddenly began shaking. His voice sounded husky as he asked: 'Want help with this?' Without waiting for an answer, he put his hands on the woman's waist, loosening the clothes and as if without intention reaching his fingers down under the trousers. 'Stop that,' Steiner said sharply. For a second Maag could not decide how Steiner meant this. But he removed his fingers. His excitement was so intense that he could feel it with an almost voluptuous pain in every part of his body. Feverishly, he wondered how he could persuade Steiner to leave the room for a few minutes. He could think of no pretext. But he made up his mind to seize the first opportunity that offered. Before we kill the women, I'll have one of them, he thought. This was the chance of a lifetime. There was no risk of making himself ridiculous here, and if it went off all right he would be rid for ever of that damnable fear that he was impotent. How could he work it? It was now or never.

Steiner had meanwhile finished cleaning the wound. He took a first-aid kit from his pocket and began laying a medication compress on the wound. Just as he finished, he heard hasty footsteps outside and Krüger, Schnurrbart and Hollerbach came noisily into the room. Steiner glanced once more at the wounded woman. She had tilted her head to one side and was keeping her eyes closed. It looked as though she had lost consciousness again. That would be best for her, he thought. He turned to the men and asked: 'How is everything?'

'Fine,' Schnurrbart said, grinning. 'Thirteen women and the billygoat too. They're right outside.'

Steiner nodded. 'Did you have any trouble with them?'

'Not a bit. They were sitting on the floor, scared to death.'

'You should have given us the lowdown,' Krüger said, his eyes studying the women. His face was twitching and he kept pulling at his nose. 'We felt like we were sitting on hot coals.'

'With your thick hide I imagine you didn't even singe your arse.' Steiner suddenly remembered something. 'Where's Kern?'

The men exchanged meaningful glances. 'Hasn't turned up yet,' Krüger said after a momentary pause. 'We saw him running across the bridge like the devil was after him. Made us think they'd cooked your goose in here. What's the matter with her?' With his chin he indicated the wounded woman. Steiner shrugged indifferently. 'She was hit. Must have been a ricochet.'

'Serves her right,' Krüger commented. 'What business have women putting on uniforms. We ought to paddle their arses so they can't sit for a month.'

'They aren't going to need to sit,' Steiner said.

Krüger frowned. 'Schnurrbart said something about that,' he murmured. 'I tell you, you can count me out.'

'I don't need you,' Steiner replied coolly.

'Are you going to kill them yourself?'

Steiner did not answer. This was the question he had been turning over in his mind for the past few minutes. The longer he thought about it, the rottener he felt. Finally he pushed it away, postponing the problem until later. If there were no other way, he would do it himself. Russians were Russians, no matter what they had between their legs. He ordered Hollerbach to search the wagons for food. When they found it, one man was to make coffee or tea; the guards on the road were to withdraw to the bridge; two men would remain in the house to guard the prisoners. For a moment he stared at the floor, considering. Then he said: 'That will be all for now. Krüger, I need you again.'

As the men filed out, Steiner turned to the women again. Their initial fear was gradually diminishing. They were still standing close together against the wall, but they were talking in whispers now and throwing curious glances at the men. As Steiner took a step toward them, they were all attention. In as rough a voice as he could muster he said: 'Ask them where they come from, where they were going and whether there are any more of them on the way here. Tell them if they lie to us we'll throw them into the creek.'

'Lots of work for nothing if they can swim,' Krüger said. He beckoned to one of the women who wore an officer's insignia on her collar. Her face expressed fear and defiance. When Krüger raised his gun, she slowly came forward. He asked her a number of questions which she answered promptly, and boldly.

Krüger turned to Steiner. 'They belong to the 34th Women's Mortar Battalion and are on the way from Maikop to Krymskaya. They are——'

'What about Krymskaya?' Steiner interrupted.

Krüger again spoke to the Russian woman. She listened attentively. Then she turned to the other prisoners and exchanged a few words with them. When she turned to Krüger again, she spoke slowly, dramatizing her words with frequent shrugs.

'Krymskaya is supposed to have been taken by the Russians last night,' Krüger said. 'But she isn't sure. Her group had to wait in Maikop for new mortars yesterday, while the battalion went down the road to Krymskaya yesterday morning.'

'How did they come to be here?' Steiner asked.

'A civilian told them about the short-cut through the woods. They arrived here last night and were intending to go on to Krymskaya.'

Steiner thought that over. The Russian woman's story might well be true, although you had to be cautious. If Krymskaya had already been occupied by the Russians, that was a hard blow. In addition to all their other troubles they would now have to detour around the city. Although he had reckoned with that possibility, he felt his earlier discouragement returning.

He heard a low cough from the doorway. Turning, he saw Schnurrbart standing there, looking weary and grim. When their eyes met, Schnurrbart said: 'So it's that.'

'What's that?' Steiner asked.

Schnurrbart shrugged. 'Krymskaya.'

Steiner growled impatiently: 'One more reason for making sure the women don't get to the city before us. Where is the other batch of women?'

'Outside. I was waiting until you were through in here. Should I bring them in now?'

Steiner nodded. 'Yes, don't forget the sentries. Are the other fellows back?'

'All here,' Schnurrbart said.

Steiner turned to Maag. 'You and Zoll stay here. If any one of the women starts anything, shoot her at once.'

'What about the man?' Schnurrbart asked. 'Should we—right away——'

'Is he young?'

'No, he's an old fellow like the others.'

'You can bring him in here for the present,' Steiner said. 'We'll take care of them all together.' He looked at Krüger, who was staring blackly at the wall. 'Don't think I'm looking forward to it,' he said. 'It makes me feel sicker than your stupid mugs, and that's saying a lot.'

They went outside, where the prisoners were lined up against the wall of the house, guarded by Zoll and Anselm. Steiner paused on the lowest step and looked at the women's frightened faces. On the left end of the line stood the wagon driver, his head hunched between his shoulders, peering at him from a pair of cunning eyes. His ugly, pockmarked face was typically Asiatic. Squat in build, he looked quite powerful still in spite of his age. When he saw Steiner's eyes upon him, he took a step forward, raised his hand pleadingly and said: 'Captain——' Steiner pointed the tommy-gun at his chest. The man reeled back, frightened, while the women screeched and ducked low against the wall.

'Take them in,' Steiner said. 'Where are the sentries?'

Schnurrbart pointed to the bridge. 'On the edge of the woods. I picked the place myself. They can see the road in both directions from there.'

'Who have you got?'

'Dietz and Pasternack.'

Steiner moved away from the steps and stood watching as Zoll and Anselm drove the prisoners into the house. When the door closed behind them, he turned to the other men. For the first time he noticed that they were all holding large chunks of Russian bread in their hands and hungrily chewing. The sight reminded him that he had not eaten for twenty-four hours. From the open window of the kitchen Dorn's head appeared for a second. In spite of his bad temper Steiner could not help grinning. It would be Dorn, he thought; Schnurrbart might have picked a better man for cookhouse duty. Kern, for instance. Suddenly he realized that Kern was still missing. He would have to discipline that idiot. Kern must be off in the woods somewhere, the piss scared out of him. Slinging the tommy-gun over his shoulder, Steiner sauntered around the house toward the wagons. On the way he remembered that he had forgotten to ask about the horses. He stopped and called to Krüger. There was no answer. Impatiently, he went back the way he had come. The East Prussian was standing with the others, gesticulating and speaking with great force. They always know better, Steiner thought with rising anger. He strode up to them and addressed himself to Krüger: 'Get hold of the man and bring the horses here. Take Anselm with you. What's the idea of standing around here making speeches? By God, we've got more important things to do.'

Krüger threw him a rebellious look. 'We're discussing something a lot more important than the goddamned horses.'

For a second Steiner seemed on the point of smashing his fist into Krüger's face. But he controlled himself. His voice tense, he said: 'What's said around here is important only if it comes from me.'

'Says your conceit,' Krüger growled.

'I'd sooner be conceited than as stupid as you. Get moving, and have those horses here in ten minutes.'

Sullenly, the two went into the house to fetch the old Russian. Steiner turned to Schnurrbart: 'Come along with me.' They went around the house and ran into Hollerbach. He was standing on one of the wagons, busying himself with some boxes. When he heard them coming, he called: 'Where the devil are you? Do you think I'm going to sweat my arse off on this stuff alone?'

Steiner went up to the wagon and looked in. Half hidden under boxes of ammunition lay two heavy mortars. Curiously, Steiner examined the calibre. 'The damn thing's murder,' Schnurrbart observed. They watched as Hollerbach tugged at a canvas cover in the back of the wagon and brought out a tommy-gun. He handed it to Steiner who examined it with interest. 'It looks brand new,' Schnurrbart commented.

'Any more of these things in there?' Steiner asked.

'Let's see,' Hollerbach said. He stooped and pulled the rest of the canvas cover aside. 'Sure, half the wagon is crammed with ammunition, and then some. What'll we do with it?'

Steiner turned the tommy-gun over between his hands. He

seemed to be struggling to make up his mind. Finally he said: 'I'll tell you, we'll take these guns along. Every man take one and as much ammunition as he can carry. The rest we'll toss into the creek. The best way, I guess, would be to push the wagons up on the bridge and turn them over into the water.'

'Not bad.' Schnurrbart yawned. He rested his arms on the edge of the wagon rack and blinked at the sun. 'But what are we going to do with our own guns?' he asked. 'We don't want to be lugging them too, on top of everything else.'

'Of course not. We'll toss them into the water too.'

'I don't know,' Hollerbach said with a worried frown. 'I grant you theirs are better than ours. But what a stink there'll be about it when we get back. Meyer will throw a fit.'

'He can throw two for all I care,' Steiner replied. 'The kind of fix we're in justifies unusual measures. Why do you want to hang on to your stinking carbines? By the time you've reloaded them the Russian tommy-guns can fill you full of holes. Besides, we've only three boxes of ammunition left.'

Schnurrbart nodded his agreement. 'As far as I'm concerned, orders are orders.' He grinned. 'I've been waiting for years for a chance to toss my rifle into a brook.'

'How do we stand on rations?' Steiner asked Hollerbach. 'Found anything decent?'

Hollerbach nodded. 'And how. Several dozen loaves of bread and a few boxes of canned stuff.'

Schnurrbart cursed. 'And I like an idiot ate dry bread. I'll bet there's canned meat in there somewhere, huh?'

'There sure is,' Hollerbach said. He put on a solemn, secretive expression. 'Guess where the stuff comes from?'

'How should I know?' Schnurrbart grumbled, angry with himself for not having examined the contents of the wagons earlier. 'It can come from Siberia for all I care.'

Hollerbach chuckled and held up a can. 'Made in U.S.A.'

Schnurrbart spat on the ground. 'Shit. What the devil are we staying here in Russia for? Just promoting international good feeling, I suppose. What a laugh: the plutocrats sending corned beef to the Communists.'

'They can get together all right if it's us they're against,' Hollerbach sighed. He sat down on the wagon shaft and let his feet dangle.

Steiner laughed harshly. 'Don't let it bother you,' he said. 'One of these days they'll be paid back for their corned beef, and more.'

They gave the matter some thought. Finally Hollerbach shook his head and with an air of profundity said: 'It's only the Jews.'

Schnurrbart clapped his hands to his ears. 'Cut it out; it doesn't sound any better on an empty stomach.'

'That's the only time I can stand politics without being sick,' Steiner said. He placed the tommy-gun on the wagon. 'Let's cut the cackle and get to work.'

'Yes, let's go.' Hollerbach jumped up and energetically rolled up his sleeves.

'What do we do first?' Schnurrbart asked.

'Let's take out the tommy-guns and the ammunition, then the food. Everything else we can dump into the water.'

They started unloading.

Dietz and Pasternack were lying on the ground near the edge of the woods, on the other side of the bridge. They talked in whispers, without relaxing their close watch. Pasternack was saying vehemently: 'It's out of the question, I tell you. Once I get back home I want to take things easy.'

He wants to take things easy, Dietz thought. A fat chance a man has to do that. He drew a blade of grass between his teeth and propped himself up on his elbows. 'It isn't any of it so simple,' he said. 'Now look——' He paused reflectively, considering how to explain why it was not so simple. 'You see,' he continued, 'back home I work as a bricklayer. I wanted to go to college, but there wasn't enough money.'

'What did you want to study?'

'Medicine. I wanted to be a doctor. I've been crazy about medicine as long as I can remember.'

Pasternack hummed thoughtfully. 'Since you couldn't make it, why didn't you go in for something else. Salesman or something.' He glanced at Dietz's thin, frail body. 'I should think bricklaying would be too tough for you.'

'It is,' Dietz said gloomily. He remembered how done in he had always been when he came home from work; sometimes he would throw himself down on his bed and weep from sheer exhaustion. There wasn't anything else, though, he went on. 'When I finished school, my old man was unemployed. I haunted the employment bureau, but it wasn't any use. One time I tried for an office job, but they didn't want me. Even though my marks in school had always been high.'

Pasternack nodded sympathetically, and Dietz looked grateful. 'It was tough,' Dietz went on. 'There just didn't seem to be anything for me. Then one day my father heard about a construction job and I went over and got it. It was supposed to be just a starter, till something better came along, but once I was in it I was stuck.'

'That's the way it always is,' Pasternack said. 'Same thing happened to me. When my old man had his accident, I went to work in the mine, and there I stayed until I was conscripted.'

They fell silent, looking out over the reeds. Dietz absently watched a small beetle crawling along the ground. When it had made off he said: 'You know, when I remember what it was like on that job, I don't know that I'm so crazy about getting home. When I think of our foreman—I tell you he was a hundred times worse than any of these birds in the army. Here you can lie down and take a snooze once in a while, but there you didn't dare take time out for a smoke. He once threw a brick at me—hit me square in the small of the back. It could have killed me.' His eyes filled with tears of resentment at the memory. He swallowed hard.

'There are bastards like that everywhere,' Pasternack said. 'We had our share of them.' He shook his head and sighed. 'The bastards,' he said bitterly.

Dietz smiled dismally. 'That's why I don't give a damn,' he said. 'Back home they go for you and here in the army they go for you. I don't know which is worse.' He picked up a dry stick and broke it in two. 'It's a poor affair anyway you look at it,' he murmured.

Pasternack stared unhappily into space. The sun was warm on his back. The stillness and the sharp tang of the reeds reminded him of days on the banks of the Oder. His father had taken him swimming when he was a little boy. Being near water always reminded him of those days—the happiest in his life.

He was gazing abstractedly at the bridge when he suddenly caught sight of Kern. The innkeeper was moving slowly toward the bridge, looking warily to all sides. Dietz, who had also spied him, called out his name. Kern turned round. Then he relaxed and walked swiftly toward them.

'What are you doing around here?' Dietz asked in surprise.

Abashed, Kern scratched his chin. He glanced uneasily toward the houses. 'I had to go,' he said hoarsely. 'Devil only knows what I done to get this upset stomach.'

Both the others grinned. While crouching with Krüger behind the machine-gun they had witnessed Kern's wild flight.

'Steiner's been looking all over for you,' Pasternack said. 'You can't just leave like that.'

'Leave?' Kern pretended to be indignant. 'What do you mean leave? I told you I had to go. Oooh!' He clutched at his belly in pretended pain. 'Never wanted to shit like this before. I can hardly stand. What's been happening, anyway? What are you doing here?

'Sentry duty,' Dietz said.

'What about the Russians?'

'Russians!' Pasternack laughed. 'You mean the women?'

Kern stared at him. 'So that's what they were!'

'The houses were full of women. Part of a mortar battalion.'

Kern paled. His chin dropped. Steiner will kill me, he thought; what an idiot I've been. He had run only a few hundred yards into the woods, then thrown himself down on the ground with a sensation of overwhelming relief. But when minute after minute passed and he did not hear the expected din of battle, he had become nervous. Torn between fear and his sense of duty, he had finally dragged himself to his feet and gone part of the way back. Then, hearing noises in the underbrush, his terror had returned with redoubled force, and he had hidden behind a tree for a long time. Discovering that the sounds were being made by some animal, he had gone on. Steiner would not believe his reason for running away, any more than Pasternack and Dietz did. The somewhat malicious expressions of the two men increased his dread.

Pasternack, who was looking up at him with amusement, yawned. 'Go on over there and tell them to send us something to eat,' he said to Kern. 'I'm hollow.'

Kern hesitated.

'They won't shoot you,' Dietz said reassuringly.

'You know how Steiner is,' Kern said sulkily, his hand touching the burned spot on his face.

Dietz laughed angrily. 'He won't try that again,' he said.

Kern stood indecisive for a few moments more. Then he squared his shoulders. 'Well, see you later,' he said.

As he crossed the bridge, he saw the others. They were pushing one of the wagons and were so absorbed in their labours that they did not notice him. Schnurrbart was holding the shaft and steering while Hollerbach and Steiner, their backs braced against the wagon, walked backwards, pushing it step by step towards the bridge. Schnurrbart looked up. Kern quickly put his fingers to his lips in a petitionary gesture, and strode rapidly toward them. When he reached the wagon, he braced his shoulder against one of the cross-pieces and began to shove with the others. In a moment they reached the bridge. Since they had to lift the wagon up a step about eight inches high, they paused. Steiner cursed under his breath and wiped the sweat from his brow. Suddenly he saw Kern standing beside the wagon. Hollerbach, catching sight of him also, exclaimed: 'Christ!' They stared at one another in silence. Then Steiner slowly walked up to the innkeeper. 'Where have you been?' he asked quietly.

Kern hunched his shoulders and did not answer. When Steiner repeated the question he stammered: 'In the woods—I had to—I had cramps—that soup must have upset my bowels.'

'I see,' Steiner said.

Kern ducked his head as though a shell were whining over him. Schnurrbart saw him begin to tremble. As always he wondered at the uncanny effect of Steiner's personality. Although Kern was half a head taller than Steiner and was certainly not inclined to be timorous, he was cringing like a schoolboy expecting a deserved whipping. Standing as he was now with drooping shoulders and white face, he looked the personification of fear, and Schnurrbart suddenly felt disgust so violent that he could taste it as a bitterness in his mouth. He had to put an end to this disgusting scene.

Turning to Steiner, he said: 'Let him alone. We were all scared stiff when we stood in front of that door. Don't forget Kern has been at the front just a few days. That sort of thing can happen to anyone.' He hesitated, then lifted his jaw aggressively. 'You went to pieces too,' he added sharply.

Steiner slowly turned toward him. When Schnurrbart looked into his eyes, he was frightened. But there was no outburst. Without a word, Steiner took his tommy-gun from the wagon, thrust two clips of ammunition under the strap of his pack, and started across the bridge. As they watched, he disappeared among the trees. The men stared at one another in alarm.

'Now we're in for it,' Kern murmured.

Hollerbach turned on Schnurrbart. 'Man, you shouldn't have said that!' he exclaimed angrily. 'You know how he is.'

Schnurrbart was still staring fixedly at the spot where Steiner had vanished. He felt like a man who has accidentally set his own house afire and is standing before the smoking ruins. He stood numbed until Hollerbach shook him violently by the shoulder and shouted in his ear: 'Go after him and bring him back.'

'It's no use,' Schnurrbart murmured. Suddenly he turned on Kern. 'It's all your fault, you idiot!' he burst out.

Kern looked guiltily into their outraged faces and did not answer.

'Here comes Krüger,' Hollerbach said. They looked toward the houses, where Krüger, Anselm and the male Russian prisoner had appeared. Each of them was leading a pair of small, rugged-looking ponies. Krüger waved to them, smiling.

'We've got them,' he called out cheerfully. 'Now we can play cavalry.' Seeing their grim faces, he turned to Anselm. 'Tie up the ponies and put the prisoner into the house,' he ordered. Then he strode swiftly toward the men. 'What's the matter, has something happened?' he asked.

Hollerbach shrugged irritably. 'And how,' he said. 'Steiner's left.'

'What do you mean left?' Krüger demanded, his heart suddenly pounding.

'Let him tell you,' Hollerbach replied, nodding toward Schnurrbart who was staring blackly at the water.

Krüger whirled around. 'What the devil is the matter? Come on, talk.'

'Damn it all,' Schnurrbart growled, 'a man can't weigh every word on a jeweller's balance.' He told Krüger what had happened.

He had barely finished, when Krüger turned upon Kern. 'You bastard,' he shouted. 'Just wait till we——'

'Cut it out,' Hollerbach interrupted furiously. 'You'll do better to try and think what we're going to do.'

There was an uneasy silence. Finally Schnurrbart said, shrugging: 'There's only one thing we can do: carry out Steiner's plans. First we'll dump the wagons into the water; then each of us will take a Russian tommy-gun and we'll clear out. Maybe he'll be waiting up ahead for us.'

'You don't believe that yourself,' Krüger growled. Again
fury overpowered him. 'If only you'd kept your silly mouth
shut.'

Schnurrbart was on the point of retorting angrily. But he felt
that Krüger was right, and on top of his awareness of having got
the platoon into this predicament came the additional sense that
all the responsibility for the safety of the group now rested upon
him. Without another word he turned toward the wagon and
began tossing boxes of ammunition into the water. For a while
the others watched him labouring. Then Krüger cursed and
unbuckled his belt. 'Don't stand there and gape,' he burst out
furiously, jumping up on the wagon. 'We're all going to croak
anyhow.' He stooped and picked up a heavy box. The others fell
to and worked like madmen.

After crossing the bridge Steiner ran into the two sentries. When
he heard his name called, his thoughts returned with difficulty to
the present sunny April morning. He stood still and stared at Dietz,
who was sauntering slowly toward him. 'Anything new?' Dietz
asked. He gave Steiner a friendly, boyish smile. 'Can't you send us
something to eat over here? We're starved.'

Steiner hesitated. Now that his initial temper was gone, he felt
uncertain of himself. Uncomfortably, he looked into the smiling
face before him. 'You'll get something to eat soon,' he answered
roughly. 'Schnurrbart will either send some stuff over here or have
you relieved.'

'Why Schnurrbart?' asked Pasternack, joining them. 'Aren't
you going back across?'

When Steiner did not reply, the two men looked worried. Dietz
began nervously fingering the strap on his rifle. 'Has something
happened?' he asked.

Steiner shook his head. He felt that it was impossible to tell the
two of them that he was leaving the platoon. 'I want to take a look
around,' he said. 'Keep your eyes open.'

They still looked doubtful. 'Did you see Kern?' Pasternack
asked.

Steiner nodded. There was a few seconds silence. Then Dietz
inquired uneasily: 'Did you hit him again?'

Steiner grinned. 'No, why should I?'

'That's good,' Dietz sighed with relief. 'I've been thinking about him. You know, Kern isn't a bad guy at all; he just isn't used to the front yet.'

'I agree.' Steiner nodded. 'Only I'm afraid he never will get used to it. He looks to me the kind of guy who feels like a man only when he's on top of a woman.' Seeing Dietz flush, he laughed and clapped him on the back. 'You're still a regular baby after all,' he said.

'Do you think we'll get out of this with whole skins?' Pasternack asked.

'I hope so.'

'But the Russians are in Krymskaya now.'

Steiner looked down at the toes of his boots. The conversation made him uncomfortable; he was anxious to end it as quickly as possible. Impatiently, he shrugged. 'We'll just have to detour around the city. We've been through worse messes.'

'You'll get us out of this,' Dietz said with eager agreement. 'Nothing to it.' There was such vast trustfulness in his voice that Steiner looked away in embarrassment. He turned sharply, made his way through the trees to the road and walked rapidly off into the woods. Dietz watched with admiration. Then he turned to Pasternack. 'He'll pull it off, I tell you; he'll get us out of here.'

'I know he will,' Pasternack repeated. They went back to their places.

The further Steiner walked away from the bridge, the less firm his pace became. Dietz's last words kept ringing in his ears. They were like elastic bands wound around his body and tied somewhere way back at the bridge. With every step forward their pull tautened; his legs began to feel as if he were up to his waist in a rushing stream and trying to advance against the current. Finally he came to a stop, turned round and looked back. It was utterly quiet. The road wound and twisted through the woods, flanked by dense undergrowth on both sides. Through the foliage overhead the sunlight speckled the floor of the forest. Steiner swallowed repeatedly. There was a hollowness in him that seemed to be spreading through his whole body, so that even his physical sensations were unreal. Wearily, he sat down at the foot of a tree, tucking the tommy-gun under his legs. He should have taken Dietz and Pasternack with him, he thought. But then he shook his head. You couldn't compromise with your conscience. For a while his thoughts dwelt on Dietz. He had sometimes tried to analyse his feelings about the little fellow, but had never really got anywhere. Dietz was a plucky little jack-in-the-box with a faithful heart and the eyes of a good dog. With the best will in the world you could not see much more in him. And yet Steiner felt he would miss Dietz more than he would miss Schnurrbart and all the others. Queer. Maybe that was it; maybe the little fellow uncovered a hidden streak of queerness in himself. The idea troubled him. He closed his eyes and thought it over. But as soon as he started to visualize the thing, he grinned scornfully. No, that was out of the question. He knew himself too well not to mistake his own feelings about such filth. Mad even to think of it.

He reached into his pocket for a cigarette and began smoking. While he sat staring with narrowed eyes at the dirt road, he reconsidered his relationship with Dietz. He recalled the many times he had favoured Dietz in ways the others would not notice. Had they really never noticed? Anything was possible. Now and then Schnurrbart had made a few remarks. But those might have been sheer chance. In any case, who cared what Schnurrbart said!

In a sudden flash of rage Steiner snapped the half-smoked cigarette into the bushes. The conversation on the bridge, momentarily forgotten, came back to him. From anyone else he could have taken that, but not from Schnurrbart. In the course of his talk with Pasternack and Dietz he had come to feel a certain detachment toward his own injured pride, but that didn't mean he was going to pardon Schnurrbart. If Schnurrbart had taken him aside to make the same point, he would not have taken offence. But the public insult could not be borne. The more he thought about it, the more determined he felt to leave the platoon to its fate.

He continued to sit for a few moments, frowning bleakly. Finally he moved; with an impatient jerk of his head he looked at his watch. It was half-past nine; there was no more time to lose. The rest of the platoon would be coming any moment. As he stood up he thought about Dietz once more and felt annoyed with himself for not having given any explanation. You're an idiot, he told himself; the way you carry on, you might be an aging spinster who feels the last stirrings of maternal feelings and goes to bed with a doll between her withered breasts. The idea amused him; for a few seconds he shook with soundless laughter and doubled over like a caterpillar. Then he jumped to his feet. As he stooped for his gun, he caught a glimpse of a large moving shadow.

All the men with the exception of Zoll were sitting in the kitchen. To gain time Schnurrbart had recalled the sentries from the bridge so that they could eat with the others before setting out. The wagons were at the bottom of the stream and the men were now armed with Russian tommy-guns. They were sipping the hot tea Dorn had brewed and eating directly out of the American tin cans. The Russian bread was moist and heavy, but they devoured it hungrily. Schnurrbart alone was scarcely eating. Until he had spoken with Dietz and Pasternack he had gone on hoping Steiner would return. But now there could be no doubt. Steiner had left the platoon. Now it was up to him to decide the next steps to be taken. For a while Schnurrbart regarded Krüger's grim face. Then he suddenly remembered the man guarding the prisoners. He turned to Maag and said: 'Hurry up; you have to relieve Zoll so that he can eat. We're leaving right away.'

Maag nodded as he gobbled a huge hunk of corned beef. Schnurrbart watched with disgust. He looked toward Krüger again, and their eyes met. Something in his face troubled Schnurrbart. He felt that they were both thinking about the same thing. What was to be done with the prisoners? Now that Steiner was gone the responsibility no longer lay in one man's hands. He knew quite well that he could not carry out the execution against Krüger's opposition. Thoughtfully, his eyes drifted over the faces of the men. Dorn, Dietz, Pasternack and Hollerbach would also undoubtedly raise a fuss. What Kern's and Anselm's attitude would be he could not decide. Zoll and Maag, he felt fairly sure, were the only ones who would mow the women down without a qualm. In any case it would not strengthen his position as leader of the platoon if he insisted on shooting the women. Left to himself, he would not have thought of it for a moment.

'What's on your mind?' Krüger asked.

Schnurrbart hesitated a moment. He glanced quickly at the door before he spoke: 'What are we going to do with the women?'

The men stopped chewing and stared at him. Although they knew this problem remained, they were nevertheless taken by surprise. They avoided each other's eyes. Dorn was the first to shake off the paralysis. He laid his fork on the table, removed his

glasses and studied the lenses as he asked: 'What do you propose?'
Schnurrbart did not reply. Dorn turned to the others. 'I don't see
that our situation will be either better or worse if we shoot them.
But in any case I am unalterably opposed.'

His downright tone aroused in Schnurrbart a spirit of contradiction. 'So,' he said irritably, 'you're unalterably opposed. May I
ask why the devil you're so opposed?'

Dorn regarded him coolly. 'You certainly may ask. I am opposed
because we are soldiers and not murderers. Anyway, I think we
are facing a far more urgent problem. Do any of you know
where the battalion is posted at present?'

No one answered. Schnurrbart shrugged. 'It's marked on the
map,' he growled.

'Right.' Dorn smiled briefly. With unwonted forcefulness he
asked: 'And who has the map?'

Schnurrbart felt a physical pang run through his body. Turning
his head, he caught Krüger's look of alarm as Hollerbach sprang
to his feet, exclaiming: 'Steiner has the map with him.' The men
stared at one another in consternation. Dorn alone remained calm;
it surprised him, how calm he was. He was as composed as a
person who has long ago understood that feeling is only a passing
intoxication of the soul which must not be taken seriously lest it
introduce needless disruption into life. Turning to Pasternack who
sat in a slump at his side, he asked: 'Didn't Steiner say anything
about the map when he talked to you and Dietz?'

Pasternack shook his head silently.

'Then we haven't got a chance,' Dorn commented tranquilly.

Krüger's repressed fury erupted all at once. He brought his fist
down upon the table with a crash and bellowed: 'To hell! To the
devil with the map. What do I need a map for? I'll show you my
map. Here it is!' He stooped quickly, picked up his Russian
tommy-gun and slammed it down on the table with all his might.
Several of the mess-kits were knocked over, spilling the hot tea in
all directions. The men jumped back out of the way and Kern, his
trousers soaked, called out angrily: 'You damned half Russian!'
Krüger whirled around, stared at him for a second, then threw
himself upon Kern with an inarticulate cry. His body hit Kern's so
hard that Kern was hurled backward across the table.

Cursing, the men jumped aside once more. 'Stop that!'
Schnurrbart roared. His words were drowned in the tumult.

Kern swung over to the other side of the table, dropped to the floor for a moment, then rose in a flash and received Krüger with a rain of furious blows. They were evenly matched. Their arms moved like windmills; they seemed to be pulling each punch from out of the air. Most of the others formed an enthusiastic ring around the fighters and cheered them on. Dietz backed trembling against the wall and watched the brawl with horror. Each time a fist landed with a dull thud in one of the men's faces, he closed his eyes and noiselessly moved his lips. When Krüger charged Kern and the two began rolling in a tangle on the floor, he found his voice again. He shouted to Schnurrbart who was standing by watching the fight with a set expression: 'They've got to stop, tell them to stop.' Schnurrbart nodded. He communicated with Hollerbach by a rapid glance and they cautiously approached the grappling men from both sides. Kern had just heaved himself up off the ground, rolled over on top of Krüger, and was closing his hairy hands around the East Prussian's neck. Hollerbach and Schnurrbart desperately tried to separate the two, but they could not get a good hold. Finally Schnurrbart attempted to seize one of the thrashing legs, but received such a violent kick in the groin from Kern that he reeled back and crumpled heavily to the ground. As he sat up, face twisted with pain, a hail of bullets from a rat-tatting tommy-gun lashed above their heads.

After Schnurrbart had called out Maag to help unload the wagons, Zoll had been left alone with the prisoners. All the while the men were at work outside, Zoll stood with his back against the door, alertly watching the women. Since there were now nearly thirty people in the relatively small room, it was closely packed. In order to simplify the problem of guarding them, Schnurrbart had ordered the prisoners to sit in rows one behind the other, legs apart and hands on the shoulders of the one in front. They had meanwhile made themselves somewhat more comfortable by using each other as supports for their backs. In the farther corner, her head upon one of the women's laps, lay the wounded woman. She was still unconscious. Although the prisoners did not yet know what was going to be done with them, their initial fear seemed to have somewhat abated. They talked in whispers, and Zoll was bothered by the feeling that they were making fun of him. He could think of no other explanation for their occasional burst of giggling. Several times he had tried to intimidate them by cursing viciously, but after looking up in curiosity and astonishment they had resumed their whispering. Finally he had given up trying to appear tough.

Towards the front, close to him, sat the solitary male prisoner. In contrast to the others his expression was worried, and Zoll observed him talking steadily to the woman beside him. What the devil was all the chatter about? Zoll wished he could pound him over the head with his machine-pistol. But after all they would be killing the man very soon now. This thought made him feel generous. Let the fellow jabber while he still had the chance. For a while Zoll listened to the flow of the unfamiliar language, feeling irritated with himself for not having learned Russian. He recalled all the tutoring his parents had forced upon him when he came home with poor marks in English and French. Where did all the cramming get you? Half of what you learned you never used, and the other half you forgot. He watched the woman the Russian was talking to. He had noticed her before. Couldn't be more than twenty, he would guess. Her thin face was rather pretty, and every time she looked up at him with her grey eyes he became restless. Sex-appeal, he thought. Too bad he was not alone with her. His eyes glided searchingly over her figure, which looked promising in spite of the shapeless uniform. Her blouse was stretched tight over high breasts, and Zoll tried to imagine how it would be if he were to unbutton that blouse. What a racket, he thought; here they had all the women they could wish for and weren't getting anything out of them. To distract himself, he glanced out of the window. The men were still slaving away at the wagons. He saw them dumping ammunition boxes and mortars into the water. They pushed the empty wagon on to the bridge, rammed it into the railing several times until the wood splintered, and the heavy wagon pitched over the side of the bridge. The water splashed high all around it. He grinned with satisfaction. That was one cart the Ivans wouldn't be using any more. He watched with interest as the men turned to the next wagon. Pleased, he saw Maag wiping the sweat from his brow. Good that Schnurrbart hadn't sent for him. He could do without an extra detail right now. He felt, to his own surprise, a touch of gratitude toward Schnurrbart. Until now he had always thought of superiors as automatically stinkers. He might as well try to get along with Schnurrbart from now on—

wouldn't do any harm. If Steiner had really gone off, Schnurrbart would be platoon leader. What luck that would be. He had felt enormously relieved a few minutes ago when Schnurrbart came into the room and told them about Steiner. He had hated Steiner from the first day he met the fellow, he reflected. Maybe because Steiner was the only man he feared.

He suddenly recalled with a surge of rage and shame their arrival that morning. That game he had played with the patches of sunlight had been ridiculously childish. But all the friction with Steiner had been to blame for that. Their nerves were shot, that was all. That bastard had been the last straw.

He had been so deep in thought as he stared out of the window that he had paid no attention to the prisoners. Now he suddenly heard a groan behind him. Whirling around, he scrutinized them suspiciously. They were sitting as still as before. Only in the farther corner, where the wounded woman lay moaning softly, had any of them turned their heads. 'Quiet!' Zoll yelled. From somewhere in the room there was a brief burst of giggles. Zoll bit his lips. Damned bitches, he thought; I ought to. . . . His hand tightened on his gun. Angrily, he looked over the rows of faces. Suddenly he stared. The woman sitting in front of him—the woman the man had been talking to so urgently—was moving ever so slightly. Head bowed, she was fingering at her blouse. The two top buttons were already open, revealing the base of her breasts. Zoll gulped and looked at the man, who sat with eyes closed, apparently dozing. The other women had stopped whispering. Most of them seemed to be asleep, or were sitting with heads drooping, staring at the floor. It was so quiet in the room now that he could distinctly hear Schnurrbart outside issuing orders. Zoll felt a peculiar sensation in the pit of his stomach. He glanced at his gun, making sure the safety catch was off. When he looked up again, his eyes met the Russian woman's. She was gazing steadily at him, and had opened another button on her blouse. As he watched her in fascination, she closed one eye in a slow wink, and smiled at him. Zoll held his breath. The thought crossed his mind that there might be some danger for him concealed behind this behaviour, only to be immediately routed by the heady rush of vanity. He ran his tongue over his dry lips and tried to look at the woman impassively. Her thin, rather dirty fingers were busy opening the last button.

Zoll threw a glance out of the window. The men were just shoving the last of the wagons over the edge of the bridge. They stared at the water for a few seconds and then turned toward the house. He heard the heavy tread of their nailed boots mounting the stairs and thumping across the hallway. Then the door was wrenched open and Schnurrbart thrust his head in. 'Everything all right?' he asked.

Zoll nodded. Out of the corners of his eyes he observed that the Russian woman was holding her blouse closed and staring vacantly at the floor.

'I'll relieve you in a few minutes,' Schnurrbart said. 'As soon as Maag has eaten he'll take over so you can eat.' His eyes roved over the rows of prisoners. 'They dozing?'

'Seem to be,' Zoll answered curtly. He was furious at the interruption; there was no room in his mind for anything but the wish that Schnurrbart would leave as quickly as possible. But Schnurrbart still delayed. Something about the women's attitude aroused his suspicions. Queer that they should be dozing, he thought, coming all the way into the room.

'What do you want?' Zoll asked impatiently. 'Everything is all right.'

'I said the women were to sit and not lie back,' Schnurrbart answered.

Zoll was aware of the swift fading of all his good resolutions. If Schnurrbart was going to be a shit like Steiner, he would have to set him back on his heels in good time. 'I don't know what you want,' he said angrily. 'Let them stay the way they are. If any of them lets out a sound, I'll let her have it.'

Their loud voices had roused the women. They sat up again, throwing anxious looks at the two men.

'There you are!' Zoll burst out in a rage. 'When they're lying down they've got less of a chance to make trouble.' He turned around and bellowed: 'Lie down!'

The Russian women looked blank. Zoll strode over to one of them, raised his boot and pushed against her shoulder, tipping her backwards. 'Lie down, I said!' he shouted again. This time the others understood. Zoll watched with satisfaction as their bodies sagged to the floor. 'Don't you think I can watch them better this way?' he said to Schnurrbart.

Schnurrbart hesitated uneasily. Finally he shrugged. 'At any rate you can't see their faces like this.'

Zoll grinned. 'What do I need to see their faces for. I prefer their arses.'

'You're a young pig,' Schnurrbart growled as he went out. Zoll kicked the door shut behind him and quickly turned toward the Russian woman. She had opened her eyes and was looking at him. Now she spread her legs apart, turning her feet outward, and nodded encouragingly to him. When he did not stir, she spread her blouse open, reached under the grey cloth of her undershirt and pressed her breast upward. Breathlessly, head crooked forward, Zoll watched the white flesh appear over the edge of the shirt. He dug his teeth into his lower lip, and his whole body tautened. But he stood still as if nailed to the spot. His eyes hung painfully, lustfully upon the brownish circles of her nipples which rose up tense and hard. When the Russian woman beckoned him with her finger, he could feel that he was losing control of himself. His eyes swept over the heads of the other prisoners, paused upon the face of the man. Although he was lying with closed eyes, just like the women, Zoll's suspicions revived. But it was crazy to worry, he told himself. The old geezer would not dare try anything. As his gaze turned back to the exposed breast, he feverishly went over the possibilities. Nothing much could happen if he went ahead. Though it would be stinking if another of the men came in. He would have to hurry. But here?

He shook himself. To provide an erotic spectacle for thirty women did not appeal to him. Besides he did not quite trust the sleepy and apparently indifferent man. The fellow might only be waiting for him to lay down on top of the woman. The thought sobered him a little. You couldn't trust any of this damned pack of Russians. Indecisive, he looked over the rest of the prisoners once more. There was nothing about their attitudes that seemed suspicious. Then he suddenly recalled that the woman who was baring herself had been the very one with whom the man had talked so excitedly. He glowered at her. As though she were guessing his thoughts, she began to smile again, and to push herself along the floor toward him. She moved in such a provocative manner that all of Zoll's compunctions disappeared. Where could he take her? Finally he thought he had found the solution. He beckoned with a movement of his head. 'Come,' he said softly, '*iddi sudda.*' She hesitated, and he noticed her glance at the man in perplexity for the briefest moment. The man seemed to notice nothing of the byplay between the two. Was he pretending? Again Zoll hesitated for a second. But by now he was in such a state of obsessive lust that he would have killed the man instantly rather than be deterred. '*Iddi sudda*,' he repeated hoarsely.

The coquettish smile on the woman's face vanished. When she looked up at him again, he saw fear in her eyes. He grinned. 'So you've decided to be coy,' he said. 'That doesn't go with me, understand, not with me.' He took one long stride up to her, stooped, grasped her shoulder tightly and pulled her to her feet. 'Not with me,' he repeated harshly.

Again he threw a glance at the man, who was still lying with closed eyes. But his face now seemed unnaturally pale. Abruptly, Zoll opened the door and pulled the resisting woman by the wrist out into the hall. Madly, he looked around. From the room behind the door opposite he heard the muted voices of the men. For a few seconds he listened, eyes narrowed, still tightly grasping the woman's wrist. If they catch me, I'm sunk, he thought. He turned toward the woman and saw that she was trying with her free hand to button her blouse. He grinned. 'Let that be,' he said, his hand darting to her breast. The touch increased his excitement. He raised his tommy-gun and wordlessly gestured with it toward the outer door. The woman stared at him, her mouth twitching. 'Come,' he said, shoving her toward the door. On the steps she tried to escape. But he had expected this and tightened his brutal grip on her arm. 'Come,' he panted, dragging her to the next house. He pushed her up the steps and into the hall. The house was just like the others, a kitchen on one side, a living-room on the other. Both doors were open. He shoved the woman into the room to the right of the hallway. On the floor lay the prisoners' blankets and equipment. As he laid his tommy-gun down in a corner, the woman suddenly broke loose and ran toward the door. In two bounds he was at her side. He threw his arm around her waist, dragged her back into the room, hurled her to the ground, and fell upon her, panting with exertion and excitement. She tried to defend herself; her small, clenched hands beat against his face, and she began to scream. Had he not been so wild with the desire to possess her, he might have wondered about her contradictory behaviour, and drawn conclusions. But he did not think. When he had stripped her naked, he dragged one of the blankets over her face and smothered her screams. She lay like an animal under him, moaning.

Vladimir Ignatiev heard the screams as he ran toward the bridge, and his heart contracted. Poor Ninotchka, he thought, tears streaming down his face, poor little Ninotchka. From the window he had watched the German pushing her into the empty house, and then he had made his break for freedom. Any moment as he ran he had expected to hear the crackle of the German's guns, their shouts, but there had not been a sound. Now he was racing across the bridge, and the forest reached out green hands toward him; the forest cried: 'Run faster, Vladimir Ignatiev.' Then he was in the shelter of the tall trees. He panted, stumbled over roots, fought with flailing arms and legs through the dense undergrowth, until he came out on the road again. For a few seconds he paused, panting for breath; then he ran on. But, as he rounded a bend in the road, he stopped, as horror-stricken as though hell had opened before him. His heart pounded against his ribs and his gasping breath seemed to have become boiling water that seared the inside of his chest.

A dozen paces away from him sat a German. It was the one he had spoken to in front of the house. The German was sitting with his back against a tree, apparently lost in thought. Vladimir Ignatiev did not dare to move. He stood with arms dangling, his thoughts tumbling over one another like skittles when the wooden balls struck them square in the centre. The forest had lost its friendly aspect; the trees stared threateningly down at him. 'Holy Saint Basil!' Vladimir Ignatiev whispered. Under his heavy wadded jacket he began to sweat; perspiration poured down over his forehead, burned in his eyes. The German did not move. But if he turned his head just a little, it would all have been for nothing. All of it, including the screams of Ninotchka who had sacrificed herself to make his flight possible. It must not, it must not have been in vain. Vladimir's parchment-like face tightened. He clenched his fists. He must kill the man, must seize his gun and make off for Krymskaya. Now, at once. As he got set to spring, he saw the German stand up abruptly, pause, and then stoop for his gun. At that moment he threw himself like a falling tree upon the German's back and pulled him to the ground.

Although the attack was a complete surprise, Steiner reacted instantly. Even as he fell he managed to half turn his body, and recognized the Russian. As the Russian's hands clasped around his throat, Steiner doubled up, reached over his shoulders and pressed his finger-tips into the man's eyes. The Russian let out a piercing scream; his grip relaxed. Like a weasel Steiner rolled over on his side, continued to roll across the road, and jumped up. He saw the man taking a tremendous leap into the bushes, rushed toward the spot where he knew the tommy-gun must be, stumbled over a tree-root and fell flat on his face. Although he recovered almost at once, he had lost precious seconds. As soon as he had laid hands on the gun, he raised it and fired blindly into the undergrowth until the magazine was empty. But when he raised his head and listened into the sudden silence, he could hear the retreating sounds of breaking branches. In a moment these were swallowed up in the depths of the woods, and the silence closed over him like deep water.

For a second Steiner stood motionless, listening still. He was so clearly aware of the hopelessness of pursuit that he did not even attempt it. To hunt down one man in these impenetrable woods would take a whole company. As he brushed out his clothing, he smiled grimly. Leading a platoon, he thought, took more stuff than Schnurrbart had in that little brain of his. Served the talkative bastard right; let him get out of this mess now. He bent over to pick up his pack, which he had lost in the fight, and as he did so a piece of paper fell out of his coat pocket. He froze. The map, he thought, the map's with me. Slowly he reached out for the piece of paper. Without the map Schnurrbart couldn't possibly find his way to the battalion. Furious, he stared blankly into the green woods, cursing his own taciturnity; he should long ago have told the men where the new positions were located. At the very least he might have informed them that the detour around Krymskaya was possible only from the north; on the south of the city they would run into swamps. The longer he considered it, the more apparent it was that taking the map with him was not in the game. Schnurrbart had to have as good chances to make it as he would have had. Yet if he returned now to bring the men the map, they would not so easily let him go off again. Most of all he feared the way they would look at him. And what would Krüger say, or Hollerbach, or Dietz? What would he read in Dorn's eyes? Yet there was no help for it; they had to have the map. What he did next would have to depend upon the situation he found when he returned to the platoon.

His next movements were swift and considered. He put a new

clip in his gun, picked up the rest of his stuff and set out at a steady trot back down the path. When he reached the bridge, he stopped and looked around. Seeing no sentry, he shook his head and looked toward the houses. They seemed deserted, and uncannily quiet. His uneasiness mounted. Inconceivable that they had not yet discovered the Russian's escape. As soon as he had crossed the bridge, he saw the horses. They were standing with lowered heads, tied to the last house. Steiner breathed easier. The men would not have set out without the horses; therefore they must still be inside. He felt somewhat reassured, although the silence was still baffling. Cautiously he approached the house where the prisoners ought to be.

As he passed the first of the buildings, he heard a suppressed moan. Quickly, he turned on his heel and peered suspiciously at the windows. The sound was not repeated. On tiptoe he stole up the steps, entered the hall and paused, listening. Now he could hear the moaning again; it was a little softer, but unmistakable. Rather out of curiosity than concern, he approached the door, pushed it open slightly and thrust his head into the room. The sight that met his eyes took his breath away. But he made no sound. When he came out a moment later his face was flushed. So that's it, he thought grimly, that's why it's so quiet here. He ran to the next building, rushed up the steps, noiselessly opened the kitchen door, and stood still, astounded. Then he raised his gun and fired.

The men, instinctively flattened out on the floor, gaped at Steiner who stood in the doorway with his gun smoking. Kern and Krüger were still lying in a tangle half under the table. But Kern's terrible grip had loosened, and as Krüger staggered to his feet, his eyes glassy, the innkeeper's heavy body rolled to the side and he lay like a stick of wood. Still bewildered, the men's eyes shifted from the motionless Kern to the tottering figure of Krüger, who reeled toward the door and straightened up, breathing heavily, in front of Steiner. For a few seconds they stared at one another without a word. Abruptly Krüger began to grin. He plucked at his nose, glanced over his shoulder at Kern, and whispered: 'Out for the count.' Steiner blinked. His initial surprise at the scene had given way to a stern suspicion. Turning to Schnurrbart, still staring incredulously at him, he demanded: 'Who is guarding the prisoners.'

It took a moment for Schnurrbart to remember. 'Zoll,' he said at last, breathing hard.

'I see. Zoll.' Steiner nodded. All at once he came to life. He sprang across the hall, wrenched open the door and looked into the room. The women were standing pressed up against the walls, their faces white. With narrowed eyes Steiner looked them over. Then he turned to the men, who had gathered in the hallway behind him. The expression on his face appalled them. 'For Christ's sake what is it?' Schnurrbart stammered.

'You'll find out soon enough,' Steiner replied fiercely. 'You idiots can't be left alone for five minutes. Get yourselves ready, and none of you leave the house.' Before they could ask him any more questions, he rushed out of the hut. As he went out Dorn, his voice aquiver with agitation, turned to Schnurrbart. 'Where in the world is Zoll?' he asked. Schnurrbart bit his lip and did not answer.

When Steiner kicked open the door, Zoll was just pulling up his trousers. The Russian woman was lying on the floor, naked and whimpering. At the sound of the opening door, Zoll whirled around. He stared incredulously at the figure of Steiner in the doorway. For a few seconds they merely looked at one another. Then Steiner came slowly into the room, and slowly approached Zoll, until he was right in front of him. The whimpering of the Russian woman stopped. With satisfaction Steiner observed the sheer terror in Zoll's eyes. He was considering whether he would run into much trouble if he shot Zoll out of hand. Did the commander of a platoon cut off in the heart of enemy country have the same rights of summary court-martial as the captain of a warship at sea? He did not know the regulations on that, but he knew that he would not tolerate Zoll in the platoon any longer. After all, there was another solution. He looked around the room and his eyes lit on the tall, single-doored wardrobe that stood beside the window, filling the entire left corner of the room. It was massively built, but seemed to have no lock; the door could be closed only by a wooden catch.

'Open the door,' Steiner said to Zoll. Zoll did not move. He was holding his trousers up with both hands, his face reflecting all the emotions that had been passing through him in these past few minutes. Steiner's order to open the wardrobe intensified his fear.

Involuntarily, he glanced toward his tommy-gun. It was out of reach in the farther corner of the room.

Steiner caught his glance. His mouth twisted. 'Don't try it,' he said icily, 'you couldn't get there. Come on, open the wardrobe.'

'What for?' Zoll asked loudly. He made an effort to speak firmly.

Steiner pointed the tommy-gun at his chest. 'You ask too many questions,' he said calmly. 'Get to it!'

Zoll stared into his pitiless eyes. He did not doubt for a second that Steiner would fire at once if he tried to jump him. Nevertheless, he made a last attempt at opposition. 'Not until you tell me why you want me to open the wardrobe.'

His resistance threw Steiner into a fury. The urge to press the trigger was almost too much for him. 'Go on,' he said hoarsely, 'go on, hurry up.'

Zoll shrank away from that naked rage. He turned quickly, went to the wardrobe and opened the door a little.

'More,' Steiner ordered.

Steiner pulled the door wide open. The wardrobe was empty inside. Steiner nodded with satisfaction. Turning his head for a moment, he saw that the Russian woman's gaze was fixed upon him. Deep within those grey eyes of hers blazed a flame that sent a shiver down his spine. If she had a gun now she would kill us both in a moment, he thought.

'Get into the wardrobe,' he said to Zoll. Zoll took a quick step to the side, his eyes widening with fear. This was taking too much time, Steiner thought; he stepped up to Zoll and whacked him across the face with the heavy barrel of the sub-machine-gun. Zoll let out a wild shriek. He let go of his trousers and pressed both hands against his nose, which streamed blood. Ignoring his cries, Steiner shoved him into the wardrobe.

'The show is over,' he said coldly. 'The applause has died down and the audience is heading for the exits. Do you know what happens then?' He saw Zoll's body tensing and quickly raised the gun. 'You don't understand. The show is over, I said. And when the show is over the curtain falls—like this.' As he spoke he had been closing the door inch by inch. Now he suddenly slammed it shut, pushed the wooden catch down, and took a step back. 'If you make a sound,' he called out loudly, 'I'll fire through the wood.'

From the side he tugged at the wardrobe until he had moved it somewhat away from the wall. He enlarged the space until he could squeeze between the wall and the back of the wardrobe. Then he braced his back against the wall, and with a mighty shove pushed the wardrobe over frontwards. The heavy piece of furniture crashed to the floor, sending up a cloud of dust, through which appeared the Russian woman's white face. She had jumped up and was staring first at the wardrobe, then at Steiner. For a few seconds there was silence. Then Zoll began to shout. When he began kicking his nailed boots against the wood inside, Steiner hammered the butt of the tommy-gun against the side of the wardrobe. The shouting stopped.

'Cut out the racket,' Steiner said loudly. 'Nothing can happen to you as long as you're inside there. I'm going to leave the woman here.' He turned upon the Russian woman, grasped her wrist and pulled her over to the wardrobe, where she crouched on the ground, trying to cover herself with her hands. Her eyes were still afire, and Steiner felt a tremor at the thought of the fate awaiting Zoll. For a moment he fought with himself. Then his face set. He picked up Zoll's tommy-gun and turned toward the door. As he went out, he stepped on a piece of clothing. It was the Russian woman's uniform. He halted. The thought came to him so suddenly that it took a while before he fully took it in. He stooped, picked up the uniform and regarded it thoughtfully. Then he went on out of the room, a triumphant smile on his face.

The men were ready to march. They stood about the kitchen looking at Kern, who lay moaning on the floor with his eyes shut. Schnurrbart was bending over him. He had unbuttoned Kern's jacket, pulled up his shirt and with both hands was massaging the innkeeper's black-haired abdomen. The others stood around discussing the jiu-jitsu trick Krüger had used. Kern seemed to be slowly recovering. His moaning stopped. All at once he opened his eyes and tried to sit up.

'Good morning,' Schnurrbart said, grinning with relief.

Kern stared blankly at him. Then he saw Krüger and his memory returned. He twisted his face in a grimace of pain and cursed. 'What the devil happened?' he said, his eyes coming to rest on Schnurrbart who was still rubbing his stomach. He could not figure it out. He had been on top of Krüger and had had a beautiful grip on his throat. And there his memory ended. Seeing the grinning faces of the others, he flung Schnurrbart's hands off him and sprang to his feet. At this moment Steiner returned. He went over to the table and spread out the Russian uniform. Then he turned to Krüger. 'You back to normal again?' he asked quietly.

Krüger straightened his cartridge-belt, brushed the hair back from his perspiring face. 'More or less,' he said.

'Let's hope it's more. Come along.' They went across the hall to the prisoners. The buzz of conversation stopped and the women looked up expectantly at them. 'Tell them to undress,' Steiner ordered.

Krüger gaped at him, thinking he had heard wrong. When Steiner impatiently repeated his order, he shrugged and spoke to the women. Their faces paled and they shifted about uneasily, but made no move to obey. Steiner lifted the sub-machine-gun and fired half the magazine into the floor. The women screamed in terror and threw their arms up in the air. 'If they don't undress voluntarily we'll strip them one by one,' Steiner said loudly, over the reverberations of the shots. 'Tell them it's their uniforms I want—nobody could take away their virginity any more.'

Krüger grinned. He did not see what Steiner wanted with the uniforms, but the business was beginning to amuse him. His voice rang out incisively as he translated Steiner's remark. This time the women complied at once. In their panic they pulled the blouses over their heads without bothering to unbutton them. When the other men, startled by the shots, came rushing into the room, they stopped in astonishment. The women had already removed their high boots and were now taking off their trousers. Their scanty and rather ragged underclothing scarcely concealed their breasts. Some of them were wearing slips; most wore men's long underwear. Half naked, they stood huddling together in front of the men, glaring at them with bitter anger. Maag ran his tongue over his lips. 'Boy, oh boy,' he murmured. The sight made his skin tingle. He glanced at the other men and saw that they were in like case. They were all standing leaning forward slightly, their faces flushed with lust.

Dorn lingered in the background, outraged. Although he understood the ugly scene no more than the others, he was revolted by the way all of them were, as he put it himself, welcoming this shameless exploitation of the weakness of the women. He elbowed his way to the front and went up to Steiner. 'What's the idea of this filthy business!' he said angrily.

Steiner regarded him coolly. 'Haven't you ever seen a female backside before?' he answered casually.

Disgusted, Dorn stared into his impassive face. Before he could reply, Krüger nudged him roughly in the side. 'If their holes bother you,' he growled at him, 'take off your glasses.'

Dorn quivered with indignation. Angrily he turned his back on the scene, went to the window and stared out into the bright daylight. So much had happened in the past few minutes that demanded explanation. Why had Steiner come back? Where was the one Russian male prisoner? Where was Zoll? What was the meaning of this disgusting undressing of the women?

The women had finished by now. Their uniforms lay in a heap on the floor, and the men's eyes slid hungrily over their bodies. Steiner, seeing the men's faces, grinned. What they were thinking was obvious, and understandable. But they had no more time to lose now. The Russian who had escaped would reach Krymskaya in three hours at most. Steiner turned to the men. 'We are going to change uniforms. Each of you take whatever fits and change over there in the kitchen. Wrap your own uniforms in your blanket and include them in your packs. Clear?'

'You mean we're to put that stuff on?' Maag gasped.

'Have you got anything against it?'

'No, of course not, but they're women's uniforms.'

'They're the same uniforms all the Russians wear,' Steiner answered impatiently. 'Have you noticed any difference?'

Maag looked at Schnurrbart beside him, appealing for aid. But Schnurrbart was just as puzzled.

'The idea in itself isn't bad,' Krüger spoke up, looking sour. 'But those uniforms are stinking filthy.'

Steiner flashed him an irritated look. 'Yesterday you yourself said we were going around like pigs. The women's uniforms are no dirtier than our own; so don't be so damn fastidious.' He nodded at the women, who were watching the bickering with apprehension. 'Ask them when they last washed. More recently than you have, I'll bet.'

There was little Krüger could answer to that. He stared blackly at the floor. Finally he looked up and asked: 'What's happened anyway? Has the Ivan escaped?'

'He would have been crazy if he hadn't,' Steiner said bitingly. 'You couldn't have made it easier for him to get away if you tried. What I've been wondering is why the women didn't skip out with him.'

'Nothing surprising about that,' Krüger said, stung by Steiner's tone. 'They were too damn scared. Incidentally, where the devil is Zoll?'

There was a sudden silence. The men looked at Steiner, who shrugged indifferently. 'Safe enough at the moment, I imagine,' he replied. 'I don't think we have any reason to worry about him.'

'Has he cleared out?'

'What would you have done in his place?'

Krüger also shrugged. They had all realized that one of the women was missing, and had figured out why. Perhaps Zoll had noticed Steiner returning and had made a dash for the woods with the woman. But then how come Steiner had the woman's uniform? Krüger wondered. One way or another the business was queer, he thought, scratching his chin.

Steiner gave them no time to think the matter over. 'Take the uniforms,' he ordered harshly. 'We're starting in five minutes.'

'In five minutes!' Maag exclaimed, looking sick with disappointment. 'What are we going to do with the women?'

Steiner did not reply. The men picked up the uniforms, went into the kitchen and began changing clothes. Steiner was the last to leave the room. At the door he glanced back. The women were standing motionless at the back of the room, a grotesque sight. They had put on their boots again and their legs emerged from the black, high tops like thin, ridiculously white sticks. As Steiner looked at their faces, he felt acutely uncomfortable. He stepped quickly out into the hall and closed the door behind him. Then he stripped off his own uniform.

Krüger had already tried on the fifth uniform. He was sweating and cursing steadily under his breath. At last he found a pair of trousers that fitted. 'What a damnfool idea,' he said aloud, staring in fury at the picture he presented. Hollerbach watched him with amusement. He had enough sense of humour left to recognize the absurdity of their situation. He also felt so relieved at Steiner's return that he would have carried out far more unpleasant orders just as cheerfully. He had found a pair of trousers that fitted him well, and as he fished a suitable blouse out of the pile of clothes he watched with a grin as the men in a frenzy of haste slipped into one uniform, turned around, took a few steps back and forth, and then—anxious not to look ridiculous—searched for garments that fitted them better.

Kern had just toilsomely squeezed into trousers that reached only just below his knees when he pulled them up to his waist. For a few seconds he looked down at himself aghast. His hand reached back and felt his behind for a while; then he turned to Hollerbach who was looking at him and barely keeping from laughing. 'You see how it is,' he said plaintively. 'I'll go off my rocker, I tell you. What a stupid idiotic idea. If the Russians see me they'll die laughing.'

'They certainly will,' Hollerbach grinned. 'From now on you have to march in the van. The Russians will laugh so hard they won't be able to shoot.'

Kern shook his head unhappily. 'What am I going to do? I can't go around like this.' He looked down at his legs with troubled gravity.

Hollerbach patted him reassuringly on the back. ''Tain't so bad. Try another pair.'

'I've tried them all. This is the only one that fits around the waist.'

'Then take the leggings and wind them around your legs. That's how I've done. It doesn't matter how you look; the main thing is if it serves the purpose.'

'As far as that goes,' Maag put in, 'do you think the Russians won't see we're not Russians?' He tugged angrily at his blouse. 'What a laugh—they're not so stupid. They only have to look at our caps or our boots.'

Hollerbach, drawing on his belt, shook his head doubtfully. 'Let's wait and see. In the dark it won't be so obvious. Don't forget we have to cross the front under cover of darkness.'

'In these rags!' Kern laughed wildly. 'When we get to the battalion our own men will mow us down. We look like a pack of Russians.'

'Don't wear your brain out thinking about it,' Hollerbach retorted. 'After all, we have our own uniforms with us.'

'Which makes another few pounds to carry,' Kern growled. 'Look at the size of this bundle.' He had begun wrapping his jacket and trousers in the blanket. The bundle was in fact distinctly bulky.

'No sense to it at all,' Maag said, cursing. As he buttoned his blouse he thought of the women with acute disappointment. He had missed the chance of a lifetime. Why hadn't he made better use of the time? He'd had his opportunity when he and Zoll were guarding the prisoners together. They could have taken turns going out with one of the women. But he had felt so damnably inhibited about broaching the matter to Zoll. Then Schnurrbart had come in later and he had had to go out and work on the wagons. But how could he have known that they would be leaving so soon? It was bad luck, that's what it was. They never let you have anything, the bastards, he thought bitterly. I always have rotten luck and one of these days Monika is going to ditch me. Gloomily, he stared down at the floor. Here you crawled in the mud and worked your arse off month after month, and when for once you had a chance at a bit of fun, nothing came of it. Filled with self-pity, he cursed Steiner; Steiner was to blame for the whole affair. Naturally that thick-skinned stud-horse wouldn't have any such difficulties. He was the kind who took a woman without complications. The thought increased his bitterness. Do they have any idea what a fellow like me has to go through, he thought. If they knew; the slave-drivers, the damned slave-drivers.

He muttered under his breath for a while until Steiner appeared in the doorway and urged them all to hurry. They regarded him in amazement. The Russian uniform had radically changed him. He looked broader, and even his face seemed different. Harder than ever, Dorn thought, studying him.

'Don't gape like idiots,' Steiner said. 'If you mess around here much longer we'll have a Russian regiment on our necks.'

The men thronged through the front door. They had wound the leggings around their calves; the long blouses fell down to their thighs; on their heads they wore their usual visored caps with the edelweiss insignia. Their swollen packs tugged at the straps. Steiner and Krüger went in to the prisoners, while the others watched, shaking their heads. They began striding back and forth, grimacing and strutting like women trying on new dresses. Hollerbach chatted with Dorn and Schnurrbart.

'I'm glad he came back,' Schnurrbart said.

Dorn looked uneasily toward the window of the prisoners'

room. 'If he shoots them I'll transfer to another platoon,' he said.

'You'll have to be back with battalion to do that,' Hollerbach reminded him. He ran his thumb along under his collar. 'To tell the truth, I don't like this business either. But I keep telling myself that we come first and the women second.' The others did not say anything. Hollerbach blinked up at the sun. 'Nice weather today,' he went on. 'It's beginning to feel a little like spring at last.'

Schnurrbart shrugged. 'If I were back home I wouldn't care if it were as cold as the North Pole.'

Hollerbach sighed. 'I'd be content if we were back with battalion. Stinking business, Zoll. What was that bird thinking of?'

Hollerbach fell silent and looked over toward the bridge, where the reeds swayed above the surface of the water. He suddenly remembered the trip he had taken to Würzburg with Brigitte. It had been a Sunday outing. After they climbed up to the old castle they sat on a bench and looked down upon the city below them. The bells of the cathedral and the Neumünster Church rang out. The hills across the Main River seemed to be rocking gently under the shadow of the vineyards, rocking up and down into the deep blue of the sky. 'I wish I could come here often,' Brigitte had said.

Hollerbach smiled a bitter painful smile as he remembered that. He had had to save every *pfennig* for over four months in order to spend this Sunday in Würzburg with Brigitte. They had had little money at home. His father lived on a small pension; his mother had been an invalid for the past three years. Now things were even tighter; his brother had been killed on the Central Front last year. Who could say how it would all end? As a boy, he had dreamed of having a great deal of money, of owning a car and seeing the world. But the world had too soon become for him a narrow funnel with its point at Mudau, and there had been no escape from it. His horizon extended no further than the edge of the woods beyond the small church, where the mountains reached to the sky and effectively blocked all yearnings. He could already see his future, sitting behind the counter of a railway ticket office as his father had done all his life, dully regarding the faces of travellers, annoyed by their stupid questions and their impatience, and having always to be at their service; and then watching them enter the train to ride out into the world, himself always remaining behind, as effectively bound to his little booth as if he were chained there.

He rubbed his eyes and looked hastily around. But no one was paying attention to him. Schnurrbart and Dorn had joined the others. The men were loading the horses with boxes of ammunition. The horses shifted restively. They had straggly manes and small, spiteful eyes. Maag picked up a stout stick of wood and began belabouring them. They kicked out, pranced wildly. Hollerbach shook his head. Those clucks don't know a thing about handling horses, he thought, and went over to take a hand. Würzburg was again 2,000 miles away.

Steiner could not have explained the impulse that made him go in to see the prisoners once more. When he and Krüger entered the room, the women were sitting on the floor, their blankets wrapped around them. They stared hostilely at him, and Krüger, too, threw a suspicious glance at his face out of the corners of his eyes. The East Prussian had no intention of playing executioner. If Steiner insisted on killing the women, he would have to do it alone. Steiner, who sensed his thoughts, smiled fleetingly. Now that the male prisoner had escaped, there was of course no point in shooting the women. Perhaps he had never seriously intended to anyway. He really did not know.

He noticed the wounded woman. The other woman had bedded her on several blankets and covered her. Her eyes were open and she was looking at him. As he approached her, the other women shrank away as though he were a carrier of the plague. He stood in front of her. 'How do you feel?' he asked.

She did not answer. He suddenly observed that she had beautiful hazel eyes, and wondered why he had not noted this before. 'When you wear a uniform in wartime,' he said quietly, 'you must not expect the enemy to treat you as a woman. Do you understand?' Although she again did not reply, he could see from her expression that she had grasped his meaning. Stubborn like all Russians, he thought, frowning, and went on: 'The rest of your uniforms are in the kitchen; you can go and get them. I imagine help will soon be sent to you from Krymskaya.'

With satisfaction he saw her pupils widening in surprise. As he started to turn away, she began to speak. 'Why do you say that?' She spoke slowly, in flawless German, her voice was low and resonant.

He looked at her in surprise. What a voice! Suddenly he felt the impulse to hear her go on talking. He took a step closer and said:

'You know as well as I that there are two missing from this room.'

With an excitement inexplicable to himself he watched her raise her head slightly. 'Vladimir got away?' she said. It sounded more like a statement than a question. But Steiner nodded anyway. 'If you mean the man who was here, yes—he escaped.'

The woman turned her head to one side and said something to the other women. Their faces brightened and they exchanged significant glances. Then she turned to Steiner again. 'You said two.'

'She is waiting next door, in the other house.'

'Is she——' the woman hesitated and her tongue licked out to moisten her lips. 'Is she all right?'

'No one ever got sick from that,' Steiner said cynically.

The woman's expression darkened. 'That is not for you to say,' she answered quietly. 'A good many have got sick from that, sick here.' She drew her arm from under the blanket and pointed at her chest.

Slinging the sub-machine-gun over his shoulder, Steiner leaned forward and asked: 'How is it you speak German so well?'

Her face twitched as she hesitated for a moment. Then she said: 'I teach the language to children—I am a schoolteacher.' There was pride in her voice.

'I see,' Steiner said. 'But why should you teach the children German?'

'Why do your children learn English and French?'

'Because we have already conquered France and are going to conquer England.'

She nodded quietly. Talking had exhausted her; her face was overlaid with dark shadows. She is going to die, Steiner realized, and the thought was painful. He pushed it away. We must all die, he said to himself, and asked: 'Well?'

She looked up at him for a second, then closed her eyes. 'You know the answer,' she said wearily.

He nodded and straightened up. 'The day hasn't come yet,' he said. 'It's still a long way to Germany.'

She opened her eyes again, and there were flickering lights in them. Slowly she turned her head, and her words reached his ears as a barely audible whisper: 'Not a long way—for us. But—for you.'

He looked down at her dying face. Then he turned and went out.

Krüger followed him. In front of the door Steiner stood still for a moment and raised his head. Beyond the bridge loomed the woods, mute and menacing. The gnarled branches had become like the lithe limbs of an octopus, scaled with green leaves and reaching dark shadows across the water to the men on the shore. Steiner shuddered. He passed his hand over his face to wipe away the image. I must be dippy, he thought. Against the sinister curtain of the woods, the dying woman's last words rang in his mind like an oracle.

There was something else that her voice rather than her words had awakened in him. His heart throbbed and memories scattered in all directions within him. There was another woodland ringing in the oval green of a forgotten meadow. The tall grass danced in the wind, the bluebells swayed, the wild pink blazed among the blossoms of the foam-flowers, while black and cream-coloured butterflies fluttered above them. Towering over the woods rose the spired mountain, grave and powerful, a circlet of white clouds around its granite neck. And a voice was speaking, saying foolish, lovely things, a soft voice, a dark voice, and meadow and woods and mountain and clouds and sky faded at the touch of an impatient mouth. Steiner stood breathing heavily, his face creased with grief. He came back to himself when Krüger placed a hand lightly on his shoulder. The men were standing near the horses; he saw their haggard faces above the Russian uniforms, and he saw the woods again. Slowly he descended the steps and beckoned with his arm. Then he started across the bridge. The men followed, falling immediately into their weary tread, and entered the green shade of the woods.

The wardrobe had been constructed of solid planks. Only on the floor side, where the door now lay, was there a crack the width of a finger, and the moulding on the bottom raised the wardrobe enough off the floor to admit fresh air. Zoll lay on his stomach, his head resting on his arms, his mouth close to the crack. About ten minutes had passed since Steiner had overturned the wardrobe. Zoll did not move. He had knocked his head against the door in falling and broken his glasses. After trying frenziedly to escape the terrible confinement of his wooden cage, he had given up. He still regarded his uncomfortable situation as one of Steiner's characteristic mean tricks and was expecting the men to arrive any moment and liberate him. He could already see their grinning faces and was framing what he would say to their jokes. Again and again he asked himself how Steiner, of all people, had happened to come into the room just at the wrong time. Perhaps Schnurrbart had only been faking and it had all been a cook-up of Steiner's just to catch him, Zoll. Just like that bastard. Zoll cursed himself for a fool for having been tricked this way. In helpless rage he clenched his fists.

Lying motionless again, he thought he heard scratching noises. He raised his head to listen. Perhaps it's the Russian woman, he thought. Steiner had said he would leave her there. Another of his rotten tricks to frighten him. Perhaps the men were already standing around the wardrobe waiting for him to scream for help. Well, he wouldn't give them the satisfaction. On the contrary. He began whistling loudly, and in spite of the pain where the butt of Steiner's gun had smashed across his face, he smiled at the thought of their astonished expressions.

The heat in the wardrobe gradually became unbearable. He felt as if he were in a Turkish bath, and although he was wearing only his shirt and trousers he began to sweat. He thought of Steiner again. He'll pay for this, the bastard, he said to himself; one of these days I'll send a bullet into his spine. Let him croak in agony, the dog.

He gritted his teeth and stared frantically into the darkness. The heat grew worse; finally he opened the buttons of his shirt, pulled down his trousers and turned over on his back. I won't let them think they can soften me up, he thought. When they get bored waiting they'll let me out. He closed his eyes and half dozed. Images and words bubbled up out of his memory. He saw himself sitting in the new Mercédès his father had given him for his eighteenth birthday. He saw the faces of the girls who followed the car with their eyes, whose walk slowed to a stop as his car cruised by, and who were only too glad to be invited for a drive. 'Where shall we drive?' he would ask, and they would always answer, 'Anywhere.' Zoll grinned at the memory. He knew a great many lonely spots which were the ideal destinations for such drives to 'anywhere'. For a while he revelled in salacious memories, and his excitement returned. He relived his recent experience with the Russian prisoner, and considered how he could have improved on it. It always goes too quickly, he thought discontentedly. He clasped his hands behind his neck and lay that way for more than fifteen minutes. Then he began to worry again. It seemed unlikely that Steiner would spin this thing out so long without the other men protesting. He pulled up his trousers, turned over on his stomach and pressed his ear against the side wall of the wardrobe, holding his breath until the strain was too much for him. It was so utterly silent that his uneasiness turned to fear. Suddenly the terrible thought struck him that the platoon might already have left. He forgot his pride and began to cry out. First he called softly, timidly, then louder and louder, until he was uttering long-drawn-out roars. He crooked his body and beat his heels against the bottom of the wardrobe. He dug his hands into the crack of the door and pulled until his fingers were bleeding. At last he lay still, panting for air. It was becoming more and more of a certainty that Steiner had left him behind, locked up in this wardrobe from which he could not escape without aid from outside.

Throwing himself on his back, he stared into the darkness. Fiery dots danced before his eyes, becoming glowing circles when he closed his eyelids, whirling madly and shooting sparks in all directions when he opened his eyes again. I must not lose my head, he told himself; I must stay very quiet now. He tried to think. Again he thought he heard noises outside. This time there was no question about it. Before he could determine their meaning, the wardrobe in which he lay began to move. Twice he was jolted hard against the wood, and then the daylight fell upon him so suddenly that he closed his eyes, dazzled. Half-stunned, he pulled himself up to a partly sitting position and blinked in surprise and terror at a crowd of mocking faces that were bending over him, at flashing eyes that sent icy chills of terror racing through his body, at rows of breasts bulging out of dirty underwear, and at dozens of hands that reached into the wardrobe, gripped his hair, his clothes, his limbs, pulled him up and hurled him to the floor of the room. As he started to defend himself, his arms and legs were pinioned, his clothes were torn off and a rain of merciless blows beat down upon him. Just above him was the face of the Russian woman he had raped. Her hair hung in tangled strands over her forehead; her eyes gleamed like green glass lighted from within. She did not strike him or berate him as the others were doing. She only stood stooped above him, staring at him in silence. And as Zoll looked into her face, as the blood ran down his forehead, bubbled out of his nose and mouth, as he jerked and writhed under the kicks and punches that struck every part of his body, as he moaned out his torment between clenched teeth and almost but not quite fainted from the pain, he saw nothing but her face above him. He saw her breasts, still bearing the marks of his teeth, her throat branded with bruises, and the pitless hot fever of her eyes.

Then a pain flashed through him that swallowed up all the other hundred pangs, that cut like a red-hot iron into his body. There broke from him a scream that no longer resembled anything human, that came down like a club upon the women's heads, so that they started back and held their ears. They clapped their hands over their ears, but the scream continued. A bestial roar, it reverberated horribly between the walls, on and on. Until one of the women shook off the paralysis of horror and with both feet at once jumped upon the bellowing, twitching, bleeding body, and then the others sprang upon him, stamping and screaming and kicking until the last twitching and the last whimpering was crushed out under their heavy boots. When they at last were done with him, and had filed out of the room, a ray of sunlight fell through the window, and the feet of the battered body lay in a pool of flickering light.

IV

CAPTAIN STRANSKY HAD decided after all not to put off his call upon Major Vogel. He set out that same evening. The 3rd Battalion's combat headquarters was located north of Hill 121.4, in the centre of a meadow that sloped off to the west. A small brook, its banks lined by dense shrubbery, flowed close by the group of bunkers. When Stransky opened the door to the commander's bunker, he saw by the candlelight that Vogel already had a visitor. Kiesel was sitting across the table from him.

Vogel stood up. 'Well I'll be damned!' he exclaimed. 'What a surprise.'

Stransky smiled, trying to conceal his discomfort at the presence of Kiesel. 'I hope I'm not intruding,' he said.

'Nonsense.' Vogel shook hands with him vigorously. 'I was expecting you yesterday; glad to see you any time.' He busied himself in a corner of the bunker and then placed several bottles on the table.

Kiesel smacked his lips. 'My respects, Vogel. Producing a 1937 Moselle here in the southernmost corner of Russia. Keep that up and you'll be besieged with visitors.'

The major gave vent to a booming laugh as he uncorked one of the bottles. 'Just takes a little organizing talent, gentlemen. Comes natural to an old soldier like me.' He filled the glasses. 'Then again, a bottle of Moselle is no more absurd in this region than we ourselves. Your health!'

They touched glasses. Stransky sipped the wine delicately. 'Splendid, Major,' he said. 'It's a long while since these parched lips have tasted nectar like this.'

The major nodded complacently and dropped a pack of cigarettes on the table. As they lit up, Kiesel, who had arrived only a few minutes before Stransky, looked around the bunker. The staccato light of the candles cast the men's shadows on the rough boarding of the walls. The major's bed, crudely knocked together out of wooden slats, was close to the door. At the head of it stood a chest, probably containing clothing. The major's submachine-gun, cartridge-belt and raincoat hung from nails.

Stransky puffed hard on his cigarette, which was not burning well. When it caught evenly at last, he crossed his legs and turned to the major. 'Incidentally, Major Vogel, why does our presence in the bridgehead strike you as absurd?'

Vogel's massive head, capped with snowy, close-cropped hair, jerked up. He pushed his glass a little to one side. 'I can tell you that, Herr Stransky,' he boomed. 'If we have to go on playing fire department, there's no sense in our being several hundred miles away from the heart of the fire. Which is where we are now. That's what makes our presence here absurd.'

Stransky frowned. 'I don't quite follow you. After all, we are here to carry out a highly important mission. It seems to me that your opinion springs from a certain prejudice. After all'—he smiled politely—'even a force that has been cut off has a function to perform. Wouldn't you say so, Herr Kiesel? Or perhaps you can tell me where our presence would be more useful. It seems to me that the tactical importance of the bridgehead is not open to question.'

Before Kiesel could reply the major's fist pounded down on the table. 'Tactical importance? You must mean decorative importance.' He leaned forward, propping both elbows on the table. 'You must be asleep,' he said rudely. 'Consider the events of this campaign up to the present day.' He laughed cuttingly. 'It's like the staggering of a blind man, going in one direction until he fetches up against a stone wall, then turning and back-tracking. Left, right, here, there. You know what it amounts to?' The major's ponderous figure seemed to swell. His eyes flashed wrathfully under his bushy brows. Stransky watched him uncomfortably. 'I'll tell you what it is. Sheer waste of strength. Waste. Muddle. Criminal stupidity.' Angrily he picked up his glass and took a long swig.

Stransky smiled superciliously. 'That's a matter of opinion,' he replied coolly. 'I do not doubt that you speak from a wealth of experience. But remember, please, that warfare has changed radically since the First World War. We no longer smash forward head-on until we're covered with blood—as at Verdun, for example; instead we seek out the enemy's weak spots. That takes mobility.'

'Bah!' Vogel swished his hand through the air. 'Spare me that rubbish. The weak spots, you say? We've picked out the strong points, not the weak spots. Prestige, big names, even if whole armies are chewed up. Look here.' He raised his hands and began counting off on his fingers. 'First the boil at Leningrad, then the bloody nose at Moscow, then the amputation at Stalingrad, and finally the carve-up of the Caucusus. And what have we achieved? Nothing, not a damn thing! Or do you think we have?'

Stransky suppressed an acrid retort. The major looked so choleric that it seemed wiser to him at the moment not to carry the argument too far.

The major refilled their glasses. 'What I'd like to know is what we've done wrong,' he said tightly.

'We have only continued what was begun by others,' Kiesel retorted. 'And now, if I am not mistaken, we are on the point of introducing our successors and stepping off the stage of world history.'

'You mean the peoples of the east,' the major asked.

Kiesel nodded.

Stransky smiled sourly. 'I'm more surprised than impressed,' he commented. 'It really astonishes me to hear such words from the lips of an active officer. After all, you have seen these Russians. How can you imagine these barbarians being capable of taking over from us?'

Kiesel grinned. 'More easily than you think. You must remember that the history of a nation is not written in decades but in centuries and millenia. Communism, for instance, is nothing but the trumpet blast awakening the eastern peoples from their enchanted sleep. In a few years it will seem obvious that it was only a brief part of their evolution, though a necessary one.'

The major seemed to feel that the conversation was reaching a danger point. To change the subject he asked about the 2nd Company's missing platoon. 'You've had no word yet?'

Uncomfortably, Stransky said he had not. The major shook his head gravely. 'I'm afraid you'll have to write them off. There doesn't seem much hope now. How many men were there?'

'Eleven,' Stransky replied reluctantly.

Vogel nodded sombrely. 'That few won't get far. I know how it is, was in a jam like that myself once. During the First World War, at Soissons. Damnable business, I tell you. When we started out we were a whole company; eight men came back.' He lapsed into morbid meditation, staring gloomily into space. Stransky seized the opportunity to steer the talk away from the platoon. Turning to Kiesel he asked: 'What do they think of the situation up at Division?'

'The general situation or our own?'

'Our own, of course.'

'The Russian preparations indicate a large-scale offensive. Our intelligence people in Krymskaya report the arrival of more and more new divisions.'

'Then I imagine we're going to be in for something,' the major remarked. 'But we'll survive this *bataille* too. At any rate they won't drive me out of my trench,' he added belligerently.

Kiesel smiled. 'Spoken like a man!' He had heard a great deal about the battle-scarred old fellow's courage. 'As a matter of fact, we have no choice. If the Russians break through anywhere, we're done for.'

Stransky nodded animatedly. 'I quite agree. Just today I spoke in precisely those terms to my company leaders. We must hold the bridgehead and we will hold it. That is my firm conviction.'

'Certainly we will.' Kiesel's mouth twisted bitterly. 'We will defend ourselves like madmen, convert the entire bridgehead into a huge mass grave, and all to the end that on X-day we can voluntarily withdraw from the heroically defended soil because the general tactical situation requires us to pull out.'

'You paint too black a picture,' Stransky objected. 'Why are you unwilling to see the positive aspects of our situation? We are pinning down strong enemy forces and relieving the crucial points of the front.'

Kiesel said coldly: 'You are talking in romantic terms, Captain Stransky. It is ridiculous to imagine that we here can ever make any important contribution toward deciding the issue of the war.'

'Bravo!' the major bellowed. 'Really now, Stransky, you're talking sheer rot. Every single man we lose is a useless sacrifice.' He had worked himself into a rage, and his eyes flashed fiercely at Stransky, who looked sulky and offended.

Kiesel tried to save the situation. 'Captain Stransky is entitled to his point of view. It seems to me'—he forced a polite smile—'it seems to me that it is good, for all our sakes, to have officers in our midst who still contrive to see some sense even in a lost position. I wish I could take a similar attitude. It would make many things easier.'

Growling, the major applied himself to his glass again. The major seemed to recall his duties as a host; he took a conciliatory tone. 'Good Lord, Stransky, don't set your jaw like a steel trap. I was just shooting my mouth off for a change. No reason for you to get huffy.' He turned to Kiesel. 'It's the ordinary soldier I'm most sorry for. You know, he's the unluckiest invention of this twentieth century of ours. I think Captain Stransky will have to admit that, at least.'

Stransky had meanwhile recovered his aplomb; his customary superior smile covered his face like a mask. 'I don't see your conclusion,' he said. 'The fact remains that every soldier suffers privations in wartime. I really don't see why the German soldier is worse off than any other.'

'You don't see that?' Again the major pounded the table so hard that the glasses jumped. 'I'll explain the reason to you, by God. Our men no longer have any ideals. They are not fighting for world freedom or for the culture of the west, nor are they fighting for the kind of government they want. They're fighting for nothing but their naked lives, for their bedeviled, unfortunate flesh. If you don't see that——' He fell silent abruptly.

Stransky regarded him coldly. 'Is that nothing?' he asked.

'Yes, it is a great deal,' Kiesel interposed. 'But it isn't everything. Otherwise our men would have deserted long ago. Perhaps' —he turned to the major—'perhaps I may add something to your line of argument. Flesh is patient, as paper is patient. It will suffer anything that is on it. It can be used, and it can be abused. And it has been abused because it has been lured with the bait of so-called ideals; it has been killed, and it has been allowed to kill until it seems to exist only for its own sake. But behind all that there is the common soldier's fundamental decency which doesn't permit him to leave his comrades in the lurch. And there is also a last glimmering spark of hope that everything may still turn out all right in the end.'

'In the present situation of our nation,' Stransky said frigidly, 'such talk borders on treason. I am a soldier and as such it is my duty to subordinate my own ideas to the interests of my country.'

Kiesel smiled easily. 'We are all doing our duty, Captain Stransky. I hope that history will some day recognize the dreadful battle which responsible German officers have had with their consciences.' He leaned forward with an expression of intense seriousness. 'To fight for a conviction does not require heroism. Heroism begins where the meaninglessness of the sacrifice becomes the last, the only message the dead can leave behind. Never forget that, Captain Stransky.'

There was a brief silence. One of the candles had burned down and the wick, sagging into the liquid wax, snuffed itself out. The major sat with clasped hands, staring into space. Suddenly he stood up. 'Getting late,' he said tightly. 'I must take another look around the positions, if you will excuse me.'

Kiesel drained his glass and slowly rose to his feet. Stransky followed his example. The major accompanied them to the door and shook hands with Kiesel. Then he turned to Stransky, his face set. 'In this regiment,' he said forbiddingly, 'there are no traitors, only human beings endowed with reason. Some use their reason and some don't. To say this may be dialectic and it may be tactless, but that is how I feel about it. Good evening, gentlemen.'

When the door had closed behind them, the two officers looked at one another. Stransky, quivering with rage, said: 'An impossible person.'

'Do you think so?' Kiesel retorted. 'My personal opinion of Major Vogel was formed long ago, and I have seen no reason to revise it. He is a first-rate soldier of the old school, and an admirable person in addition. It is interesting to hear your opinion of him. Good evening.' He bowed formally and strode off.

Stransky started up the hill, possessed by a fury which made him incapable of any consecutive thoughts. The land lay motionless at his feet, dark and still as a beast with a crooked back, and Stransky felt cold shivers prickling his skin. The rude comforts of his bunker seemed very good to him and he hastened down the south slope. Half-way down he stopped abruptly. Out of the stars broke a whining noise that swelled rapidly to a fearful roar. Stransky threw himself to the ground instantly and pillowed his face on his arm. The shell exploded with a shattering boom. A fiery blast of wind swept along the ground, carrying with it the ugly odour of burnt powder. Stransky lay numbed, holding his breath and waiting faint with fear for the next impact. When the whining in the distance came again, he dug his finger-tips into the sandy soil and closed his eyes. But this time the whooshing sound passed high over his head and ended in a dull rumble beyond the hill. Then all was quiet. These were the first shells to fall upon Hill 121.4.

For a while Stransky remained lying where he was. But when minute after minute passed without incident, he pulled himself up, blew the sand from his lips and felt his limbs. It seemed a miracle to him that he had not been hurt. Never had death been so close to him.

For a few seconds longer he stood still dazed. Then he ran with giant strides down the hill, stumbled into the ravine, hurried along the brook, and slowed down only as he approached his headquarters. A few paces before the bunkers he was hailed. One of his men emerged from the shadow of the fruit trees. As soon as the soldier recognized Stransky, he clicked his heels and rattled off a report. Back in his bunker, Stransky threw himself down on the cot. For a long while he lay still, staring open-eyed at the ceiling. Each time his recollections came around to Kiesel, a blaze of rage obliterated cool thought.

He began to seek excuses for his conduct. The period in France softened me up, he thought. I'm not the man I was. Certainly those two years in Paris had left their traces upon him. He had been commander of a garrison battalion and uncrowned lord of several thousand civilians. Those feasts at the colonel's villa, the French wine, the ladies of easy virtue—he closed his eyes and enjoyed his recollections for a while. Then he saw the colonel's mocking look when he informed him of his decision to ask for a transfer to the eastern front. His parting words rang in Stransky's ears as if they were being spoken at the moment. 'I can't stop you,' the colonel had said, 'since I am convinced that without you the eastern front would collapse in a matter of days. Go ahead, in the devil's name, you heroic fathead.' His other friends and acquaintances had shaken their heads in bewilderment, as if he were a man exchanging a mansion on the French Riviera for a straw-roofed kraal in the Congo.

And now after only ten days here, he was wishing he were back in France. Fortunately his connections were good enough to enable him to transfer back at any time he wished. But it was too soon as yet. First there was the little matter of filling out the empty space on the front of his tunic. Eyes closed, he tried to picture the look of the Iron Cross on the grey uniform cloth. An oval face appeared before his eyes, a hand touched his arm lightly, and a bewitching voice whispered words that stirred his blood and confused his mind: 'I love brave men, men who have more courage than it takes to pay compliments, men who have lain with death as well as women——'

At the sudden knock on the door he jerked around sharply. 'Yes!' he called in a strident voice. Lieutenant Triebig entered, pausing in the doorway with a respectful smile. 'Forgive me for disturbing you at this late hour, sir,' he said. 'I'm sorry, but there are a few things for you to sign.'

'Let me have the junk,' Stransky said crossly. As he glanced through the papers and signed his name, Triebig continued to watch him with his soft eyes, the smile remaining fixed on his face. Stransky, finishing the batch, pushed the signed papers toward him and looked up quickly. This bird cannot look you straight in the eyes, he thought. Time I found out a little about him. After all, it was of some importance to know what kind of creature lived inside the skin of his adjutant. Gesturing toward a chair, he tried to inject a cordial note into his voice. 'Sit down, won't you? We really have had no chance to exchange a personal word until now.'

'Unfortunately that's true,' Triebig replied politely.

Stransky offered him a cigarette. 'How long have you been here—with the battalion, I mean?' he asked.

'Four months. The battalion was at Tuapse when I joined it.'

'Where had you been stationed before?'

'In the south of France—Bordeaux,' Triebig said, his voice softening.

'Oh!' Stransky raised his head in surprise. 'What unit?'

'The 312th Infantry Division. Guarding the coast.'

'Then being transferred must have come hard, eh? Why were you transferred, anyway?'

The question caught Triebig off balance. Officially, the transfer had come by his own request; unofficially, there had been a small incident he preferred not to mention. At an impatient little cough from Stransky he quickly pulled himself together and replied: 'I voluntarily applied for a transfer, sir.'

Noticing his embarrassment Stransky began to look at him suspiciously. 'How interesting,' he drawled.

In the ensuing pause Triebig moved his head restlessly. With mounting apprehension he waited for Stransky to speak again, and was almost overcome with relief when the captain dropped the awkward subject and began to talk about the lovely countryside of southern France. 'Believe me, I have seen a good deal of the world; but whenever I visit that region I am enchanted all over again. A beautiful country; its charm is in the very air. One can almost scent it; perhaps it is the closeness of the sea.'

Triebig nodded eagerly.

'Yes,' he said, 'that is exactly how I felt.'

He gazed dreamily into a corner of the bunker. It was all present to him again: the undulating blue of the water, the white pebbled beach, the flickering brightness of the caressing air, the deep, moist green of the palms. With a little sigh he said:

'All of southern France is like one garden. We lived in real mansions right on the beach. Swimming at any hour, day or night. It was indescribable: the sea, the palms, the beaches, the people, everything——' Overwhelmed by his memories he stopped. Stransky was astonished to see him swallow with emotion. With a knowing smile he winked and said:

'The women, you mean.'

Triebig raised his head inquiringly:

'I beg your pardon?'

'I said, the women—I mean, in referring to the people you meant, of course, the women?' Stransky repeated.

Triebig shrugged indifferently. 'Not so much that. I am—that is——' he became confused. 'I didn't have much time to think about women.'

'Come now,' Stransky raised his finger jokingly. 'Occupation duty and no time for women—I've been in France myself!'

Triebig tried hastily to correct his slip.

'Of course, there were opportunities now and then,' he said. 'But to tell the truth, I had other worries.'

He felt at once how unsatisfactory this explanation sounded and watched the commander's face uneasily.

Stransky's eyebrows rose:

'Other worries. You mean to tell me you had worries in *France?*' And suddenly Stransky became keenly alert. The story of voluntary transfer sounded fishy. Anyone who talked so enthusiastically about France was unlikely to volunteer for service in Russia. Triebig didn't look the type who would risk a hero's death for the sake of a few medals, and Stransky remembered the man's reluctance to answer when asked the reasons for his transfer. He decided to probe a little further.

'If you had worries in France, that is your affair. It is not my habit to intrude on any man's private life. It is——' He stopped abruptly. The relief on Triebig's face was so patent that for a second Stransky lost the thread. But he caught himself quickly and continued in an even, casual voice: 'Are you married?'

Triebig shook his head. 'No, sir. When would I have had a chance to marry? I was only twenty when I started at Officers' Training School. That didn't leave much time for anything like that.'

'I suppose not,' Stransky agreed. His next question was a cautious generality: 'Do you like soldiering?'

'Certainly,' Triebig declared with emphasis.

Stransky nodded patronizingly. 'I am glad to hear that.'

'It is like living in an altogether different world,' Triebig added.

The candle had burned down. Stransky rose and lit another. Then he sat down again and folded his arms across his chest. 'It would interest me,' he said slowly, 'to hear your definition of the differences between this world and the world of the civilian.'

Triebig smiled, abashed. 'Hard to say, sir. I suppose it's something in the environment, in the atmosphere.' He shrugged. 'I really don't know.'

'You are a keen observer,' Stransky remarked innocuously. 'But after all isn't it always the people who make the environment, who provide the atmosphere.'

'Certainly,' Triebig agreed.

Stransky lit another cigarette and dropped the burning match to the floor. He waited until it went out; then he raised his head. The suspicion he had been nursing during the past few minutes began to assume a definite shape.

'It is indeed a very different world, the one we live in,' he now said. 'A world of danger and a world of men, a world without women. You know, Triebig, we experience it in ourselves. Things that seemed simply impossible in the past, in ordinary civilian life, happen here.' He laughed. 'For example, in the army it becomes apparent that men are not absolutely dependent on women after all. It's an old idea of mine that we men can get along, even without women. Dependency upon women seems to me a regrettable flaw in the male character. I tell you, man's truly natural destiny is not only to breed children, but rather to be free, to rule, and fight—in other words, to lead a man's existence in which women are no more than a fancy but superfluous dessert. Or do you disagree?'

Triebig looked up at him in great confusion. For a moment Stransky wondered whether he had not gone too far. But no, he had nothing to fear from the man. The bait was good; if his suspicion proved correct, Triebig was sure to bite.

He was momentarily disappointed. Triebig remained extremely reserved. His innate sense of caution, sharpened by a good many bad experiences, had been alerted by Stransky's remarks. Intertwining his fingers, he regarded his thumb thoughtfully. 'I don't think I disagree, sir.' He hesitated. If Stransky was seriously feeling his way to an offer, he must not put obstacles in the way. He had played this nerve-wracking game of words dozens of times and thought he could trust himself to risk a step further. Forcing himself to adopt a tone as innocent and casual as possible, he said: 'This seems to me an individual matter. There are men who simply cannot live without women, and others who never have been dependent upon them.'

'And which class do you feel you belong to?' Stransky asked.

Triebig hesitated again. 'That depends,' he said tentatively. 'I think that if I have to, I can live without women.'

'I'm pleased to hear that,' Stransky declared. For a moment he studied the burning tip of his cigarette. Then he looked up quickly. 'In other words, you prefer the company of a man to that of a woman?'

Triebig, eyes half-closed, scrutinized him. He felt himself breaking into a sweat, and he shifted uneasily about in his chair. From here on every word could turn into a booby-trap. 'It depends on the situation,' he muttered.

'Really?' Stransky smiled. When Triebig did not reply, he shrugged. 'Wearing a uniform does not relieve you of the obligation to display a certain amount of ordinary, everyday courage. But if it will help you, I shall put your thoughts into words for you.' His smile broadened. 'You prefer the society of men to that of women in any and all situations.'

The words hung in the silence of the bunker in all their brutal nakedness. Triebig retreated into himself like a snail sealing itself up in its shell. His chin trembled and he stared with mingled fear, assent and hope at Stransky's face, which still registered nothing but friendly interest. Afraid silence might be interpreted as agreement, Triebig murmured, 'I did not say that, sir.'

Stransky nodded reassuringly. He felt convinced that he was on the right track, and decided to risk everything on a single card. Softly, insistently he said: 'Certainly you did not say it, but I wish you would.' He grinned confidentially. 'Let's drop the hide and seek. By God, man, you don't have to put on a front with me, of all people. What I said is true isn't it? Say yes, man, for heaven's sake.'

Triebig felt his mouth opening. He wanted to stop himself, but the word was already said. The smile on Stransky's face went out at once. He dropped back into his chair, staring at Triebig as though seeing him for the first time. His eyes filled with contempt. 'How very, very interesting, Lieutenant,' he drawled. 'Extremely interesting indeed. To tell the truth, I've never had dealings with one of your kind before.'

Triebig stared at him appalled, his mouth partly open as though he were on the point of screaming. 'I don't understand, sir——' he stammered.

'You understand me well,' Stransky replied savagely. 'Do you take me for a fool. You said yes, didn't you?'

Triebig, lips quivering, did not answer. Stransky sprang to his feet and stepped directly in front of him. 'Speak out,' he bellowed. 'You said yes. Don't you dare lie to my face. You said yes, didn't you?' At the sight of the enraged face only inches away from his own, Triebig closed his eyes in terror. When Stransky gripped his shoulders and shook him, he nodded feebly and whispered: 'Yes.'

At once Stransky released him, took a step back, and ordered: 'Stand up!' Trembling, Triebig obeyed. Slowly Stransky looked him up and down. His voice was under control again as he said: 'I can assure you of this: if I catch you trying any of that stuff, I'll have you hanged, remember that! Now get the hell out of here and keep out of my sight for the next twenty-four hours. Get out!' He suddenly shouted as Triebig stood immobile. For a second Triebig looked at the commander's distorted face. Then he wheeled round, stumbled across the threshold and vanished into the night. Stransky remained standing in the same spot for several minutes. Then he fished for a cigarette, lit it and began to grin. For the first time in a week he was completely satisfied with himself and with the world at large.

Triebig stood in front of the bunker gazing wild-eyed at the trees. From the trenches came the occasional hammering of a machine-gun. Isolated rifle-shots sounded disturbingly close, and tracer bullets whished in fiery trails above the dark hills. For a long while Triebig stood unmoving, incapable of a coherent thought. He felt his whole being trampled upon, humiliated, reduced to a pulp. Finally he moved off toward his bunker on unsteady legs. He stumbled down the steps, closed the door and dropped on to his cot like a stone. I must shoot myself, he thought; I must shoot myself at once. He groped for his pistol. But as soon as he felt the cool steel against his forehead, he lowered his arm, and with a sudden, violent movement hurled the gun to the floor. Then he turned over on his stomach, pressed his face against the blanket and began to sob unrestrainedly.

He made up his mind to kill Stransky.

V

LATE IN THE afternoon they came upon the Russians. They had just skirted a sizeable patch of swamp when the horse led by Dietz suddenly broke loose and galloped wildly off between the trees. The men stopped and looked accusingly at Dietz, who was staring in a daze at the place where the horse had last been. Since it was carrying part of their rations on its back, they felt the loss keenly. 'Idiot!' Krüger exclaimed in a fury.

Steiner came striding toward them. 'Can't you keep hold of a rope?' he shouted at Dietz. 'You get that horse back or I'll show you something.'

Dietz stared for a second at his enraged face. Then he turned and dashed after the runaway horse. His feet were covered with blisters; for the past few hours he had only barely managed to keep going. But now he forgot his pain and exhaustion. He must make good his carelessness, he felt, and bring back the horse. He ran on among the trees and underbrush, stumbling, falling, picking himself up, scratching his face and hands on thorns and twigs till the blood ran. Still he panted on. Then he could no longer keep going. He leaned against a tree and dug his clenched fists into his heaving chest, while tears streamed down his face.

It was beginning to grow dark among the trees, and the woods were formidably silent. Turning his head a little, Dietz suddenly caught sight of the Russians. They were standing about a dozen yards away from him, not moving, just staring at him. There were five men in long overcoats, with sheepskin-banded caps, their tommy-guns pointing at him. Dietz gaped. But he felt no fear, nothing but a vast astonishment that gradually seeped throughout his entire body and transformed his legs into wooden posts buried deep in the earth. Movement was impossible. Then he suddenly remembered the platoon. He must tell Steiner about the Russians at once, must warn the men. How surprised they would be. They would certainly forgive him the loss of the horse. This thought so comforted him that he almost forgot the menace of the Russians. When they began coming slowly toward him, he pulled his numbed legs out of the ground and rushed away blindly. At his back he heard a shout and he hunched his head between his shoulders. How surprised the others will be, how surprised they'll be, he thought. His face was contorted, but he smiled expectantly at the thought of the impression his news would make. The shouting behind him grew louder. It bothered him, made it hard to think, but did not seem to mean very much. Suddenly something hit him in the back and threw him forward on his face. Above his head sounded the hysterical hammering of several sub-machine-guns at once. At first he thought someone had thrown a rock at him, and he remained lying where he was, startled. Above him the bullets hissed, slapped into the trees, hummed through the air as they ricocheted. Why are they firing like crazy lunatics? Dietz thought. He tried to get up. Then he realized that his body no longer obeyed him. His arms felt dead, and there was a dull, painful pressure against his back. With great effort he managed to slip his hand underneath his pack, but he could feel nothing in particular. When he tried to turn on his side, a fiery pain shot through his chest. He let his face sink to the ground and began to whimper.

After Dietz ran off in pursuit of the horse, the men sat down on the ground, their heads bent with weariness. Steiner remained standing near the other horses, pondering. It would soon be dark, and the end of the forest was nowhere in sight yet. During the march he had discovered that the horses were a hindrance rather than a help; their obstinacy constantly made for delay. He would long ago have released them and chased them off if he had not been worried about the condition of the men. They had been marching almost without interruption, and were completely exhausted. Under normal conditions they should have covered three times the distance they had managed to march. But the ever-recurring barricades of thorny undergrowth, the miles of swampy ground, the many narrow streams, had forced them to swing in countless wide detours, and eaten up their strength. Their original intention to use the road had to be abandoned, since the Russian's escape meant it would be guarded. They had followed it only for a few hundred yards beyond the brook, then struck out by compass in a south-westerly direction, straight across the woods. Since the road wound and turned, they had quickly diverged from it and were now somewhere in the heart of the pathless forest.

Cursing under his breath, Steiner glanced at his watch. Three minutes had passed since Dietz had rushed off after the horse, and Steiner suddenly felt an intense uneasiness. He turned to the men: 'I'll see how he's getting along,' he said. As he struck out in the direction Dietz had taken he reflected that his order had been idiotic. Once a horse started running a man could not catch up with it, anyway. He increased his pace. Since orientation was impossible in these dense woods, he relied on instinct. He had gone no more than 300 yards when off to the right he heard voices calling. He stopped as abruptly as if he had run head-on into a tree, and raised his head to listen. The calls became a furore of shouts, but he could distinctly hear single words. Russians, he thought with a stab of alarm. He peered into the darkening woods.

When the firing began, he doubled over, leaped behind a tree and raised his tommy-gun. The air was suddenly filled with a wicked hissing; ricochets slapped into the tree trunks, buzzed by his head like humming-birds and landed with a dull patter on the soft forest floor. It might be too late if he waited to fetch the men, he thought. If Dietz were still alive—and the Russians wouldn't be shooting if he weren't—there was not a second to loose. Scurrying from tree to tree, he covered about fifty feet. Then he began firing at random, holding the muzzle of the gun high. Once he thought he glimpsed a dark form among the trees. But since it might be Dietz, he did not dare fire at it. Then he realized that the fire of the invisible enemy was concentrating upon him. Bullets hissed over his head. Cursing, he darted behind a tree. He was in a bit of a fix. If the Russians realized they had only a single man to deal with, they would surround him quickly. Even as he thought this his fears were confirmed. From the right side a sub-machine-gun began hammering away, breathtakingly close. He swung round and began answering the fire—disregarding all caution, exposing himself to his previous opponents and blazing away blindly between the trees. Then he tumbled rapidly a few yards to one side, behind the next tree, and raised his head. The flanking fire had stopped; perhaps he had hit someone by chance. The rattling of the guns was continuing only from in front, where a strip of dense underbrush cut across the woods. He tried in vain to make out the flash from the hidden enemy guns, but it was still too light.

For a while he lay motionless, watching the cone of fire high above his head. They'll strip the leaves from the trees, if they keep firing like this, he thought, and rolled a few yards away.

His excitement began to subside. He had survived worse situations, after all. Had he not been worried about the platoon, he would have felt almost serene. In another ten minutes it would be too dark for the Russians to do anything. Flattening out behind the shaggy trunk of a black birch, he looked around alertly. The random fire of the Russians continued to lash through the leaves high up. He did not answer it. What could have happened to Dietz? He hoped the boy had not been hit. It didn't seem likely, since his uniform would have confused the Russians momentarily. Undoubtedly he was crouching somewhere among the trees, waiting for full darkness to come. Where could the others be? Even as he thought this, hell broke loose behind him.

When the din of the skirmish started, the men had leaped to their feet and looked about them in shocked surprise. Krüger stammered, 'Steiner,' and looked at Schnurrbart. Schnurrbart silently took the tommy-gun from his shoulder, his hands shaking. 'Bring the horses with you,' he said to Pasternack. 'Take the ammunition off them.' He began pulling boxes of ammunition from the horses and issuing curt orders which the men obeyed in feverish haste. A few seconds later they rushed forward toward the increasing clatter of rifles and sub-machine-guns. When the first bullets began whistling over their heads, they scattered and began answering the firing.

Suddenly they came upon Steiner, who had sat up facing in their direction. Maag noticed him first and shouted. The men stopped firing and Steiner came dashing toward them. As soon as they recognized him, they felt an enormous relief. 'Have you been lucky!' Krüger bellowed. He slammed Steiner on the shoulder. 'What'll we do?' he asked hastily. 'Where's Dietz?'

'We'll have to look for him,' Steiner said. The firing from the other side had stopped abruptly.

'They've cleared out,' Anselm declared. 'How many were there?' he asked Steiner.

'I don't know.' For a moment they stood inconclusively, until Schnurrbart grunted with impatience. 'Think we should follow them?' he asked.

Steiner shook his head. 'What for? We'll look for Dietz and then get out of here as fast as possible. Where are the horses?'

Schnurrbart jerked his thumb back, where Pasternack had just appeared, leading the horses.

'Let's start,' Steiner said. 'He must be somewhere nearby.'

They scattered among the trees and began searching the ground. Since the Russians might still be lurking in the vicinity, they moved with extreme caution. After a while they risked calling. It had grown much darker, and the search became increasingly difficult. Once or twice Steiner thought of sending up a flare, but it seemed to him too dangerous. His foreboding mounted. If Dietz were anywhere nearby he should have heard them calling. Perhaps it would be better to spend the night in this vicinity and continue the search next morning. Suddenly he heard his own name called. He recognized the Professor's voice and hurried toward it. As he approached he made out the rest of the men, gathered in a cluster and watching him.

'What is it?' he asked hoarsely.

There was a moment of silence. Then Krüger spoke up: 'Here he is.' A dark bundle lay on the ground. In spite of the gloom Steiner recognized Dietz at once. He knelt down beside him, removed his pack and turned him over on his back. Krüger switched on a shielded flashlight and Steiner unbuttoned Dietz' coat. The men leaned forward as Steiner opened the little fellow's shirt. There was a low sigh of relief as they saw no sign of a wound on chest or stomach. Then their features froze, mouths open. Steiner had turned Dietz over and was staring incredulously at two holes the size of hazel-nuts below the right shoulder-blade. There was no trace of blood, just a pink circle around the edges of the wounds. 'Damn it all,' Krüger whispered. The flashlight in his hand shook.

'Is he dead?' Anselm asked.

Steiner did not answer. He placed his arm around Dietz' waist and raised him up. Then he began rapidly bandaging the wounds. Dietz' heart was still beating, though rapidly and irregularly.

'Bring the horses,' he said curtly.

They tied the two horses close together, made a litter of ground-sheets, and cautiously raised Dietz to the backs of the horses. Not a word was spoken all the while.

'We must get out of here,' Steiner declared. He turned to Krüger.

'You and Schnurrbart follow at a distance. Make sure the Russians aren't following us.' He slung his gun over his shoulder and started back in the direction from which they had come. Pasternack and Dorn led the horses; the others walked behind to guard against Dietz falling off. It was pitch dark. Stars shone now and then through the leafy roof. The crack of dried branches under their boots sounded alarmingly loud. Schnurrbart and Krüger followed at a considerable distance, stopping now and then to look back. The woods appeared deserted. 'They've cleared out,' Krüger murmured. He sighed. 'It would be Dietz; that's all we needed.'

Schnurrbart nodded. 'That's only the beginning,' he said. 'The Ivans have picked up our trail now; just wait till daylight comes.'

'The devil,' Krüger said. He suddenly thought of Zoll. 'That dirty bastard,' he growled. 'If only I could lay hands on him.'

'Who?'

'Who do you think—Zoll, of course.'

'Oh, him.' Schnurrbart fell silent for a moment. 'He got his, don't worry.'

'How come?'

Schnurrbart shrugged.

'The whole forest must be swarming with patrols by now,' Krüger murmured. 'And when we get out of the forest, what a reception they're going to give us.'

Schnurrbart sighed.

Dietz was walking last in line, leading the horse by the reins and suffering terribly from thirst. Suddenly the horse pulled loose and Steiner came raging toward him. From that menacing face Dietz fled into the woods, running behind the horse. Often it was so close he thought he could reach out and grasp it. But it was always faster than he and escaped each time. He stretched out his arms, called and sobbed. Suddenly the horse stood still. But as he approached he was horrified to see that it had turned into a Russian with five heads, glaring at him with ten fiery eyes. He began to scream and the five-headed Russian began to scream, and as he stared at those malignant faces they merged into a single huge face with gaping maw, shouting at him, and suddenly he recognized it as the foreman stooping to pick up a monstrous brick. He turned and ran as fast as he could, making off among the trees, and the screams behind him grew worse, until something hard struck him in the back and threw him to the ground where he lay sobbing.

Then it seemed to him he was being lifted up. Somewhere sweet voices were singing a song of unearthly beauty. He raised his head, incredulous, and a happy smile passed over his face. Someone told him he must sing also. He opened his mouth and sang: 'Oh, the mountains, oh, the valleys.' Tears streamed down his cheeks; he could no longer sing because he was sobbing so hard. But he closed his eyes and listened, deeply stirred, until the song faded away. When he opened his eyes again, his first impression was of a gentle rocking motion that lulled him and aroused pleasant memories. He saw himself at home in Eger, walking through the streets of the older part of the city, going on down to the river bank and skipping flat stones over the water. He got into a boat and rowed upstream until he tired. While he let the current carry him back, he gazed dreamily at the green woods of the Fichtelgebirge and saw himself hiking among the quiet valleys and out-of-the-way villages. The boat rocked over the still water and the sun shone warm and pleasant upon him. But suddenly his mother's harsh, complaining voice rang out, scolding him, calling him a good-for-nothing for loafing around instead of working. Now he felt sad again; bitterness wrapped him in a black mantle that grew heavier and heavier, dragging him down to the ground, burying him.

A long while later, years afterwards, it seemed, he opened his eyes and saw Steiner's grave face bent over him. He tried to sit up, but Steiner held him firmly and said: 'Lie where you are, Baby; you must lie very quiet.'

'Lie very quiet,' Dietz whispered obediently, and nodded. Steiner glanced at his watch. It was an hour after midnight. He turned his head and looked over toward the men. All except the sentry were wrapped in their blankets and sound asleep. The horses, necks lowered, were standing among the tall, grim trees that surrounded the little clearing. They had reached this place after two hours of trudging through the dark woods, and Steiner had decided to stop here for the night. After arranging the order of sentry duty, he had sat down beside Dietz, pillowed his head on his arms and spent the time in anguished vigil. When Dietz began to stir, he had switched on his flashlight and examined his face. He knew that expression; he had seen it hundreds of times before. There were dark hollows under the cheekbones; the skin was drawn taut and waxen over the jaw, and the eyes were sunk in deep shadows that seemed to be spreading out slowly, consuming the rest of the face. Dietz would not live through the night. And since Steiner had realized this, something inside him had snapped. But he was unable to feel grief.

A while later, when Dietz opened his eyes again, he bent over him and asked: 'Are you in pain?' His own voice sounded grating. Dietz stared at him wide-eyed. Then he moved his head slightly and murmured: 'Thirsty.' He drank from the canteen Steiner held to his mouth and sighed gratefully. 'Enough?' Steiner asked.

Dietz nodded. He was fully conscious now and struggling to seize the broken thread of memory, to find some explanation for his present strange situation. He was conscious of the cold water running down his throat, filling his stomach, spreading through all the channels of his body. But the events of the day just passed were tangled in an inextricable knot with the fading of his recent delirium. Turning his head slightly, he asked: 'What's the matter with me?'

Steiner did not answer at once. Dietz' voice took on a plaintive note: 'Tell me what's the matter with me. Why won't you tell me?'

Steiner swallowed. 'Nothing much,' he said roughly. 'You were creased by a bullet, that's all.' He hesitated, and then added with forced cheerfulness: 'That's all, really.'

'Is it bad?'

'No, just a crease, I tell you. Nothing to worry about.'

'That isn't true,' Dietz stated. There was such certainty in his voice that Steiner caught his breath.

'What isn't true?' he asked helplessly.

'That it's nothing much. Don't lie to me; I can feel myself that my whole chest is smashed.'

'There's nothing wrong with your chest,' Steiner said. 'You were just nicked in the back, that's all.' He felt the perspiration starting on his forehead. 'Tomorrow we'll fix up a stretcher on the horses, and take you to the battalion. By the day after tomorrow you'll be on the hospital train and headed for home.'

Dietz did not reply. As soon as Steiner mentioned the horses, he remembered what had happened. Raising his head, he whispered: 'I'm sorry, I mean about the horse, that it got away from me. I——'

Steiner interrupted him. 'God, don't worry about the bloody horse. We meant to get rid of it anyhow.'

'You mean that?'

'Of course I do or I wouldn't say it.'

Reassured, Dietz closed his eyes and thought hard. He had been running behind the horse and had not been able to catch it. Then he had stood still, and then. . . . He opened his eyes wide and let out a terrible cry. The men started up, dazed and alarmed. The scream continued to issue out of Dietz like an endless coil of sound unwinding and unwinding from his throat. The men haltingly drew nearer. 'He'll have the Russians on our necks,' Kern said anxiously.

Steiner held the flashlight close to Dietz' face. 'Be quiet now, there's no need to be afraid, we're all with you,' he repeated. At last the screaming stopped. 'If only we had a medico with us,' Steiner said. 'He ought to have a shot of morphine.'

'He wanted to be a doctor,' Pasternack said. And after a pause he asked: 'Do you think he'll make it?'

Steiner did not reply. At last he looked up and said: 'You fellows better lie down again.'

'Lie down yourself,' Schnurrbart said. 'I'll relieve you. You have to get a few hours sleep too.'

Steiner shook his head. 'I'm not tired.'

The men returned to their places. When Steiner noticed that Schnurrbart was still standing beside him, he frowned. 'What's the matter?' he said irritably. 'I told you I'm not tired.'

'Don't be so pig-headed,' Schnurrbart said.

Steiner opened his mouth to reply angrily, but Dietz spoke first. Neither of the other two had noticed that his eyes were open and that he was watching them. 'You musn't bicker,' he said softly. 'Why are you bickering again?'

Steiner turned swiftly toward him. 'We aren't bickering,' he said.

'You are bickering. Make it up, please, make it up.'

Steiner switched off the flashlight. 'Please,' Dietz whispered. Steiner glanced at Schnurrbart, who stood motionless beside him. He could feel Dietz reaching out for his hands in the darkness, and soothingly ran his palm over the boy's damp forehead. 'Please.' The word was barely breathed. He nodded. Then he realized that Dietz could not see the movement of his head. Leaning over him, he framed the words, 'I will.' When he looked up again, he saw Schnurrbart softly walking away. Dietz lay motionless. Steiner looked down at the bright oval of his face. The woods were very still. Then a rustling began among the trees, and as it grew stronger the dying man's face underwent a strange transformation. The lines narrowed, became thinner and more delicate. The eyebrows arched high beneath a clear, white forehead; the ears were hidden in an abundance of wanton, chestnut-brown curls. Breathless, Steiner bent over him. Dark rings danced before his eyes, but he could see the face before him with great distinctness. . . .

Lips, red and softly parted, reveal small, shining teeth, and big dark eyes bent upon his in utter despair. His strength is giving out. He sees the snowflakes upon her face, and his bare hands ache unbearably in the frightful cold. A few minutes before she slipped on the narrow, steep mountain trail. He threw himself forward and grasped her outstretched hands. Then he slid, slid until he managed to hook his feet on something. Now he lies pressed flat against the ground, her face directly below his. She is dangling free over the cliff, while his fingers dig into her arms. He knows she is lost, and he stares into her face. She opens her mouth and speaks, but her words do not penetrate to his mind. It is as if he were dead and seeing nothing but her eyes. . . .

'You have no heart, Anne.'

'Yes, I do, Rolf. Here, I'll show you I have.' She places his hand on her small breast. It is always this way. When he becomes importunate, she disarms his impatience with a 'no' and a simple gesture.

He shakes his head: 'You don't know how hard this is on me.'

'I do know, Rolf.'

'A lot of good that does, then.'

'Be patient with me.'

He sighs, takes her face in his hands and examines it. His eyes rest upon her lips, and he says: 'Your mouth.'

'What about my mouth?'

'I don't know——' He laughs, abashed. 'You see, once a fellow kisses it he never gets over it.'

'Don't talk that way, Rolf. It sounds so strained and——' Her eyes avoid his, and she looks grave. 'And so sad,' she adds. Suddenly she throws herself into his arms. Pressing him close to her, she exclaims: 'Will you always be fond of me?'

'What would I be without you?'

When he tries to sit up, she holds him fast by the hair. 'That isn't an answer. Promise me.'

It is still and warm. Above the meadow the air quivers, and the trees reach up toward the sun. A butterfly wings past them and vanishes in the grass. Slowly he gropes out for her hand, brings it to his mouth.

'Always,' he says, 'always.' When she laughs happily, he draws her head to his chest and whispers: 'I must tell you this: you are everything that is lovely.' He gazes over her head at the woods, where the mountain lunges toward the sky, and goes on: 'You are like the air above the glaciers, and you are all the things I cannot understand because I am dazzled when I look at them. You are yourself, and ever so much more.'

Slowly she turns her face toward him, and he sees her tears. 'Say that again,' she whispers.

But he shakes his head. 'That sort of thing can be said only once, as all good things can be really experienced only once.'

She leans her head against his chest again and says: 'You talk like my father.'

He smiled. 'And you still behave like a child of fourteen.'

'Why do you say that?'

He places his hand on her firm, slender thighs, whose nakedness he can feel through the thin white skirt. 'That's why.'

For a few seconds they are silent. Then she brushes a strand of dark hair away from his forehead and says: 'Let us save the best for later.'

'How do you know it is good at all?' he asks quietly. 'Some people say it is ugly.'

She leans against him, and in a confusion of feeling he is conscious of the pressure of her breasts against his shoulder. 'It must be,' she says pensively. 'If it weren't, it would not mean so much to you.'

Her wisdom is such that he has to shake his head. 'You're an incredible girl.' He frowns. 'Before I met you I did not know what the human being could be.'

'And now you do know?'

'Yes.'

'Oh, Rolf!' She presses against him. 'Sometimes I'm so frightened.'

He looks at her in surprise. 'Frightened. You, Anne? For heaven's sake, what are you afraid of?'

For the space of a few heart-beats she looks down at the ground, hesitant. Then she lifts her shoulders. 'You're right, of course; I'm silly. But you see, you're going away again the day after tomorrow, and last night father said there might be a war and then you'd certainly go into the army and then you and I would——' Suddenly she begins sobbing. When he tries to kiss her to comfort her, she shakes her head violently. He waits until she is calmer. Then he says:

'Your father is foolish. Even if there were a war, it would be over in a month.'

There is a note of forced confidence in his voice, and she looks up quickly. 'Would you promise me something, please?' He looks at her questioningly. 'If there is a war you must come to our place, in Zurich. Father can get you a job and you can stay with us until the war is over. Promise me that?'

'That's impossible, Anne,' he says, gravely and firmly. She turns away, disappointed, and he places a hand on her arm. 'Be sensible, sweet. A man cannot simply desert. You can escape the law and the guardians of the law, but you can't escape your own conscience. I can't, anyway,' he adds, in a lowered voice.

She looks down at the ground, pouting, affronted. 'But you can escape from me, can't you? You can go away from me, perhaps for years, just on account of your miserable war. I don't matter to you. That's what you mean to say, don't you?'

'You're being so unreasonable,' he says, troubled. 'I've never known you to be like this. Look——' He lies down again and draws her down beside him. 'You must understand. If I go away from you I know that we will be parting only for a short time. But if I desert from home, I can never go back again. I'd have to remain an exile, an outcast. Is that what you want?'

She does not answer. His eyes rest upon the gathering clouds in the sky. It is going to rain, he thinks, and turns his head. Anne is lying beside him, eyes shut. He sees that her shoulders are quivering, and gently takes her hand. 'You must understand that,' he says softly. 'And you don't want me to be a fish out of water. You can't want that, Anne; you're not so selfish.' When she shakes her head, he kisses her. They lie close together, looking up at the silvery cone of the mountain top. Suddenly Anne sits up and says: 'But I have one thing to ask that you musn't refuse.'

'If it's something I can do, certainly.'

'I want to climb up there again tomorrow. Up our mountain once more.' Seeing his worried frown, she bends over him and looks pleadingly into his eyes. 'We can take the first train tomorrow morning. We'll be here by four o'clock, and there'll be plenty of time.'

'The weather is changing,' he says, eyeing the clouds.

She shakes her head wilfully. 'Tomorrow will be fair.'

It is hard for him to refuse. There is fresh snow on the peak and he knows how unpredictable the weather is at this time of year. Still. . . . Indecisive, he sits up. The political situation has been going from bad to worse these past few weeks; war is no longer so unimaginable. Although he has said nothing to Anne about his own fears, he knows she is right. This may be their last chance to be together for a long time. And if we do not reach the peak, it doesn't matter; we can turn back, he tells himself. It is 'their' mountain. That was where they had met two years ago, at the peak. . . . As she kisses him, he nods assent. . . .

Again and again he tries to find some support for his elbows, to draw in his arms, pulling her back up. But he no longer has the strength. She is still holding her head up, her eyes fixed upon his face. The wind is letting up, but the snow continues to fall in big wet flakes. His arms and hands are numb, insensible. Lying face down on the slope, his head lower than his body, has brought a rush of blood to his head; there is a dull roaring in his ears. He is aware that he is gradually losing control over his body. Her face is wet. He sees the snowflakes thawing on her skin, and wants to reach out a hand and wipe them away; he sees her lips twitching; sees the mortal fear in her eyes; and he gasps words that are intended to comfort her and that are only the inarticulate utterance of his horror. When she suddenly closes her eyes, he realizes that the grip of his hands has loosened. . . .

The roaring in his ears went on with unremitting intensity. Steady, monotonous, it seemed to fill all the air, beating its way into his consciousness, bringing him back to reality. When he sat up, he felt the dampness on his back and lifted his face in bewilderment. It was raining. The crowns of the trees were whipping about in the wind, but he knew this only from the sound; the trees themselves were lost in darkness. For a few seconds he peered about him, uncomprehending. Then he realized that his hands were clutched around something soft that felt strangely cold and lifeless. With a surge of disgust he let go and stood up. His clothes were soaked to the skin. He shivered. What has happened? he wondered. Then he came back to the present. The forest, the platoon and . . . Dietz. He knew at once that Dietz was dead. Feeling along the ground until he touched the flashlight, he snapped it on and directed the beam at Dietz. Dietz's mouth was open and the whites of his eyes gleamed under half-shut lids. He was already scarcely recognizable. With horror Steiner thought that he had been clutching Dietz' hands all this while. Quickly he stooped, tugged the woollen blanket from under the dead man, and covered his face. Then he looked over toward the sleeping men.

When he saw Schnurrbart walking slowly toward him, he switched off the light. He could feel nothing at all. The forest panted and groaned under the assault of the wind which shook the trunks of the trees and lashed them with rain. 'He's dead,' Steiner said. The storm wrenched the words from his lips. He held his face up to the rain, listened for a moment with closed eyes. Then he nodded his head and repeated: 'He's dead.' Gripping Schnurrbart's arm, he drew him across the clearing to the shelter of the trees. Then he slung his pack off his back, unbuckled the blanket and ground-sheets, and spread them out on the ground. They drew the canvas over their shoulders and stared into the shuddering darkness. Later, when the storm had let up somewhat, Schnurrbart said. 'There was no saving him.' Steiner nodded in the darkness. He had known that wounds like that were hopeless. 'And it's really best for him,' Schnurrbart went on. 'We would have had somehow to carry him all the way, and then try to get him across the Russian line. Couldn't have been done.' Steiner nodded again. Schnurrbart laid a hand on his arm. 'We mustn't let it get us down,' he said beseechingly. 'Don't forget what we still have before us. We've never been in anything like this before—not as bad as this.'

'I know,' Steiner answered.

Schnurrbart peered worriedly, trying to see the expression on the other man's face. The tone of Steiner's voice bothered him. 'Then you have to keep your chin up,' he said. 'Wish I knew what's been the matter with you lately. You used to be a lot different, Rolf.'

'I know,' Steiner said again. A gust of wind shook the leaves above them and sent huge drops of rain on their heads. Schnurrbart felt at his wit's end. Much as he disliked Steiner's cynical, superior attitudes, he wished at the moment that Steiner were like that again. Steiner had been on his mind for the past few hours. In the past, in similar jams, Steiner had always seemed to grow more confident as the difficulties mounted. His present state was incomprehensible; not even the death of Dietz could explain it, Schnurrbart thought. Still, that might be a factor. He would see. 'Sooner or later we all get it,' he said experimentally. 'Doesn't matter much who comes first and who last.'

Steiner did not answer. Schnurrbart went on: 'I always liked the kid, but damn it all——' He spat on the ground and stared grimly into the darkness. Steiner turned so abruptly that Schnurrbart started.

'Do you believe in God?' he asked.

It gave Schnurrbart a start, from which, however, he recovered quickly. The answer to that question had been given him in his childhood, and he had carried it with him ever since. It was beyond discussion. 'Do I believe in God?' he repeated slowly. 'Of course I do. At any rate, I believe we are dependent on someone who decides our fate.'

Steiner smiled savagely. It was the answer he had expected. 'You make things easy for yourself,' he said. 'I had the same idea once. But if there is a God, he's a sadist. That's my firm conviction.'

'You're crazy,' Schnurrbart murmured, alarmed by the blasphemy. He shook his head. 'You really are. Otherwise you'd see that all creation doesn't indicate sadism but—I suppose the word for it is love. Can you deny that?'

'I won't go into that,' Steiner said contemptuously. 'What about the other side? If I'm dying of thirst and someone gives me a pail of water, that's love, would you say?'

Wondering where this was leading, Schnurrbart nodded half-heartedly.

'Good.' Despite the darkness Steiner had detected the movement. 'So that's love. But if this someone takes the pail of water away from me when I've only had a swallow or two, that's love too, isn't it?' When Schnurrbart did not reply, Steiner leaned closer to him. 'You haven't an answer to that one, have you? I'll tell you the name for it, though. It's sadism, dirty rotten sadism, the kind of trick a real brute would think of. That's my opinion, anyway; you can like it or lump it.'

Schnurrbart closed his eyes, confused, groping for the right rejoinder. For a while there was no sound but the swish of the rain. When Schnurrbart spoke again, his voice cracked with repressed agitation: 'That's what you say. Speak for yourself. I'll tell you this: there are certain people who go on for so long hankering for a pail of water that's disappeared that they die of thirst, when all the while a brook is flowing past them a few feet away. Good night.' He stood up abruptly and walked off.

The following morning they buried Dietz. It was still raining, and the clouds hung low in the sky. The men dug a rectangular hole and stood around, soaked and shivering. A cold wind blasted across the clearing. When Steiner stepped up to the hole and looked down, the others silently approached. They had rolled Dietz in a tent canvas; he lay in the deep pit, small and inoffensive. The men held their short-handled spades in their hands and looked impatiently at Steiner.

'What are we waiting for?' Kern asked irritably.

Steiner sized up their dirty, unshaven faces. 'Maybe I intend to hold a funeral service,' he replied hoarsely. He wiped the rain from his face with his sleeve. 'It's something we don't usually bother with,' he went on, 'not out here. If Dietz had died at home, a few score, maybe even a hundred people would be standing around his grave, in their best dark clothes. Some would be crying because they really felt sad, and others because it was the thing to do.' He wiped his face again. They stared morosely at him. 'And if they met again later on they would say: so young; it's always the best who go first. And would look sanctimoniously down at their bellies and be glad they still had bellies—the god-damned overstuffed brutes,' he suddenly shouted. The men started. Schnurrbart, standing beside him, noticed that his shoulders were heaving.

'A few weeks later they would have forgotten him,' Steiner went on. 'I hope that none of you will forget him. I should be sorry for anyone who did.' He stooped and threw a handful of the black earth into the grave. Then, wordlessly, they all set to work closing the grave.

An hour later they set out, tent canvas over their shoulders, for the rain had not abated. They were still leading two horses, on which they had loaded the machine-gun's heavy ammunition boxes. The other horses they had driven away. Since they might run into Russians at any moment, they held their guns at the ready and moved cautiously ahead, keeping a sharp look-out to all sides. Schnurrbart talked in whispers with Dorn.

'That was a funny business before, but typical Steiner.'

Dorn nodded gravely. 'The strangest funeral oration I have ever heard. He's an original, no matter what else you may think of him.'

'You can think a lot of different things about him,' Schnurrbart said.

'That's so, but it's hard to judge him fairly. He must once have suffered a real trauma, a mental shock; that's the only explanation for his oddness.'

Schnurrbart turned his head suspiciously. 'Did he ever tell you anything?'

'Not directly,' Dorn said. 'But I gathered a little from things he said.'

'I see.'

For a while they walked along in silence. Schnurrbart considered whether he should tell Dorn anything about Steiner and Anne. He decided to keep his background material to himself. If Steiner ever found out, he would be through with him for good.

There was a halt up at the front of the line. The men were looking at a dense line of shrubbery about a hundred yards ahead. Beyond, the woods thinned out, and a steep incline rose sheer and grey. As Schnurrbart and Dorn drew closer they saw that what they had ahead of them was a hill.

'We're there,' Steiner said, glancing at his watch. 'We'll wait here until dark. Come along.' They went toward the bushes and forced a path through their tangled stems. On the other side of the hedge was an open field overgrown with tall grass. The chain of hills which began about a hundred yards further on was almost bare of vegetation. Half-way to the first hill a brook flowed across the meadow. It did not look wide enough to be a serious obstacle. The men stood close around Steiner, gazing in silence at the prospect before them. In thought they travelled back over the long trail through the forest. Fifty-five hours ago they had seen in the distance the silhouette of these hills which now lay close before them in this rainy noon hour. A promised land then, the hills presented a sad and dreary sight to the nearer view. The men thought of Dietz. A cold wind was still whipping the rain into their faces. Again and again the hill-tops were enveloped in drifting tag-ends of mist, and the sky was piled high with ledge-like cloud formations, grey and black. Steiner raised his head and listened to the hollow sighing in the trees. Then he turned to Schnurrbart. 'Tether the horses. We'll let them go this evening. One sentry will be enough; he can watch the meadow and the hills. I don't think we need fear any trouble from the rear. The rest of you find a good place in the bushes and keep out of sight.'

The men silently followed his instructions. A relatively dry spot in the heart of the thicket was covered with groundsheets. Anselm posted himself as sentry on the edge of the woods. The others began unpacking canned food and bread. After eating they stretched out on the ground and smoked.

They spent the afternoon sleeping. The weather continued the same, and it grew dark very early, so that they were able to set out again by six o'clock. They left the horses behind. As soon as they began crossing the meadow they discovered that the ground was extremely marshy in places, and within a few minutes their boots filled with water. The brook was small. As Steiner indifferently stepped into it—he was so wet already he could not be wetter—he was still wondering which direction to take. For the tenth time he tried to recall the position of the city as he had seen it from the distance two days ago. But the outlines had been too vague then, although he did have the impression that some isolated hills rose out of the mist to the south of the city.

Just as he was about to step out on the bank of the brook, he stopped abruptly, his feet still in the water. The others, too, froze in their tracks. About 500 yards away, above the hills, a white flare rose vertically into the air, paused for seconds as though hanging by an invisible thread, and then slowly fluttered down upon the meadow and faded out among the grass. Then it was as dark as before.

Steiner slowly climbed up out of the water and squinted toward the hills. The invisible soldier who had shot up the flare was stationed half-way towards the right, approximately in the direction of Krymskaya.

The others had all waded through the brook and came clustering around him in the high grass.

'What shall we do?' Schnurrbart whispered.

'Keep a sharp eye out,' Steiner replied. 'And stay close together.' He had made up his mind. As he slung the tommy-gun from his shoulder he said: 'If you see anything, fire at once without challenge. Clear?'

Carefully they made their way toward the hill and began climbing the slope. The bare ground was smooth underfoot; now and again one of the men would slip and slide back several yards, then get to his feet, cursing, and wipe his hands on his trousers. At last they reached the top and stopped to catch their breath. They could not see five paces ahead of them. The wind was no longer so violent, but the rain beat steadily against their faces, soaked their uniforms and seeped, cold and clammy, down their sweaty backs. Steiner waited a few moments until all had stopped panting; then he led the way due west. Within a few steps they were going downhill again. But the dip did not continue for long. They crossed a flat hollow and began climbing once more.

Suddenly a cry rang out of the darkness: '*Vnimanye*.' The men started as if a shell had exploded a few yards away. The call struck them so unexpectedly that they felt it like a physical blow that knocked them off their feet and froze their blood. They threw themselves flat and peered up the slope. Steiner looked back toward where Krüger must be and ordered in a whisper: 'Answer him, you idiot, answer him.'

It took a moment before the East Prussian understood. He raised himself up, funnelled his hands over his mouth and shouted: '*Tovarishchi—tovarishchi*.'

They held their breath. Not a sound came from in front of them. If the Russian had a flare gun with him now, things would happen fast. Steiner crawled on his belly until he reached Schnurrbart. He whispered: 'Crawl a hundred yards farther, over to the right, and wait there.' As the men slithered by him, he moved over beside Krüger. They lay close together, staring tensely into the impenetrable darkness. 'I don't understand it,' Steiner said. Why doesn't he do something?'

Krüger chuckled softly. 'I must have made it sound right,' he said. 'What do we do now?'

'Keep going,' Steiner decided. 'But we have to be more careful. Don't make so much noise. They must have heard us; they couldn't possibly see us. Come on.'

The platoon followed him like a many-limbed animal tensed to spring. For over an hour they went up and down the hills without incident. The monotonous tramp over soft ground, the steepness of the slopes that seemed to stretch on for ever into the nocturnal rain, their tops never visible until they were reached, the constant menace of the enemy who might confront them at any moment, drained the men. Their caution gave way to apathy. Not even Steiner's occasional sharp rebukes could shake them out of it.

Even Krüger and Schnurrbart were done in. Krüger was limping. For the past half-hour he had been feeling a stabbing pain in his right heel which grew steadily worse. Must be a blood-blister, he thought, and wondered whether he ought to take off his boot to look. But Steiner would not order a rest on account of a blister. Krüger cursed him fiercely under his breath. For a while he tried walking on tiptoe, but then the water in the boots was doubly unpleasant; at every step it bubbled between his toes and made smacking noises. I would get a blister, he thought, infuriated. It seemed to him incredible that his feet, so hardened to marching, should play such a trick on him—as though he were a raw recruit. His wet socks must have bunched up at his heel, and the skin, softened by water, have reacted to the chafing. The pain became unbearable. His shoulder, sore from the weight of the heavy machine-gun; the painful tugging at his hips, which bore the brunt of his pack with all its troublesome but indispensable equipment; the soaking uniform on his steaming, sweating skin; the plodding over soft ground where every step was an effort; the gloom and rain and uncertainty—all these other burdens vanished before the torment of his smarting heel. Suddenly he stopped and dropped the machine-gun to the ground. Its thud reached Steiner up at the front of the line. 'You're crazy,' Schnurrbart muttered to him. Krüger did not reply. He simply sat down on the wet ground and began untying the laces of his boot. He took off boot and sock and felt the soft swelling at his heel. When Steiner came over and looked down at him in silence, he did not even look up.

'Mamma's boy got a sore footy?' Steiner asked, his voice dripping scorn. Still Krüger did not reply. He stretched out his foot, held the painful heel up to the rain, and groaned with relief. Steiner's frown grew fiercer by the second. He stooped, picked up the machine-gun and asked: 'How long are we supposed to wait for you?' Stubbornly, Krüger held his tongue. The men had come closer and were grinning broadly.

Suddenly they fell flat on their faces as though all had been kicked in the back. In front of them, about at the spot they would have reached by now but for Krüger's breakdown, the night exploded like a ball of fire. A crashing roar broke over them, forcing their mouths open. Steiner lay with his face on Krüger's back. Krüger had forgotten his painful heel. The roar continued with undiminished violence. At last Steiner raised his head cautiously; he had realized that he was unhurt, and his analytic faculties, schooled by three years of war, returned to him. A moment later he had grasped the situation. The platoon was no more than fifty yards from the emplacement of a heavy Russian battery which must be up ahead in one of the innumerable hollows of this terrain.

Steiner slowly got to his feet and looked up at the battery, which was firing without pause. The others, too, got up one after the other. Only Krüger, Kern and Pasternack remained sitting on the ground. The East Prussian was clutching his boot and sock in his right hand, and his bare foot stood out as a bright shape against the dark ground. Steiner regarded him silently. Then he laid the machine-gun across Krüger's legs and said: 'Put on your boot before you catch cold.' The men's shoulders began quivering; they bit their lips and shook like saplings in a wind. Ignoring their amusement, Krüger carefully laid his footgear on the ground beside him, used both hands to draw his foot up above his left knee, and with his finger-tips felt his abused heel. Then he raised his head. 'Anybody got a needle?'

Silently, Steiner reached under his belt, fumbled for a moment, and brought forth a large safety-pin. 'Hurry up,' he said, not harshly. Krüger nodded. As he pressed the pin into his flesh, he felt the lymph spurt out over his fingers. 'More water in there than in all your heads put together,' he said. He carefully pressed out the blister, took a packet of bandages from a pocket, and bound up the heel. 'There,' he said contentedly, put on his torn sock and his sopping boot, and quickly stood up. As he did so the artillery fire stopped.

'A short cease-fire,' Schnurrbart murmured. 'They'll be——'

'Sh!' Steiner interrupted him savagely. They raised their heads to listen. Somewhere, surprisingly near, the shells were falling, and the men looked meaningfully at one another. Krüger turned philosophical. 'If we were over there,' he said. 'Over there where they're landing, we'd be where we want to be.'

They were still quaking inwardly from the shock and surprise, but they grinned and looked almost tenderly at Krüger. At this moment each of them felt about the others as he felt about himself. No better and no worse. They were very close.

They made a wide detour around the Russian emplacement. Their apathy had altogether vanished, had given place to an abnormal alertness. They started climbing again, and this time the ascent seemed to go on for ever. When Steiner suddenly stopped for no apparent reason, they raised their heads in alarm. The rain pattered evenly down upon their weary faces. They saw that Steiner was staring fixedly up the hill. 'What is it?' Kern whispered excitedly. Steiner pointed toward the darkness in front of them. For a few seconds they stared at the sky without understanding. Then they all saw it. For brief moments the outlines of the hill stood out, clearly visible against the rainy darkness; then it seemed to fuse with the darkness again, like water that is poured into a bottle of ink. At irregular intervals the same phenomenon was repeated. Before they could grasp the meaning of it, Steiner hurried on.

A few minutes later they reached the top of the hill and stood still again, panting for breath and shivering with emotion. At their feet the terrain fell away steeply to the south. Far below them stretched out what appeared to be a broad plain. An endless chain of dimmed headlights was moving from east to west. The whole of the western horizon stood in the spectral illumination of white flares. The men fought in vain against the emotion that tightened their throats and filled their eyes with moisture. They began to swallow and rub their hands over their damp faces. 'The front,' Maag whispered almost reverently. 'The front,' Kern repeated, placing his hands one over the other as if he wanted to pray. They stared fascinated toward the west. Steiner raised his arm and pointed to the row of lights. His voice thick, he said: 'That's the road to Krymskaya. The battalion must be dug in to the left of it. Fix it in your minds, in case we get separated.'

Schnurrbart threw him a glance. He was the first to realize the significance of the heavy traffic on the road. 'Man, something's going to be popping down there.'

'So what?' Steiner said, shrugging. 'Once we reach the battalion others can worry their heads about it.' He crouched down on the ground. 'We'll take a short rest here.'

Schnurrbart looked around uneasily. 'Isn't this place dangerous?'

'Not especially. At least from here we can see what's going on. Sit down. The final sprint comes next.'

'How do you figure to get through?' Krüger inquired. 'There are whole armies rolling along down there.'

Steiner grinned. 'Then us few Russians won't make much difference.' He looked at his watch. 'It's half-past nine now. We have plenty of time. There's no sense trying to cross before three o'clock—too much doing down there.'

The men sat down and began talking in whispers.

'Not a chance we'll get through there,' Kern protested. 'We must try it in some other place. Imagine what it's going to be like when we try to cross the Russian trenches. Why, it's mad!'

'Don't get so alarmed,' Steiner retorted contemptuously. 'We've made it this far and we'll make it the rest of the way, you can depend on that.' He turned to Dorn. 'Won't we, Professor?'

Dorn looked shiftily down at the ground. He thoroughly agreed with Kern and could only think with horror of what lay before them. On the other hand he did not want to provide Steiner with fresh food for mockery. He limited himself to a silent shrug. Steiner watched him out of the corners of his eyes. Then he laughed curtly. 'You seem to think differently. As you like. To tell the truth this whole business amuses me, amuses me enormously. Damn it all, what do you want? This is a bit of a change from sitting around in a filthy mudhole and waiting till one of those blasted things goes off over your head and turns you into fresh hash. Isn't it?'

He looked around at their abashed faces. Listening to the overtones of his own words, he felt a serene satisfaction because they had arisen out of his deepest convictions. The sense of being dependent only upon his own instinct for all decisions increased his boldness, gave him a feeling of immense confidence. Suddenly, in contrast to his usual manner, he grew quite garrulous and came out with a long string of cynical remarks. The men did not know what to make of Steiner in this new mood. Finally Krüger looked up angrily. 'Now cut it out,' he said. 'I'd like to know what's so funny. Was what happened to Dietz a big joke, eh?'

Steiner started as though he had touched a hot iron. Grief welled over him, along with a profound astonishment that he had not thought about Dietz for so much as a moment during the past few hours. Could the boy have meant so little to him that he was able to forget him within so short a time? The question was answered by the aching pain within him, which grew in intensity from second to second, washing away all his high spirits and arousing a dull rage that was directed solely against Krüger. The men were aware of the sudden change, and Schnurrbart gave Krüger, who was sitting in front of him, a furious shove. Krüger bit his lips. The words had slipped out involuntarily and he was already regretting them. Dorn, too, was distressed; it seemed to him that a harmless, casual conversation was being needlessly dramatized. He tried to stop the avalanche: 'Let's not weigh every word on a chemical balance,' he said. 'I think we all agree that war is horrible in all its manifestations.'

With a look of disgust, Steiner stretched out on the wet ground. Conversation stopped.

Later, when they began ascending the hill again, the incident was forgotten. Steiner centred his whole attention on the difficult terrain. Although the front in the main ran due west, there was a deep salient at one point, a wedge that appeared to expand far to the east. The flares which rose at regular intervals along the line gave him a fairly accurate picture of the course of the front, and Steiner vainly tried to understand why in defiance of all tactical rules the German commanders had permitted this extension of the line. Probably the reason lay in the character of the terrain, which he could not judge properly from his present position. They had reached the foot of the hill meanwhile and were now moving toward the front. They kept close to the line of hills until these turned off at an acute angle toward the north and the terrain opened up on all sides. The ground turned mucky and walking again became difficult. The front was closer than ever now. The men could already hear the boom of mortars and occasionally the hollow, heart-stirring chatter of machine-guns. During the past few minutes Steiner had been slowing their marching tempo. Now he moved forward toward a dark barrier that crossed the land in front of them. When they reached it they discovered that it was a shoulder-high line of thicket running along both sides of a narrow brook. The water was not deep, but the current was surprisingly strong.

On the other bank, Steiner stopped abruptly. He had bumped his head into an obstruction which proved to be the wire of a telephone line. It crossed the brook a few yards away and ran between the bushes toward the front. Thoughtfully he slid his fingers along the wire and stared into the night. The men thronged around him, and Anselm asked: 'Shall we cut the wire?'

'You're out of your mind,' Hollerbach said. 'We'd only bring the Russians down on our necks.'

Steiner considered. The moment he had touched the wire he had perceived how the platoon was going to cross the lines. He looked at his watch. It was shortly before midnight—too early to carry out the plan. He turned to the men: 'We'll have to wait two hours. Shortly before dawn will be the best time. Take a rest.'

They slipped their packs from their backs and crouched down on the bank of the brook, as deep in among the bushes as they could get. Steiner stood by for a few seconds; then he vanished softly as a cat into the darkness.

After following the wire for nearly half a mile, he came upon a Russian sentry. He fell flat to the ground, eyes fastened on the dark silhouette of the man, who stood motionless some seventy feet away. In spite of the distance he could hear the Russian whistling idly under his breath. The man's back was turned to him, so that there was no great danger of being discovered, and Steiner crawled a few feet closer. I should have taken Krüger with me, he thought. The original plan was better. The front line seemed almost within reach from here. Every time a flare rose up toward the sky, the figure of the sentry stood out plainly against the dark background. With satisfaction Steiner noticed that the direction he was taking led straight to the point of the protruding salient in the German front, which fitted in neatly with his intentions.

When he had got it all straight in his mind, he crawled slowly backwards, careful to make no noise at all, until he was far enough from the sentry to stand up without risk. As he approached the line of bushes he looked to his left, toward the road, and found confirmation of his earlier observations. At a particular spot the headlights of the vehicles were extinguished and it was no longer possible to see their course. He guessed that the Russians must be assembling their material at this spot. Probably there was a small village down there. The distance was too great for him to see anything more in the darkness, but his map would probably show. When he reached the men, he dropped to the ground and disregarding their eager silence took the map out of his pocket and studied it by the shielded light of his flashlight. His guess was correct. About a mile and a half south of the road was a fairly sizeable village, and off to the west, approximately in line with the front line, lay a wooded area, its northern edge bordered by the highway. As he examined the immediate vicinity of the wooded area he came across a number that attracted his attention: 121.4. He frowned thoughtfully. Possibly that indicated a hill, which would explain the puzzling wedge in the front line.

He looked up from the map and briefly outlined his plan to them. Concluding, he said: 'Of course we first have to find out how many bunkers there are. If you don't mess it up, it ought to work. Only you have to act fast, and with as little noise as possible. Close the doors behind you when you shoot, and don't miss.'

'The firing will be heard,' Schnurrbart remonstrated.

Steiner shrugged impatiently. 'There's always firing going on at the front. As I've said, be sure you close the doors behind you. Can you think of any better plan?'

They did not answer. Now that they were facing the decisive test, their excitement began to die down. Steiner's bold plan no longer seemed so fantastic, and the more they considered it the more hopeful it began to look. They talked in whispers. Kern, eyeing the front, remarked: 'This seems to be a quiet area. No artillery or nothing.'

'Why shouldn't our company come in for a quiet sector once in a while,' Krüger replied.

Schnurrbart grinned: 'If this is a quiet sector you won't find our company here. Take a look at that torchlight parade over there. Do you think they're laying Easter eggs?'

'Hell, no,' Maag said, looking down at the road, where the headlights of vehicles still showed.

'Our artillery is sound asleep again,' Kern said grimly. 'That stuff down there would be a sure target for a forward observer. They ought to be able to see what's going on here.'

'Shortage of ammunition,' Schnurrbart replied. 'You mustn't forget that our supplies have to come in over water. We'll need what we have when the big show starts.'

'When it starts!' Maag laughed cynically. 'When it starts our wires will be cut and the batteries blown up. There's something going on back there right now, and it's not a little show either.' He gestured toward the south where constant flashes lit the sky and a low rumble hung steadily in the air.

'Where would that be?' Krüger asked Steiner.

Steiner shrugged. 'I don't know. Maybe near Novorosisk. Won't matter to us, anyway.'

'I wouldn't say that,' Schnurrbart commented. He shivered and drew his groundsheet closer around his shoulders. 'If the Russians break through over that way, we're sunk. They'll reach the sea and we'll be right in the trap.'

Krüger nodded. 'If we lose the war then, do you think you'll ever get home again?'

Schnurrbart did not answer. He thought of Erika. She would marry someone else and he would spend the rest of his life pounding stone or working in a mine. His head drooped and he stared down at the ground between his legs.

'Its horrible which ever way you look at it,' Maag said gloomily. 'Whether we win the war or lose it, we're left holding the bag anyway. Do you think we'll get back into civvies, even if we do win the war? Don't you believe it!'

'Rot,' Krüger said irritably. 'What the hell would they do with all us soldiers when the war is over. They'll be glad when they don't have to pay us any longer.'

'They certainly will,' Maag replied excitedly. 'To win the war we'll first have to beat half the world, and if we do beat half the world we'll have to keep it occupied afterwards. Who do you think is going to do that job? The Party, maybe? They'll have enough to do celebrating the victory.'

'Don't talk to me about the Party,' Krüger growled. 'When the war is over they can do what they like with their Party and their army.'

Maag grinned cynically at him. 'You don't believe that yourself. What are you going to do when the war is over? Raise radishes?'

'None of your business whether I raise radishes or herring. The main thing is to get out of this stinking uniform and be a free man again.'

The other men had been only half listening to the conversation. The artillery fire in the south was dying down, and they saw a row of red flares mount into the air. 'Now they're attacking,' Anselm said excitedly. 'I hope they get a bellyful.' They gazed toward the south, where the sky was slowly beginning to redden as though dipped in blood. 'Something's burning there,' Anselm commented. 'What a show's going on down there. Attacking in this weather— just like the damned Ivans.'

Krüger turned to Schnurrbart and whispered: 'It's getting late. What the devil is he waiting for?'

'Don't worry, you'll have it coming soon enough,' Schnurrbart said indifferently.

'We'll see about that. Before they get me I'll knock off a few dozen of them, as sure as my name is Krüger. What do you think about the idea?'

'What idea?'

'The bunkers. We don't even know how many there are. And maybe the wire leads right up to the trench.'

'So much the better. We'll make it all the faster.'

Krüger shook himself. 'Damn this rain. I'm soaked to the skin. And on top of it all this darkness.'

'You'll be glad it's dark in a few minutes. I think we're starting now.'

Steiner had slowly got to his feet.

'Are we going?' Maag asked.

'Yes,' Steiner said.

The men rolled up their groundsheets. Then the platoon started off. Krüger stayed close beside Steiner, who went over his plan again. 'And when you know where you stand,' he went on, 'shake hands with him. I'll take care of the rest.'

The men stared tensely into the darkness and moved forward crouching. Everything would depend on the next few minutes, they realized. The rain spraying their faces with fine droplets made seeing difficult. Steiner began to be anxious. Had he mistaken the direction? He paused and peered uncertainly into the darkness. Suddenly a voice called to them. They were prepared for it and did not start. Steiner dug his fingers into Krüger's arm and whispered: 'Go on, answer him.'

Krüger took a deep breath. Then he shouted: '*Potselui menya v shopu—iddi zudda.*' Nothing moved. He took a step forward and said sharply: '*Biuda*!' Nervously, Steiner gnawed his lips. The men, breathing hard, held their guns ready to fire. Somewhere nearby a Russian machine-gun chattered; the noise plucked at their nerves, seemed to go on for ever. 'Damn,' Maag whispered, and took two steps back. Krüger, too, turned his head uneasily and looked at Steiner, who was already making up his mind to resort to force.

At this critical moment a figure emerged out of the darkness and slowly approached. Steiner swallowed; his relief was so intense that for a second he felt as if his body were no longer subject to the law of gravity. He lowered his gun and stared at the Russian, who had stopped a few paces away and was regarding them with curiosity. He was a lean fellow; his head protruded from the long Russian coat as though he had been stuck into a sack which was tied under the chin. He was carrying his tommy-gun loosely under his right arm, the muzzle pointed at the ground. '*Kuda*?' he asked. His voice was high-pitched and a little hoarse; it was evident from his tone that he was so far without suspicions.

Krüger went up to him. Reaching into his pocket he took out a single cigarette and held it out. '*Papirossa*?' The Russian nodded gratefully. The others could see only a little of his face. He put the cigarette carefully into his coat pocket and said: '*Spasiba*.' He was looking hard at Steiner, who began to wonder whether their caps were arousing his mistrust. But he turned to Krüger again and repeated: '*Kuda*?'

Krüger waved his hand vaguely and replied that they were going on a patrol up to the front. 'Where do you belong?' he asked.

The Russian began to speak freely, with the volubility of a person who is pleased to find something to break the monotony and wants to keep his visitor in good humour. By interjecting a few adroit questions Krüger learned that the man was guarding a Russian battalion combat HQ located in a bunker about a hundred feet away. But when the Russian went on to indicate that there were four bunkers, Krüger began to feel anxious. He looked at Steiner, who was standing beside him, half listening to the noises from the front. Their glances met and Krüger blinked. He exchanged a few more words with the Russian, then held out his hand, saying: '*Dosvidanya*.'

That was Steiner's cue. As the Russian shifted the tommy-gun to his left hand and held out his right, Steiner took a rapid step to the side and raised his own gun high. The Russian caught the movement. Terrified, he twisted his head round and tried to escape the steely grip in which Krüger held his hand. He opened his mouth to shout, but before he could utter a sound the heavy barrel of the tommy-gun struck him in the back of the neck. It had all Steiner's weight behind it. There was a horrible, cracking noise. Krüger caught the lifeless body and carefully lowered it to the ground. 'He's done for,' he said to Steiner.

'Move back,' Steiner said.

'He's done for, I tell you,' Krüger said as he stepped back.

'Better to make sure,' Steiner said coldly. He picked up the Russian's gun and swung it twice. Then he hurled it far away. The men approached, their faces white. 'Horrible,' Dorn whispered.

'You'll see things a lot more horrible in the next few minutes,' Steiner said. He turned to Krüger. 'What did he say?'

'This business isn't so easy,' Krüger replied hesitantly. 'There are four bunkers. A battalion HQ'—he detailed hastily everything he had learned.

Steiner shrugged. 'We'll have to do it anyway. Two men to each bunker. One will stay outside and stand guard.' He turned to Dorn. 'That's a job for you.' Dorn nodded, relieved. 'Let's start,' Steiner said. He assigned each man a bunker. 'Remember, no prisoners,' he whispered. 'And don't spare ammunition. Let's go.'

They moved forward again. After a few yards they saw dark mounds of earth rising above the ground, and a feeble gleam of light. The bunkers were scattered, not in a straight row as he had assumed. They were connected by a deep trench that led, with many windings, toward the front. The gleam of light came from the crack under a door. In spite of the darkness they could see telephone lines leading from all directions to one of the bunkers and disappearing into a rectangular opening near the door. 'Communications centre,' Krüger whispered.

Steiner scrutinized the bunkers. They were covered with freshly dug earth and seemed massively built. He turned to the men. 'I'll open fire. As soon as you hear the first shot, go in and close the doors behind you. Are your flashlights working?'

They nodded. 'Good. Depending on how many Russians are inside, one of you can hold the light and the other fire. Clear?' He turned to Dorn. 'You stay outside. If anybody comes along, fire at once, even if it's Stalin in person.'

They divided up in pairs and began climbing down into the trench. As Krüger stepped to the edge of the trench his foot slipped on the wet earth. He tried to throw himself backward, but the weight of the machine-gun hindered him. Anselm, close at his heels, reached out to grab him, but it was already too late. The bunker was directly opposite and Krüger fell heavily against the door. It yielded and he tumbled headlong into the interior of the bunker. For a few seconds he lay dazed. When he started to get up, a glaring beam of light fell upon his face and an incisive voice rang in his ear. Anselm, who had jumped down into the trench after him, stared over Krüger's body at the half-dressed figure of a Russian who was holding a battery lantern and shouting in fury at Krüger. At that moment the muted but fully audible hammering of tommy-guns began. The Russian flashed his light toward the trench. Krüger, who had recovered from his first shock, instinctively reached out and grasped the Russian's high leather boots.

'An officer,' he thought. With a powerful jerk he pulled the man off his feet. He saw Anselm raising his gun. 'Don't shoot,' he panted. 'Hit him on the head, on the head.'

Anselm hesitated. There might be other Russians in the bunker. Across the two men grappling on the floor he peered into the room. There was a candle burning on the table, a cot in the background, and blankets scattered around the floor.

'Hit him!' Krüger groaned.

The Russian fought desperately. His lantern had rolled into the trench and illuminated the scene. At last Anselm grasped his hair and slugged him on the head with the butt of the tommy-gun.

Krüger quickly got to his feet and shook himself like a dog emerging from the water. 'How's it going?' he asked quickly, stooping for the machine-gun.

'I don't know,' Anselm gasped excitedly. 'It's so quiet.' He looked down at the Russian, who lay motionless. 'What should we do with him?'

'I don't know. Maybe we can use him.'

He looked around the bunker. The Russian's tunic and coat were hanging from a nail. Krüger nodded with satisfaction. 'A captain. Must be the commander. We're sure in luck.'

'If he isn't dead already,' Anselm said. 'But Steiner said no prisoners.'

'We can always kill him later,' Krüger replied brusquely. He stooped over the Russian and took his wrist. 'There's still a pulse-beat.' He listened. The firing had stopped. No more than two minutes had passed since his tumble into the trench. He dropped the Russian's arm. 'We'll have to see what's going on. It's——' He broke off. Someone came running down the trench. They crouched, then recognized Schnurrbart and Kern. 'All right?' Schnurrbart asked, glancing at the Russian.

'How about your bunker?' Krüger returned the question.

'Four men.'

'Dead?'

'Yes. They were asleep. Nothing to it.'

'What about Hollerbach and Steiner?' Krüger asked nervously, mopping his damp face with his sleeve.

'I don't know,' Schnurrbart replied. 'We'll have to go and see.'

Krüger turned to Anselm. 'Watch the Russian.'

'Is he still alive?' Kern whispered.

'Yes,' Krüger said. The three of them hurried down the trench.

Steiner had picked the communications bunker for himself. Maag at his side, he pressed the door open inch by inch. The first thing he saw was the back of a man sitting on a chair, head drooping, dozing. Then he heard loud snoring and thrust his head in so that he could see the whole of the spacious bunker. There were six bunks in two tiers, each tier at right angles to the other. They filled the rear long wall and the right side wall of the bunker. On each of them lay a Russian wrapped in a brown woollen blanket, sound asleep. Most of them had their backs to the door. The man sitting on the left had in front of him a box containing a switchboard. Guns hung from a wooden pole driven into the earthen wall. The room was lit by two candles. Steiner closed the door again and turned to Maag. 'You take the beds on the right——' he started to say.

A low thud in the trench interrupted him. Aghast, they looked to the left where a loud voice suddenly bellowed incomprehensible phrases. 'Russians,' Maag gasped. For the fraction of a second Steiner hesitated. Then he swung round, kicked open the door, and stepped in. The Russian at the switchboard had jumped to his feet and was staring at him in surprise. Steiner forced himself to smile. He kept smiling and waited until Maag had slipped into the bunker. Then he slowly closed the door behind him. Out of the corners of his eyes he detected movement in the bunks. But his attention was wholly taken up by the Russian standing before him. He was a tall man with a mournful face under a shaved head. As he opened his mouth, Steiner shot from the hip. He saw the pupils of the man's eyes start to widen with horror, but his face did not have a chance to express the sudden emotion. The astonishment remained suspended in his eyes as he turned from the force of the bullets and toppled forward. Steiner whirled round. The beds had come to life. He saw jerking limbs, eyes goggling with the terror of death, heavy boots swinging through the air, blankets fluttering to the floor. Then there came a loud bellow of fear that was silenced at once by the hammering of his gun. Maag fired also. He stood crouching slightly, his back against the door, his face contorted. They braced the butts of their tommy-guns against their chests, took their stand with legs wide apart and squinted over the shaking barrels of their guns at the beds. The rapid succession of bullets tore scraps of wood from the bunks, caught leaping bodies and dropped them to the floor like sandbags, transformed open-mouthed, frightened faces into shapeless, bloody clods of flesh. Steiner acted in a fever. Objects swam before his eyes. The insane roar of the two sub-machine-guns in the confined space almost robbed him of the remnants of consciousness. When from one of the upper bunks a dark shadow moved and came flying toward him in a gigantic leap, he instinctively crouched and thrust the barrel of his gun into a face of which he saw only the blood-shot eyes and gaping mouth. Then the Russian's heavy body threw him to the floor and knocked the wind out of him. Abruptly, there was silence. From somewhere came the alarmed voice of Maag, calling him by name. Groaning, he tried to free himself from the weight on his chest. Then the Russian's body was pulled to one side, and turning his head he recognized Maag's smoke-blackened face. Pushing with both arms, he managed to sit up.

'Were you hit?' Maag asked in dismay. Steiner slowly shook his head and looked around. The Russian lay close beside him. At the sight of the man's face Steiner suddenly felt sick, and threw up. The gush of vomit was so violent that he was thrown forward. Spasm after spasm racked him, and he felt as if he were choking in his own slops. He writhed on the floor, snorting, struggling for breath. Maag stared down at him in helpless fright.

The door was kicked open and Hollerbach, followed closely by Pasternack, came rushing in. They stopped dead, stunned by the sight of Steiner on the floor. Before Maag could explain, Schnurr-bart and the others appeared. A few seconds later the whole platoon, except for Dorn and Anselm who had not left their posts, were gathered round Steiner and bending anxiously over him. Their concern was unfounded. Steiner had by now recovered sufficiently to be aware of what was happening around him. He still felt wretched and had to be helped up by the men, and his legs shook as he staggered to his feet. But then he saw the open door, angrily pushed aside the helping hands and cursed. 'You idiots, close the door, damn it!'

Krüger grinned. 'I thought so. There's still some bile in him, even though half of it is on the floor. How are you feeling, General?'

Steiner rubbed his mouth with the back of his hand and glared. After Maag had closed the door, they looked around. 'A regular slaughterhouse,' Schnurrbart exclaimed in disgust. 'This god-damned lousy war!'

Steiner picked his tommy-gun up from the floor and replaced the empty clip.

'Where do we go from here?' Krüger said with some imperativeness. 'We're apt to have visitors soon. They must have heard the racket we made.'

'So what,' Steiner said. 'There's room enough for more corpses here. What happened in your bunkers?'

The men reported. Hollerbach and Pasternack had had the easiest time of it. The two officers sleeping in their beds had never had a chance to wake up.

Steiner turned to Krüger. 'Is the commander in a condition to be questioned?'

'When I left him he was still taking a snooze,' Krüger replied. 'I can go and see.'

'You do that,' Steiner said. Krüger left the bunker. Steiner reached into his pocket and produced a pack of cigarettes which he silently passed to Schnurrbart. He took a cigarette for himself, stepped over the bodies lying on the floor and with the cigarette in his mouth leaned forward to the burning candles. As he stooped one of the dark-brown jacks on the switchboard dropped and a muted buzzing sounded. The men's heads jerked around and they looked at Steiner, who had frozen in the midst of his movement and was staring at the telephone jack. The buzzing stopped.

Schnurrbart came over to Steiner's side. 'What'll we do? If nobody answers they'll be coming to see what's the matter.'

'Get Krüger,' Steiner snapped, taking the cigarette from his mouth. Schnurrbart rushed out of the bunker. Steiner examined the apparatus. If was similar to the type of switchboard used in the German army. As he stared at the bright brass plugs he was struck by a thought at which he first shook his head, then involuntarily grinned. He turned toward the men and encountered anxious glances. Maag opened his mouth to say something. But at that moment the buzzing resumed, and instead of speaking he glanced impatiently at the door.

'Any of you know how to say "wait" in Russian?' Steiner asked.

All shook their heads.

'I'll see what's keeping them,' Kern exclaimed. As he opened the door, Schnurrbart and Krüger appeared. Schnurrbart had already told Krüger the latest development. The East Prussian went directly to the switchboard, picked up the hand-set and pressed the button above the jack. He brought the mouthpiece closer to his lips and said: '*Da.*' The men watched the tense expression on his face slowly disappear. With his free hand he reached out for the crank on the telephone box, turned it vigorously several times, and said: '*Kharshov.*' As he replaced the receiver, the jack sprang up. 'What is it?' Steiner asked quickly.

Krüger grinned broadly. 'What a laugh. Some fat-headed signalman decided to test the line.'

Steiner sighed with relief. 'He ought to be shot for that.'

The door was thrust open again and Anselm appeared, pushing the tall figure of the Russian officer into the bunker. The man's lean, pale face looked distraught. He caught sight of the dead bodies and swallowed. They could see his adam's apple bob up and down above his shirt collar. He turned still paler, and swayed from side to side, his eyes fixed upon a single point. Involuntarily, the men followed the direction of his gaze. From one of the upper bunks dangled the corpse of a Russian. He hung head downward; his finger-tips seemed to be reaching for some invisible object on the floor. The head was a dark blob from which blood was dripping on to the wooden floorboards. Already there was a large pool of blood. Schnurrbart felt an impulse to say something obscene. 'Like a virgin after defloration,' he commented.

'What the hell's that?' Maag asked.

'What?'

'That word you just used. Defloration, or something.'

Schnurrbart tore his eyes away from the corpse on the bunk and grinned. 'That's the fate worse than death that a virgin always lives through.'

The men guffawed, and the spell was broken. Steiner turned to the Russian again and studied him. Then he asked Krüger: 'Who told you to take prisoners?'

'You can kill him any time,' Krüger retorted.

Steiner shook his head. 'I've changed my mind, but in the future obey my orders, understand?'

Krüger fell into sulky silence.

'Come on, we'd better get out of here,' Schnurrbart said impatiently. He was suddenly filled with an acute dread which was only intensified by the sight of all the dead. But Steiner waved his protest aside. 'Five minutes more or less don't matter,' he said. 'We have a little more to do here.' He turned to Krüger.

'Did you find any maps?' he asked him.

'I had other things to worry about,' Krüger replied indignantly.

'Well, go and look now. Since this bird is the commander there must be maps of these positions in his bunker.'

Krüger went out.

'What have you got in mind?' Schnurrbart asked.

'You'll find out in a moment,' Steiner replied. He beckoned to the Russian. 'Come here.' The Russian raised his head; he was still standing by the door. The men had given him no time to put on his tunic. His high-collared shirt was smeared with mud. Steiner regarded his set face thoughtfully. The fellow did not look the type to yield easily. They would have to soften him up good and proper. Kern pushed him roughly forward, bellowing: 'Didn't you hear?' Steiner saw the Russian glare at Kern and clench his fists. 'Bring him over here,' he ordered. Kern gripped the Russian's arm and pulled him across the bunker to where Steiner was sitting near the switchboard. 'The bastard is still cheeky,' Kern said, frowning fiercely at the glowering prisoner. 'Should I smash his ugly mug for him?'

'Maybe later on,' Steiner said. He watched as the other men cleared the bodies out of the way, tossing them unceremoniously on to the bunks. For a few seconds he fought down a renewed impulse to vomit. Luckily, the door opened and Krüger came in with several sheets of paper. He dropped them on the telephone switchboard. 'That's all there were,' he said.

Steiner unfolded the maps and studied them. Then he smiled with pleasure. 'Nice work. Meyer will be glad to see this stuff.' With his finger he traced the lines. The map was distinctly better than his. The course of the front line was marked in red pencil, and the sectors of the different companies were neatly divided up, although there were no indications of the numbers of the companies. The battalion combat HQ was marked by a red circle. Steiner also found the explanation for the peculiar salient in the main line of resistance at this point. He turned to Schnurrbart, who was peering inquisitively over his shoulder. 'You see that? There's a ridge in front of us, and I'll stake my head on it that our company is over there. The line runs out around here'— his finger pointed to the area marked out with brown crosshatching. 'Now we know just where we stand.'

Finger on the map, he considered for a moment. It would obviously be best to try to get through right at the point of the salient. This route was shortest and easiest. He turned to Krüger. 'Now let's see what you can do. What I have in mind depends on you, because it depends on the Russian. Look here.' Krüger bent over the map. 'You see the point of this angle here?' Krüger nodded. 'Good. That's where I want to cross. Now I have to know which company is stationed there.'

'Which Russian company?' Krüger asked.

'Of course. What's on the other side of the line doesn't interest me until we get there.'

Schnurrbart took the pipe out of his mouth. 'Isn't that marked on the map. Which company, I mean?'

Steiner shook his head. 'If it were, I wouldn't have to ask the Russian.'

'Well, let's see,' Krüger said. He turned to the Russian, who had been listening darkly to the conversation. When Krüger held the map up in front of him and spoke to him, he turned his head aside and set his lips. Steiner raised his hand. 'He wants to play the hero,' he said. 'But we can knock that idea out of his head.' He stood up and looked at the Russian officer. The man was wearing his trousers without a belt. Steiner reached out so quickly that the Russian's defensive gesture came only after the buttons had given and the trousers slipped down to the floor. For seconds the Russian stared at the grinning men, his face contorted with fury. But when he stooped to pull up his trousers, Steiner struck him in the face so brutally that he fell over backwards and lay groaning on the floor.

'That was only the beginning,' Steiner said fiercely. 'Undress him completely.'

The men stared at him in astonishment. 'Hurry up about it!' he snapped at them. Silently, they obeyed. The Russian's initial resistance quickly ceased. A moment later he lay naked on the floor, panting from indignation and struggle. Steiner sat down again and regarded him coldly. 'Stand him up,' he ordered curtly. As though he had understood the order, the Russian sprang to his feet of his own accord. Without clothing he looked spare and helpless. His mouth and nose were bleeding; he rubbed the back of his hand over his face. 'I never knew a man who was ready to be a hero in his birthday suit,' Steiner drawled.

He took his bayonet out of his belt and threw it skilfully across the bunker so that it stuck in the wooden floor close to the Russian. 'If he doesn't talk, we'll castrate him,' Steiner said. He spoke urgently to the men. 'Everything depends on him. If he tells us lies or refuses to talk, we're going to have a damned hard time of it, understand?'

They looked at Steiner's set face, and then at the Russian. Steiner was right, they felt, and the idea of falling into the hands of the Russians now that they were so close to safety drove all mercy out of their heads. Kern rubbed his finger-nails on his coat sleeve and growled: 'I'll cut him up piece by piece if necessary.'

'Then we agree on what we're to do,' Steiner said. 'Tell him, Krüger.'

Krüger spoke harshly, gesturing repeatedly at the bayonet on the floor. The Russian's face reflected in turn shame, fear, rage and resolution. Steiner, studying him closely, thought he could guess his reaction in advance. He was right. When Krüger stopped talking and held the map up in front of the Russian, the skin tightened over the man's cheekbones and he said in a firm voice: '*Nyet!*' There was a collective groan in the room. The men moved threateningly closer to the prisoner. Steiner got up and slowly approached him, taking each step with deliberation. When he came up to the man, he stooped, pulled the bayonet out of the floor and toyed with it. 'So you don't want to,' he said softly. Then he took a step backward and ordered: 'Lay him down.' They threw him to the floor. When he tried to scream, Krüger slapped his mouth. They knelt on his arms and legs and held him fast. His eyes were fixed upon Steiner with an expression of mortal terror. Steiner clenched the bayonet in his right hand and slowly bent over him. When he raised his arm, a babble of words burst from the Russian's lips. Krüger listened expectantly. When the Russian stopped, he turned to Steiner, grinning. 'Good enough. He says it's the 3rd Company at the point, the 1st and 2nd are on the left and right respectively.'

The men looked at Steiner with visible relief. Steiner was still frowning fiercely at the Russian. Before anyone could stop him, he brought his boot forward and stepped heavily between the man's legs. The Russian let out a piercing scream and doubled up in agony. 'You're crazy,' Krüger growled. The others looked at Steiner with outrage in their eyes. Steiner tossed his head impatiently and said: 'This bird wasn't nearly softened up enough for what I intend to do with him.'

'You've already got your information,' Krüger protested angrily.

'Sure, but that's only a starter.' They looked blank. He smiled and said: 'Take him over to the switchboard.'

They pulled the Russian to his feet again, dragged him across the bunker and plumped him down in the chair. Steiner leaned over the switchboard and studied the numbers over the contacts.

'What are you up to?' Schnurrbart asked impatiently.

'You'll see,' Steiner said. He turned to Krüger. 'We're going to call up the 3rd Company.'

They looked at him as if he had gone out of his mind. He let them thresh for a few seconds, enjoying their consternation. Then he said: 'That's right, we're going to telephone the 3rd Company. This bird'—he indicated the Russian, who sat doubled over on the chair, hands between his legs—'this bird is going to tell the company commander that a reconnaissance patrol is on its way.'

'A reconnaissance patrol!' Schnurrbart whispered. Suddenly he slapped his thigh and burst into laughter. Kern had not yet understood. He looked at Krüger, who excitedly plucked at his nose, and wrinkled his brow, until all at once a broad smile of understanding spread over his face. 'Why that's—I'll be damned—what a mad—what a——' He pounded Steiner on the shoulder. 'You're the maddest man I ever met,' he declared admiringly. The others still looked baffled. 'Don't you understand yet, you idiots,' Krüger boomed. 'This Russian will tell his company commander that a reconnaissance patrol is going to cross the lines, so the boys have to keep quiet and not shoot.' Laughing, he turned to Steiner. 'They'll give us a guard of honour, I tell you, a guard of honour.'

Steiner twisted his mouth in a thin smile. 'I think we had better dispense with that,' he said. 'It might be too much of a good thing.' The smile vanished. 'You've got to realize that if the Russian says one wrong word he can bring the whole company down on our necks. Keep tabs on him.'

'You can depend on that,' Krüger said fiercely.

Krüger told the Russian what was expected of him. If he were sensible, he said, they would take him with them as a prisoner—and he would be a lot better off than if he lay here mutilated and slowly bleeding to death. Intimidated, the Russian nodded.

Schnurrbart hooked up the second telephone and blew into the receiver several times. 'It works,' he said to Steiner. 'We can try it.'

He placed the receiver in the Russian's hand. Kern stepped up behind the man and almost tenderly placed his hands around his throat. The Russian hunched his head between his shoulders and pressed the receiver to his ear. Steiner exchanged a glance with Krüger. Then he pressed one of the black buttons and turned the crank. There was a dead silence. Steiner drummed his fingertips on the wooden case that housed the switchboard. In a moment they would see whether he was risking too much. All at once the plan seemed to him crazy and impossible. He wished he could stop the call, but it was already too late. The prisoner began to speak. He spoke slowly; only a very attentive listener would have detected the excitement in his voice. The men kept their eyes on his face; their fists were clenched and they held their breath. Anselm stood with eyes closed. It can't work, it just can't, he kept thinking. He was so convinced that the telephone call would end badly that he still held his eyes closed when the prisoner's voice had stopped and Krüger sighed with relief and replaced the receiver on the hook. 'It worked,' he said. Anselm opened his eyes in astonishment and saw around him the men's white faces.

'Nobody will believe us when we get back,' Pasternack whispered. 'If only Dietz had lived to see this.'

Steiner turned slowly toward him, his mouth twitching. Suddenly Schnurrbart laid his hand on Steiner's shoulder. 'If it hadn't been for you,' he said impulsively, 'we never would have got out of here. Never, believe me.'

'No laurels in advance,' Steiner said roughly. 'We aren't out yet. Besides'—he looked at Krüger—'without you there would have been no way to pull this off.'

'Right,' Anselm exclaimed. He stepped up to Krüger and shook his hand vigorously. 'You really handled that swell. We were lucky to have you with us.'

Krüger was taken aback. He tried to conceal his pleasure and play modest. 'Oh, hell,' he said. 'What good would my Russian do me if Steiner didn't have the ideas.'

'Do your back-slapping later on,' Schnurrbart said. 'It seems to me high time we got out of here.'

They looked at Steiner for further orders. 'We'll take the Russian with us,' Steiner said. 'Better put him in one of the dead men's uniforms so he doesn't attract attention. He'll march between Krüger and Kern. If he attempts to escape, hammer him. Don't shoot. Krüger, tell him that if he opens his mouth on the way he's done for. He can make trouble for us, but it won't do him any good.'

While Krüger translated, the men stripped one of the bodies. Steiner tucked the Russian maps carefully into his coat pocket. He watched as the prisoner donned the bloodstained uniform. Before they left the bunker they dropped the switchboard and telephones to the floor and trampled on them. Then each of the men took a souvenir—the Russian officer's uniform on the floor was almost torn to pieces. Maag, Hollerbach and Dorn joined them at once, and Steiner explained in a whisper what had been happening. Then they set out along the trench leading toward the front line.

It was still raining, a thin, even drizzle. The front had quieted down all along the line. But flares still rose, hung trembling against the clouded sky, fluttered noiselessly down to the ground and went out. Schnurrbart followed Kern. He had slung his tommy-gun over his right shoulder, buried both hands in his trousers pockets, and walked with head drooping in thought. Soon the trench became shallower, and ended in a grassless plain that sloped slightly upward. 'Quite a bit of construction for two nights,' Maag, walking behind him, whispered.

Schnurrbart nodded. The Russians must have worked like

moles, he thought. But undoubtedly they had mobilized the entire civilian population of Krymskaya; were it not for the rain the platoon probably would have run into a construction crew by now. That would have meant more trouble. As it was there were dangers enough to pass through before they reached the German trenches. Suddenly something occurred to him. He hurried past the file of men until he came up with Steiner. 'Do you think all the Ivans have been warned we're coming?' he asked.

'Yes,' Steiner said. 'Look up ahead. Don't you notice anything?'

The other men had caught up with them, and all looked, but they saw nothing in particular. It was impossible to see more than a dozen paces ahead anyhow, and the occasional glow of flares above the trenches was swallowed up in the darkness before it reached them. 'Dark as the inside of a black cow's belly,' Kern whispered.

Steiner raised his hand impatiently. 'Don't you see anything?'

'Sure,' Schnurrbart nodded, 'if you mean the flares.'

'I do mean them,' Steiner replied with a scornful undertone. 'Not the ones you see but the ones you don't see.'

Schnurrbart shook his head. 'That's too much for me.'

'Not for me,' Dorn said.

The men looked at him. 'We know you're smart,' Schnurrbart growled.

'You don't have to be particularly smart to see this,' Dorn replied evenly. 'If you look close you'll notice that the Russians directly in front of us are not firing any flares; all of the flares are coming from the other side.'

'Right,' Steiner said approvingly. 'So the Russians are just waiting until we come through. Stay close together from now on. In case we're spoken to, Krüger knows what to do.' He slipped the gun from his shoulder and went up to the Russian. 'One word from you, you bastard,' he said threateningly, 'and we'll tear you to pieces!'

'He can't understand,' Kern said.

'He understood that, don't worry.' Steiner turned away and moved forward, taking long resolute strides. According to the map, the distance between the battalion command post and the positions of the 3rd Company was about a mile. They must have covered at least half that distance by now. The men moved in a knot. Kern was walking so close behind the prisoner that their bodies touched. He was acutely conscious of the responsibility resting upon him, and he wanted Steiner to be satisfied with him. At the first suspicious movement on the Russian's part he was determined to kill him, even if he himself were killed in the process. The thought filled him with pride. Suddenly he felt a part of the platoon, as though he had been with it for ten years. It's a damn fine thing to belong to a crowd like this, he said to himself. We all belong together. All for one and one for all. He no longer remembered where he had picked up the phrase, but it sent strange chills down his spine, plucked strings in him that momentarily made his eyes fill with tears. It was a great thing to have comrades. As he listened to the crunch of the gravelly earth underfoot and the stirring noises from the front, he was more and more overwhelmed by this emotion. Comradeship is everything, he thought. It didn't matter if you pitched into each other once in a while; what mattered was that you could depend on the others when you were in trouble. And by God you could depend on these fellows here. You really could, and he was damned glad to be in their platoon and not in some other. Later, when the war was over, he would invite them all to come to his inn. The idea enchanted him. He turned his head and glanced almost with tenderness at Dorn, who was stumbling along behind him. The longer he thought about it, the more enthusiastic he became. He'd keep them for two weeks; they could eat all they had room for, and sleep in his bedrooms, and he would hang a big sign on the door: *Closed for veteran's reunion.* Yes, by God, he would do it, and every night he would bring up the best stuff in the cellar and they'd talk about the past, how they had marched through this damned dark night and through the goddamned woods and how they had undressed the women and almost run head-on into the Russian artillery emplacement, and how they had all been scared stiff. He could see the whole scene: all of them sitting around the big round table in his inn, laughing, slapping each other on the back, the glasses tinkling as they touched. Then he would stand up and make a speech, a fine speech in plain words, and at the end they would stand up and bow their heads and think of Dietz, of Dietz and . . . oh, well. . . . He ran his sleeve over his face, wiping away the picture.

Meanwhile they had come so close to the line that they had to fall flat as each flare went up. While the Russians up ahead of them remained absolutely quiet, machine-gun and rifle fire from the other side often passed close over their heads, so that for stretches they had to crawl on all fours. 'Idiots!' Krüger whispered indignantly. He stuck close by Steiner's side.

At the moment Steiner was flattened out on the ground, peering ahead.

'You should have sent them a postcard that we're coming,' Steiner growled. 'But you're right, they seem to be awfully nervous over there. They might be getting nervous because the Russians are so quiet.'

He concentrated on the ground before them. The ground was still rising. It was muddy now, and made progress difficult. But the rain had stopped. On the other side, about 200 paces away, another flare was shot up. For a few seconds all the features of the terrain could be seen. In front of them, a good stone's throw away, a dark wall rose above the ground. Steiner guessed that it must be the rampart of the Russian trench. The eastern slope of the hill was also distinctly visible. The German line must run somewhere along over there. When the flare went out, he glanced briefly back at the men. They were lying flat on the ground, motionless. Wearily, as though the burden of the pack on his back had suddenly increased many times in weight, he straightened up. For a few seconds he stood indecisive. 'What is it?' Krüger whispered. Steiner did not reply. His original intention of leading the platoon in a body across the no-man's-land, across these damned crucial hundred yards, now seemed insane. Frowning, he considered the situation. There seemed to be only one way to keep the platoon from being mowed down by their own machine-guns.

He beckoned the men to him and explained in a whisper. 'And suppose you get hit?' Krüger asked uncomfortably.

'With a little luck it ought to work,' Steiner said. 'But if I am, Schnurrbart must try it next. We haven't much choice. You come with me now. We must first find a place where you can cross afterwards without being stopped. Then you go back and wait for the flares. If nothing happens in fifteen minutes, Schnurrbart had better set out. I——' He threw himself to the ground. A chilling howl hurtled toward them, and they pressed their faces into the damp earth. Then came the frightful crash of the explosion, and a few seconds later a hail of large and small lumps of earth pattered down on their backs. They waited with bated breath until the wicked hum of the splinters stopped and the silence washed over them like water. Steiner raised his head and shook off the paralysis of shock. All year long they have no ammunition, he thought fiercely, and they have to pick this moment to throw the stuff around.

The men came to life again. Schnurrbart wiped his muddy face and began to curse softly. 'There'll be more,' Krüger warned. 'They never fire only one shell.'

'They always fire just one shell,' Schnurrbart answered. 'Ever since I've been in this bloody army they fire one shell and hit their own men with it.' They listened fearfully to the darkness.

'Calm down,' Steiner said. 'If any more come, we can't do anything about it.' He turned to Krüger. 'We have to start. Everything clear?'

'Clear as mud,' Krüger said gloomily.

He passed the machine-gun to Maag, who stood beside him. The prisoner was sitting on the ground, crouching forward, motionless. 'Keep a close watch on him,' Krüger said to Kern. 'If he makes a sound now, we're sunk.'

'He won't,' Kern promised, spreading his fingers significantly.

'Good luck,' Schnurrbart whispered uneasily.

Steiner nodded. As he and Krüger disappeared into the darkness, the men stared anxiously after them. They cowered on the ground and waited.

Flattened out, the two crawled up to the Russian trench. They were within a few yards of it when Krüger suddenly hissed softly and clutched Steiner's foot. Steiner turned toward him and breathed: 'What?' Silently, Krüger pointed to the left. For a few seconds Steiner peered; then he saw the Russian. The man was standing in the trench, his helmet rising shapeless above the mounded earth. 'To the right,' Krüger whispered. With infinite caution they crawled over the slippery ground. They moved about fifty feet parallel to the Russian trench before Steiner abruptly turned. Panting, Krüger crawled up beside him. Their uniforms were pasted to their bodies, their faces and hands smeared with mud.

'Do you see anyone?' Steiner whispered.

'No.'

Steiner hesitated. Then he stood up and walked on, crouching. When he reached the trench, another flare rose from the German lines. He dropped quickly to his knees and looked up and down the trench. It was not occupied here. He waited until Krüger came up beside him, then whispered: 'Not this place. This is where you must cross. Right here, understand?' He straightened his belt. 'You can take my tommy-gun. I won't need it any more.'

'Why?' Krüger whispered anxiously.

Steiner looked across the trench. Somewhat to the right a German machine-gun was firing tracer rounds. He watched them fade out in the darkness like shooting stars. The flare was dead now; no-man's-land stretched before him, black and hostile.

'Because deserters don't carry weapons when they cross the lines. Go back now.'

Krüger hesitated. Then he reached out for Steiner's hand and pressed it hard. 'If anything happens to you,' he said fiercely, 'I'll kill them all.'

'Too damn many of them,' Steiner murmured. 'Get going.'

He watched Krüger crawl off until the dark shadow on the ground was absorbed by the surrounding gloom. Abruptly he felt terribly isolated. For a while he stood staring across the trench, jaw set. He wished he could turn back and take one of the men with him. One of the men. . . . He remembered that they were waiting for the signal, and pulled himself together. Cautiously he climbed up the other side of the trench, clambered over the rampart, and waited until the next flare came. When it faded, he straightened up and tensed his body. His heart suddenly began to pound like mad, and he sank back on the ground. 'Stand up, you fool,' he chided himself. 'Stand up.' His legs were trembling violently; he panted, gasped for air and dug his fingers into the soft earth. For a few seconds he fought desperately against his fear, against the sheer terror that pinned him to the ground and threatened to crush his will. His face was contorted, and he stared wide-eyed at the height where the German line must be located. Groaning between clenched teeth, he tried to force his body into motion. But the night lay with a frightful weight upon his hunched back. It clutched at his throat until he felt that he was choking; a sound like a death-rattle emerged from his mouth, and spittle trickled from his lips on to his hands. He fought against himself. Suddenly the whole area was illuminated again. This time there were two flares sent up from different spots; they rose almost vertically, drifted sideways, driven by a faint breeze, and wrapped in their bright light sailed down toward the ground. At that moment he pulled himself up, braced his shoulders against the returning darkness and charged forward, mouth wide open. He saw nothing, heard nothing. His feet churned the ground; in a few seconds he had crossed the level space and was flying as if hurled out of a catapult up the slope. He had come within about twenty yards of the German line when the next flare arose. Then he threw his arms up and began to shout.

VI

Meyer waded through the water in the bottom of the trench, feeling the rain patter down on his face. He stumbled over something, and fell. Cursing, he got up and groped for the obstacle. It proved to be a length of wood that had jammed between the walls of the trench and in spite of all his efforts would not move. Irritably, he kicked at it. Then he noticed an opening in the left side of the trench, and when he cautiously climbed into it he found that it was a well-constructed machine-gun emplacement, provided even with a convenient bench for sitting. As he straightened up he knocked his head against a ceiling beam. He glanced through the wide embrasure, but the darkness was as impenetrable outside as in. Nevertheless, he felt a certain sense of comfort in here, and the feeling was intensified by the pattern of the rain outside. Sighing, he dropped on to the bench, hunched his shoulders and listened to the monotonous, lulling sound of the rain. He closed his eyes. A long while afterwards—he did not know whether minutes or hours had passed—he was startled by a noise. He heard a voice, and when he opened his eyes he thought he detected the shadow of a man moving in front of the dim rectangle of the entrance. 'What's the matter?' he snapped.

There was a silence outside. Meyer was wide awake now. Automatically he reached for his pistol-holster, and sprang to his feet. Then he heard a voice which was unmistakably Lieutenant Gausser's saying: 'What little beast's crawled into this nice burrow?'

Momentary embarrassment made Meyer duck his head. But his sense of humour came to his rescue and he answered jokingly: 'If you mean me, Lieutenant Gausser, I must insist upon a more respectful tone toward a fellow-officer.'

From outside there came an exclamation of surprise. Then Gausser's lean figure appeared. 'Meyer,' he blurted, 'how the devil did you get into this cave?'

'Through the entrance, Gausser, through the entrance, even as you yourself.' They stood facing one another in the darkness, unable to see more than the blurred outlines of their bodies. Meyer explained. 'I must have fallen sound asleep,' he concluded. 'After all, it doesn't matter much whether I spend the night here or in my bunker. But what brings you out at this hour? I would have thought you'd gone to sleep long ago. Whom were you talking to outside there?'

'Too many questions at once,' Gausser said. 'I stumbled over that wood in the trench just as you did. Was just making a tour of the positions. I wasn't talking to anybody, just cursing to myself. I suppose that woke you. Shall we sit down?'

'Why not?' Meyer said. They moved close together and lit cigarettes.

'Miserable weather,' Gausser growled.

Meyer nodded. 'If it lasts much longer,' he said, 'the bunkers and trenches will collapse on us. I would never have thought the rainy season could go on for so long.'

They fell silent and looked out through the loophole. Now that he had recovered from his initial surprise Gausser began to consider the reason for Meyer's presence here. Undoubtedly he was waiting for his platoon, he thought. Perhaps he had intended to wait until dawn. He was conscious of a warm admiration for Meyer. Meyer must think a good deal of his men to stay awake night after night on their account. For a while he wondered whether he ought to bring up the subject again. But since Meyer remained laconic, he decided not to say anything. After a while they began chatting casually, occasionally taking surreptitious glances at their watches. Although they could scarcely keep their eyes open, neither of them wanted to be the first to admit it. But they spoke less and less; their conversation faded into dull monosyllables that scarcely rose above the monotonous patter of the rain. At last it petered out entirely.

Third Company's positions ran around the eastern tip of Hill 121.4. It had stopped raining about an hour before. The front was quiet. In one of the advanced weapon pits stood Private Faber behind a machine-gun. His tour had begun at three o'clock in the morning. He was a broad-shouldered fellow who never did much talking. But the other men in his platoon felt that when he did speak there was little to be added to what he said. He picked his words painfully, and his thoughts often struck his fellows as deep and mysterious, like the still lakes of his native province. Faber came from the Black Forest district. Before the war he had been a woodcutter, and the pathways through the dense pine-woods were as familiar to him as the wrinkles on his mother's face. Three years ago, when he had been called up, he had donned his uniform without enthusiasm. At that time he had been twenty-four. Since then he had remained in Lieutenant Gausser's 3rd Company and was well thought of by his superiors. A steady, reliable man. Now he stood motionless, alert in the chest-deep MG position, his eyes probing the dark landscape before him, his ears attentive to every sound. The noises, however, were always the same: the suppressed coughing of the man in the foxhole nearby; the metallic clank when the lever of a machine-gun was moved; the smacking suction-noise of boots on the muddy bottom of the trench. He was aware of these sounds only on fringes of consciousness. Nevertheless, he had become more alert during the past fifteen minutes. At first he could not have said himself what had shaken him out of torpor during the first few minutes of his watch and produced a mounting uneasiness. Then he had realized that it was the unnatural silence in the Russian positions opposite.

Now he was suspicious and tense. He used his flare-gun frequently, and the men in the nearby weapon pits were also shooting off flares at shorter and shorter intervals. But strain his eyes as he would, he could detect nothing to give him grounds for concern. Every time one of the flares hit the ground and went out, he closed his eyes in order to ease the shock of the returning darkness. As he reloaded the flare pistol, he wondered whether it might not be best to communicate with his platoon leader. He had half made up his mind to go over to the adjoining sentry and ask his opinion when he suddenly started and his hand flashed out again to send up another flare.

From the right came a warning cry, and as the flare mounted he saw the bent-over figure of a man come tearing up the slope, saw him stop abruptly and throw up his arms. Then a shout reached his ear, words in German. Faber took his hands from the MG and stared bewildered at the Russian who stood some twenty yards away. But then Faber displayed a presence of mind in keen contrast to his usual slow-moving temperament. He called hastily to the men within range of his voice, and before the flare had gone out he ordered the Russian who was shouting that he was Corporal Steiner to approach the trench slowly, with hands raised. He was quite conscious of the risk he was taking; the whole business might be a clever Russian trap. For that reason he kept his finger on the trigger of the MG and waited until the man was close enough so that he could watch his every movement in spite of the darkness. Then he ordered him to jump into the trench. From the neighbouring weapon pits men hurried up; they thronged into the MG emplacement with rifles at ready to receive this strange visitor. Suspiciously they stared at him as he stood before them, panting and doubled over, leaning his back against the wall of the trench for support. Faber meanwhile sent up another flare; only after he had made sure there were no more unexpected visitors on the way did he turn to the men who were pouring out a torrent of words at the new arrival.

'Quiet a moment,' Faber said, thrusting his broad frame into the midst of the group. For a few seconds he studied the Russian silently. Then he said quietly: 'So you're Steiner.' The man nodded. Faber switched on his flashlight and illuminated the man's face. It was smeared with mud, unshaven and unrecognizable. 'Where are the others?' he went on.

'If you waste any more time,' the man in Russian uniform replied irritably, 'you can pay them a visit in Siberia. They're waiting for the signal, green and white flares shot up in succession. Hurry up, damn it all.'

Faber hesitated. He had seen Steiner only a few times. If this man should happen to be a double who was playing the part of Steiner, the pre-arranged signal might bring a horde of Russians down on the position. The other men were equally wary. They had been in the company only a few weeks, and when Faber asked whether any of them recognized Corporal Steiner, they remained silent.

Their hesitancy was legitimate but nevertheless disastrous, Steiner realized, yet a lethargy prevented him from doing anything. The moment after he had reached the trench and recognized the men as members of 3rd Company, the furious energy which had propelled him across the 300 feet of no-man's-land and up the slope to the German positions had left him like a fountain turned off at the source. The reaction set in: he felt like closing his eyes and falling promptly asleep. But out there in the night his platoon was waiting. He pulled himself together, explained the meaning of his masquerade to the men, tore open the pack on his back and produced his own uniform. 'Don't be asses,' he said with some return of his former vigour. 'If Meyer or anyone else from my company were here, they'd let you know who I am, by God. But we can't take the time to rustle up one of them. If I were a Russian——'

He broke off. The men had not noticed that as he spoke these last words Faber had turned and fussed with his flare-pistol for a few seconds. He moved fast, and before anyone could stop him a green and right after it a white flare rose into the sky.

'Are you mad?' one of the men exclaimed angrily. The others stared in alarm over the rim of the trench. Faber stood squarely behind his MG watching the flares sink to the ground and go out. Then he turned his head. 'Go back to your posts. If there's any need for shooting, leave the first shot to me.'

'You should have waited till I went for the sergeant,' one man protested.

Faber shook his head. 'If what the corporal says is true, we have no time.'

'And suppose it isn't true?'

Faber glanced at Steiner. Evenly, he said: 'Then this fellow will be the first to get a belly-full.' He spoke to Steiner. 'Go out there.'

'Where?' Steiner asked in amazement.

Faber waved his hand toward the rim of the trench. 'You sit down over there. Right in front of the MG, three paces away from the barrel. When the others come along tell them to enter the trench one by one and without their weapons.'

'Suppose I don't,' Steiner drawled.

'If you don't I'll fire as soon as the first man appears.'

As Steiner wordlessly clambered out of the trench and sat down in the assigned spot, the other men scurried back to their places. The next few minutes were trying. Through his clothes Steiner could feel the damp of the ground. Anger filled him as he stared into the darkness. But his irritation was soon gone. The man's prudence impressed him, and he grinned as he reflected that this was the first time he had obeyed a private's order without protest. The boy is all right, he said to himself; he's handling a ticklish business skilfully. If only he would not lose his nerve at the last minute. A ribbon of MG bullets in the back would be devilishly uncomfortable. He turned his head and saw the stocky figure like a dark log behind the machine-gun. 'What's your name?' he asked.

'I'll tell you later; you shut up now.'

Steiner raised his eyebrows. Then he shook his head and suddenly began to chuckle. 'You're priceless,' he whispered, 'really priceless.' Shaken with amusement, he kept looking at the man's face, which was visible only as a white blur.

It was the hour before dawn. The night still clung darkly to the hill, lay upon the trenches and weapon pits and filled every hollow of the land. In the east, however, the face of the night was turning sallow like the skin of a dying man, and above the still invisible horizon a gash in the sky had opened, through which trickled yellowish light. Steiner drew his feet close to his body and turned his eyes ahead again. The men ought to be showing up any second now. He suddenly felt a keen sense of happy anticipation. There no longer seemed any reason to worry. The loud shouts by which he had announced himself might have made the Russians suspicious, and there was always the possibility that they had seen him standing with arms raised in the light of the flares from the German trenches. But the absolute silence on the other side was reassuring. Several times he thought he heard distinctly the rattle of weapons. But the noises might have come from the trenches behind him; he could not be sure. Again and again he glanced at the radiant dial of his wrist-watch. It seemed impossible that only four minutes had passed since the green flare rose into the sky. His uneasiness mounted.

He was about to turn and say something. But the man at the MG made a hissing sound. Steiner was amazed at the keenness of the fellow's hearing, for several seconds passed before he also heard the noises. First there was a vague, dull thudding; then he was able to distinguish gasping breaths and a tinny rattle. The darkness in front of him suddenly took on life, a stirring and scurrying that abruptly ceased when a flare rose behind his back, flooding the area with harsh light. Half-way up the slopes, about sixty feet from the lines, he saw his men. He recognized Schnurrbart and Krüger at once, standing side by side, necks thrust forward, peering up the hill. Behind him the voice of the machine-gunner cracked out a few words. Steiner raised his arm. He ordered his men to drop their weapons and come up to the lines one by one, at intervals. As soon as the flare died Schnurrbart appeared. 'What's the idea?' he panted. He stood looking angrily down at Steiner. 'Why the devil are you sitting here? What's the matter?'

Before Steiner could answer, Faber spoke up. As soon as he heard Schnurrbart's voice he had taken his hands from the machine-gun. Now he climbed up out of his weapon pit. 'Don't take offence,' he said apologetically. 'You understand we had to be sure.'

Steiner slowly rose to his feet. Sighing, he rubbed his stiff back. 'There are easier ways to be sure, my boy,' he said. 'A telephone call to Freiburg would have done it. That's my home town.'

The other men had come up one by one and were thronging around Steiner. He could scarcely fend off all who wanted to shake hands with him. From foxholes on both sides sentries came hurrying up, and word of the successful return of the platoon spread like wildfire up and down the lines. 'Now for half a bottle of schnaps,' Krüger said ambitiously. The men of the platoon laughed and nudged each other with their elbows.

Steiner turned to Schnurrbart. 'Was everything all right?'

'Yes,' Schnurrbart said contentedly. 'There was a while there when we had butterflies in our stomachs because it seemed so long, but as soon as those flares went up we started out like an express train, let me tell you. On the way——' He babbled on about the details of their trip across the no-man's-land, and Steiner listened with only half an ear. He was gazing out into the distance with the queer feeling that he had lost something irrecoverable. But he did not know what it was.

Faber stood watching him in silence for a while. Then he went up to him and remarked: 'I think it would be better if you went on another ten paces before looking back.'

Steiner slowly turned to face him. 'What do you mean by that?'

'As a boy I once got lost in the forest,' Faber said. 'Maybe you know what it's like. Anyway, my father found me next morning. When he brought me home, that is what he said to me.'

Steiner shook his head. 'Quoth the raven,' he exclaimed. He hesitated for a moment. 'Would you care to come over to me—I mean join my platoon?'

'I think so.'

'Good,' Steiner said. 'I'll talk to Meyer about it.' He suddenly reached out for Faber's hand and shook it strongly. Then he turned to the others. 'Let's go. We'll rout out Meyer.' He grinned. 'I don't think he'll be annoyed when we disturb his beauty sleep.'

They groped their way forward to the main trench.

When Gausser awoke, it took him a while to realize where he was. At his side he heard Meyer breathing deeply and evenly. He shook his head. Here they had both gone to sleep in an MG emplacement instead of seeking the comparative comfort of their beds. Along with astonishment at his own conduct he was aware of intense uneasiness as he found himself wondering what had so suddenly awakened him. As a rule he slept soundly during the most intense artillery barrages; an uncomfortable position never bothered him. It must be late; he glanced at his watch and saw that it was already four o'clock. Day would break before long. For a moment he considered waking Meyer. But Meyer was sleeping so soundly that he could not bear to.

He got up, intending to look around. Suddenly he heard noises. In two rapid strides he was outside, and his eyes widened in surprise. Through the greying darkness of the trench came a long line of men, led by a man of his company. Cheerfully the man raised his hand: 'Oh, there you are, sir! Corporal Steiner is back.'

Incredulously, and with just a touch of alarm, Gausser stared at the men in Russian uniform. He did not quite take it in until one of the newcomers raised his hand to his cap with studied careless-ness and stood appraising him rather insolently. Without a word Gausser stooped and went back into the MG emplacement, where Meyer still slept. He gripped the other man's arm roughly and pulled him to his feet. 'Come on out,' he shouted in his ear. 'Come on out, Meyer, you have visitors.'

He dragged the recalcitrant, still sleeping company commander outside, where the grinning men awaited them. Meyer suddenly jerked angrily away and snapped: 'Are you going out of your mind, Gausser—what the devil——' The words froze on his lips as he caught sight of the men in Russian uniforms. Involuntarily his hand flashed to his side. Gausser seized his arm. 'Calmness does it, Lieutenant Meyer. Man, you're hard to satisfy. First you can't wait until your platoon comes back, and now that your Steiner is here you're all ready to take a pot-shot at him.'

'Steiner!' Meyer's mouth flew open; he rubbed his eyes and

shook his head unbelievingly. Steiner, who had been watching him with amusement, suddenly felt a wave of emotion which clamped his lips shut and sent a prickly sensation up his back and through the nape of his neck into his face; the corners of his mouth twitched and he had to dig his teeth into his lower lip to keep himself from saying something silly. When Meyer gripped his hand and held it clenched in his for a long while, he closed his eyes for a few seconds. Gausser quietly departed.

The shrill ringing of the telephone awoke Stransky from his soundest sleep of the night. As he stumbled to his feet in the darkness, he bumped into the chair on which he had placed his clothes, and knocked it over. 'Blast it,' he cursed, kicked out at it vindictively, and cursed again because he had hurt his toes. The ringing went on. Face twisted with pain, he hobbled to the table, lifted the hand-set, and trembling with rage bellowed his name. When he recognized Meyer's voice, his first impulse was to hurl the telephone to the floor. But the company commander's first few words brought him wide awake. What was he saying? That Steiner was back, had brought a prisoner, wiped out a Russian battalion command post. Why that was. . . . 'Is this an actual fact?' he demanded suspiciously.

The jollity went out of Meyer's voice. 'I am not in the habit of playing practical jokes, sir!' he replied sharply.

Stransky instructed Meyer to bring the prisoner and the platoon to his bunker at once. He hung up. For a while he sat lost in thought, unable to decide how to act. The return of the platoon presented him with a number of problems he would sooner not have dealt with. Chief of these was his promise to promote the corporal. Naturally, he told himself, he could simply pretend to have forgotten his conversation with Meyer on the subject. But Meyer would undoubtedly make a point of reminding him. The thought of Meyer's temerity was even more unpleasant than the promotion as such. What irked him was not only that Meyer had been right, but also that he, Stransky, would have to pay tribute to Meyer's rightness by promoting Steiner. The longer he considered this the deeper grew his antagonism toward his company commander.

He lit a candle and dressed. He would look this man Steiner over carefully. If the regimental commander thought so much of him, it would certainly not be out of order for himself to make a good showing by displaying generosity and jumping Steiner a grade. That was it: he would promote him to master sergeant.

He had just finished buckling his belt when there was a knock at the door. Quickly, he stepped to the little window and looked out. Day was breaking. Above the rim of the trench stood several men; he could see only their heads. Their faces looked grey and weary in the cold light of the morning.

When he stepped outside, he found Meyer before him. Stransky bit his lips at the triumph in Meyer's face. He mounted the steps and silently inspected the men. They were standing close together, their heads held high, and he sensed that this was a great moment for them. They were still wearing the Russian uniforms. Stransky's eyebrows shot upward in surprise. When he turned for explanation to Meyer, the lieutenant nodded, smiling. 'I forgot to mention the uniforms, sir. You see——'

Stransky waved his hand impatiently. 'I'll hear the explanation later. Which of these is the prisoner?'

Silently, Meyer pointed to the Russian, who stood in the background watching alertly. The men of the battalion staff had meanwhile come out of the other bunkers. Stransky turned to Triebig, who had just appeared: 'Put the prisoner in a bunker and see to it that he is well guarded,' he ordered.

Meyer felt obliged to point out the Russian's rank. 'He is a captain, sir.'

'At the moment he is a prisoner of war,' Stransky replied coldly.

He looked at the men again. 'Which one is Corporal Steiner.'

Steiner took a step forward and slackly came to attention. Stransky studied him, disappointed. From all that he had heard he had formed another picture of Steiner—a vague one, but resembling in no way the man who stood before him and met his gaze with insulting unconcern. He felt Meyer eyeing him and stiffened. 'You are promoted to master sergeant, promotion to be effective at once!' he declared loudly. He watched Steiner's face. But again he experienced a disappointment. It was as if he had spoken to a tree. Steiner betrayed no sign of surprise, and only the manner in which he flexed his arms slightly indicated that he had heard at all.

Stransky frowned. Then he turned abruptly to Meyer. 'Come in, you and the sergeant.'

As Steiner followed the two officers down the steps to the bunker, he suddenly felt his knees shaking from exhaustion. In spite of the half-dozen shots of schnaps he had drunk in Meyer's bunker, he was shivering with cold.

The men of the platoon watched him go. It was a chilly, disagreeable morning, the air filled with mist, and the muddy slopes stretching upward on all sides making the scene even gloomier. Schnurrbart stretched, his teeth chattering. He turned to Krüger. 'Some reception, huh? I tell you, if Brandt were still here——' He glared down at the commander's bunker.

'This one looked like a stinker to me the first time I laid eyes on him,' Krüger growled.

They stood in a huddle, cross and cold, answering in monosyllables the questions bombarded at them by the men of the staff. Their exuberant mood had been thoroughly quelled. Standing around in filthy, soaking wet clothes did not improve their humour; all they could think about was their need for sleep. After a while they accepted the invitation of the signalmen and scattered among the men's bunkers to await Steiner's return.

Meanwhile the newly-appointed master sergeant was sitting at the regimental commander's table reporting in short, clipped sentences the events of the past few days. Meyer, who had already heard most of the story, remained silent, but Stransky kept interrupting with questions. Steiner at first answered these patiently, but gradually grew more and more irritable. He had difficulty keeping his eyes open, and Meyer, well aware of his condition, finally thought the time had come to put an end to the conversation—all the more so since the main events had been covered. When Stransky wanted to know what had happened to their original guns, Meyer cleared his throat. 'Wouldn't it be possible to discuss these matters at some later time, sir?' he suggested. 'It seems to me that Sergeant Steiner is too exhausted to go into more detail. Besides, the other men are waiting outside; they'll catch their deaths in those wet clothes of theirs.'

Stransky's eyes flashed angrily. But since there was little objection he could raise, he nodded with a hypocritical sympathy. 'You should have remarked on this sooner,' he said. 'But after all I must have some of the details in order to make my report to Regiment.' He crushed out his cigarette and turned to Steiner with a patronizing smile. 'I have been in the habit of interrogating men in the uniform you are wearing, not receiving reports from them. A new experience, really. Take your platoon back to Kanskoye. Until tonight you may catch up on some sleep. I shall expect you back when the supply column comes over, since there are several points I am still unclear about.' He let his eyes travel over Steiner's filthy uniform once more. Then he smiled harshly. 'See to it that you transform yourself into a German sergeant by then. Incidentally, the uniform looks very well on you; were you an actor before the war?'

Meyer raised his head, alert to the insult in the words. Steiner showed no change of expression as he replied: 'Not before the war.'

Stransky folded his arms. Something in the man's intonation did not please him. 'You seem to emphasize the word "before,"' he said.

Steiner appraised him. Then he shrugged. 'If I did, it was accidental.'

'So?' Stransky scratched his chin in vexation. There was something wrong with the fellow's attitude; he seemed to think that he was talking to an equal. The fact that he was discreet in his choice of words and overstepped the limits Stransky had mentally set for the rank of an NCO only in his tone, made it all the more offensive. Stransky made up his mind to cut him down to size: 'I have the feeling, sergeant, that you somewhat overestimate your importance,' he said.

A little colour rose in the grey of Steiner's exhausted face. His eyes darkened, turned almost black. But there was no change in his voice as he replied: 'At the moment I am free of any such illusions.'

Stransky stared at him more in astonishment than indignation. In a voice just a shade colder he said: 'You are in the habit of speaking your mind, I see, but I would nevertheless suggest to you not to underestimate your present company. At any rate never forget that everything you are and may become is dependent upon that present company.'

'I don't think I will forget that,' Steiner replied coolly. 'Although I may add that a man generally becomes what he feels himself to be.'

Stransky pushed his chair back and rose. His face looked sallow and apathetic. The candles on the table flickered tiredly in the dim of the bunker, though the daylight was seeping in through the window with increasing brightness. The air was heavy and stale.

Steiner felt a craving to get outside into the open air. As he, along with Meyer, followed the commander's example and rose, fatigue suddenly almost toppled him; he had to lean on the table for support. Stransky picked up the maps Steiner had brought and spoke to Meyer. 'I will inform Regiment; see to it that the prisoner is taken to Kiesel at once.'

He turned again to Steiner. 'For my part you can feel as you like. But as long as you talk with me do not forget that you are wearing a uniform. In the future you keep that in mind.' He reached for the telephone and Steiner decided that he had been dismissed.

As he stepped outside, Meyer laid a hand on his shoulder. 'A useful tip,' he said. 'Remember from now on that we have a different battalion commander.' Steiner did not answer. They collected the men from the bunkers and Meyer shook hands with each one of them. 'Get yourselves plenty of sleep. I'll see to it that you're given a few days rest.' He turned again to Steiner and explained the route they must take to Kanskoye. 'You'll be there in twenty minutes. Fetscher will take care of you. I've had him informed. Well, then——' He hesitated and lowered his voice. 'Don't forget by tonight what I've just said.'

The platoon watched him walk off toward the bunker where the prisoner had been put. Schnurrbart clicked his heels and rasped: 'Pull your arses together from now on; we have a master sergeant for platoon leader.' They laughed, crowding around Steiner and pounding him on the back. 'Now you're somebody,' Anselm said flatteringly. 'Do we have to say "sir" when we talk to you?'

'Shut up, idiot,' Steiner replied with mock fierceness. 'I've just been told in there'—he jerked a thumb toward the commander's bunker—'how important I am.'

'Why, what was wrong?' Krüger asked curiously.

Steiner gestured wearily. 'Not now. There'll be a better time to——' The rest of the sentence trailed off into an indistinct murmur. 'Was there something he didn't like?' Schnurrbart asked sourly.

Steiner shrugged. He slung the tommy-gun over his shoulder and said: 'Let's get to the village. I'll be glad to get out of these wet clothes.'

They descended into the ravine and followed the winding brook. Although the sky was still clouded, it felt as though the rains were over. The sight of the bushes that lined the brook, their fresh green contrasting with the barrenness of the dead clay slopes, revived the men. Their thoughts hurried on ahead; they could see themselves already resting in comfortable, dry quarters beyond the next or at most the next but one turn in the path. One of them began to sing. Hollerbach took up the song, and a few moments later the echo of their voices boomed boisterously down the gorge:

> We, we are the huntsmen of the plains,
> The starvelings of the nation.
> For three years now, in snow and rain
> We've marched on dehydrated rations.
> Forward, you huntsmen of the plains,
> Forward, to do your fighting all alone.
> For the others come in cars when the battle is all done.
> Forward, you huntsmen of the plains.

Up ahead, through a cluster of trees, the first houses appeared. A minute later they were surrounded by a crowd of admirers who slapped them on the back, shook hands and hurled so many questions that it would have taken hours to answer all. Finally the massive figure of a first sergeant thrust through the crowd, cursed furiously for silence, and stood shaking his head at the appearance of Steiner and the others. He was a powerfully-built man with rugged, honest features; it was easy to imagine him pacing slowly behind a plough. Several times he started to speak but was so surprised by the sight of the Russian uniforms that he could not say a word. Steiner grinned. He had always got on well with Fetscher. Slowly he brought his heels together, performed a caricature of standing at attention, raised his hand to his cap and said: 'Beg to report, sir——' The sergeant's face turned red. Suddenly he found speech again, and the rest of Steiner's report was drowned out in a series of obscene curses.

'Come up for air,' Steiner said at last. 'You've used up two week's stock of swear words. Better show us our quarters.'

Fetscher continued to mutter under his breath for a moment, but then he roused himself and displayed such admirable efficiency that within a few minutes the men were being guided by members of the supply column to comfortable houses. Steiner followed Fetscher to his own house. As soon as he stepped inside he slipped the pack from his back and hurled it to the floor. Fetscher was meanwhile talking. 'There's a warm meal waiting for you all, new clothes, rations for two days. You certainly deserve it. Congratulations, too—I mean about your promotion—you were bound for promotion soon anyhow. High time, too. You've got to tell me all about it—how the hell did you——'

Steiner clapped his hands to his ears. 'Hold your horses; I want food and sleep and first of all I want to wash. Any water in this place?'

'More than you need,' Fetscher said complacently. 'I've got a tub full for you in the kitchen. It's even hot—thought of everything.'

'That's all you've got to do is think,' Steiner said. He looked around the room. For Russian conditions it was pretty decent. In one corner the big stove built of clay; under the windows a green-painted bench and two huge beds big enough to sleep half a company. Fetscher smiled with pride. 'Not a bad place, eh? Almost like home.'

'Like your home maybe,' Steiner chaffed him.

Fetscher turned to the door. 'I'll see how the other fellows are getting on. Incidentally, where did you—I mean, what became of your own pea-shooters?'

'Just what Stransky asked me. In the summer offensive, I'll show you the spot.'

'You don't mean you——?' Fetscher asked in alarm.

'I do,' Steiner replied indifferently. 'I'll tell you about it later. Let me alone now.'

Fetscher went out. Later, when Steiner came out of the kitchen, freshly washed and shaved, his mess-tin stood on the table, filled to the brim with stew. He sat down. Strangely enough, he no longer felt hungry, and his weariness seemed to have washed away in the hot water. He felt depressed and ill-humoured without knowing why. All right, so they were back with the battalion. Meyer had been as giddy-glad as a kid on Christmas morning, he himself had been promoted, looked and smelled like a human being again—everything seemed fine, and still. . . . He propped his chin on his fists and stared out the window where fragile rays of sunlight played upon the fresh green of the trees. He recalled the conversation with Stransky and snorted contemptuously. So that was the sort of fool. . . . Well, he would see what came of it. . . . Stransky was only one of the many battalion commanders he had survived; he would survive Stransky, too. A stupid self-important ass—no need to take him seriously. What the devil were they so proud of, those arrogant idiots. Of their ancestry? It wasn't their doing. Of their money? They'd inherited it. Of their educations? They'd had time to get one. He laughed and pushed the mess-tin aside. Then he stood up, walked slowly to the window and looked out. Maag was just passing, a new uniform over his arm, his face reflecting contentment. Steiner watched him trudging along until he disappeared into the house across the way. Undemanding and shallow, he thought bitterly. They're glad to be back with the battalion. Here they felt at home, safe, sheltered. But he himself, where was he at home? Certainly not back in Freiburg, where for the last two years there had been no one waiting for him. He leaned his forehead against the cool window-pane and closed his eyes. If only there were still Anne, he thought. Anne! For the first time he felt that he had lost her for ever.

At Regiment HQ the news of the missing platoon's return was a bombshell. Brandt sent for Kiesel at once. Kiesel had rarely known the commander to be in such high spirits. In spite of the earliness of the hour, Brandt had a bottle on the table in front of him and invited Kiesel to have a glass with him—of genuine Black Forest kirschwasser, he emphasized. Kiesel declined; he could not take alcohol on an empty stomach he said.

'You're an ascetic,' Brandt declared, filling the water glass. '*Prost!*' He drained his glass in one swig. 'I told you right off,' he said, 'that Steiner would come through. What a boy, Kiesel, what a boy. If we had a few hundred like him the Russians would never have a peaceful moment.'

'Have you heard any of the details?' Kiesel asked.

'Yes! I made Stransky cough up the story. He didn't like it a bit; it's my feeling that we'll have to watch him for a while. You keep an eye on him, Kiesel.'

'I don't quite understand,' Kiesel said in surprise.

'You will soon enough. Remember that Stransky has already had some difficulty over Steiner, and remember the type Stransky is. He has a damned loose tongue on him anyway,' Brandt added cheerfully.

'Stransky?' Kiesel exclaimed.

'Don't be silly. Steiner, of course. So watch sharp. And now get an earful of what that hellhound has done.'

He began on the story of the platoon, repeatedly bursting into laughter and pounding the table with his fist. 'And do you know what I'm going to do?' he concluded.

'Promote him, of course,' Kiesel guessed.

'He has already been promoted. Stransky did that right off—even jumped him a grade to master sergeant. A lucky stroke by the way, or I would have made a point of asking him to. No, I was thinking of something else. Sending Steiner to Gursuf for two weeks. What do you think?'

'He deserves it,' Kiesel answered. Gursuf was a small spa on the southern coast of the Crimea where the division operated a rest camp. It was part of Kiesel's job to allocate space in the camp among the various units of the regiment. He took a notebook from his pocket and turned through it for a few seconds. Then he said: 'The next transport goes in ten days. I'll put Steiner down for it.'

'Ten days!' Brandt gave a scornful laugh. 'What do you mean, ten days? Steiner is to leave at once—tomorrow!'

'The place is all filled up,' Kiesel protested.

'You take your damned red tape and do what you know with it. They'll have a room free down there, and if they don't I'll see abuot it personally.'

Kiesel suddenly recalled a letter he had received in the last post. He took it out of his pocket. 'If you don't mind, I have a personal favour to ask this morning. I have a letter from my brother-in-law, Lieutenant März.'

'What about him?'

Kiesel hesitated, then gave a chagrined laugh. 'He insists on a transfer to the front, and to the eastern front of all places. Right now he's a company commander in a Leipzig garrison. You know how these young chaps are. Think they're missing something if they don't get out here. He's set his heart on it, and if I know him he'll keep at it until he's where he wants to be.'

Brandt nodded. 'I take it you want to keep him near you.'

'Exactly. I would feel a good deal better about it. Perhaps it would be possible to ask for him through Division.'

'Will do,' Brandt said, making a note of the matter. 'How old is he?'

'Twenty-four. He comes from Villingen in the Black Forest—the family owns a watch factory out there.'

Before Brandt could inquire more there was a knock at the door and a soldier reported the arrival of Lieutenant Triebig with Steiner's Russian prisoner. Brandt nodded to Triebig as he entered the bunker. 'You can return immediately,' he said. 'Tell Stransky I want to congratulate him on the return of his platoon, and tell him furthermore that I will expect Sergeant Steiner here at six o'clock. Have you the captured maps?'

Triebig laid the maps on the table and withdrew. On the way back he studied the terrain carefully. From the hill behind which Regimental HQ was located there was an excellent view of the surrounding countryside. Beyond the ravine rose the crooked ridge of Hill 121.4. The trenches and weapon pits could be seen clearly. Every detail of this terrain must be equally visible from the enemy positions, Triebig thought, and involuntarily walked faster. He did not slow down again until he had reached the ravine; then he returned to his sauntering pace. In the past few days he had thought a great deal about his conversation with Stransky and had come to the conclusion that he could not have handled his end of it more foolishly. But his nervousness had by now dissipated. His resolve to kill Stransky had already dwindled down to a mere wish, of no more intensity than his desire to spend one of these spring days strolling through the streets of Cologne again. He had decided not to act too hastily in any dealings with Stransky. Perhaps something would turn up; he would keep his eyes open for opportunities.

When Steiner set out shortly after five o'clock, the Russian artillery was sending occasional nuisance bursts into the ravine. He avoided the direct road and made a wide detour around the dangerous area. As a result, it took him nearly an hour to reach Regimental HQ, and he arrived a few minutes late. As he approached he admired the skilful arrangement of the bunkers. They had been built into a part of the slope that rose almost vertically, so that it would be virtually impossible for the enemy guns to reach them. Steiner asked his way to the commander's bunker, which had no outward marks to distinguish it from the rest.

Brandt came striding forward to meet him and pressed his hand vigorously. 'So there you are,' he said loudly. 'Unpunctual and unsoldierly as ever.' He laughed and propelled Steiner into a chair.

Steiner looked up at his smiling face and shrugged regretfully. 'The way was longer than I thought; I had to——'

'No need to apologize,' Brandt interrupted, taking a seat opposite him. 'If that sort of thing bothered me I would have seen that you changed your ways long ago.' He laughed again and shook his head. 'What you've pulled off this time beats all. I wouldn't have thought you could do it.'

'We were lucky,' Steiner replied.

Brandt crossed his legs. 'If luck was all there was to it,' he said quietly, 'you wouldn't be sitting here. Now tell me all about it. Don't leave anything out.' He took a pack of cigarettes from his pocket and handed them across the table. Steiner thanked him, lit up and began his report. Brandt listened in silence. When Steiner came to the encounter with the Russian women, he took a few notes. After Steiner had finished, he said: 'You've done a wonderful job, Steiner. It's a long time since I've felt as pleased as I do today; we know each other well enough for me to be able to say that to you. Your report is enormously valuable; I intend to transmit it personally to the general. I hope it gives him a thing or two to think about. You know the big brass think we're in a rest camp down here; maybe they'll see what's brewing when I tell them about the material you saw rolling down that highway.'

Steiner watched him in silence. His relations with Brandt had been good from the start, without his having made any effort. Both men had felt drawn to one another, and since the incident at Studenok the commander had displayed an understandable interest in him. After becoming commander of the regiment Brandt had suggested that he stay with him, and had offered him a quiet staff post. But Steiner had politely asked permission to remain with his men. He could still see how disappointed Brandt had looked. Asked for his reasons, he had referred to his feelings of solidarity with the men. It would have been difficult to explain to the commander that he did not want to be dependent upon anyone, let alone a regimental commander, no matter how good a fellow. Since that time he had not seen Brandt, and he was relieved to find that the commander did not seem to hold his refusal against him. Yet he could not stifle a slight sense of uneasiness, and he waited impatiently to be dismissed. When Brandt thrust some papers across the table and told him that beginning tomorrow he was to start two-week's leave in the Crimea, he could not rise to the occasion. In fact he found himself raising various objections to the leave. However, when it became apparent that the commander was beginning to be seriously displeased, he shrugged his acquiescence. 'If it's your command, sir—You see, the reason that I don't feel easy about it is that every man in my platoon deserves this leave and it will make a bad impression if I——'

'As far as I can recall,' Brandt interrupted him sharply, 'you have never given a hang about the impression you were making anywhere and at any time. You are going on leave tomorrow, and that's all there is to it. I have already informed your company commander.' He rose quickly. 'Sometimes, Steiner, you make it hard for me to forget that I am your superior.'

'I often wonder why you try to forget.' Steiner also stood up and looked expectantly at the commander. Brandt's mouth began to twitch and his voice shook as he shook hands. 'You're the most impertinent man that's ever come my way. If you aren't gone by tomorrow I'll have you chased away from this front at bayonet point.'

He gripped Steiner by the shoulders and ushered him out of the door. A little bewildered by the treatment he had received, Steiner began ascending the slope and almost failed to notice an officer who was coming down the path toward him. The officer looked him over carefully. Steiner recognized the regimental adjutant. 'You are Steiner,' the officer said, stopping. Carefully, so that the slackness of his reaction would not be overlooked, Steiner placed his feet together and nodded. A fleeting smile passed over the captain's stern features. 'So I thought,' he said. He continued on up the hill and vanished into the commander's bunker. Steiner looked back after him with a startled expression. Then he continued on his way, whistling.

He was due at the battalion command post at eight o'clock. Since the Russian fire had stopped toward evening, he reached the headquarters without incident. He had more than half an hour before his scheduled interview with Stransky, and he dropped in on Meyer first. The lieutenant gave him a hearty greeting and congratulated him on his impending leave.

'I've already informed the captain,' he said. 'He doesn't seem altogether delighted, but orders are orders and not even Captain Stransky can scotch them.' He produced cigarettes and schnaps.

'The two weeks will do you good. I'm afraid, though, that things will be popping here by the time you return.'

'Really?' Steiner asked.

Meyer nodded gravely. 'I'd say that the Russian preparations indicate a big offensive in the making. Since we're right in a salient, I imagine we'll be hit hard. That damned hill,' he added uncomfortably. From somewhere outside came the dull thud of exploding shells. 'Do you hear that? Must be a 17.2. They're bringing in new guns every day over there.'

'They have plenty,' Steiner said, shrugging.

Meyer leaned across the table. 'I did want to tell you this. Be careful with Stransky. He seems to have taken a dislike to you. He's sure to make a stink about the weapons you discarded.'

Steiner waved that away. 'That doesn't worry me. I've already reported the matter to Colonel Brandt. He let it pass without a word.'

'That's good.' Meyer was visibly relieved. He glanced at his watch. 'You'd better be on your way; it's nearly eight.'

Steiner finished his glass and reached for his cap. As they shook hands Meyer said: 'Don't forget us while you're on leave.'

'I've been in your company too long for that,' Steiner said.

It was dark outside, with stars gleaming among scattered clouds and a soft breeze blowing over the hill. Steiner took a deep breath. It was starting to feel like spring. At home the last patches of snow would be melting among the pine trees. He stood still abruptly, listening with astonishment to his own thoughts and emotions. Was this homesickness? Perhaps—a homesickness for memories. Violently, he started forward again and went toward the battalion headquarters by the shortest route, without bothering to use the trench.

When he entered the commander's bunker, Stransky was sitting over a map. He looked up and said: 'Here you are. Sit down. You're three minutes late.'

'Dark out,' Steiner explained laconically, taking the offered seat. Stransky took a cigarette case from his pocket, removed one cigarette, tapped it carefully on his thumbnail several times, and finally put it between his lips. Steiner watched him impassively. There was the outside chance that Stransky would offer him a cigarette—as this was the last thing he wanted, he put on an expression of refusal. But Stransky came promptly to the point.

'I've sent for you in order to clarify certain obscurities,' he said. 'Principally I should like to hear again how your casualties occurred. You lost two men?'

'I've been over that,' Steiner said curtly. This was a subject he preferred to steer clear of. After Schnurrbart had pointed out that even if Zoll had funked, they ought to conceal the fact, out of consideration for Zoll's parents, they had all agreed on a new version of the story. Zoll was simply to be reported missing. This was the story Steiner had given in his first report and Stransky's inquisitiveness endangered it. 'That time we ran into the Russians,' he went on reluctantly, 'it was already dark in the woods. Dietz received two shots in the back, while Zoll simply vanished.'

'Did you look for him?' Stransky asked.

Steiner shrugged impatiently. 'We had no time to lose. It would have been mad to risk the safety of the entire platoon for the sake of one man. I'm glad we came out of it as well as we did.'

'You will have to make a written report,' Stransky declared. 'There ought not to be any missing men in such cases. But let us drop that for the moment. There is another matter I cannot understand. What prompted you to exchange weapons? As you surely know, the weapons are entered in the men's pay-books and each man is responsible for the equipment entrusted to him. You know that, don't you?' He did not wait for an answer. 'Furthermore, you must also be aware that the quality of our arms is far superior to that of the Russians and——'

When Steiner shook his head, he broke off. 'Yes?' he asked, raising his eyebrows.

'On the contrary,' Steiner said. 'In our opinion the German sub-machine-gun is not nearly as good as the Russian. Ask any of the men in the trenches. They'll all tell you the same thing.'

'That is stupid, loose talk,' Stransky retorted sharply. 'The weapons as designed by our engineers and produced in German factories are superior to any others. You have every reason to be grateful for the fine equipment that the Fatherland puts into your hands at the cost of countless sacrifices.'

Steiner could not quite suppress a grin as he replied: 'I never asked for the stuff to be put in my hands, you know.'

Stransky took a deep breath. 'I request you for the last time to mind your tone. I haven't asked you here for a discussion. I have told you that our equipment is far superior to that of the Russians and I do not wish——' The rest of the sentence failed to reach Steiner's consciousness. He had no desire to bicker with Stransky. Let him talk, he thought. For his part he let himself drop down into the bottomless weariness which still filled his body, in spite of the rest he had had. From far away Stransky's voice sounded like the troublesome buzzing of a fly. Steiner looked down at his hands and tried to move his fingers. But they remained stiff and motionless, and he wondered why. Disturbed, he moved his legs, tensed his biceps and concentrated wholly upon his hands.

Then he heard the commander's voice again; it was violent now, had risen almost to a shout. Uncomprehending, Steiner lifted his head and looked at the captain. He realized that Stransky was now standing; his face was red and his eyes, ordinarily so icy, were flaming. What was this about, Steiner wondered. Active passivity, he thought; I've been able to do something without doing a thing. He was still considering this when he suddenly felt himself gripped by the arm and jerked to his feet. With more astonishment than indignation he blinked at the commander's excited face. Then he pulled free, and reached for the Russian tommy-gun hanging from the chair. Without another look at Stransky he turned to the door. As he stepped out into the night, the stars came rushing at him. For a second he closed his eyes. Tomorrow evening, he thought, tomorrow evening you'll be in Gursuf.

He tried to think of the mountains, of the endless swells of the sea and the white beach. Then he opened his eyes and looked about him. The bunkers, dark and apparently deserted mounds, lay scattered among the trees. It was beautifully still. Absorbed in thought, he followed the path down the ravine and along the brook.

It was shortly after nine o'clock when he reached Kanskoye. When he entered Fetscher's house he heard the men's voices. They stopped talking as he opened the door. The whole platoon was sitting around the big table, bottles and glasses in front of them, looking at him. Schnurrbart pointed to an empty chair and said: 'Have a seat.'

Steiner looked at them in astonishment. 'Why so solemn?' he asked. He sat down and looked around expectantly.

Krüger stood up sheepishly. In a somewhat hoarse voice, he began: 'Fetscher told us that you were leaving tomorrow, so we thought we would give you a good send-off. Fetscher's a pretty good hand at rounding up things to drink. Now I'm not much of a speaker and two weeks are a long time, but the fellows here wanted me to say something.' As he hesitated, Steiner gave him an encouraging nod. The men grinned. Krüger glared at them and went on: 'As I was saying, two weeks are a damned long time, a hell of a long time, I tell you, and we hope you'll come back and we're still here, we hope, and as I was saying——' He frowned and plucked agitatedly at his nose. 'The devil take this war, but if this war gets us first we hope you're with us——' He became aware of the broadening grins of the men and began to stammer. 'I don't mean by that that I want us, I mean that I want to be—but that all of us, all of us sitting here together, if we're with you and——' He stumbled to a halt, his face flushed. Abruptly he smashed the table with his fist and turned to the men, quivering with rage. 'I told you I couldn't do it, you idiots.' He reached for his glass, and gulped down its contents, at the same time sneaking a look at a bit of paper he held in his palm. It was done so clumsily that everyone saw him.

'If I were you I'd start from the beginning again,' Schnurrbart proposed innocently.

Krüger glowered at him. 'You know what you can do?'

Schnurrbart nodded soberly. 'I know. You've made that suggestion time and again.'

'Have I now?' Krüger leaned far across the table toward him. 'Then go ahead and do it,' he bellowed. 'Why don't you do it, you big talker——' The rest of his explosion was drowned out in the roaring laughter of the men. Krüger dropped into his chair and stared bitterly at his glass. Steiner placed a hand on his shoulder and quickly stood up. The men fell silent.

'There are things that ought not to be talked about,' he said quietly. 'We know one another and don't have to say anything. The fact that this fancy oration didn't turn out so well'—he smiled at Krüger—'isn't the speaker's fault; it's because of the subject. There are all kinds of things that make bonds between people—love, respect, habit, and so on. That sort of thing can be talked about. But the bond among us isn't anything of the sort. Certainly our uniform isn't a bond; it only brought us together.' He paused and looked into their earnest faces. There were four candles on the table, half burned down, and for a moment he watched with his mind empty of thought as the hot wax dripped down the candles' sides. Then he raised his head. 'Sometimes we feel what it is. But if we wanted to talk about it, it would sound silly. Better to keep it to ourselves. If we want to show one another what our mutual feelings are, there will certainly be better occasions than this. Let us just hold on to those feelings.'

They remained silent a long time after he had sat down again and filled his glass from one of the bottles. The sporadic conversation which commenced again here and there around the table, had none of the usual brashness about it. Steiner said little for a while. He felt that something had gone wrong; something strange and disturbing had taken place within him which he could not relate to any of his previous experiences. And the queerness was not only inside him; there was something wrong all around him also. Pondering, he stared into space. His life ever since, since then—hadn't it been like slowly toiling through an almost endless tunnel? Walking on and on toward a distant glimmer of light? The thought came as a vision, and for a few seconds it seemed to him that he need only open his eyes abruptly in order to see clearly where he was. But his eyes were open. He held his glass between both hands, his breathing came hard. He struggled toward the lucidity which lay just ahead, just around the corner. Finally, disappointed, he slumped back in his seat. It's hopeless, he thought; you can be almost on the point of grasping it and then. . . .

He turned to the Professor, who sat at his right, and said: 'No philosophy tonight, but there's one question I want to ask you.'

'Go right ahead,' Dorn said. He adjusted his glasses and was all attention.

'It don't cost anything to ask,' Steiner said. He lowered his voice, and the flippancy disappeared from his tone. 'Is there anything one can do to help oneself forget?'

Dorn's thin face became grave. He looked away from Steiner and his glance lingered on the wine goblets. They were part of a precious table service; more than once in the course of the evening he had marvelled that things of this sort existed in Russia. Carefully, he picked up one of the thin-stemmed glasses, drank the remaining wine, and raised it to the candlelight. He turned it swiftly between his fingers. The polished crystal sparkled. Then he put it down on the table and met Steiner's eyes. 'There's the answer,' Dorn said. 'Live and be alive, see and be seen, and a few er things—but you know that yourself.'

The conversation at the table had revived. The men were growing boisterous now. Anselm filled his glass and turned to Steiner:
'What did the old man want of you?'

'Nothing in particular. I had to finish my report.'

They spoke disparagingly of Stransky for a while. 'We'll see to
him,' Anselm boasted. 'Just wait till he's been here a few weeks;
we'll trim him down. Anyway, you don't have to worry about him
for the next two weeks. What's the name of the place they're
sending you to?'

'Gursuf,' Steiner replied.

Anselm sighed enviously. 'Must be some hot women there,
eh?'

'Maybe, I don't care. I want to recuperate.'

Launched now on their favourite topic, the men talked about
women through the next few bottles. Later they began to sing.
When the general boisterousness had reached its height, Steiner
went out of the house. Slowly he strolled along the dark road,
taking deep breaths of the clear night air. After a while he heard
footsteps behind him. He turned and recognized Dorn, who came
up quickly and stopped. 'Am I in the way?' he asked.

Steiner suppressed a rude reply and thrust his hands into his
pockets. 'Hardly. What brings you out?'

'I needed a little air.'

They walked side by side back toward the house. 'We might sit
down for a while up there,' Steiner said, indicating the hill that
rose up behind the house. Half-way to the top they dropped to the
ground and looked silently down at the buildings. The men's loud
singing reached their ears. Steiner closed his eyes.

> Im Feldquartier auf hartem Stein
> Streck' ich die müden Glieder
> Und sende in die Nacht hinein
> Der Liebsten meine Lieder.

As he listened to the time-honoured soldier's song, he felt a
beneficent tiredness that neutralized all the bitterness within him
and restored a profound sense of peace. The mild night air stirred
memories, aroused nostalgia and a rare gladness. For the first time
he felt pleasure at the thought of two weeks of rest in the Crimea.
An impatience to be there took hold of him. To see the sea stretching before him—he could hardly wait. Again he gave ear to the

singing. Hollerbach's tenor rose distinctly above the voices of the others:

> Vielleicht werd' ich bald bei dir sein,
> Annemarie.
> Vielleicht scharrt man schon morgen ein
> Die ganze Kompanie, die ganze Kompanie.*

The song ended. The two men sat together in silence. In the sky the stars sparkled, and the houses lay bedded down among the still trees, sleeping. They slept, and everything was strangely close and vast. Steiner looked down below and the song ran through his head, the song and the men who sang it. The predatory Nazi hordes, the Huns and barbarians—his comrades. When Dorn suddenly gripped his arm, he started up. 'What's the matter?'

He knew at once and hunched his head between his shoulders. An ear-splitting roar filled the air, mounting with incredible speed, and seconds later the deafening detonation shattered the night air. Several more shells followed, striking somewhere in the vicinity, but the two sitting on the hill did not stir. They sat close together, their eyes fixed at the houses huddling under their straw roofs. At last Dorn turned his head and looked back. 'That was close,' he said softly.

The brief flurry of shelling seemed to have done no damage. But the air still hummed with the ugly buzz of splinters, until they pock-pocked into the ground. Dorn's body jerked at the sound. He felt as if a fragment of hot, shattered steel had penetrated his own flesh, and frantically ran his hands over his legs and chest. 'Our evensong,' Steiner said. His words restored Dorn to his senses. He shook his head over his own nervousness. 'One never gets used to it. Did you hear those splinters? A gruesome sound.'

'Hearing them isn't so bad. It's worse to feel them. I've been wounded five times and never had a bullet hit me yet. Shell splinter every time. Damn the stuff.'

'You've had lots of luck,' Dorn remarked.

Steiner glanced around. 'A few more holes in the landscape,' he commented. 'In another month this area will look like the surface of the moon. It's a good thing the earth is so patient.'

* In bivouac, on stony ground I stretch my weary limbs, and into the night I send my songs for my sweetheart.
Perhaps I will be with you soon, Annemarie, perhaps by tomorrow they'll be dumping in the grave the whole company, the whole company.

'It certainly is,' Dorn nodded soberly. 'It really is patient, the good old earth.'

Steiner smiled. 'Sentimental, Professor?'

'Perhaps.' Dorn clasped his arms over his knees. 'Perhaps I am sentimental, but to me the earth is a creature like ourselves. She endures us and our unreason as a mother endures her sorrows.'

'Go on,' Steiner said teasingly. 'I like the topic. The patient earth.' He closed his eyes for a moment. 'Though she does become impatient sometimes, doesn't she?'

'When we carry on too rottenly,' Dorn said, looking up at the stars, 'she shakes her broad back and seas pour over the continents, islands sink and volcanoes come to life.'

'A nice image,' Steiner said. 'Go on.'

Before Dorn could continue, a band of light appeared among the trees down below. Someone had opened the door. Steiner recognized the silhouette of Schnurrbart on the threshold, who took a few steps away from the house and looked around, apparently searching. 'They're getting worried about us,' Dorn said.

'I expect so.' Steiner stood up and called out in reassurance. Schnurrbart went back inside. When the door closed and the darkness flooded back, Steiner turned to Dorn again. 'And what do human beings do then?'

'Human beings?' Dorn laughed bitterly. 'They climb upon mountain peaks or hide in caves and wait in terror until old Mother Earth has calmed down again. Then they return and work heroically to save the lives and property of the victims so that a little later they can take away the same lives and property in far more bestial fashion.'

Steiner chuckled. 'Wonderful, Professor—pour it out. After all, we are the only creatures who know precisely what we are about.'

'So we are, and how proud we are of it. But the earth endures our pride just as she endures our laughter and our tears. Not that anyone thinks about her; we have so much more important things to do. We dig holes and fill them up again; we build cities and burn them to ashes; we create life and kill it; and we talk about God and think of ourselves.'

He fell silent. Steiner turned on his side and looked at him as though he were meeting him for the first time. 'I did not know,' he said slowly, 'that we had so much in common, Professor. But you've left one thing out. Do you know what I mean?'

'I know,' Dorn replied. 'It endures us patiently because it is obedient to the meaningful laws of creation as we are obedient to the meaninglessness of our human laws. But if that were not the case, who would be able to say what is human and what divine.'

'That's it,' Steiner said. 'That is our comfort.' Impulsively he laid his hand on Dorn's arm. 'We must talk more when I come back.'

'When you come back,' Dorn said. Down below, in the house, the men had started singing again. Steiner hummed the melody under his breath. Then he stood up and drew Dorn to his feet. They stood in silence for a few minutes longer, looking out over the dark hills.

'By himself, a man is scrap-iron,' Steiner said roughly.

Dorn nodded. As they walked down the hill, Steiner kept his hand on Dorn's shoulder. His hand was still there as they entered the house.

After Steiner left the bunker Stransky returned to the table and dropped heavily into a chair. His face was burning with shame, and every time he recalled how Steiner had turned his back and walked out the door, his hand flew to his throat which felt almost choked with humiliation. His helpless rage was all the greater when he realized that he could not undertake any serious punishment of Steiner without arguing with Brandt. A succession of wild plans ran through his head, to be dropped each in turn as soon as he began to think them out seriously. After a while he began to regret his passion. How could he possibly have let himself go like that? He lit a cigarette and forced himself to reason calmly. In his three years as an officer in the Wehrmacht he had often run into resistance, and had broken it by the usual methods. But an episode such as the one he had just been through was something he would have thought impossible in the army. Taken by surprise, he had bungled the thing, had failed to hold Steiner down, as he should have done, there and then. Now, of course, it was too late. The bold-faced brute would not fail to cover himself by obtaining support from Brandt. Perhaps he was already on his way back to see the regimental commander.

This idea aroused a sudden suspicion. Suppose Brandt or Kiesel were behind the whole business. He recalled Triebig's telling him that the sergeant had been ordered to report to regiment at six o'clock. The longer he pondered the matter, the more convinced he became that the whole incident had been pre-arranged. Perhaps they wanted to trap him, in order to get rid of him as battalion commander. He smiled grimly. If that were the case, that pair had underestimated him, underestimated him sorely. He must try to turn the point of their weapon against them—and he would find a way. Above all he must find out everything there was to know about Steiner's background and personality. He made a note. Then he began to undress. Long after he had blown out the candle he lay on his cot with hands clasped under his head, gazing into the darkness.

VII

TOWARD NOON, TWO days later, Steiner reached his destination, after a long ride in the heavily-laden back of a truck. He stood somewhat dazed on the cobbled pavement, watching the truck rattling away down the road. Now that he was no longer cooled by the wind of its motion, he could feel how searing hot the sun was. The heat was doubly unpleasant because of the heavy camouflage suit he wore over his uniform. Fetscher had thought it best for him to take all his stuff with him—one never knew. Fetscher had also swapped his Russian tommy-gun for a German one. 'As long as you're on leave,' he had said self-importantly. 'Any MP would arrest you on the spot if he saw you carrying that thing. You're going back to rear-echelon, don't forget that, my boy.' He was right, of course, and so Steiner had set out with his pack loaded and festooned with all the regulation equipment.

He slung the straps of his pack over his shoulders and stood for a few minutes longer with an air of perplexity. The street was still and deserted. Apparently the inhabitants of the little resort kept to their houses at this time of day. The houses, which lined both sides of the street, were set among gardens of tropical lushness. The village lay at the foot of a mountain slope which seen from this point seemed almost vertical. On his right the restless sea gleamed with the same blueness as the sky. Low pines and tall palms bordered the pebbly white beach, and out of the water gigantic rocks rose like petrified fountains above the white surf. Steiner tore his eyes away from the peacefulness of it and set out down the street. He soon came across a soldier lounging about under the arch of a garden gate. He was dressed only in shirt and trousers. When Steiner spoke to him, he barely moved his head. But he was awake enough to point out the way to the Divisional Rest Home. It was only a short distance away, a huge building close to the beach, with tall windows and marble pillars in the façade, set in the midst of spacious grounds. The flat roof was shaded by a large grove of pines. As Steiner approached the door opened. A sergeant and a Red Cross nurse came out. Steiner sauntered toward them. He did not like the sergeant's leathery face, nor his brand-new uniform with the knife-like creases in the trousers. He was only too familiar with that type from back in the barracks.

The sergeant scrutinized Steiner from top to toe. 'What do you want?' he asked.

Steiner thrust his thumbs under his pack straps and stared coolly at the man. 'Do you mean me?' he retorted.

The leathery forehead flushed. Steiner ignored the angry sergeant and looked at the nurse. She had a pretty insipid doll's face with bright, watery eyes.

'Who do you think you are?' the sergeant bellowed. 'What are you doing here?'

Steiner grinned. 'Looking for a room with running water, central heating and a view of the ocean. Anything of that sort available, my man?'

The sergeant gaped at him, while the nurse giggled foolishly. Steiner reached into his pocket and handed the sergeant his papers. The man turned through them for a moment, and the expression on his face slowly changed. When he handed them back, there was embarrassment in his voice. 'You might have said so right off. How's a fellow to tell who's inside one of those damned monkey-suits you've got on.' He turned to the nurse. 'Where can we put him? All the rooms are taken.'

'Is he to stay here?' she asked in surprise.

'Yes. Master Sergeant Steiner—two weeks leave.' He laughed irritably. 'The devil only knows how they figure it. We always receive our men by groups, each group to stay ten days. The whole place is filled up.'

Steiner was growing impatient. 'You must have a closet empty. Otherwise I'll look for private quarters.'

'There's a regulation against that,' the sergeant replied quickly. He thought for a moment.

'We could put him upstairs,' the nurse said with sudden eagerness.

The sergeant looked at her. 'You mean upstairs?'

She nodded. He hesitated. Then he turned to Steiner again. 'We do have one room for special people, but it's on the third floor.'

Steiner scrutinized his face and then the nurse's. 'For special people?' he asked. Then he noticed the nurse blushing and grinned. 'I'll take it. I don't suppose you have a lift?'

The sergeant laughed. 'The servants didn't have it as cushy as that. You see,' he went on conversationally, 'the house used to be the summer residence of some Russian government big noise. The upper rooms were for the servants. We'll get that room ready now. You can wait on the bench there. We won't be long.' He pointed to a white bench under the trees. Then he beckoned to the nurse and went back inside. Steiner slung his pack from his back, unbuttoned the camouflage jacket and dropped on to the bench with a sigh. He looked out over the sea. Somewhere out there, beyond the horizon, lay Turkey, Syria, Arabia and the Indian Ocean: the great wide world, adventure and distance, the islands and dreams of youth, longing and its fulfilment. He looked at the white beading of the surf. There was an almost unnatural silence here, broken only by the rhythmic slapping of the waves. Eyes half-closed, he let the song of the sea lull him. Pleasantly weary, he felt grateful now for the warmth of the cloudless April day. Now and then a cool breeze wafted across the water; then the pines would be stirred out of their immobility and their shadows would dance across the gardens.

He completely forgot where he was. When he heard a voice in his ear, it took him a while to recover awareness of his surroundings. The nurse was standing at the door, her face under its white cap turned toward him. He stood up slowly, picked up his pack and walked toward her. 'Had you fallen asleep?' she asked.

'No, but I was pretty close to it. The room's done already?'

'Yes. You'll like the room.' As they mounted the stairs side by side she talked steadily. 'You're really in luck. The other NCOs are two or three to a room. This is the first time anyone has arrived here so irregularly. Incidentally, your room is right next to mine.'

He glanced at her face out of the corner of his eye and said: 'I hope you don't snore. I'm very sensitive to noise.'

They had reached the third floor. She went up to one of the many doors. 'This is it,' she said, letting him go ahead of her. On the threshold he paused for a moment and studied the room. At the left stood the bed, its head beneath the large casement windows. In the centre of the room stood a small table and two chairs. The right wall was taken up by a wide couch with several cutely arranged cushions. Steiner turned and saw the nurse's face close behind him. 'Do you like it?' she asked. He nodded, went over to the table and laid his pack on it. Then he stepped to the window and looked out. 'You can see the sunset every evening from here,' she said, still right behind him.

As he turned to face her, he found his arm brushing her breast. He wrinkled his brow and asked: 'Can the sunset be seen from your room, too?'

'Of course.' She laughed. 'I told you mine is right next to yours.'

'That's good,' he said coldly. 'It would be a bother if you had to watch your sunset from here.'

As he slipped off the camouflage jacket, the nurse glared at him. Her face was hot and her voice trembled as she said: 'There are lots of other rooms in this building.'

'I don't doubt it,' Steiner said. 'I wouldn't be surprised if you knew them all. Where's the roster here?'

She was already on her way to the door. In the doorway she turned and looked at him with fury. 'We don't have any roster and we don't have ranks here, either; we have a house schedule and guests are supposed to follow it. It's posted here.' She angrily indicated a printed card on the wall and went out, slamming the door behind her. Steiner grinned. Then he went over to the schedule and studied it carefully. From one to three was a rest period. That explained the peculiar quiet in the building in which, he guessed, seventy or eighty men must be housed. Supper was served in the dining-room at half-past six. He looked at his watch. It was not yet half-past three and he decided to take a swim. After stowing away his belongings, he left the room and strolled slowly down to the beach. There he undressed and dived in. With vigorous strokes he swam to a rock that rose out of the waves about 150 feet from the beach. From the top of it there was a good view in all directions. The coastline was full of indentations, and the shifting surf lined the beach like a silvery girdle. The town itself stretched in a single line for about half a mile. From his perch on the rock the sharp slopes of the mountain seemed to loom directly over the houses, threatening the safety of the town.

Steiner was absorbed in the view when he heard a loud call. He looked down and saw a man thrashing the water energetically. He reached the rock at last and climbed up, panting and shaking himself like a wet poodle. 'Well, my friend,' he said. 'This is the life.' He beat the water out of his red bathing trunks, brushed it out of his blanched blond hair, and finally settled down on the rock close to Steiner. His body was on the puny side, but he had a good head with blue, cheerful eyes and rosy cheeks. 'Wonderful!' he went on talking gaily. 'Couldn't be better. The upper crust of the socialist worker's state certainly knew how to appreciate the good things of life. Don't you think?'

'They would have had to be idiots not to.'

The blond boy nodded. 'They would! Where are you staying? I haven't seen you before.'

'Just arrived an hour ago,' Steiner said.

'Has a new shipment come?' the boy asked in surprise.

'No, I came alone.'

'Oh. Well where are you staying?' He made no attempt to conceal his frank curiosity.

Steiner pointed to the Division Rest Home.

'A lousy place,' the towheaded fellow said contemptuously. 'A fine front and nothing behind it.'

'What do you mean?' Steiner asked. 'There are at least seventy troops staying there.'

'I don't mean the men. You ought to come over to our diggings. Six houses down the street. Not such an elegant building, but we've got a canteen that's first class.'

'Is that so?' This boy talked a little too much and he wanted to be left alone. To get rid of him he nodded and said: 'Perhaps I'll drop in tonight.'

The boy slapped him on the back. 'Fine. Don't forget. By the way'—he leaned confidentially closer to Steiner—'we have some women there who are really worth seeing. Especially two of them. There's one of them wears her breasts as I would wear the Iron Cross.'

'Women?' Steiner queried.

'Yes, the nurses. High class, let me tell you. Swell girls. They come to all our parties.'

'All?'

'You can go the limit with them. Only the one with big breasts is reserved for Lieutenant Mannheim, the paymaster. Nobody else gets a chance at her.' He sighed and gazed gloomily over the water. 'It's always the same; if there's anyone around with a pip on his shoulder, we don't get a look in.'

His chagrin seemed so genuine that Steiner smiled. 'If so, you aren't missing much,' he said contemptuously. 'I'd sooner have a decent glass of wine or beer than a dozen of these illegal whores.'

'Whores?' the blond chap protested indignantly. 'They're not whores. When you see Gertrud you'll change your mind.'

'Don't go on about it,' Steiner replied irritably. 'I'll take a look at your canteen tonight. If I needed women I wouldn't have to go six houses down the street.' He nodded good-bye, dropped into the water and swam back to the beach. As he dressed he wondered whether he had been too sharp with the boy. Then he recalled his conversation with the nurse and grinned. That kind were the same everywhere. He'd make it up to the blond kid this evening over a bottle. After all, he should be grateful for the tip about the canteen. As he thought of it, his mouth watered. It was a long time since he had last tasted beer. He frowned. Had the blond chap said anything about beer? He couldn't recall, and shrugged impatiently. He would see; a canteen without beer was no canteen.

The swim had wonderfully refreshed him, and the act of having rid himself of the dirt of the road seemed to bring back the mood of bygone Saturday nights, when, still a civilian, he had washed and shaved and gone out. As he approached the house he saw several men talking in loud voices. They were standing by the door; when they caught sight of him they fell silent and studied him with curiosity. For a few seconds he was undecided whether to join them or not. Then they apparently recognized his rank, and their faces set. He went on past them, answering their salutes with a brief nod. When he reached his room he lay down and promptly fell asleep.

It was already dark when he awoke. He lay for a while staring up at the ceiling with eyes half shut. He began thinking about the nurse, and regretted having told her off so roughly. Cursing under his breath, he got up, combed his hair and slipped into his tunic. Glancing at his watch, he saw that it was high time for supper. He hurried downstairs. The dining-hall was a long, lofty room. Three rows of tables took up nearly half of it. Most of the chairs were already occupied and Steiner had difficulty finding a seat in the further corner of the room. He squeezed in between chairs and noticed that the men stared curiously at him, then put their heads together and whispered. When he started to sit down, someone said: 'You'll be served up front; this section is for privates.'

'Then this is where I belong,' Steiner said, sitting down beside the man who had spoken. The soldier looked at him in astonishment. Then he grinned and resumed eating. The faces of the other men brightened and they moved closer together so that he had more room. Since the place in front of him was not set, Steiner looked around. The food was being served in big bowls. Steiner waited until one of the nurses approached and asked her for a plate and cutlery. She shook her head and pointed to the other end of the table. 'You'll have to go up there. That's where sergeants and corporals are served.'

'As you see, I am a master sergeant,' Steiner said sharply. 'Bring me a plate or I'll get one for myself.'

Their interest piqued, the men all raised their heads. The nurse set her bowl down on the table, her pretty face flushing with temper. 'If you want to change the regulations,' she said defiantly, 'tell Sergeant Maier, not me.' She started to turn away, but Steiner held her by the arm. There was a sudden silence in the room. The clatter of spoons stopped and all eyes turned inquisitively toward him. Steiner looked down the table and caught sight of the leathery-faced sergeant, who sat at the other end of the table, with a half-dozen NCOs, staring hard at him. Steiner raised his voice. 'In the first place I don't like your tone, miss, and in the second place I don't intend to be told where I have to sit to choke down your dehydrated rations. Now bring me a plate.'

Helplessly the nurse turned her head toward the NCOs' table. The sergeant stood up and strode rapidly toward them. 'There are regulations here,' he said angrily, 'and even a master sergeant has to obey them. You sit up front with us. No one gets special treatment, understand?'

Steiner took a deep breath. He released the nurse's arm. 'What regulations say I must?' he asked quietly.

'There's a copy of them hanging in your room,' the leather-skinned sergeant replied curtly.

'In all the rooms?'

'Of course.'

'Really.' Steiner tapped one of the men in front of him on the shoulder. 'Bring me the regulations from your room.'

The man stood up and hurried to the door. 'I'm not out for special treatment,' Steiner declared coolly. 'This is a matter of principle and we're going to settle it right now.'

The sergeant's voice was thick with rage. 'You'll find out soon enough what it's a matter of. Don't think you can play the big shot here.'

'That's a part that suits you a lot better than it does me,' Steiner replied coldly. The scene disgusted him, but on the other hand he did not want to give in now. He looked over toward the door where the man was returning. He made a wide circle around Leatherskin and came over to Steiner. 'Here it is, sir,' he said.

'Thank you very much,' Steiner said, taking the printed card from his hand. He looked the regulations over again and noted with satisfaction that he had not been mistaken. The sergeant regarded him darkly. When Steiner passed the copy of the regulations to him he looked up and asked: 'Well?'

Steiner smiled scornfully. 'Do you think I'm an illiterate?' The smile vanished abruptly. He glanced briefly at the men, who were listening in eager suspense. 'There's not a word here about NCOs having to eat separately. Is there?'

'That's taken for granted,' Leatherskin replied violently. 'It doesn't have to be specifically mentioned.'

Steiner frowned. 'There's only one thing I'd take for granted: that the enlisted men here are being diddled with unwritten as well as written rubbish. I came here to rest up, not to be reminded of the barracks and the drill-ground.' He snatched the card from the speechless sergeant's hand and slapped it down on the table. 'You can just pull in your horns. If I am not served right here tomorrow morning, I'll see that I get my rations elsewhere.' He strode through a wall of icy silence to the door. As he passed by one of the windows outside, he saw that everyone in the dining-hall was still sitting motionless and silent. His appetite was thoroughly ruined by now, so he fetched his cap from his room and left the building.

He counted the houses on the left side of the street. The sixth house lay in the midst of large grounds. The building was hidden far back among the trees. He went up a paved walk toward the brightness of its windows. On the threshold of the open door he collided with a fellow who was hurrying out, and at once recognized the tow-headed boy of his afternoon acquaintance. He gripped his arm roughly and announced himself. 'Well, here I am.'

The boy stared at him incredulously. Steiner laughed. 'What's the matter? Have you forgotten me already?'

'No,' the boy stammered, confused. 'I didn't know that you—I mean, sir——' He gulped, and sweat actually started out on his face at his sudden discovery of Steiner's rank.

Steiner gave him a poke. 'Drivel! If we always knew the whole truth about other people, sooner or later we'd turn hermit. Where's this canteen of yours? My throat is dry as a hot stove-lid.'

'We can take care of that.' The boy laughed, at ease again. He led Steiner inside. 'I was just going out to look you up,' he said. 'Things are getting gay downstairs.' As they descended the stairs he told Steiner that the canteen was intended only for the use of occupants of the house and their guests. 'If you came alone they'd throw you out. Otherwise the mob in this town would drink us dry in two days.'

At the bottom of the stairs was a long corridor which led to a door from which a din of laughter and singing sounded. 'Sounds good,' Steiner murmured and followed the boy in. It took a few seconds for their eyes to adjust to the dense cloud of cigarette smoke which enveloped the whole of the large room. Some two dozen men were sitting around small round tables, bottles and glasses in front of them, loudly singing to the harsh notes of an out-of-tune piano in the rear corner opposite the door. Steiner followed the boy to the bar. A soldier in rolled-up shirt sleeves was acting as bartender. He scowled at Steiner. Towhead leaned forward and whispered a few words that Steiner could not make out, but the man's face cleared. He nodded and asked: 'What will you have?'

'What have you got?'

'Red wine and beer.'

Steiner chose beer. When the man set two bottles on the counter, Steiner opened his eyes wide in astonishment. 'Pilsner in Russia!' he exclaimed, overpowered by emotion. 'This is a dream. Give me five bottles.'

'The two of us will finish them off in good shape,' Towhead said serenely.

'The two of us!' Steiner laughed harshly. 'What do you mean, the two of us? I'm going to drink these five alone. What do you think I am, an infant? I've been waiting for this moment for six months. You guys don't know what it's like to go without beer for six months. I don't know what the stuff tastes like any more.'

'It's three marks a bottle,' the bartender said.

'I wouldn't care if it was a hundred,' Steiner replied. 'What good is this drivel in my pocket? Here!' He brought out a roll of big notes. 'Six months pay and not a chance to spend the stuff.' He tossed a note on the counter, tucked the bottles under his arm, and strode over to a table. Sitting down, he lined the bottles up in front of him. Towhead followed, shaking his head, and sat down beside him. There were two other men at the table, so absorbed in a game of chess that they scarcely noticed them. Steiner picked up a bottle, regarding the label lovingly. His mouth was parched as if he had not drunk for days. As he opened the bottle, his hands shook.

'Here's your change,' Towhead said. 'You had five marks coming to you; you left it on the counter.'

With the back of his hand Steiner swept the bill off the table. He disregarded the glass and set the bottle to his lips. As he drank, he closed his eyes. 'You can stow it away,' Towhead said enthusiastically. 'I've never seen anything like it.' He laughed. 'That stuff will knock you over, believe me. It's pre-war beer.'

Steiner wiped his mouth and grinned. 'The first three bottles won't, and after that it doesn't matter.' He opened the second bottle.

'Here are your five marks,' Towhead said, holding out the money which he had picked up from the floor. Steiner took it from him, cursed and tore the bill to pieces. The boy stared at him in dismay.

'What's wrong with you?' he asked.

'Another word about money tonight and I'll hit you over the head with a bottle. What the hell is it good for? To drink myself to death?'

'But you can always send it home,' Towhead stammered.

'Home!' Steiner laughed insultingly. The two chess players lifted their heads. He paid no attention to them, raised the second bottle to his lips and drank half of it. 'Do you send your money home?'

'Of course.'

'Why, may I ask?'

Towhead shrugged. 'So it will be there for me later, when I get home.'

'Later! You mean so they can put up a tombstone for you? With your name on it, and under the name "Died for Nation and Fatherland", and all that rubbish?'

Towhead shifted uncomfortably in his chair. Steiner leaned across the table toward him and fixed him with his eyes. 'Don't worry; I don't get plastered on a bottle and a half. I'm still cold sober; it takes me at least five to get going. I want to tell you this. Later, when you're walking barefoot over the heavenly prairies you won't need your money, and if you're shovelling coal in hell you certainly won't.'

'No need to get so pessimistic,' Towhead replied crossly.

'Sure. Maybe you'll be lucky enough to pound rock in Siberia or clear ruins at home and shout Heil Hitler.'

'Be quiet,' Towhead said anxiously, glancing at the two men who had turned back to their chess game, but who must be hearing every word. Steiner snorted. He was starting on the third bottle by now. 'We're all poor lousy bastards,' he said vehemently. 'We're all sick and scared to death of it, all of us.' He spat on the floor.

'I like that—coming from you,' Towhead commented, throwing a somewhat envious glance at the decorations on Steiner's chest.

Steiner caught the look and laughed contemptuously. 'You mean on account of those things. If you only knew——' He broke off and stared darkly down at the table. 'Why aren't you drinking? Go on, get yourself something to drink.' He tossed money across the table and watched Towhead go over to the counter and return with two bottles. 'Now we're really getting started,' Steiner said, opening the fourth bottle. More men had come into the room meanwhile. The pianist was worn out and had taken a seat at a nearby table. Among the uniforms the white of a nurse's costume gleamed, and Towhead began shifting impatiently in his chair. 'Piles bothering you?' Steiner asked maliciously.

Towhead shook his head. 'I'm just wondering where Gertrud is.'

'Is she the breasty one?'

'No, that's the other one. I'm speaking of Gertrud.'

Steiner took out his cigarettes. He passed them across the table. 'I don't smoke,' Towhead said.

Lighting one for himself, Steiner smiled pityingly. 'You don't smoke and you hardly drink and you send your money home. What do you live for?'

Towhead shrugged. 'I'm satisfied. As for the money, they can use it at home.'

'Your parents.'

'Yes.'

Steiner glowered at him. 'I'm sure they can use it. That's what I thought two years ago. I wrote to them to take a holiday, to have a good time with the money I was sending them.' He stared down at his hands and his lips quivered.

'Well?' Towhead asked. 'Did they do it?'

'Oh, they went off on their holiday all right,' Steiner said. His voice was hoarse.

Towhead leaned forward, intensely curious. 'And then?'

Steiner puffed at his cigarette. His face was red and his forehead beaded with tiny drops of sweat. He picked up the bottle and finished it off. 'And then,' he said, 'and then—ah——' He snapped the cigarette to the floor, and opened the last bottle. 'Shut up,' he said roughly. 'You ask too many questions. You ought to drink, not ask questions. Drink, drink.' They drank in silence. After a while Towhead went back to the bar. He walked unsteadily, touching a chair for support now and then. Milksop, Steiner thought, watching him; these children can't take it. He began mumbling to himself, and rested his head on his hands. The sounds in the room reached his ear in a vague, distorted manner. Someone started to sing. The pianist was playing again: 'Underneath the lamplight, by the barrack gate. . . .' Steiner hummed the melody. All at once he felt a gentle indifference. The canteen began to sway; the walls rose almost imperceptibly; all the harsh, sharp angles disappeared and everything became soft and round as a woman's breast. When Towhead returned with several bottles, Steiner slapped him on the back. He was in high spirits. 'Them and them and more to come; today we drink, today we swill.'

'Today we swill,' Towhead said thickly, opening a bottle with a loud pop. 'In four days,' he went on, 'I'll be on my way back into it again, back to Smolensk. Ever heard of the place?'

Steiner nodded. 'Birthplace of Shakespeare. Everything comes from Russia, everything stays in Russia. Everything.'

They guffawed and clinked bottles. The chess players dumped their pieces into the box and moved closer. Steiner thrust two bottles toward them. 'That's it; why wear your brains out. The game is lost either way.' He suddenly began to sing, pounding the table with his fists in time to the music.

Auf der Strasse nach Tuapse
Marschiert ein Bataillon,
Und das sind die Reste
Von unserer Division.

There was a silence at the other table. Laughing, the pianist turned his head and looked over toward them. In one corner someone joined in, then a third voice followed, and when it came to the refrain almost all of them roared out:

> Wir konnten schon Tuapse sehn
> Und mussten wieder stiften gehn
> Wie einst Napoleon.*

The song faded out. The men raised their glasses, drank thirstily and started another song. As Steiner opened the second bottle, a voice behind his back roused him. Towhead stood up quickly, exclaiming: 'Gertrud, here you are. Come over here, sit down. I'm so glad you've come.' He dragged a chair over from the next table. His face was radiant; he was so excited that he seemed almost ridiculous. Steiner placed his bottle on the table and slowly turned his head. He looked into a pallid face, a face which kept its distance and knew its worth. A wealth of chestnut hair gathered in a bun at the nape of the neck emphasized the high arched forehead. The girl's large, almond-shaped eyes had a look of great self-assurance in them. There was a fineness and regularity about all her features, and the corners of her soft mouth were disturbingly sweet. Steiner stared at her and slowly lifted his hands from the bottle. He watched with narrowed eyes as she sat down opposite Towhead and greeted the other men with a friendly smile. Then she turned to Towhead. 'You've drunk too much, Klaus,' she said. She had a throaty voice, and Steiner suddenly felt a painful stabbing sensation around his heart. He bent over a little and pushed his chair back as though intending to get up.

At the reprimand in the nurse's tone Towhead had looked guiltily down at the floor. He seemed absurdly embarrassed. He raised his head, shrugged in comic despair and said to Steiner: 'This is Trudel, the finest girl I ever met. But when she sees a fellow sitting over a bottle, she behaves as if he'd thrown away his chance for Paradise.'

Steiner coughed lightly. He felt out of control and bad-mannered and tried to steady himself by lighting a cigarette. But the seven bottles of Pilsner were taking effect. His face, he felt, had become a

* On the highway to Tuapse a battalion is marching. And that is all that's left of our division. We had a glimpse of Tuapse and cleared out again, like Napoleon long ago.

stupid mask, and he rubbed his hand over his mouth. Hoarsely, he muttered, 'Perhaps she reads the Bible too much.' As soon as the words were out he was sorry he had spoken. The nurse looked at him. He saw her face as a vague whiteness through the smoke of his cigarette, and reached for the bottle again. To hell with her, he thought; what do I care what these uniformed whores think of me.

He finished the bottle and rapped it down on the table. The nurse continued to look fixedly at him, and his insecurity intensified. Angrily, he thrust out his lower lip. 'Don't you like what I say?' he asked sharply.

She pretended not to have heard. Turning to Towhead, she asked: 'Who is this?'

'An acquaintance,' Towhead replied, abashed. He looked imploringly at Steiner.

'I'm surprised,' the nurse replied coolly. 'Where did you pick him up?'

Steiner had had enough. Before Towhead could answer, he used both arms against the table to push himself to his feet. 'You sound as if I was a new pair of his pants,' he said. 'But if I was, I'd prefer to be on the part of you where pants belong. Good night, everybody.' He staggered to the bar and dropped a fifty-mark note on the counter. 'Two bottles; the rest is for you.'

The man behind the bar stared unbelievingly at him. 'Do you mean that?'

'Of course. And you can do me the favour of wiping your arse with it one of these days.' Paying no attention to the man's baffled face, he picked up the bottles and made his way among the tables to the opposite end of the canteen. Out of the corners of his eyes he saw Towhead speaking earnestly with the nurse. He grinned.

Passing by the piano, he stopped. For a few seconds he watched the man's fingers moving over the keys. Then he gripped his shoulder and said: 'Play the Volga song. Do you know it?'

'I do. I played it only five minutes ago.'

'Did you now?' Steiner pondered that. Then he shook his head. 'I don't remember; play it again.'

The man nodded. 'Often as you like.'

Steiner found an empty seat at one of the rear tables. The other men at the table fell silent and looked at him. He set his bottles down and said: 'Don't you like my mug? Sorry, it's the only one I have.' He sat down and opened a bottle. The men laughed and drank to him. Through the noise, bits of the Volga song could be heard. 'Be quiet a minute,' Steiner said. He tilted his head and felt his heart beating in short, hard thumps. Although he was completely drunk, he had not entirely lost mastery of himself. He looked across the room to where the nurse was still sitting with Towhead. For a brief moment their glances met. She quickly looked aside. Steiner lit another cigarette. I shouldn't have drunk so much, he told himself. But then he promptly shook his head in anger. What did he care about the woman—and a nurse at that. He grinned scornfully. Had he come so far that he thought every skirt was another Anne. He puffed hard at his cigarette, thinking. You had to have something you could cling to. Something real with meaning because you felt it, not something you imagined just because you wanted something meaningful. His head was growing heavier and heavier. With a terrible effort he forced his eyes open, emptied the last bottle and pushed his chair back. As he stood up, the canteen began whirling around him. He compressed his lips and took a deep breath. The other men at the table laughed as they watched him. He became aware of them and stiffened his body. Then he steered toward the door, left the canteen and stumbled up the stairs.

In front of the building he stood still for a moment. The fresh night air, far from making him feel better, affected him badly. Reeling, he found his way down the path in the direction of the sea. With a vague idea of cleansing himself, he set out toward the beach. On the way he stumbled and fell so awkwardly that he cut his forehead and lay where he had fallen, half conscious. Suddenly he heard a voice: 'How could you get yourself in such a state?' He rose on his knees and began to curse. When someone gripped his shoulder, he struck out wildly with his fist. He heard a suppressed cry of pain. 'Clear off!' he panted. 'Go away or——' He staggered to his feet and plodded on, blood running down his forehead and into his eyes. Half-blinded, he reached the sand and stripped off his clothes. As he was about to plunge into the water, someone held his arms and again the voice, imploring and insistent, spoke in his ear: 'Are you mad? You're in no fit condition to——' He whirled around and stared into the anxious face of the nurse.

It was a bright night. A full moon hung like a round lamp in the sky, shedding yellow light. The waves were rolling heavily up against the beach, digging into the pebbles and flattening out as though a crack in the earth were absorbing them. Steiner wiped the blood out of his eyes. 'You touch me again,' he said hoarsely, 'and I'll throw you into the water. What do you want anyway? Anything special about me that interests you?' He looked down at her and suddenly laughed. 'From what I hear a man's no good when he's drunk anyway,' he added.

She looked steadily at him. He saw the disgust in her eyes. But she stood her ground. 'Clear out!' he said roughly. He strode forward up to his waist in the water, drew up his legs and let the waves carry him. After a while he swam against the tide and did not return to the beach until he could feel his arms and legs growing stiff and numb. From far out in the water he could see that she was waiting for him, standing like a statue against the background of the dark garden. As he emerged from the water, his teeth were chattering. Before he reached his clothes, he felt sick. He turned quickly, dropped down with his face in the water and vomited. His body heaved; he could feel all the air leaving his lungs, but he allowed himself to slide deeper and deeper into the water. Suddenly he was gripped by the feet and pulled back. Struggling for breath, he lay on the ground and saw her horrified face above him. 'What are you doing?' she stammered. 'My God, what are you doing?'

He turned over on his back and looked at her. Abruptly he felt a surge of rage and shame. The repulsive taste of vomit was on his tongue, and he felt his stomach drawing together again. But he fought down the new fit of vomiting. Blood began streaming down his face afresh. Suppressing a groan, he sat up. When she tried to support him, he knocked her arm back. 'Are you still here?' he growled. 'If you don't go away I'll smash——' He broke off and stooped for his clothes.

Suddenly something else occurred to him. He glanced at the chest-high wall which surrounded the garden only twenty feet away. Heavily, he went over to it, pulled himself up and dropped to the soft ground on the other side. Before the surprised nurse could follow him, he crawled a few yards forward into the darkness of the garden, flattened out on the ground and looked back. He waited with bated breath. If she went to the canteen to fetch help from the men, he would have to clear out in a hurry. The thought worried him, and he raised himself slightly off the ground. Now he could distinctly hear her footsteps as she ran along the wall. She must have reached the little gate by now. He tensed his muscles. Although he was trembling violently in the cool night air, he did not move from the spot. The trees almost shut out the moonlight. Nevertheless he could see her white uniform nearing; she was evidently looking around for him. He pillowed his head on his arms and began to moan softly. A moment later he heard her voice in words of concern, and then she was close beside him.

He moved so swiftly that he smothered her resistance and her outcry before she could recover from her initial horrified numbness. He pulled her to the ground, brutally threw himself upon her, pulled her skirt over her head and pressed his knee between her legs. Then he suddenly released her and stood up. He stood watching her as she slowly sat up, rearranged her clothing and stared at him without speaking.

'Why did you follow me?' he asked in a low voice.

She did not answer. He shook his head slightly. 'You are reckless, Nurse Gertrud. In the future keep your humanitarian paws off drunken men. It might be misunderstood.'

'You're mad,' she murmured. Her face was as white as her uniform, and she was breathing heavily.

'We are all mad,' he replied tranquilly. 'We are living in an age of absolute madness; the few normal people are safely behind barbed wire because they have failed to understand that it's no longer worth being normal.' He laughed and felt the wound on his forehead. 'Our century is changing everything. What was thought bad in the past will be thought good in the future, and what was good once will become bad. We will no longer lie on top of but under women, and some day we'll reach the point where the men will bear the children and the women go out and earn the bread.' He tittered. 'We're heading for a great age, nurse; madness will be total and the insane asylums emptied.' He took a step toward her and lowered his voice. 'You're just as mad as I am, because if you were normal you'd stay home and darn socks and study cookbooks instead of coming to places where every man has two glands too many. You get me?'

'My father is a doctor,' she replied calmly.

'So much the worse. Then he ought to know what comes of leaving his daughter to a horde of two-footed billygoats. If I were your father, I would have pounded your backside black and blue and locked you up in the cellar.'

He turned away abruptly, climbed over the wall and found his clothes. He was dead sober now, but his head ached as though it were locked in a vice. Dressed, he went over to the wall once more and looked into the garden. The nurse was still standing motionless in the same place. Her face seemed dark now, scarcely distinguishable against the background of the night. For a moment he was tempted to say a friendly word to her. Then he shrugged, turned away and strode along the beach until the massive structure of the divisional rest home appeared among the trees. With few exceptions the windows were dark. He remembered that ten o'clock was tattoo. It must be within a few minutes of ten. He hurried, found the front door open, and slowly mounted the stairs. In front of his room he hesitated. Then he went softly to the next door and leaned forward, listening. He glanced up and down the hall to make sure no one was there, and slowly depressed the latch. As he entered the dark room he heard a hasty sound and a sleepy voice asked: 'Who's there?'

'Three guesses,' he said, closing the door behind him. For a few seconds there was a dead silence. Then he heard a sound like that made by a blanket being thrown back. His eyes had grown accustomed to the darkness meanwhile and he saw a figure in white get out of the bed and hesitantly approach him. She seemed to recognize him, stood still and said indignantly: 'Leave my room at once.'

'You've got that out of the cinema,' he said. 'But don't worry; I just wanted to ask you whether you have any aspirin. I've got a frightful headache.'

She came two steps closer, her long nightgown trailing around her ankles. 'You're drunk,' she said with disgust.

He regarded her speculatively. 'Not any more. I got rid of it all in the water. Have you aspirin?'

She hesitated. As she turned toward the door, he gripped her shoulders and held her tightly. 'Were you going to turn on the light?' he asked.

'Yes.'

'You don't need any light,' he said, feeling along her arms. The nightgown had slipped off her right shoulder and he knew that she had slid it off deliberately. But she defended herself and panted: 'Let me go. I'll scream. I will scream.'

'Sure, you will scream,' he said.

Her breasts were firm and soft. When she tried to kiss him, he turned his face aside and laid her on the bed.

Later, when they were lying side by side, he mused about Gertrud. Why, he wondered, had she not run to the canteen for help. There was no doubt that she was a different sort, different from this girl beside him, whose name he did not even know. In the darkness he smiled and asked: 'What is your name?'

'My friends call me Inge.' When he said nothing, she pressed close to him and stroked his chest. 'Don't you like the name?'

'Why, of course I do; why shouldn't I like it?'

'How many girls have you said that to?'

He laughed. 'Up to this moment I've never met a girl named Inge. At least not in bed,' he added.

He tried to sit up. She held him tight. 'Where are you going?'

'To bed.'

'But you can sleep here with me,' she said, disappointed.

He shook his head. 'I wouldn't be able to sleep.'

Vexed, she pulled the blanket up under her chin and watched him dress. When he was finished, he came over to the bed once more and said: 'Good night.'

'Aren't you at least going to kiss me?' Her voice was quivering with anger. He stooped and casually kissed her shoulder.

'Is that all?' she asked.

'Isn't it enough. Do you want to be paid?'

She started up as though the pillow under her back had become a hot iron. Then she threw herself face down on the bed and began to sob wildly. Steiner stood for a moment looking at her in embarrassment. Then he slowly withdrew, closing the door behind him. For a while he stood in the corridor with eyes closed. When the sobbing stopped, he went to his room. For a long while he stood at the window, staring out at the sea. He felt oddly wakeful and not at all tired. Dispiritedly, he undressed again. His headache was almost gone, but the cut on his forehead throbbed painfully. He took out his pocket-mirror and by the light of a candle examined the narrow, blood-encrusted slit over his right eyebrow. Irritably, he shook his head. Then he threw himself down on the bed and closed his eyes. The candle burned down and went out. Outside the open window the sea breathed, gasping, rolling blindly up on the beach, and the moon hung above the water like a savage mask, grinning like a faun.

Steiner awoke early next morning. He felt as fresh and rested as if he had slept for twenty-four hours without a break. Carefully, he washed the encrusted blood from his forehead, put a bit of adhesive over the wound, and appeared punctually in the dining-room. As he approached the private's table he saw that a place was set for him. Several of the men were already at the table; in response to his greeting they winked significantly. The one who had fetched the card of regulations for him last night pulled out the chair for him, saying: 'Congratulations, Sergeant.' 'You gave it to them,' another man commented. 'What did you do to your forehead? Been rubbing elbows with the big chief?'

Steiner sat down. 'No, just rubbing noses with the ground.' He leaned back comfortably in his chair. 'Here come their lordships,' someone said. Everyone turned to look at the door, where the NCOs were entering. Leatherskin came last. They sat down without so much as a glance in Steiner's direction. Later Steiner noticed Inge serving at the NCOs' table. After breakfast he went up to his room, straightened it up and then set out for the beach. In spite of the early-morning chill he decided to take a swim, and drifted about in the water for a long time. Suddenly he caught sight of Towhead sitting on a bench and apparently watching him. Steiner pretended not to notice him; he swam back to where his clothes lay and dressed. He suddenly felt the impulse to talk with somebody about Nurse Gertrud, and the only person to talk to was Towhead. He began sauntering idly in his direction and stopped in pretended surprise when his name was called. 'Well, what are you doing here so early?' He sat down on the bench.

'What happened to your head?' Towhead asked.

Steiner touched the adhesive. 'Slight accident,' he said casually. 'Did you stay long?'

'In the canteen?'

'Yes.'

They looked out over the water. After a while Towhead asked: 'Did you see Gertrud later last night?'

'How come?' Steiner asked, feeling his way.

'Oh, I was just wondering. She went out after you. Said you were so drunk you had to be watched.'

'Why didn't you come with her?'

Towhead laughed in vexation. 'She said I was so tight myself I wouldn't be any help. I waited over an hour in the canteen, but she didn't come back.'

'Well,' Steiner said pensively.

Towhead regarded him suspiciously. Then he stooped, picked up a pebble and skipped it over the water. 'At any rate,' he went on maliciously, 'she was awfully queer this morning.'

'Just one of her days, I guess,' Steiner said.

Towhead shook his head vigorously. 'No, it's something else. I'm not usually nosy, but I'd give a lot to know what happened last night.'

'You can ask her.'

They sat in silence. The beach was gradually coming to life. Alone and in groups men were appearing. Most of them headed straight for the water. Others stretched out on the pebbles in the sun. Since it was obvious that he would get no further information out of Towhead, Steiner stood up. 'I have things to do.'

'Won't you be coming over this evening.'

Steiner shook his head. 'No, thanks. I've had enough for the present.'

'But you haven't even met the other girl yet,' Towhead said insistently. 'The breasty one. She wasn't around last night. There's a girl for you.'

Steiner raised his eyebrows. 'I thought the paymaster had reserved her.'

'God, what would that mean around here. A man like you would put that old barrel-belly in the shade.'

'Too strenuous,' Steiner said, grinning. Towhead's jealousy was all too obvious. He was surprised to find himself slightly pained by the thought that there might be something between Towhead and the nurse. What did he care? Nevertheless, as he walked along the beach, his early-morning good humour was gone.

After supper Steiner decided to take a walk through the town. He strolled aimlessly down the street between the spacious lawns whose scent mingled with the tang of the water. A strange mood had taken possession of him, and he stopped frequently to gaze up at the massive mountain slopes, or over the sea. He had the feeling that he was walking upon a narrow path that led between the heights and depths, between serenity and restiveness, to the intersection of all roads; and he smiled bitterly at the thought that there should be a new road from there, one going in a different direction. There was only one road for him, and it was the road taken by all the men who stopped in this resort for a brief breathing spell—the road back to the front. For a moment he closed his eyes. Better not to think about that, he told himself. Every such thought was like a razor-edged knife cutting another sliver off the little time remaining to him.

From the windows of the houses light flowed upon the dark yards. Steiner turned his steps toward the beach. Like a barrier of black clouds the mountains towered up against the sky. They seemed to be staring westward, breathlessly, where the last embers of the day rent the heavens. Steiner shuddered. He felt an acute need to talk to someone, to make contact with some human being and he was pleased when he saw Towhead coming towards him. At the sight of Steiner, he hailed him excitedly, 'There you are!' and broke into a run. 'I've got her, I've got her all organized for you,' he said excitedly.

'Got whom?'

'Anne,' Towhead said hastily. 'You know——'

At the mention of the name Steiner started. He gripped the boy's shoulder hard and whispered tensely: 'Anne? Who is Anne?'

'The breasty one,' Towhead said eagerly wrenching away. 'She's right on my heels.' Although the moon was overcast, it was possible to see a long way down the beach. Steiner noticed a figure approaching and recognized the white uniform of a nurse.

'Listen, I don't want——'

'Have fun.'

Before Steiner could finish, Towhead had freed himself and was running off into the night. Slowly the nurse came up to Steiner. He pulled his cap down low over his forehead. It's crazy, he told himself, there are a million girls named Anne. But when he heard her voice, he suddenly began to tremble. He pulled his flashlight out of his pocket and flashed it full in her face. She closed her wide, dark eyes, but her mouth was smiling. 'Turn out that light,' she raised her hand to her dazzled eyes. 'I can't see.'

Without a word he switched off the flashlight and thrust it into his pocket. 'Do you study all girls so thoroughly?' she asked. Her voice was flat and rather common. Turning his face to one side, he murmured: 'Excuse me. I always like to see who I'm dealing with.'

She gave a cooing laugh. 'Are you satisfied?' He glanced quickly to the right and left. Then he nodded. He reached out so fast that before she could make a move to defend herself, he had pulled her close to him. His face was right above hers. She was still smiling. He took off his cap, quietly stuck it into his coat pocket, and said: 'Good evening, Anne.'

Her smile froze.

'And how I'm satisfied!' he said. He laughed hoarsely, dangerously and held her more tightly. 'Nothing is lost,' he said. 'Nothing is lost and the past is never so dead that we may not meet it again.'

She tried to pull away. Her face was twisted into an ugly grimace and she groaned under the hard pressure of his arms. Suddenly she went limp and sank to her knees. He let go of her and she slid slowly to the ground. He stooped over her. She lay still, with face averted, her mouth open and twitching. My God, he thought, my God. It still seemed to him that he was dreaming. But this was no dream, this was reality. He closed his eyes. Thirteen months had passed, more than a whole year since. . . .

He straightened up, and saw that her eyes were open and fixed on his. 'Get up!' he ordered harshly. His voice was so imperative that she obeyed at once. She made no resistance as he led her to a bench a few yards away. 'Sit down,' he said curtly. He sat down beside her. For the moment he did not know what he ought to do. The meeting had come too unexpectedly. With unsteady hands he pulled out his cigarettes and lit one. For a while he stared at the glowing tip of the cigarette, until he heard suppressed sobs at his side.

'Tears, Anne?' he said. 'Why? More to the point if you'd done your crying last time.'

She turned toward him and spoke with unbending fury: 'You brute!'

He laughed, liking her courage. 'Is that what I am?'

'Yes,' she said violently. 'You always were a brute. You don't know how to treat a woman.'

'When a woman forces her way into a man's bed,' he said coldly, 'she must expect something of the sort. Sooner or later she'll find herself lying alone in it, or be thrown out the other side. That's the fate of all whores,' he added brutally.

She quivered. He noticed it and grinned. 'You didn't used to be so sensitive about words,' he said. 'You're slipping, Anne.'

As she made a move to spring to her feet, he gripped her arm hard. 'Stay here; we haven't finished with one another yet.' He tossed the cigarette away. 'You know how that little romance started. I didn't want it. I grant you that I learned something from you. But all there was to learn I found out the first night, and I knew there wasn't any more.' He laughed cynically. 'A man can't forgive himself for his clumsiness with his first woman, especially when she's as experienced as you. I told you what I thought of you that third night. Two nights were enough to bring me to my senses again.'

Suddenly his fury returned. He would never forget the expression on the face of the staff doctor, Major Dietrich, who had searched the room, assisted by several nurses and medicos, and had found the watch among his things. The rest had been an ugly dream. The court-martial, the sentence, the countless humiliations that he had undergone up to and all through the period in the penal battalion. At the recollection he clenched his fists, faint with hatred. It had not been a chain of unfortunate accidents; he knew that. It had been rigged from start to finish. He wanted to hear the confirmation from her own lips.

She shook her head. 'I don't know what you're talking about.' She tried to make it sound genuine, but he heard the waver in her voice and smiled malignantly.

'So you don't know,' he replied softly. 'Of course you don't know. You weren't present that morning—at least not while the comedy was going on. But we have plenty of time now. You'll remember before this evening is over. In the next room a wrist-watch was stolen from a patient. Next morning it was found among my clothes, wasn't it? There was only one person who could have put it there, Anne, and that was you.'

In spite of the darkness he could see the unnatural wanness of her face. She tried to laugh, but produced so strange and forced a sound that she stopped abruptly. 'You're crazy,' she said at last. 'Why should I have done a thing like that?'

'Why?' He laughed wildly. 'Because on that third night I told you I was a human being, not a stud horse. That's why.'

She did not answer. It was gradually growing lighter. The moon had risen above the mountains and seemed to be hesitating before taking the leap over the sea. Steiner took his pay-book out of his pocket, turned through it until he found a piece of paper which he placed on his knee. Then he switched on his flashlight. Anne was watching his movements nervously. As he bent over the paper and began writing with a stubby pencil, she asked: 'Are you writing me a letter now?'

Her light tone sounded false. He said nothing until he was finished. Then he read through what he had written and nodded with satisfaction. 'That will do,' he said quietly, placing the pencil and paper on her lap. 'Now sign this.'

'What is it?'

'Your confession. I want it in writing.'

Suddenly she jumped to her feet and tried to run. But he was prepared. He caught up with her in two strides. She kicked him and pummelled him with her fists. Her blows prompted him to harsher measures than he had intended. He dragged her down to the water, waded in knee deep, and thrust her head under water. Then he pulled her up by the hair and asked: 'Will you sign now?'

She coughed and struggled for breath. When he carried her back to the bench, she lay utterly defeated in his arms. He set her down, picked up the paper and pencil, and flashed the light into her face. Water was dripping from her hair down her forehead and on to her hands. 'That was unnecessary,' he said quietly. 'You might have spared us both the unpleasantness. In bed you were superior to me, but not here.' He placed the paper in her lap again and put the pay-book under it for a hard surface. 'If you don't sign, I'll duck you again—and for good this time, believe me.' He watched as she signed her name with trembling hands. When she was finished, he took the paper and the pay-book and carefully pocketed them. Then he switched out the flashlight. 'You may go now,' he said.

She did not stir. 'You may go,' he repeated sharply.

Unsteadily she got to her feet. She looked up at him. 'You're going to report me,' she said tonelessly.

He nodded.

'God,' she stammered. 'God, what am I going to do?'

He shrugged. Slowly she turned away. He watched as she walked off, her wet skirt clinging to her long legs, her head bowed, shoulders twitching. He felt no pity at all. For a while he stood staring across the water. Then he reached into his pocket, took out the sheet of paper and held it close to his eyes. In spite of the wavery handwriting the name was quite legible. Annemarie

Baumann. He was struck by the realization that he had never known her surname. For only a moment he hesitated. Then he tore the paper into tiny scraps and tossed them into the water. He watched them being carried out on the waves, dancing and scattering until they vanished from sight. Then he set out for his quarters. He recalled a phrase he had once read somewhere: that the person who could not forgive carried his unhappiness across his own shadow. He thought about this for a while as he lay in bed, but could not quite understand it.

Next morning as he strolled through the town he saw across the street a nurse was coming in his direction. He recognized Gertrud immediately and crossed the street. When she noticed him, her steps swerved; she seemed to wish to pass him by. He blocked her way and said: 'I wish I were meeting you for the first time now.'

She stood still, the corners of her mouth quivering, but when she spoke her voice was cool and distant. 'You will have to accept things as they are. Wishes don't undo what is done.'

By daylight her face seemed even better-wrought than he remembered, and he suddenly realized that she was lovely—more than that, she was beautiful. His hands felt awkward and he thrust them into his jacket pockets. 'Perhaps you are right,' he said quietly. 'But what is done can sometimes grow or diminish in importance, as one likes.'

She shook her head firmly. 'I see things as they are, not as I might like to see them afterwards.'

He listened to her voice with delight, and smiled. 'You are a person with principles. But just between the two of us, wouldn't you rather like to see our first encounter as different from what it was?'

'I was speaking generally,' she replied coolly. Her face flushed slightly, like a glacier at sunrise.

'If I were a woman,' he said genially, 'I would never talk in generalities.' He changed the subject abruptly. 'As for the Pilsner in your canteen, my compliments. I'm going to drop in this evening. Will you be there?'

She shook her head. 'No.'

'I won't drink more than one bottle.'

'I would recommend a water cure for you.'

She walked swiftly past him. Somewhat taken aback, he watched her until she was out of sight among the trees. Then he set out for his quarters, thoughtful and a little sad.

VIII

Staff Sergeant Fetscher had worries. He sat in his office staring grumpily out of the window without the slightest awareness of the brilliance of the spring day. At irregular intervals a low, long-drawn-out rumble broke the noonday quiet, and each time he raised his head uneasily, cursed at length and relapsed into gloomy brooding. At last he got up and went out. He gave a wide berth to several ugly craters that had meanwhile appeared in the street and walked slowly toward one of the buildings. As he approached he noticed a group of men busy digging a hole behind the wall of a house. They raised their heads expectantly.

'You'd better stop,' Fetscher said morosely. 'You have to go back up front tomorrow morning.'

'So soon?' Pasternack exclaimed. 'I thought we had a full week back here.'

'So did I,' Fetscher growled. 'Commander's orders. You're going to be assigned to the battalion headquarters.'

Krüger climbed out of the hole and shook the dirt from his clothes. 'Those bastards,' he griped. 'They promise us a week of rest and send for us after three days.'

The rest of the men angrily tossed their tools aside. 'What does Meyer say about it?' Schnurrbart asked.

Fetscher shrugged. 'How should I know? It wouldn't matter anyhow.' He turned to Dorn, who was cleaning his glasses. 'They want to see you, too, about officers' training. Triebig wants to talk to you.'

Dorn opened his mouth to reply; then appeared to change his mind and said nothing. Hollerbach grinned. 'Well, well,' he said. 'Before long you won't know us.'

'Don't be silly,' Dorn said curtly.

Krüger lit a cigarette. 'If we had only known,' he said to Fetscher, 'you would have had to dig your bunker yourself.'

Fetscher shrugged regretfully. 'Not my fault,' he said. 'Besides, the bunker was meant for you, not for us. You know we have our own.'

Krüger turned to the others. 'Don't matter much whether we're here or at battalion HQ. Since Ivan's got the range it's getting uncomfortable here. I wonder what we're supposed to do there.'

'Same thing,' Fetscher said.

'You mean dig bunkers?' Kern asked.

'Yes.'

'But they already have theirs,' Anselm said.

Fetscher grimaced. 'The commander thinks he needs a deeper one.'

'He's got the jitters,' Schnurrbart sneered.

Fetscher looked disapproving. 'That's his order and that's all there is to it.' He turned to go.

'What'll we do now?' Schnurrbart called after him.

'Whatever you like for the rest of the day. Do up your uniforms.'

Back at his desk, Fetscher sat down, sighing, and turned unhappily through a sheaf of papers. For the tenth time that day he told himself that there must be some special significance to it when a battalion commander asked for the personal papers of a platoon leader. Two days ago Stransky had called him up and ordered him to send Master Sergeant Steiner's service record book up to the battalion command post. He had sensed trouble at once, and his feeling had persisted even though the papers were returned the following day. Of course Stransky now knew that Steiner had once been broken. Fetscher had long known all about this black mark on Steiner's record, and had formed his own opinion about it. But he had guarded his knowledge carefully and had made sure the incriminating papers never were seen by anyone else. Why Stransky's knowing should disturb him so acutely, he could not say. He wondered whether he ought to write to Steiner about it. Then he realized that the letter would reach Gursuf too late. He could only let things take their course, and be prepared for a talk with Meyer, who would certainly get wind of the matter before long. Cursing again, he tried to concentrate on the papers in front of him. But the work went miserably. Two hours later, when he left the house to find the clerk, he had with him the recommendation for Krüger's promotion to corporal.

'Say what you will,' Schnurrbart remarked, 'the calm in this sector here isn't going to last another week; I feel it in my piss.'

Four of them were sitting in their quarters, smoking. Krüger spat on the floor and turned to Dorn. 'If you're smart, you'll clear out. If Ivan starts getting nasty here, we're done for. Don't be silly. By the time the training course is over the war will be over too, and when the war is over it won't matter a damn to you whether you were an officer or a private.'

'I cannot reconcile that with my conscience,' Dorn said.

'Conscience!' Krüger puffed contemptuously. 'When you're a stiff you can stick your conscience up your arse. You're married, aren't you?' Dorn nodded silently. 'Well, then what is there to consider? Think of your wife. You have some children too?' Dorn nodded again. Krüger turned to Schnurrbart, who was sucking vigorously at his pipe. 'What do you say to such an idiot? Has a wife and children and refuses to leave this rat-trap because he can't "reconcile it with his conscience" to be one of Adolf's officers.'

'He's mad,' Schnurrbart said quietly.

'Insane,' Anselm agreed. He was sitting on a wooden box, a harmonica in his hands.

They all looked at Dorn who sat with drooping head and did not answer them. It was late evening. In the east the front continued to rumble; for seconds at a time the sky was bathed in red light. Schnurrbart asked a question: 'What is your wife's name?'

Dorn raised his head. 'Maria.'

'And the children's?'

'Betty and Jürgen,' Dorn murmured.

Schnurrbart nodded. He removed the pipe from his mouth and spoke in an oddly hoarse voice. 'If I had a Maria and a Betty and a Jürgen, I would seriously ask myself whether I had the right to determine for myself alone what was to become of me and of them. That's what I'd think about, and to hell with my so-called conscience.'

Krüger looked at him with admiration. 'You sound like a preacher, but you're right.' He turned to Dorn again. 'It doesn't matter to me what you do. Principles are neither here nor there. But I'll tell you this: if you decide to play the hero again, I'm finished with you till the next ice age. Remember that.'

Dorn raised his head dolefully. Everything the men were saying he had considered himself. If it were only a matter of overcoming his distaste for an officer's career, he might long ago have given in. But there was something else. He made the effort to convey it to them: 'You make the matter out as more simple than it really is. After all, we have grown used to one another and——'

There was a moment's silence before Krüger growled: 'That's sheer sentimentality. You're mad, man.' He waved his arms violently in an effort to conceal his real emotion. 'I want to tell you something. One of these days every one of us sitting here will be laid out stiff as a poker. What good will it be to you then, eh?' He leaned toward Dorn and fixed him with a fierce gaze. 'Not a damn bit of good, that's what. If you clear out now, at least you won't have to watch them chop us into mincemeat. And they will, let me tell you.' To reinforce his declaration he let out a fart so loud that it elicited from Schnurrbart a respectful grunt. Then he stood up. 'I'm going to sleep. Tomorrow morning the circus starts again.'

Schnurrbart also stood up, yawning. 'Think it over,' he said to Dorn. 'You won't miss us like your children are going to miss you. Good night.' He followed Krüger into the house.

As Dorn was about to get up also, Anselm placed a hand on his shoulder. 'Hold on a minute, please,' he said. 'There's something I want to ask you.'

Although Dorn felt little inclination to converse, he nodded encouragingly. There was a long pause as Anselm pondered how to begin. At last he asked: 'You're a Catholic, aren't you?'

'Yes,' Dorn answered in surprise.

'Are you a good Catholic?'

'I hope so.'

Anselm clasped his arms across his chest. 'I thought you were, but I wanted to make sure. I've been meaning to talk with you for a long time. But now that you may be going away I don't want to put it off any longer.'

The elaborate preface aroused Dorn's curiosity. Trying to catch an impression of Anselm's face in the darkness, he said: 'By all means tell me what's on your mind.'

'It isn't easy to talk about,' Anselm stammered. He pulled himself together and went on: 'You see, I'm Catholic too. Maybe you have a low opinion of me on account of the stories I've told about women and so on.'

Dorn shook his head. 'We all have our weaknesses,' he said quietly.

Anselm nodded, relieved. 'A fellow can talk with you,' he said in a pleased tone. 'Anyway, it isn't half as bad as it sounds; I mean, a fellow likes to boast a bit.' He laughed abashedly. 'Of course I've done a lot in that field, but it was always just the way things turned out, and after all a fellow is only human.' Dorn's continuing silence revived his uncertainty. He scratched his throat and lowered his voice. 'I don't know whether you as a married man can understand that. But when a fellow gets to a certain age and has no chance to marry, it's damned hard to get along without it. Or don't you think so?'

'Of course it is hard,' Dorn said, looking down at the ground.

Anselm moved closer, and his voice took on a pleading note. 'I want you to believe what I say—I've always gone to church and to confession gladly, but since the first time I had a girl there was just no sense to it. I confessed it twice. Lord, you should have heard what a pig he made me out to be, talking about irresponsibility and sinful lust of the flesh and so on. He took on like it was high treason, and then I just stopped going, so of course then there wasn't any sense in going to church any more.' He fell silent and looked uneasily at Dorn, whose head was still bowed. The topic was not new to him.

Dorn placed his hand on Anselm's shoulder. 'You yourself must know how strong you are.'

Anselm laughed contemptuously. 'What good does my strength do me if I can't sleep at night and go crazy when I see a woman. I've thought about it often, believe me. It would be different if I could say today that in one year or two I would marry, and if I could begin saving up for a house. But even then it would tear me apart. My body needs it, that's all, and when I don't have it I don't feel human.'

Dorn sighed. Without conviction he said: 'The human body finds a way to cope with it.'

'I know that,' Anselm nodded. 'But you must admit that afterwards it's only worse. When you get to the point where you start dreaming about it at night, you're really off your rocker next morning. Besides'—his tone became scornful—'what is it you dream about? Heaven? Or hell maybe? No,' he shook his head vigorously, 'it's lucky you're not supposed to take your dreams to confession. It would be funny if it weren't so sad.'

There was little point saying anything, Dorn knew. As he thoughtfully lit a cigarette, he wondered how many men had lost contact with the church on this same issue. He was aware of Anselm's eyes upon him, and shrugged. 'I cannot help you,' he said quietly. 'I married fairly young and can only sympathize, but not really know how you feel.'

'But you studied philosophy,' Anselm said helplessly.

Dorn smiled painfully. 'Yes, I studied philosophy, but this is a problem you would do better to take to a priest. He will be able to discuss it with you far more sensibly than I can. Try our divisional chaplain one of these days. He is a man with both feet firmly on the ground. Tell him everything, and he won't just condemn you; he'll give you some guidance to help you along.'

'I've had enough of all of them,' Anselm said in disgust.

'You ought not to say that,' Dorn replied gravely. 'Perhaps you ran into a priest who was particularly stern in his judgments. Not all priests are alike. If you feel the need to find your way back, it is always open to you. But in God's name you must also give up your prejudices.'

'I'll think it over,' Anselm said. 'Are you coming in?'

'I'll stay out a while.'

Anselm said good night and walked off swiftly. Dorn sighed again. He tossed his cigarette away and remained sitting under the clear April sky for a long time. Should he become an officer? The longer he thought about it, the more difficult it was to decide. He recalled his wife's last letter: that he must not worry and that all were well at home. At home. . . . He clasped his hands over his knees and lifted his face to the stars. Home, he thought, and felt his eyes filling with tears. It was long past midnight before he went into the house.

They set out early next morning and reached the battalion command post in good time. Schnurrbart went into the adjutant's bunker to report the arrival of the platoon. Triebig received him in his shirt sleeves, his face lathered and his razor in one hand. He turned his head, annoyed at being disturbed so early. Recognizing Schnurrbart, he asked him to wait. When he had finished shaving, he went outside with Schnurrbart and gave the men their instructions. 'And be snappy about it,' he said. 'The bunker must be ready by tomorrow night. You can ask the signals platoon for tools.'

He beckoned to Dorn and went back into the bunker with him. Offering Dorn a cigarette, he came to the point at once. 'We don't want you to feel pressed,' he said in a friendly tone. 'But a man of your abilities must know himself where his place is. At any rate I cannot imagine that you feel comfortable in your present situation.

We need officers, men who are above average, and I really see no reason why you hold back. In a few days you can be on your way back home, that surely would be a treat for you. Moreover, it's a chance of getting out of Russia for good. I assure you, I would not hesitate for a moment if I were in your position.'

Dorn hunched his shoulders in torment. Although he had scarcely closed his eyes during the night, and had been turning the matter about in his mind the whole night through, he had not yet been able to decide. Triebig talked with him a while longer and spread out a number of papers on the table. 'All you need do is sign. Naturally you will be given some leave first and can be back home with your family for Easter.'

'I don't know,' Dorn murmured, staring at the papers.

Triebig rose. 'I'll give you a few hours more to think it over. Come to see me again around two and let me know.'

Dorn nodded and slowly rose to his feet. 'I really don't understand you,' Triebig said irritably. 'Anybody else would be overjoyed.'

Dorn suppressed an unfriendly remark, saluted and left.

The men had meanwhile begun their work. They were digging a large rectangular pit somewhat to one side of the other bunkers, in the centre of the orchard. Ten feet deep, the signals platoon leader had said; those were the commander's orders. As Krüger fiercely wielded a sharply-filed spade, driving it viciously into the tangle of roots in the ground, he poured out a steady stream of curses, until even Schnurrbart had had enough. He straightened up from his stooped position, wiped the sweat from his brow and said: 'Save your breath, will you. Your grousing is beginning to get on my nerves.'

The others also stopped work and looked reprehendingly at Krüger. But Krüger went right on. 'Ten feet deep!' he snarled furiously. 'Have you ever heard the like of it. This isn't a bunker, it's a mine, I tell you. First thing you know we'll be putting in an elevator shaft. That bastard of a captain is scared shitless.'

He would have gone on railing if Dorn had not returned, looking as if he had seen a ghost. Schnurrbart called out: 'What's the matter? Have they been raising a stink about something?'

Dorn shook his head mutely and began removing his tunic. 'What is it?' Anselm insisted. 'Aren't you going?'

'Yes, I'm going,' Dorn replied sombrely.

Krüger grinned. 'Well, at last you've come to your senses. By your face one would think you were going to your own funeral, but you'll get used to the idea. Once you're sitting in the train bound for home, you'll feel better.'

Since Dorn offered no comment and picked up a spade without a word, they resumed their work, and by midday had dug a hole chest-deep. 'Chow,' Schnurrbart said, tossing his shovel away.

Stiffly they clambered out of the hole, unpacked the rations they had brought with them, and scattered among the trees. Dorn sat by himself. After a while Anselm joined him and tried to strike up a conversation. But Dorn answered in monosyllables, and Anselm at last fell silent and concentrated on his end of sausage. Although there were some scattered clouds in the sky, the sun burned down on them fiercely. The front was quiet, the silence broken only now and then by the thud of heavy mortar shells or the agitated chatter of a machine-gun. Dorn sat with lowered head, staring down at the ground, like a person who has lost something precious for ever. He forced himself to think of his family again, reached into his pocket and took out his wife's latest letter. His features softened as he studied the toilsomely drawn letters at the bottom of the paper: 'Dear Papa come home soon.'

He let his hand drop and chanced to turn his head and look over at the other men. They were lying flat, pressed against the ground. What is the matter, he had time to think, and tried to do as they did. But it was already too late. The earth exploded. The blast knocked him backwards and he lay staring up at the sky. His expression was unchanged; the quiet joy had lingered on his face, though his glasses lay with shattered lenses beside his head.

The black pillar of smoke began to collapse. The torn branches of the trees emerged again, stripped of their leaves, and the men came to life. Faces pale with fright, they sat up. By the side of the crater Anselm and the Professor lay as though sleeping. Schnurrbart was the first to recover; he approached slowly. Seeing the red flesh among the remnants of the Professor's uniform, he turned away. Then he knelt beside Anselm, who lay on his belly, his fingers dug into the ground. As soon as Schnurrbart turned him over on his back, he let go of him. Anselm had no face left.

The others had come over, too. They stood beside the two dead men, looking down on them in silence. Over at the bunkers men were stirring also. Stransky appeared for a few seconds, glanced over toward them, and vanished into his bunker immediately. A few minutes later Triebig came over. He asked: 'Dead?' They nodded. His face was chalky. He ran his tongue over his lips. 'Let them lie there until tonight,' he said. 'The supply column can take them back.' He walked a few steps further on and looked at the shell-hole. Then he turned back toward his bunker.

'That one came like a flash of lightning,' Kern said.

'It always comes like lightning,' Schnurrbart said tonelessly.

They looked down at Dorn. His lifeless eyes seemed to be staring through the twigs up at the fragile ribbons of cloud. 'He was a fine chap, the Professor,' Kern said tightly. 'This stinking, this miserable war—just to kill like that—a man of his learning.' He wiped his eyes and swallowed. Pasternack, standing beside Krüger, suddenly turned away and walked over to a tree. He pressed his forehead against the tree trunk and stood motionless.

'What are you turning weepy for?' Krüger growled hoarsely. 'You think any of you are going to make out better? You make me laugh.' He turned sharply, went back to the pit, picked up his spade and began digging furiously. Hollerbach followed him in silence.

'What are you waiting for?' Schnurrbart said to the others.

'Are you going to let them lie like this?' Maag asked.

'I'll cover them up. Let's get through here.'

Hesitantly, they moved off. Schnurrbart stood beside the bodies for a while. Then he went to the Professor's pack, extracted groundsheet and blanket, and spread them over the two dead men so that only their heavy nailed boots could be seen. As he started to put Dorn's right arm under the blanket, he noticed the piece of paper in the clenched fist. With some effort he pulled it away and discovered that is was a letter. Slowly he straightened up. His eyes rested fascinated on the boots. German army boots, size forty-two. He suddenly recalled that these were the boots of a man who had joined the company shortly after Dorn, and had died under a hail of machine-gun bullets. At that time the boots were relatively new, and Dorn, who had been equipped with uncomfortable clodhoppers, had asked Fetscher for the boots. The nails had since become worn down and the soles were full of holes. What a long way those boots had come since their nails first rang challengingly upon the cobblestoned street of a small Czech town and the March sun was reflected in the high polish of the uppers. They had trodden the clean highways of Slovakia, the sandy paths in Poland, the corduroy roads of the Ukraine, the crushed flowers of the steppes, the lonely forest paths of the Caucasus, and more. In light and dark, on hills and valleys, over land and water. And the road had always been there. Dust and searing heat had dried the leather and cracked it. The boots had slogged through rain and bottomless swamps, through cold and deep snow. With a kind of insane clarity Schnurrbart calculated: perhaps 6,000,000 footsteps lay behind them. Now they had reached their final destination and were resting: unsightly, used up, worthless, lying with the warm sun upon the cracked leather. They lay waiting patiently, patient as the hide of which they were made. Schnurrbart suddenly became aware of the tears streaming down his face. Now Private First Class Dorn had left his boots and his body behind; for the road he was marching on now, he would need boots no longer.

In the evening the men of the supply column would load the flesh and the boots upon a horse. Somewhere among the hills was an army burial ground. There the earthly remains would be put under, and a simple wooden cross would be all that was left—that, and the grief of a wife and a Betty and a Jürgen.

Schnurrbart looked at the letter, and then back at the boots. It occurred to him that he had forgotten something: the philosophy and its unrest. But then he told himself that Doctor of Philosophy Dorn must at last be recognizing the ultimate meaning of his existence and the relationships among all things, for death solves many questions. Perhaps he was now in possession of an understanding that had no need of knowledge because it was terrifyingly simple, like all great matters. Slowly he thrust the letter into his pocket. He noticed Pasternack still leaning motionless against the tree. Going over to him, he placed a hand on his shoulder. 'Come,' he said softly. They joined the other men.

It was the last evening in Gursuf. They sat on a bench by the beach looking over the water. Steiner, his elbows propped on his knees, his chin in his hands, tried in vain to fight against his melancholy. The fourteen-day dream had come to an end. He would have to answer the call of the front as the others had, as had Towhead, who more than ten days ago had been absorbed by the boiling cauldron of the central sector. The front forgot no one.

Well, he had known that from the start, and the knowledge had scarcely troubled him. It would have mattered to him as little as everything else. The prospect of seeing the men of his platoon again would certainly have overlaid the trivial regret at leaving this island of rest and peace—the present was always overshadowed by the demands of the next day. But something had happened since that extended from the present into the future. Ten days ago such a possibility would have seemed preposterous to him. But now. . . . He looked at the sea and the choking sensation in his throat grew stronger. When he was gone from here, the melody of the sea would still sound; the waves would pound on the beach, the pines rustle in the sea breeze, and the sun sink into the sea as it did every day at this time. All would remain, remain behind. He felt a hand touching his arm and turned his head. 'You must not think about it, Rolf.'

He smiled bitterly. 'It is so close now,' he said softly. 'I can't help thinking about it, whether I want to or not.'

She sighed and laid her head on his shoulder. 'Yesterday it was still so far off,' she whispered. 'As far away as the stars.'

He drew her close. 'The stars are often closer to us than human beings; tomorrow you'll be thousands of light years away from me.'

'How far is that?' she asked seriously.

'How far?' He wrinkled his brow. Then he nodded his head in the direction of the water. 'If you walk across the sea until you are so tired that your feet can no longer carry you, you've taken the first step.'

'And how many steps are there?'

He raised his face toward the sky. 'As many as there are stars.'

'Then it is far,' she breathed.

He nodded. After a while he placed his arm around her waist and studied her face. 'You shouldn't have come into the canteen that evening,' he murmured.

'Would you have liked that better?'

'If you had asked me that yesterday I would have said no.'

'And today?'

He smiled tormentedly. 'Today I no longer know what to say.'

'I didn't want to come.'

'But you came anyway.'

'Yes.'

'You don't know how I waited for you, and I really did drink only one bottle.'

She kissed him quickly and ran her hand over his hair. 'You kept your word,' she said solemnly.

They fell silent. Steiner thought about that meeting. Even now he still felt a certain surprise at how quickly she had agreed, that evening, to go walking with him on the beach, although her experiences should not have encouraged her to take such risks. They had spoken little, but next night they had met again, and each time there had been more between them. Each through the other discovered new things in their surroundings, things they had not noticed before, and as they drew closer to one another his own front of cynicism dropped away without his even noticing the change. Whenever, alone in his room, he thought over their last meeting and the things she had said, he felt a quiet joy that quelled the bitterness within him and uncovered long buried, deeply overlaid feelings.

And yet, he suddenly realized all this had taken place and yet when he came right down to it, he knew very little more about her than her name. The thought bothered him, and he said: 'I know so little about you.'

She smiled at him. 'It isn't good for a man to know too much about a woman.'

'I don't see that.'

Her voice dropped lower. 'Knowledge is often quickly forgotten.'

He still did not understand. 'I think you and I are talking about two different things,' he said cautiously.

She shook her head firmly. 'No. Why do you want to know more about me?'

'That's simple. Because I want to see you again some day.'

'And why do you want to see me again?'

His face hardened. Seeing this, she quickly took his hand. 'We are both sensible enough and old enough,' she said, 'to know that there has to be more between a man and woman than walks by moonlight and an occasional kiss.'

'Why do you talk like that?' he asked quietly.

She hesitated, avoiding his eyes. Then she lifted her head. 'Because,' she explained firmly, 'I don't want you to go on feeling until the last hour that you have something to make up to me.'

Breathlessly, he stared at her. 'Is that feeling unjustified?' he asked at last.

'Yes.' When he looked down at the ground, she added: 'If it

were justified, we would not have met again.' Her voice became stronger. 'I don't want you to misunderstand me. I know less about you than you do about me. But what I know is basis enough for what I said.'

He thought he understood her now. He nodded and drew her head tenderly against his chest. 'It's all right, I know what you mean. Perhaps it was because things need time to develop and time was just what we haven't had.'

'Perhaps we have not used it properly,' she replied pensively, 'or perhaps this is the way it had to be.'

'You sound like the Professor and Schnurrbart,' he said.

'Who are they? You've never told me about them.'

'I know,' he said. 'You'd have to actually know them; it wouldn't be any good describing them. Perhaps I would never have come to know you if it had not been for them.'

'You're talking in riddles.'

'There are no such things. What we call riddles are only the inadequacies of our minds.'

'That is philosophy,' she said gravely.

He began to laugh, stood up quickly and drew her to her feet. 'Come,' he said softly.

The last embers of the day sank in the west. A dark shadow trailed across the sky and only on the margin where the sea plunged into the blackness a strip of bright light clung, trembled for a time, and then shrank up like a dead man's face, scattering as it was extinguished a rain of blinking lights upon the water, until the shadow fell over the horizon like a black curtain, hiding everything beneath it. Arm in arm, they walked along the beach. Steiner regarded her face from the side. Later they went out to the tip of a narrow sandbar that extended far out into the water, and sat down. He felt her body close beside his, and when he put his arm around her she let herself fall back against it. 'Why must that be?' she whispered.

'What?'

'The war and all these terrible things.'

'Perhaps so that we could meet one another.' He sat up a little.

'Do you believe in fated meetings?'

'I don't know,' she answered thoughtfully, her finger following the lines of his mouth. 'I don't know what I believe and I don't know what you want me to say. But it's obvious that many things had to come together so that we two could meet.'

He nodded. Her words sounded echoes in him. He leaned over her so that he could feel her breath upon his face. 'And where will we meet again?'

She closed her eyes and whispered: 'Somewhere above or below the stars. Perhaps——'

He closed her mouth with a long kiss. When his hand felt for her knees, she started and opened her eyes. Then she threw her arms around his neck and sighed. Her skin was smooth and firm; he began to undress her slowly, with great care and tenderness. She did not resist, and he felt her trembling under his hands in the cool night air.

A long while later they walked back the way they had come. When they reached the wide grounds around the building where they had first met, Steiner stopped and drew her close. 'I still don't know all about you,' he said softly.

'I'll write to you.'

He nodded. 'As you like. Don't forget the address.'

He looked across the low wall at the building. 'I'll be leaving very early and won't see you again. Perhaps we'll not meet until the war is over. Why won't you tell me where you live?'

'I'll write you all about it,' she murmured, leaning her head against his chest. He could not understand her strange conduct and looked down upon her, frowning. When he took hold of her chin to see her face, she turned her head aside quickly, whispering: 'No, please don't.' Suddenly she wound her arms around him and kissed him wildly. Then she broke loose and ran off.

He watched her until she disappeared in the darkness of the lawns. He wanted to call out to her, but his voice would not obey him. Unsteadily he staggered forward a few steps, then stood still. At his back the surf roared, monotonous, heavy and mournful. For a while he stood peering among the trees. Then he turned away. Slowly he returned to the beach and walked with bowed head toward his quarters. At the gate he stopped for a moment and looked up at the mountains. They crouched blackly under the weight of the sky. Over their bent backs hung the moon, its face cold and expressionless. Steiner hunched his shoulders and moved his lips. His voice sounded strange to himself as he said, like a prayer: 'As you like.' Then he went in and up to his room.

IX

Easter passed almost unnoticed in the monotony of their existence. Spring they were scarcely aware of. Only now and then, when they went out of the dugouts and bunkers and stood in the deep trenches, lifting their weary faces to the warm sunlight and closing their eyes, did they forget their surroundings for a few minutes. Until somewhere in the vicinity a shell exploded and the dark cloud of smoke and dust rolled over their heads. Then they crouched like beasts and their faces turned hard and angry. They cursed and went back into the bunkers where they sat longingly looking up at the narrow strip of blue sky that showed above the edge of the trench.

The expected Russian grand offensive had not yet begun. But more and more big guns were raining shells down on their positions. The hill was veiled in the dust of detonations all day long, and at night heavy bombers flew so close over the positions that the men in their bunkers hunched their heads between their shoulders. Uncertainty as to when the enemy offensive would come hardly bothered them. For months and years they had been learning the art of waiting. They moved about their trenches and weapon pits like acrobats, for any false step, any awkward movement, could swiftly put an end to all movement. But they did so with the skill and indifference of long practice. The daily artillery fire upon the positions, the reconnaissance attacks of strong Russian patrols almost every night, and the heavy bombardment of the rear positions, cost the battalion more and more casualties. Scarcely a day passed without some dramatic incidents. While the soldiers, thousands of miles from home, under a cloudless sky in that decisive spring of 1943 waited for the Russian general offensive, they learned in helpless despair that the war, in a new and terrible form, was being carried over the front lines into their homeland. The familiar faces around them grew rarer; more and more they felt that their struggle was meaningless, and they grew steadily quieter and more hopeless.

Second Company's bunkers were dug deep into the walls of the trench at intervals of seventy-five to a hundred feet. The men who were not on duty lay dozing on the hard plank beds. Steiner was with them again. The previous week he had rejoined the battalion. Immediately after his arrival Fetscher had called him in for a long talk and had gravely warned him that he would be better off accepting the regimental commander's offer and transferring immediately to the headquarters staff. Shaken though he was by the news of Dorn's death, Steiner had flatly rejected the sergeant's well-meant advice. It would take more than a dozen Stranskys to make him leave the company, he had said.

The reunion with the men of the platoon had been subdued and rather grave. Schnurrbart and Krüger were already wearing their corporal's insignia and received his congratulations with somewhat dreary smiles. 'What good does this nonsense do me,' Krüger said bitterly, 'if a month from now none of the bastards I always wanted to order around are left.' They had not yet got over the deaths of Anselm and Dorn. Steiner, too, was soon affected by their mood, which only deepened the depression he would feel whenever he reflected upon Gertrud's strange evasiveness. But luckily he had little time to think too much about that. He had redivided the groups and was devoting most of his energy to training the new replacements who had been brought in only a few days before. He instructed them in the possibilities and perils of positional warfare and sketched for them the probable phases of the impending battle, so that they would not lose their heads when the time came.

His thoughts were with them now as he sat at the table in his bunker, absently watching Faber conscientiously divide up his meagre piece of sausage. Faber's big, earnest face with its vigorous nose, cleft chin and thin lips was concentrated upon his task; he held the knife poised as though picking the next spot on a tree before swinging his axe. His eyes were a deep lake-blue. Faber's transfer from the 3rd to the 2nd Company had been accomplished only over Lieutenant Gausser's resistance. Gausser had been unwilling to release his reliable machine-gunner, and it had taken all of Meyer's persuasiveness to move him. Later Meyer had told Steiner that next time he wanted a man, he'd better go out and capture one from the Russian lines. But the transfer had gone through at last and Faber was now machine-gunner in the 2nd Platoon.

Five men were lying on the cots in the bunker, snoring loudly. Of the five, Kern was the only former member of the platoon. Maag and Pasternack were assigned to Krüger's group in the next bunker; Hollerbach and Schnurrbart shared the next but one bunker with four replacements. Although the platoon now numbered over thirty rifles, the 'old boys' had not been particularly enthusiastic about the reinforcements because it meant that the regulars were split up. Hollerbach had been emphatic about sticking together with Maag and Pasternack, but Steiner had pointed out that it would not be fair to the new men to leave them without front-line veterans. In any case, Krüger had remarked sarcastically, within another two weeks it would be possible to stow the whole battalion away in a single bunker.

The Black Forester had meanwhile finished his meal. He wiped his fatty fingers on his trousers. Looking up, he caught Steiner thoughtfully regarding the men on the cots. 'Not much to them,' he remarked laconically.

Steiner, startled out of his thoughts, looked up distractedly. Then he nodded. 'I know, but what can we expect? Those infants have picked a bad time to come out to the front. Four weeks training and right smack into the soup. I'm afraid we're going to have trouble with them.'

'So am I,' Faber said. 'Even a tree must learn to bow at the right time. If it doesn't, it breaks in the first storm.'

Steiner grinned. 'Do you always talk in terms in trees?'

'Almost always,' Faber replied quietly.

Steiner took out his cigarettes and held them across the table. 'Do you smoke?'

'No.'

'Oh, well,' Steiner said, shrugging and lighting a cigarette.

He had talked with Faber several times and knew that his parents owned a small farm near St. Blasien. But the woodsman was so taciturn that he had not found out very much more. Only once had Faber dropped his reserve somewhat. They had been talking about trees, which was the one subject Faber really seemed to know and care about. Thinking of this, Steiner took up the conversation again. 'I've never been one to hear the grass growing, and as for your trees, all I know about them is that they look pretty and are useful for lumber. I guess I can stand learning a bit more about them.'

Faber's face remained expressionless. He laid his big hands on the table and said: 'When it comes to trees, a person can always learn a little more about them. Back home in our valley there was a man who wanted to know how many trees there were in the forest. He wanted to know exactly, and he counted them.'

'Counted the trees?' Steiner exclaimed incredulously.

'Yes. He took a brush and a pot of white paint and went into the woods. Every tree he counted he marked with a white cross.'

'He was insane.'

Faber shook his head. 'He was living on a pension and was sixty-five years old when he started his work. For over fifteen years he walked in the woods painting his crosses on every tree.'

'He should have been put in a lunatic asylum,' Steiner said, somehow angered.

'That's what some people said,' Faber continued, 'but he had influential friends who saw to it that he was let alone; he had been a university professor and a famous astronomer. When people tried to persuade him to stop his senseless work he only smiled and said he had spent his whole life investigating the stars but didn't know how many trees there were in the forest.'

'The story is pointless,' Steiner said. 'That was a fellow who stared up at the sky so long he lost touch with the ground under his feet. What became of him?'

'He died a few years ago.'

'Best thing he could do. How many trees did he count in those fifteen years?'

'He kept that to himself. But one day he came home and said that now he knew exactly how many there were. The trees told him, he said. He passed on not long afterwards.'

'Peace to his ashes,' Steiner said. 'I suppose we ought to feel sorry for a fellow like that. I hope to spend the last fifteen years of my life more profitably. When I get to the point where I hear the trees talking, I'll drink a bottle of nitroglycerin and jump off the Jungfrau. But seriously, do you believe any of that?'

Faber stood up slowly. 'The peasants where I live have their work and they have their beliefs,' he said quietly. 'They know the trees have their own language and they believe what the trees tell them, because what the trees have to say is sure and steady and our peasants are like the trees.'

Steiner wrinkled his brow. 'Sounds to me that you're saying something about us—I mean, about us city people.'

The ghost of a smile passed over Faber's grave face. 'You are the leaves on the trees.'

'Are we?' Steiner studied him suspiciously. 'Well, that's something; what would a tree be without leaves!'

'A tree without leaves is still a tree,' Faber said. 'But a leaf without a tree is a withered nothing, and the leaf always dies before the tree.' He left the bunker.

Maag and Pasternack were in the MG emplacement, sitting on empty ammunition boxes and peering through the loophole at the woods. It was warm and they had taken off their tunics. At regular intervals they heard the dull explosion of heavy mortars firing. Plop, plop, plop. It sounded like the hammering of a woodpecker. The shells landed somewhere on the hill at the back of them. Pasternack sighed. 'I wonder how long this war is going on?'

Maag twisted his freckled face into a grimace and spat on the floor. 'Until final victory,' he declared pompously. 'One of these days we'll turn the tide, all right.'

'I can't believe that any longer.'

'Neither can I,' Maag said. 'But what the hell, who cares? The cart is stuck in the mud and that's all that matters.'

Pasternack shrugged impatiently. 'That's ridiculous,' he replied crossly.

'It isn't ridiculous,' Maag retorted. 'It's better for it to be stuck in the mud than to go on rolling over the cliff. But that's politics and I'm sick of it.' He spat again. Then, seeing Maag's troubled expression, he clapped him reassuringly on the shoulder. 'We'll get through one way or another. I just want to live through this war; that's all I care about. As long as the cart stays in the mud, I'll stick with it; when it starts rolling again, I'm jumping off.'

'A good way to break your neck.'

'True enough, but I'll jump carefully, you can depend on that.'

Several shells landed close in front of them. They flattened out on the floor. Acrid black smoke entered through the loophole. When the vision cleared, Maag got up, groaning, and looked at the crater. 'Those stinking mortars,' he growled. 'Another ten feet and it would have made our bones rattle.' He turned to Pasternack with a sudden thought. 'Maybe those women from the bridge are firing at us now. I said right off we should have killed them.'

Pasternack pounded the dust from his clothes. 'What would have been the use? They have plenty of replacements. Women are women, in or out of uniform.'

Before Maag could reply, Schnurrbart appeared. Maag grinned at him. 'What's new, Corporal?'

Schnurrbart drew an ammunition box up for a seat. 'If you say corporal again, I'll throw you out of the trench.' He filled his pipe and voluptuously puffed smoke at the ceiling. 'What could possibly be new?' he said at last. 'You know already that we're losing the war.'

Maag dug the tip of his boot into the sand. 'There's no proof of that,' he said ill-humouredly.

'Any map proves it,' Schnurrbart replied.

They sat in silence for a while, looking out through the loophole. At last Maag cursed. 'So what? Any army can retreat. So maybe the others will win the war, but it's nothing to boast of. Dozens against one country. Our allies don't count. Except for the Japs, they're good for nothing.' He was hit by sudden fury. 'Today they shake hands with you, all smiles, and next day they kick you in the behind. The devil take them.'

'Who?'

They turned their heads and saw Krüger, who had come up quietly and was now standing, head ducked, in the entrance.

'All of them and you too,' Maag growled.

Krüger threw out his chest. 'You are talking to your superior officer.'

'In that case come over here and kiss my arse.'

Krüger's face flushed. 'One of these days somebody's going to let out a howl,' he threatened.

Schnurrbart raised his hand. 'Cut the bickering,' he said mildly. His glance fell upon an earthworm that was wriggling across the floor. 'Learn from this lowly creature,' he said with mock solemnity. 'It lies in slime all the time and yet it doesn't grumble about it.'

They all stared at the worm, and Maag shook his head in aversion. 'Disgusting things,' he said. 'I wonder what they exist for.'

Krüger studied the worm thoughtfully. 'Still and all,' he commented deliberately. 'If you cut off its head, the rest of the body goes on living.'

'Too bad that isn't the case with a certain type of corporal,' Schnurrbart observed.

Maag chuckled, and Krüger glared at him. Then he turned to Schnurrbart and said frostily: 'You might refrain from such remarks in the presence of the men.'

Schnurrbart swallowed the wrong way and coughed, while the others regarded Krüger's flushed face half in astonishment, half in amusement. Krüger paid no attention to them. He stepped forward quickly, crushed the worm under his heavy boot and turned toward the entrance. 'One of these days you'll find yourself thinking of me,' he said.

Schnurrbart nodded. 'Often as you like—in the latrine.'

Krüger made off. Maag turned to Schnurrbart. 'What's eating him? He was only joking, wasn't he?'

'Certainly,' Schnurrbart said, looking down at the crushed worm, which was still twitching. He stood up. 'Everything's a joke,' he declared, and also went out.

Maag shrugged. 'They've got trench fever,' he said angrily. 'They can stick it up.'

Pasternack said nothing. He was thinking of home in Breslau, and everything suddenly seemed much harder and far more hopeless.

In the evening they sat around in their bunkers. Steiner lay on his bunk without interest turning the pages of his volume of Eichendorff. He felt an uneasiness he could not explain. Faber was sitting at the table writing a letter. His big, hairy paws covered most of the sheet of paper; now and then he would stare absently into the candlelight for a while, then carefully set down a few more words. Beside him, using the other half of the table, Kern and two of the other men were playing cards and exchanging comments in murmurs. For a while Steiner watched their faces. Then he decided to look in on the other bunkers. He stood up. At that moment the door was opened and the broad face of the company commander appeared. As the men started to rise, he waved his hand. 'Don't let me disturb you.' He turned to Steiner. 'You can accompany me through the positions.' His voice sounded so impersonal that Steiner was taken aback. Without a word he picked up his tommy-gun and went out behind Meyer.

The night was warm and still. They inspected the MG and

sniper positions. Meyer remained uncommunicative; he received the sentries' reports without his usual word or two of encouragement. When they reached the right wing of the company's sector, he turned about and started back. Abruptly he stopped and looked over the top of the trench. 'If the Russians keep pushing their trench in the direction they've been doing, they will land just about here,' he said.

Steiner nodded. He had known for two days that the Russians were working hard on an assault trench leading from the edge of the woods across the open field straight toward 2nd Company's positions. 'When they get close enough,' he answered offhandedly, 'we'll pay them a visit. But they won't be finished before the day after tomorrow.'

'Let's hope so,' Meyer said. He took a step back, and Steiner felt that the company commander was scrutinizing him. Meyer's odd behaviour was beginning to get on his nerves and he was on the point of asking what it was all about when Meyer himself spoke. 'A nasty business,' he said uncertainly. 'I ran into Triebig this afternoon. He says you were degraded a year ago. Is that true?'

Steiner closed his eyes for a moment. He had reckoned on this eventuality, but it was coming sooner than he had expected. Stransky works fast, he thought, his mouth twisting in contempt. He answered frigidly: 'It's true.'

Meyer nodded. 'And why were you degraded?'

'I assume you already know,' Steiner replied calmly.

Meyer nodded again. His face hardened. 'I've heard one side of the story; now I'd like to hear the other. You see, I hope you have something to say about it.' As he spoke these last words, his voice took on a tone of command.

Steiner frowned. 'I see no reason to,' he declared icily. 'I owe explanations to no one, including my company commander.'

Meyer started back. 'Do you mean that, Steiner?'

'I damn well do, if you want to know.' His voice sounded ruthless and unyielding. They stared at one another for a few seconds. Then Meyer turned away without a word and strode off. Steiner stood motionless, his lip drawn back, chuckling scornfully into the darkness. Idiot, he thought contemptuously, you damned idiot. After a while he began to whistle softly. He felt a grim amusement that extended into his fingertips and produced a whirling sensation in his head, as though he had been drinking. Pilsner, he thought with a spasm of sickly laughter. Suddenly the chatter of a Russian submachine-gun burst out of the night, and the bullets whistled so close over his head that he involuntarily dropped to his knees. cursing wildly. But his fright lasted only for a second. Then he rushed with huge bounds to the next MG emplacement, squeezed in through the shaft and in the darkness bumped into a man who was trying to get into the trench. He recognized Maag's voice and clutched his shoulder. 'Where to?' He had to shout to make himself heard.

'To fetch reinforcements,' Maag stammered, unhinged by the sudden encounter.

'Leaving your post for that?' Steiner bellowed angrily, pushing Maag before him back into the hole. As he felt for the MG in the darkness, he went on berating Maag.

He peered through the loophole. The Russian fire had stopped. A few shells whined through the air and exploded nearby. 'I wish I knew——' Steiner murmured. He interrupted himself, turned to Maag and snapped: 'Where is the flare gun?'

'Here.' Maag handed it to him. As Steiner fired a flare through the loophole, there was a rattling against the metal of the MG and the hideous noise of ricocheting bullets buzzed around their heads as though they had stumbled into a beehive. 'They must be right in front of us,' Maag gasped. 'In the shell holes down there.'

Steiner recalled that there were a number of big craters on the slope below the MG emplacement; Maag's guess must be right. 'Go get the other fellows,' he ordered. The firing had diminished somewhat in the past few seconds, and Steiner considered what to do. Before he could take any action he would have to inform Meyer, although the thought of doing so, so soon after their interview was distasteful. The arrival of the other men turned his thoughts in a different direction. Schnurrbart squeezed into the emplacement first. 'Nice evening, everybody,' he said cheerfully. 'I'll take bullet stew, if you please. Where's the field kitchen?'

Steiner waited until Krüger and Hollerbach had come in. Then he briefed them on the situation. 'We've got to get them out of there,' he said. 'They could be on top of us before we started shooting. We'll have to——' He broke off. From the entrance came Meyer's incisive voice. The lieutenant squeezed into the hole and went up to him. 'What's happening?' he asked.

In silence he listened to the report. When Steiner finished he stood frowning for a few seconds. Then he raised his head. 'Signal for a barrage,' he ordered. 'I'll inform the commander.' He hurried out. Steiner picked up the flare gun again, took the cartridges that Maag handed him, and followed the company commander out into the trench. He sent up the first flare, and then the second. Watching as they burst in the air, shedding red and green light as they sank to earth, he hoped the artillery observers would see what they illuminated. In his mind he followed the action a few kilometres back of the lines as the men rushed to their guns and began loading the big shells. He waited with bated breath. Minutes later, just as he heard hasty footsteps and the figure of Meyer reappeared, a hollow roaring sounded above their heads, swelling rapidly to a mighty moan. A moment later the heavy detonations came. Steiner followed the lieutenant into the MG emplacement, where the men were waiting impatiently. 'Commander's order,' Meyer said. 'The 2nd Platoon is to undertake a counter-attack at once. You are to occupy the craters and take as many prisoners as possible.' He turned to Steiner. 'You will command. How are you going to proceed?'

Steiner considered briefly. 'We'll attack from three sides: Krüger from the west, Schnurrbart from the east and myself from the south.' He outlined his plan hastily. 'When the firing starts we'll need artillery support. But only on the Russian positions at the edge of the woods. That's all.'

Meyer nodded. 'Good in theory; let's hope it works out in practice.'

Steiner ordered the men to get ready. Before he left the MG emplacement, he turned to Meyer again. 'Who will take over our positions?'

'The 1st Platoon. I've already given the order. One moment, Steiner.' He waited until the other men were out and came up close to Steiner. 'I wish you all the luck in the world in this business,' he said hesitantly. 'But before you go I must tell you that it is often hard to understand you.'

'That may be,' Steiner replied. 'That may be.' He followed the men. The artillery fire had ceased. The air was saturated with the smell of burnt powder. As he walked down the trench, he felt his heart beating faster. In his bunker he hooked four reserve clips to his belt, exchanged a few words with Faber, and urged the men to hurry. Shortly afterwards the platoon was ready to go. There was an air of nervous tension about them all. The clatter of weapons persisted, and Steiner had to remind them several times to tone it down. Now and then a Russian sub-machine-gun hammered away, and the bullets whipped harmlessly over their heads. Krüger grimaced discontentedly. 'Haven't you got anything better for me to do? That's a mad job to lie out on the slope and do nothing.'

'Be nice if that were all,' Steiner said. 'When Schnurrbart attacks and I turn up in their rear, the Russians will only be able to retreat to the east. You'll probably find all hell letting loose in your direction before it's over.' He turned to Schnurrbart, who had come up behind him. 'All clear?' Schnurrbart nodded. From somewhere Meyer's muted voice could be heard. 'Let's go,' Steiner said. He waited until Krüger's voice disappeared in the darkness. Then he raised his arm. The rest of the men followed him. He led them about a hundred yards westward down the communication trench. From there they cautiously descended the slope. When they reached the level field, he gave them final instructions. 'You wait here,' he said to Schnurrbart. 'Attack in exactly five minutes. As soon as the first shots are fired, we'll come in. Clear?'

'All clear,' Schnurrbart growled, shaking hands with him.

'Good luck.' After taking leave of Hollerbach also, Steiner led his men across no-man's-land in a south-easterly direction. Schnurrbart watched them go. Then he turned to the others in his group. 'Stick close together and don't save on hand grenades. Remember, the eyes of the entire German nation are upon you.'

The men chuckled low, and one of them said: 'Shit.'

Schnurrbart looked at him. The man had come in the last group of replacements—a pale eighteen-year-old. 'Sorry, pal,' Schnurrbart said, 'you can't now. You probably will anyway when the shooting starts.'

'I don't see why we should start the thing,' another spoke up. 'I say we ought to wait here until the sergeant gets to the Russians.'

Schnurrbart whirled around. 'You shut your trap, my boy. Any more of that silly stuff and you'll be sorry.'

'We weren't born yesterday,' the man replied rebelliously.

'Day before yesterday, I guess,' Schnurrbart said, looking at his watch.

'It ought to be time,' Hollerbach said. Schnurrbart put the watch back into his pocket. 'One minute more.' He turned his head in the direction in which Steiner had disappeared. Suddenly his eyes widened. He raised his arm. 'Someone's coming,' Hollerbach breathed. In spite of the starlit sky there was almost impenetrable darkness here at the foot of the hill, but they thought they could make out dark shadows slowly moving toward them. The men dropped soundlessly to the ground, pushed the steel helmets back from their foreheads and scarcely dared to breathe. The shadows took on visible forms, and now they also heard the harsh tingle of arms. They pressed flat against the ground and settled the butts of their rifles against their shoulders.

Steiner and his men had marched toward the clump of woods. They were coming close to the Russian assault trench when Steiner suddenly dropped to the ground. To one side of them, marching from the south in a north-easterly direction, appeared a long row of dim forms moving cautiously through the darkness. Steiner realized that if they continued in the same direction they would pass by only a dozen paces away. He hastily began crawling along the ground. His men did likewise. They covered a considerable distance, until the Russians were out of sight; then they sat up and stared back. 'How many do you think there were?' Steiner whispered.

'Hard to say,' Faber answered. 'I would guess a hundred.'

'They're going to run smack into Schnurrbart.'

Faber nodded. 'What should we do?' he whispered.

Steiner hesitated. They were really in a jam. On the one side was the woods, the outlines of the trees vaguely visible in the darkness, and on the other side the Russians—so large a force that if they encountered Schnurrbart they would roll right over his dozen men. Schnurrbart ought to be warned. But firing prematurely would endanger the whole counter-attack. Agonized by the urgency of a decision, he clenched his teeth and felt the sweat start on his forehead. Behind him he heard Kern's voice murmuring words he could not make out. The others were standing motionless, staring tensely toward the north, where fighting would surely flare up any moment. Steiner started forward. But at that moment an inferno broke loose back toward the German trenches. Steiner threw a hurried glance toward the edge of the woods, then back at the spot where a few carbine shots were almost drowned by the hammering of several dozen sub-machine-guns. Then he started to run. They raced back the way they had come. Abruptly light flooded the area. Above the battalion's positions, five or six flares rose simultaneously. The air was suddenly filled with loud shouts and the crackle of rifle fire. They've broken in, Steiner thought in dread, they've broken into the trenches. Abruptly, he stood still. A howling roar swelled above their heads. They dropped flat, pressed their faces into their arms. Then they realized that it was their own artillery firing upon the edge of the woods. They sprang to their feet and ran on. Steiner's thoughts were a turmoil. When from a distance he saw several dark bundles on the ground, he turned aside from the direction in which he had been running and ran straight up the slope. In the trench they came upon the Russians. The platoon had the advantage of surprise on their side, and a dozen well-aimed hand grenades created wild confusion among the Russians who had broken through. Faber settled behind the MG and began firing. But the Russians adjusted to the new situation with amazing speed. Their resistance stiffened. Then Steiner saw two of his men rolling down the slope like wooden dummies. He decided to break off the unequal combat. But at that critical moment they received unexpected aid.

Krüger had reached the assigned spot with his group. They crouched on the ground and talked in whispers. 'The plan is cockeyed,' Maag said crossly, tugging nervously at the strap of his sub-machine-gun. Pasternack disagreed. 'Why? Seems good to me. It'll give those Russians a turn when we suddenly start firing on them from the rear. They won't be counting on that.'

They looked over at Krüger, who was peering alertly into the darkness. 'What do you think?' Maag asked. The East Prussian shrugged. 'Wait and drink tea. Anyway, you'd better keep your traps shut and your ears open. It's going to start in a minute.'

'Let it,' Maag growled, trying to appear superior.

Krüger glanced impatiently at his wrist-watch. 'I don't want any of you shooting up the air,' he said to the replacements. 'When the Ivans start coming, I'll fire a flare and you can pick them off at leisure.'

There was an uncomfortable silence. He looked at his watch again. His uneasiness was infectious, and several of the men stood up. He was about to snap at them when there was an outbreak of furious rifle fire. 'Here it goes,' Maag whispered excitedly. Krüger sprang to his feet and stared in dismay at the trenches, which were suddenly bathed in light. 'They're crazy,' he exclaimed. 'What are they shooting flares for?'

'Giving it all away,' Maag stammered. Krüger raised his hand for quiet and listened. But then the artillery barrage began, and the mighty explosions drowned the noise of rifles and tommy-guns. 'Something's up over there,' Maag shouted through the noise. 'Those were Russian guns.'

Krüger thought feverishly. If the counter-attack was going wrong, as seemed to be the case, they would be needed. For a moment he was sorely tempted to stick by Steiner's order. He could stay right here and let the other fight, whatever it was, go on without him. Then he thought of Schnurrbart. He suddenly felt that everything up there in the trenches was hanging by a thread. Choking with a sudden onset of apprehension, he shouted orders. The men obeyed reluctantly, holding their guns ready to fire. They began advancing toward the shell-holes. Flares were still rising steadily from the trenches, throwing dancing shadows over the bare terrain, chiselling details out of the darkness with merciless clarity. They had come within thirty paces of the shell-holes when a hail of rifle fire roared at them. Krüger had a chance to see Pasternack sink to his knees with a groan, and another man reach into the air with both hands as if trying to grasp some invisible object, then whirl round and round and topple heavily to the ground. Then he raced forward with huge strides, hurled one, two hand grenades at several heads which showed just above the ground, as though their owners were buried there up to the neck. He scarcely waited for the thunderous detonations to reach their end; seconds later he jumped with both feet at once into a deep hole. He stumbled over a twitching body, fell, rolled over on his back and raised his tommy-gun. He saw the stooped backs of two Russians disappearing over the edge of the crater, heard the lash of several rifle shots, then there was silence. As he staggered up he heard Maag shouting his name. He tried to answer, but his voice would not obey him, and instead he clambered out of the hole. The men were standing in a knot a few yards away. Seeing him, they haltingly approached. 'Where are the rest?' he asked hoarsely. Maag gestured silently over his shoulder. His right arm was dangling stiffly, and Krüger asked him: 'What's the matter with you?'

'My arm. I don't know.' He turned his head and looked back. Then he said dully: 'Pasternack got it.'

'Dead?'

'Yes. Right through the chest.'

Krüger began blinking as though a grain of sand had got into his eye. From the shell-hole came a loud moan. As the men started toward the hole, Krüger held them back. 'That one won't bother us. We'd better look through the other holes.'

'No need,' Maag said. 'All the bastards made tracks. There couldn't have been many. What are we going to do now?'

'Look for Steiner and Schnurrbart,' Krüger said firmly. 'Where are the other fellows?'

'Wounded. They're lying over there. Should we take them with us?'

Krüger considered for a moment, then shook his head. 'There'll be time for them later. How many are there?'

'Five,' Maag answered.

'Good enough. Maybe there'll be a few more; that will make it worth while picking them up.'

They stared at him outraged. One man came a step closer and said: 'Now look here——'

'Shut up,' Krüger ordered sharply. 'None of you has any reason to jabber. Why did you stop instead of following me?'

They evaded his menacing glance and did not answer. The artillery barrage had stopped meanwhile. But further to the west the noise of fighting continued; they distinctly heard the shattering explosions of the hand grenades. Loud shouting rang out from the top of the hill, where more and more flares were being fired. Krüger beckoned to the men to follow him. They climbed the hill and ran into men of the 1st Platoon, who shouted excitedly at him. Cursing wildly, Krüger silenced them long enough to ask a question. 'What's going on up there?' One man explained that the Russians had got into the trenches and that Meyer was gathering all available men for a counter-thrust.

'Then let's go,' Krüger declared, and started forward. The 1st Platoon men joined his group. They had covered about a hundred paces when there were several violent explosions in front of them. At the same time they heard loud cheers. On the run they reached the spot where the Russians had broken in. A few dark figures clambered out of the trench and ran forward, stooping. For a moment Meyer's powerful voice could be heard. Then an ear-shattering hammering began. A large number of fleeing Russians came tearing down the slope. Krüger fired until his magazine was empty. As he reached for a new clip he caught sight of Steiner, standing beside Faber only a few yards away. For a second they stared at one another in amazement. Then Krüger cursed. 'Where the hell is Schnurrbart?' he asked. Steiner looked down the slope. Singly and in groups, pursuing Germans were coming back. Meyer appeared among them. Seeing Steiner, he came toward him swiftly. 'What's up?' he asked tensely. Steiner shrugged. The question seemed superfluous.

Krüger took a step forward. 'We cleaned out the shell-holes,' he said.

'Really?' Meyer swung round. 'And you only tell me that now?'

'Haven't had a chance to before,' Krüger growled.

'How did all this happen?' he asked curtly.

Steiner reported laconically. 'I was just about to withdraw when your show started. If you had attacked later we——' He stopped abruptly, recognizing the man standing over there as Hollerbach. Hastily he pushed through the others and asked Hollerbach: 'Where is Schnurrbart?'

'He must still be lying down there,' Hollerbach replied softly.

'Down where?'

Stammering, hesitant, Hollerbach began to explain: 'First we fired till our magazines were empty, and then the Russians came on at us and we ran up the hill. But I saw nothing of Schnurrbart.'

'So.' Steiner glowered at him. Then he turned and started down the slope again, followed by several men, including Krüger, Hollerbach and Faber. They found Schnurrbart at last, lying on his face, and Steiner looked down at him for long seconds before he knelt beside him and quickly examined him. Then he raised his head. 'He's alive,' he said hoarsely. 'Let's get him to the infirmary.' They lifted Schnurrbart carefully and toiled up the steep slope with him.

The infirmary bunkers were jammed. The medicos had their hands full, and it was some time before they found a doctor to look at Schnurrbart. Meanwhile Steiner looked round. The severely wounded men lay side by side on the floor. He saw many familiar faces. Most of the wounded men were already bandaged. Near the door lay one man with his torn abdomen exposed. His face was so smeared with blood as to be unrecognizable. Looking at him, Steiner had to clench his teeth to fight down the sickness that threatened to overpower him. It seemed incredible that a man with such gruesome wounds could still be alive. Quickly he turned his head away and looked at Schnurrbart. They had laid him on a blanket and Krüger was unbuckling the chin-strap of his helmet. Suddenly he cried out in horror: 'Head wound.' Steiner closed his eyes. He had avoided examining Schnurrbart because of his fear of what he would find. For a second he stood paralysed with agony. Then he heard Faber saying: 'Don't be silly! It just grazed him, that's all.' Steiner took a deep breath. He opened his eyes. The men had cut open Schnurrbart's trousers and Krüger was saying: 'He's been hit in the leg, too.'

'In the calf,' Hollerbach said. 'Shot went clean through.'

Steiner now had the courage to look at Schnurrbart's face. From his temple a red streak ran down to his chin, where it vanished in the thick growth of beard. His face was pale, dirty, sunken-cheeked; all its familiar character had been erased. The sight of that alien face aroused a dull pain in Steiner. He could feel a choking, burning sensation rising in his throat. The noises in the bunker, the suppressed moans of the wounded men, the lowered voices of the medical personnel, the soft clinking of instruments, the curt instructions of the doctors, who worked with rolled-up shirt-sleeves, the flickering light of the candles—all of it merged into an unreal, stagy background. But close to him was this mask-like, bearded face of a man who had been at his side through all these months and years.

A violent dispute caught his attention. One of the medicos was arguing with Krüger, waving his hands angrily. 'You've got to clear out,' he asserted angrily. 'This isn't a hospital ward.' He turned to Steiner. 'I'm sorry, Sergeant, but you must realize we need the room.'

Steiner ordered the men to wait outside. They left reluctantly. 'I'll go as soon as you tell me what the story is,' he said to the medico, gesturing at Schnurrbart.

'We'll be ready for him in a minute,' the man said.

The doctor had approached meanwhile. He wiped his blood-stained hands with a piece of gauze, attended to a man who was lying in front of Schnurrbart, and then stopped before Steiner. 'Wounded?' he said curtly.

Steiner shook his head. 'Not me. I want to know what's wrong with this man here.'

He watched with outward calm as the doctor bent over Schnurrbart and felt the bloody welt above the right temple. Then he looked up. 'Wasn't the man wearing a helmet?'

'Here it is,' Steiner said. As he picked up the steel helmet his eyes widened. 'Look at that,' he said, pointing to a round hole on the back of the helmet. The doctor took it from his hand and examined the spot curiously. 'Was he lucky!' he said slowly. 'The bullet came from behind, penetrated the metal and bounced around inside until it fell out. Incredible luck.'

'Is it bad?' Steiner asked.

The doctor stooped over Schnurrbart again. 'Not a bit. Slight concussion of the brain. He'll come to soon.'

'And the leg?'

'I don't know yet. If the bone isn't injured, he'll be on his feet in a month.' He turned to the next patient.

'Well?' Hollerbach asked outside.

Steiner waved his hand. 'Luck. He may be back here in four weeks.'

They sighed with relief. 'The idiot,' Krüger cursed cheerfully. 'I always told him to watch out for that silly head of his. Do you know that Pasternack got it?'

'Dead?' Steiner asked hoarsely.

'Yes.'

Steiner bit his lip. 'Who else?'

'Maag,' Krüger answered. 'He's on his way to the rear already. Half the platoon is knocked out. Incidentally, Meyer is looking for you. We said you would be right along.'

'He can wait,' Steiner growled.

Captain Stransky had put some exciting experiences behind him. Originally he had intended to await the outcome of the patrol action in his bunker. But soon he was seized by uneasiness and, accompanied by Triebig, had set out for the 2nd Company's sector. They had reached the first foxholes when the enemy break-through occurred. Stransky had turned about promptly and raced back to his bunker, Triebig close at his heels. As soon as he recovered sufficiently to issue orders, he had commanded his frightened adjutant to take up positions in front of the bunker with all the men attached to the staff. Then he had placed telephone calls to the combat train and to Regiment. First Sergeant Fetscher was ordered to start marching everybody who could carry a gun to the battalion command post at once; to the worried regimental commander he gave a vivid description of the events, weaving into his report phrases about resistance to the last cartridge. Shortly afterwards, just as Sergeant Fetscher arrived with a heavily armed group of communications personnel, Lieutenant Meyer telephoned him that the positions had been retaken from the enemy and the bomb craters cleared. The result was that Fetscher and his men, cursing but visibly relieved, started back and the regimental commander received a report calculated to warm the cockles of his heart. Now Stransky sat in his bunker waiting impatiently for Meyer, whom he had ordered to bring Steiner with him. Meanwhile, he explained to his adjutant the proper way to meet any repetitions of such unfortunate incidents as he called them. 'Everything depends on keeping calm and acting quickly and precisely,' he was saying.

There was a knock at the door and Meyer and Steiner came in. Stransky greeted them curtly and then, turning to Steiner, asked him to describe the course of events in sequence. As Steiner spoke the three officers listened closely, and Stransky repeatedly gave vent to low exclamations of disapproval. Steiner studiously ignored them. When he had concluded his report, Stransky turned to Meyer. 'Bad business. The penetration of the trench could have been prevented.'

'Under normal conditions certainly,' Meyer said. 'But in the first place the positions were weakly held, and in the second place the men did not know what to expect, since their own men were out there in front of them. By the time they realized the men coming up the hill were Russians, it was already too late.'

'All the same,' Stransky retorted testily. He picked up a candle from the table and rolled it several times between his hands. Then he turned to Steiner. 'You should have taken into consideration such a possibility,' he said sternly. 'A shock troop leader must count on all eventualities.'

Meyer sucked in his breath indignantly. But Steiner answered before he could intervene. 'My assignment was to clear the bomb craters,' he replied coolly. 'An encounter with a hundred Russians was not expected by me or anyone else.'

'You should have attacked the Russians right off,' Triebig interposed. 'If you had done so, they would never have got so far.'

Steiner threw him a contemptuous glance. 'The reasons why I did not,' he said, 'are so obvious that an explanation is unnecessary.'

Stransky pounded his fist on the table. 'I cannot agree with you,' he said savagely. 'In fact, it is perfectly clear that you are not up to coping with such situations.' He turned to Meyer. 'It would have been better after all if you had led the patrol. Apparently I overestimated your platoon leader's abilities.'

Meyer exchanged a rapid glance with Steiner. In spite of the harsh words between himself and Steiner earlier, his sense of justice was outraged by Stransky's attempt to fix the blame. His anger was apparent in his voice as he said: 'I disagree, sir. As I see the situation, I would have acted precisely as Steiner did in every detail.'

Stransky regarded him without expression. 'It grieves me to hear that,' he retorted. 'If you equate your qualities as a leader with the sergeant's, that is your affair, of course, but it suggests regrettable conclusions.'

Triebig spoke up. 'I must agree with the captain,' he said softly. 'Such situations call for not only a high degree of coolness, but certain traits of character. Whether Sergeant Steiner possesses them, you would know. Certainly there is reason to doubt that he does.'

There was a silence. The eyes of the officers were upon Steiner, whose face was drained of colour. Meyer stood up quickly. 'Perhaps you are an authority on character, Herr Triebig,' he said scornfully. He turned to Stransky: 'Have you any further orders for me?'

Stransky, still seated, looked up at him, his light eyes holding a glint of mockery. 'Not at the moment. You can inform me about your casualties tomorrow. I shall expect your written report at nine o'clock. You may go.'

Outside, they had gone some distance from the bunker when Steiner suddenly stopped. 'There's something I have still to take care of,' he said tightly.

Meyer scrutinized him. In the darkness he could scarcely see Steiner's face, but the tone of voice gave him concern. 'You'll get into a mess,' he warned him. 'Don't do anything foolish.'

Steiner shook his head. For a moment Meyer still hesitated; then he nodded. 'All right, see you later. Come to my bunker.' He walked away swiftly.

Steiner waited until he had vanished in the darkness. Then he stole back quietly. He detoured around the command post, and found a good spot among the trees, where he could not be seen. There was a sentry in front of the commander's bunker. Steiner prepared for a long wait. He thought over every detail of his plan. It was relatively simple. It would only be necessary to work up a suitable alibi. That was easy: Krüger and Hollerbach would swear to high heaven that he had been with them all during the time in question.

Minute after minute passed. Suddenly a light fell from one of the bunkers. A man came out slowly and looked around. Then he closed the door behind him, exchanged a few words with the sentry, and disappeared among the trees. Steiner stepped behind a crooked trunk and peered again. The sentry shifted his carbine to the other shoulder and began pacing back and forth. Finally he turned to the right, went over to the western edge of the orchard, and again stood motionless. He was only dimly visible now. Steiner was about to step out from behind the tree when he heard a sound. A dark shadow emerged from the trees, stood poised for a while, approached with footsteps silent as a cat's and disappeared noiselessly into the bunker which Steiner knew belonged to Triebig. Steiner shook his head in wonder. But another ten minutes passed before Triebig appeared. He came from the commander's bunker and went straight to his, without glancing right or left. As he descended the steps and opened the door, Steiner stretched his head forward. But to his amazement no sound of conversation broke the silence. The glimmer of light from the small window beside the door went out. What was going on here? At last curiosity overcame caution. After making sure that there was no immediate danger from the sentry, Steiner carefully approached the bunker, felt his way down the steps and paused for a moment at the door, listening, his tommy-gun tucked under his arm. Nothing stirred inside. Inch by inch he pushed the door open until he could squeeze in. Then he stepped quickly across the threshold.

He heard hasty movements; then there was silence. Slowly, he closed the door behind him, pressed his back against it and tried to make out something in the absolute darkness. He switched on his flashlight. On the low cot lay two men. It took a moment for him to recognize one of them as Triebig, who held his pistol in his hand and was staring wide-eyed into the light. The man beside Triebig he knew only by sight—a member of the battalion staff. Steiner took a step forward and placed the flashlight on the table. As he did so, he saw the clothing strewn on the floor. The silence became agonizing. He walked round the table, the Russian sub-machine-gun held like a club in his hands, and stopped in front of the bed.

'Put that down,' he whispered, indicating the pistol which Triebig was still clutching. Triebig did not stir. The waxen pallor of his face was suddenly washed away by a rush of blood that mounted to the roots of his hair and seemed to flow even into the whites of his eyes. He uttered an inarticulate sound and tried to pull the blanket over his naked shoulders. But Steiner's hand flashed forward, caught a corner of the blanket and wrenched it off the bed. He tossed it behind him on the floor. 'Stand up·' he said to Triebig. When the lieutenant did not obey, Steiner gripped his wrist tightly, took hold of the pistol and laid it and his own gun beside the flashlight on the table. Uncertainly, Triebig stood up. The other man pressed against the wall, drawing up his legs. His childish face reflected such abysmal terror that for a moment Steiner felt sorry for him.

'You should have barricaded the door,' Steiner said. 'Then you wouldn't have been caught, you swine.'

'What do you want?' Triebig whispered. They were the first words he had spoken since Steiner had entered the bunker.

'I almost forgot,' Steiner said, smiling savagely. 'Thanks for reminding me.'

Triebig backed away from him. Steiner followed until the man was brought to a stop by the wall and stood still, trembling. 'I meant,' Steiner said, 'to beat you up for what you said over at Stransky's bunker. The problem would have been to keep you from shouting for help. Now I'm going to give you that beating and you won't shout.'

'I will,' Triebig stammered.

Steiner shook his head. 'No you won't,' he declared grimly. 'If you do, you'll be heard, and if you are heard people will come and see what's going on here. What do you think Stransky will say if he finds you in this state?'

Triebig moved his lips without making a sound. Suddenly he propelled himself from the wall, ran to where his clothes lay and stooped. As he reached out his hand, Steiner brought his nailed boot heavily down on his fingers. Triebig opened his mouth to scream. But only a low moan emerged. 'So you're keeping that in mind,' Steiner said hotly. He lifted his foot and pulled Triebig up by the shoulder. 'For all I care you can stick a handkerchief between your teeth. Only you'd better keep quiet. It will cost you your neck, remember.'

He struck abruptly. His clenched fist hit Triebig squarely in the face. Triebig tried to defend himself, but Steiner gave him no time. His blows followed one another mercilessly, with all his strength behind him. He pounded the man until his fists ached. Then he picked him up and tossed him on the bed. The other man pressed even closer against the wall.

'What's your name?' Steiner snapped.

The man did not answer.

'What's your name?' Steiner repeated sharply.

'Keppler,' the man whispered.

'Are you his orderly?'

The man nodded.

'Get up, get dressed and get out. If you tell anyone about this, you'll be up against a court-martial yourself. Clear?'

The man nodded silently. He stepped over Triebig and got off the bed. Steiner picked up his tommy-gun. He glanced at Triebig. The fellow had passed out. It would be a while before he came to again. Without another word to Keppler, he left the bunker. Cautiously, he climbed the steps and peered about.

The figure of the sentry was outlined indistinctly in the darkness. Steiner watched him for a while. At last he was able to make out that the man had his back turned to him. Hastily, crouching, he stole among the trees to the trench and started up the slope. It was the hour before dawn. Night still lay blackly over the land. Beyond the hill, isolated rifle shots cracked away. The light was ebbing tiredly out of the stars. Reaching his bunker, Steiner paused, wondering whether he should go to see Meyer. But the company commander must be asleep by now. Indecisively, he looked over the rim of the trench. He felt soiled.

Suddenly a glow passed over his face. He raised his head in astonishment. In the east the heavens were cracking open. The horizon became a darting sea of flames, and a few seconds later a roar like a monstrous wave surged over the positions. He jumped down the steps, kicked open the door and found half a dozen horrified faces staring at him. A candle was flickering on the table. He shut the door behind him and looked at his watch.

'It's just three o'clock,' Faber said quietly.

'Yes,' Steiner murmured. 'Just three.'

X

LIEUTENANT-COLONEL BRANDT was sitting on his bed, half-dressed. As he reached for his shoes, still dazed with sleep, he fiercely cursed the unreliability of the intelligence people in Krymskaya who had predicted that the Russian offensive would begin in the middle of May. If you got to the bottom of it, he thought angrily, you'd probably find they were hand in glove with the Russians and deliberately feeding us misinformation.

He had got his shoes on, but sat for a while with drooping head. Outside there was a rumble as loud as a hundred trucks passing over a cobblestoned road. Objects in the bunker vibrated; the window glass hummed and the light of the candle dipped and flickered and threatened to go out. Suddenly the telephone buzzed. Brandt picked it up and recognized Captain Kiesel's voice. 'It's starting, sir.'

'Never stopped,' Brandt growled. 'Come over here in five minutes.' He replaced the receiver and remained bent over the table for a moment. The enormous barrage had startled him out of deep sleep. He had been dreaming vividly that he was at the opera. But he could no longer remember what opera was being played. Perhaps the 'Marriage of Figaro', he thought, closing his eyes.

There was a knock. He quickly slipped on his tunic and turned to face the door as Kiesel, tall and energetic, stepped in. At the same moment the telephone buzzed again. As Brandt lifted the receiver, Kiesel came over to the table. 'The general,' Brandt murmured, winking at Kiesel and pressing the receiver tightly against his ear.

The smile vanished. He listened, nodded thoughtfully. 'Of course, *Herr General*. I shall issue the appropriate orders at once.' He dropped the telephone and turned to Kiesel. 'Drum fire along the whole line. All available reserves have already been alerted. The general thinks this is the greatest massing of artillery the Russians have yet achieved. It really looks like the expected offensive.' He turned the telephone crank and exchanged a few words with the operator. 'There we have it,' he said irritably. 'Communications with the front are already broken.'

'We have radio,' Kiesel replied.

Brandt nodded. 'They're busy establishing connections now.' He made a few more telephone calls. Then he went to a corner of the bunker, produced a bottle of kirschwasser, and filled two glasses. 'You'll make an exception of your rule today,' he stated. 'We have a warm day before us and are going to need a tonic.'

Kiesel nodded. They drank. Brandt set the glass down hard on the table and looked at his wrist-watch. 'Twenty past three,' he noted. 'The overture will last another two hours at least. Send the other officers in to me.'

Kiesel went out and shortly afterwards returned with the rest of the staff officers. The conference lasted only an hour.

The radioed reports coming in from the battalions were increasingly disturbing. Stransky reported loud motor noises from the edge of the wooded area. Kiesel shook his head as he read the message. 'If Stransky can hear motor noises while this barrage is going on, the tanks must be right in front of his bunker,' he said. Shortly afterwards telephone communication with the battalions was restored and Brandt had a chance to say a few words to the commanders. He tried to reassure them by pointing out that an assault regiment was on its way up front as reinforcement. Shortly afterwards the wire was broken again. The signals officer informed Brandt that in attempts to restore the line more than half his men had fallen. Brandt ordered him to give up trying; radio communication would be good enough until the attack began, he said. The officers, with the exception of Kiesel, returned to their bunkers. Slowly, the sky grew brighter. The barrage had increased in violence and seemed to be drawing closer. Brandt raised his head, listening. Then he looked at Kiesel who was standing by the door, smoking a cigarette and looking calmly out of the window. 'We'll take a look at the show from outside,' he said to him. 'Do you feel like it?'

Kiesel smiled. 'Even if I did not feel like it I wouldn't admit it. In ninety-nine out of a hundred cases our courage is nothing more than an expression of common politeness or sense of duty.'

'And in the remaining case?' Brandt asked.

Kiesel opened the door up a crack and flipped the cigarette out. 'An expression of our insanity,' he replied tersely.

It was already light enough for them to have a good view of the steep slope. The dull grey of the sky was shot through with silvery threads, and the stars were fading rapidly. Beyond the hill the artillery fire rumbled on undiminished. An inferno, Kiesel thought as they plodded up the slope. When they reached the brow of the hill, they both stood still at one impulse. Toward the east, as far as the eye could reach, a volcano was raging. The horizon had been transformed into a writhing dragon that lunged, stretched and twisted its giant length, spewing yellow flame over the land, puffing fiery clouds, never pausing for a moment. Between the blue-black hills there still hung pockets of darkness into which torrents of sparks were showered. The knife-edged ridges of the hills stood out distinctly against the burning sky. Far to the west the moon stared down like the half-shut eye of a cyclops. Brandt gripped Kiesel by the shoulder and their eyes met.

They walked on a short distance to a trench which had been dug a few days earlier at the commander's order. It was intended for observation and provided with a number of solidly built dugouts with broad look-out slits. In one of the dugouts they found Lieutenant Spannagel, the forward observer of the 2nd Artillery Battalion. He had a radio section with him, and was visibly delighted by the unexpected visitors. Since he also had a telephone connected to the regimental switchboard, Brandt informed the communications platoon of his whereabouts and ordered all messages and telephone calls for him to be switched to the forward observation post. Then he questioned Spannagel about the situation. The lieutenant said that the guns were ready to fire, radio communications were intact, and the supply of ammunition should be adequate to hold the Russians.

Brandt then turned to the artillery officer's telescope and studied the opposite hillside. Meanwhile Kiesel talked in low tones with Spannagel. In spite of his sanguine words, the thin-faced, likeable young lieutenant seemed nervous. He kept shifting his weight restlessly from one leg to the other. 'If I had only half the stuff the Russians are throwing away over there, I'd make things hot for them,' he said.

'I thought you said you had enough ammunition,' Kiesel remonstrated.

'Oh, I do, I do, but I'll need it when the attack starts. As long as the Ivans are hiding in the woods there's not much sense wasting my shells. The battalion has let me have 500 rounds. You have no idea how fast they use up.'

'True enough. How many guns would you estimate they have on the other side?'

Spannagel shrugged. 'Hard to say. I've been with the battalion since the start of the Russian campaign, but I've never seen anything like this. Just listen to it. You'd have to go back to the First World War to find a parallel for this kind of squandering of material.'

'Which goes to show how seriously the Russians are taking us,' Kiesel commented. 'They seem to know they're facing the crack divisions of the southern front.'

'Not much consolation in that. I just wonder what's left of our front lines.'

Kiesel gave a worried nod. He looked at his watch. 'It's been going on for two hours already. Before long their bombers will come.'

'And then their tanks. They couldn't ask for better terrain.'

Brandt turned to them. 'The fire seems to be concentrating primarily on 121.4. I don't think the Russians are going to attack along the road. They'll try to take the hill. If they succeed in that, our tank barrier on the highway will be worthless and they'll pay us a visit from the rear.'

'They must not take the hill,' Kiesel said gravely. 'If they do, we're done for.'

They stepped over to Brandt's side and followed his gaze out across the landscape. With the sky's dull grey taking on more and more colour, the frightful glare on the horizon waned under the cold light of the new day. Slowly the light moved from the east over the hills, almost imperceptibly drawing the gentle lines of the terrain out of the dusk. The greyish-black cloud of dust hovering above the churned-up hills became more and more visible, and a huge banner of smoke blocked all vision to the more distant east.

Kiesel suddenly raised his head and listened. At first there was only a delicate humming that set the air in the dugout vibrating; then the sound swelled to a drone that seemed to fill the whole of the sky above their heads. Their faces paled. 'The second phase,' Brandt declared coolly. 'Planes.'

The shrilling of the telephone made them all jerk around. Spannagel picked up the receiver and said a few words. Then he turned to Brandt. 'The general, sir.'

Brandt took the telephone from him, and his body involuntarily stiffened. 'Herr General?'

'How do things look out your way, Brandt?' The voice sounded thin, remote, as though coming from a distant planet.

'Unchanged,' Brandt replied. 'Violent artillery fire on the trenches. I'm afraid the casualties will be high.'

Outside a penetrating howl approached a crescendo. Out of the corners of his eyes Brandt saw Kiesel and Spannagel press their bodies against the walls of the dugout. The radio section men were lying flat on the floor. He pressed the receiver to his ear. 'Herr General——'

The voice at the other end sounded concerned. 'What's the matter? Brandt, what——'

The dugout began to sway. A deafening crash drowned every other sound. With his free hand Brandt clung to a prop and stared at the ceiling of the dugout. The buzzing in the receiver stopped. Dark smoke poured through the look-out slit. He heard Kiesel shouting something. Sand trickled between cracks in the plank ceiling, and the doorless opening vanished in white smoke. Brandt coughed. He had let the receiver drop; now his legs sagged and he slid to the ground, with his back against the wall, gasping for air. A few minutes went by. The crash and roar of explosions gradually slackened, moved off into the distance, and the air slowly cleared. Brandt stood up and stared at Kiesel who was still standing near the entrance, his hand covering his eyes. Spannagel was sitting on the floor at his feet.

Kiesel took his hand from his eyes, wiped the tears from under them and blinked vigorously. When their glances met, he nodded. 'The third phase,' he said loudly. 'The barrage is rolling over the communications zone now.'

As if on command they stepped over to the look-out slit and peered out. The sound of motors hung in the air. Scattered heavy detonations indicated that the bombardment was not yet over. The officers stared at the white pall of fog that was spreading over the entire landscape. Kiesel recalled reaching the peak of a mountain several years ago, to find himself standing high above a solid bank of clouds. He felt the commander's hand grip his arm. 'Smoke,' Brandt exclaimed. 'They've fired smoke shells.' He took two strides to the field telephone and turned the crank. But the line was dead. He started toward the door and bumped against a man who was just coming in. The man clicked his heels and gasped: 'They're attacking now, sir. Radio message from the 2nd Battalion: tanks approaching; request artillery.'

Brandt turned his head in the ensuing silence. The radiomen were already at their apparatus, headsets over their ears, looking at Spannagel, whose nervousness had entirely disappeared. He was standing beside Kiesel at the telescope. Now he straightened up. His voice sounded calm, sure, distinct as he said: 'Firing command.'

'Firing command,' one of the radiomen repeated in a monotone. Spannagel leaned forward over the telescope again. 'Entire battalion: fire!'

The attack took place on a thirty-mile front, with the main blow directed against the positions west of Krymskaya. Little ground was gained, although the Germans estimated that between twenty and thirty Russian assault divisions were employed. The spearhead was formed by several tank brigades which rolled over the smashed trenches under cover of the smokescreen and in spite of the vigorous German barrage reached the peak of Hill 121.4. The army communiqué that day reported a grand Russian offensive against the Kuban bridgehead, with an expenditure of material comparable to the battles of the First World War. Local penetrations, the communiqué went on to say, had been sealed off and thrown back by counter-attacks and the offensive had been halted by the concentrated fire of the German defenders.

That morning, however, a few minutes after the Russian barrage had rolled back to the rear areas, to the men on Hill 121.4 it scarcely seemed that there was any serious resistance to the surging tide of Russian infantry. The survivors of the artillery barrage rushed in wild flight down the battered trenches and tried to reach the battalion command post. Those who got through were assembled by Triebig for the defence of the command post. Steiner's men stayed at their positions, wondering how long these posts, already as good as lost, would go unscathed. They had sat in dull apathy through the three-hour barrage, smoking countless cigarettes and scarcely exchanging a word with one another.

The moment everything abruptly fell silent outside, and even the drone of airplane motors faded in the distance, Steiner had picked up his sub-machine-gun, slid the strap of his steel helmet under his chin, and climbed up into the trench, followed by Faber, Kern and the others. White swaths of smoke blotted out everything; the men had to grope their way to the next MG emplacement. Now they were standing around the loophole, staring in perplexity into the impenetrable smoke that covered the terrain. Steiner slung the tommy-gun over his shoulder. 'I'll look for Meyer,' he said. 'Set up the MG; it's going to start soon.'

Faber hunched and dropped his shoulders. 'I'm afraid you won't find anyone. Where do we meet if things go wrong?'

'Battalion command post,' Steiner replied. 'But not until you've used up all your ammunition.' He lingered for a moment watching the woodsman place a belt in the machine-gun. Kern crouched down on the ground, his face twitching. His nerves seemed about gone. Besides Kern and Faber there were three other men in the dugout. They seemed somewhat calmer, although they had come with the latest batch of replacements. A bit rough for a starter, Steiner thought, regarding them with pity. It suddenly occurred to him that Schnurrbart was no longer here. Lucky he was out of this. But Hollerbach and Krüger must. . . . Concerned, he did not finished the thought. Quickly he climbed into the trench and took a look round, listening. You could not see ten feet in front of you. Isolated rifle shots sounded feebly from all directions. And the noise of motors could again be heard. He could not be sure whether the sounds came from the air, or from the slope of the hill below. For a few seconds he stood motionless, wondering which way to go. Since Hollerbach's bunker was on the way to the battalion command post, Krüger must be somewhere to the left, near the company command post. The noise of the motors was growing louder and he realized that he had little time for reflection. He decided to look for Krüger first; that way he might be able to contact Meyer at once. Crouching, he began hurrying down the trench. Here and there the sides had collapsed, and in many spots huge craters blocked the way. The rifle-pits he passed by were unmanned. His uneasiness increased. Suddenly he came across a man lying in his path. The head was separated from the body and had lodged among clumps of earth a few paces farther on. The mouth was opened for screaming, as if the head wanted to shout to him to come back. Steiner closed his eyes and stepped over it. A head, he thought, just a head. He felt his whole body trembling.

The trench made a sharp turn to the left. The company command post ought to be beyond the next turning. Involuntarily, he speeded his steps. Then he stopped abruptly. Before him yawned an enormous crater made by a bomb. Out of the black earth protruded splintered bits of beams and wood siding; the smoke had sunk thickly into the pit, forming a pool of whiteness at the bottom. Steiner dug his fingers into the hard earth of the trench wall. His legs felt oddly numb, lifeless. The company command post, he thought. Lieutenant Meyer. For a few seconds he stood unable to move. Then he detoured around the crater, stumbled into the continuation of the trench, and felt his way slowly forward. The smoke was even denser here; it clung viscously to the ground. He passed another roofed emplacement and glanced in. He did so without intention, without hope. Then he stood still in astonishment. He saw a back, a broad, uncannily familiar back. His mouth opened to call, could not produce a sound. But when the back moved, he crawled into the hole and laid a hand on that familiar shadow. The man turned round and he found himself staring into Krüger's face. They looked at one another in silence. Then Krüger turned his face to the loophole. 'They're coming now,' he said. His voice was strange, low and toneless.

'Tanks,' Steiner whispered. He stepped to the other side of the heavy machine-gun and looked through the slot. The sound of the motors had risen to a horrible drone that filled the air and inexorably drew nearer. The steely clank of the treads was clearly audible. Visibility was gradually improving. The smoke-screen was sliding down the hill, so that it was possible to see a few yards of the precipitous slope. Further down, however, it lay like thick soup, lazily drifting eastward toward the sun which was just beginning to rise.

'If they have infantry with them,' Steiner said, 'we won't get out of here.'

Krüger nodded. His set, mask-like face did not change.

'Where are the others?' Steiner asked.

'I don't know. When the bombs started falling they were in the bunker.'

'And where were you?'

'I was right here.'

'Through the whole barrage?' Steiner exclaimed.

Krüger nodded. 'We were waiting for you,' he explained, speaking slowly and with effort. 'Me and Hollerbach. When you didn't get here by half-past two Hollerbach left and I'—he shrugged—'I didn't feel like sleeping. So I relieved the infant who was at the MG here, and then it started. I couldn't get out any more so I just sat, and later the bombs fell and the bunkers blew sky high and——' He fell silent.

'It was horrible,' Steiner said.

Krüger turned his head slowly. 'What was horrible was that I sat here for four hours all alone. There's nothing worse than being alone. I know that now.'

They listened to the roar of the motors. The sound was so near by now that they wondered why they could not see the tanks, although they were peering fixedly through the loophole. Krüger was standing, legs spread wide apart, behind the machine-gun.

'That's something I've known for quite a while,' Steiner said. 'We learn it sooner or later, and the sooner we get used to the idea, the better off we are. There's no sense fooling ourselves.' He placed his tommy-gun beside the MG, continuing to stare through the loophole.

He raised his head to listen. A roar passed overhead, swelled and dimmed as it plunged into the swaths of smoke below them. 'Our barrage,' Krüger commented at the top of his voice. They watched as a black cloud surged up down below, smothering the noise of the tanks. They should have started sooner, Steiner thought. Why did they wait so long, those idiots. With a kind of mad satisfaction he watched as out of the turbulent cauldron below a long barrel appeared and a tank with churning tracks and steel-plated sides rolled up the slope, a dozen Russian infantrymen clinging to its broad back. T.34, he thought—always these damned T.34's. Apathetically he watched Krüger swing the MG around and begin to fire. The men on the tank tumbled off like so many stones and rolled down the steep slope, where they were swallowed up by the boiling smoke. The tank continued on and vanished from sight. It had not fired a shot. But behind it another appeared, and behind that one still others. Krüger pulled the MG off its pedestal and shouted: 'Let's go.'

Steiner barely nodded. A terrible numbness was creeping over him; he could not stir. 'Come on,' Krüger cried. At the same time the tanks opened fire. The sharp crack of their cannon was louder than the barrage; the explosions resounded menacingly up the slope. The hammering of several dozen machine-guns was suddenly interrupted by many voices bellowing: 'Oorraaaay.' Krüger and Steiner crouched down on the floor and stared at the entrance to the dugout. The Russians must already be in the trench. The German barrage moved back, pounded for a few seconds on the trenches, and then rolled on up the hill. They've given us up, Steiner thought. 'We won't get through now,' he said. His words were drowned out in the din. 'Too late,' Krüger bellowed in his ear. Steiner nodded again. Emotionlessly he looked at the white lines in Krüger's blackened face. He ought to wash, he thought, he ought to wash up right away. Becoming aware of the absurdity of the thought, he grinned. At that moment he saw a shadow in the trench, and from a sitting position fired several rounds. The shadow disappeared. Steiner imagined the Russians' next actions. Now the hand grenades would come, several explosive blocks tied together. There was nothing to do but shut your eyes and wait until you were blown to smithereens. Holding their breath, they stared into the trench, the upper half of which was already flooded with dawnlight. Waiting in wearied resignation for the end, Steiner thought of Gertrud. Perhaps the supply column would bring a letter from her tonight. It would be returned to the sender as undeliverable, and Fetscher would note on it in red pencil: 'Fallen for Greater Germany'—as he had done with innumerable letters before. The meeting in Gursuf would remain an episode on the margin of the war.

The waiting became unbearable. Krüger had risen to his feet and was crouching forward, peering into the trench. It was quieter outside now. The racket of motors sounded farther away, and the firing also seemed to proceed higher and higher up the slope. Only now and then could a German MG be heard. The artillery barrage had stopped. The two men listened. Then Krüger slowly, with terrible slowness, moved toward the entrance, paused motionless for a few seconds and finally stuck his head out into the trench. Steiner, watching his back, saw his tenseness relax. He stepped quickly up to him, tommy-gun held high. 'Nothing here,' Krüger whispered in bewilderment. The trench was deserted; there was no trace of the Russians. But suddenly, from the left, came a new sound, like that made by several dozen boots thumping at a run along a trench. 'Russians,' Krüger stammered.

Steiner dropped to his knees and raised the barrel of his gun. The steps came closer; they heard panting breathing, and the men came in sight—not Russians, but men of the 3rd Company. They were running for all they were worth, one behind the other, most of them without weapons, with tattered uniforms, contorted, blood-smeared faces. Krüger groaned with relief. When the last of them passed, he wanted to run after them, but Steiner held him back. 'Wait,' he whispered sharply. 'Not with the crowd.' They listened. Suddenly, terrifyingly close, a motor whined, several terrified screams rang out; then a tank cannon cracked and violent MG fire began. The screams died, and a series of shattering crashes that could only have come from hand grenades completed the unseen drama.

'They ran right into the Russians,' Krüger whispered when the noise stopped. Steiner wet his dry lips with his tongue. The temptation to glance over the rim of the trench was enormous, but he controlled himself. Krüger stared at the MG in his hands as though it were somehow the key to their desperate salvation. Finally he shrugged. 'No sense,' he murmured. 'We can't go back; we've got to stay here.' His perplexed helplessness made Steiner smile, but the smile flitted over his face as if it did not belong to him. Although he had no illusions, he suddenly felt that the worst was behind them. His head was clearing rapidly.

'We can't stay here,' he said firmly. 'The Russians will be here any minute. They must be rolling up the whole trench. What do you think those men were running from?'

Krüger plucked at his nose. 'I don't know. If we stay here they'll come to us, and if we go out we'll come to them. We'll get it just like those others did.'

'We've got to try,' Steiner said. 'Stick close behind me.' He turned to the right and began walking, crouching low, along the trench. Krüger shifted the MG to his right hand. They reached the bomb crater under which the ruins of the company command post lay, climbed down into it and scrambled out the other side. It was so quiet now that they had to walk on tiptoe to muffle the crunching of their boots. Only above them, on the brow of the hill, some random rifle shots were still being fired.

After a dozen paces they reached Steiner's bunker and glanced in briefly. The door was open. No one was inside. Now came the hardest part of the way; they continued forward on hands and knees. As they turned a corner of the trench they came across a man who had been pinned to the bottom of the trench by a heavy bomb. The bomb fin protruded from his back like a ventilator, the metal red and gleaming dully in the sunlight. Went right through his back and chest and into the ground, Steiner thought. He closed his eyes and crawled over the man's guts. Krüger followed close behind him. Their faces were filthy, the sweat pouring down their foreheads and into their eyes. But they moved steadily along over discarded equipment, pieces of uniform and human limbs scattered about the half-collapsed trench, as though the barren soil of Hill 121.4 had suddenly become a womb bearing waxen faces, clenched fists and bloody rags. They crawled over three men who had been mashed into a single heap of flesh, their mouths open in death, as if to scream curses at a sky that now arched velvety blue above the hills. As Steiner wiped a ghastly, sticky mess from his fingers, a cry above their heads threw them flat on their faces. '*Stoi!*' They lay numbed. A Russian sub-machine-gun hammered above them. At the same moment Steiner sprang to his feet, fired blindly over the wall of the trench and raced on. Stumbling, panting, Krüger ran behind him. Hand grenades exploded in their rear; loud shouts sounded down the trench. From somewhere to one side of them a dark face under a fur cap appeared for a few seconds. Steiner fired without taking aim. The face withdrew. In its place a dark object rolled up to their feet, hissing meanly. Eyes widening with terror at the sight of the hand grenade, Steiner was about to throw himself backward. But he could already hear Krüger's panting breath right at his neck. Instead, he took a leap he did not know he was capable of over the grenade, dashed several yards further on to the next turn in the trench, and threw himself flat. The detonation came just as a heavy body fell right on top of him. Then he heard Krüger's voice again, felt his hands pulling him up, and stared unbelievingly into his contorted face.

'Keep going,' Krüger groaned, 'keep going, keep going.'

Exhausted, they stumbled ahead, heard the shouts and the firing behind them growing feebler. Abruptly, they stopped. Some thirty feet away, diagonally across the trench, stood a Russian tank. 'This is it,' Krüger said tonelessly. They stared at the monster as the turret slowly swerved around until the cannon was pointed directly at them. Then, with an inarticulate cry, Steiner hurled himself forward, and Krüger followed him as though they were one body.

Things were happening fast at the regimental command post. As soon as the barrage ended, Brandt had hurried to the message centre, run through the reports that had meanwhile arrived, and then talked by radio with Division. He had described the tactical situation in the blackest colours and persuaded the general to give him the support of a Stuka wing. Shortly afterwards Kiesel had come into the bunker and reported that the Russian assault had apparently bogged down in front of 2nd Battalion's positions, but that it was rolling steadily up the hill over the trenches of the 1st Battalion. Meanwhile alarming radio messages from Stransky had come in. He reported that dispersed remnants of the 2nd and 3rd Companies were reaching the battalion command post. There could no longer be any doubt that the line had collapsed on Hill 121.4. Through the artillery observer's telescope Brandt had personally verified the disastrous situation. Now he was standing in his bunker bent over the maps, with Kiesel and two other officers of the regimental staff at his side.

Brandt raised his head. 'The breakthrough must have come at Gausser's part of the line,' he said gloomily. 'We have no time to lose. By the time the assault regiment arrives it will be too late. Look here.' The officers stepped closer and bent over the map. 'Vogel was almost untouched,' Brandt went on. 'He's still holding his positions. If the Russians have reached the top of the hill, they'll turn up in his rear.'

'How is Körner's company?' Lieutenant Mohr, the communications officer, asked.

'Körner's holding firm,' Brandt replied. 'He's in the least danger. His right flank is covered by Stransky, who is gathering the dispersed soldiers at his command post and will attack in ten minutes.'

'With the assault regiment?' Kiesel asked.

'No. If we wait for that to arrive, Vogel will be encircled. I've already radioed orders to him and Stransky. Vogel will abandon the positions as far as the battalion command post and attack from the south up the hill, where he'll meet Stransky.'

'I see.' Kiesel nodded. 'Then the line will no longer run around the hill but over it. A simple rectification of the front.'

Mohr spoke up. 'That seems all clear to me,' he said. 'But it looks as though advanced Russian sections—mainly tanks, I should think—will already be west of the point where Stransky and Vogel are supposed to close the gap in the line.'

'That's true,' Brandt said, rubbing his unshaven chin. 'But those isolated Russian forces will run into the assault regiment which is attacking from Kanskoye. If it makes you feel any better, that regiment has ten self-propelled assault guns with it.'

The gloomy faces around him brightened. Brandt tapped his knuckles on the table. 'Once the assault regiment gets here, we'll take the hill back, you can depend on that. We'll attack with Stuka support and the comrades will find things a bit hot for them.'

The other officers were partly convinced by his confidence. They consulted their watches, and discussed the situation in low voices while Brandt conducted several telephone conversations. Lieutenant Stroh, regimental special-missions officer, was less optimistic than some of the others. 'The attack on the hill will not be easy,' he brooded. 'Think of the artillery the Russians have massed over there. As soon as our men appear on the hill there'll be a barrage that will make them reel.'

Kiesel glanced at Brandt, who was sitting at the table talking over the telephone. 'I assure you,' he replied quietly, 'that the commander is aware of that. But after all it's the commander's duty to show optimism even against his better judgment.'

'Has there been any news of the company commanders?' Mohr asked.

Kiesel nodded sadly. 'Yes, some. Meyer is presumably dead. Merkel and Schwerdtfeger wounded. There's no trace at all of Gausser.'

Stroh sighed. 'In other words, the 1st Battalion is without officers.'

'Except for Stransky and Triebig, yes. Körner has also lost two of his company commanders. It's pretty raw.'

They looked up eagerly as the commander rose to his feet. 'Good news,' he said. 'Division reports that the attack was beaten off almost all along the line. Small penetrations here and there, most of them already cleared up.' He turned to Mohr. 'Radio message to Stransky and Vogel. The counter-attack is to be postponed ten minutes. The Stukas ought to arrive at any moment. I don't want our own men coming in there just when the bombs are falling. That would be all we need.'

As Mohr hastened out, Brandt turned to Stroh. 'Inform Spannagel and get in touch with Potzenhardt. I need every one of his guns. As soon as the Stuka attack is over, have him put covering fire on the hill until he doesn't have a round left.'

'Is he still with Vogel?' Stroh asked.

'Yes, his observation dugout is near Vogel's command post. Try to reach him through his battalion. The wire to Vogel is still out.'

Stroh went tearing out. 'And now,' Brandt said, 'a little refreshment. I feel we've earned it.'

He filled the glasses and pushed one across the table to Kiesel, who had silently seated himself. They drank. Kiesel set down the glass and searchingly regarded the commander's exhausted features. 'May I give you my frank opinion?' he asked quietly.

Brandt settled back in his chair with a groan. 'I can't remember ever saying that you couldn't,' he replied grumpily, 'though you've never asked permission before. What is it?'

'We won't recapture that hill,' Kiesel said incisively.

Brandt regarded him from half-closed eyes, his broad face expressing thorough lack of sympathy. Suddenly he smiled unpleasantly. 'Are you giving me advice, Kiesel?'

'I should like to remind you of the several hundred guns on the other side.'

'Do you imagine I've forgotten about them?'

Kiesel shrugged. There was a silence for a few seconds. Then Brandt reached for the bottle and refilled his glass. His voice rang out clear and cold. 'Division has ordered me to throw the Russians back to their starting point at all costs. The general thinks it is possible.'

'The general?' Kiesel asked hesitantly.

Brandt drained his glass at one swallow. Then he leaned across the table. 'I want to tell you something, Kiesel. If you as my adjutant try to impose your personal views upon me, you are at liberty to do so. All you are risking is my good feelings toward you and perhaps your position as adjutant. But if I as regimental commander want to prove a point of mine with the general, I can do so only by bleeding the whole regiment to death.' His voice rose. 'My regiment, Kiesel, and because my regiment consists for

me not of figures but of men, and because that fact is with me
every minute of every day, because I have to think not only for
myself but for 4,000 men, I find it just too goddamn much to have
to sit and listen to your damned ideas.' He fell silent.

Kiesel, seeing the revelation of agony on that lined face, bit
his lips. He bowed his head. 'I beg your pardon,' he faltered.

'None of that!' Brandt commanded sharply. His face looked
more normal again. Noticing that Kiesel had scarcely drunk, he
urged him to finish his glass.

'The thing is,' Brandt went on in a somewhat lower voice, 'you
have to be either up at the very top or down at the very bottom,
either a private or commander-in-chief, not one of these thrice-
damned middlemen like us who have no breathing space to the
right or left, who neither produce nor consume, but simply
receive and pass on. Ah——' He clenched his big hands in disgust.

Kiesel folded his arms over his chest and nodded assent. 'The
purchase price was too high,' he said quietly. 'Can you still
remember what your uniform cost you?'

'Is that a joke?' Brandt asked sharply.

'The subject is too grave for joking. We did not buy our
uniforms; we swapped them. Swapped them for our consciences,
and now we'd like to take back the swap, but it is too late.'

'Too late?' Brandt whispered.

'Too late,' Kiesel repeated boldly. His eyes flashed. 'It was
already too late when we raised our hands and took the oath for
Fuehrer and Nation and for something else—we knew at the time
what it was, although we did not have the guts to admit it to
ourselves.'

Brandt's face was chalky. 'Shut up!' he barked. 'For the last
time I order you to shut up, Kiesel. I won't permit you to talk that
way; do you hear, I won't permit it!'

He sprang abruptly to his feet and paced back and forth.
Finally he came to a stop at the table again. 'Even if it were
true,' he said, 'as long as our men are bleeding and dying out
there, you have not the right to talk like that, you have no right
and I have no right. Here'—his hand came down heavily on the
maps scattered over the table—'here is my job; here is my regiment's sector and here is where the Russians have broken through.
Nothing else interests me, not today and not tomorrow, not at all.
If this war is lost I'll be able to stand before any mirror without

spitting in my own face, and I will not permit anyone to work with me who cannot say the same for himself. Have I expressed myself clearly?'

'Unequivocally,' Kiesel said. He had listened in perfect calm to the commander's outburst. Obviously this was an inappropriate moment for such a discussion, and he made up his mind to return to the subject some other time. But he could not forbear to remark that he personally would prefer not to look in any mirrors at all, since it might well be that his better judgment would be grinning scornfully over his shoulder, awakening doubts that he could easily escape by keeping his eyes shut. At that Brandt left the bunker without another word. As he did so, a swelling drone in the sky announced the arrival of the expected planes. Kiesel also went outside in time to see about a hundred of the thick-set dive-bombers flying in a gigantic V and heading straight for Hill 121.4. They disappeared beyond the brow of the hill. Seconds later the air was filled with a volley of thunderous detonations; the sound waves battered their ears as they listened in breathless exultation.

The officers were all standing in front of their bunkers, their faces expressing grim satisfaction. Kiesel wondered whether he should follow the commander, who had started up the hill to watch the counter-attack from the observation post. Then he decided it would be better to leave Brandt alone with his thoughts, and he went into his bunker. For several minutes he sat pensively at his table. Then the telephone rang. He lifted the receiver and recognized the voice of Sergeant Hüser, the signals platoon leader, who asked where the commander was and informed Kiesel that a radio message had just come in reporting the success of the counter-attack. He also said that communications with the 3rd Battalion had been restored. Kiesel sighed with relief. 'I'll inform the commander,' he said. 'If any further messages come in, we'll be up at the artillery OP.'

Hüser also reported that telephone communication with the 1st Battalion would be restored shortly. Kiesel hurried out, climbed the hill, and found the commander at the observation post, as he had expected. Brandt was standing behind the telescope, apparently following with tense concern the events on the hill opposite. The radiomen were at their apparatus, and the artillery officer was standing beside Brandt, peering through the loop-hole. Kiesel spoke. The two heads jerked round. 'They're up there,' Brandt said happily. 'They've made it, Kiesel; the gap is plugged. Here, see for yourself.' He drew him by the arm over to the loophole and pointed. He looked like another man, and seemed to have entirely forgotten their bitter exchange of a short while ago.

As Kiesel peered through the telescope, he reported the radio message from the 1st Battalion. Brandt rubbed his hands gleefully. 'A pity you weren't here,' he said. 'In all Russia I've never seen an air attack like this one. A hundred planes.' He gave a booming laugh. 'Wouldn't have thought we had that many left.' He turned to Spannagel. 'You can start now. The assault regiment ought to be along any minute now.' He drew Kiesel along outside the shelter. 'Maybe the line has been repaired by now,' he said. 'I must talk to Stransky.' In silence they returned down the hill, and on the way encountered Sergeant Hüser, who was hurrying up toward them. 'The wire is restored,' he reported hastily. 'Captain Stransky wishes to speak to you, sir. The assault regiment has arrived.'

'Good, good.' Brandt joyfully patted him on the shoulder, hurried on into his bunker and picked up the telephone. Kiesel stood close by and could hear Stransky's voice, loud and seemingly excited, but he could not make out any of the words. He tried to read the gist of the conversation in the commander's face, but found nothing to indicate any reason for further worrying. Finally Brandt nodded several times and said: 'Very well, Stransky. Start at once. We will give you ample artillery support. Follow close behind the assault regiment and occupy the positions again. How are things over your way, otherwise?'

As he replaced the receiver, the smile had vanished from his face. 'So it's true,' he turned to Kiesel. 'Stransky has no officers left. Do you know who led the counter-attack on the hill?'

'Triebig,' Kiesel guessed.

Brandt shook his head. 'No, it was Steiner. The boy was wounded in the course of it. In the arm.'

'Steiner?'

'Yes.' Brandt pondered for a moment and then suddenly inquired about Kiesel's brother-in-law.

'He ought to be arriving within the next few days,' Kiesel replied uncomfortably.

'We'll give him the 2nd Company,' Brandt said, nodding.

'Today I'm going to put in an urgent request for replacements. The 1st Company is practically wiped out and——' He fell silent. Kiesel, too, raised his head to listen. Outside violent artillery fire had begun abruptly. 'It's starting,' Brandt said with enforced calm. 'Come along, we'll watch from up above again.'

Kiesel followed him.

Steiner acted without thinking. It was as if he were being propelled forward. Krüger, too, had lost all his faculties, as though the black muzzle of the tank cannon had been a telescope showing him a ghastly pit that made the blood freeze in his veins. Nevertheless he reacted a fraction of a second faster than the invisible gunner inside the tank. As the explosion of the cannon struck like a club against their ears, they were lying on the ground about ten feet away from the tank, pressing their faces into the moist earth. Behind them the trench vanished in a dark cloud of smoke. But even before the hail of earth stopped pelting down on his back, Steiner crawled forward on all fours. Between the crushed walls of the trench he discerned a narrow crack. He squeezed his body into it, closing his eyes as he did so. Thirty-four tons, he thought, thirty-four tons above me. And he crawled underneath the thirty-four tons, followed so closely by Krüger that he could feel the East Prussian's hands touching his legs. Every second he expected to hear the motor roar, he imagined he felt the masses of earth starting to shift, starting to crush his body. His head, arms and shoulders bumped and pushed desperately at some soft, dark obstacle in the way. Suddenly it gave. Then the ground sank beneath him and he took a fall of several yards. He lay motionless until a heavy body slammed into him and the sound of Krüger's voice made him open his eyes wide. Panting, trembling with exhaustion, they gaped at each other. They were lying in a deep bomb crater, and Steiner noticed that his hands were still clutching hard at the soft obstacle that had nearly stopped him. It was the body of a man, and felt strangely spongy. From neck to knees it was nothing but an empty, bloody sack. He let go and looked up, where the tank still stood unmoving. Then he saw that the right-hand track hung slack on the wheels, ripped in two. Steiner groped for his tommy-gun, which he had dropped in falling, and stood up. He noticed that Krüger no longer had his MG, but asked no questions. They clambered out of the crater, crawled into the trench and went on without turning their heads. They moved slowly. From somewhere on the hill came the sound of firing. Isolated shells whined high above their heads from left to right and right to left. But they paid no attention. They were utterly weary and had no feeling left at all.

They reached the fork where the branch trench led off to the battalion command post, without having run into any Russians. Their way led downhill now, and the sun shone warmly in their faces, but they scarcely felt it. Their legs moved as though no longer part of them; it was as if they were dead. But the sun shone warmly and it was a lovely spring day.

The men lay behind their rifles on the edge of the orchard. Their faces were marked by the experiences of the past several hours. Hollerbach was staring vacantly at Faber, who sat beside him with eyes closed. Kern, carrying a canteen, came up to them and tossed the canteen on the ground, muttering a curse under his breath. 'None?' Hollerbach asked.

Kern shook his head and dropped down beside them. 'Nobody has any,' he said grumpily. 'The water down there is too filthy for me. Corpses in it. I'd rather go thirsty.'

'We'll have to wait till the field kitchen gets here,' Hollerbach said.

Kern gave a fierce laugh. 'By the time it comes we won't need anything. By that time the whole battalion'll be able to feed out of one mess-tin.' He looked up the hill. 'They won't be coming any more,' he murmured. 'They should have been here long ago.' He turned to Faber. 'We should have looked for them.'

'It was too late,' Faber said. 'You know yourself it was too late. The Russians were in the trench and we were out of ammunition.'

'Not a round,' Kern said.

Hollerbach sighed. 'I never would have thought Steiner could get it,' he said. 'I still can't grasp it.'

'Neither can I,' Kern said blackly. 'A man like him should have realized what was happening.'

'Death isn't something you realize,' Faber said. 'It comes like the night. When the twilight falls among the trees, it's there already and you can't avoid it.'

'What a way to put it,' Kern said, strangely moved. He hunched his shoulders as if he were cold. Four men came by carrying a wounded soldier. His legs dangled at an odd angle over the edge of the canvas. They watched as the stretcher-bearers and their burden disappeared among the trees. Kern removed his steel helmet and scratched his head. He felt his mournful sense of loss deepening. And even now he was being pierced by the shock he had experienced when the tanks had appeared. He recalled how Faber had kept firing at the onrushing Russians until a man came dashing into the emplacement shouting that the Russians had broken into the trench on the right. For all that, Faber had stuck by the gun; they had not started to retreat until the last belt of ammunition had been fired. On the way they had encountered Hollerbach and his men, and had reached the battalion command post together. But neither Steiner nor Krüger had turned up. They would have to assume that the two were lying somewhere in the trench and would never return. The longer Kern thought about this, the more painful the dull throbbing in his chest became. Recollection of past ugly scenes between himself and both the missing men did nothing to abate his grief.

Suddenly Hollerbach produced a sound half-way between a squeal and a shout. Kern looked up in time to see him carrying on like a madman, jumping to his feet and throwing his hands in the air. Faber, too, was staring up the slope. Above them, in the chest-high communications trench, two figures appeared, trudging along with bowed heads as though there were nothing in the world that could ever arouse their interest again.

'Steiner,' Kern murmured incredulously. The orchard was suddenly full of excited men pressing forward, calling out to the two. Almost half an hour had passed since the last straggler had arrived at the command post; no one was expecting any more survivors. As Kern and Hollerbach rushed forward to meet them, someone brought news of the return of Sergeant Steiner to the commander's bunker. A staff courier promptly appeared with orders for Steiner to report to the commander's bunker at once. Steiner took his time. He exchanged a few words with Faber and the other men before following the courier down a lane of inquisitive faces.

When he entered the commander's bunker, he found Stransky bent over a map. Stransky's face looked aged and expressionless. Silently, he pointed to a chair. Steiner sat down. Arms clasped behind his back, Stransky strode about the bunker several times, finally halting in front of Steiner. 'You've come from up above?' he asked curtly.

Steiner nodded. He made an effort to conceal his dislike, and looked down at the floor.

'How do things look?' Stransky asked.

The question seemed pointless to Steiner. He shrugged apathetically and replied: 'Unchanged.'

'What does that mean?' Stransky asked sharply. His eyes became narrow and spiteful.

'The Russians are still holding our positions,' Steiner said quietly.

Stransky suppressed an angry retort. He went over to the map. 'We are going to undertake a counter-attack,' he declared. 'The purpose is to restore contact with the 3rd Battalion.' He outlined briefly the plan of the counter-attack. 'The Stukas ought to be along any minute now. I need a man to lead the counter-attack. Would you like to?'

Steiner had been expecting something of the sort and had already planned his answer. 'I don't think I would like to,' he said slowly. 'I don't believe I have the qualities needed to cope with such a situation.'

Stransky turned abruptly, stalked to the door and looked out of the little window for a few seconds.

'You are forgetting one thing,' he said over his shoulder. 'You forget the fact that actually it doesn't matter at all to me whether or not you would like to. May I suggest that you examine your mind to see what, if anything, justifies your attitude.'

'What makes you think that I haven't done that?' Steiner asked coolly.

Stransky leaned his back against the door. 'I make that assumption because of your total lack of discipline and——' he hesitated. Then he went on: 'And because young people do not take the trouble to think when they know that if need be, someone else will do that thinking for them.'

Steiner frowned.

'I don't understand.'

'I can put it more clearly,' Stransky said scornfully. 'You need not be honest toward me. I am quite accustomed to having my subordinates lie to my face. But for once be honest with yourself.'

Not knowing what he was getting at, Steiner shrugged impatiently. 'I try,' he said, somewhat contemptuously.

'Good. Then perhaps you can answer this question: isn't your display of independence based simply on the fact that you have—I'll put the thing in terms of civilian life—that you have an influential uncle.'

As Steiner started to rise angrily, Stransky raised his hand quickly. 'No one likes to be reminded that his so-called individualism depends on having powerful backing——'

Having delivered that insult, he fell silent. Steiner leaped to his feet and stared balefully at him. 'You wanted to talk about the counter-attack,' he said loudly.

'Right,' Stransky said. 'I'm coming to that in a moment. You see, Steiner, even if we did have something in common, there is one highly essential difference between us.'

'Your rank,' Steiner interjected.

Stransky smiled superciliously. 'I was not referring to that,' he said quietly. 'If I were to proceed from that angle, I assure you that our conversation would take an entirely different course. I have already told you, and I should like to repeat with emphasis, that you overestimate yourself. Granted, you have had luck so far, and you have connections which stiffen your backbone. But there's no personal merit in that and it doesn't raise you above the average. I assure you, in spite of your connections, I could apply pressure that would make your life thoroughly miserable.'

'Then why don't you try?' Steiner asked slowly.

Stransky grimaced, but his voice remained patronizing. 'You are very young. I don't doubt that in my position you would not hesitate to throw into the scales your authority as a superior officer. The fact that I forbear ought to give you something to think about. Perhaps this alone demonstrates the nature of the difference between us.'

Steiner regarded his amiable face with distrust. Then he laughed aloud. 'You overlook a few facts. In the first place, those good connections you harp on didn't come about by chance and are not unmerited. In the second place, I never angled for them and have made a point of never making use of them. If I had, you would scarcely have any chance to give me orders at all. As for——'

He broke off. Stransky had raised his hand for silence. A low drone filled the bunker. 'The Stukas,' Stransky said hurriedly.

'We'll have to continue our conversation some other time. Look here.' He bent over the maps and sketched briefly the details of the counter-attack. 'When you reach the hill,' he went on, 'wait until the assault regiment arrives and follow behind it into your old positions. All clear?'

Since the bombing began at that moment, Steiner merely nodded briefly and left the bunker. The men were standing in a knot staring up at the hill, where a dark cloud of smoke was mounting to the sky.

Steiner stood for a few seconds watching the planes dive vertically and release their bombs. The sight gave him grim pleasure, and he clenched his fists. For Meyer, he thought, for Meyer and Pasternack and Dorn and all the others lying dead up there.

A loud voice reached his ear. As he turned his head he saw Krüger striding toward him. 'What's up?' the East Prussian asked.

'Shit.' Steiner growled, and ordered Krüger to assemble all the NCO's. When they were gathered around him, he explained what they were to do and began dividing up tasks among the various platoons. Then he turned to Krüger, who stood gloomily plucking at his nose, and said: 'You stay near me. You and Hollerbach and Kern and Faber.'

'The bastards,' Krüger cursed fiercely. 'They don't give a man ten minutes rest.'

'When you've got six feet of ground over you you'll have more rest than you like,' Steiner said mirthlessly.

He looked over the group of about a hundred men. They were holding their weapons, and intent on the signal from him. Raising his hand, he started up the slope. As the hum of aeroplane engines faded away in the west, the men spread out in a skirmishing line and followed the point group up the hill over the shell-torn terrain. Not a shot had been fired yet. Steiner walked with bowed head, wondering what they would do if a Russian tank turned up. Although most of the tanks were undoubtedly somewhere beyond Kanskoye, raising cain in that area, there might still be a few stragglers on the hill. Even one would be enough. Steiner had no illusions about that; he knew that the men, exhausted as they were and with their morale at zero, would run back in wild flight at the first sound of motors.

As he circuited a large crater, Hollerbach came over to him. He had evidently been considering the same question. 'What are you going to do if tanks come?' he asked, with a testy note of challenge in his voice.

Steiner shrugged indifferently. 'How do I know?'

The hill was steep, and they panted with the climb, but the top was now slowly drawing nearer. Steiner glanced back to reassure himself that the men were following, and for a moment he felt a grim satisfaction and pride that he was leading the whole battalion. Then he grinned ironically. He had no more than half a company there behind him. For a few seconds he thought of Stransky; it should have been the captain who was heading the line, not some low-down platoon leader. Remembering their talks, he smiled cynically. The conceit of the bastard, he thought with infinite contempt. The hill was flattening out and they could already see part of their old positions, which ran along the hill on the left. Nowhere was there any sign of life. It looked as if the Russians had long ago advanced behind the hill, further to the west. There was hardly any incline now, and they speeded up.

'They'll start shooting in a minute,' Krüger panted. As though set off by his words, violent sounds of skirmishing suddenly broke out far ahead of them. They stood still and looked around. The scorched earth, still covered by swaths of smoke in many places, seemed to stretch on all the way to the horizon, where several white flares were now rising.

'That's the Third,' Steiner said. And in answer to Krüger's uncomprehending look he explained: 'The 3rd Battalion is attacking from the other side of the hill. We must send up flares.' He took the pistol from Faber's hand and shot up two flares in succession. Looking back, he saw far below the orchard where the command post was situated. Behind stretched the long ridge on whose other side the regimental command post must lie. The sky was quite cloudless; visibility was splendid back that way.

The noise of fighting to the north increased. Most of the men had dropped into shell-holes, their steel helmets protruding above the ground like huge dark mushrooms. 'What are we waiting for?' Krüger asked, looking down uncomfortably at the barren moonscape beneath their feet.

Kern was sitting on the ground, his legs dangling over the edge of a bomb crater. Faber, crouching somewhat, was standing beside Hollerbach, leaning on the machine-gun.

'Why the hell should we pull the others' chestnuts out of the fire,' Kern growled. 'What's the sense of rushing on.' He turned to Steiner. 'We've reached the top; we can wait here until the men of the Third get to us.'

There was something tempting about the proposal. The men looked at one another significantly. 'If we go on,' Hollerbach said, 'they're going to see us from the woods, and then there'll be hell to pay.'

Steiner turned his head indecisively. Kern kept close watch on him. He had made up his mind to disappear into a shell-hole at the first shot and wait until the fighting was over. He'd had more than enough for the day; a man should not push his luck too long.

'I tell you what,' he went on when the others remained silent. 'It seems to me we've carried out our orders, and now they can just stick it, the goddamned idiots. What the hell do they think they're doing, sending us against tanks without anti-tank guns.'

Faber, listening in silence, had been watching two of 1st Company's NCO's. They were sitting about a dozen paces away, taking in the whole incident. He suddenly had the uncomfortable feeling that they were amused by Steiner's indecision. He thumbed his steel helmet back on his head. 'I think we'd better go on,' he said quietly, indicating with a half-gesture the sounds of battle. 'We've got to help them, and those are our orders.'

Steiner frowned. 'You don't have to tell me what our orders are,' he said hoarsely. 'Are we on top of the hill or aren't we?'

'We aren't,' Faber replied firmly, and Steiner thought he detected a trace of disdain in the woodsman's blue eyes. He opened his mouth for a retort. But then he set his lips, turned his back on Faber and started forward, making huge strides, toward the sounds of fighting. Faber and Hollerbach followed him at once; Krüger remained standing, looking after them with annoyance. But when he saw the other men clambering out of their holes, he turned to Kern. 'Let's go.'

'I'll be along,' Kern growled, not stirring.

Krüger took a step closer and glared down at him. 'Aiming to be a slacker, eh?'

'None of your business,' Kern replied rebelliously. But he

picked himself up, pounded the dust from his trousers and cursed furiously. 'Trouble with you bastards is, you can't wait till you're dead,' he wound up grimly.

'I'll be glad to have it over with,' Krüger said.

They joined a group of men who were moving forward slowly, crouching low. Kern's rage evaporated. His face had grown grey with fear, but he kept close beside Krüger, who moved along with bowed head as though nothing mattered. They advanced several hundred yards. With growing alarm Kern noted that with every step the horizon around them moved back several kilometres. He did not dare to turn his head because he knew that they were now visible from the edge of the woods, where the Russians had their artillery emplaced. For a while he clung to the desperate hope that the Russian artillery observers would, from the distance, be unable to distinguish the German infantry from their own men. But he felt like a man walking naked in front of a crowd. Although there were several dozen others all around him, it was as if he were entirely alone, a solitary target for the Russians. Suddenly he stopped dead. In the distance a series of dull explosions sounded; instinctively he bent his back. Then there was a howl over their heads, dark mushrooms of smoke burst up out of the earth, and they lay pressed against the ground with their eyes closed in terror. Steiner dived into a crater beside Hollerbach. It seemed likely that they were in for a long and systematic shelling. Suddenly he recalled that Fetscher had once insisted that shells never struck twice in the same place. Nonsense. But then he began listening alertly. As suddenly as it had begun, the shelling stopped. It took Steiner a while to credit it. Still sceptical, not trusting the quiet, he clambered out of the hole. But when nothing happened, he tore into action. Even before the thick veil of dust and smoke could disperse, he shouted to the men at the top of his voice. Seconds later they were running after him, taking grotesque leaps over obstacles.

The encounter with the Russians was a surprise to both sides. Unexpectedly, the ground suddenly sloped off to the north, and as Steiner and his men reached the top of the hill, they stood still for a few seconds, staring at the scene before them. The steep slope below them was, like all the rest of the terrain, pocked with innumerable shell-holes. Almost all of these were occupied by Russians. They lay side by side, firing steadily at some invisible enemy further down the slope below them. The sight of those backs turned unsuspectingly toward the top of the hill was so utterly fantastic against the vaporous background that the men were momentarily stunned. They stood in a long chain on the edge of the incline, utterly motionless. Then, out of the corners of his eyes Steiner observed Faber setting up the heavy MG with almost reverential care. He crouched down behind it. The others came to life also. When Steiner raised his fist into the air, a deafening roar of concentrated rifle and machine-gun fire rolled like an avalanche. down the slope. Steiner had time to notice the Russians turn around in their holes and throw agonized glances up the slope, while below them a white flare rose triumphantly. While he blindly emptied his magazine he felt an intoxicating, nameless gratification that made him forget to take cover. When the painful blow twisted his body around in a quarter turn, he did not become aware of its meaning until the sub-machine-gun dropped from his hands and a cry of alarm reached his ears. He staggered back, sank to his knees with face contorted by pain, and grasped his right shoulder. Krüger was at his side in a moment. Anxiously, he bent over Steiner and shouted something which was lost in the din of the firing. Hollerbach and Kern came rushing over. They carried him back several dozen yards and laid him on the ground with infinite care. 'Is it bad?' Krüger asked worriedly. Steiner shook his head. He felt the need to reassure them. 'Flesh wound or something,' he said tightly, looking at his shoulder, where his tunic was gradually darkening. The pain was bearable, but he had a queerly numbed feeling in the whole top part of his body.

Up ahead the men of the battalion had vanished as though a sudden gust of wind had blown them down the slope. He recalled that it was his duty to lead the attack. But before he could say anything, loud shouts, then cheers came from down below. 'Got them,' Krüger exclaimed. He raced ahead to the spot where Faber was still lying behind his MG, and peered down the slope. 'They've met the Third,' he shouted back. 'You ought to see the Ivans with their hands up.' After a while he returned. 'We'll have you at a dressing station in a shot,' he said to Steiner. 'But first let's see what you've got.'

Carefully, they removed the tunic and cut open the blood-soaked shirt. 'Shoulder wound,' Krüger delivered his verdict. 'The bullet must still be in there. Let's hope it didn't touch the bone.'

They put an emergency bandage on the rapidly bleeding wound. Steiner's face was grey, but he was able to stand on his feet fairly well. While Krüger and Kern supported him on both sides, Hollerback picked up his light assault pack, slung the Russian tommygun over his shoulder and followed them. Since they did not want to go back by the exposed route over the hill, they cautiously descended the slope where the men had their hands full gathering in the prisoners. Within a few minutes they reached the 3rd Battalion's command post. Only then did they notice that Faber had trailed along with them.

Krüger turned to one of the men hastening past and found out that the dressing station was in a hollow a few hundred yards further to the west. As they walked on, Steiner reflected with satisfaction that the counter-attack had been a complete success. They could set up the switch position now and wait quietly for the assault regiment to arrive. He felt somewhat better; aside from the dull throbbing in his shoulder, he was all right. The terrain before them began to drop. Shortly afterwards they came upon the dressing station bunker, hidden in the midst of dense shrubbery. Several men with minor wounds, wearing white bandages on their heads or arms, were standing or sitting around.

Steiner's shoulder was freshly bandaged. The doctor advised him to wait here until darkness, since it was inadvisable to take the risk of going on to the clearing station while Russian tanks were prowling around. 'I'll just give you an injection,' he said, 'and you can go back tonight with our supply truck. They've established the clearing station in Kanskoye for the past hour.'

Steiner hesitated. Then he shook his head. 'I'd rather get started right away,' he said. 'I can manage the walk to Kanskoye.'

'You'll have to go over the hill,' the doctor warned.

'I know. But I'll try it over to this side, and further to the rear.'

'As you like. You need only follow the brook till it turns north, and then go straight over the hill. You can't miss the way.' He nodded and returned to the bunker.

Steiner turned to his men, who were standing gloomily around, looking down at the floor.

'I'll be back soon,' he assured them. 'Don't put on such expressions. You're really glad to be rid of me!'

'Who's glad?' Krüger demanded loudly, plucking furiously at his nose.

Steiner grinned. 'You more than anybody.'

Krüger gasped angrily and shouted: 'Me!'

'Yes.'

'Take it easy,' Hollerbach advised. But Krüger was working himself up into a rage. 'You know what you can do for me?' he bellowed still louder.

Steiner nodded. 'You'd love it, wouldn't you?' he said amiably.

Hissing between his teeth, Krüger turned and stalked away past the medical bunker. He disappeared in the bushes.

'You shouldn't have said that,' Hollerbach reproached him.

'Rot,' Steiner replied, himself a bit irritated. 'He's as thin-skinned as a girl, but in five minutes he forgets all about it.' He turned to Faber, who was standing, silent and grave, beside them. 'If I get back to Freiburg,' he said to him, 'I can look up your family. Shall I?'

'They'd be glad,' Faber replied. 'Tell them not to worry about me. And if you see Barbara, say hello to her for me.'

'Who is she? Your girl?'

A faint, mischievous grin passed over Faber's face as he answered: 'A birch, a sapling birch.'

It was hot and still now, as if there were no war at all, no Hill 121.4. A narrow stream wound westward, through green bushes, and the landscape stretched on for mile upon mile. Steiner felt the sadness of parting as if it were a harmless but troublesome disease. You never ger used to it, he thought. It's always the same and always new. He stretched his good arm. 'Maybe I'll meet Schnurr-bart somewhere. If he comes back before me, tell him to look after all you babies.' He hesitated. Then, impatience and emotion in his voice, he began rapidly shaking hands all around. Hollerbach offered to accompany him to Kanskoye.

'Drop us a line once in a while,' Kern said. His watery eyes were sad. With surprise Steiner saw that the corners of his mouth were twitching. He turned rapidly away.

Krüger was waiting for him and Hollerbach a short distance away, glowering fiercely at Steiner.

'You can bring something for me. When you come back, I mean.'

'A gravestone?' Steiner asked.

Krüger curled his upper lip, exposing his fine set of teeth. 'I'll get one of those for you some day,' he retorted. 'No, I mean something else. You can bring me a bottle of Cologne water.'

'What for?' Steiner asked suspiciously.

'Just in case we have to live in the same bunker again,' Krüger replied, covering his mouth with the back of his hand.

Steiner nodded. 'You mean because my nose is so sensitive?'

'Who's talking about your nose?' Krüger growled.

Steiner shrugged. 'Well, you know,' he said innocently, 'they say people can't smell themselves.'

There was no answer to that one. 'You have no idea what a relief it'll be not to have to see you for a while,' Krüger said malevolently.

Hollerbach chuckled in advance and looked at Steiner, who delivered his calm reply: 'No, you're wrong, I do have an idea. I so often feel the same way myself.'

Before Krüger could speak again, Steiner started off. 'Take it easy,' he called loudly.

Krüger stood looking after them. They had gone quite a way before he funnelled his hands over his mouth and shouted: 'Come back soon.' Steiner raised his sound arm and waved.

For a long while Steiner and Hollerbach walked in silence side by side. Hollerbach glanced at him now and then. He's tough, he was thinking, to be able to walk this distance with his wound. After a while he caught himself wishing that he himself would not have to go back.

'I'd like to be going with you,' he said.

'Where to?' Steiner asked.

'Home, of course.'

They slowed their pace. Steiner looked off toward the hills. 'Home?' he repeated softly. 'Where is that?'

'What do you mean?'

'Do you know where your home is?' he asked.

'I'm not an idiot.'

'That's a moot question.' Steiner grinned. Then he became serious again. 'You're at home where you're happy, isn't that so?'

'Of course.'

'And were you happy at home, really happy?'

Hollerbach hesitated. Steiner nodded. 'So you weren't. Being at home is nothing more than crude habit and the pitiable knowledge that we don't have to worry where we're going to spend the night.

It's being with a few people you like, and when you lose those few, you can't stand the place any more because everything around you reminds you of them. And being at home means giving up voluntarily all the things you don't have at home. It's the damned commonplaceness of existence and an infernal mirror that shows you the wrinkles coming in your face. Believe me, of all the illusions in our lives the biggest is the idea that somewhere is home for us. There isn't any place really where you can keep your balance without dancing like a tightrope walker. Do you see what I mean?'

'No,' Hollerbach said.

Steiner frowned. 'No wonder. There's a lousy clever system in it. From childhood on they put blinkers on us so we won't see to either side of us. Every time, just before you're about to see, they toss you a bone like you were a dog. You can sink your teeth into that and forget about it all for a while. The older you get and the more demanding you become, the bigger the bone. But when the time comes that you're sick of it all—school, job and so on— then they throw you the biggest bone of all. That's the one that really does the trick; it's guaranteed to wear your teeth down because it keeps you busy even in bed, so that you don't have a minute to spare to think about other things. Ah . . .' He waved his sound arm disgustedly.

'What is it you really want?' Hollerbach asked.

'I don't know,' Steiner answered tonelessly. 'You always think you no longer have any illusions. But believe me, the biggest illusion of all is believing you're without illusions.'

They had covered somewhat more than a mile by now, and his shoulder was beginning to ache viciously again. They ought to be level with Kanskoye soon, and it was getting to be time to cross over the hill. He looked up along the road, marked by the tracks of innumerable vehicles. It ran almost due west and disappeared in the distance beyond a gentle undulation in the landscape. Probably it led to Kanskoye, swinging in a big arc around the hill. On their left, about twenty yards away, the brook turned sharply off toward the north and appeared to lose itself in an endless plain. This must be the spot the doctor had mentioned. Steiner came to a stop and looked up the hill.

'What's the matter?' Hollerbach asked, wiping the sweat from his brow.

'We have to cross over here,' Steiner said. 'But let's have a cigarette first.'

They dropped to the ground where they were, and Steiner swung off his tunic, which he had hanging loosely over his back. He was glad to see that the bandage was not yet soaked through with blood. As they lit their cigarettes, Hollerbach looked down at the ground with a troubled expression.

'I'm not sure I follow you,' he said. 'You're always talking about somebody tossing us bones. Who the devil is this "they" of yours?'

'If I knew that, I'd know everything,' Steiner replied. 'But it isn't something you can prove; you just believe it or don't. Maybe some day I'll get to the bottom of it.'

He looked at the other man. Hollerbach's face was flushed and dirty. He had removed his steel helmet and his blond hair straggled over his forehead. How little I know about him, Steiner thought suddenly. We never have time for each other; we lie in the same mud for three years and hardly know more than each other's names. It's a shame.

'It's a shame,' Hollerbach said.

Steiner grinned at the apparent harmony of their thoughts and asked: 'What?'

'It's all a shame,' Hollerbach explained. 'Everything. In the old days I always wanted to get away from Mudau, my home town, and now I'm away from it and I wish I were back. Then when I think of working my arse off for the lousy railway, I'm not so sure. Why the hell does it have to be like that?'

'It's always a mistake to do more thinking than we're supposed to,' Steiner said thoughtfully. He felt his shoulder and went on: 'They say man is the perfect creature when he's nothing more than a pretty poor compromise between an animal and something better than himself. A contradiction, dreaming of nectar and ambrosia and eating pig's flesh, talking about love—and whoring around every chance he gets, talking about goodness—and being beastly to the other fellow. Not much good.'

He suddenly felt no inclination to go on with the discussion, and frowned into the distance. Hollerbach started to answer. But at that moment a succession of violent crashes sounded behind them. The rolling echo rumbled above their heads, weird and heart-stopping. 'Tanks,' Hollerbach exclaimed.

Steiner nodded. They sat motionless, listening. Those first explosions seemed only the beginning of a regular battle. The cannonade grew in intensity, and interspersed between the louder explosions came the crackle of rifle fire. 'That must be the assault regiment,' Steiner said. He recalled Stransky's mentioning anti-tank guns.

They could hear motors now also. Hollerbach glanced over at the underbush that grew beside the brook. It would afford good cover. But they sat still, staring up the hill. From where they sat they could see only a little of it because the initially steep slope flattened out somewhat higher up.

By the time they saw the Russian tank tearing down the slope, it was less than two hundred feet away. Steiner uttered a warning cry, turned instantly and made for the underbrush as fast as his legs could carry him. Hollerbach followed at once. But he had taken only a few steps when he remembered Steiner's pack still lying where they had been sitting. He turned, snatched it up and then ran with desperate leaps after Steiner. He saw that Steiner had come within a few yards of the brook and wanted to shout to him to stick to the left, where the brush was somewhat thicker. At that moment a shattering roar sounded behind him; the earth burst open and he plunged to the ground like a felled tree. He could feel nothing at all, but was still conscious. His eyes remained open and he saw Steiner stop abruptly, turn and stare toward him. And he shouted to him to go on running and throw himself into the brook. But although he shouted as loudly as he could, he was unable to hear his own voice, and astonishment at this fact occupied his mind so completely for the next few seconds that he forgot everything else. His attentiveness returned only when Steiner's figure disappeared behind a cloud of smoke that suddenly appeared between them as though fallen from the sky. Then he saw that Steiner was lying on the ground and behaving strangely. He seemed to be crawling like a crab, and it struck Hollerbach as astonishing that he was not moving forward so much as a yard. It looked so funny that he giggled. Then it occurred to him that there was a stillness all about. He turned his head, and his eyes froze.

Steiner, too, was quite conscious. Although he felt as though every inch of his body had been pierced by splinters, and although he was quite faint with pain, he tried to crawl over the ground toward the motionless Hollerbach. He was completely unaware of the senselessness of his efforts. From the moment he had seen the advancing tank heading straight toward the helpless Hollerbach, he had lost all sense of what he was doing; he writhed like a madman, eyes popping, foam dribbling from his mouth. His arms and legs flailed wildly around his body like ripples around a point where a stone has been thrown into water, self-consuming and ineffectual. At last he lay still like a body already dead, only his eyes burning in a white face. The tank had approached within ten yards of the motionless body, and Steiner saw Hollerbach turn his head. Then Steiner opened his mouth and screamed. He screamed so that the land heaved and a storm rose that carried the hills before it as though they were skyscraper-high waves of water stretching from horizon to horizon. When he looked up he saw the space between sky and earth beginning to fill, darkening with a horde of withered leaves that whirled closer and closer and showered down upon him like snow. He saw without seeing the tank pass over Hollerbach's twitching body, mashing it into the ground and leaving a bloody track upon the hard soil as it moved off toward the east. The landscape lay unchanged under the hot noonday sun. Only where the bushes crowded up against the narrow stream a few paces beyond Steiner's still body a few dry leaves were strewn, and beyond the underbrush there yawned between sky and earth a fearful void.

XI

Somewhere in the East.

DEAR ROLF,

I am sitting on an old sandbar, tanned like a South Sea islander, dangling my feet in the water. And those feet need it, by God. Last night a Russian gunboat tried to make a landing. Krüger happened to be on guard and drove it off with his carbine. So he says. He spent two hours diving today and found two old leather boots, both of them for the left foot. Krüger insists they belonged to the captain and first mate of the boat. We chucked them back into the water. (The boots, of course.) It's about time you were coming back. For the past three weeks we've been stationed here on the Black Sea, heroically battling against boredom. We snooze all day long, and sleep all night. What a life, I tell you. It's a pity you're not with us. None of these birds can play chess, just when we'd have plenty of time for it. Have I written you that Maag is back again? He really stuffed his belly while he was back home; he's put on lots of weight. Faber looked at his calendar yesterday and discovered that it's exactly three months since you were wounded. Time flies. This is all for now. Writing a letter in this heat is tough work. Krüger and Kern are looking over my shoulder and both of them say I have a handwriting like an old goat. But my beautiful style makes up for it, don't you think? Keep well and watch out that they don't pick you up and stick you in some other unit when you start back for here. Things are supposed to be pretty hot back on the main front. All the best.

Your old friend

SCHNURRBART

Steiner's hands holding the letter sank to his lap. He looked out of the train window. Three months, he thought. It seemed to him that ten times three months had passed. Thrusting the letter back into his breast pocket, he closed his eyes. He had been wounded at the beginning of May, and now the hot August sun was searing down upon the parched earth of the bridgehead. He had hoped the division would be in the Crimea by the time he returned to it. But although the front in the north was daily shifting further to the west, although the situation was growing more precarious with every passing moment, no move had been made to abandon the Kuban bridgehead. More and more people were predicting another Stalingrad. He looked out of the window again, abstractedly watching the telegraph poles sweep by. The monotonous song of the wheels on the rails was lulling. Most of the other men in the compartment were sitting with heads drooping, eyes closed, slumped into queer positions on the uncomfortable seats. In a state half-way between sleeping and waking and dreaming of the end of this interminable trip—he had been travelling for almost ten days now—he went over the events of the past three months.

He recalled the moment when he had come to again in one of the dirty cots at the clearing station—the first stage of his journey back home to Germany. He had never learned how he had got there. Perhaps some men of the 3rd Battalion had picked him up that evening. During the night he was operated on, and when he awoke again from deep anæsthesia he was already on the way to a field hospital. Two days later he was sent in a hospital train non-stop as far as Przemysl and ended his journey in a hospital back home in Passau.

He had recovered with surprising speed. The nasty splinter wounds all over his chest, arms and legs had begun to heal without complications. Nor did the wound in his shoulder prove troublesome.

About a month after his arrival in the hospital, the first letter from Schnurrbart had come, reporting with disappointment that he had not got as far as Germany. Schnurrbart's wound had only been good for a trip to Odessa, and a month later he had been sent back to the division as fit for service. He wrote that the attack of the assault regiment had been stopped by Russian artillery fire and the line now ran definitively straight across the hill. He spoke of rumours of relief, of new replacements and a new company commander, and said that all they needed to hold the bridgehead was Steiner's presence.

Three more letters had come from him since. The rumour was confirmed and the division moved to quiet positions on the coast for a few weeks rest. The last letter, the one Steiner had just been reading, had reached him on the day of his departure. When he reached Kerch, he learned that the division had meanwhile been transferred to Novorosisk. There could only be a few miles more to go. The big, boxlike passenger car had poor springs and Steiner was often startled out of his thoughts when the wheels thumped hard over switches, or when a shrill whistle from the locomotive shrieked through the glassless windows.

He studied the faces of his fellow travellers. All of them seemed to be veteran soldiers, probably returning from leave to judge by the indifference with which they occasionally opened their eyes and glanced out of the window, only to slip back into a doze again. Slumped in the corner opposite Steiner sat a corporal. He, too, had his eyes closed, and with every jerk of the train his head bobbed about on a neck of unusual length, as though on a coil spring. His big-boned face looked weary and lifeless.

Suddenly he opened his eyes and their glances met. 'We should be almost there,' Steiner said.

Stretching, the man threw a look out of the window. Then he nodded. 'Another ten minutes.' He yawned. 'We're coming to a long tunnel now,' he added. 'Once we're through that, we're there.'

'Have you often come this way?' Steiner asked.

'Yes. Courier.'

Steiner regarded him with interest. Nice job, he thought; I'd like that. 'Is the station in town?' he asked.

The man grimaced. 'Station is good. You'll have an hour's walk into town. But the road is good, and if you're lucky some truck will pick you up.'

'What's the place like?' Steiner asked. 'This is my first time there,' he explained.

The corporal shrugged. 'A nice quiet position. The main thing is there's plenty of champagne. All you can drink.'

'Champagne!' Steiner exclaimed in amazement.

The man nodded. 'Haven't you heard about it? Tremendous champagne vaults there. The war could go on for ten years before the stuff is drunk up.'

'I'd just as soon it didn't,' Steiner replied dryly.

The locomotive let loose two piercing whistles. 'The tunnel,' the corporal said. 'Here we are.' He stood up and reached his things down from the baggage rack. Steiner followed his example. The others in the compartment started up, dazed from sleep, and foraged for their baggage. A moment later they rolled into the tunnel and everything grew dark. When daylight flooded in through the windows again, the train braked swiftly and finally came to a stop with a sharp jerk. The men tumbled over one another and cursed. 'They act as if they've got cattle aboard,' one man said. The man at his side laughed. 'What else do you think we are?'

Steiner opened the door and jumped to the platform. Since he wanted to shake off the corporal, he pressed rapidly through the crowd to the barrier. After his pass was checked, he stood for a moment and looked around. The railroad station consisted of a few small buildings. To judge by the many trucks, the place must have been a shunting yard. He glanced back at the train. The locomotive was being uncoupled, and for a moment he felt a faint stabbling sensation in the pit of his stomach. He took several deep breaths. This is the way you wanted it, he told himself. You could be back home in Freiburg now if you had not refused to take a convalescent leave.

He started off rapidly down the road, and in a few minutes had left the last of the buildings behind. The road led straight westward, and he hit a smart pace. Apparently the corporal had not exaggerated. The highway was flanked by vineyards. The ripe grapes were of a size and sweetness he had tasted only once before, in southern France. Again and again he stopped to pick some. Looking around, he saw the rest of the train's passengers following in loose formation. He walked faster. Here and there, between the green of the grapevines, gleamed the white-painted walls of a small house. Everything about the region seemed neat and orderly; it was more like the landscape south of the Loire than anything he had seen before in Russia. The scent of the nearby sea was unmistakable and grew steadily stronger as he approached closer to his destination. Silhouettes overcast with a yellowish shimmer gradually emerged out of the bright-blue mist on the horizon. Later he was able to see them as the precipitous slopes of a mountain range. He stretched his head forward and peered, trying to make out details. He was so absorbed in looking that he did not hear a truck bearing down on him from behind, and stood still only when a loud voice reached his ears. The truck stopped a few feet away from him and a good-natured face under a forage cap appeared at the window. 'Where to?' the man called out.

'Freiburg,' Steiner said.

Without a flicker of a smile, the man opened the door. 'That's where I'm going. Climb in.'

Steiner shifted his pack from his back and clambered up to the seat. 'I don't usually give rides,' the man explained as he shifted gears. The truck started forward. 'Not that I'm hard-hearted,' he went on. 'But I've been careful ever since a couple of bastards snitched two boxes of sausage from me.'

'Are you in the supply train?' Steiner asked.

'Yes, I'm sorry to say.'

'Why are you sorry?'

The driver laughed. 'You've got no idea all the responsibility and trouble we have.'

'Why don't you transfer?' Steiner said.

'Where to?'

'To us. We just sleep in nice warm bunkers.'

The man laughed again. 'I'm not as mad as that. It's no good wherever you are. The devil take this army.'

The houses to either side of the road were becoming more numerous. Apparently these were the outskirts of the town. Steiner leaned out of the window. The road led gently uphill, and when they reached the top he saw the sea before him. The memory wrenched so hard that he pressed his hands against his heart. Two weeks ago he had imagined that it was all over and done with, that he had come to terms with it, and now he realized how he had been deceiving himself.

He tried to distract his mind by studying the view of the city. The mountainous coastline formed a deep indentation, and the city spread out around this bay in a semicircle. The terraced construction reminded him of Zurich. Most of the houses were painted white.

The driver's voice startled him out of his thoughts. 'Last week the civilians were evacuated,' the man told him. 'A pity, too— you should have seen the women that lived here.' He discussed this for a while, then asked about Steiner's unit. 'You'll have to get out here,' he said. 'First street to the right. They're posted down near the waterfront, I think.' He stepped on the brake.

Steiner offered him a packet of cigarettes, but he waved this aside. 'Hell, all the supplies pass through our hands. Good luck.'

Steiner watched the truck until it turned a corner. The houses, some of them as much as four stories high, were quiet in the hot noonday sun. His nailed boots thumped loudly on the deserted street. On the way he met an MP and asked directions.

The company was quartered in a neat row of houses near the waterfront. Steiner encountered a man who, as soon as he saw him, clicked his heels and raised his hand to his cap. Steiner stopped and asked: 'Where do you belong?'

'Second Company,' the man replied.

Steiner looked him over. He had never seen him before. 'What platoon?' he asked.

'Second platoon.'

It seemed odd to Steiner to be speaking with a man of his own platoon, who was a stranger. Dropping his official tone he asked: 'What is your platoon leader's name?'

The answer was snapped out like a pistol shot: 'Corporal Schnurrbart, sir.'

With difficulty Steiner repressed a grin. Schnurrbart's real name was evidently lost for good and all. He asked the man to take him to Corporal Schnurrbart.

The houses were set in the midst of small yards, ringed by walls and fences. The man led Steiner to one such green-fenced dwelling which was Corporal Schnurrbart's. The yard was planted with fruit trees which might have been battered by a hurricane, so ripped were their leaves. The flower beds were thick with weeds; only the gravel-strewn paths looked tended. Steiner slowly opened the chest-high gate and entered the yard, walking on tiptoe, careful not to make any loud noises. Seeing the front door of the house closed, he walked a few paces past it. As he turned the corner, he stopped abruptly. On a bench, facing the water which was about a hundred yards away, sat Schnurrbart, his face to the sun, his eyes closed, his pipe inevitably in his mouth. He looked as if he had been sitting there for ever, and he looked as he had always looked, thin, wiry, heavily bearded. Steiner felt his heart thumping; he smiled and wiped his eyes. Till this moment he had never realized how fond he was of Schnurrbart. Quietly, he went over to him, slipped the pack from his back and sat down on the bench beside the other man. Dropping his arms over the back of the seat, he looked at Schnurrbart's face from the side. Schnurrbart did not open his eyes. He took the pipe from his mouth, threw his head back a little and said: 'Have you men had a good rest?'

'Yes,' Steiner said, watching his face. At first it showed no change. Then suddenly all his features began to move. He blinked opened his eyes slowly and turned his head. They looked at one another, silently, searchingly, with unnatural calm. Finally Schnurrbart turned his face back to the water and said: 'In this weather the fish bite.'

Steiner nodded. There was a long pause. The garden sloped down toward the water's edge, and beyond the green pickets of the fence piers stretched out into the oily surface of the sea.

'Although,' Schnurrbart commented, 'when it rains they bite too.'

Steiner yawned ostentatiously, holding his hand over his mouth.

'In point of fact, they bite in all weathers,' Schnurrbart said stubbornly.

'No doubt about it,' Steiner murmured. He felt very content.

'We weren't expecting you yet,' Schnurrbart said abruptly. 'How was it back home?'

Steiner reached into his breast pocket and after some fumbling brought out a sheet of paper. He placed it on Schnurrbart's lap. 'Read that,' he said tersely.

The letter was short. 'Dear Rolf,' Schnurrbart read, 'I am sure you will not understand my behaviour, but I could not help myself. When we first met in the canteen, I was very angry with you. Then I felt pity for you, and later I loved you. I hoped that some day I would be able to free myself. You see, Rolf, I'm married and I thought I loved my husband. It was a proxy wedding, because he wanted it so much. After that last night together I decided firmly to get a divorce. But a week afterwards word came that my husband had been seriously wounded. They have had to amputate his right leg. I struggled with myself, but now I know that I have no right to leave him. Please don't think too badly of me. I was not honest with you, but I loved you and couldn't bear to lose you. Forgive me. Gertrud.'

Schnurrbart handed the letter back. Steiner was staring vacantly across the water. 'So her name was Gertrud,' Schnurrbart said after a while.

Steiner nodded.

'Where did you meet her?'

'In Gursuf.'

Schnurrbart looked up in surprise. 'In Gursuf, of all places. And why didn't you go back home?'

'How do you know I didn't?'

'You wouldn't be here so soon if you had,' Schnurrbart replied with assurance.

Steiner leaned forward, propping his arms on his thighs and letting his head droop. 'What would I do at home?' he asked wearily. 'After I received that letter at the hospital, I didn't feel like it.'

Again it occurred to Schnurrbart that Steiner had never spoken of his family. But he did not dare to ask about it, and the opportunity passed when Steiner suddenly changed the subject and asked about Krüger and Kern.

'They're snoozing,' Schnurrbart said. 'Taking their siesta. Since we've been here I've never seen either of them really awake.' Schnurrbart then imparted some general information: that he was sharing this house with Krüger; that Kern, Faber and Maag were quartered next door. Stransky was trying to introduce regular barracks discipline and drill. The new company commander, Lieutenant März, had been raised on dynamite. When Steiner asked about the front, he jerked his thumb to point across the bay. 'We're dug in out over there, half-way to the right, near the big factory. With binoculars you can see the barbed wire. It's quiet here, except for an occasional 17.2 around noon.'

'Who held the place before?' Steiner asked.

Schnurrbart waved his hand contemptuously. 'A marine unit. Were those boys in clover.' He warmed up, and before long had told Steiner virtually all the news. Both of them shied away from speaking of Hollerbach. Finally Schnurrbart lit his pipe and stretched his legs. 'It's so nice sitting in the sun,' he said. 'Once I get back home I'll just spend several weeks in the sun and be glad that everything is so.'

'What do you mean by so?' Steiner asked.

'Just so,' Schnurrbart waved his hand vaguely. He drew violently on his pipe and looked across to the opposite shore of the bay. 'You know what I think,' he said at last. 'I think we've just forgotten to live in the present and it seems to me that the present is our life and the future is what we hope for, and I'll pull my own beard out by the handful if we don't pass life right by when we do it the other way.'

'Hold on,' Steiner said. 'I didn't quite follow that.'

'I'll have to spill it out again,' Schnurrbart murmured. He sat pondering. 'Now I don't know any more,' he said irritably. 'Yet I knew just what I meant. I could have wrote it down for you, I had it all so clear in my mind.'

'I can tell you what you meant,' Steiner offered. 'You mean that the present is real and the future is illusory, and if we take it the other way around we pass life by.'

'That's it,' Schnurrbart said. 'That's exactly what I meant.' Now that he heard his own thought repeated he was amazed at it; for a few seconds he felt as though he had discovered a wonderful trait in himself which he had never before suspected. Seeing Steiner's eyes resting upon his face with a curious expression, his sense of having pronounced a profound philosophical maxim grew stronger, and he felt very proud of himself. 'That's the way it is,' he repeated emphatically.

It suddenly occurred to him that he had omitted something. 'I haven't told you the queerest business yet,' he said excitedly. 'Happened a couple of days ago at Regiment. Krüger and I had to go see Captain Kiesel.'

Steiner raised his eyebrows. 'Kiesel? What did he want?'

'Damned if I know. He asked us whether we saw Stransky with us the night I was wounded. Did you see him?'

Steiner shook his head in bewilderment. 'How could I have? He stayed at the command post.'

'So I thought,' Schnurrbart growled. 'We said we hadn't seen him, and then Kiesel said he would have to wait till you got back.'

'Funny,' Steiner murmured. Frowning, he considered the matter. But he could make nothing of it, and shrugged impatiently. 'I wish they'd leave me alone. They start hounding a man the minute he comes back.'

Schnurrbart tapped his pipe out on the ground and stood up. 'Want to come along?' he asked. 'I'll wake Krüger.'

'I'd want to be in on that,' Steiner said. He picked up his pack. They entered the house and walked down a long hallway. At the last door Schnurrbart stopped, slowly pressed down the latch, and opened the door slightly. 'He's in dreamland,' he whispered.

Steiner looked in. Krüger was sprawled out on a bed, snoring loudly. As Schnurrbart started into the room, Steiner restrained him. Schnurrbart watched in puzzlement as he took a small bottle out of his pack and held it aloft, winking. 'What's that?' Schnurrbart whispered, 'Liqueur?'

Steiner shook his head. He opened the door quietly, cautiously approached the sleeping man, and sprinkled his hair and uniform with the contents of the bottle. The remainder he poured into the boots standing beside the bed. With a happy smile, he tiptoed back to the door. 'We can wake him now,' he said.

Schnurrbart sniffed. There was a sweetish odour which grew stronger from second to second. Steiner identified it, 'Scent,' he said.

'It stinks something awful,' Schnurrbart whispered. 'Where did you get the stuff?'

'Liberated it,' Steiner replied. He handed him the empty bottle. 'Fill that with water, will you?' Schnurrbart went out, while Steiner stood watching the sleeping man. Krüger moved restlessly, then turned over on his other side. Schnurrbart reappeared carrying a dozen china dishes. 'What's the idea?' Steiner asked. Schnurrbart chuckled. 'Wake him up. There's plenty of the stuff in the kitchen.'

Steiner took the refilled bottle from him, and they entered the room. 'Ready!' Schnurrbart whispered. Steiner nodded. He watched Schnurrbart raise the pile of plates high. As they crashed down on the floor he uttered so piercing a scream that even Steiner jumped.

The sleeping man started up as though an aerial mine had exploded beside his head. Before he could grasp what had happened, Steiner stepped up to him quickly, held the bottle under his nose and said: 'I couldn't get any Cologne water, as you asked, but this stuff is better still.'

Krüger stared at him, his face turning alternately red and white. Then he wrinkled his nose and stammered: 'Ugh!' He caught a glimpse of the pile of broken crockery on the floor and suddenly understood. As he sprang to his feet, he bumped into Steiner. The bottle fell to the floor and poured out over the floorboards. Krüger let forth an inarticulate cry of rage.

'Have you come back for that?' he roared. 'Why the devil did you come back at all, why didn't you stay away?'

Steiner smiled into his burning face. 'I was homesick,' he said. 'Homesick for you.'

Krüger seemed on the point of swinging wildly at him. Then he snatched up his tunic, stepped into his boots and stormed from the room. They followed him. As he sulkily sat down on a garden bench, Schnurrbart and Steiner sat down to his right and left.

'He hasn't improved at all,' Steiner said.

'He never will improve,' Schnurrbart said. 'A hopeless case.'

Krüger groaned and clenched his fist. Steiner laid his hand placatingly on his arm. 'Come on, make it up, old fathead.'

His voice sounded so gentle that Schnurrbart raised his head in astonishment. He had never heard such a tone from Steiner before. It did not fail to take effect upon Krüger also. He went on growling for a while, but his rage seemed to withdraw more and more into itself like a snail into its shell.

'That's better,' Steiner said. They sat in silence, looking out over the water. Three men in torn uniforms sitting close together on a bench, blinking peacefully up at the sun. Three good friends.

'Let's drink to your homecoming,' Schnurrbart said enterprisingly. He stood up. 'I'll get the others.'

They returned to the house. Steiner looked around. The three big rooms were comfortably furnished. Apparently the civilian populace had not been permitted to take their furniture with them, and everything still stood as it had been. As Steiner entered the living room with Krüger, he heard hasty footsteps in the hallway. The door flew open and Kern appeared, with Maag and Faber behind him. For a few seconds they stared at him without a word. He saw their familiar faces, their twitching lips, the pleasure in their eyes, and he was suddenly overcome by an emotion he had not felt for a long, long time. 'So there you are,' he said hoarsely.

'Don't start bawling,' said Schnurrbart, coming in behind them with several bottles in his hands. He pushed the others into the room. Kern was the first to go up to Steiner and give him a long handshake. Maag followed. As Steiner turned toward Faber, he saw the woodsman's eyes resting on him with a curious look, and he suddenly recalled his promise to visit Faber's family. 'Sorry to disappoint you,' he said quietly. 'I didn't go home.'

Faber nodded. 'I received a letter from Barbara yesterday,' he said. 'She wrote that you hadn't come yet. They were looking forward to meeting you.'

'Looking forward?' Steiner smiled bitterly. 'To meeting me?'

'I wrote them about you,' Faber said.

Steiner smiled with gratitude and embarrassment.

'Didn't you have any leave?' Maag asked.

Steiner shook his head, but gave no explanations.

Schnurrbart had meanwhile arranged the bottles on the table. 'Sit down,' he called noisily. 'What do you say to that?' Proudly he pointed out the half dozen bottles of champagne, watching Steiner's face for a reaction. When Steiner remained blank, he shrugged. 'Doesn't anything impress you?' he said in disappointment.

'Why should it?' Steiner said, grinning. 'Every schoolboy knows Novorosisk is full of champagne.'

They sat down. Since Schnurrbart had brought no glasses, they drank straight from the bottles. Kern made a face. 'The stuff is too warm,' he commented. 'I'd sooner have beer. You know . . .' He broke off and sniffed ostentatiously.

'What's the matter?' Maag asked.

'Something stinks of scent.' Kern declared, glancing suspiciously back and forth between Steiner and Krüger.

'I thought I smelled it,' Maag said.

Seeing that all eyes were turned upon him, Krüger smiled maliciously. 'That's Steiner,' he said.

Kern sniffed again. 'No, that isn't Steiner. It's you.'

'You're mad,' Krüger growled. 'Get yourself a new smeller. The old one isn't any good.'

Schnurrbart intervened. 'Don't bicker,' he said. 'We all stink.' He raised his bottle. 'Here's to the champagne-guzzling German army.' 'Here's to the mass grave,' Maag toasted. They emptied the bottles. Kern wiped his mouth. 'Open the window,' he growled. 'Open it yourself,' Maag retorted. But then he stood up and pulled the casement windows wide open. Returning to the table, he paused behind Steiner and stooped over him. 'It isn't him,' he said loudly.

'Of course not,' Kern said emphatically. 'It's just as I've always said. There are men who just can't stand promotion. Soon as they get a little rank their true colours come right out. Goddamn fairies.' He threw a significant look at Krüger. Krüger's face slowly reddened. He reached for an empty bottle. 'Another word,' he threatened, 'and I'll rap this thing over your bean.'

Kern made a placating gesture. 'Take it easy. I've got more practice with bottles than you have. Still and all, you stink like a whore.'

'I don't stink,' Krüger bellowed. 'It's Steiner who stinks.'

The men began to giggle, and a fleeting smile passed across even Faber's grave face. They all looked at Steiner, who shook his head reprimandingly.

'I beg your pardon, Corporal Krüger,' he said gravely.

His calmness infuriated Krüger. And when Steiner added that, friendship aside, this was no way to talk about a superior, he sprang to his feet and shouted: 'You can stick your goddamned rank. This isn't a question of rank, but of stench, I tell you, of naked stench.'

As he paused to catch his breath he noticed Schnurrbart scribbling something on a sheet of paper he had produced from somewhere. 'What are you writing?' he asked suspiciously.

'Always learning something new,' Schnurrbart replied dourly. 'Naked stench. Pretty good.'

Krüger thrust out his chin. 'So what?' he said challengingly. 'Do you think a stench has clothes on it?'

'No.' Schnurrbart grinned. 'But your clothes have a stench on them.'

A lieutenant entered the room, erect in his bearing, firm in his movements. His lively grey-blue eyes scrutinized the men. They had jumped up and come to attention. 'As you were!' the officer said tersely. He strode toward them. 'Drinking parties so early in the afternoon?' he stated rather than asked. His glance fell upon Steiner, who was standing at ease across the table. 'Who is that?'

Steiner placed the tips of his shoes together and replied: 'Master Sergeant Steiner, back from hospital.'

The lieutenant's eyes widened in surprise. 'Steiner?' he repeated. Then he nodded and held out his hand across the table. 'I am your company commander, Lieutenant März. Have you heard about me?'

'A few things,' Steiner said.

März raised his eyebrows. Then he smiled. 'So have I about you. Some good and some not so good. You will resume command of the platoon at once. Order and discipline. I don't stand for slackness. If there are any misunderstandings, tell me to my face, but don't talk about them behind my back. Clear?'

Steiner nodded, taken by surprise. The boy has the temperament of a young colt, he thought.

März turned to the other men. 'Inspection in one hour. By the commander in person. I don't wany anybody slipping up.'

He was standing close to Krüger now, and suddenly raised his head. 'Who's been dousing himself with scent?'

Krüger threw a sideways glance at Steiner and grinned. 'I mean you, corporal,' März said sharply. 'Are you a queer?'

Krüger did not know what to think. But since the lieutenant was looking straight at him, he raised his shoulders helplessly and stammered: 'It's not me.'

The company commander's eyes suddenly flared. 'Really,' he said, and with a rapid movement passed his hand over Krüger's hair. Then he held his hand under his nose. 'Smell that!' he ordered.

Aghast, Krüger sniffed. He looked so thunderstruck that Steiner began feeling intensely guilty.

The lieutenant's voice rang out sharply. 'If you want to smear scent all over you like a woman, that's your affair, but if you lie to me it's my affair. Remember that!'

Before Krüger could recover from his dismay, the company commander was gone. Krüger stared at Steiner's neutral face.

'You really do smell awful,' Steiner said. 'How could you be so foolish as to deny it to the lieutenant's face.'

Krüger had come so close to him now that their bodies were touching. He gripped Steiner by the lapels. 'You know what I'm going to do to you!' he growled out.

'Nothing reckless, I hope,' Steiner replied calmly. 'It might cost you your stripes.'

Krüger let go of him. 'I don't know what's going to happen in this war,' he choked. 'But I can tell you what's going to happen to you.'

Steiner raised his eyebrows, courteously attentive. 'What is that, my good fellow?'

'I'm not your good fellow!' Krüger roared, beside himself.

'As you like. What's going to happen to me?'

'I'll keep it to myself,' Krüger declared menacingly.

'I'll die of the uncertainty,' Steiner said.

'Go to the devil!' Krüger shouted at him.

Schnurrbart stepped up to them, raised his head and inhaled

the scent with sham delight. 'What a lovely fragrance,' he whispered, closing his eyes.

'Like a rose,' Kern said.

'Like a prickly rose,' Maag added.

Krüger tore out of the room.

The battalion command post was in a small group of houses about eight hundred yards from the waterfront. The company commanders were gathered in Stransky's office for a short briefing. Lieutenant März sat in a comfortable basket chair listening with boredom to Stransky's explanations. First Lieutenant Moninger, commander of the First Company, stared absently out of the window at the cloudless August sky. Beside him Lieutenant Hahn, commander of the Third Company, tried to conceal a yawn behind his palm, while First Lieutenant Stallmann studied his fingernails with deep interest. If only he'd wind it up, März thought, watching Stransky with veiled eyes. Stransky, standing behind the table, was throwing a great deal of emotion into his voice. But he now seemed to become aware of the officers' lassitude, and spoke more loudly. 'We are in the unfortunate situation of having been forced over from the offensive to the defensive. The momentary calm must not be allowed to lull our alertness, I consider it more important than ever to keep the men well in hand. Tight discipline is the prime factor in keeping a battalion in battle-trim and tip-top shape.' He emphasized his words by pounding vigorously on the table. 'I require my company commanders to root out every type of undisciplined behaviour. See to it that the roster is drawn up accordingly. Now is the best time for the men to put their equipment in order. I shall personally look into this matter.' He glanced at his gold wrist-watch. 'Inspection begins in fifteen minutes. I shall make spot-checks on the condition of weapons.' He turned to Triebig. 'Have we anything else?'

'I don't think so, sir,' Triebig replied obsequiously.

Stransky blew an invisible grain of dust from the sleeve of his tunic. 'Then that will be all for today.'

While the others left the room, März came over to Stransky and asked: 'Where do you intend to begin, sir?'

Stransky was on the point of replying sharply when he recalled that März was the regimental adjutant's brother-in-law. He smiled slyly: 'With your company, Lieutenant März.'

'Then I'll have the company fall in at once.'

Stransky nodded casually. When März remained posted in front of him, he asked: 'Is there anything else?'

'Nothing important,' März said casually. 'I only wanted to inform you that Master Sergeant Steiner returned to the company an hour ago.'

Although Stransky made an effort to master his feelings, März saw his eyelids flutter rapidly. The evenness of his voice sounded quite forced as he said: 'Steiner?' He looked down at the floor, then raised his head again. 'Very well. Send the sergeant to me at eight this evening.'

März saluted and left. As he emerged from the command post, there was a thin smile at the corners of his mouth. Stransky watched him through one of the big triple-casemented windows as he crossed the street. Then his eyes suddenly widened. A tremendous, swelling roar filled the air. He had time to see März leap with giant strides into the nearest house. For his part he threw himself instantly to the floor. A terrible impact shook the house to its foundations. The window glass shattered and fell inward; plaster broke from the ceiling and shrouded the room in white dust. Stransky lay with bated breath until outside the pattering rain of brick, wood and fragments of stone stopped. Then he shook off the paralysis of fear and stood up. His knees were quivering. He looked out through the empty window frames. Across the street one of the houses had collapsed. A huge blackish-yellow cloud of smoke was billowing out of the ruins and drifting slowly toward the waterfront. Stransky realized that the house was the messengers' quarters.

He saw März come rushing out of the house next door and stop, horrified. Behind him several men of the signals company appeared, their faces white. Suddenly they threw themselves to the ground. Stransky drew in his head. Once again that horrible hum filled the air. But it was higher in pitch this time, and did not have the same sense of fatal abruptness. Far behind the houses, in the midst of an open field, the shell exploded. Another dark cloud of smoke shot up into the sky. The noise of the detonation was so painful that Stransky clapped his hands to his ears.

He watched while the men got up and, led by März, disappeared into the wrecked house. He wondered what calibre the shell had been. Perhaps one of those notorious 21 cm. Russian mortars about which he had heard so many ghastly tales. He waited for a few minutes. When no more shells came over, he sent for Triebig and ordered him to cancel all roll-calls at once and set the men to work digging bunkers near their quarters. 'Inform the company commanders,' he added, 'and see to it that a strong dugout is built behind my command post. You can use the signal men.' He became aware of Triebig's distressed look and asked: 'Were there casualties?'

'Three men,' Triebig replied hoarsely. 'Dudek was one of them.'

'Dudek?' Triebig nodded silently. Stransky bit his lip. 'Really unfortunate,' he said at last. 'I was highly pleased with him. Couldn't have asked for a better orderly.'

'I feel exactly the same,' Triebig said softly. 'Keppler was one of them too.'

'Dead?' Stransky asked.

Triebig nodded. 'All three.'

There was a long pause. Stransky went over to the window, hands clasped behind his back, and watched the men of the signal platoon working to get at the victims, whose bodies were trapped under the ruins. 'Steiner is back,' he said abruptly, without turning round. As a result he did not notice the sudden pallor that spread over Triebig's face. 'I've sent for him for this evening. As soon as I have his signature I want you to transmit the paper to Regiment at once.'

Triebig had recovered from the immediate shock, though his face remained unnaturally pale. He moistened his lips with his tongue. 'I had not expected him back so soon. I hope he doesn't make trouble.'

'Bah!' Stransky laughed contemptuously. 'I'll soften him up, rest assured.' He looked at his watch. 'Getting late. Inform the company commanders and see to it that new messengers are detailed. I'll look around for another orderly.'

Triebig saluted and left the room. As he crossed the street, his face was set and hard. When he reached his quarters he telephoned the companies, informed them of the new situation, and ordered them to detail a messenger each to battalion. Then he drew a chair over to the window and sat staring absently at the white limestone slopes of the mountain. He felt as if a suppurating sore inside his chest had broken open and was poisoning his blood. Steiner's return struck him like a physical blow. All the past few months had been a torment; every time the telephone rang the sweat had started on his forehead. He had trembled before every meeting with Stransky, and the constant fear had brought his nerves nearly to the breaking point. Although it looked as if Steiner intended to keep quiet, the threat remained, and it would remain until Steiner had been silenced for good and all.

As he was considering rather hopelessly how that could be done, Triebig remembered that Steiner was to see Stransky that evening. He knew about the antagonism between the two men. Couldn't that be put to good use? There must be some way.

He laid his arms on the window-sill and half closed his eyes. It will depend on how the interview turns out, he thought. If his estimate of Steiner were correct, Stransky was going to be in for a disappointment. For all he too was implicated in the success or failure of the interview, he felt malicious joy at the thought of the tight spot Stransky had got himself into. This business could lead to anything. Pursuing that thought a little way, he became worried. You shouldn't have let yourself in for it, he thought; now you're going to have to figure out some way to slip out of the whole affair.

The thing had started because Stransky, in his report on the events of the night before the Russian offensive, had somewhat overdone it when he described his own part. According to his account, it was only due to his initiative that the unexpected Russian penetration into the positions of the second company on Hill 121.4 was repulsed. The report had pictured Stransky, accompanied by his adjutant, appearing at the last moment among the fleeing men, stemming their panic and leading them into the counter-attack. Stransky had candidly told his adjutant that he counted on an Iron Cross as the reward for this report. 'Of course you must confirm the details if you're asked, Triebig. It's perfectly safe. You are the only witness. Meyer is dead so no one can prove it wasn't so. This is the way everybody does it, and if the nomination goes through, you'll get the Iron Cross Second Class for it.' The temptation was great, and in any case Triebig was in no position to oppose Stransky's wishes.

Next day the report had been sent on to Regiment. Brandt had comprehended the point and had informed Stransky that he was entitled to the Iron Cross First Class for his part in the counter-attack. But he had also pointed out that in such cases two witnesses were required; he would have to have the signature of the company commander in addition to Triebig's. Stransky had pointed out that Meyer was dead. In that case, Strauss suggested, he should apply to Meyer's deputy at the time. In case the latter could not be reached at the moment, he was to table the nomination until the witness was available. Although Steiner's name had not once been mentioned, Stransky realized at once whom the regimental commander meant. 'A ticklish affair,' he had said to Triebig at the time. 'But we can't back out now. There's too much at stake.'

The more Triebig thought about it, the more pessimistic he became. But Stransky was right. Their retreat was cut off, and the affair had to be fought right on through Regiment. And it seemed highly likely that Steiner would refuse to give his signature. In that case Stransky would be forced to get rid of him as a person who knew too much. How—that was Stransky's affair. It shouldn't be too difficult to manœuvre a hothead like Steiner into a situation where even Brandt could no longer protect him.

XII

Wʜᴇɴ Sᴛᴇɪɴᴇʀ ᴀᴘᴘᴇᴀʀᴇᴅ at the command post, Stransky received him with marked restraint, and asked him to sit down. The sergeant did not take up this invitation. 'You may sit down,' Stransky repeated impatiently.

'If you order me to,' Steiner said.

'Consider it an order,' As Steiner reluctantly drew up a chair, Stransky moved the kerosene lamp so that he himself was sitting in darkness. He crossed his legs casually and asked: 'Do you recall our last conversation?'

Steiner nodded silently.

'As a result of your wound,' Stransky went on, 'we were unable to conclude it. I don't like to do things half-way and should like to follow it up.' He continued in a completely colourless voice: 'You are still quite young. That is why I prefer to excuse your past behaviour. But I can do so only if you recognize that I am being tolerant.'

'Are you referring to my switching tommy-guns?'

Stransky frowned. 'The matter of the sub-machine-gun is only one phase of the subject,' he murmured. 'When I speak with you, I assume a certain amount of mental agility on your part.'

Steiner shrugged. 'Maybe you're assuming too much, then. But leaving that aside, certain things can be talked about only man to man, not superior to subordinate.'

Stransky studied him speculatively. 'You would naturally think that,' he said with an attempt at a smile. 'But even if we leave my rank aside, this still remains a conversation between a superior and an inferior. You are quite aware that in civil life a distinction is made between people and personalities. Or haven't you ever been aware of that?'

Steiner bit his lips. So that's what you're getting at, he thought. Evidently Stransky was bent on humiliating him. He forced an ingenuous sunny tone to his voice. 'I have never thought much about such matters. But I'm sure you can explain the distinction to me.'

'I can,' Stransky said. He folded his arms over his chest, his long face with its silvery temples forming the very portrait of a distinguished man. 'The difference is a matter of ethical and intellectual superiority and comes about whether you like it nor not, from class differences. Those who are reared in dirt will never or rarely emerge from it because they have never learned to see dirt as dirt. Isn't that self-evident?'

Steiner shook his head. 'I disagree,' he said. 'What experience I have had has shown me that talent, sensitivity and character are not privileges of the upper classes. If I remember rightly Kant was the son of a saddlemaker and Schubert's father was nothing but a poor schoolmaster. I'm sorry my scanty education makes it impossible for me to add a whole lot of big names to the list, because at eighteen I had to drop my schoolbooks and pick up a spade in order to dig useless holes in the ground, instead of developing myself into a personality.'

He had spoken swiftly, in a low voice. Now he fell silent and looked past Stransky into the dark reaches of the roon. There was a pause.

'We were talking about general concepts,' Stransky parried.

'We are still talking about general concepts,' Steiner said quietly. 'I might add that useful plants and weeds grow on the same soil everywhere. Or are things different in East Prussia?'

Stransky's voice had become less urbane. 'May I ask in which category you count yourself?'

It was an open challenge, precisely what Steiner had feared. He straightened in his chair. 'This talk was going to be about general concepts,' he said. 'Before we go over into personal matters, I'd like to clarify one question.'

'What is that?'

'To go back to the beginning: is this conversation taking place between two equal human beings, or between a superior and his subordinate?'

'I see no reason to throw the weight of my rank into the balance.' Stransky declared haughtily.

Steiner nodded with satisfaction, feeling the sharp delight of the chess player who sees the game is his. 'In that case,' he replied quietly, 'I am free not to answer your tactless question.'

There was a silence, such a dead silence that for a second Steiner felt as if he were alone in the room. He watched the change in Stransky's expression. He felt himself like a man who has tossed a pebble down a slope and stands and watches it start a roaring landslide. Yet Stransky did not stir from his seat. The fury showed only in his eyes as he whispered: 'You are forgetting yourself, Steiner.'

For a moment Steiner quailed before that fury. But he shook off his fear, the product of years of military discipline, and raised his head. 'You are forgetting our agreement,' he said coldly. 'If you feel insecure about standing on grounds of equality, we can easily go back to our regular relationship.'

Stransky looked down at his hands. 'Your impertinence can only arise from stupidity,' he said softly. 'If it came from courage, I might punish it, but I would also admire it.' He stood up brusquely and paced about the room several times. Then he came to a stop in front of Steiner, who sat and looked up at him. 'I have encountered more than one person of your type.' he went on, 'and I have always crushed them like repulsive vermin. At our first meeting I told you that you overestimate your own importance. If you think you can impress me, you are very much mistaken. I consider you nothing more than an insolent lout with criminal tendencies who cannot keep his hands off his comrades' property.'

Steiner stood up slowly. He looked down at his hands and was glad to see that they were steady. 'You'll regret that,' he said quietly.

Stransky wiped his sleeve with his right hand. 'For that remark alone,' he replied, 'back home I would have had dogs chase you over the countryside until your feet were bleeding straps.'

'We're not back home,' Steiner replied.

'You'll wish you were before long.' He turned his back on Steiner, strode over to the table, picked up the telephone and called Triebig.

'Come over here,' he ordered curtly. Turning round, he saw that Steiner was leaning easily against the wall. 'Stand at attention.' Steiner took a half step forward and let his arms dangle. 'You'll learn that too,' Stransky snapped. At that moment Triebig entered. At the sight of Steiner blood rushed to his pallid face. 'You called me, sir,' he said to Stransky.

Stransky lit a cigarette, placed the used match carefully in an ash tray, and nodded. 'How far has my bunker progressed?'

'The men have started,' Triebig reported. 'It's slow work; the ground is very hard.'

'How deep is it now?'

'About a foot and a half.'

'The bunker is to be ten feet deep. Sergeant Steiner will work on it tonight until that depth is reached.'

'Tonight?' Triebig exclaimed, astonished.

'Tonight; in fact he is to begin at once. Give him the necessary tools. I shall hold you responsible for having that bunker ready by tomorrow morning.'

'Yes, sir,' Triebig stammered. Steiner had listened with an impassive face. Now Stransky turned to him. 'You wait outside.'

He remained silent until Steiner had left the room. 'I intend to play a different tune with that fellow now,' he said then.

'Did he refuse?' Triebig asked in alarm.

Stransky shook his head. 'I've changed my mind. We are going to call the whole thing off. You go to see Kiesel tomorrow morning. Listen carefully.'

While he explained his plan, he kept striding back and forth in the room. Triebig listened attentively, and the worried expression slowly passed from his face.

Outside, Triebig found Steiner standing with hands in his pockets, a cigarette drooping from his lips. 'Come along!' Triebig ordered him. They walked around the house to the back garden.

'You'll find tools here,' Triebig said, pointing to a spot along the wall of the house. In spite of the darkness Steiner could see freshly turned earth and a dark rectangle in the ground. He went up to it and glanced in. Then he turned to Triebig, who was watching him uncertainly. 'What are you staying around for?' he asked without removing the cigarette from the corner of his mouth.

'I want you to know that I have nothing to do with this business.'

'That's fortunate for you,' Steiner murmured. Since Triebig made no move to leave, Steiner took a step toward him. 'I've heard that you suffered a terrible loss today,' he said. 'But bear up. There are plenty more of that type around.'

Triebig stared at him with hatred. His voice shook as he said: 'I have only one wish, and the commander shares it. We could court-martial you or get rid of you some other way. But we want to have the pleasure of seeing you croak.'

Steiner smiled. 'You'll have to take good care of yourself if you want to outlive me.'

'You're an idiot,' Triebig said hoarsely, 'an idiot and a stupid fool.' His voice dropped to a whisper. 'Do you think anyone would believe you?'

'Brandt would,' Steiner said. 'But if I wanted to tell tales, I would have done so long ago.'

'And if you had, it would be your word against mine, and you may be sure an officer would be believed rather than you, of all people.' He laughed contemptuously. 'You lost your chance, Steiner. You had me until you left the bunker and not a second longer.'

'That may be,' Steiner replied. 'But you're too insignificant to be worth jawing about. You're so insignificant you're not worth the bullet I'm going to send through your filthy hide one of these days. Not worth it, but I'll have to do it sooner or later. Go on, get out of my sight.'

Triebig clenched his fists in helpless fury. 'Thank you for the warning,' he snarled.

'You're entirely welcome,' Steiner said coldly.

Triebig stood for a second leaning forward as though he were going to topple over, or spring upon Steiner. Then he turned on his heel and stalked off. As Steiner looked round he saw to his surprise two figures emerge from the dark background of the garden and come toward him. He recognized them immediately.

'Where are you two coming from?' he asked, shaking his head.

'Over there,' Schnurrbart replied, jerking his thumb over his shoulder.

'It was highly interesting,' Krüger murmured, lighting a cigarette.

'Did you hear what we were talking about?'

'Not quite,' Schnurrbart said. 'But it was interesting anyway. Are you coming along?'

'Not at the moment,' Steiner said. 'I have to dig out the commander's bunker tonight.'

The two stared at him unbelievingly. 'Who says?' Schnurrbart asked softly.

'The commander.'

'Well, what do you know,' Krüger growled. 'This gets more

interesting by the minute.' He turned to Schnurrbart. 'I'll get the fellows.' Without waiting for an answer, he sped off.

'What's the idea?' Steiner asked.

Schnurrbart hunched his shoulders. 'Do you think we're going to leave you here alone? Six will do it a lot faster.'

'You're mad,' Steiner muttered, swallowing hard. 'What were you doing here anyhow?'

Schnurrbart sat down on the ground. 'Seemed as if you'd been gone a long time and we got to wondering. Krüger thought we ought to take a look around here, so we started out. Just as we reached the house we saw you and Triebig going round the back. That looked funny, so we waited until Triebig left. That's all.'

'That's a lot,' Steiner said, taking a deep breath. He fought against the impulse to place his hand on Schnurrbart's shoulder.

'They'll be right along,' Schnurrbart said, fussing with his pipe. Steiner looked at his watch. It was shortly after ten. Suddenly they heard a voice speaking loudly in the street. Schnurrbart jumped to his feet. 'That's März,' he said worriedly. 'What's he doing here.'

Hasty footsteps sounded along the path from the street. A moment later five men appeared around the corner of the house. Steiner recognized the foremost as Lieutenant März. 'What's going on here?' März inquired sharply. Behind him came Faber, Maag and Kern, anxious looks on their faces. Krüger stepped up to Schnurrbart and answered his questioning look with a shrug. 'We ran into him on the way,' he whispered. 'When he heard what it was about, he insisted on coming with us.' He looked at Steiner, who was answering the company commander's question. He merely repeated the commander's order.

'And why was such an order given?' März asked curtly.

'I don't know. We were having a pleasant chat.'

'By chat you mean——?'

Steiner smiled. 'A private conversation.'

'With the commander's approval?'

Steiner rubbed his chin. His smile broadened as he murmured: 'I am cautious by nature.'

März considered for a few seconds. Then he ordered Steiner to begin work and turned to the others. 'You return to your quarters.' Seeing their disgruntled expressions, he added: 'If it turns out that the sergeant needs you, you'll be informed.'

The men grinned significantly at one another. With encouraging nods to Steiner, they straggled off. März stayed long enough to see Steiner jump into the pit and pick up one of the spades. Then he turned away and went out along the garden path to the street.

Back at his headquarters, he telephoned Kiesel at once. The conversation took some time, since Kiesel had to check with Brandt. When März laid down the receiver, he smiled with satisfaction. He waited a little while. Then he picked up the telephone again. Stransky answered sleepily. März apologized for disturbing him at this late hour; he had received a telehone call from Regiment, he said. 'I hear that Steiner is supposed to be with you now,' he went on. 'The lieutenant-colonel wants him sent to regimental headquarters at once.'

He fell silent, raising his eyebrows and listening intently. It was so still at the other end of the line that for a moment he thought Stransky had hung up. Then he heard Stransky again, speaking tensely and with effort: 'Very well, he will leave immediately.' März heard several noises he could not interpret. Then the hum in the receiver stopped. The indifferent voice of the operator asked: 'Are you through?' März listened, not answering. 'Are you through?' the voice asked again. Then, after a short pause: 'I am disconnecting.'

März turned to the window and looked out across the water. The mountains gleamed as though coated with frost, towering gravely into the star-sown sky. The night upon the mountains wore a sparkling diadem above a dark face, and stooped low over the sea, over the still surface of a curved mirror. As he saw, with a strange, constricted feeling in his breast, how sky and earth held one another in close embrace, he was conscious of a mute melancholy. Never before had he been so painfully aware of the banalities that filled his days to the very brim.

Triebig was startled out of sleep by the persistent shrilling of the telephone. Cursing, he groped his way unsteadily to the table. He came wide awake as soon as he heard Stransky's voice. 'Come over here!' Stransky ordered him. 'At once.'

Triebig stammered something and began dressing with feverish haste. He was so frightened that he was still trembling when, a few minutes later, he left the house. Before he entered the command post he tiptoed around the corner of the house and made sure that Steiner was still working. Then he went in rapidly. Stransky received him in a state of agitation such as Triebig had never before seen him display. He stood behind his desk, leaning forward with arms braced and shouted in a voice altogether out of control: 'Where the devil have you been? Didn't I say to come at once.'

'I had to dress,' Triebig replied, shaking.

Stransky's face flushed. 'Dress!' he bellowed. 'A soldier is always dressed, even when he's in bed with a woman. Come over here! Where is Steiner?'

'Working at your bunker, as you ordered,' Triebig whispered, hesitantly stepping closer to the captain.

'You are to take him to Regiment at once,' Stransky said. 'Regiment wants to see Steiner today, now. At'—he looked at his watch—'at eleven o'clock. Do you know what that means?'

Triebig moved his lips soundlessly. He was so stunned by the news that he was unable to speak. In one sudden vision he saw disaster descending upon his own head. 'It must be the report.'

Stransky nodded fiercely. 'Certainly. Brandt must somehow have got wind of what happened tonight, and I'll lay ten to one that that damned sneak März is behind it.'

'You should have expected that,' Triebig said tonelessly.

Stransky threw him a scornful look. 'Of course I expected it; do you think I don't know that I'm spied on every step of the way here?' He laughed sarcastcially. 'Those gentlemen underestimate me. I'll show them that a captain is a captain and a sergeant still a sergeant no matter how many times he crawls behind the back of the regimental commander.' He began pacing the room.

Triebig moistened his lips with his tongue. 'What do you intend to do?'

'I need time,' Stransky replied. 'No matter what, you must speak to Brandt before Steiner sees him. Tell Brandt that I prefer to forgo the Iron Cross because it is beneath my dignity to have a decoration depend on the signature of a subordinate whose undisciplined conduct has bordered on open mutiny. Tomorrow I intend to send a written report to Regiment on his behaviour. You will also tell the commander that it is asking too much to expect me to seek a favour of a man with a criminal record who has every reason to wish me ill because a single word from me would suffice to put him where he has long deserved to be: up against a wall.'

Triebig gasped. 'The lieutenant-colonel will . . .'

Stransky cut him off with an angry wave of his hand. 'The lieutenant-colonel,' he said loudly, 'will not be able to ignore the justified complaint of a battalion commander. I am thoroughly sick of being treated like a stupid boy by a sergeant who thinks he's under the protection of the regimental commander. If my complaint is not accepted, I shall disregard channels and address myself directly to Division. I want you to repeat what I have said to the lieutenant-colonel word for word.'

'Wouldn't you prefer to give it to me in writing?' Triebig asked anxiously.

Stransky sneered. 'I should think not. They're quite capable of twisting a noose for me out of anything written. It will be quite enough documentation for me to present my complaint on Steiner in writing tomorrow morning. And now repeat what you are to tell the lieutenant-colonel.'

He sat down at the table and while Triebig, acutely uncomfortable, repeated his words he made brief notes on a sheet of paper. When Triebig finished, he nodded his approval. 'In general outline that is what we discussed this afternoon in case Steiner refused his signature. Put a bit more strongly, but that does no harm. One must not allow oneself to be intimidated; it's essential to keep on the offensive. Start at once.'

Triebig left hurriedly. He returned first to his quarters, then went round to Steiner, who was standing up to his chest in the pit. Steiner looked up indifferently when he was spoken to. 'Come along! You're to go to Regiment.'

Steiner concealed his surprise, although he could not understand what Brandt could possibly want of him at this late hour. Since Triebig did not explain and strode rapidly ahead, he asked no questions. He regretted being weaponless, especially since Triebig was wearing his pistol. But then he smiled scornfully. As long as he did not turn his back on Triebig, the fellow would take care not to reach for his gun.

They had meanwhile passed through a good dozen black tunnels of streets, and he was gradually losing his sense of direction. At rare intervals they encountered a bored sentry who stood in front of a door and regarded them inquisitively. Their way led finally out of the confusion of tenement houses into a dark street lined by trees on both sides. Steiner glanced at his watch and discovered that they had already been walking for more than twenty minutes. At that moment they were hailed sharply. 'Regimental command post?' Triebig asked. Steiner saw the dim silhouette of a man who approached and asked for the password. 'Kuban,' Triebig returned, adding: 'The commander is expecting us.' By now the sentry had apparently recognized the officer's uniform; he clicked his heels. On the right a wall loomed up out of the darkness; they passed through a gate guarded by another sentry. A short flight of steps led to a front door, and they entered a long hallway. 'Wait here,' Triebig said.

Steiner thrust his hands into his pockets. He was quite calm now, and observed with disdain the nervous timidity with which the lieutenant knocked on the door. But no one called to him to come in. Instead, Kiesel suddenly appeared on the threshold. Seeing Triebig, he raised his eyebrows in surprise. Then he caught sight of Steiner. For the fraction of a second a faint smile seemed to pass over his face. But since Steiner was not sure of it, he slowly took his hands from his pockets.

'Did you want to see me?' Kiesel asked Triebig.

'Captain Stransky has sent me,' Triebig said. 'I must speak with the commander.'

Kiesel's expression became reserved. 'Concerning what?' he asked in a stiff official tone.

'Concerning . . .' Triebig glanced quickly at Steiner and fell silent. Then he gathered up his courage again. 'I request permission to speak personally with the commander in regard to an official matter.'

'One moment,' Kiesel said, and went back into the room, closing the door behind him.

He was unusually long about returning. At last he reappeared and with a silent movement of his head indicated that Triebig was to come in. Before he followed he turned to Steiner. 'The commander asks you to be patient for a few minutes more.'

'Gladly,' Steiner said. Kiesel turned swiftly. But before the door closed behind him, Steiner thought he caught a glimpse of a sardonic grin in his direction. Standing, Steiner looked down at his soiled boots. I should have polished them, he thought. But then he realized that there had been no chance to.

The wait proved long. To break his boredom Steiner wandered along the corridor, which was lit by two candles. At the end of the corridor was a flight of steps covered by a thick runner. He sat down on the lowest step and stretched out his legs. Suddenly he became aware of his weariness, and closed his eyes. The hell with it all and with all of them, Stransky, Triebig, Brandt and all the rest. He began whistling under his breath. Again he noticed his dirty boots. The sight of them troubled him, and he began wiping them off with a corner of the carpet. Then he settled back contentedly and tried to think of nothing at all. It was hard for him to keep his eyes open, and he began blinking. If I close them, he thought, I'll fall asleep.

Suddenly a loud voice startled him. He stumbled to his feet, straightened up jerkily, and stared blankly about him. Kiesel was standing in front of him. 'I think you fell asleep,' he remarked.

'Seems like it,' Steiner murmured, rubbing his eyes.

Kiesel looked at him, shaking his head. 'I wish I had your conscience. Come this way.'

They entered the room, and for a moment Steiner stood stock still in confusion. It was so stuffed with furniture that he did not see where the commander was until he heard his booming voice. Brandt sat behind a huge, clumsy desk piled with all sorts of useless objects, holding a lighted cigarette between his fingers. 'So there you are,' he said loudly. 'Next time you're wounded, give me a week's notice that we're going to lose you, haha. How are you, Steiner?'

'I can't complain,' Steiner murmured weakly, feeling that he was acting the fool. But Brandt did not seem to think so. He stood up and shook hands heartily with Steiner. Then he gestured toward a chair. 'Make yourself comfortable. I've heard that you've worked a great deal today.'

'A man does what he can,' Steiner muttered, cursing his sleepiness. As he sat down and took a cigarette from the case Brandt extended across the desk, he noticed that Kiesel had also taken a seat on an old-fashioned couch in the back of the room, and was looking on curiously. He suddenly realized that Triebig was not in the room. He lit his cigarette and looked attentively into the commander's face.

'How was it in the hospital?' Brandt began.

Steiner smiled politely. 'Pretty good,' he said laconically. Apparently Brandt was in good humour, to judge by his expression. But it seemed unlikely to him that the commander had sent for him so late at night merely to ask how he was. Besides, why had Triebig accompanied him, and where was Triebig now?

The commander spoke again. 'Tell me about your wound, won't you? I hear that you were wounded again on your way back to Kanskoye.'

'That's right,' Steiner said, and began to tell the story, keeping it as short as possible. While he spoke, the commander listened gravely. 'Yes, that was a bad business,' he sighed, when Steiner had finished. His face darkened at the memory of the several hundred men who had fallen in the unsuccessful counter-attack of the assault regiment.

Steiner puffed at his cigarette. The presence of Kiesel bothered him, for he felt that the captain was staring at him all the time. 'I was afraid that would happen,' he said. 'I was glad not to have to cross over that hill a second time.'

They went on talking and had reached their third cigarette when Brandt suddenly leaned forward, elbows on the desk, and casually asked whether Steiner knew that Captain Stransky had led Second Company's counter-thrust that night just before the beginning of the big Russian offensive. Steiner looked at him in surprise. He recalled that Schnurrbart and Krüger had also been questioned, and became alert. 'The counter-thrust was led by Lieutenant Meyer,' he stated. 'Captain Stransky was nowhere in sight at any time.'

He caught Brandt exchanging a glance with Kiesel, and Kiesel now asked whether he was sure of that. 'Absolutely,' Steiner affirmed. 'In the first place I would have seen him, and in the second place, directly after the business Lieutenant Meyer had to report to the captain what had been happening in the lines.'

'How do you know that?' Kiesel asked.

'I was there myself when he made his report,' Steiner replied.

Brandt gave an exclamation. 'When was that?' he asked.

Steiner, not understanding the cause of his excitement, looked in puzzlement at his flushed face. 'Right afterwards,' he declared, and began sketching in the order of events.

When he finished, Brandt let his head droop and sat thinking. Something in his expression warned Steiner to step cautiously.

But whatever the threat was, it apparently was not directed toward him, for when the commander looked up again there was a faint smile around his mouth. He turned to Kiesel. 'Fetch Triebig,' he ordered sharply. While Kiesel was out of the room, Brandt remained silent.

Triebig bit his lips when he came into the room with Kiesel and saw Steiner sitting so much at ease beside the desk. It was, he felt, alarmingly quiet in the room.

When Brandt spoke, his voice sounded unusually soft and low. 'You gave your name, Lieutenant Triebig. Were you present when Captain Stransky led the counter-thrust?'

Triebig hesitated. He seemed to be struggling to come to a decision. Finally he hunched his shoulders and spoke. 'I accompanied the commander to the hill and saw him calling several men around him. Then he sent me back to the command post.'

'Why did he do that?' Brandt asked.

'He thought someone ought to be in the command post in case you called, sir.'

'Then how do you know that Stransky really led the counter-attack? You signed a statement to that effect as a witness, Lieutenant Triebig.'

Triebig's reply came without hesitation this time: 'I learned of it from wounded men who were returning.'

At this point Kiesel intervened. He turned to the commander. 'Will you permit me to ask a question, sir?' When Brandt nodded, he addressed Triebig: 'Can you give me the name of one of these wounded men?'

'They weren't staff men but company men,' Triebig replied evasively. 'I knew them only by sight. Besides, it was pitch dark when I spoke with them. I saw no reason to doubt their statements.'

'You should have noted their names,' Kiesel said.

Triebig shrugged. 'In all that confusion?' he murmured. 'I'd practically lost my head myself.'

'You may yet,' Brandt said icily. 'I want you to know, Lieutenant Triebig, that I have been having your statements checked. Captain Kiesel will now inform you of the results of our investigations into this matter.'

Steiner had been listening to the conversation with mounting wonder. He watched as Kiesel took a sheet of paper out of his pocket, studied the contents for a moment, and then raised his head. 'Our investigation so far,' he stated placidly, 'have disclosed that at the moment there are forty-two men in Second Company who took part in the aforementioned counter thrust. They declare unanimously that the attack was led by Lieutenant Meyer. None of them saw Captain Stransky and none of them heard that he was even with the company at the time the attack was launched.'

'Very well,' Brandt said. He turned again to Triebig, who looked as if he were standing against a wall watching an execution squad line up in front of him. 'You are not going to try to tell me that all this is a matter of sheer chance. If it should turn out that Captain Stransky has deliberately sent in a false report, I shall take the matter up with Division. In that case, Lieutenant Triebig, you yourself would have to jusify your conduct before a court of honour.'

Steiner, watching Triebig from the side, noticed the fine beads of perspiration on his forehead. But he felt no sympathy at all. Now that he had wind of what was going on here, he could feel nothing but contempt. Iron Cross hyenas, he thought, and recalled that neither Schnurrbart nor Krüger wore any special decorations, although they had earned them a hundred times over.

Triebig seemed to have recovered somewhat from his funk. He attempted to lend firmness to his voice as he said: 'I acted out of my deepest convictions, sir.'

'Whether you acted out of deepest conviction is not in question.' Brandt replied coldly. 'You can only corroborate what you yourself saw, not what was allegedly told to you. To my mind there is nothing more contemptible than snatching the laurels that properly belong to a man who fell on the field of battle. I shall abide by Sergeant Steiner's testimony. He was in the immediate vicinity of Meyer. If he stands by his statement that Captain Stransky was not with the company during the time in question, I shall be compelled to institute disciplinary proceedings against the captain.'

He turned to Steiner. 'Do you stand by your statement?'

There was a deep silence in the room. Steiner hesitated, torn between his knowledge of the truth and the feeling that it would be unfair to dispose of his enemy in this cheap and easy manner. He disliked the idea of others intervening in the contest between himself and Stransky. It was his business.

'Would it be possible for me to think that over for a few days? he asked Brandt.

Brandt was taken aback. 'Think it over?' he said, anger and disappointment in his voice. 'What is there to think over? Did you see Stransky? Yes or no!'

Steiner bit his lips. But at this juncture he unexpectedly received aid.

Kiesel had stood up and came swiftly over to them. 'I think Sergeant Steiner is right,' he said to Brandt, who sat glowering behind his desk 'A question as important as this one ought to be considered very carefully.'

Brandt jumped to his feet. 'Are you starting the same nonsense. Common sense ought to tell you that . . .' He broke off abruptly. Kiesel had been furiously winking at him. He turned to Triebig and Steiner and ordered them to wait outside.

As soon as they were gone, Brandt asked sharply: 'What's this nonsense all about?'

'Of course it's nonsense,' Kiesel said. 'Steiner knows perfectly well where Stransky was during the counter-attack.' He took a few strides about the room, then turned swiftly. 'You have two alternatives,' he said quietly. 'Either you can pursue the matter and perhaps bring Stransky up before a court-martial. But then Steiner would have to appear as a witness. That is a rôle he is not going to love. Perhaps that's why he wants to stall.'

Brandt rubbed his chin. 'We could leave him out of it,' he said reluctantly, after a long pause.

Kiesel shook his head dubiously. 'Stransky would wonder,' he retorted. 'If we don't bring up the principal witness against him, he'll think about it and probably draw false conclusions. It wouldn't be a good idea for us to leave ourselves open that way. Moreover, we can't load forty-two men of the second company on a truck and transport them God knows where as witnesses.' Observing the gathering frown on the commander's face, he stepped closer to him and argued pleadingly: 'If I were you, I would avoid doing anything that might bring Steiner into a tussle before a court-martial for the second time. Stransky would certainly refer to Steiner's past, and we'd be in for ticklish complications. And the question still remains: would we succeed in convincing the judges?'

'That's ridiculous!' Brandt thundered, pounding on the table. 'He can't pull a trick like this on me and get away with it!'

'Not at all,' Kiesel replied. 'I spoke of two alternatives. You can administer a much more thorough slap to Stransky if you accept my proposal.'

'Well, what is it?' Brandt asked.

Kiesel dropped into a chair and crossed his legs. 'I have been watching Steiner this evening, and I think I know something about men's reactions. I can well imagine that he not only wants to avoid testifying before a court-martial, but that the idea of being the principal witness against Stransky is also distasteful to him.'

Brandt shook his head. 'Why, in Heaven's name? To judge by what März has said, he must have every reason to want revenge.' He laughed itrriably. 'That's sheer fantasy, Kiesel. Steiner must wish him in hell. Incidentally, I'd be curious to learn what happened this evening.' He rubbed his chin again. His voice sounded reproachful now. 'I told you right off there would be trouble between those two.'

Kiesel shrugged ruefully. 'It's been hard to know what was going on every minute. In the future I'll be able to keep tabs on the two of them much more easily because my brother-in-law will keep me better informed than Meyer did. But you must remember that I can't be present unobserved at every run-in between Stransky and Steiner. To see the whole clearly, we must understand the motives.'

'I'll find them out from Steiner,' Brandt retorted forcefully.

Kiesel smiled. 'I hardly think so. My impression is that he regards his differences with Stransky as a private matter. And as for Stransky, he would talk about the effects but not the causes. What will you do if he sends in his recommendation that Steiner be disciplined?'

'Let me worry about that,' Brandt replied. 'If he dares to make good his threat and contact Division behind my back, he'll find he's bitten off more than he can chew.'

'He seems to have good connections,' Kiesel reminded him.

'Connections!' Brandt waved his hand contemptuously. 'If I convict him of presenting a falsified report, the best connections in the world won't do him any good. But we're digressing. You had a plan, you said.'

'Right,' Kiesel said. He had finished smoking his cigarette and now stood up in order to walk over to the desk and crush out the stub in a crystal bowl. Then he began explaining his plan. When he finished, there was a prolonged silence.

'Only you could hit on that idea,' Brandt delcared at last. He sat for several minutes with drawn face, thinking it over. Then he raised his head and said: 'Bring the two of them in.'

He turned first to Steiner. 'I've thought it over. I agree. You may think the matter over for a few days. You know what it is about?'

'I can guess,' Steiner replied.

Brandt nodded. 'So that there will be no misunderstandings about it, it is this: Captain Stransky claims that he led 2nd Company's counter-attack. For that he would receive the Iron Cross, First Class. But I want the action confirmed by two signatures, as is proper. The first was supplied by Lieutenant Triebig; the second should come from the company commander. Since Lieutenant Meyer was killed, you, who were his representative at the time, are the only possible person to give his signature. Any questions?'

Steiner shook his head. Brandt turned to Triebig. 'I want you to inform Captain Stransky about this conversation. As for his promised report on the insubordinate conduct of one of his platoon leaders, you may tell him that I leave it to his imagination whether such an action might not refresh the memory of the person in question in a manner disadvantageous to Captain Stransky.'

Kiesel barely repressed a smile at the carefulness of Brandt's wording. Triebig held his head bowed. But his relief was obvious. 'I shall inform the captain,' he murmured.

Brandt glared coldly at him. 'That is an order,' he informed him. 'You are no longer needed here.'

He waited until Triebig had left the room. Then he sat down behind his desk again and looked at Steiner, who had remained standing in the middle of the room. From the back of the room, where Kiesel sat, came a repressed cough, and Brandt suddenly felt his presence as disturbing. But since he could not very well send him away, he forced himself to take a distant tone as he asked: 'Why were you set to digging Stransky's bunker tonight?'

Steiner compressed his lips.

'I asked you something,' Brandt said loudly.

Tempted though he was to retort sharply, Steiner only murmured: 'I would rather not talk about it.'

'And suppose I order you to?'

Steiner raised his head. Their eyes met, and Steiner felt a dull rage mounting within him. 'Do you want to hear lies?' he asked rebelliously.

Brandt placed the tips of his fingers together and leaned forward somewhat. 'I want to tell you something, Steiner. In the vicinity of this house there is room for several hundred bunkers, and it might occur to me to keep you busy for two or three weeks, just to keep you where you don't make any more trouble for me. Do you know that Stransky intends to recommend disciplining you?'

'If I were he I wouldn't lose a minute about it,' Steiner growled.

Brandt turned to Kiesel, who had been listening attentively. 'What do you say to that? I really think it would be better for me to place a guard over him and have him dig holes until he's blue in the face.'

'A poor cure for obstinacy,' Kiesel joked. 'Besides, why try to revise the decisions of Providence?' Since he did not want to say anything more in front of Steiner, he shrugged and fell silent. Brandt peered questioningly at his face. Then he turned to Steiner, and his voice took on the timbre of sternness. 'Listen to me. You know quite well that I have always shown a great deal of understanding for you. But I am gradually beginning to get tired of battling with your superiors over you.'

'I didn't ask you to,' Steiner replied with a defiant stare. It was the greatest liberty he had ever permitted himself with Brandt, and as soon as he had said it he was frightened at his own foolhardiness. But he met the commander's eyes firmly and observed with an almost voluptuous excitement the way Brandt's expression changed. Brandt drew himself up sharply and propped his arms on the desk top. 'Didn't ask me to!' he repeated, hoarse with rage. 'You didn't ask me to? Have you gone clean out of your mind? Do you have any idea what you're saying?'

For a second Steiner closed his eyes. The anger surged up in him so suddenly that afterwards he could not explain it. The bitterness locked up inside him for months spilled out with such violence that his whole body felt emptied, discharged. 'I do know,' he snarled. 'Ever since I've been wearing this damned uniform I've known that there are two kinds of human being. One kind are the Stranskys and Triebigs and other commissioned officers, and they're all the same, as much alike as one arse is like the next, and I'm glad I've said it to you at last.'

He fell silent, shaking. His face was twitching like the restless surface of a lake, and there was so much contempt in his eyes that Brandt was stunned. The commander uttered a low groan. Then there was a dead silence in the room. A clock could be heard ticking. The commander was breathing heavily. His unsteady hands groped across the top of the desk. Several times he started to speak. When at last he brought out a whisper, his voice sounded broken. 'Get out. Get out of here at once!'

Steiner abruptly came to his senses. Staring at the commander's grief-stricken face, he suddenly felt such remorse that his eyes filled with tears and all the objects in the room swam. Staggering, he moved toward the door, turned around once more and looked back helplessly. Then he went out.

When the door closed behind him, Brandt dropped into his chair and looked down at his big hands until he heard a shuffling sound at his side. He raised his head and saw Kiesel standing stiffly, watching him with a strange expression.

'Why didn't you spare yourself that?' the adjutant said slowly.

Brandt looked blankly at him.

'You should either have ignored his first impertinence or punished the last,' Kiesel went on quietly. 'You were inconsistent. You can raise up a wildcat, but don't count on it for gratitude. The species is unpredictable. To tell the truth, I'm worried.'

'About Steiner?'

'No, not about Steiner. I'm worried about Stransky. For the past five minutes I've felt convinced that I would not like to be in his shoes.'

He watched as the blood flowed back under the commander's skin, washing away the dumbfounded expression. Brandt nodded. 'You're right,' he said.

'In that case it would be better for you to transfer Steiner to another battalion at once, or bring him up here to Regiment.'

Brandt stared down at his hands again. When he raised his head there was an inscrutable expression on his face. 'I wouldn't think of it,' he said slowly. 'A few minutes ago you yourself advised me not to revise the decisions of Providence. It seems to me that was for once a wise remark on your part.'

'The case is somewhat different now,' Kiesel retorted uncomfortably.

By now Brandt had recovered completely. He smiled somewhat mockingly. 'I disagree. If you tried to mend a hole in a spider's web, you'd tear the whole web, no matter how skilful your fingers were. I am going to keep my hands off matters as delicate as this.'

He stood up and began striding about the room. 'Perhaps I've treated Steiner wrongly.' he said reflectively. 'The relationship between superior and subordinate presupposes a distinct barrier. I thought that in this case I could dispense with it.'

'Why so?' Kiesel interjected.

Brandt ignored the question. 'It's hard to find the proper tone.' he went on. 'I don't want my men to lose touch with me, and at the same time I can't have them taking the liberties Steiner does,'

'It's a matter of sensitivity,' Kiesel said.

Brandt laughed harshly. 'Don't give me any of that. If I started being sensitive, I should have to apologize for every order I gave my men, saying it wasn't from me but from Division. No . . .' He shook his head passionately. 'It's something else, and it's the thing I worry about most of the time.' He halted in front of Kiesel, his face flushed. 'I'll tell you what it is,' he declared in an unnaturally loud voice. 'It's the damned fear we carry around all the time, the fear of exposing any of our weaknesses, of losing our nimbus. That's it, Kiesel. That's why we don't dare tolerate any personal contact with the men. If we discuss our love affairs, say, with a subordinate, we've shown ourselves in our underwear and can no longer ask him to run blindly head-on into a tank cannon while we hang medals on our chests.'

'Not always.' Kiesel smiled. 'You're right, though. In reality it is nothing but the attempt to maintain an illusion—the illusion that the officer occupies a special position. If you permit closer relations, you are letting the other fellow understand that you respect him as a human being. In doing that you bolster his self-assurance, and that way you run the risk of his feeling himself your equal. Letting down the barrier can be the equivalent of surrender.' His smile broadened. 'We are like actors who don't dare appear without our grease-paint.'

'I didn't put it quite that drastically.'

'But that is what you meant,' Kiesel answered.

They stood silent for a few moments, until Brandt went over

to the desk and sat down with a groan. Face twisted in pain, he clapped his hand to his hip. 'This damned rheumatism. I can't seem to get rid of it any more.'

'We're getting old,' Kiesel said equably.

Brandt looked at him suspiciously. 'Is that directed at me?'

'At your rheumatism,' Kiesel said.

The conversation between them had bogged down once more. Somehow, Kiesel could not understand Brandt. There were too many contradictions in his personality which at the moment he could find no explanation for. He recalled how a few months ago the commander had emphasized that his regiment did not consist of figures, but of human beings. And now came this strict repudiation of any such feelings. He decided to explore along this track.

'Stransky must have made the same mistake you did,' he said. 'He was too sure of himself when he started discussions with Steiner.'

'Don't overlook the difference in our motives,' Brandt growled.

'I've thought of that,' Kiesel replied. 'Stransky's I know. He received a setback to his morbid arrogance that he will have to chew on for a long time. Incidentally, that sort of arrogance seems to be a specifically German trait.'

Brandt waved his hand impatiently. 'That's sheer prejudice,' he said irritably. 'We are no worse than others.'

'But perhaps more peculiar,' Kiesel countered. 'There's no denying that our country swarms with frustrated despots. For their own self-esteem they need someone's back to step on, just as a short woman needs high heels to feel self-respecting. They're frustrated, of course, only so long as they're not in uniform.'

'You're an anarchist,' Brandt said.

Kiesel shrugged. 'I lack the courage to be an anarchist. I am just one of the many who know very well they're in the wrong pew and do nothing about it.'

'It's not worth the doing.'

'Not for the sake of others,' Kiesel agreed. 'But perhaps for our own sakes. What are you going to do with Steiner?'

Brandt looked up into his face. 'You certainly are prying,' he said rudely. 'Why are you concerned?'

'For your sake,' Kiesel said earnestly.

Brandt seemed on the point of replying in the same gruff tone. Then he suddenly compressed his lips, reached into his breast pocket and took out a worn leather letter-case. From it he removed a picture and sat for some moments staring at it. At last, still without a word, he handed it to the captain. In astonishment Kiesel studied the snapshot of a man in officer's uniform who unmistakably looked like Steiner. Only on closer examination could he detect where the face varied. And something else now struck him. For the first time he became aware of a resemblance between Steiner and the commander. It was particularly recognizable around the eyes. His hand holding the snapshot dropped and he looked questioningly into the commander's composed face.

'I don't quite understand.'

'I'm not surprised,' Brandt said, taking the picture from him. 'This is my son. He was killed four years ago, in Poland. The first time I saw Steiner I thought I would go out of my mind. The resemblance, you understand. And the same sort of obstinacy besides. Steiner lost both his parents—did you know that?' Kiesel shook his head silently. 'Two years ago. In an accident. He lost his parents and I have lost my son. On top of that the resemblance and . . .' His voice had been fading steadily. Now he fell quite silent and let his head droop. Shocked, Kiesel looked down at him, waiting. But as minute after minute passed and Brandt remained immobile, he turned and went softly to the door.

The sun had set beyond the peaceful swells of the sea. Faber was sitting in his quarters reading for the second or third time his letter from Barbara. At last he folded it carefully and placed it in his breast pocket. Thoughtfully, he went over to the window. His gaze wandered from the mountains down to the waterfront, trying to connect the appearance of this city with the information Barbara had supplied. Her data must have come from their old village schoolmaster. He wrinkled his broad forehead. Could 95,000 people possibly have lived here? He tried to imagine the number, and shook his head in astonishment. However, the big factories Barbara mentioned were here—he had seen them. The grain mills and cement works, the elevators and oil refineries—these stood. But on the waterfront there was none of the busy activity she spoke of, no sign of the many ships. What a Babel of tongues there must have been along those piers. But now the port lay still like a choked spring, and the city had been transformed into a stony wasteland at the foot of the mountains; it could not have seemed more silent and lifeless if it had lain at the bottom of the sea. A city without human beings. It was like a Black Forest without trees, unthinkable and unreasonable.

He opened the window and leaned far out. The sky was studded with stars. But they did not seem near, as they were at home when he saw them above the trees. Here they were inconceivably remote. He recalled how often at this time of day, when the sun sank beyond the trees and the clangour of bells rang across the mountains, he would sit down on top of a hill somewhere, fold his hands and murmur an Ave Maria. And think of Barbara. Barbara with her quiet, grave face who wore her braid of fair hair into a crown about her head. He could hear her voice in his ears so distinctly that for a second it seemed to him she must be standing at his side, and he looked back into the dark room. Then he sighed and closed the window. Were it not for the war, he thought, we would have been married long ago.

Since it was still too early to go to sleep, he decided to take a stroll. Kern and Maag were with Krüger, playing cards. Buckling on his belt and plumping his cap over his unruly hair, he left the house. Outside he encountered Maag.

'Game over already?' Faber asked.

'No,' Maag said crossly. 'I just got sick of it and quit.'

'Were you bickering?'

Maag shook his head. 'No, not that, I'm just sick of letting Steiner get under my skin. He's at it again. Since that business last night he's been in a stinking mood.'

'When did he get back?' Faber asked.

'I don't know. Schnurrbart says he went to the regiment command post during the night. Schnurrbart and Krüger waited up for him till two and then went to bed. He was back this morning. But won't say a word about it all. Are you on duty?'

'No, not today. Tomorrow morning at six.'

'Bloody time for sentry duty,' Maag murmured, lighting a cigarette. 'I'd sooner have it at night. Then at least I can sleep in the morning.'

They walked together across the street, Faber remained taciturn. Although Maag tried several times to induce him to talk, he could not get a decent conversation going. Finally he stood still, saying: 'I'm going back home. I have to stand sentry in an hour. Till then I can catch a bit of a nap.'

'Hardly worth it,' Faber said. 'Your head just feels heavy when you have to get up.'

Maag looked around. They had wandered a considerable distance beyond the company sector into a district strange to them. All around stood four-story houses, apparently unoccupied. 'We might take a look at those dives from inside,' he said enterprisingly. 'Maybe we'll come across something worth taking.'

'That's forbidden,' Faber replied. 'You know a special order of the day has been issued about plundering.'

'What's plundering in a place like this? It doesn't matter much whether the stuff's smashed to bits by shellfire or whether I pocket it.'

'In the one case it's plundering, in the other fate,' Faber said firmly. 'I won't have anything to do with it.'

Maag shook his head in disgust. 'What a man you are,' he said irritably. 'Haven't you ever liberated anything?'

'Not unless it was absolutely necessary for me, no. Besides, it's pitch dark in the houses.'

'I have a flashlight with me.'

'The MPs are constantly patrolling,' he said. 'If they see a light in a window, they'll investigate and you'll be in for a rough time. Take some good advice and keep clear of that kind of thing.'

'The bastards,' Maag cursed the MPs automatically. He knew quite well that Faber was right. After a few more resentful murmurs, he turned to go. Faber joined him and they retraced their steps. 'I'll be glad when we're back in regular positions again,' Maag said. 'This here gets me. Half front and half rear-echelon. And the brass so bored they spend all their time thinking up ways to annoy us.' He spat on the ground and added threateningly: 'When things start getting hot here, they'd better keep out of my way. I might take a notion to puncture his spine for him.'

'That's just talk.'

'What do you mean?' Maag suddenly flared up. 'You don't know me very well.'

'We don't know each other at all,' Faber replied thoughtfully.

Their pace slowed. 'What's that about we don't know each other?' Maag asked in astonishment.

Faber thrust his hands into his pockets. 'Of course we don't know each other,' he said quietly. 'About all we do know is each other's names.'

'I suppose that's true,' Maag said, taken aback. After a pause he asked: 'Do you happen to be married?'

Faber shook his head. 'No, the war interfered.'

'For me too.' Maag nodded gloomily. 'The damned war. If it weren't for the war I'd have . . .' He stopped abruptly.

'What?' Faber asked.

Maag laughed in embarrassment. 'That's something else again. You see . . .' He hesitated until they had crossed a street. 'I have a girl. You too?'

'Yes.'

'What's her name?'

'Barbara.'

'Nice name,' Maag said. 'My girl's named Monika.'

They walked on in silence, Maag turning over the idea that had suddenly occurred to him. He had never spoken about his impotence to anyone, for fear of ridicule. But there was something about Faber's quiet manner that made Maag think he might be helpful. The difficulty was beginning. Several times he started to speak. Finally he stood still and grasped Faber's arm. 'A fellow can talk with you, can't he?' he asked uncertainly.

Faber looked at his face, whose freckles showed through the pale skin even at night. 'I think so,' he said.

'That's good.' Maag sighed. 'I suppose you've been with your Barbara, haven't you?'

'Been with her? What do you mean?'

'You know what I mean.' Maag gave an embarrassed laugh. His uncertainty was increasing and he already regretted having brought up the subject. But he made a last try. 'I don't know how you say it in your district. I mean, when you go to bed with a woman.'

Faber's expression hardened. 'In my district you don't go to bed with a woman until you're married,' he declared with emphasis.

Maag gaped at him. He realized his mistake and tried to cover up. 'That's what I mean.'

'That's not what you mean,' Faber replied. 'I told you I wasn't married.'

'I forgot,' Maag mumbled.

Faber studied him silently, then turned and walked on. Maag followed him, downcast. There just isn't anybody, he thought bitterly. A fellow can't talk to any of these idiots. Head bowed, shoulders slumping, he trotted along behind Faber, his feet leaden, his soul heavy with disappointment.

Faber walked swiftly. Even after years in the army conversations of this sort still filled him with disgust and annoyance. They can never talk decently about a woman, he thought, repelled.

They were approaching their company sector when Faber suddenly paused. From a house on the right side of the street had come a strange whining sound that cut one to the heart. It was not something you could miss or pass by.

Maag, too, had stopped. They looked across the street toward a dark shadow in front of a door. The shadow started moving slowly toward them. 'A dog,' Maag whispered in surprise. It was in fact a big watch-dog that limped across the street toward them, its right hindpaw held up in the air.

'Damned mutt,' Maag said, raising his fist threateningly.

'Let him alone,' Faber said sharply.

The dog stopped and whimpered. Faber held out his hand toward it and began coaxing it. 'Come,' he said again and again, 'come over here.'

'What do you want with the filthy beast?' Maag asked irritably.

Faber did not reply. He went up to the dog, which raised its head trustfully and began licking his hand. 'I have to go,' Maag said. 'My tour begins in five minutes.'

Faber looked around at him. 'Nobody's keeping you.'

For a moment Maag glared angrily. Then he turned on his heel and stalked off, offended. They'll feel sorry for a dog, he thought bitterly. All the sympathy in the world for a dog!

Faber examined the dog's forepaw. As he ran his fingers carefully over the leathery skin, he came upon a thorn buried deep between the pads. The animal seemed aware that he wanted to help it, and held still. When he gripped the thorn between his fingernails and pulled it out with a jerk, the dog's body twitched and it whimpered softly. 'There, it's done,' Faber said soothingly, patting the moist snout that rubbed gratefully against his hand. He wondered whether he should take the dog along to his quarters. But perhaps the others would object. And he did not know where he could get food for it. Rations here in the bridgehead were not exactly generous. On the other hand, he could not leave the poor creature to its fate.

Hoping it would follow him, he walked on a few steps. But when he turned around, he saw that the dog had stood still and was watching him go. Now it hobbled across the street to its old place in front of the door, crouched down and whimpered softly. Faber went over to it and sat down on the doorstep beside it. He drew his knees up, and the dog laid its narrow head on his lap and began eagerly licking his hands. Tenderly, Faber stroked the shaggy hide. The street was dark and silent. After a while man and dog sat still. It occurred to Faber that they had much in common. The only difference was that he knew he was homesick and the dog only dumbly sensed it. There was some comfort in their being here together, comfort for the man from the valleys of the Black Forest and for the forgotten dog who had been driven by homesickness back to the threshold of a deserted house. . . .

The dog kept its eyes closed. It felt the hand upon its back, and its whimpering stopped. Now and then, Faber saw, it raised its head and looked at the door. But there was no one here to let it in. Nor were there any of the familiar faces, the loved smells. Everything was strangely different, and the dog was mournful because of that. When Faber stood up, it watched his every movement with anxious attentiveness. Its eyes seemed to be begging, and Faber felt his heart grow heavy. 'I cannot help you,' he said softly. 'I am as forlorn as you.' When he turned away at last and walked off, the dog's head dropped down on its paws, and it whimpered. Faber bit his lip and hurried away. A great, helpless rage was in him.

XIII

IT WAS OCTOBER by now, and the order for departure came as a complete surprise. It snapped the men out of the reflective quiet of the preceding weeks. But they were accustomed to such changes and quickly adjusted to the idea. During the night they were relieved by a marine unit and marched east over the dark roads. Steiner walked at the head of the second platoon, alongside Lieutenant März, who occasionally threw a glance back at the company behind him. They said little to one another; each was busy with his thoughts. Steiner was in a bad humour. That morning he had had a talk with Fetscher who opined that to his mind the divisions in the bridgehead had already been written off by the army. 'There'll be a second Stalingrad,' he had said. 'The Russians are already close to Melitopol, and in a few days they'll reach Perekop. The Crimea is lost, and us along with it.'

Steiner tried to shake off these gloomy thoughts. Out of the corners of his eyes he looked at the face of his company commander. Steiner had spent a good deal of time with him of late. Once it had developed that März was a passionate chess player, they had whiled away a good many evenings in the company command post, playing chess and afterward talking of this and that. In the course of their talks it had come out that März was related by marriage to the regimental adjutant. This information had rather disturbed Steiner, reminding him as it did of his last encounter with Kiesel and the ugly scene with Brandt. Although several weeks had passed since that night without any gesture from Brandt, and although Stransky was letting him alone, he still had the gnawing sensation that the hardest contest still lay before him. As he studied the lieutenant's face he again became aware that März had never remotely referred to the incident in the regimental command post, although Kiesel must certainly have told him about it. There was some method behind this silence, Steiner thought. He looked back along the line.

'How far do we still have to go?' Schnurrbart asked. He was

marching beside Krüger and Kiesel in the first row of the platoon, his pipe in his mouth. März, who had caught his words, shrugged. 'I've no idea. There's supposed to be a truck column somewhere that's going to pick us up.'

'Truck column?' Krüger growled. 'As soon as I hear that I feel sick to my stomach. That means all hell has let loose somewhere.'

März tramped out his cigarette butt and nodded. 'That may be. But not in the bridgehead, for sure. At present our whole sector is quiet.'

'Ivan's had a bellyful,' Schnurrbart muttered, spitting sideways on the ground.

In the darkness Steiner tried to regain his sense of direction. They had already been marching for four hours, and it must be way past midnight. This area was strange to him. They had not followed the highway leading westward, but a country road tending more in a south-westerly direction. The road rose and fell endlessly over hilly country that reminded him of the area around Krymskaya. Everything seemed black, monotonous, limitless and terribly abandoned. Under their nailed boots fine sand squeaked and in spite of the darkness they could see the kicked-up dust that hung like a translucent veil above their heads and made breathing difficult. Up ahead in the ranks of the first company a song was started. But it did not catch on, and faded wearily away amid the dull tramp of boots. Occasionally a man stood out of the line of march with his back to the road. They passed by him as though he were a tree. Weariness crawled from their legs into their brains, making them dead-sleepy. The three behind Steiner had locked arms and were marching with closed eyes. Alternately one of them would open his eyes to see the direction, and would gently press the others toward the middle of the road, so that they would not stumble into the ditch. That was a technique they had developed over thousands of miles. It enabled them to march half-asleep; their legs seemed to separate from the rest of the body and become independent units which kept moving automatically. Steiner walked with drooping head, staring at the shoes of the company commander beside him, who took long strides and whistled under his breath. Once again Steiner found himself thinking about Brandt. The more time that passed since that interview, the more conscience-stricken he felt about it. The devil must have got into me, he thought, shaking his head. He could not understand himself.

Several times he had wrestled with the thought of sending a letter of apology. But there was a stubborn defiance in him that forbade such a step. Least of all could he understand the commander's conduct. The longer he thought about that, the more inexplicable it seemed. He would have accepted any punishment with a shrug, accepting it as the natural result of his insolence. But this mysterious silence on the commander's part tormented him; it simply did not fit in with what he knew of the way superiors acted. Altogether, it was a queer business.

When März spoke to him, he looked up vacantly. 'We're there,' the lieutenant said.

'Really?' Steiner asked. Now he became aware that the road before them terminated in a broad highway where a line of big trucks stood. At the same time a loud call came down the column, ordering the company commanders up front. 'Bring us good news!' Steiner said. März nodded and hurried off. The men dropped leadenly by the roadside, lit cigarettes and talked in muted voices.

'I wonder where we'll drink our next champagne,' Schnurrbart remarked.

Krüger grinned. 'In Siberia. Where else?'

'How late is it?' Maag asked. He sat with legs drawn up, chewing a piece of bread.

Steiner looked at his watch. 'Half past three. We marched for five hours.'

'Twenty miles,' Schnurrbart said, looked at the trucks. The drivers were asleep at the wheels.

Five minutes passed. Then März returned.

'Where are we going?' Steiner asked.

März hooked the map-board to his belt and grinned. 'Guess.'

They regarded him curiously. 'Italy?' Steiner said hopefully.

März shook his head.

'Crimea?' Schnurrbart guessed.

'No.'

They suggested various possibilities. Finally März said: 'You'll never guess it. We're going back.'

'We've been doing that for the past year,' Steiner growled. 'You don't mean back to dear old Germany?'

'No, back to Novorosisk,' März stated.

They stared blankly at him. Steiner rubbed his eyes and

murmured: 'Somebody's dippy.' Suddenly he grinned. 'Then we can go on with our chess match.'

'We'll have to play against the Russians,' März said. 'Tonight they landed at five points on the waterfront. Two hours after we moved out. Does that give you any ideas?'

Steiner gasped. 'Treason!' he murmured.

'You could call it that,' März replied equably. 'But it sounds better if you say intelligence. In that area we have still something to learn from the Russians. Last week a radio station of theirs was discovered right in the heart of the city. Probably there were others.'

'Incredible,' Schnurrbart whispered.

März twisted his mouth into a mirthless smile. 'We'll have to get used to the idea. All right, into the trucks.'

Cursing, the men got up and scattered among the vehicles. Minutes later the trucks started up. Schnurrbart sat beside Steiner, holding his tommy-gun in his hands. 'What a stinking mess,' he grumbled. Steiner nodded.

They sat in silence until they reached the outer suburbs of the city. The trucks covered the distance of the five-hour march in barely an hour. It was already so light that the road could be seen. Above the city hovered huge clouds of smoke: dull detonations rolled over the roofs; and as the men jumped down from the trucks they noticed that the street was full of splintered glass, scraps of wood and fragmented stone. 'You'd think there was a war going on here,' Krüger said, gazing with disgust at the black shell-holes.

Steiner looked toward the one-story buildings which seemed to be cowering in terror behind the garden fences. Then he recalled there was something he'd wanted to ask about. He went over to März, who was supervising the unloading of the vehicles, and put his question: 'Where were we going?'

'The Perekop Peninsula,' März replied.

'And what were we supposed to do there?'

'Defend the Crimea.'

Steiner nodded. 'Then I guess there's no harm in my having sent my letter.'

'What letter?' März asked in surprise.

'My last will and testament,' Steiner said, and returned to his men. He felt somehow relieved. They waited until the last of the soldiers had clambered out of the vehicles, then watched the trucks drive off as though the devil were behind them. Krüger picked at his nose and watched them go thoughtfully. 'If I ever come into this world again . . .' he began, but Steiner interrupted him. 'You'll be a truck driver, I know. But I imagine you'll take care not to come into the world again.'

From somewhere sounded violent rifle skirmishing. Schnurrbart raised his head to listen. 'That's on the waterfront,' he commented. 'Must be going hot and heavy down there.'

'If it weren't they wouldn't have sent for us,' Maag growled.

Kern sighed. His unshaven face twitched as though pricked by nettles. He wished he could crawl into one of the houses and wait until the show was over. Glumly, he watched the head of the first company start forward. The men formed squad columns, leaving large intervals between them. They had exchanged their alpine caps for steel helmets and were walking crouched, with heads tilted.

'I wonder whether this area is exposed to observation,' Maag remarked uneasily.

Krüger shrugged. 'I doubt it, or we'd have smelt powder by now.'

'Just give it time,' Schnurrbart said, hitching up his belt. 'I don't like this quiet.'

'You call this quiet!' Krüger grinned, nodding toward the waterfront where a series of heavy explosions rumbled one after the other. The air was smoky, and the cool breeze from the sea carried the smell of burned powder to the street. Steiner saw März place himself at the head of the first platoon and raise his fist into the air. The company started forward. They passed down several streets which were swathed in dense smoke and had been partly converted into rubble heaps. 'Mortars,' Schnurrbart commented, glancing distrustfully up at the cloudless sky, which was gradually colouring with the promise of a fine day. After a quarter hour's march they had come so close to the centre of the city that the noise of battle seemed to be raging beyond the next street corner. They could easily distinguish machine-guns and hand grenades. Isolated shells passed high above the roofs and exploded with thunderous crashes. Up front there was a pause. Steiner observed the men scattering among the houses as März hurried on, crouching as he ran.

'What's going on?' Schnurrbart asked.

Steiner shrugged. 'Dunno. Probably a briefing at battalion. Let's get off the street.'

He sat down on a doorstep, lit a cigarette and looked at the houses across the street. The top stories were already receiving the light of the rising sun. A curtain swayed in and out of an empty window frame. The sight was somehow homelike, and Steiner felt his heart grow heavy. Damn it all, he thought, absently puffing on his cigarette. Behind him he heard the voices of Kern and Krüger, who were sitting in the vestibule of the house, talking loudly. Suddenly they fell silent. The even noise of rifle and machine-gun fire was drowned out by a long dull thunder that reverberated menacingly over the streets, plucking at the nerves. 'Artillery salvo,' Schnurrbart murmured. They had all jumped up and cowered in the doorway. The detonations followed in quick succession somewhere along the waterfront. 'They'll blow our arses off,' Kern whispered, white-lipped. They were all pale, unshaven, sleepworn. Their steel helmets hung down low over their eyes.

'You know what we'll have,' Krüger asked. He laughed savagely. 'The same shit as in Kharkov, I tell you. Fighting from house to house and room to room. When we throw them out on one side they'll come in again on the other, and when we're in the cellar they'll be in the pantry. I can do without it.'

He stared darkly out at the street, where März had suddenly turned up and was coming toward them swiftly. He went over to Steiner, who rose and looked inquiringly at him. 'It's starting,' März said laconically. He turned to Kern. 'Bring the other platoon leaders here.'

Kern went off and returned shortly with Sergeants Schulz and Stober. Steiner knew the two men only slightly. They had come with the latest batch of replacements, and he had exchanged a few words with them just once or twice. They entered the vestibule of the house and looked expectantly at März, who held a map in his hand and was studying it attentively. Now he looked up at him. 'We're attacking. The goal is a big machine-tool factory on the waterfront. The Russians have raised a red flag on the factory tower. We're to take it down. Express order from the battalion commander. Special assignment for you, Steiner.'

'That's idiotic,' Stober murmured.

März ignored the remark and continued: 'The first and third

companies are advancing toward the waterfront to our left and right. The attack is set for eight o'clock.'

'How far is it to the factory?' Steiner asked.

'Above five hundred and fifty yards. We'll be there soon.'

'And the line?' Schulz asked.

März scraped his chin. 'Things seem to be confused. In places the Russians are already deep into the city, and at other places they haven't got beyond the waterfront.'

'I don't get it,' Stober murmured, shaking his head. 'What are we doing on the waterfront if they're inside the city already?' He had an angular face with deep hollows in his cheeks and eyes that seemed made of glass.

März spread the map out on the floor and the men stood looking over his shoulders. 'Here's the waterfront. When we get there, we'll advance along the shore and take the Russians on the flank. They seem to be bent on establishing contact with their units on the other side,' März pointed to a spot on the map. 'Here is Novorosisk and here is our southern flank. The line begins on the other side of the harbour. If the Russians succeed in breaking through, they'll advance along the seacoast as far as Anapa and seize the ferry-landings.'

'I see,' Stober said. 'By landing on the waterfront he's taking us in the rear. It's like cutting the string on a stretched bow.'

'Pretty much,' März replied. 'If we want to hold the bridge-head we've got to get the Russians out of here. So you know what's at stake.'

Schulz straightened up. 'That's idiotic,' he declared discontentedly.

'What?'

'That about the factory. How big is the place?'

'I don't know,' März replied. 'I've never been in that part of town. We'll soon see.'

A man came in from the street. 'The first company is leaving, Lieutenant,' he reported.

'I know. They have further to go than we.' He folded up the map and thrust it into the map-board hanging from his side. Then he turned to Steiner. 'You and your platoon will follow me at the head of the company. In front of us are parts of a marine unit. We will relieve them and then attack at once. Order the men to fall in.'

Steiner had a few more words with the two sergeants. Schulz had thrust his hands into his pockets and was glaring furiously at the lieutenant, who was already outside. 'Wants to earn the Iron Cross, the stinker!' he said with an ugly sneer.

Steiner looked at him with reproof. He did not like the man. His face appeared extremely brutal. From temple to chin ran a deep scar. The man's brows grew together over the base of his nose, and his broad mouth was embedded in ugly folds. 'Mind your own business,' Steiner said sharply, and followed the lieutenant out. The men streamed out of the houses and stood waiting in a long row on the right side of the street. Steiner glanced rapidly around to assure himself that Schnurrbart and the others were close by him. März raised his hand. 'Keep a good distance between you,' he ordered. 'I don't want any casualties before the show starts. March!'

As they moved down the street, keeping close to the row of houses, the artillery fire above their heads increased. The din of battle in front of them went on without pause. The district they were now in must once have been the business centre of the city. On both sides of the street gaped the empty frames of huge show windows; the insides of the shops were strewn with plaster and broken glass. In many places the pavement on the street had been torn open by shells, and as Steiner, following März, went round a heap of rubble, there was an explosion behind them that threw them to the ground and showered large and small pieces of stone on to the street. When the hail stopped, März stood up and dusted his clothes. 'That's the start,' he said calmly. 'Increase distances.'

Steiner passed the order on and observed the men come out of their frozen positions. Then he followed März, who was displaying an astonishing coolheadedness. Steiner had to smile as it struck him that the lieutenant was walking as though he were out for a Sunday stroll in a peaceful garrison town. März, happening to turn his head at that moment, caught the grin and stood still.

'What amuses you so?' he demanded.

'You,' Steiner replied, wiping the grin from his face. März opened his mouth. Steiner, hearing the shell a fraction of a second before him, pulled him to the ground as he dived. The street vanished under a cloud of smoke. Again a wild hail of stone hurtled against the walls of the buildings. Glowing splinters of iron darted with a horrible hissing noise into the wooden frames of the shop windows. The men lay flat on the ground, pressing their faces into their arms. The next shell exploded a long way ahead of them.

März got up. 'I asked you a question,' he said to Steiner, who was rubbing an aching elbow.

Steiner shook his head irritably. 'Maybe you were going to ask me something.'

März looked thoughtfully at him. Then he nodded. 'Right. I wanted to ask you what amuses you so about me.'

Steiner looked back and noticed Schnurrbart's uncomprehending expression; he was standing right behind them, listening to every word. Steiner turned to März again. 'Are you fishing for compliments?'

'If that's all it is, you can keep it to yourself.' März strode on again. They made a detour around the fresh shell-hole. When they reached an intersection they saw that the street dropped steeply to the waterfront, and that it seemed to be blocked off at the end by a board fence. Coming closer they were able to see a cross-street running along the fence and in a wide curve around the harbour. 'We're here,' März said. 'Send the men into the houses. I'll go to the battalion command post.'

'Where is it?' Steiner asked.

'Around the corner here somewhere. I'll be right back.' As März trotted off around the corner, Steiner turned and signalled to the men to take cover.

'What's up?' Schnurrbart wanted to know.

'You're to wait here,' Steiner ordered. 'Get out of sight.' He lit a cigarette and walked slowly forward toward the intersection.

The waterfront street was built up only on one side. On the other side was the six-foot-high fence. As Steiner turned the corner someone called out to him: 'Watch your step, man!'

He looked up and saw the face of a man glaring indignantly down at him. 'What's worrying you?' Steiner asked.

The man had by now recognized his rank, and his face showed emabrrassment. 'You must be careful, here sir. It's all under enemy observation.'

Steiner looked around. Close to the window was a door into the building. He went through it. On the steps of the front hallway stood three men in dark-blue uniforms, their faces bearing the marks of fear. 'What unit?' Steiner asked curtly.

'Marines,' one of them replied. 'Are you the relief?'

When Steiner nodded, the faces of all three brightened. 'Thank God!' the second man sighed. They reached for their carbines, which were leaning against the wall. Steiner climbed up the four steps to them and asked: 'Where are you going?'

The men grinned. 'Back,' the first of them answered. 'We've got a bellyful.'

'Not any more than we have,' Steiner replied with animosity.

'You've no idea,' the man said. 'You should have been here last night when it started.'

Steiner scrutinized him with contempt. 'You crawled into the cellar anyhow; if you hadn't the Russians wouldn't have been able to land. And now we've got to clean up your shit.'

They glowered at him, and the first speaker said: 'We're not infantry.'

'That's obvious,' Steiner said, his dislike mounting steadily. 'What's been going on here?'

'Just about everything,' the man replied. 'There's that factory over there, where at least a regiment of Russians have squatted. If they attack, we're finished.'

'You boys would be,' Steiner growled. 'Can the factory be seen from here?'

'Sure. You must have seen the tower already.'

Steiner went back down the steps and stepped to the doorway. 'Careful!' one of the men warned him. Steiner shrugged contemptuously. He saw the tower at once. At the very top of it was a pole from which hung a red cloth that fluttered in the wind. He stared up at it for a few seconds. The marines had come up behind him, and one of them said: 'That beats all. They've got their nerve with them.'

'We're supposed to take it down,' Steiner murmured. He smiled grimly at their looks of wonder. 'Wouldn't you like to help us do it?'

They shook their heads in horror, and his grin broadened. 'I'll see how it looks from up above,' he said, and went back into the house. Upstairs, a door led into an apartment. From the window he could see the whole area. The factory consisted of a block of connected eight-story buildings in the shape of a triangle open toward the waterfront. The tower was on the south wing. The longer Steiner looked the place over, the more hopeless the impending attack appeared to him. From the fence there were some five hundred feet of factory yard completely without cover, offering every opportunity to the defenders and none to the attackers. He leaned out of the window to glance at the south elevation of the factory, and jerked back abruptly. Over his head there was an ugly hiss and then a thud as though a board were struck against a stone. A cloud of dust whirled down toward him. Simultaneously a Russian machine-gun began hammering away from the factory. Steiner stepped quickly away from the window, cursing under his breath. They were keen as watchdogs. But he had had time to notice that the chances for an attack from the south side were somewhat better, since there the fence approached to within a hundred feet of the building. Moving cautiously, from the side this time, he approached the window again and looked down at the street. To his surprise, he saw several men of the second company running across the pavement and scattering along the fence. He recognized März among them. Quickly, he left the room and ran down the steps.

The marines had disappeared. On the street he caught sight of März again, leaning with his back against the fence and watching the company crossing the street in small groups. He saw Steiner and raised his hand. 'Where have you been?' he called impatiently. Steiner crossed over to him and gestured back over his shoulder with his thumb. 'Getting our bearings.'

'You'll take the right wing,' März directed briskly. 'We'll start in a moment. We have artillery support.'

'Ten rounds,' Steiner growled, slipping the tommy-gun from his shoulder.

'I beg your pardon?' März asked in astonishment.

'Ten rounds,' Steiner repeated. 'It won't be enough to disturb the Russians at their second breakfast.'

'You take too black a view.' März reached into his pocket, took out a pack of cigarettes and offered it to Steiner.

'The only colour for it,' Steiner murmured morosely, holding the burning match under the company commander's cigarette. As he tossed it away, he caught sight of several men kneeling on the ground and using their bayonets to pry the slats of the fence from the lower bar. He took a step forward. The rest of the company was engaged in similar work. 'What's the idea?' he said to März, who was equably puffing away at his cigarette.

'What idea?'

'That,' Steiner said impatiently, gesturing at the men.

'You can see for yourself,' März replied. 'Do you imagine we're going to climb over the fence?'

Steiner stared at him. 'Does that mean we attack from this point?' he asked incredulously.

'Of course,' März said.

They stood in silence. From the direction of the factory a Russian machine-gun chattered now and then. Further to the south a violent skirmish seemed to be going on. Heavy artillery detonations boomed in unbroken succession. Before the mountains loomed dark clouds of smoke that stretched higher and higher, dirtying the cloudless sky. Steiner looked at the houses across the street. Their white stucco showed ugly wounds; they glistened starkly in the cold morning sunlight. An uncomfortable sensation crawled down his spine. 'It's mad,' he murmured. 'I hope you realize what our chances are.'

'I do.' März nodded indifferently. Steiner looked at the men. They were working away eagerly, as though the fence were the last obstacle between them and a storehouse full of provisions. The thought amused him so much that he laughed aloud. März looked up at him in astonishment. 'What's the matter with you?'

'Nothing. I just thought of something funny.'

'Of yourself, by any chance?'

'For once no. I thought of a stupid rat desperately looking for a way into a trap.'

'That certainly is funny,' März replied. His face was deadly earnest.

As Steiner started to turn away, the lieutenant gripped his shoulder. 'Don't forget the flag. The commander wants it.'

'He can use it to be wrapped in at his funeral,' Steiner growled. He went over to his men. They were sitting on the ground about sixty yards away.

'How's it look?' Schnurrbart asked. He held his cold pipe clenched between his teeth. His face looked sunken and weary. Steiner sat down beside him without replying. He leaned his back against the fence and stared across the street. 'Are we supposed to attack here?' Kern asked anxiously.

Steiner nodded. Krüger propped himself up on his right elbow. 'We won't get across,' he said definitely. 'We'll all be finished in this business, you can depend on that.'

'Maybe luck'll be on our side,' Maag murmured. It was evident from his voice that he did not believe his own words.

Faber said nothing. The machine-gun tucked between his legs, he stared absently at the ground. Suddenly they all jerked at once. Above their heads, so close that they imagined they could feel the wind of their passage, a series of heavy shells swished by and exploded behind their backs in the factory yard. 'It's starting,' Steiner murmured. They turned on their stomachs, pushed the slats somewhat to one side, and watched the barrage. The next round drummed against the factory walls, and they saw the walls burst apart. The building vanished behind a yellow-black cloud of smoke that slowly mounted upward. Ineffective, Steiner thought. The building was solid; there was no reason to think that a dozen holes in the walls would seriously weaken the enemy's resistance. His glance fell upon a small black beetle that crawled under the fence and disappeared into a tiny hole. He swallowed. We're too damn big, he thought. As he stared at the ground, aware that he was envying a beetle, he suddenly thought of Anne, and his throat contracted so that he had difficulty in breathing. The hellish report above his head continued. Insanely loud, the shells howled above the roofs, cleaving the air and crashing into the factory. Hooeeee-vumn, hooeeee-vumn. It went on and on. He turned his head and saw beside him Kern's sallow face. Kern lay on the ground, lips twitching, steel helmet pressed against the fence. Faber was squatting on his heels, the machine-gun clutched in his hands, his eyes shut. Krüger and Schnurrbart were peering through the cracks in the fence at the factory yard, the skin over their cheekbones so taut it seemed on the point of ripping. Maag was on his other side, the freckles on the white skin of his face like drops of blood on snow.

Then there was an abrupt silence. Somewhere a piercing cry rang out. Steiner saw the men jump up, reach for the slats of the fence and tug at them. The big nails in the wood squealed as though several dozen doors were moving on rusty hinges, and the boards thumped to the ground. Then the yard lay before them. Smooth, flooded with sunlight. A slaughtering yard, Steiner thought, and began running. Two hundred steps to the factory. Two hundred ridiculous steps to the grey basalt walls behind which the Russians lay. He felt his heart pounding against his ribs, sweat streaming down his face. He panted. Two hundred steps, twenty seconds. Since Anne plunged over the cliff two thousand years had passed, or was it more? Twenty seconds; it was ridiculous. He heard his breath whistling, saw the scurrying shadows of the men to his left and right, felt biting dust in his eyes and stumbled and ran and gasped. They had covered half the distance when machine-gun fire blazed in their faces. They had taken a hundred steps, and fell to the ground as though they had stumbled over a wire. Within ten seconds the company lay like a writhing, many-limbed animal in the factory yard, and somewhere a man began to scream as though he had three voices. Seconds later a second began, and then another, then many. They lay screaming on the ground, and over them and into them pelted the bullets from half a dozen Russian machine-guns. And then came the artillery fire. The yard was transformed into a forest of darting fountains of smoke, as though the earth had broken open in a hundred places, and the screams of the wounded and dying men were drowned by the garish explosions. Steiner lay two paces away from Kern and stared at the one-time innkeeper, whose right arm stuck up into the air like a post, fingers curiously outspread. Steiner lay beside the dead man, and two paces farther on Maag had his freckled face pressed against the ground as though he had discovered there a shaft leading through the earth, with the blue sky above the Azores on the other side. Steiner lay between the dead men and felt clods of earth raining down on his back, felt the hot breath of steel fragments hissing by, and in his head was nothing but a roaring which made him scarcely hear the infernal din in the factory yard. In the cemetery, he thought, closing his eyes. He heard a voice calling his name, but did not stir. He stayed still, his thoughts flying amid swooping in great circles, and he heard another voice saying: '. . . And none of you will go without his reward . . .' But it sounded unreal and remote. It must have been in a barracks yard, he thought. A voice ringing out across a barracks yard in which stood eight hundred men in new uniforms and shining boots. How far away was that? Six million steps and more, and across the factory yard it was only two hundred.

He raised his head and looked toward the road. A hundred paces from the fence, he thought; only half the distance. And he saw several dozen men running in between the detonations of the shells, running, throwing themselves to the ground, picking themselves up and racing on, until they vanished from sight. Suddenly he realized that it had been Schnurrbart's voice calling his name.

At that he pushed himself up. He pushed himself away from the ground and for a moment stood upright. As he turned around he saw März. The lieutenant came stumbling across the yard, eyes wild, mouth open, arms dangling slackly at his sides, and Steiner heard him shouting. But he could not understand a word, When a shell struck near März, he tipped over as though his legs had been knocked from under him, and Steiner ran toward him. He looked neither to right nor to left and ran over to him. For a second he stared down at him, then slung the man over his shoulder and stumbled blindly through the fire. He ran like a machine, utterly without sensation, eyes closed, thinking: You will all receive your reward. All of you. He tripped over bodies, slid heavily into shell-holes that opened before him, panted through dark clouds of smoke, until suddenly he saw the fence before him. The weight of the lieutenant seemed to increase tenfold. As Steiner ran across the street, his knees threatened to give in. He saw several men in a doorway shouting at him, saw a familiar face as Schnurrbart came running toward him, and then the tons of weight fell from his shoulder and he plunged into the vestibule of a house, where he lay groaning and half unconscious. You will all receive your reward, he thought again, and closed his eyes. There was a great stillness within him.

Toward evening Kiesel entered the commander's room. He found the lieutenant-colonel studying some papers which he quickly laid aside on perceiving Kiesel. His face expressed uneasiness and concern as he asked: 'Well?'

'He was lucky,' Kiesel replied, sitting down. 'I found him at the clearing station. He had already been operated on and was out of ether when I came. But now he is probably . . .' Kiesel glanced at his wrist-watch. 'At this moment he must be on his way to the ferry. In a few days he'll be in a hospital back home.'

'I'm glad for him and for you,' Brandt said heartily. 'What do you think your sister will say to that?'

Kiesel stared reflectively at the floor. 'She will thank his lucky star,' he replied. 'His lucky star and Steiner.'

The commander's head jerked up. 'Steiner? What about Steiner?'

'If it were not for Steiner he would have lain there and bled to death. Steiner carried him back. März told me about it himself.'

'Can you guess what I am thinking?' Brandt asked softly.

When Kiesel said nothing, he turned and slowly approached his adjutant. 'I am thinking of what would have happened to März if I had accepted your recommendation and transferred Steiner. I can't help thinking of that now.'

'I have already thought of that,' Kiesel said.

Brandt looked down at him. 'Do you still remember what you said about providence?'

Kiesel nodded silently. For a while Brandt stood motionless, looking over his head into a corner of the room. Then he returned to his chair and sat with head bowed.

Kiesel looked over at the tall windows. The ruins of the city towered into a fiery sky. The light of the setting sun flooded in through the window panes, casting bars of brightness on the intricate pattern of the rug. He watched as the sunlight neared the wall, flowing over the white-painted wood of the baseboard and almost imperceptibly crawling up the wallpaper. On an antique chest stood a plaster bust of Lenin staring pop-eyed at the leggy china-closet on the opposite wall, in which a delicate Biedermeier tea service was arrayed. Rendezvous of the centuries, Kiesel thought, feeling an odd sense of grief. The commander picked up a sheet of paper and raised his head. 'Captain Morlock was here.'

Kiesel raised his eyebrows expectantly. Captain Morlock was Chief Operations Officer of Division. He seldom came down to the regiment; when he did, it was always on something of special importance. Controlling his curiosity, Kiesel waited. He watched Brandt consult the sheet of paper again. Finally he thrust it into a drawer which he carefully locked. 'Top secret, for commanders only,' he said tersely.

Kiesel regarded him with bright, intelligent eyes. Then he said: 'We're evacuating.' It was not a question, but a statement.

'How do you know?' Brandt asked.

'A guess. It's been in the air a long time.'

Brandt nodded wearily. 'The day is still secret.'

'And why are we attacking?' Kiesel asked.

'Camouflage tactics. As long as we keep on attacking the Russians won't expect us to evacuate the bridgehead. It has to be done, senseless as it seems.'

'When do you think we'll go?'

'Today, tomorrow, the day after.' Brandt shrugged. 'We're waiting for the cue. The evacuation has been prepared down to the last detail. What bothers the big brass is the unexpected invasion of the Russians in Novorosisk. They think it important for that to be cleaned up first.'

'We're too weak,' Kiesel said.

Brandt, who had been pacing the room, paused in front of an engraving in a gilded frame on the wall. He stood studying the print for a moment. Then he turned toward Kiesel again. 'Morlock holds the same opinion. But we dare not leave anything untried. There's too much at stake. According to information reaching Division, the Russians have been concentrating their strength for months. It's going to be a race with time, and everything depends upon whether we can carry out the step-by-step evacuation as planned. Novorosisk is the first monkey-wrench in the machinery.' He went to the table and leaned over the map. 'Vogel has reached the waterfront. Körner is still fighting around the centre. Stransky is stuck in front of the factory, while his first and third companies are brawling with the Russians somewhere and sending alarming radio messages. My picture of it is beginning to be quite a mess.'

Kiesel stood up and looked over his shoulder at the map. 'What is Stransky going to do?'

'I've ordered him to occupy the factory after dark. Triebig will lead the second company's attack. Let's hope they have more success than they did this morning. As long as the Russians hold the factory they'll be able to keep their little bridgehead on this side. There seem to be four or five warships in the harbour.'

'Hopeless,' Kiesel murmured. He asked a few more questions, which Brandt answered laconically. After a while they sat down at the table again and discussed the situations of the other battalions.

'Körner worries me most,' Brandt remarked, rubbing his chin. 'He hasn't advanced a yard and on both sides has exposed flanks which . . .' He was interrupted by the urgent shrilling of the telephone. 'That may be Körner now,' he said eagerly, answering. Then he frowned and looked up. 'It's from Vogel. What . . .' He fell silent and listened intently. Kiesel saw his features stiffen. He laid back the receiver and spoke dully: 'Vogel is dead.'

'Dead?' Kiesel changed colour.

'They caught the battalion staff,' Brandt said. 'Suddenly broke in from the back of the house. Nobody knows where they came from.' He leaned forward, probing Kiesel's pale face. 'What are we going to do when we lose the war?'

The question was such a bolt from the blue that Kiesel started. He shrugged wearily. 'Start life all over again,' he said softly.

A dark frown passed over the commander's face. 'You may, but not I. I'm too old to start life all over again.' His big head drooped. 'It's no longer worth it.'

'There are ways,' Kiesel murmured without conviction.

'Certainly.' Brandt nodded absently. 'Certainly there are ways. Being a salesman, for example. Going from house to house and door to door. Can you imagine it?'

Kiesel did not reply. Several painful minutes passed, until Brandt laughed harshly. His whole body stiffened. 'Perhaps we are thinking further ahead than is really necessary. There are other solutions. A hero's grave, for example, or Siberia, or the National Committee. What do you think about that?'

Kiesel saw mingled rage and anguish in his face, and something of the commander's hopelessness affected him. 'I would prefer the first,' he answered.

'That surprises me,' Brandt replied loudly. 'I would have thought the last.'

Kiesel felt that he was looking for a quarrel, and shook his head. 'You misunderstand me. That would be an escape into self-deception, and in the long run you can't go on deceiving yourself.'

'What about your ideology?' Brandt asked scornfully.

Kiesel looked down at his cigarette and remained silent. When the commander drummed his fingers impatiently on the table, he raised his head. His voice was cold as he spoke: 'I'll put it this way: in principle I can't enjoy a full dinner when others sitting beside me are hungry, especially when they wear the same uniform and have sworn the same oath as I have.'

'I'm glad to hear that,' Brandt said. His face relaxed. 'There is no excuse for the Committee,' he said harshly. 'They call upon our men to desert, although they know perfectly well what is awaiting them on the other side. Filthy scoundrels.' He fell silent and began kneading the skin above his cheekbones.

To divert his thoughts, Kiesel spoke of Steiner. 'I'd like to find out his home address. März asked me for it.'

'Fetscher will have it,' Brandt growled. 'Staff Sergeant Fetscher.' He was scarcely paying attention, and quickly turned the conversation back to personal matters. 'I've never thought about that before,' he went on. 'But for several weeks now it's been weighing on me. I really don't any longer see what I'd do with myself if I should take off this uniform today.'

'You're still a fine figure of a man,' Kiesel said cautiously.

Brandt laughed twistedly. 'You mean I might marry again? Are you mad? I was forty when my wife died. Twelve years have passed since then, and I've become an inveterate bachelor. Don't bring that up.' He lit a cigarette and tossed the match to the floor, where it went on glowing and burned a hole in the rug. They watched it without moving. Their eyes met, and Brandt laughed bitterly. He pointed to the ugly black spot in the vivid design of the rug and said: 'If I were a married man, I wouldn't do that sort of thing. But I'm too old to adjust to domesticity. Too old and full of idiosyncrasies.'

'You would have to find the right woman,' Kiesel replied.

'That happens only once. You know that as well as I. Why haven't you ever married?'

It was a challenge that struck Kiesel to the quick. He bristled as he said: 'Don't you know?'

'Yes, I do know. There's more talk about you than you have any notion of. The division is full of gossip about it. If what they say is true, you were studying for the ministry until you got mixed up with some girl, who later threw you over. Is that so?'

'They are well informed,' Kiesel replied coldly.

'You should expect that,' Brandt said. 'You may think me tactless for saying it to you so bluntly. But I'm not one for this damn beating around the bush. When I talk with somebody, I want him to know where he stands. You've escaped into the uniform just as I did, and now that we are probably on the point of losing our uniforms, we're right back where we once were. And I tell you frankly, I don't look forward to it.'

Kiesel regarded him expressionlessly. 'You can shoot yourself,' he said brutally.

He saw the commander's eyes widen for a moment. But his voice was perfectly tranquil as he replied: 'The thought is not new. Perhaps I shall some day take it up.'

There was something in his face which Kiesel had never seen before, and which aroused his concern. 'You mean that?'

'What do you think?'

'That's no solution,' Kiesel said harshly.

Brandt shrugged. 'It's no better or worse than the others. It's just—shall I say, more final.'

'At first sight,' Kiesel said.

Brandt waved that aside.

'At last sight, which is what gives the idea its peculiar appeal.' He leaned forward across the table. 'Listen to me carefully, Kiesel,' he said in a controlled voice. 'You have your philosophy and I have mine. Of late I have had occasion to note that we have a great deal in common. But the point on which we fundamentally differ—you know as well as I. I may envy you for your illusions, but I cannot take them seriously.'

The patch of sunlight on the rug had meanwhile travelled to the ceiling where it clung to a corner, shrinking and fading. Kiesel sat rigidly in his chair. His eyes under half-shut lids were fiercely alert as he asked: 'What do you mean by illusions?'

Brandt nodded as though primed for the question. 'For heaven's sake, don't start splitting hairs with me. I had illusions, too, Kiesel, but they possessed form and substance. I had my eye on one thing and another, until finally I picked the uniform. That was the greatest folly of my life, not that you could have told me so at the time. It was not that I had no other opportunities. There was a family business—you understand—but it wasn't enough for me. I had ambition, wanted to make a career. Well, did I succeed or not?' He laughed stridently. 'Didn't make it to general, as I had hoped, but still regimental commander isn't bad. There hasn't been time to go any further.' He fell silent, rose quickly and went over to the window where he stood with averted face, gazing out over the roofs.

'You can regard it as an episode,' Kiesel said quietly.

Brandt shook his head emphatically. 'That sort of thing is not an episode. It's what I have to show for my life. The top step, where I intended to rest, and I have spent fifty-two years reaching it.' He turned around, propping his arms on the window-sill. His face seemed shattered, but he was smiling. 'Fifty-two years. I don't know anybody who started at the beginning again at the age of fifty-two. Not when all bridges were burned behind him.'

'There are examples . . .' Kiesel began.

The commander cut him off. 'Don't give me any of that. Public welfare case or monk or something. I'm not the type. I'm sick of

it all, damn sick of it.' At that moment the telephone rang. He
went to the table and picked up the receiver. His body stiffened.
'Herr General!'

The four of them sat around the table in silence. Schnurrbart
was holding a worn letter-case in his hands, turning aimlessly
through a number of papers. The only window in the room was
shielded by a ground-sheet so that no light would fall into the
street. The flickering candle cast leaping shadows on the walls
of the room. Now and then a machine-gun chattered.

Schnurrbart lifted his head. 'What'll we do with this stuff?'

'You can give it to Fetscher,' Steiner replied. He sat with feet
on the table, smoking. Now he held out his hand. 'Let me see.'
As Schnurrbart handed the letter-case to him, a picture fell out.
Krüger leaned forward with interest. 'Who's it of?'

'A girl,' Steiner said, holding the picture up to the candle and
studying a merry face with tight curls framing a clear forehead
and crinkles of laughter around the mouth. 'Nice bit,' Krüger
murmured. 'I wonder what she'll do when she gets the news.'

'What's there for her to do,' Schnurrbart replied grumpily.
'She'll buy herself a nice-looking black dress, and by two weeks
she'll have forgotten him.'

Faber shook his head in reproof. 'That's no way to talk. You
don't know how they feel about it.'

Steiner had turned the picture over. He read the words written
in a rather childish handwriting on the back. 'For my dear Kurt.
Monika.' Curious that his name was Kurt, Steiner thought. 'Did
any of you know his first name was Kurt?' he asked.

'Who?' Krüger asked.

'Maag, of course. I don't think I ever heard his first name.'

'Neither did I,' Schnurrbart said. 'Was it?'

'Here it stands,' Steiner said.

Krüger plucked at his nose. 'He never said a word about it.
Monika. Interesting name. Reminds me of somebody.'

Steiner replaced the picture in the letter-case and turned to
Faber. 'Have you Kern's things?'

'No. They've already taken him away. He must be over at
1st Company. When I went, Maag was the only one lying there.'

'Rotten business!' Schnurrbart shook himself. 'You know what
surprises me?' They looked up questioningly at him. 'That they

gave the job to the 1st platoon instead of us.' He turned to Steiner. 'You must be in good with Triebig.'

Steiner frowned. 'That *is* funny. I'll bet there's something behind it.'

'I've got that feeling too,' Krüger said. 'It's a suicide job, picking up the wounded and dead. The Ivans keep kicking up the dust with their MG's in the yard.'

'At any rate the attack has been called off,' Schnurrbart said.

'How come?' Krüger asked, pausing in his vigorous scratching of his head.

'It's obvious,' Schnurrbart said. 'If we were going to attack again, we wouldn't have to fetch the dead because we could do that a lot better once we were in the factory.'

The reasoning seemed cogent. 'Let's hope you're right,' Krüger said. 'I wouldn't like to run across there again. I was thinking we were all done for when the shooting started.'

The memory of that wild flight through the artillery fire marked dark shadows upon his face, and the faces of the others darkened also. 'It was sheer madness,' Schnurrbart growled bitterly, 'It serves them right, the goddamned heartless slave-drivers. Why didn't they try it from the other side?'

'Higher strategy,' Steiner said. He crushed out his cigarette. As he was about to stand up, the door opened and Triebig appeared. They stared at him without rising. He turned to Steiner. 'How many men do you have left?'

Steiner gave him a look of disgust. 'I haven't counted them yet,' he murmured.

'Then do so at once. You will attack in fifteen minutes. With a shock troop, and from the south. When you are inside the factory, fire a green flare. That will be the signal for me to follow with the rest of the company. Order of the battalion commander.'

There was a silence in the room. Triebig saw the masklike faces of the men and shrugged slightly. 'Order of the battalion commander,' he repeated in a somewhat softer voice. After a moment's hesitation he added: 'Before I forget: you must bring down that flag. The commander wants the flag.'

'To wipe his arse with?' Schnurrbart asked loudly.

Triebig whirled around. 'What are you thinking of! Stand up when I talk to you.'

Steiner, at the lieutenant's last words, had put his feet up on the table again. He lit a cigarette and let it droop from the corner of his mouth as he spoke. 'You don't have to play the big shot here. Besides which I'd advise you not to get on Schnurrbart's nerves. Since that last wound in his head he's got into the habit of firing at anything stupid enough to cross his path. Don't forget that he'll be in the factory before you.'

'What has that to do with it?' Triebig asked sharply.

Steiner wagged his head pityingly and glanced at Schnurrbart, who was glaring narrow-eyed at the lieutenant. 'Simple enough,' Steiner explained. 'If we get to the factory before you, you'll get there after us, and it just might happen that a stray bullet would meet you in the darkness.' He watched calmly as Triebig's face turned pale. With his tongue he shifted the cigarette from the right to the left corner of his mouth. Triebig stared at him. This was the first time Steiner had taken this tone to him in the presence of subordinates. To preserve a last remnant of authority, he would have to do something effective. But his fear of Steiner was even greater than his agitation, and he chose the worst imaginable way to reassert his authority. 'I'll inform the commander of that statement, you can depend on it.' His voice was shaking and he felt as though he might burst into sobs at any moment.

Steiner stared him down. 'I don't know what good you think that will do you,' he said. 'Do you imagine you'll find anyone here to confirm your charges?' He turned to Krüger. 'What were we talking about?'

The East Prussian grinned. 'About the shock troop action.'

'There, you see,' Steiner said, turning to Triebig again. 'You're an officer, aren't you? What do you need a big brother for?' His voice was full of contempt. Triebig started to speak several times. Then he stared into the faces of the men as though imprinting them on his mind. 'Very well,' he whispered, and left the room. After the door had closed behind him, there was a silence for several minutes. At last Faber spoke up. 'If I hadn't been here, I wouldn't have believed it. There's going to be a big fuss, I imagine.'

Steiner shook his head contemptuously. 'There won't be a big fuss nor a little one, but something else entirely, and very soon.' He stood up and turned to Krüger. 'How many of us are left?'

'About twenty.'

'That's enough. Get ready.'

As he went out of the room, the men reached for their gear. Krüger cursed. 'What a damned swindle. How are a few poor bastards like us going to occupy that whole factory? It's madness, I tell you.' He had slung his assault pack on his back and now stood with his clenched fists leaning on the table. 'Are you mad?' he asked. They looked at him blankly, and he laughed furiously. 'First Dietz, then Anselm and the Professor, then Hollerbach and Pasternack, and today Kern and Maag. You know what I think?' He looked at each of them in turn. 'I don't think a single one of us poor bastards is going to come out of this bridgehead alive. That's what I think.'

Schnurrbart nodded. 'I've known that for a long time. That's nothing new.'

'So it isn't,' Krüger whispered. He stood motionless for a few seconds. His glance fell upon a crystal vase that stood on the table beside the candle. Suddenly he picked it up and hurled it with all his might to the floor. It shattered into a thousand pieces. He picked up a chair and hurled it at the sideboard filled with glasses and dishes. Fragments shot in all directions. But as he started to pick up the table, Schnurrbart jumped at him and held his arms. 'Stop that,' he roared angrily. 'I don't see what good this does, you damned idiot.' He pounded him hard on the chest. The blow brought Krüger to his senses abruptly. He dropped like a log into his chair. When he looked up, he met Faber's eyes; the woodsman had been sitting motionless at the table all the while, face expressionless. Now he spoke. 'You can't fight against it. You can see it coming, but you can't do anything about it, and that is good.'

'That is good,' Krüger aped him, raging. 'What's good about our dying, what?'

'It's good no matter how it comes,' Faber murmured. He said no more. Krüger stared at his wooden face, biting his lips. Like a gravedigger, he thought. The guy looks like a gravedigger. He bowed his head. They sat in silence until Steiner returned. He merely glanced at the wreckage in the room, did not waste a word on it, and beckoned the men to follow him.

The others were waiting in front of the house. They stood close together, wearing steel helmets and assault packs, talking in whispers. When Steiner appeared among them, they fell silent. In a low voice he gave them instructions. Before they started, Steiner tied ten stick grenades into a bundle. The platoon moved forward. The men kept close to the fence and followed the street around the factory yard. It was about eleven o'clock. Above the roofs hung a narrow crescent moon, the huge mass of factory buildings towered black and threateningly toward the stars. Further to the south artillery explosions rumbled steadily. Now and then tracer shells hissed past the gleaming white limestone slopes of the mountains which were lit to their very tops by the glare of tremendous conflagrations. The line of houses past which the men were marching looked like an abstract stage-set, the vacant windows gaping blackly out of the whitewashed walls. Schnurrbart stayed beside Steiner. He was so fearfully tired and indifferent that even the impending assault could not wring any emotion out of him. He held his right hand over his gas mask so that it would not knock against his mess tin and said: 'You'd think Triebig would have turned up again.'

'What do you want with him?' Steiner replied irritably. 'I'm happy not to see the bastard.'

'Sure, so am I. But we ought to have discussed the details with him. He doesn't know where we'll be waiting for him.'

Steiner snorted. 'Do you know?' he demanded. 'He'll see where the flare comes from.'

Schnurrbart glanced speculatively across the street. It turned sharply to the west at this point; they ought to be at the place for their assault in a moment. The fence on this side had been shattered by many shells and they could see the factory building ominously close at hand beyond the crazily dangling pickets. Luckily it was so dark in the street that movement behind the fence could scarcely be detected. After another fifty yards, Steiner stopped and waited until the men had closed ranks. Krüger pressed through the group to him and whispered: 'What now?'

'The place is right,' Steiner answered. He turned to the men and explained his plan. 'I don't know what it's like inside, but I imagine there'll be one long room. Perhaps with machinery in it. Once we've got ourselves established in the first floor, we'll fire the flare and wait for the others.' He spoke to Schnurrbart. 'You stay here with the boys. I'll try to get under the window and throw this thing in.' He indicated the bundle of hand grenades which he carried in his right hand. 'When it goes off, come over, and then in we go. Clear?'

'Clear enough,' Schnurrbart said unwillingly. 'But wouldn't it be better for us to go all together?'

'Rot. If they discover us, we're all sunk. Besides . . .' He dropped abruptly to the ground. From one of the lower windows a flare rose, hissed over their heads and smashed into the wall of a house. It dropped down and burned out on the ground. The men lay motionless, pressed up against the fence. When all was dark again, Steiner turned his head and brought his mouth close to Schnurrbart's ear. 'Did you notice which window?'

'I can see without glasses,' Schnurrbart muttered. 'Must be an MG there.'

'Must be,' Steiner agreed. He rose to his knees. The men shifted restlessly. Anxiously, they eyed the silent factory front. 'Damn shit,' Krüger muttered, watching Steiner sling the tommy-gun around his neck, grasp the bundle of grenades in a throwing position and cautiously crawl through the damaged fence. He continued on all fours. Halfway to the building he reached a deep shell hole. He dropped carefully into it and waited for the next flare. His shirt was sticking damply to his back and he had to clench his teeth. Never before had he felt such intense fear. When he laid his head on his arms, his whole body shook. Blast this hero's death, he thought, closing his eyes.

XIV

AFTER THE HOT EXCHANGE of words with Steiner, Triebig
made his way straight to the battalion commander. Quivering
with fury, he spilled out his story. 'It's an impossible relationship,' he concluded angrily, forgetful of his customary servile
manner.

Stransky sat at his desk, face indifferent, puffing easily at his
cigarette. When Triebig finished, he shrugged disdainfully. 'You
know as well as I why the fellow takes such liberties. Legally there
isn't much I can do about him. Legally, Lieutenant Triebig.' He
smiled malignly. 'But there are other ways. Happily there are
other ways.' He asked Triebig to sit down and looked thoughtfully up at the ceiling. During the pause in the conversation Triebig examined the furnishings of the room. After the unsuccessful
attack of that morning, he had looked around very carefully for
a suitable command post, and had finally decided on a third-floor
flat facing the courtyard of a group of houses. 'The higher the
better,' he had decided. 'We don't know how the business will
turn out, and if the Russians undertake a counter-attack it's better
to have them under us than over us.'

The pause was prolonged. Finally Stransky seemed to have
come to a decision. His voice sounded vexed as he said: 'I would
rather you had avoided that clash with Steiner.' As Triebig opened
his mouth to defend his conduct, Stransky raised his head soothingly. 'Never mind. What's done is done. I don't like it, but it
can't be changed now. You will have to be all the more cautious.'
He glanced at his watch. 'We don't have much more time. Steiner
will start in five minutes, and you must follow him at once with
the rest of the company. Whether or not he gets into the factory
is his business. But you must make it yours to see that he never
leaves it again. If you succeed, you'll be first lieutenant in a few
days, as sure as my name is Stransky.'

'Do you mean that?' Triebig asked dubiously.

Stransky smiled maliciously. 'When I make such a statement,
you have no reason to doubt it. Incidentally, I may as well tell

you that I have already taken steps to have myself transferred from here back to France. I expect the order to come through any day now. Perhaps'—his smile deepened—'perhaps I can also do something for you in that connection. Or would you have any objection to continuing on as my adjutant in some French city?'

The news took Triebig so much by surprise that for a moment he merely gaped. This moment erased all the humiliations he had suffered from Stransky. The prospect of transfer made him slightly giddy. 'You don't know how grateful I would be to you for that,' he stammered at last.

Stransky nodded patronizingly. 'You will have the opportunity to prove your gratitude—promptly.' His voice changed; it rang like steel. 'Get that creature Steiner off my neck and I guarantee that you will survive this war. He must not come back, not even if you have to kill him with your own hands. I want to know that he's dead, *dead, dead.*'

Triebig involuntarily shrank from the savage expression on his superior's face. 'I'll do everything possible,' he said hastily.

But Stransky shook his head violently. 'You must do more than everything possible. You must stop at nothing, and the more daring you are, the higher I will value your achievement. Only manage it cleverly, so nothing is apparent. Bear in mind that I cannot cover you if the story should come out.'

Triebig hesitated. He did not like the idea of bearing the whole responsibility, and the more he thought about it the more worried he became. But Stransky gave him little time for weighing the matter. He stood up quickly, went over to the lieutenant and placed a hand on his shoulder. 'You have no cause to be concerned,' he said quietly. 'I'll make the business easier for you, as far as is in my power. Once you are in the factory with him, there will be a hundred opportunities; it will be up to you to seize one of them.' His voice became persuasive. 'In any case it is the lesser evil. I know from reliable sources that the men in the bridgehead have been written off. There is no longer any intention of evacuating. Within at most two weeks the Crimea will be a sack with a closed neck. The Russians are close to Perekop now, and everyone south of Perekop will suffer the same fate as the Sixth Army. Do you want to be here then?'

'How do you know that?' Triebig stammered through bloodless lips.

'I know. A relative of mine is in the Army High Command. Before that day comes I shall be on my way to France. France...' He shook Triebig by the shoulder. 'Do you know what that means? It means life, Triebig, in Biarritz or Arcachon or Mont de Marsan or Paris. Think of it, man. Paris, Notre Dame, Champs Elysées, Montmartre . . . What the devil is there to consider?'

Triebig stared up at the man's flushed face, which seemed irradiated by an almost hysterical rapture, and swallowed hard. He felt his scruples being swept away, and when Stransky went on to describe the fate that probably awaited Triebig if he remained here in the bridgehead, the lieutenant clapped his hands over his ears and jumped to his feet.

'No, no,' he exclaimed, closing his eyes.

Stransky studied him with satisfaction. 'You have the choice,' he declared quietly. 'You can either go to the dogs somewhere in Siberia or guzzle champagne in France. Which do you prefer?'

'Steiner will not come back,' Triebig said softly. 'I am counting on your word: that you will take me with you to France. But may I know one thing?'

'What is that?'

Their eyes were locked as Triebig asked it: 'Why is it so important to you? If you are leaving here in a few days, it shouldn't matter to you what happens to Steiner.'

There was a brief silence. Stransky stepped over to the window and stared down into the dark courtyard. 'What happens to Steiner,' he said at last, 'is more important to me than whether we win or lose the war. But you will not understand that. It's my personal affair, Triebig. Go now. Otherwise you'll be too late. And don't neglect to keep me informed constantly by radio.'

He waited until the door closed behind Triebig. Then he picked up the telephone and called the communications platoon leader. There were no new messages either by radio or telephone from the other companies. Biting his lips, he laid down the receiver. It's sickening, he thought.

Ever since Triebig had returned from the regimental command post that fatal evening, Stransky had had the feeling that he was sitting on a volcano. The regimental commander's threat had been so definite that in the past weeks he had not dared to do anything against Steiner. The consciousness of his impotence had given him some terrible moments. He could do nothing but wait for the proper time, but that time seemed to have come at last. Six feet underground—that was where Steiner belonged. Once this account was settled Stransky could leave the East behind, even without the Iron Cross. At bottom it was Steiner's fault that he was not already wearing one.

So absorbed was he in his painful thoughts that it took several buzzes from the field telephone before he started up and absently reached for the receiver. But as soon as he recognized Kiesel's voice he became keenly alert. He listened attentively to the adjutant's words, and his face paled. What was the fellow saying? Call off all attacks immediately, set up defences along whatever line had been reached and await further orders. And then: 'Has Triebig started yet?'

'No,' Stransky stammered. 'That is . . .' He fell silent and thought feverishly. Kiesel's voice rang coldly in his ears. 'Beg pardon?'

'I'll check,' Stransky said hastily. 'One moment please.'

He dropped the receiver to the table, rushed with huge strides out of the room to the hallway and into a room facing the street. As he leaned out of the window he saw a number of men standing together, barely recognizable in the darkness. Then he heard Triebig's voice issuing muted orders. Stransky opened his mouth to call. Then he compressed his lips and watched stony-faced as the company started moving, marched across the street, and seconds later disappeared from sight. He brushed the back of his hand over his forehead and felt the moisture. Then he hurried back into his room and took up the telephone. 'The attack has already begun,' he said in a controlled voice. 'I can't stop it now.' He heard Kiesel exchanging hasty words with someone. Then the hated voice was in his ear again: 'Are they advancing?'

'I have no information yet. As soon as I know details, I'll inform you.'

'The commander wishes you to. What do your other companies report?'

'For the past half hour I've had no news from them,' Stransky replied. 'Couriers are on the way. The last reports said that the third company was close to the waterfront, while the first has scarcely advanced at all; it's practically fighting in the assembly area.'

'Very well, Captain Stransky. Make sure that the companies are informed at once. It's of prime importance that they establish contact on their right and left. If it should turn out that the factory cannot be taken, withdraw your second company to the street and inform us.'

As Stransky laid down the receiver, he thought he heard the sudden blaze of guns. He stepped quickly to the window. He had not been mistaken. 'It's at the factory,' he murmured to himself. The attack had begun.

Some three minutes might have passed when Steiner heard a soft pop such as was produced by the firing of a flare. Without opening his eyes, he waited the necessary period. Then, with the yard in darkness again, he crept cautiously out of the shellhole. Now that the decisive moment was only a few seconds away his excitement had abruptly vanished. As he crawled forward foot by foot toward the black factory wall, his senses were keyed to a pitch of alertness. His eyes were fixed on the dark window opening behind which he guessed the Russian machine-gun was posted.

He had come within ten paces of the building when a piercing cry rang out, so unexpectedly that he pressed himself against the ground and froze. Then followed a succession of hasty words, and before Steiner could recover from his initial start of terror the factory yard was bathed in the merciless light of a flare which hung like a great arc lamp above him. Simultaneously, a machine-gun began to chatter. The fearful sound of steel-jacketed bullets hissing by, gashing the dry, sandy soil around him, speeding past his head with an ugly whine, pierced into his consciousness and revived all his reflexes. Before the traversing fire from the invisible machine-gunner could touch him, he bounded across the last few yards, slammed heavily into the stone blocks of the factory wall, and with all the strength of despair hurled the concentrated charge of ten hand-grenades through the yawning void of the narrow window above his head. Then he dropped full-length on the ground, pulled the strap of the tommy-gun over his head and waited. The machine-gun fire swept wildly across the factory yard; it must be coming from one of the windows farther to the west.

Above his head he heard several loud shouts that seemed to be passing down through the entire factory. In his excitement he bit his lips till they were bloody. He was beginning to fear he had not pulled the fuse cord of the concentrated charge properly when, inside the building, there was a crash as though the roof had fallen in.

Before the last rumble of the blast had ceased, Steiner swung himself up on the window-sill, jumped off into space, though how high the window was he could not estimate, and landed safely beside a huge machine. The ends of the long hall were lost in darkness. The room seemed to be occupied by a large number of machines of the most varied types, and by several dozen small lathes installed along the row of windows. The machine-gun fire had stopped, but from the further end of the hall he could hear the hasty tramp of nailed boots along the stone blocks of the floor. The sound mounted to a wild drumming as Steiner emptied the magazine of his tommy-gun in that direction. While he reloaded he heard loud shouts from the yard and leaped to the window. Here they came, running shoulder to shoulder, rifles held high, gasping mouths under swaying steel helmets, at their head Schnurrbart and Krüger. Seconds later they poured in through the windows, stumbled over the lathes, in the darkness knocked each other against the machines and shouted all at once, until Steiner's incisive voice restored some order. He issued his commands precisely and swiftly, and while the last of the men were still climbing into the factory he rushed, followed by the others to the far end of the long hall. They reached a door which led to a narrow corridor on the long side of the room, and a few minutes later the entire first floor of the south wing was in their possession without their having encountered any serious resistance.

'You'll get the Knight's Cross for this,' Schnurrbart said. He was standing beside Steiner, in the doorway, scanning their immediate neighbourhood. 'What a place!' He pointed to the long corridor which ran parallel to the machinery room. 'I wonder where that leads.'

'Must go to the yard,' Steiner replied. 'Up at the front end must be the tower. Perhaps a stairway leads up.' He glanced speculatively at the dozen windows in the left side of the corridor and went cautiously up to one of them to see what lay outside.

But as soon as he moved a few steps away from the door a Russian machine-gun let loose. The bullets rattled through the windows. The men dropped to their knees and crawled hastily back through the door into the main hall, where the others had meanwhile distributed themselves along the windows.

'Nothing for it,' Schnurrbart growled, glumly rubbing his hairy chin. 'At any rate they can't get in again.'

'And we can't get out,' Steiner said. 'Let's fire that flare.'

After sending up the agreed signal, they made a thorough inspection of the room. There were two doors, one on either end, each leading out to the corridor. Although they examined every nook and corner, and even looked under the machinery by the beams of their flashlights, they found no trace of any Russians. Steiner was about to return to the windows to await the arrival of Triebig when a man came running up to him and informed him that there was an elevator in the right-hand corner of the hall. He followed the man. Behind an iron double door, both leaves of which stood wide open, yawned a dark shaft. When Steiner flashed his light down into it, he observed a massive platform hanging in iron guide rails on both sides. It was operated by strong steel cables. His attention was immediately attracted by a row of steel rungs attached at intervals of a foot or so to the front face of the shaft. They extended both up and down until they were lost in darkness, and they were covered by a thick layer of dust. He flashed the light upward, but could not see to the top of the shaft. However, there was no time to study the elevator shaft more closely, since the rest of the company had by then arrived. In a caustic voice the lieutenant inquired about the state of affairs. 'We have to occupy the windows and investigate the corridor,' Steiner declared. 'How strong are we?'

'About fifty men,' Triebig replied. He stood with his back to a window, his eyes wandering uneasily up and down the hall.

'Not much,' Steiner said. 'I would suggest that we secure the hall with half our men and use the other half to see where the corridor leads. Perhaps we'll run into a stairway leading to the upper floors.'

'That's silly,' one of the men objected. Steiner recognized Sergeant Schulz.

'Have you any better ideas?' Steiner asked coldly.

'I'm for our sticking together,' Schulz replied. 'We won't get far with twenty-five men, and we can never occupy this factory if we had a lifetime.'

'We must keep our retreat open,' Steiner declared. 'It's sure we can't hold this building permanently with fifty men. Once the Russians find out how weak we are, they'll make things hot for us.'

Schulz growled something under his breath, but when Triebig agreed to Steiner's suggestion he fell into an angry silence. He sat down on a machine and let his legs dangle.

Steiner turned to Triebig. 'I would suggest that you post an MG outside by the fence. If the Russians should get there before us our way across the yard will be cut off.'

Triebig rejected the suggestion. 'We have only three MG's. I can't spare one of them. Besides, I don't think it will occur to the Russians to do that. They need their men to occupy the other floors.'

'Whatever you think. I've warned you.' Steiner looked around until he caught sight of Schnurrbart, who was standing nearby with Krüger and Faber, attending closely to the discussion. 'Get your men together,' he ordered them. 'We'll take a look at the situation now.'

'What about the elevator?' Schnurrbart asked.

'That comes later. First we'll try the stairs. If that doesn't work, we can always break our bones on the iron ladder.'

'Nice prospect,' Krüger grumbled. He looked around the room. All the windows had been occupied by sentries meanwhile, and the company stood round Triebig, who was talking rapidly with Sergeant Schulz.

'Well, let's try it,' Schnurrbart said, and called over the men of his group. While Krüger did the same, Steiner went to the door on the right and peered out into the corridor. All was still out there. Through the corridor window he could see into the back yard, where several trucks were parked. Undoubtedly they were not usable; they must have belonged to the factory. He turned to the right. Here he could not use his flashlight, since the glow of it could be seen from the yard. Groping his way forward in the darkness, he kept close to the left-hand wall. He had gone about thirty feet in this manner when the hall ended in a closed door. By feel Steiner decided that it would open outward.

'Watch out,' Schnurrbart warned him. He kept close behind Steiner and watched anxiously as Steiner reached for the latch.

The rest of the men stood pressed against the wall, holding their weapons ready to fire. Something about the unnatural stillness throughout the entire factory made Steiner nervous. Instead of proceeding cautiously, he kicked out violently at the door, knocking it wide open, while at the same time he threw himself to one side against the wall.

The consequences were breathtaking and frightful. Through the pitchblack doorway half a dozen Russian tommy-guns barked. The cone of fire whipped down the corridor, whirling the men away from the wall as though the rough stone paving blocks of the floor had suddenly been transformed into smooth ice. While the men toward the front were protected by the dead angle, those further back were helplessly exposed to the fire. The animal screams of men who had been hit sounded down the corridor. Steiner huddled to the wall. Although he had half reckoned with such a possibility, he was for a few seconds paralysed by fright. Then he feverishly pulled a hand grenade out of his belt, unscrewed the safety cap and pulled out the button. He waited a full three seconds before he tossed the grenade through the door. Out of the corners of his eyes he saw Schnurrbart also throwing a grenade. The detonations rumbled so violently in the narrow corridor that Steiner clapped his hands to his ears, deafened for a moment. Paying no attention to what was going on behind his back, he leaped into the doorway and began blazing away blindly into the darkness. The Russian machine-guns had stopped firing. He thought he heard hasty cries. From somewhere sounded a dull thud such as might be produced by a heavy door being slammed shut. Then silence in front of him. When he switched on his flashlight, he saw several steps leading down into a continuation of the corridor which was here at a slightly lower level. In front of him lay the twisted bodies of two Russians. Raising the beam of his flashlight, he saw that the corridor made a right-angle turn and apparently continued on toward the yard. For a second he stood indecisive. Then several loud explosions sounded behind him. He whirled around and bumped against Krüger, who shouted: 'They're throwing hand grenades in through the windows.' Schnurrbart also came up behind him and urged him to hurry. Steiner grasped the latch and drew the door closed behind him. 'Back to the big room.' he said.

From the yard the Russian machine-gun began firing again,

raking the line of windows. Further ahead two or three hand grenades exploded. Several men were working feverishly to get the wounded back out of the corridor. When Steiner reached the main hall, he saw Triebig standing excitedly at one of the windows, barking out a succession of meaningless orders. He caught sight of Steiner and swooped down upon him. 'What the devil have you done?' he shouted wildly. 'Half your platoon is knocked out, do you know that?'

'If you'd been leading them, not one of the bastards would have come back,' Steiner snapped. 'Am I the company commander or you?' He left him and turned to Schnurrbart. 'Where is Faber?'

'At the front door with his MG. What'll we do?'

Steiner turned his head and saw his men still busy with their wounded. They were being laid on the floor between two big machines. There were eight or ten stretched out there.

'Shall we try the elevator?' Schnurrbart urged.

'We can't get into the yard,' Steiner said. He shrugged. 'There's no other way, although it's insane. If they're up above, they can pop us off as we climb.'

'The whole attack on this coffin is insane anyway,' Krüger declared. He laughed savagely. 'And that fool has already sent off a big-breeches radio message. Factory taken and so on.'

'Who?' Steiner asked quickly.

'Triebig. We have a radio section with us, you know. They're up there in the corner and communicating with Battalion.'

'I didn't know that,' Steiner said. He again went over to Triebig, who was bickering with Sergeant Schulz. 'You need not tell me what to do and what not to do,' he was saying. 'We have orders to take the factory, and that's all there is to it.' He caught sight of Steiner and fell silent.

'What do you think?' Schulz asked Steiner violently. 'Do you think we can take this building?'

'With several tons of dynamite and a hundred Stukas, why not?' He addressed Triebig. 'We're going to try it up the elevator now. Four of us at first. If we reach the top, I'll signal.'

'And if you don't reach the top?' Triebig asked.

'Then you can order us a state funeral. But don't rejoice too soon.' He went over to the elevator shaft where Schnurrbart and

Krüger were waiting for him. They stood by the opening, craning their necks as they stared up. 'Who's coming with us?' Krüger asked.

'We four. Get Faber.' Steiner slung the tommy-gun around his neck and collected a bunch of hand grenades from the other men. Then he felt for the rungs. All the men who were not posted as sentries thronged round the shaft and watched breathlessly as he slowly started climbing. Someone called after him: 'The lieutenant says you're not to forget the flag.'

'The lieutenant can kiss my arse,' Steiner retorted. He paused and looked down. Then, seeing Schnurrbart swing himself into the shaft, he reached for the next rung. He felt as if he could not tell up from down. It was so dark that he shut his eyes and depended wholly upon his sense of touch. But as yet he felt no fear.

Surprised and instantly on his guard, Stransky greeted Kiesel coldly. It was unusual, to say the least, for the regimental adjutant to call upon him at his command post.

'Do sit down,' Stransky said, gesturing toward a chair. 'To what do I owe the honour? Have you news from the other battalions?'

'No,' Kiesel said curtly. 'What news I have is so confused that it would be of little use to you. The latest reports make grim reading. We are trying to disengage, but the Russians are keeping us busy.'

'And the city?'

Kiesel shrugged his broad shoulders. 'We may as well write it off. It has become a secondary issue. I have orders for you. May I see your map?' Stransky spread the tactical map out on the table. Kiesel took a pencil from his pocket and began explaining. 'You will withdraw this morning at four o'clock to this line.' He traced the line with his pencil. 'About five miles north-east of here, at the western exit of the big tunnel. Do you see?' Stransky leaned over the map and nodded. 'To your right is the third, to your left the 2nd Battalion,' Kiesel continued. 'As soon as you have occupied this position, the lieutenant-colonel will expect you at Regiment. Inform your companies. What is your second company doing?'

Stransky picked up a sheet of paper from the table. 'The last bulletin came in ten minutes ago. See for yourself.' He handed the message form to Kiesel.

'Factory building occupied without losses,' Kiesel read aloud. 'Mopping up has begun. Triebig.' He nodded approvingly and laid down the sheet of paper. 'They are not to take any more needless risks. Send a radio directive to that effect. We must conserve our forces. What is the situation with your other companies?'

'Somewhat more stabilized. Only they can't really make contact. The gaps between the companies are too large to close with available manpower. At night practically impossible.'

'The eternal evil. Huge sectors and no men to occupy them. If we had one battalion more it would be . . .' He broke off, for the telephone was ringing. Stransky lifted the receiver. After the first few words Stransky's face creased into lines of vast astonishment. He laid down the receiver. 'It was the artillery observer who has been watching the factory through his night glasses. He has just seen the flag pulled down from the factory tower. I wouldn't have thought it possible.'

'What?' Kiesel asked quickly.

Stransky realized that he had made a mistake. He gave an embarrassed laugh. 'The whole thing,' he answered evasively. 'I wouldn't have thought Triebig would succeed in getting as far as the top of the tower.'

Kiesel studied him closely. 'What makes you think it is Triebig?'

'Lieutenant Triebig is in command of the company,' Stransky replied aloofly.

'Indeed. Had you given orders for the flag to be taken down?'

'Would that be so odd? The flag was undoubtedly a control point for the Russian artillery. I had no idea we were going to pull out and thought it essential for the flag to come down.'

'But you assumed it was impossible?'

'As troop commander one gives the right orders irrespective of their feasibility. If offensive action always depended on its probable outcome, we would never attack at all.'

'You are partly right,' Kiesel said. 'But there is a difference between operations undertaken for strategic significance and those undertaken merely for prestige. Did you by any chance order Sergeant Steiner to fetch that flag?'

The bluntness of the question caught Stransky off balance. 'What makes you think that?' he parried.

Kiesel's voice was hard as he answered: 'A guess, Captain Stransky. I will tell you something. There are two persons in this world who mean a great deal to me, and Sergeant Steiner saved the life of one of them.'

'I don't know what you may be referring to,' Stransky said. 'Are you speaking of your brother-in-law?'

'Yes, my brother-in-law, Lieutenant März. You know that he was wounded. Steiner carried him back. It surprises me that you have not yet heard about it.'

'Lieutenant Triebig did not mention it,' Stransky said, shrugging. It took him a moment to adjust to the new situation. When he spoke, his tone was reserved and he chose his words carefully. 'Sergeant Steiner is to my knowledge platoon leader in Second Company. What orders he receives come from Lieutenant Triebig.'

'That may be so,' Kiesel said frostily. 'But in case it really was Sergeant Steiner who brought down that flag, I hope that the assignment was not given to him with a certain intention.' He stood up.

'Will you express yourself somewhat more clearly?' Stransky asked.

Kiesel shook his head. 'If my interpretation is correct, I spoke clearly enough. I might at most add a general suggestion.'

'Directed toward whom?'

'Answer that yourself,' Kiesel said contemptuously. 'My point is that it is risky to play Providence. Many a nasty wish has boomeranged.'

Stransky rose slowly to his feet, his face betraying the intensity of his effort to control himself. 'That sounds like a threat.'

'I never bother to threaten,' Kiesel retorted. 'Justice does not require advance notice.' On the way out he turned briefly. 'You will be informed of the position of the new regimental command post.'

He let the door slam behind him. Back at the command post he seized the first opportunity to talk with the commander. He urged the immediate transfer of Steiner with such forcefulness that Brandt could not conceal his astonishment.

'I don't know why you are so agitated,' he said, shrugging. 'Frankly, I no longer care to meddle with the business. I've given

Steiner a chance and I've given Stransky a chance. Let them now settle with one another. What made you go to see Stransky, anyway? I needed you.'

The commander picked up the telephone, called Captain Körner and had a brief talk with him. Then he turned to Kiesel again. 'It looks as though we have switched parts,' he said harshly. 'At least in our relationship to Steiner. I don't want to tell you what to do, but I assure you, it isn't worth it. Believe me, it isn't worth it. Steiner has already come to the point that it has taken me fifty-two years to reach. You'll have no more success with him than I have had, and you'll be kicked in the teeth, besides.'

The commander ceased speaking, his eyes fixed blankly at some spot far beyond Kiesel. Then his sagging shoulders straightened. 'Take four or five men, drive to our new command post and get the quarters ready. We will follow in two hours. Send the car back to me.' When Kiesel did not respond immediately, Brandt snapped: 'Did you hear me?' Kiesel nodded, but did not move. 'What are you waiting for?' Brandt asked, frowning.

Somewhere in the vicinity several heavy shells exploded, and Kiesel waited until the din had faded before he spoke. 'Permit me one question,' he said.

'Yes?'

'What point has Steiner reached?'

Brandt studied him, his own expression non-committal. Then he picked up his belt which lay on the table with pistol holster attached. 'This,' he said tersely, slapping the leather holster. 'Just this. Is there anything else you want to know?'

'Thank you,' Kiesel murmured. He left the room, his face grey.

Steiner had counted one hundred of the iron rungs when his hand, groping for the next, failed to find it. Carefully, he felt the wall on his left until he encountered a depression which must be a doorway. He called down in a whisper to Schnurrbart, whose panting breaths were growing louder beneath him, and waited until he felt Schnurrbart's hand touch his boot. He told Schnurrbart to switch on his flashlight. As the bright beam cut the darkness, he was able to orient himself. About six feet above his head was the roof of the shaft, to which the heavy elevator mechanism was attached. On his left, an easy step away, he saw the foot-wide base of the iron door. The door resisted the pressure of his hand.

It was undoubtedly bolted from outside, and for a few seconds Steiner was in a quandary.

'What's the matter?' Schnurrbart whispered. He stood with his right arm hooked around a rung, still holding the flashlight. Steiner glanced down. Seeing that Krüger and Faber were immediately below, he ordered them to climb back as far as the next floor and wait there. Then he took two stick grenades from his belt and unscrewed the safety caps. 'We'll have to blow it open. Buckle yourselves to the rungs with your belts.'

'The stuff will fall on our heads,' Schnurrbart objected.

'The hell it will. You're safe if you press close to the ladder. The door will blow open outward. Get down.'

Grumbling, Schnurrbart climbed downward. He was sweating and the air in the shaft was stale. When he thought of the yawning depths below him, he had to close his eyes to press back a feeling of giddiness. A warning cry from below indicated that he had reached the others. 'What's up?' Krüger wanted to know.

'He wants to blow the door open,' Schnurrbart growled, flashing the light up to where Steiner was leaning over and laying the hand grenades at the foot of the door.

Krüger cursed. 'Mad, he is,' he muttered.

'That's what I said.' Schnurrbart took the flashlight in his mouth, unbuckled his belt and drew it around a rung. The others followed his example. When Steiner called down to ask whether they were ready, Schnurrbart answered crossly: 'We're as ready as we'll ever be. You'll finish us off with your wild ideas.'

Suddenly Steiner came racing down the ladder like fury and pressed himself against the rungs just above their heads. The explosion will be heard throughout the building, Schnurrbart had time to think. Then there was a booming crash as though the shaft were collapsing. Above their heads scraps of iron hurled against the walls, and the air blast threatened to wrench their cramped fingers from the rungs. But they could already see Steiner swarming up, and before they could detach their belts from the rungs he had disappeared into the wall of the shaft. Seconds later they stood panting and excited beside him, staring into a broad corridor with large windows through which the reflected light of the burning city shone. On their left were doors probably leading to offices. Steiner quickly tried these and found them locked. Meanwhile Krüger was examining the door of the shaft. The force of the explosion had torn the bolting device right out of the concrete blocks and blown the door outward. The trick had worked, and now that the worst lay behind them, they quickly regained their confidence. Only Krüger was still worried. He turned to Steiner and asked: 'What do you want to do now?'

Steiner looked thoughtfully out of a window at a fantastic vision. All along the waterfront and in the centre of the city burning houses stood like gigantic torches against a star-studded sky. The artillery fire had quieted down. But through the smashed window-panes rifle fire could be heard distinctly, rising and falling in intensity and seeming to come from all parts of the city.

Steiner turned around. 'We'd better call the others. Until they get here, we can't do anything.'

They went back to the shaft and Schnurrbart moved his flashlight in circles. The signal was immediately answered from below. Krüger felt as if he were stooping over a bottomless well, and at the bottom of the pitchy darkness there was a dancing light that seemed to come from another world. 'They've seen it,' he breathed. 'We're lucky bastards.'

They waited in suspense. A few seconds passed. Then a dull thud reached their ears, at first inexplicable. There followed suddenly so piercing and frightful a cry that they reeled back from the opening. They had heard many kinds of screams. They knew how a man roared when the glowing hot iron of a shell splinter struck into his flesh, when a bullet tore away his intestines or shattered his genitals. But the sound that came up from below was not one of these. There was no longer anything human about that scream. It filled the entire shaft and did not stop until it was cut off by the chatter of a Russian tommy-gun. Then abruptly and terribly there was utter silence.

'What was that?' Schnurrbart whispered. None of the others answered. Steiner took several steps back and went to a window. He peered down into the courtyard. Finally he turned to the men. 'We'll have to find the stairs. We won't get back down that shaft.' He began running with catlike steps down the corridor. The men followed him. They passed a number of closed doors and came up at last against a wall. On their right a staircase led down, while behind an open door on the left a few steps were visible; probably these went up to the tower. Steiner stood hesitant. Then he told himself that the five minutes more or less would not matter.

Without a word of explanation he went through the doorway and scaled the narrow winding staircase. Schnurrbart followed at his heels. Although they tried to move quietly, their footsteps echoed with dreadful loudness on the stone steps, which went on and on, winding upward through impenetrable darkness. Finally Steiner stood still and called out a whispered order for the men to wait until he came back. Then he went cautiously on. Suddenly he heard an indistinct murmur that evidently came from further up. He dropped to his knees and crawled, careful not to make a sound. The murmuring became louder and more distinct. He could already make out individual words. Grey light trickled into the narrow tube of the stairwell, and after one more turning he saw above him a door which was closed except for a narrow crack. He raised himself to his knees, slipped the tommy-gun from his neck and listened. For a moment he wondered whether he ought to turn back and forget the flag. But no, he would not give up now that he was so close to the goal. With infinite care he pushed his head against the crack in the door. The room was rectangular, quite bare, with windows running around three of the sides. The glass in most of them was intact and reflected burning houses. On the right side stood four figures in Russian uniforms looking down at the city. They were talking unconcernedly in loud voices. Two of them were evidently officers; they wore caps and rain-coats under which their high boots were visible. Now that his eyes had grown accustomed to the dim light, Steiner made out two small boxes on the ground. Obviously radio apparatus. Advance artillery observation post, the thought flashed through his mind. All his keyed-up tension gave way abruptly to a sense of relief that affected him deceptively like gaiety. With a kind of eager curiosity he raised his tommy-gun to firing position. For the fraction of a second he felt inhibited; those backs turned un-suspectingly to him somehow troubled him, and he could not refrain from uttering a hissing noise that fell like a noose around the Russians' heads and pulled them around. He saw the mask-like planes of their faces, had time to observe the drawing-in movements of their necks and their arms, and then he pressed the trigger. The lifeless steel in his hands changed into a roaring, jerk-ing creature that sent the bodies of the Russians spinning as though an invisible lash had struck into their midst. Steiner wondered at the way they died without a sound. Like animals, he thought, and lowered his tommy-gun. He felt sick. As he kicked the door in, a frantic trampling sounded on the staircase behind him, and Schnurrbart's voice cried out his name. A second later they came rushing around the next winding of the stairs, weapons held high. Steiner called out that everything was under control, and Krüger let loose a string of relieved curses. 'Always the same,' he griped as he mounted the last few steps behind Schnurrbart. 'The bastard was just trying to scare us again. I'll bet there wasn't . . .' He fell silent. They had reached the doorway, and as they entered the room they saw the dead Russians. Steiner was standing with his back against the row of windows, his eyes fixed upon a narrow iron door in the rear wall. That, apparently, was the opening to the peak of the tower.

The men stepped closer to the bodies and looked down at them, shaking their heads. 'A radio section,' Schnurrbart said. He looked over at Steiner, who was changing the empty magazine of his gun. 'Nice shooting. Didn't they see you?'

'It was too dark for me to introduce myself,' Steiner replied. He strode over to the iron door and tried it. It was unlocked. 'We'll get that flag now,' he said. 'Schnurrbart can come with me. You two wait until we're back; you have to keep our retreat open.'

'What do you want the stinking old flag for,' Krüger remonstrated. 'If the Russians catch on to what's happening up here, we'll never get back down.'

Schnurrbart sided with Krüger, urging that they find the quickest way down again. But Steiner would not listen. 'It isn't the flag that matters; it's something else entirely. If you feel things are getting too hot for you, you can run for it. I'm not keeping you.' He turned away and went through the door. 'Damned mule,' Schnurrbart grumbled, following him.

They found themselves again on the worn steps of a winding staircase even narrower than the other. The stairs rose steeply into a pitch dark room. Steiner sent the beam of his flashlight sweeping hastily around it. The room was windowless and circular, the floor coated with dust. In the centre was an iron ladder with wide flat rungs which led to a rectangular opening in the ceiling. At the top of the ladder Steiner encountered a wooden trap-door which yielded to the pressure of his hands. He raised it, and a moment later they stood on the roof of the tower, with the stars above them. The roof was flat, ringed by a knee-high wall. In one corner, fastened to the wall by iron clamps, the creaking flag-pole pointed toward the sky. The flag fluttered clumsily like a big, dark shadow in the fresh breeze that blew from the sea and cooled their hot faces. Quiet had settled over the city. All was still and dark. Only here and there were fires still smouldering, casting a glow into the gloomy gorges of the streets and now and then raining sparks upon the roofs. From the elevation of the tower the fires seemed altogether harmless, and the red window openings looked like lanterns. The mountains reached toward the stars, and the Milky Way blazed in a bright arc from horizon to horizon.

'I wonder which one is ours?' Schnurrbart said.

'Which what?' Steiner asked.

Schnurrbart waved his hand at the sky. 'Which star, I mean. My mother always used to say each of us had one.' He fell silent. Then he asked: 'Have you still a grudge against me?'

'What about?'

'Oh, anything. I thought maybe about that business at the bridge, back in the woods.'

'I don't know what you're talking about,' Steiner said.

'You're just saying that,' Schnurrbart muttered sceptically.

'We're not children any more,' Steiner said curtly. 'A lot of water has passed under the bridge since then. I've forgotten about it. I've forgotten a great deal.'

'That's good,' Schnurrbart whispered. And obeying a sudden inspiration he added: 'Anne too?'

A few seconds passed before Steiner answered: 'No. Not her. Never.'

Schnurrbart averted his eyes. 'What she must have meant to you.'

'That's enough!' Steiner said. With both hands he pulled down the flag. The rusty rollers screeched, and he had to tug hard at the cloth before he could separate it from the wire. They folded it carefully. Then Steiner strapped it to his assault pack and returned to the trap-door.

In the lower room Krüger and Faber were waiting impatiently for them. Quietly they descended the winding staircase and reached the corridor below without encountering any Russians.

Steiner peered toward the elevator shaft at the other end of the corridor. Not a sound reached their ears. Slowly, they went down the stairs to the next floor. Here, too, they paused for a few seconds, listening hard for suspicious sounds in the darkness. Steiner was about to continue on down when Schnurrbart suddenly held him back. Muffled, but distinctly audible, the din of violent shooting reverberated in the stair-well.

'That must be from the yard,' Steiner breathed. 'They're attacking the company.'

Schnurrbart relaxed his tight grip on Steiner's arm. 'What do we do?'

'We must get down. If Triebig runs for it, we'll be stuck in this trap. Let's go.'

Disregarding caution, they pelted down the stairs. Suddenly a sharp outcry dropped like a stone at their feet. They glimpsed the outlines of a Russian on the landing below. He stood motionless, looking up at them. Without thinking Steiner raised his tommy-gun. The staircase resounded with the cracking of the shots. The Russian tipped over. The four of them raced across his body. Simultaneously the whole corridor came to life. Doors flew open, men shouted, boots thundered over the paving blocks, and then a random salvo spattered over their heads. Ducking, they raced on down the stairs, tearing their clothes on the banisters as they rounded the turns. Behind them the racket grew more terrifying from floor to floor. Then they reached the end of the staircase. It was blocked by a door that must lead out into the yard, and Steiner desperately tugged at the latch. But the door was locked. Behind them footsteps boomed like an avalanche down the stairs. The searing beams of flashlights ate into the darkness and scraps of words in Russian shrieked in their ears. Panting for breath, they stood still, their eyes frantically searching for a way out.

Krüger saw the door first. A corner behind the stairs, a big wooden box, and beside it a narrow door. Unlocked. Beyond it more steps led into a black tunnel. As they plunged on down, the total darkness wrapped them like a blanket. Steiner switched on his flashlight. To left and right ran a long, narrow underground corridor. A few iron pipes attached to the low ceiling. Doors on both sides. And in the background impenetrable darkness. But there was no time to consider. The Russians had reached the entrance to the cellar, and Steiner turned to the right. They raced with giant strides down the narrow tube of the corridor, the cones of light from their flashlights severing the darkness. Behind them several shattering explosions boomed. Hand grenades, Steiner thought. He ducked even lower. Any moment now the Russians would be down here with their tommy-guns, and this corridor seemed to go on for ever. No branches, nothing but doors, doors, doors. Every one of those doors concealed a rat trap, and Steiner knew it. Once they were caught in one of those holes, the Russians would have no trouble smoking them out. It was hopeless. He halted in his tracks so suddenly that the others bumped into him.

'What?' Schnurrbart panted.

'Shut up,' Steiner whispered. 'Put out your lights and keep going.'

'What about you?'

'I'll follow you; go on, damn it.' As the men ran on, he flung himself flat on the ground and began firing blindly into the darkness. Schnurrbart wanted to stop again. But Krüger's fist caught him hard in the back. 'Go on, go on!' They continued running until, in the darkness, they slammed up against a wall.

Their hearts jumped. The corridor turned at a right angle here and led toward a patch of light against which the shadowy outlines of several men could be seen. They were standing in an open doorway, and they wore steel helmets. German steel helmets. Schnurrbart uttered a cry of disbelief. Then he rushed toward the men, shouting: 'Sergeant Steiner here, don't shoot. It's us—Sergeant Steiner.' He ran out of the darkness toward the light. With every step he took his jubilation grew; he could think of nothing but: saved, we're saved. Already he thought he could distinguish Triebig, standing in the midst of the men and raising his hand. But Schnurrbart overlooked the motion. He saw only the familiar uniforms, and he thought of the captured flag and that Steiner was the luckiest bastard born and with him by you a fellow could fetch the stars from the sky. By God, the luckiest bastard born. Joyously, he threw up his arms. The stars, he thought, the stars from the sky. Then something fell at his feet and he staggered. But he managed to remain on his feet and tried to regain his balance. 'Damn it all,' he stammered, throwing his head back, uncomprehending. With abrupt horror he felt something striking his body. It was as though his chest, his abdomen, were being torn open, and fiery pain darted up to the roots of his hair. They're mad, he thought, sinking to his knees. The rumbling stopped and he saw innumerable shimmering points plummeting towards him. The stars, he thought again. Then he suddenly heard his mother speaking to him; he knew instantly it was her voice. While he tilted forward from the waist, he laughed wildly. The stars gathered together, formed big, glowing-hot discs that became a face. He recognised Erika. Or was it his mother still? It's all one, he had time to think. Then a black wall fell across his brain.

XV

CORPORAL NONNENMACHER was leader of the radio section in the signals platoon at Regiment. He was a stocky, powerful man with a ruddy face and good-natured blue eyes that regarded the world with quizzical intelligence. Sitting in his headquarters on the second floor of the regimental command post, he casually twisted the dial of the radio set. At the back of the room the men of his section were snoring. Nonnenmacher listened to them for a while. Then he fooled with the dial again. But nothing special seemed to be happening to either the first battalion or the others, and Nonnenmacher yawned mightily. He glanced at his watch. Another hour and a half, he thought. How slowly the time passed. As he idly continued to turn the dial, listening to the unchanging drone of the ether waves, he wondered what their new quarters would be like. Undoubtedly not as comfortable as these, he thought gloomily, and sighed. Russia was bearable only when you were established in a big city. Novorosisk had had some conveniences they were going to miss. He stared into the quiet flame of the lantern and sighed again. It was a dreary business, these eternal retreats. When he thought of the imminent winter, the stark snow-covered hills whipped with icy wind, when he remembered the two thousand miles that lay between him and his home in Karlsruhe, an unnameable sadness and hopelessness came over him.

A sudden noise in his ears interrupted his broodings. Automatically he adjusted the headset over his ears and leaned forward, intent. His fingers glided skilfully over the knobs beneath the dial, and a voice shouted so loudly out of the earphones that he pulled back in alarm. As he regulated the volume, a tense expression settled upon his face. He reached hastily for paper and pencil and began copying down the words. Glancing at the pad in front of him, where the call numbers were listed, he noted that the second company was sending a message to Battalion. The contents of the despatch were dramatic enough to command attention. When the voice stopped and a few moments later a second

417

voice repeated the words, Nonnenmacher muttered an exclamation that startled the snoring men from their bunks. Sleep-dazed, they reeled toward him. 'What's going on?' one of them asked.

'Read that,' Nonnenmacher said, handing him the slip of paper. 'Cannot hold the factory any longer,' the man read aloud. 'Sergeant Steiner killed. Request orders.' The man let the paper flutter out of his fingers. 'That would happen just before we're withdrawing,' he murmured. 'What are you going to do?'

Nonnenmacher shrugged. 'It isn't really any of our business. They'll report it directly to Regiment. I suppose we might inform the commander. Then if he wants he can . . .' Nonnenmacher abruptly broke off. The voice he had heard before sounded in the earphones again, a breathless, distraught voice, and Nonnenmacher's pencil skipped across the pad as he copied down the words. Then he wrenched the headset away from his ears. 'The Russians are attacking,' he told the anxious group around him. 'They're signing off now, but asking First Battalion to stay on their frequency. Get the other set and keep check on the other battalions. I want to hear how this thing turns out.'

While the men brought another set from the back of the room, and hooked it up, Nonnenmacher again listened at the earphones. Minute after minute passed without any further messages from Second Company. He grew increasingly anxious and wondered again whether it might not be best to inform the commander. But the report must already have been telephoned in from the first battalion, he thought. He waited. At last, when more than fifteen minutes had passed, a loud whistle-tone sounded in his ears. 'They're switching to CW,' he said to the men. Again Nonnenmacher picked up his pencil and waited. The call signal came: dah, dit, dit . . . dit, dit . . . dah, dah. Reception was feebler than before. 'They must be asleep,' one of the men said impatiently.

Nonnenmacher turned to him. 'Were you listening in?'

The man nodded. 'It's loud enough. QSA 3, I'd say. David, Ida, Mike—that's the Second. But Battalion doesn't answer. Have they changed frequency?'

Nonnenmacher shook his head. 'They're coming in on the same frequency. I wonder what the hell is the matter with Battalion.'

Several more minutes passed, during which the call signal came in regularly at shorter and shorter intervals. Finally Nonnen-macher's patience gave out. 'I'm going to answer,' he said. 'May-be 1st Battalion's transmitter is on the blink.' He placed his thumb and forefinger on the bug, switched the transmitter to CW and gave a continuous tone. Then his fingers flew on the bug. The men watched him with admiration. Nonnenmacher was un-deniably the fastest operator in the regiment; you had to be damned good on the other side to copy him. The answer came. First the call signal and confirmation, then a succession of staccato whistling tones. Nonnenmacher nodded with satisfaction. 'They've got us. We're to wait; they're sending AS.'

Two or three minutes passed in silence. Then the call signal came again, and after Nonnenmacher had answered, the men heard the familiar and exciting signal that preceded every urgent message.

'KR,' Nonnenmacher murmured, leaning forward over his pad, frowning with concentration. For a while nothing but the Morse signals could be heard. Then Nonnenmacher sat bolt upright. 'I can't see what's going on here,' he said helplessly. 'Take a look at this.' As he turned back to the transmitter to acknowledge, the men studied the message with equal puzzlement.

'Take it to the commander,' Nonnenmacher ordered. 'Imme-diately.'

One of the men hurried out and raced downstairs to the com-mander's room. Lieutenant-Colonel Brandt was busy stowing his personal belongings into a large canvas bag. His head whirled around in annoyance as the radio man came in. 'What is it?' he asked harshly.

The man clicked his heels. His voice rang like a trumpet as he said: 'Radio message from Second Company to Regiment.'

Brandt turned around to face him. 'Well?'

'Second company surrounded in factory cellar, underneath tower. Lieutenant Triebig dead.' The man hesitated. Then he added: 'Signed by Sergeant Steiner.'

With three long strides Brandt reached the man and snatched the sheet of paper from his hand. 'Any more messages?'

'Yes, sir.' The man spilled out an explanation: that they had picked up the first message and had finally answered when Battalion remained silent. Brandt heard the story out before he asked: 'Have you the text of the first message?'

'Corporal Nonnenmacher has it.'

'Bring it here at once,' Brandt ordered. 'And inform Second Company that we will come to get them out. Hurry up.' He waited a moment until the door closed behind the man. As he went to the telephone there was a dangerous light in his eyes. 'Get me Lieutenant Stroh,' he barked.

When the prearranged light signal flashed at the top of the elavator shaft, Sergeant Schulz turned his head. 'They've made it,' he said to Triebig, who was standing behind him. He signalled into the shaft with his own flashlight. He then asked the lieutenant, who stood nervously fingering the strap of his tommy-gun: 'How many men do you want to send up there?'

Triebig looked around indecisively. 'Ten will be enough,' he ventured. 'The rest will stay with me. You too, Sergeant.'

'Yes, sir!' Schulz addressed the men standing nearest him. 'Up with you, and make it snappy.' One after the other they entered the shaft and began climbing. 'Speed it up,' Schulz called impatiently. He took a step forward, and craned into the shaft. The fourth man had just swung on to the ladder when a strange noise came from up above. There followed a scream that sent the other men reeling back from the doorway. Seconds later a body plummeted past their horrified faces and struck with a dull thud at the bottom of the shaft. Schulz started forward to shout to the other men on the ladder to come back, but as he opened his mouth a Russian tommy-gun began roaring up above and the other three plunged also, slamming with a hideous sound upon the iron platform of the elevator. A hissing rain of sparks from hand grenades danced past the doorway; four or five shattering explosions reverberated in the shaft; and then there was a deadly silence.

'We can write them off,' Schulz said hoarsely to Triebig. 'Them and the others with them. If we don't instantly . . .' He fell silent, for Triebig had suddenly sped off down the long hall, running in the aisle between the machines. Schulz chased after him. He caught up with him in front of the lathe on which the radio men had placed their apparatus. Triebig loudly telling them: 'Report to battalion that we cannot hold the factory another five minutes; we must pull out at once and . . .' He hesitated. 'Report that Sergeant Steiner has been killed. Are you connected?'

'They're on permanent reception,' one of the men replied. He was wearing a throat microphone, and as he spoke he slipped the headset away from his ears.

Triebig nodded, gratified. 'Send that right away,' he ordered. 'I'll wait until you receive an answer.'

As the radio men bent over their apparatus, Schulz stepped up to Triebig's side. 'Isn't it premature to report Steiner killed?' he remarked.

Triebig shrugged impatiently. 'It's a dead certainty the Russians have already got him. Lord knows what went on up there.'

Dubious, but not minded to dispute the matter, Schulz remained silent. He watched with interest as one of the two radio men spoke into the microphone. Unthinkingly, he put his hand into his pocket to take out a crushed cigarette. Halfway through the movement he froze. Through the window a fiery rain sprayed. A deafening rattle of gunfire followed. Schulz dropped to the ground. Beside him he saw Triebig, who was shouting something. But he could not grasp the words. Innumerable darting, bluish flames were dancing in the big room. They're shooting explosive bullets, Schulz thought. He forced himself to his knees and crawled to the windows, where the men were huddled on the floor shouting something to him. The din grew louder. Cries of pain came from the wounded men. From the direction of the corridor hand grenades burst, and as Schulz looked toward the right-hand door he saw the sentry there run back into the hall. He turned and crawled back to Triebig. 'They're attacking from both sides,' he shouted in Triebig's ear. 'We've got to get out of here. We're trapped.'

Triebig jumped to his feet and ran down the aisle between the machines to the other end of the hall. He stooped in front of the elevator shaft and waited until Schulz caught up with him. Several other men joined them there. Triebig leaned over the shaft. 'One man go down there,' he ordered, his voice trembling. 'Perhaps there's a cellar door below. Go on, Sergeant.'

Schulz hesitated. But since hand grenades were already flying in through the windows of the hall, he fished with his foot for the rung of the ladder below the door. For a few seconds he remained suspended, peering upward. Above him all remained still. Squinting, he descended the ladder until his foot encountered something soft. As he tried to feel along the wall, his hands encountered nothing and he felt a draught of cool air in his face. He kicked aside a body lying in his way, and made sure that the opening actually led into a room. Then he swarmed rapidly back up the rungs. The shaft stretched above him, a column of blackness. When he reached the main floor, the full violence of the battle struck his ears. He jumped out of the shaft and landed in front of the group of men. Triebig gripped his shoulder. 'How is it?'

In breathless haste he reported what he had found. The men groaned with relief. 'Everyone down there,' Triebig rapped out the order. 'Is the radio section here?' One of the radio men replied, and Triebig turned to Schulz. 'Call the men away from the windows. They're all to come down to the cellar.'

'What about the wounded?' Schulz asked. But Triebig was already swinging down the ladder in the shaft. Schulz bit his lips. A dirty deal, he thought. Then he shrugged. He raced across the room, which was by now saturated with dust and smoke and an insane roar. At one of the windows he found two men kneeling behind an MG, firing into the yard. He slammed the first man on the back and shouted: 'Into the shaft, into the shaft and down to the cellar.' Then he rushed on, to the next window and the next.

But then he recoiled. In the fore part of the hall great shadows poured through the windows, jumped over the lathes, landed on the floor and scattered with phantom movements in all directions. For a second Schulz stood rigid. They're here, he thought. The Russians are here. Then he whirled around and sped blindly back between the machines, stumbled over a body, felt two hands clutching at his coat, heard a gruesome, despairing bellow, and with a jerk pulled free. The wounded, flashed through his mind. But there was no time for him to take any other path. They lay side by side, filling the narrow aisle between the machines. His boots dug deep into the lushly soft carpet of their writhing bodies. He tripped over outstretched arms, until at length his foot caught somewhere; he plunged full length on his face, and several hands held him fast. He saw a face in front of his, a mouth stammering something. Gasping for air, he raised his tommy-gun and struck out blindly with it. He got to his feet again, was pushed from behind and thrown forward. 'Kill him,' a voice roared, and many others took up the cry: 'Kill him, kill him.' He defended himself like a wild beast, and when he realized that he was making no progress he pulled the trigger and fired until his magazine was empty. The shouts died away into groans and whimpers and helpless sobbing; the hands fell away from his torn uniform. Free, he took three huge leaps, reached the firm pavement of the flooring, dashed with aching lungs toward the shaft, while behind him a single voice continued to shout, each word striking him like a blow: 'Yellow, bastard, traitor.' He dropped the tommy-gun and pressed his hands to his ears as he continued to run. But the shouting went on. When he got to the shaft he was shaking so violently that he could scarcely stay on his feet. He saw a knot of men struggling in front of the door, pushing each other back from the shaft, behaving like madmen. For a moment he halted and stared with bloodshot eyes at the scene. Then he gathered himself and crashed with all his weight against the living wall that blocked his way, and carried it down with him into the shaft. He fell about fifteen feet, landed on a clump of intertwined bodies, instantly rolled away from them, leaped to his feet and pelted on. The shouting behind him sounded more muted. He rushed down a narrow corridor toward a glimmer of light until he noticed a door on his right, and heard a harsh voice. A few seconds later he came face to face with Triebig, who stood in the middle of a room. As he recognized Schulz, Triebig slowly lowered his raised tommy-gun. There were about fifteen men in the room. Some were holding flashlights. Blinded, Schulz closed his eyes. Then he remembered the Russians and shouted: 'Keep going; they're coming; the Russians are coming, Lieutenant.'

Triebig jerked around, shouting orders. The men stormed toward the back of the room where, Schulz now noticed, another door opened out. As he followed he suddenly realized that other members of the company would be coming. He stood still and looked back.

'What are you waiting for?' Triebig screamed impatiently. Schulz silently pointed to the opposite entrance as two more men came running toward them. One of them shouted: 'Hold it there.' He collided with Triebig, who violently pushed him back. 'What are you yelling for?' Triebig asked loudly. 'What's the matter?'

The man recognized the lieutenant and snapped to attention. 'More of the fellows are coming, sir,' he panted, jerking his thumb back over his shoulder.

'Have you seen Russians?' Triebig asked.

'And how!' the man burst out. 'They must be in the shaft by now and . . .'

'Why didn't you say that right away?' Triebig cursed. He sprang to the door. 'In with you,' he shouted. 'Come on, we can't lose another second.' He shoved the men violently inside. The door was made of solid sheet steel and had two big bolts that could be shut from inside. As Triebig slammed and locked the door behind him, fists thudded against the steel from the other side and several voices roared: 'Open up, open up!'

'For God's sake open that door,' Schulz stammered. The men on the other side now seemed to be kicking against it with their nailed boots. Triebig did not open it. As Schulz tried to force past him, Triebig placed both hands on his chest and pushed him away. 'Keep your hands off, you goddamned idiot!' he screamed.

'But you can't . . .' Schulz whispered.

'Shut up!' Triebig commanded, glaring at him. 'I know what I'm doing. Better they than the whole lot of us.' He stepped away from the door and he and Schulz ran after the others. The corridor turned at a right angle and terminated, about a dozen paces farther on, in a large room that was piled right to the ceiling with boxes. They flashed their lights over every corner of the room and discovered a second door. Schulz turned to the lieutenant. 'We have to keep our rear open,' he panted. 'If we set up an MG at the corner there, nobody can get through the door and we can take our time about looking around.'

Triebig agreed. He ordered the radio men to set up their apparatus. Meanwhile he had the men drag four of the heavy boxes, which were filled with machine parts, over to the right angle where they were stacked on top of one another. 'No bullet will go through that, I tell you,' he said with satisfaction. 'You're as safe behind those boxes as in a tank.' He waited until the MG crew had taken up positions behind the improvised barricade, and peered hard in the direction of the door. But not a sound could be heard. Presumably the locked-out men had run back into the corridor—God knew where it led to. Perhaps they had run straight into the hands of the Russians. He felt an enormous uneasiness as he thought of the way Triebig had left them to their fate. Bad enough about that business with the wounded. . . .

Shame and horror welled up within him as he remembered. Suddenly it also occurred to him that he no longer had a gun. He cursed himself for having failed to take one from one of the dead men in the shaft. But who in such a situation would be likely to think that far ahead? Weaponless, he felt naked. He decided to ask round among the men; perhaps one of them would be carrying an extra gun. As he turned toward the storeroom, where the men had sat down on the crates and were smoking, he tried to figure out what part of the factory they were now under. Beneath the tower, he decided.

Triebig was standing beside the radio men, impatiently watching as they fussed with their set. As Schulz came in they were setting up the long rod antenna. 'I hope we'll have some kind of reception here,' one of them remarked. 'Not a window anywhere in this damned cellar—I don't know.'

'Do you need a window?' Triebig asked anxiously.

The man nodded. 'You do with these sets. They're not much good except in the open. We'll see.' He turned the dial. 'Not a whisper,' he complained. 'I'd better try CW right away.' As the radio man reached for the bug, Schulz went round among the men until he found one who had a pistol in addition to his carbine. 'I'll give it back to you later,' he assured the man, examining the weapon.

The soldier waved his hand generously. 'What the hell. You don't seriously think we'll ever get out of this tomb, do you?'

Schulz shrugged. He went over to Triebig who was still standing beside the radio man, shifting his weight tensely from one leg to the other. 'That's just a waste of time,' he said. 'I'd suggest we first see where the corridor over there goes. We have to know what we're up against.'

Triebig nodded, but did not stir. When the men looked questioningly at him, some of them with their mouths twisted in an expression of mockery, Triebig pulled himself together. 'Take a few men with you,' he said to Schulz. 'If you discover anything special, send a man back to me.'

The sergeant shook his head firmly. 'It will be better if you come along,' he declared in a loud voice. 'It may prove necessary to make a decision that I couldn't take upon myself as long as there's a company commander around.' There was undisguised mutiny in his voice. The men had all stood up, and as he looked at their hostile faces Triebig realized how serious his mistake was. He dared not risk angering them any further. Perhaps his life would depend on every one of them in the course of the next hour. Suppressing his impulse toward rage, he said: 'If you are afraid, Sergeant, I'll go with you.'

'It isn't a question of being afraid,' Schulz said bitingly. 'The men here can tell you exactly who is afraid and who isn't.' He looked around. Seeing the agreement in all their faces, he grinned spitefully. 'We have eyes in our heads, Lieutenant, good eyes: we know what's been going on here.'

Triebig felt that he was losing control of his temper, in spite of his resolve. To avoid bringing the quarrel to a head, he turned without a word and went out through the door. Some ten yards down, the corridor suddenly turned at an angle and ran on. Triebig paused and checked the direction by his compass. Then he turned to Schulz, who was moving the beam of his flashlight up and down the corridor. 'Leave one man here,' he ordered curtly. 'In case we have to come back quickly.'

Schulz nodded. 'I don't understand why the building has no cellar windows,' he said. 'If we could find a window we could try getting out.'

'If there are they'll be barred,' Triebig said. 'We can check that later. But right now we must know where the corridor goes.' They continued on until they reached a door that led into a chamber in which was a large array of machinery, boilers and enormous pipes that disappeared into the high ceiling. 'Heating plant,' Schulz declared with the air of an engineer. He flashed his light around. They began searching the room. Toward the rear they came upon a pile of coke reaching to the ceiling. There was an opening in the wall which proved to be the entrance to the coal cellar.

'Now it's getting romantic,' Schulz muttered. Triebig watched him climb over the coke and disappear through the opening. 'Be careful,' he called out, and was about to follow. A sudden noise stopped him in his tracks. He turned his head and saw several men run across the cellar and stop in front of a door he had not noticed earlier. The noise grew louder; now he heard the chatter of a tommy-gun. He jumped off the pile of coke to the floor and ran after the men. They were gathered in front of a dark corridor. Before he could order them to switch off their flashlights, a voice rang out in front of them. Triebig staggered back as from a blow. 'Sergeant Steiner here, don't shoot. It's us—Sergeant Steiner.' Incredulous and aghast, he saw a man come running toward them out of the darkness, arms upraised, while behind him the roar of the tommy-gun continued with undiminished insistence. Triebig's thoughts were in turmoil. No more than the outlines of the approaching man's body could be seen as yet, but Triebig took it for granted that it was Steiner. Steiner whose death he had already reported to Battalion; Steiner who had climbed up to the factory tower and was now appearing in the cellar like a ghost; Steiner whom he hated more than anyone he had ever before encountered in his life; and Steiner who stood between him and the future that Stransky had promised: Biarritz, Arcachon, Mont de Mersan, Paris, Montmartre. . . . And Triebig forgot where he was. He forgot the men of his company who stood on both sides of him, breathless and incredulous; and he forgot himself. By the time he raised the tommy-gun and pulled the trigger, the man had approached within ten paces of them. Triebig saw him stumble, sink to his knees and tumble forward on his face. Then he felt hands dragging his arms down, heard voices clamouring in his ears, received a punch in the waist that took his breath away. Someone roared at him: 'That was one of our men!'

Triebig did not answer. He watched with a strange feeling in his chest as the men ran toward the soldier on the ground, and he swallowed. This was the first human being he had ever shot. The first, he thought. Then a wild sensation of triumph rose up within him, staggering him by its very force and distorting his face to a horrible grinning mask. Behind him he suddenly heard the voice of Schulz, and at the same time Triebig became aware that the hammering of the Russian tommy-gun had stopped. The sergeant pressed close to him. 'What happened?' he asked. Triebig shrugged and remained silent. Vacantly, he watched three more figures appear out of the darkness of the corridor and move toward the group who were still occupied with the man he had shot. He saw them stop, bend over the body, and his heart abruptly began to pound so hard that he clutched at his chest with both hands. Schulz, eyeing him from one side, now pushed past him and went over to the others.

Then he noticed Steiner kneeling beside the man on the ground. He had unbuttoned the other's shirt and was looking down at him, lips compressed. Steiner raised his head and asked Krüger: 'How did this happen?' He spoke in so low a voice that it was barely possible to understand him.

'I don't know,' Krüger murmured dully. 'When we turned the corner, he went on running toward the light. I wanted to run after him, but Faber held me back. And then . . .' He hunched his shoulders and stood helplessly among the men.

'And then?' Steiner demanded.

But Krüger did not reply. Faber spoke for him. 'And then someone fired. We dropped to the floor until the firing stopped.' He shook his head. 'I don't get it.' he said, 'They couldn't help seeing it was us.'

Steiner nodded. He suddenly saw with great clarity what must have happened. For a long while he looked down into Schnurrbart's face, which was crumbling into shapelessness like ruined masonry. Then he slowly straightened up. 'Who fired?' he asked. He was certain he knew the answer. The men remained silent, but their glances all flew in one direction. Steiner raised his flashlight. The beam struck a bloodless face, picked out a pair of nervous eyes, and every sound in the cellar ceased abruptly. 'Take a couple of men,' Steiner said to Krüger. 'You must hold the corner; the Russians will be along in a moment.' Then he stalked toward the lieutenant. The men followed him as if they had slivers of glass in their shoes. 'Why did you shoot?' Steiner asked. He stood in front of Triebig, fixing those evasive, flickering eyes. Triebig made no reply. When Steiner repeated the question, he blinked to escape the probing of the flashlight. 'Shut up!' he barked.

Steiner could feel the skin of his face tautening and his eyes smarting. Grief knotted his throat like a noose; he panted for breath as he said: 'You damned swine.' At that moment several tommy-guns began roaring down at the corner of the corridor, where Krüger and the other men lay. The shooting boomed like cannon fire in the confined space. The men came to life. They tried to get past Steiner, toward the rear, but he blocked their way. 'Stay here!' he shouted. As he raised his gun and aimed it at them, they pressed themselves against the wall in terror.

'Stay here!' Steiner repeated. He saw Triebig on the point of running. A leap brought him to the lieutenant's side, and he held him fast. Triebig fought. He dropped his gun and struck out at Steiner with his fists. Taken by surprise, Steiner staggered back for a second. His flashlight hampered him. He thrust it into his pocket. In the darkness the men ran past him, although he again shouted to them to remain. Triebig flailed away at him like a madman. He was breathing so hard that in spite of the roar of gunfire Steiner could hear each gasp, and he had difficulty fending off the man's blind swings. At last he lost patience. He raised the barrel of his gun in both hands and struck brutally, once, twice, thrice. When he pulled the flashlight out of his pocket, he saw Triebig lying on the floor. The skin had opened up from his right eye to his chin, and blood was pouring into his mouth, which he had opened to scream. Steiner gave him no time. He gripped the other's tunic and pulled him to his feet. 'Come on!' he said. Disregarding the man's outcry, he pushed him along in front of him toward the corner just as Krüger and the others retreated toward him. 'They're coming,' Krüger shouted. He stopped and looked at the screaming lieutenant, from whose shattered nose blood spurted. 'What's the idea?' he asked in horror. Steiner shoved him aside. 'Get back!' he said. Simultaneously he gave the lieutenant a violent shove forward. Krüger tried to catch his arm. With a movement almost playful in its agility Steiner ducked under his hands and thrust the barrel of the tommy-gun into his stomach with so much force that Krüger lost his balance and fell. As he straightened up, face working with pain, he saw Steiner driving the lieutenant on toward the Russians. 'He's mad,' one of the men cried; he had come from the corner, and was watching the scene, too shocked to do anything. They shouted at Steiner, but he paid no attention. He kept pushing Triebig ahead of him like a ball. When the lieutenant attempted to resist, he slammed the barrel of the tommy-gun into his back. He kicked Triebig alternately in the legs, in the buttocks, in the back, repeating over and over: 'Keep going, keep going.' They came within ten feet of the corner. Rifle fire was still clattering into the walls, tearing down the plaster. Ricochets whistled around their ears. Then there was a crashing explosion in front of them.

Steiner had time to see Triebig reach both hands into the air, reel to the side and plunge heavily to the floor. He paused long enough to fix the sight in his mind. Then he turned and dashed back. The flashlight fell from his hands and shattered on the floor. Without pausing he ran on until in the darkness he stumbled over a body and plunged full length. He cursed. Then it occurred to him that this must be Schnurrbart. With one mighty effort he managed to heave the lifeless body on to his shoulder and ran on, gasping for breath. He reached the furnace room where the others were waiting tensely for him.

'Which way?' Krüger asked. Schulz pointed to the door opposite. Krüger turned to Steiner. 'Let me have him,' he said, and took the dead body on his own broad back.

They pressed into the corridor and ran into the next room, where the men who had remained behind received them excitedly. Schulz waved his hand impatiently to stop their torrent of questions. 'Not so much talk. We have to block this side with boxes too. The Russians are coming.'

In feverish haste they began barricading the second corridor also. Steiner had meanwhile looked around the place. The room seemed ideal for withstanding a siege. From both sides the Russians would have to run down a long corridor completely without cover; they would easily be stopped by the heavy machine-guns and could be held off far enough so that their hand grenades would do no damage. As Steiner ran from one corner to another he felt silent vexation at observing the men whispering to one another, throwing meaningful glances at him. As soon as he came near them they stopped talking. Krüger and Faber behaved in the same way. They sat on a box, their faces chalky, watching him. Behind them lay Schnurrbart. They're all scared stiff, Steiner thought contemptuously. The stinkers are scared stiff. He noticed the radio men in a corner. As he approached, one of the two men raised his head. 'We have communication with Regiment now,' he said.

'What about Battalion?' Steiner asked.

The man shrugged. 'They don't answer. God knows what's wrong there.'

'I can tell you what,' Schulz put in as he joined the group. 'They've written us off, the brutes. As far as they're concerned we're through. Dead and gone.' He looked up at the dirty-grey arched ceiling that curved above them like the lid of a coffin. 'Shut up,' Steiner said with disgust. To the radio men he said: 'How did you get here?' As one of the men explained, Steiner stood with closed eyes, trying to reconstruct the diagram of the cellar. Finally he nodded. 'We've run around the sides of a square and come out under the tower again. If they don't fight through to get us out, we'll have to try it ourselves. Get in touch with them,' he ordered sharply.

The radio men slipped on their earphones.

After receiving the alarming radio message from Triebig, Stransky sat at his desk in a mood of blankness. The news of Steiner's death brought him none of the inner rejoicing he had anticipated, and he wondered why this was so. The feeling suddenly swept him that a vast cloud of danger was gathering around his head. If they are wiped out by the Russians, he thought, things will be bad here. For a moment he thought of removing the First or the Third Company from its position and ordering it to the defence of his command post. But Brandt would have to approve such a step. At last he lifted the telephone and spoke with the signals platoon leader. 'Get all your available men and take up position in front of my command post,' he ordered. 'If anything should happen, send a courier up to me.'

For a moment there was a dead silence at the other end of the line. Then Hüser exclaimed in dismay: 'I need at least four men for the switchboard and radio communication, sir.'

Stransky bit his lips impatiently. 'One man is enough for communication,' he said imperatively. 'The Russians may be on top of us at any moment. You will need every man down in the street below the command post. Once the danger is past, I'll inform you and you can have your men again and resume communications. How many are you?'

'Only six at the moment,' Hüser replied, his uneasiness plain.

Stransky frowned. 'How is that? Your platoon is fifteen men strong.'

'The others are out taking down the telephone lines to First and Third,' Hüser explained.

'Then take the couriers also, and hurry up about it, man.' He replaced the receiver and lit a cigarette. But after the first few puffs he dropped it to the floor in disgust and ground it out with his boot. The silence in the room intensified his nervousness. He tried to win a little pleasure by turning his thoughts to his transfer back to France. If what his cousin had written were accurate, the transfer ought to come through any day now. His cousin could be relied on, he thought, grinning.

Now and then he glanced impatiently at his watch. The battalion was due to start its withdrawal in one hour. The other companies, except for Second, had been informed and would evacuate their positions according to plan. Lieutenant Moninger had sent a message that he was in communication with Third and that all was peaceful on both sectors. Peaceful? Stransky smiled grimly. Nothing reassuring about this peacefulness; it plucked at the nerves and was harder to bear than all the racket of yesterday.

Unable to banish his gloomy thoughts, he went over to the window and looked down into the dark back yard. 'There is no peace,' he murmured to himself. 'One is a hunted animal.' His thoughts returned again and again to his Second Company. It was really time now to order it to withdraw. Perhaps it will be better after all, he told himself, if I send a courier over there. Was Triebig still alive? He was not eager for Triebig to come back, but he could not put off issuing his order much longer. Glancing at his watch again, he saw that nearly an hour had passed since his conversation with Hüser. It was twenty minutes to four now. As he reached for the telephone it occurred to him that the house was deserted except for the communications platoon out front. He started for the door. Suddenly he recalled the radio message from Triebig. Since he had deliberately failed to report this message to Regiment, he returned to the table and carefully burned the message slip over the candle. Then he turned toward the door again. At that moment it flew open and Stransky found himself confronted by Kiesel. The adjutant's face bore an expression of anger and harshness such as Stransky had never seen before in him. Without a word Kiesel strode past him into the room, sat down at the desk, reached into his pocket and accusingly laid a sheet of paper on the desk. The silence became unbearable; it stood like a wall between the two officers. At last Stransky pulled himself together, managed a dim smile and murmured: 'You. Herr Kiesel?'

'As you see, Herr Stransky. I have something to say to you.' He waited until Stransky had taken a seat. 'The commander has sent me. What is the situation of your Second Company?'

Stransky moistened his dry lips with his tongue and tried to keep his voice on a casual, even note. 'The last radio message came from Triebig. But you know how Triebig is.' He assumed a sardonic air that dissolved at once under Kiesel's icy gaze. 'I didn't take his assertions too seriously,' he added rather vaguely. As Kiesel persistently did not speak, Stransky's discomfort mounted. He passed his hand nervously over his temple. 'What makes you ask?' he murmured.

'The last radio message came from Sergeant Steiner,' Kiesel

replied, picking up the sheet of paper he had laid on the desk. 'He says that Triebig has been killed and the company is surrounded in the cellar of the factory. Didn't you know that?'

His eyes probed Stransky's corpselike face. Stransky's lips moved without making a sound. At last he whispered incredulously: 'Impossible.'

Kiesel regarded him impassively. 'You didn't know that?' he asked in mock surprise. 'But you have radio communication with the company, Herr Stransky.' He spoke now with naked scorn.

Stransky fought to restore some order to his thoughts. To gain time he lit a cigarette. But his fingers were trembling so hard that he feared Kiesel would notice his state, and he laid the cigarette on the edge of the desk. 'I don't understand that,' he murmured weakly.

There was a knock on the door and a tall, broad-shouldered man in lieutenant's uniform entered. He paused at the threshold and snapped his hand to his cap.

'You're a little earlier than I expected,' Kiesel said, rising. 'Do you know Lieutenant Gollhofer?' he asked Stransky. When Stransky shook his head, he continued: 'He has been commanding the engineer's platoon for the past eight days. Lieutenant-Colonel Brandt has ordered him to go to the relief of Second Company. I have no more time to spend talking with you. You are to take the rest of the battalion as planned to the new position. The commander will expect you in his command post at nine o'clock.'

He had spoken very rapidly. Now he swept the lieutenant out with him into the hall. Side by side they ran down the steps to the street. There several dozen men were huddling close to the wall of the building, talking in whispers. 'You know what to do?' Kiesel asked. Gollhofer nodded. They looked beyond the fence at the shadowy outlines of the factory. Kiesel bit his lips. Then he shook hands with the lieutenant. 'I hope you are successful. The business must not take too long, or you'll lose contact with us. Good luck.' He stood watching as the men disappeared into the shadow of the fence. Then he hurried on to the next intersection, where his car was waiting. 'Back,' Kiesel snapped, swinging into the seat beside the driver. He ordered him to drive fast.

It seemed to Kiesel that he had been doing little else but ride in this car for the past two hours. He had reached the new command post and sent the car back. Half an hour later it returned with Lieutenant Stroh who told him that Brandt wanted to see him at once. Turning the task of arranging quarters over to Stroh, he had driven back to the old headquarters to find Brandt in a state of intense excitement. 'I've deliberately refrained from getting in touch with Stransky,' the commander had told him. 'I want you to go there and find out for yourself what has been happening.' Then he told Kiesel about the radio messages and his order to Gollhofer to relieve the factory. 'Drive over to Stransky at once,' he concluded. 'I want to see him at the new command post at nine o'clock. If he has tried any more slimy tricks, I don't intend to let it pass this time. I'll wait here for you.'

The commander's hunch had been entirely right. Meeting the battalion communications platoon leader in front of Stransky's command post, Kiesel had learned that the radio station had been left untended and communication with the second company broken off on Stransky's orders. That will cost him his head, Kiesel thought grimly as the car drew up in front of the regimental command post. 'Wait till I come back,' Kiesel ordered the man at the wheel. He bounded up the steps.

The candles in the hallway were still burning, but almost all the doors stood wide open, and his footsteps echoed loudly through the deserted building. The commander sprang to his feet, irritated and impatient, as Kiesel entered the room. 'You can tell me about it while we drive,' he said quickly. 'I must get to the new headquarters. Since the communications men have left I've been up in the air here. Where is the car?' Without waiting for a reply he snatched his baggage and hurried out. On the way down to the car he told Kiesel that the rest of the staff had left half an hour ago. 'I put them all on trucks,' Brandt said. 'It will be light in an hour. The time for the withdrawal was set much too late. I don't understand the general.'

'Neither do I,' Kiesel agreed. 'The battalions will reach the new line in broad daylight.'

Sighing, Brandt settled on the seat. 'Get started, man,' he barked at the driver. He turned to Kiesel, who had sat down beside him. 'It's four sharp now. I hope there was no last-minute hitch with the withdrawal.'

'Let's hope so,' Kiesel murmured. Brandt watched indifferently as the car barely by-passed a fallen telegraph pole. 'You can turn on your headlights now,' he called to the man at the wheel. Unhappily, he eyed the greying sky. Then he turned to Kiesel. 'Now let me have it.'

Silently, he listened to Kiesel's report, while the car gathered speed, left the last houses of the city behind, and reached the highway. When Kiesel finished, there was a long quiet. Finally Brandt looked up, shaking his head. 'He must have gone stark raving mad,' he said. 'In the language of military law there's only one word for that: sabotage. And the rope is the penalty for sabotage. Stransky knows that as well as I. I'd like to know what he could have been thinking of. He must have reckoned on the possibility of this foulness coming out.'

'Certainly,' Kiesel said. He looked back. The silhouette of the city was beginning to emerge gradually from the darkness, black against the grey of the sky. 'Of course he must have reckoned on the possibility,' Kiesel repeated absently. Suddenly he turned to face Brandt. 'I feel like a deserter.'

'So do I,' said Brandt, 'but we have done all in our power. H-hour couldn't be postponed on account of a single company. The bridgehead has begun to move and will go on moving until the last man has reached the Crimea. A moment of historic significance.' He smiled bitterly. 'We are making history once more.'

Still holding its smile, his face suddenly convulsed. 'Drive faster, damn it all,' he shouted at the driver. Frightened, the soldier hunched his shoulders as though he had received a blow, at the same time pressing the accelerator to the floor. 'But we are like the sorcerer's apprentice,' Brandt continued in an easy conversational tone. 'We have forgotten the magic word for stopping the flood. Or do you perhaps know it?'

'Capitulation,' Kiesel said.

Brandt dismissed that with a wave of his hand. 'The time for that has passed. What would we get out of it now?'

Kiesel shrugged.

'There you are,' Brandt said. 'Incidentally, I want to have everything on this business with Stransky in writing. Don't forget any of the details, including those radio messages. I'll need them as evidence.'

'Are you intending to start so soon, tomorrow, on . . .?' Kiesel asked hesitantly.

Something in Kiesel's voice alienated Brandt. His own tone became more reserved. 'As soon as I know how the affair in the factory turns out,' he replied crisply.

Kiesel bowed his head. For all his outrage at what Stransky had done, he suddenly felt rotten at the thought of contributing toward bringing the man before a court-martial. But did Stranksy deserve anything better? He pursued this thought until the commander's voice, louder and somewhat sharper now, made him conscious again of the upholstery and the sway of the speeding vehicle. 'You are unstable,' Brandt said challengingly. 'You are unstable and should never have been permitted to wear a uniform. A person like yourself ought to be careful about entering a sphere where justice is not meted out by the hand of God. In military life there's no time to wait for that kind of justice. But you cannot change your spots any more than I can. If I find fault with you for anything, it's for not perceiving sooner the nature of the individual you work for. If you have perceived it, you should by now have accepted it. *J'y suis et j'y reste.* Since I have been commander of this regiment I have sent several men up before a court-martial, not because it amused me, but because I happen to be commander. In Stransky's case, too, I shall do what is my duty. That's all there is to it.' He pressed further back into his corner and fell into a profound silence.

In the beam of the headlights several houses flew past, the shadowy outlines of a railroad yard, tall poles, tracks. The road spiralled up a steep slope that seemed to go on forever. Brandt asked: 'How far to go yet?'

'Ten minutes,' Kiesel replied, consulting the illuminated dial of his wrist-watch. They seemed to have reached the top of the climb now. The road ran on almost in a straight line along the barren ridge of a series of hills. A few miles further on it turned toward the north and dropped precipitately into a narrow valley, in whose lap stood a small cluster of buildings. 'We're there,' Kiesel said, pointing to the houses.

The driver steered the car around a last curve and braked sharply in front of a longish building. The door of the building was flung open and a man came running toward the car. Kiesel recognized him as Lieutenant Mohr, the regimental communications officer. 'What's the news?' Brandt asked as he stepped out of the car.

'The general has already called you three times,' Mohr hastened to report.

'I'm not a magician,' Brandt grumbled. 'Did he want anything special?'

'I don't think so, sir. He asked how things were going. I told him that the withdrawal had all gone according to plan so far, the battalions were on the way to their new positions.'

'And Gollhofer?' Brandt asked with apparent casualness. Kiesel waited tensely. Mohr gave his news: 'Gollhofer's already on his way, with the second company. Radio message from him just ten minutes ago.'

'What's that you say, man!' Brandt exclaimed loudly, snatching the sheet of paper with the report from his hand. There was already enough daylight for him to read the hastily scribbled notation. He read it through twice. Then he turned to Kiesel. 'What do you say to that?' he exploded, and suddenly burst into cheerful laughter. He crumpled the paper in his clenched fist and thrust it into his pocket. 'You're a damned gloomy raven,' he said to Kiesel. 'I hope you'll admit it.' Disregarding Kiesel's blank expression, he asked Mohr: 'Where do I hang my hat?'

Mohr gestured toward the door. 'Here sir. There's someone waiting to see you already.'

'Who?' Brandt asked.

'A Captain Killius,' Mohr replied. 'He's come direct from the High Command and says he's to replace a battalion commander; the name of the man he replaces is in a letter which he wants to hand to you personally'

Brandt exchanged a brief glance with Kiesel. Then he followed the lieutenant. As he entered the room which was now his new headquarters, a stocky figure rose from a chair. 'Captain Killius,' the man said, clicking his heels. 'I . . .' But Brandt cut him off with a brusque gesture. 'I've heard,' he said curtly. 'You have orders for me?'

Plainly depressed by this frosty reception, the captain laid a sealed envelope on the table. 'I have, sir,' he said stiffly. While the commander tore open the letter, Kiesel watched his face; it had suddenly lost all expression and looked like a whitewashed wall. For a while Brandt stood staring over the head of the officer. Then he quietly asked Kiesel: 'Didn't you once mention Captain Stransky's good connections?'

Kiesel nodded. 'There is a Major-General Stransky, attached to Army High Command, South. He is, I believe, a cousin of Captain Stransky.'

'I see,' Brandt said slowly. Grimacing, he tossed the letter on the table. 'You can guess what that is, can't you?' he said, indicating the letter as if it were some offensive filth.

'His transfer, of course,' Kiesel replied calmly.

'Exactly,' Brandt said grimly. 'Herr Stransky is to report to the staff of a battalion in Paris within a week. I believe it is the very assignment he held before he came out here to us.'

There was a brief silence in the room. Lieutenant Mohr made bold to murmur: 'Miracles still happen.'

'You may be right about that,' Brandt growled. 'But the miracle is going to be a bit different from the kind Herr Stransky expects.' He turned to Killius, who had been attending to the conversation in a total fog. 'I'm happy to welcome you among us,' he said cordially, shaking the new man's hand. 'Things are rather hectic at the moment and I must ask you to bear with us. Let me introduce you to everybody. Oh yes, you already know Lieutenant Mohr.' Kiesel was obliged to smile at his superior's sudden shifts of mood.

The telephone shrilled. 'That must be the general,' Mohr said. His guess was apparently right. When Brandt hung up, after a brief conversation, his expression had become very grave. 'We're staying here only till tonight,' he said to the officers. 'A courier is on the way with important orders. Let's get to work, gentlemen.'

XVI

IN THE CELLAR nothing had changed. The men perched idly on the boxes, smoking and talking in muted tones. Their spirits were at low ebb, their faces sallow under the steel helmets. Steiner, too, was sitting on a box, head drooping, eyes empty.

Krüger muttered a curse. He dropped his cigarette to the floor and ground it out. 'We have to do something,' he said loudly. 'This business of sitting around gets on my nerves. Just look at the silly faces on all these mutts.'

He had spoken to Faber, who hunched his shoulders indifferently. 'What do you want to do?' he asked quietly. 'We just have to wait until they come for us.'

'Until they come!' Krüger laughed wildly. 'By the time they come they can scrape us off the walls.' He strode over to the radio men's corner. 'Nothing new yet?' he asked.

One of the men shook his head. 'They signalled QRX 30,' he said. 'They're moving to new positions and we're to wait thirty minutes. There are still ten minutes to go.'

'They've cleaned out on us,' Krüger said. 'That's what they've done. They've given us up, the bastards, that's all.' His loud voice disturbed the trance of the other men. Schulz and several others trotted up to him. 'What's happened?' Schulz exclaimed.

'Don't ask such stupid questions,' Krüger replied violently. 'How much longer are we going to sit around on our arses? Any of you think they're going to dig us out? You can wait till you're blue in the face, I tell you.'

He had only put their own fears into words. Schulz nodded emphatically. 'I think so too,' he declared hoarsely. 'We're wasting precious time. As it is I don't understand why the Russians haven't come yet.'

'You mayn't, but I do,' Krüger snorted. 'They'd be idiots to run head-on up against our machine-guns. They know they can have us cheaper. All they have to do is wait till we've got nothing to eat, and we'll come crawling right up to them, wagging our tails.'

'Right.' Schulz turned round and looked toward Steiner who still sat in the same attitude.

'Let him alone,' said Krüger, guessing Schulz's thoughts. 'Let him alone, I tell you.' He lowered his voice. 'You don't understand that.' He stretched and said in a loud voice: 'Left or right?'

Schulz grasped his meaning at once. He swung round and indicated the door on the right. 'There, I'd say. Maybe we can get back up through the lift shaft.'

Although most of the others looked sceptical, Krüger took up the plan. 'We'll block up the door with boxes,' he declared. 'That way we have our rear protected and don't have to leave anyone here.'

Schulz nodded. Glad to throw off the crushing burden of inactivity, the men set to work. The machine-gunners were pulled back, the door locked, and they piled a dozen of the heavy crates in front of it. Another dozen were stacked behind the first row, so that the entire doorway from floor to ceiling was shielded by their immovable mass. 'That ought to do it,' Krüger panted, studying their work with satisfaction. He went slowly over to Steiner and announced: 'We're going to try to break out.'

'All right,' Steiner said without raising his head. Krüger squinted down at him, his face drawn. Something was impeding his tongue so that he could hardly talk. 'Perhaps we can get up through the lift shaft,' he managed to say. Turning his head, he observed that the men were all standing impatiently behind him. 'Once we're in the hall,' he said in a somewhat louder voice, 'we're as good as away.'

Steiner stood up heavily. 'Take Schnurrbart along,' he said. As Krüger looked into his eyes, a shudder passed through him. He turned to two of the men and ordered them to carry Schnurrbart's body. Then he followed Steiner toward the barricade at the other end of the corridor. They moved the boxes aside to make a small opening through which they could crawl, and cautiously went on toward the next door. Schulz suddenly recalled the men whom Triebig had locked out. In a whisper he told Krüger about it. 'Damn dirty trick it was, but I couldn't do anything.'

'He's had his,' Krüger said. They watched Steiner move the bolt back. 'Lights out!' Schulz whispered. Instantly all the men switched off their flashlights. Up ahead the darkness was impenetrable. A faint creaking indicated that Steiner had opened the door. At the same time they felt a fresh stream of air against their faces; it was like something from another world. In the intensity of his excitement Krüger bit his lips until they bled. There's no chance of it, he thought. If we . . . He recoiled in fright as someone touched his chest. Then he heard Steiner's voice right in front of him: 'Leave your lights out. Where is Schulz?'

'Here,' the Sergeant breathed.

'Come along,' Steiner whispered, and Schulz felt a hand taking his arm. They tiptoed down the corridor, feeling their way along the walls, until they reached a door. Schulz whispered: 'That's a cellar room. The door we want is on the other side, and then the corridor runs left to the elevator.'

'Let's go,' Steiner whispered.

The nails of their boots scraped on the stone floor. At last they came up against a wall. After some searching they found the door. 'Get the others,' Steiner said. He turned to the left. A few yards farther on he stumbled on a body that lay across his path. He stepped over it. The current of fresh air was even stronger here. Steiner straightened up somewhat from his hunched position. The last few yards he walked erect until his foot encountered something hard. It was a step. His hands groped over the two leaves of an open door, and he reasoned that this must be the elevator shaft. For a moment he hesitated. But since he could not hear a sound anywhere, he took the risk and switched on his flashlight. The bright beam revealed the crumpled bodies of about a dozen men who lay piled one on top of the other, their faces horrible to behold, blocking the entrance. There was a noise behind him. Steiner turned and saw the rest of the men. 'What is it?' Schulz whispered. Then he caught sight of the bodies and his mouth twisted in sick horror. 'Upstairs there will be worse sights,' he said.

Krüger joined them. 'How do you make it out?' he asked. Since Steiner gave no reply, Schulz asked: 'What?'

'That the Russians haven't let out a sound,' Krüger answered impatiently. 'Good Lord, they must be hiding somewhere.'

Schulz shifted uneasily, 'It's funny,' he remarked. 'And what the hell's happened to the others?'

'What others?'

'The ones Triebig locked out.'

'Shit,' Krüger whispered. They fell silent. Krüger pressed his fist against his right knee which was suddenly beginning to quiver like a gear shift. His reason rebelled against the unreality of the situation. He felt the sweat starting on his forehead. The men remained motionless, watching Steiner. Steiner switched off his flashlight, clambered over the dead bodies and groped for the ladder. Slowly he pulled himself up, rung by rung. He reached the first floor. On his left he saw the rectangle of the doorway shimmering dimly, and for a few seconds he hung on the ladder, peering incredulously. Then he carefully moved his leg sideways until his foot found support, and swung over into the opening. Before him lay the machinery hall, dark, silent and lifeless. Through the high windows dull light trickled down upon the machines which filled the room like petrified primordial monsters. For no reason he had a feeling amounting to certainty that there were no longer any Russians inside the room. Carelessly, he walked forward several yards and looked around. Then he returned to the shaft and called to the men to come up. Krüger appeared first. He thrust his powerful frame through the doorway and stopped in amazement. Behind him came Schulz, and then the others followed one by one, pushing each other ahead impatiently, and equally incredulous as they saw the empty hall.

'What the hell does it mean?' one of them said.

'They must be waiting for us outside the windows,' Schulz said hoarsely. 'It's a trick, that's all.'

'It is,' another man whispered. 'They can't have run away.'

Krüger shook his head impatiently. 'Don't wear your brains out thinking,' he snapped morosely. He turned to Steiner. 'Now what?'

Steiner looked around. 'Where were the wounded placed?'

'Over there,' Schulz said, pointing to a spot between two machines. Steiner walked toward the area, until his foot encountered something soft. He switched on the flashlight and stood rooted to the spot. Behind him a suppressed groan arose. Krüger whispered: 'My God!' the men lay scattered over the floor like lumps of raw meat, naked, their uniforms stripped off, abdomens slit open, faces smashed in, bodies bestially mutilated. The floor was red from pools of coagulated blood that had also run underneath the machines. Steiner switched off his flashlight. 'Where is Schnurrbart?' he asked.

'They have him,' Krüger replied hollowly.

'Wait,' Steiner ordered. He went over to a window. They

watched as he swung up on a sill, paused for a moment and then jumped with both feet into the yard. 'He's crazy,' Schulz stammered. They ran to the window and peered out into the grey twilight of dawn. Steiner ran erect across the yard. He kept his head forward, and they heard his gas mask knocking against his mess tin. Then his figure faded and vanished against the dark wall of the fence. 'He's got there,' Krüger breathed. When a green light flashed along the fence, Krüger climbed on to the window sill. 'First those two men with the canvas,' he ordered. He waited until the men had lifted Schnurrbart's body down.

Then they ran across the yard. They felt as if bells ought to be ringing somewhere as they ran, holding their faces up in the fresh morning air. Schulz, a short distance ahead, had come within a few yards of the fence when he stopped abruptly. He thought he had heard voices behind the fence. Krüger caught up with him and panted, 'Go on, go on.' At that moment they saw several of the slats of the fence being pushed aside. Steiner appeared in the gap and called impatiently to them to hurry. When they reached him they were stunned to see an officer standing beside him, addressing him with many shakes of the head, and behind the two stood several dozen men in German uniforms. 'I'm seeing things,' Krüger murmured. He turned to Schulz and Faber, who stood frozen beside him, and whispered: 'I'm going mad.'

'I'm mad already,' Schulz said.

The outlines of the factory were now rising more and more distinctly out of the dissolving darkness. The building presented a black bulk against the paling sky. The men moved heavily toward the officer who was shaking his head again and saying: 'The case reminds me of something that happened just about a year ago. Maybe the Russians realized that we were evacuating. In any case, I can't understand their fighting it out in the factory when they'd already dug in right in the heart of the city. They would have finished you fellows off today in any case.'

He thrust his steel helmet back from his forehead. 'You've had unbelievable luck,' he declared happily. 'We were supposed to dig you out and were just going to cross the yard when your sergeant came out of the window. 'I'm glad we didn't fire wildly.' He caught sight of the two men with the canvas and asked: 'Wounded?'

'No. dead,' Schulz replied.

'What are you dragging him along for?' the lieutenant asked in surprise. 'Do you expect to carry him six miles?'

'Six miles?' Krüger exclaimed.

The lieutenant nodded and looked at his watch. 'It's five to four,' he said urgently. 'We must hurry. We're evacuating the city at four.' He laughed at their astonished expressions. 'That's the way it is. If I hadn't got on the track of you right off, or the Russians had put up a hard fight, I would have had to leave you stuck there in the cellar. Then God knows what would have become of you. So let's go.' The lieutenant hitched up his belt. 'Leave the dead man here. We have no time to carry him along.'

'Who says so?' Steiner asked. His voice sounded on the point of breaking.

Gollhofer raised his eyebrows. 'I do. Have you a different opinion on the matter?'

'Yes,' Steiner retorted. He turned to the men. 'Who'll help me?'

'Me,' Krüger said. Faber stepped up beside him. The other men held back. 'One more,' Steiner said loudly. No one stirred. Steiner gripped two ends of the canvas. 'Three can do it.'

'Hold on a moment,' Schulz said. Without feeling any eagerness for this task, he suddenly felt that he had something to make up for. He took his place beside the other three. Gollhofer glared at them. He considered simply ordering them to let the dead man lie. But something about Steiner's face restrained him. Raising his hand, he placed himself at the head of the column. As they marched with long strides down the street they kept looking back through the battered fence at the factory which seemed to be watching them through the empty sockets of its windows. At last they crossed the street near the former battalion command post and left the factory behind them. They marched up a dark canyon between towering walls of buildings.

Gollhofer had meanwhile noticed the radio operators and instructed them to contact Regiment. 'Report that we're on our way. That will give them something to chew,' he added humourously. The knowledge of having carried out a difficult mission so easily filled him with elation.

Suddenly he thought of the men who were carrying the dead soldier, and his gleeful mood gave way to guilt. He waited until they had gone two blocks further. Then he ordered the company to halt and walked back to the rear where Steiner and the other three had taken advantage of the rest to lay their burden on the ground. They stood beside it, panting.

'I'll have you relieved,' Gollhofer declared so loudly that the rest of the men could not help hearing. 'I hope there will be volunteers,' He looked his men over, waiting. 'As you like,' he said after a brief pause. His voice took on a tone of command. 'Line up four abreast.'

The long column began to move. The men obeyed sullenly, while Gollhofer spoke to Steiner. 'Take five or ten men and march a hundred yards ahead of the company as advance guard. I'll give you a man who knows the way.' Then he went to the head of the line and ordered the first row of four to carry the dead man. 'After five minutes you'll pass him to the next, and so on to the end of the line. Then start over at the beginning again.'

While the first four were carrying out the order, Steiner selected his men. Krüger whispered to Faber: 'I couldn't have held out much longer.' He rubbed his aching arms. 'Never knew he was so heavy,' he added sadly. He turned to Schulz. 'That was damned decent of you. Did you know Schnurrbart?'

Schulz nodded. 'I did! Who didn't know him? God, don't mention it: I couldn't leave you to do it all.'

They covered a long distance in silence until they reached a street that sloped somewhat uphill. 'Do you know this district?' Schulz asked.

Krüger looked around speculatively. 'Seems familiar to me. Weren't we here yesterday morning?'

'Yes. Over there, in the next house or the one after, März told us about the attack on the factory.'

'Right,' Krüger said. His big face started to work; he swallowed, wiped his face with his shirt-sleeve and fought vainly against the grief that clawed at his heart. He knew it, he thought. Schnurrbart knew he wouldn't come out of it. The mist of moisture over his eyes grew more and more opaque; he forced his eyes wide open so that he could see where he was going. Their street ran now between a lane of trees into the brightening grey of daylight. Suddenly he felt that he must have a few words with Steiner. He caught up with him and asked: 'Where are we going?' He had to repeat his question twice before Steiner reacted.

'Doesn't matter,' Steiner said.

'Right,' Krüger said. 'Nothing matters now.'

Beyond the trees were one-story houses, small grey cubes each ringed by its green-painted garden fence. 'Here's where we got out of the truck,' Krüger said. Steiner remained silent. 'Yesterday morning,' Krüger said. Steiner remained silent. But abruptly they all stood still and looked back. In the west a number of low detonations sounded, and a few seconds later a steady rumble thundered up from the city. 'They're starting again,' Krüger commented.

Schulz grinned. 'A waste of ammunition.' His shoulders twitched with soundless laughter while he held his sharp face turned toward the sky.

'They should have realized we've cleared out,' Krüger commented.

'They haven't,' Schulz said. 'Why do you think we left so late? That's strategy. The Russians are used to us leaving around midnight when we retreat. By four o'clock in the morning they thought we wouldn't be going.'

His reasoning sounded convincing. 'Lucky we're not there,' someone said. 'We really would have been in for something.'

The rest of the company had drawn up closer meanwhile, and Gollhofer came running toward them. 'What are you loitering for?' he said impatiently. 'Let's get out of here or we'll get ourselves a dose of the Russian matins.' He grinned. 'They're going to be in for a surprise when they attack.'

They continued on at a smarter pace, and a few minutes later left the outlying suburbs of the city behind. Steiner looked back once more. It was not yet light enough to distinguish more than the grey cones of the mountains suspended in the sky—like clouds. The skyline of the city, embedded in the ambigious dusk of morning, was already almost visible. The sight produced no emotions in him. It was as if all his feeling were frozen and lifeless. But his mind circled incessantly and with great concentration around a single point. He had to settle the account; there was no help for it. Stransky was the real culprit. Triebig had only been his tool. The tool had been eliminated. The hardest task was still ahead. What happened to himself did not particularly matter, so long as he gave Stransky what he deserved.

He considered how to do it. Shoot him, he thought. That was the simplest way. The only question was where? That question he could not answer until he was back with the battalion.

Gollhofer came running up calling out his name. 'For you, Steiner,' he said loudly, holding out a scrap of paper. 'Radio message from Regiment,' he went on respectfully. 'You're to go directly to Regiment.'

As Steiner indicated neither curiosity nor any other sign of interest, the lieutenant disappointedly thrust the paper into his pocket. 'This probably means you're due for the *Ritterkreuz*,' he said with forced gaiety. Steiner shrugged. The summons troubled him, although he told himself that it could not possibly have any connection with Triebig's death. His expression of sourness deepened. Gollhofer studied him in wonderment. 'What's the matter with you, man?' he asked impatiently. 'You've deserved a decoration. Even if you already have a dozen of them plastered on your chest.' Steiner still remained stubbornly silent. The lieutenant laughed crossly. 'You're a queer fish,' he said. Out of sorts, he stood still, waiting for the company to come up with him. Then, as a thought occurred to him, he called out: 'You can stay with us; we're going straight to the regimental command post also.'

Steiner nodded without turning his head. Faber was marching at his side, and it suddenly struck him that he had not exchanged a word with Faber for hours. The kind of man who never says anything but who's always there when you need him, he thought.

The summons from Regiment continued to prey on his mind. If only he knew what lay behind it. Finally he gave up trying to imagine. By now it had grown so light that the terrain on both sides of the highway was visible. The familiar vineyards had a melancholy air. The leaves on the harvested vines were already aglow with the colours of autumn, as though they had been dipped into the hot embers of a fire, and as Steiner raised his head he saw the purple veil on the horizon slowly lifting, drawing after it the blue-black shadows of a chain of hills. It looked as though the highway ended in an unearthly radiance that the earth herself was shedding like a lamp. With an oddly cramped feeling in his chest, Steiner watched the sunrise. He looked back and saw the faces of the men washed with a pale yellow glow as though they were the souls of the dead marching on the great highroad to heaven. The impression lasted until a blaze flashed across the horizon, and the rim of the sun became visible beyond the hills. With silent might it thrust higher, showering light over the last shades of the night. Day had come.

A quarter of an hour later Lieutenant Gollhofer ordered the company to halt. He went up to Steiner. 'Your men must continue on from here,' he directed. 'They'll do best to stick to the railroad embankment until they reach the tunnel. As far as I know the battalion is somewhere over there.'

'Where are we going?' Steiner asked.

Gollhofer indicated a mud road that branched off the highway on the left and disappeared among the vineyards. 'We're taking a short cut. The highway leads to the command post also, but it takes a detour and winds around the hills. We'll be there in an hour, if the map is right.' While he was speaking he happened to notice Steiner's pack, and asked: 'What's that you have there?'

At first Steiner did not know what he meant. Then he recalled the captured flag which he still carried strapped to his assault pack. He had forgotten all about it, 'A memento,' he said tersely, and turned to Krüger. 'Take him to Fetscher,' he said hoarsely. 'Tell him to make the grave level. Tell him that. So level that nobody will ever spot it as a grave. Clear?' Krüger nodded. 'I hope one of you will be able to be present,' Steiner went on. 'Faber or you. Try.'

'Yes,' Krüger said. Steiner hesitated. Then he went over to the men who were carrying Schnurrbart's body. They had laid him down on the road, and no more of him but his nailed mountaineering boots could be seen. These protruded from the canvas as though they were things in themselves. Krüger stood beside Steiner, his lips so tightly compressed that they looked like a white streak across his face. Stiffly, clumsily, Steiner reached over his shoulder and fingered a strap until the red flag fell to the ground. He rolled it up and placed it on the canvas under the dusty boots. 'Tell them to cover him with that,' he said. They stood side by side, looking down at the dead man. Gollhofer had quietly come up to them and was watching the scene, a curious expression around his mouth. 'A friend of yours?' he murmured. Steiner turned on his heel, crossed the highway and started up the track between the vineyards. There was a startled silence, until Krüger spoke. 'He was his brother,' he said. Thin-lipped, Gollhofer watched as they picked up the body and marched off toward the railroad embankment. None of them looked back. When the last man had disappeared beyond the embankment, Gollhofer turned round and said: 'Engineers platoon, march!'

Their way led across a treeless plateau extending westward as far as the eye could see. Suddenly Steiner, who was walking some five hundred yards ahead of them, disappeared as though swallowed up by the earth. Only then did they realize how sharply the land dropped ahead. The valley appeared at their feet so suddenly that they stood amazed. From up above the dip in the land was so extreme as to form what was practically a ravine. Cleft and uneven, the steep slope was almost barren, with only an occasional bush which clung to the rock. A few hundred yards to their right they saw roofs, and caught sight of the highway again winding down in four huge spirals. They scrambled down the rough incline. Steiner was waiting for them near the first house. Gollhofer sadly observed the dirty-grey walls of the houses and the boarded-up windows. A regular den for bandits, he thought.

A man came running toward them. 'The lieutenant-colonel wants to speak to you at once, sir,' he said to Gollhofer. The lieutenant nodded. As he pounded the dust from his uniform he asked where the quarters for the engineers platoon were to be. The man pointed to a barnlike building. 'There, sir.' Seeing the frown of chagrin on Gollhofer's face, he laughed. 'Not as comfortable as Novorosisk. But it doesn't matter; we'll be moving on again tonight.'

'Oh!' Gollhofer exclaimed. His face brightened. 'Where to?'

'I don't know. But it's certain that we're evacuating the bridge-head.'

'That's what counts,' Gollhofer said. He looked around. 'Where is the commander?'

'In the long building there. I'll take you to him now.' The man turned to Steiner. 'You are to come too, Sergeant.'

In the commander's building they had to wait several minutes in the dark, dirty vestibule until the man came back out of a room. 'You may come in now, sir,' he said to Gollhofer.

'What about me?' Steiner asked.

'Captain Kiesel says you are to wait a little while,' the man replied. He wore the chevrons of a staff corporal and had a weary, bored expression.

'If you need me, I'll be in front of the house,' Steiner said indifferently.

He went out again. Here in the ravine the shadows had not yet lifted. Only the upper half of the western slope was tinted with a pink which slowly seeped into the gorge. The houses of this village formed two rows, with a lane between. Their chimneys were half crumbled and their slate roofs full of holes. Behind the eastern row of houses the slope was deeply eroded. The ugly ruts led to the dried bed of a stream which was undoubtedly a torrent during the rainy season. Several vehicles stood on the highway. One of them bore the divisional standard. At the wheel sat a driver, dozing. Steiner slowly wandered about among the houses. Perhaps it was on account of the early hour—it was shortly after six—that so few men were about. At the end of the row of houses, a sentry watched in boredom as three men of the signals platoon laid a cable. Steiner turned about and walked toward the other end of the settlement. The gorge led straight for about fifty yards, then bent sharply eastward. The highway, too, following the bed of the stream, disappeared beyond that corner. The last of the buildings stood somewhat at a distance from the others and seemed uninhabited. Glancing in through the glassless windows, Steiner saw bundles of straw lying on the bare floor. Behind the house a deep channel wound its way up the western slope of the ravine. In three places the highway cut across this channel. Accustomed to thorough analysis of the most trivial aspects of his surroundings, Steiner traced its course up to the rim of the ravine.

For a few minutes he stood gazing vacantly upward. Then he started back. As he approached the command post he saw the staff corporal standing on the steps, looking around. The man caught sight of him and called: 'The captain is waiting for you.'

As he entered the room, Kiesel came striding toward him and held out his hand. 'I'm so very glad you're back!' he said with a cordiality that took Steiner aback. 'Make yourself comfortable. You really have been through something. The commander is occupied at the moment, therefore I'm delegated to listen to your story. We may as well get right to it. Smoke?' Steiner looked at the pack of cigarettes Kiesel held out to him, the while he tried to fathom the captain's intentions. He nodded and accepted a cigarette. 'First of all I'd like to discharge an obligation,' Kiesel went on. 'I wouldn't have delayed so long except that you've been, shall we say inaccessible, for quite a while. You saved my brother-in-law's life, and I want to thank you for it. I regret being able to do so only in words, but you've never cared to accept favours from anyone, Steiner, and I hope you understand my feelings.'

Steiner shrugged uncomfortably. But his relief was so great that he was able to smile as he replied: 'He happened to be in my way, so I picked him up, that's all.'

A touch of Steiner's new geniality passed over into Kiesel's grave face. The captain nodded as though he had expected some such answer. 'We'll drop the subject for the present. Would you mind outlining the events inside the factory from the beginning.'

'If you like.' Steiner gave him a summary account. Kiesel scribbled brief notes on a sheet of paper. At the mention of Triebig's death, the captain interrupted: 'A hand grenade, you say?'

'Hand grenade,' Steiner assented, scanning Keisel's face vainly for traces of suspicion. 'The lieutenant was standing no more than two feet in front of me, and toppled over.'

'Dead?'

'I hope so,' Steiner said coldly. 'For his sake,' he added as Kiesel raised his eyebrows. 'If he was not killed the Russians will have butchered him as they did the wounded men whom the lieutenant abandoned to their fate.'

Kiesel blanched. 'How did that happen?' he asked quickly.

As Steiner went on with his story, the captain's face set in harder and harder lines. Finally he stood up with an awkward movement. 'I know you're tired, but we may still need you. Captain Stransky has been ordered to see the commander at nine o'clock. It is possible that in connection with their meeting the commander will have a few more questions for you. Why don't you take a nap until then. Tell the sentry where we can find you. Incidentally . . .' He hesitated, and an edge of curiosity crept into his voice. 'What did you do with the flag?'

'Threw it away,' Steiner replied curtly. 'It was a nuisance to carry.'

'Really?' Kiesel's voice expressed doubt. But he asked no more questions and accompanied Steiner to the door, stressing again that he must hold himself in readiness to be called at nine o'clock. 'That gives you two and a half hours,' he said. 'Time to get a bit of rest.' He nodded goodbye and opened the door.

As Steiner stepped out on the street he wondered whether it had been a mistake to expurgate his story. Originally he had not intended to conceal the manner in which Schnurrbart had been killed. Yet when he came to that part of his report something had compelled him to pass over the matter, although it was highly unlikely that Brandt or Kiesel would infer the connection between the lieutenant's apparent error and his subsequent death. Perhaps the reason had been simply that talking about Schnurrbart at all was still too painful.

But this problem was insignificant in comparison to the vital information that Keisel had unwittingly given him. As he crossed the street a plan began to form in his mind. With every step it grew clearer. Suddenly a key detail occurred to him. He turned on his heel, and went back along the street until he met the sentry. 'If they look for me,' he told the soldier, 'I'll be taking a snooze in the last house over there. Tell your relief, remember.'

The man clicked his heels and said: 'Yes, sir.' Steiner headed straight for the house, pleased to note that the sentry was watching him with curiosity.

The house consisted of three small rooms so filthy that Steiner grimaced with disgust. The largest of them had apparently been used on and off as a latrine and stank fearfully. The second room was in somewhat better shape. It was in the centre of the house and had a window on the rear. Steiner decided to stay there. With the butt of his tommy-gun he hammered the bolt of the door shut and then went to the window. Opposite, a few yards away, the land sloped up toward the highway. He found himself looking directly into the erosion gulley. It was six feet deep on the average and from ten to twelve feet wide. Undoubtedly there were more like it in the vicinity, but this was the one for him since it was within a few steps from the window. The only danger points were the places where the highway crossed it. But it would take a considerable coincidence, Steiner told himself, for anyone to observe him at those points.

Having thought the matter out thus far, he slipped his pack off, laid it on the floor and sat down on it. Now that he was apparently going to have a chance to settle accounts with Stransky far sooner than he had hoped, he was filled with a violent impatience. Waiting seemed intolerable. Nevertheless he forced himself to sit still for a while.

Then he swung himself out of the window and began climbing the slope. He stayed in the gully, keeping his head low. The ground had been soaked by the rain; it was slippery and made hard going. Panting, he worked his way up to the first winding of the road. There he paused to catch his breath and look back. The roofs of the houses were already a considerable distance below him; he could see the rents in the slates. From above the gorge struck him as romantically wild. The road crossed the gully on a stone embankment about ten feet high. Steiner climbed over the stones, scurried across the dusty highway, and ducked down into the continuation of the gully again. He had hung the tommy-gun across his back in order to leave his hands free. After he had crossed the two other highway embankments he slung it over his shoulder once more, ready to hand, and climbed the rest of the way up the slope. The houses had vanished from his field of vision, but he could survey the ravine for more than a mile. He took a short breather and then followed the road. Since he could see a considerable distance in both directions, he was safe from unwanted encounters. The land was undulating here, rising somewhat to his left and forming a low ridge which would provide good cover if necessary. He had to avail himself of this cover sooner than he had expected. Turning around for a moment, he thought he saw a cloud of dust rapidly approaching, He sprang up the slope as fast as he could run. At the top he threw himself flat on the ground and watched the approaching vehicle. As it came closer he recognized the divisional car. The driver was wearing goggles which made his face almost unrecognizable. In the back sat two officers who seemed engaged in an excited discussion. Before he could recognize their rank the car disappeared again behind the billowing dust.

He lay where he was for a few minutes, considering. The regimental command post was still too near. He decided to go on another half-mile. As he got up, he wondered about the direction the divisional car had taken. If it kept going at that pace for another half-hour, he thought, it would run smack into the Russians. Instead of returning to the road, he continued swiftly on along the top of the ridge, carefully watching the terrain to his left. It fell off gently on the other side, then rose again after a few hundred yards to form another ridge. The ground was sandy and slowed him down. After ten minutes he stopped and looked around. The place seemed ideal for his purpose. Here the land dropped off more steeply from the crown of the ridge and he would have to go only a few paces in order to be completely invisible from the highway.

He unbuckled his belt, took his spade out of its leather case, and with the sharp edge marked a large rectangle in the sand. Then he set to work. The ground under the layer of sand was hard and forced him to take many rests. But he made good progress. Now and then he ran to the brow of the hill and peered westward where the road crawled under the veiled horizon and vanished. Then he returned to his hole and resumed work. Sweat poured down his face and his shirt stuck wetly to his back. After a while he took off his tunic and rolled up his shirt-sleeves. He worked until he stood chest deep in the ground. Then he stopped. Contentedly he looked at his pit; he remembered that a few weeks ago he had done a similar job for Stransky. Only then the purpose was different. As he climbed out of the hole there were grim lines around his mouth. He got into his tunic, buckled his belt on and picked up his tommy-gun. He lay down flat on top of the ridge and waited. It was fifteen minutes past eight.

After dismissing Steiner, Captain Kiesel went into Brandt's office. The commander was sitting with two officers discussing the details of the impending transfer of the regiment to the Crimea. As Kiesel entered all turned their faces toward him. 'All done?' Brandt asked.

Kiesel nodded and sat down. 'It's fortunate that Herr Morlock is here,' Brandt said, rubbing his sharp chin with the back of his hand. His eyelids fluttered rapidly. 'We'll discuss the case afterwards,' he continued. Then he turned to Captain Killius, who sat grave-faced beside him. 'You know all about it now, so there's no need for you to be here for the conference at ten o'clock. You can set out for the battalion at once and relieve Herr Stransky. Is my car here?' he asked Kiesel.

'You gave it to Lieutenant Stroh,' Kiesel reminded him.

'Damn it, so I did,' Brandt ejaculated. He turned in explanation to the fourth officer, who had said nothing as yet. 'I sent Stroh to the Third. As you know, Major Vogel is dead. There's a competent company commander taking his place, but I want to play safe. . . . Sorry, Captain Killius, I'm afraid you'll have to walk it. If you keep up a good pace you'll be there in less than an hour. It's a quarter to seven now. In case Herr Stransky hasn't left yet, you can explain the route to him.'

Killius stood up quickly. 'I need to stretch my legs anyhow,' he said.

'Have you baggage?' Brandt asked.

Killius shook his head. 'I left it with the supply column. If I need it I'll send for it.'

Captain Morlock, operations officer of the division, had been listening with interest to the brief exchange. As Killius was about to bid goodbye to the commander, he raised his hand. 'One moment, please. If I'm not mistaken I can give you a ride, Captain Killius.' He bent over the map in front of him. 'Yes, you see, here is your road. I drove this same way with the general a few weeks ago. About a mile and a half west of here your road branches off from the highway, runs north for a while and then intersects with the highway again beyond the ravine. For me it will be the smallest detour, while it will save you a good forty minutes.'

'I don't want to put you to any trouble,' Killius protested.

'Nothing of the sort, Captain Killius. Besides it will give us a chance to swap some more news.' He turned to Brandt with a smile. 'Captain Killius comes from the same town as myself, it seems. We discovered that yesterday when we first met at divisional headquarters.'

'Then by all means make the most of your chance to talk,' Brandt said. 'Who knows when you may have another. Perhaps in the Urals,' he concluded bitterly.

For the fraction of a second the captain's face changed as a landscape does when the shadow of a cloud passes over it. Then his smile returned, reinforced, and he said: 'I do not think our leadership is continuing to entertain such far-reaching goals. We would be content with Baku, sir.' The undertone of reprimand in his words was barely perceptible, but Kiesel detected it. The dark-haired, thin-faced divisional operations officer was well known and feared for his straitlaced ideology. In their occasional meetings Kiesel had strictly avoided anything like a political discussion. Brandt, too, had always been on his guard with the man and had never so much as touched on subjects outside the line of duty.

But now the devil seemed to have entered Brandt. His bass voice rumbled dangerously. 'Don't misconstrue what I said, Herr Morlock; I don't like having my words twisted. For the past year our goals have been determined not by ourselves, but by the Russians. You know that as well as I.' He shook his big head and snorted. 'You at Division should be able to see that more clearly than I can.'

'Undoubtedly,' Morlock said coolly. The shadow had returned to his face. As he spoke he looked at his hands which he had placed palms down on the desk. 'Undoubtedly,' he repeated. Uneasily, Kiesel noted the tightening lines around his mouth. 'Precisely because we can see the whole situation more clearly,' Morlock went on somewhat more loudly, 'we beg to differ with you, sir. I believe the general would be very much surprised to hear your views. Rightly surprised, if I may add my personal opinion.'

Brandt looked back at him with an amused twinkle in his grey eyes. 'I'll tell you something,' he said, glancing at Killius, who had sat down again and was taking in the talk with obvious discomfort. 'I don't know where the blinkers are made that so many people wear over their eyes. As long as they don't blind me, I don't mind them. But only as long.' His tone had suddenly become chilly. Now he stood up. The leather of his boots squeaked loudly in the silence as he went to the window and stood there with averted face, looking out. With feelings of mingled admiration and nervousness Kiesel looked at his broad back, and then at the frozen face of the operations officer who was sitting rigid and unstirring, again studying his hands.

Morlock looked up when Brandt abruptly crossed the room in three big strides, pulled the leather strap of binoculars from the nail in the wall, returned to the window and held the glasses to his eyes. Since he said nothing, none of the other men ventured to ask a question. Killius, leaning across the table to Kiesel, whispered: 'Planes?'

'We'd hear them,' Kiesel said, shrugging. Brandt was leaning forward eagerly now, pressing the binoculars to his eyes. His peculiar behaviour was highly disturbing. At last Kiesel could not refrain from asking: 'Anything unusual?'

Brandt did not reply. He remained at the window for a moment more, slowly lowering the binoculars. When he turned around there was an expression of deep wonderment on his face. But he did not explain. Instead he said to Killius in a tone of forced calm: 'There was one more thing I wanted to say to you. I would appreciate your not mentioning Herr Stransky's transfer to him. I should like to surprise him. I'll send for his baggage.'

'Of course,' Killius said, rising.

'Didn't you also want to talk with me about Herr Stransky?' Morlock asked.

Brandt looked at him for a moment out of half-shut eyes. He shook his head. 'There's time for that later. I must talk with him first.' He turned to Kiesel. 'You accompany the gentlemen to the car,' he said, and shook hands vigorously with Killius. He took leave of Morlock with a curt nod. When the door had closed behind them he went to the window and watched the car start up the winding highway, wrapped in a cloud of dust.

Kiesel returned immediately. The manner in which he sat down again expressed so much concern and incomprehension that Brandt drew up his mouth in a scornful smile. He stood with folded arms, looking at the captain with an air of challenge. At last, in the face of Kiesel's persistent silence, he said: 'Well?' The ironic undertone could not be missed.

Kiesel's lined face flashed a variety of expressions. When he spoke, it was with an almost pedantic carefulness. 'You pose riddles,' he said quietly. 'Perhaps I am exceeding my privileges when I tell you that as an adjutant I am uncomfortable being kept on the fringes of a discussion that concerns me just as much as it does the other participants. Would you be surprised if I should ask you to replace me?'

Brandt's face reflected in rapid succession indignation, disdain, and finally vexation. The superior expression which had lain like patina on his skin withdrew to the depths of his eyes. 'I don't think I would be surprised,' he retorted coolly. 'You know perfectly well that I would not let you go. Not because you are indispensable—you aren't, any more than I am—but because I might land a creature like Morlock for adjutant. You get on my nerves at times, but I've grown accustomed to that, and I have the right to ask the same of you—that you get used to me.'

Kiesel tilted his head to one side. 'It was only a theoretical question,' he said serenely. 'If I couldn't stand you as my superior officer I would have one consolation: that my problem will soon be over. Another conversation like the one you've just had with Herr Morlock and there's likely to be a violent solution to the problem. I'm not so sure I would enjoy that.'

'I see,' Brandt said. He smiled. 'Are you afraid?' he asked slyly.

'A person is only afraid for himself,' Kiesel replied, shrugging. 'After all, it's not my neck you were risking with your loose talk.'

Brandt frowned. 'Is that all you have to say?'

'No.' Kiesel shook his head. 'Perhaps I have a favour to ask of you,' he added gravely.

Brandt went over to his desk and looked absently down at the papers strewn over it. 'We can talk about that later,' he said. 'What did you learn from Steiner?'

'A fascinating story!' Kiesel said, and retold it. The commander listened to him in silence, his face expressionless. 'A certain imprecision about the report,' Kiesel said. 'I have the feeling that Steiner concealed one or two details. It might be a good idea to question another participant.'

'What for?' Brandt asked.

Kiesel shrugged. 'I suspect that Steiner is still trying to cover up Stransky.'

'I doubt that,' Brandt said forcefully. Kiesel looked up at him, startled by the emphasis in his voice. Brandt gave an odd smile. 'Where is Steiner at the moment?' he asked.

'In the house next door, I suppose. I suggested that he sleep for a couple of hours, until we would need him.'

'Does he know Stransky is coming here?'

'I think so,' Kiesel said, considering. Then he nodded. 'Yes, I remember, I mentioned it.'

'You mentioned it!' Brandt repeated. He broke out into hysterical laughter that shook his whole big body. 'You're priceless,' he said, gasping for breath. Then he became serious so abruptly that Kiesel could scarcely follow the alternations of mood. He sprang to his feet again and went to the window once more. For a while he stood looking up the slope of the ravine. When he turned around, there was a grim sparkle in his eyes. 'I told you this morning that you were unstable, Kiesel,' he said. 'But you are not only unstable, you are naïve. Do you know whom I observed with my binoculars a while ago?' His face suddenly looked alien and brutal to Kiesel. 'I saw Steiner. Steiner whom you think is next door taking a couple of hours of well-deserved rest. What a fool you are, Kiesel.' He chuckled and folded his arms across his chest. 'Steiner is a product of our times,' he went on, and Kiesel thought he detected a trace of satisfaction in the commander's voice. 'Do you recall what I said to you about justice? Of course you do. And I should like to add that a man like Steiner makes no bones about correcting Providence when the powers above bungle things. What is more, he'd be a thrice damned fool if he let a good chance slip by because he trusted in heavenly justice. The justice of Heaven is a dream of the weak, Kiesel, and it's about time you absorbed that idea.'

He fell silent and began pacing the room. When Kiesel rose without a word and started toward the door, Brandt blocked his way. 'Where are you going?' Kiesel did not reply, but his pale face was answer enough for Brandt. 'You have more imagination than I thought,' Brandt said coldly. 'But I cannot do without you for the next hour. The march routes for the battalions have to be settled and I'll need your help.'

'I'll be back in ten minutes.' Kiesel's voice sounded muffled, tense and resolute.

Brandt shook his head mockingly. 'You will stay here,' he declared firmly, 'Do you understand me?' Again Kiesel did not reply. Brandt returned to his desk and bent over the maps. 'Come here,' he said sharply. Kiesel continued to stand immobile at the door. The commander's tone changed. 'In case you are not yet aware of it, I have given you an order.'

'I know,' Kiesel said. His voice thickened with rage as he added: 'You are making me guilty as an accomplice.'

Brandt straightened up. 'I am on the point of leading my regiment into a cul de sac from which it has not the slightest chance of escaping. To what sort of guilt are you referring?'

It was a clever move. But Kiesel would not concede defeat. 'That is still no excuse for this other thing.'

'You are evading my question,' Brandt retorted. 'As matters stand, I have no time for philosophical debate when there are these important decisions to make. Now will you kindly drop the question and attend to business.' He sat down at the desk. 'Let's start with Killius's regiment,' he said crisply.

XVII

Iᴛ ᴡᴀs twenty minutes to nine when a dark spot crawled up over the horizon of the road and slowly drew nearer. Twenty minutes to nine; this must be Stransky, Steiner thought. He laid the tommy-gun ready to hand on the ground beside him and peered with narrowed eyes along the grey ribbon of road that wound so forlornly across the undulating landscape. The highway seemed utterly out of place in the context of the scenery; the telegraph poles looked like big posts stuck into the ground for no reason at all. The dark spot in the distance increased in size. Steiner regretted having no binoculars with him. He continued to lie flat. In spite of the early morning hour he felt the warmth of the sand through his uniform. Tiredness trickled down from his brain all the way to his toes. He figured it out: fifty hours since he had last slept. As long as that, he thought in astonishment, and again turned his attention to the dark spot, which had meanwhile come much closer. Still he could distinguish nothing more than a formless something that moved with tortuous slowness down the highway. Often it seemed to stand completely still for minutes at a time. Gradually, however, Steiner made out the figure of a man striding forward at a vigorous pace.

At last he was convinced that the man was Stransky. With a relieved sigh he tucked the tommy-gun under his arm and crawled back a little way, so that he could no longer be seen from the road. Now that the decision was nearing, silently and steadily, he felt that his face was covered with a thin layer of sweat that ran, salty-tasting, into the corners of his mouth. His throat felt all choked up. His hands twitched restlessly. He crawled back a little more, then instantly worked forward again and remained lying still as a stone. Stransky had by now come within some two hundred yards of him. With every step the man took Steiner's face changed like a sandbar under the wind. At last it froze into a mask in which only the eyes remained alive, burning. The oiled steel of the gun lay cool and firm in his hands. As he pushed back the safety-catch, he did so with so utter a lack of feeling that he was not even conscious of the movement.

Suddenly the upper part of his body shot up as though snapped by a spring. For a few seconds he disregarded all caution. Stransky was not alone. To one side of him there appeared the figure of a man who must have been marching along behind the commander all the while. Steiner stared at this person as though he had fallen from the sky. He had thought of some such possibility, but only fleetingly. What should he do? If he shot Stransky, the captain's companion would have to share his fate. Otherwise the man would run straight to Regiment with his tale. There was no way out. As Steiner watched the two of them he became aware, with grim contempt for himself, of how much value he was placing upon a perfect alibi, how careful he was being to cover his tracks. A few hours ago he would have maintained that he didn't care. He had thought he was finished with himself, with everything. That had been a mistake.

With a gesture of finality he braced the butt of the tommy-gun against his armpit. The two men swiftly approached, Stransky walking with that peculiar, rather rocking gait of his, his right hand resting lightly on his hip, while his companion trotted along apathetically behind him, head drooping. He was a stranger to Steiner. Probably he had come with the last batch of replacements, Steiner thought; perhaps he was the captain's orderly. He could distinctly see Stransky's face now. It wore an expression of gloom, and the manner in which he stared at the ground also suggested that his thoughts were none too happy.

By now they had come within fifty paces, and Steiner knew it was time for him to act. But still he held back. Something in the bearing of the man tramping behind Stransky troubled him, made him unsure of himself. It was a man like any other, with a face like all the faces which had permanently peopled his surroundings for so many months—haggard, weary and utterly indifferent. The man's arms hung loosely, his body seemed to be following the movements of his legs with reluctance. A dusty, unpressed uniform without insignia of rank, a visored cap under which a few strands of hair protruded, and a carbine slung diagonally across his back. At every step tiny puffs of dust whirled up from the ground, and the man's boots looked as though they had been wading through chalk.

Were there really two men marching along the highway? Wasn't there just one? He was marching on a road without end, a road that ran on over the horizon as though there were no horizon, a straight, dusty-grey, merciless road. A weary, apathetic, hopeless man. And looking at his face Steiner told himself that the man would never reach the end of the road, for the road had no end. The longer he stared at that face, the more familiar it seemed to him. Suddenly he realized that it was Dietz. He opened his mouth to scream, but his voice did not obey him; and then, suddenly, numbed, he thought he recognized Dorn, but then again it was not Dorn but Hollerbach, Hollerbach who . . .

He groaned and stirred. Part of his conscious mind noted the movement with which he rose up beside the road. Then reality leaped at him once more. Stransky was there in front of him. Stransky, who had seen him now and was standing petrified. They confronted one another, motionless as the telegraph poles behind them, no more than ten paces separating them.

As Steiner raised the barrel of his gun, the two walkers held their breath. Steiner's face was frightful to behold. Stransky saw only his face, like a white disc, and the meaning of this meeting burst upon him. He made no attempt to reach for his pistol which hung, ludicrously small, at his belt. Nor did he think of his companion who stood beside him, open-mouthed, stunned. Stransky simply ran. His right hand had dropped away from his hip, and he ran down the road ducking his head so low that only his back could be seen. His feet drummed a rapid tattoo on the gravel, and Steiner followed him with his eyes. He watched him without moving, turning his head just enough to keep Stransky in view. He saw Stransky's companion start forward and run after the commander, the dust spurting up under his boots. Then he slowly let the barrel of the tommy-gun slide down toward the ground. They won't make it, he thought. He watched as their figures became smaller and smaller. They were still running, desperate and tireless as hunted game, and Steiner murmured, 'It's pointless' without any awareness of what his words meant.

He suddenly felt unutterably tired, and sat down. The idiots, he thought, shaking his head. He had the feeling that he had missed the greatest opportunity in his life. But he did not feel unhappy about it, and wondered why.

After a while he set out along the road to rejoin his company.

Stransky did not stop until his feet began to stumble and fiery needles were pricking his brain. Gasping for air, he looked back. About fifty yards behind him his orderly came running through the dust like a lame horse, his head jogging from side to side with every step. There was no longer any sign of Steiner. Endless, dusty, deserted, the highway ran due west, and for a moment Stransky was inclined to think that he had been the victim of an hallucination. But he rejected the idea at once. Although his nerves had been subject to great strains of late, he knew he was not so far gone. Steiner's face and the Russian tommy-gun in his hands, the whole horrible encounter was still so vivid in his mind that there was no pretending it had been an illusion. He became aware that his whole body was trembling, and he pressed his hands against his chest to still the irregular thudding of his heart. Still half mad with terror and shock, he looked at his orderly, who had slowed his pace and was shambling along unwillingly. The man's haggard face had an expression of outrage, and deep within those colourless eyes Stransky thought he detected contempt mingled with astonishment. In a flash Stransky became aware of how frightfully foolish his behaviour had been. What must the man be thinking of him?

He turned swiftly so that they could not look at one another, so that he would no longer be exposed to that scornful scowl which shot arrows into his mind. Without a word of explanation, he continued on his way. The longer he thought about the encounter, going over the wretched rôle he had played, the more depressed he became. I'm disgraced, he thought, disgraced forever. Rage flickered up in him and quickly faded as he realized soberly that what had happened could no longer be undone. He had run away from Steiner like a whipped dog; he had no proof at all that Steiner had intended to kill him. He could feel his ego crumbling piece by piece, as though it were the bark of a dead tree.

He walked the rest of the way without paying the least attention to his surroundings. Not until the road dipped into the ravine did he recall the painful interview he was facing. But even the thought of this failed to produce any emotion in him. All through the morning he had pondered it so steadily that now, with the clash immediately before him, he was capable only of apathy. He was simply at the end of his rope. He had become psychologically sterile.

When he reached the regimental command post, he instructed the orderly to wait outside, and went in. For a few seconds he stood in front of a door through which the commander's booming voice could be heard. He knocked. The conversation stopped and someone said loudly: 'Come in.' Stransky opened the door. Directly opposite him he saw Kiesel, who started up from his chair by the desk so suddenly that Stransky flinched. The commander remained in his seat. He was looking up, and his face was printed with a mingled surprise and disappointment that Stransky found utterly perplexing. The odd look persisted as he opened his mouth and exclaimed: 'You!'

Stransky struggled for composure. This fantastic reception aroused again that thumping of his heart which he felt down to his fingertips. He closed the door behind him and blinked alternately at the faces of the two officers. The difference in their expressions only increased his bewilderment. While the commander's face grew steadily angrier, Kiesel's seemed to lighten and lighten —still further baffling Stransky, who had been expecting a particularly frosty reception from the adjutant. It was Kiesel, too, who broke the already embarrassing silence. With a mysterious twinkle in his clear eyes he said to the commander: 'You made an appointment with Herr Stransky for nine o'clock.'

Brandt slowly turned his head. With mounting uneasiness Stransky witnessed the exchange of looks between the commander and his adjutant. Stransky had to lean against the wall to suppress the sudden weakness in his legs. The movement did not escape Brandt. He turned his head. 'You are punctual,' he said softly. He pointed to a chair. 'Sit down.' As Stransky obeyed, Brandt, with set features, studied a large map on the table before him. Finally he raised his head. 'Get me Killius,' he said to Kiesel. A few minutes of tormenting silence passed until Kiesel handed the telephone across the table. 'He's on the line now.' Brandt nodded. Leaning both elbows on the table, he asked a few questions; Stransky was disturbed to note that his name was mentioned several times. 'Very well, Captain Killius,' Brandt said at last, and laid down the telephone.

'You missed Captain Killius,' he explained to Stransky. 'Captain Killius reached your former battalion without meeting you. Didn't you go by the highway?'

Former battalion, Stransky thought. He said former battalion.

His voice hoarse with agitation, he replied: 'Only part of the way. We took a short cut for the first mile or so.'

'Who is we?' Brandt asked quickly.

Stransky moistened his dry lips. 'I have my orderly with me,' he said with an effort. 'He's waiting outside.'

'I see.' Brandt studied him out of slitted eyes. Suddenly he turned to Kiesel. 'Bring the man in.'

As Kiesel left the room, Stransky shifted about in his chair. There was no need for my saying that, he thought. The idiot will tell the whole story and . . . The idea took his breath away. My God, he thought. But Kiesel was already back. Sheepish, cap in hand, Stransky's orderly followed him into the room. He clicked his heels resoundingly and lifted his eyes timidly to the commander's face. Brandt waited until Kiesel had taken a seat. Then he asked the orderly: 'Anything happen on your way here?'

The man threw a shamefaced look at Stransky. Unaware that Brandt was watching him, Stransky blinked his eyes violently at the orderly. At the sound of the commander's incisive voice Stransky whirled round in panic. 'If you can't keep your eyes still,' Brandt said, 'I'll have you stand in a corner.' He turned to the soldier again. 'Speak up, man, and don't you dare lie to me or hold back. Is that clear?'

'*Jawohl*!' the man said, terrified. Kiesel, catching the expression of shame and embarrassment on Stransky's face, once again felt admiration for the commander's sure instinct.

'Well, what happened?' Brandt asked.

The man dropped his eyes. 'All of a sudden he was standing in the road,' he mumbled awkwardly.

'Who?' Brandt snapped.

'The sergeant. He stood there with a Russian tommy-gun in his hand, and the captain ran away.'

'Ran away?' Brandt repeated incredulously, leaning across the desk.

The man nodded. 'He just ran,' he said helplessly. 'And then I ran too, I don't know . . .'

He glanced nervously at Stransky. Kiesel bit his lips. He suddenly saw the scene and found it hard to keep a straight face. Even Brandt's glowering features twitched as he asked: 'And why did you run away?'

Again the man threw a perplexed glance at Stransky, who sat still, head lowered, 'I don't know,' the man faltered. 'The sergeant was holding his gun in such a queer way.'

'Did he fire?' Brandt asked quickly.

The man shook his head. 'He was one of our soldiers,' he said in surprise. 'How could he have fired at us.'

'Right.' Brandt got up, went to the window and stood there for more than five minutes, face averted from the three in the room. Finally he turned. 'Go back to your battalion,' he ordered the man. He waited until the door had closed behind him. Then he went to his desk, picked up a letter, and sat for a few seconds looking down at it. Kiesel watched him breathlessly. He could not have said why, but suddenly he had the feeling that he was witnessing a magnificent scene. He was not mistaken. With an inimitable gesture that expressed all at once contempt, superiority and pity, Brandt tossed the letter across the desk so adroitly that it fluttered down into Stransky's lap. Stransky reached for it with both hands. Before he could begin to read it, the commander's icy voice lashed him to his feet. 'Examine it outside,' Brandt said. 'I don't want to see any more of you. Run, you little shit!' Stransky stared open-mouthed at that stony face. When he did not stir, Brandt said to Kiesel: 'Open the door for him.'

Kiesel obeyed. At that moment he felt that he could embrace Brandt like a brother.

'Go,' Kiesel said. He avoided looking at Stransky's face as the man lurched past him to the door. Then he went over to Brandt's side and watched with him as Stransky stepped out on the street and there stood still. He read the letter, but his face remained expressionless. Finally he thrust the sheet of paper almost carelessly into his pocket and moved off down the street, shoulders drooping, growing smaller and smaller until he disappeared from sight around a turn in the ravine.

'What I cannot understand,' Brandt said hoarsely, 'is why this creature is the one to escape. Stransky, of all people!'

Shaking his head, he returned to his desk and dropped heavily into a chair. Kiesel remained at the window, his intelligent eyes fixed on the commander. 'Why do you say that?' he asked softly.

'Why?' Brandt laughed bitterly. 'You know as well as I what

awaits us. Hundreds of times we've escaped; hundreds of times we've been caught in the trap and each time found a way out somehow. But this time . . .' He bit his lips. 'This time there is no way out,' he finished glumly.

Although Kiesel knew how right he was, he tried to find something encouraging to say. 'It isn't as bad as all that. Things may still turn out.'

'Don't fool yourself,' Brandt said surlily. 'When they pick on us as the last division for the Crimea, the meaning is another Stalingrad. Even if we should succeed in reaching Sebastopol, we won't find so much as a rowboat to take us off. No, this time our number is up, Kiesel, and perhaps it's just as well. I really think it is just as well.'

Kiesel felt a sudden sinking sensation. He looked out of the window at the hovels that made up this village, and clenched his teeth. Brandt's remarks were certainly not the product of exaggerated pessimism. Rather, they represented the logical conclusion to be drawn from what Morlock had said. The Russians were already established west of Melitopol and were pushing toward Perekop with strong armoured forces. If the intention actually was to evacuate the Crimea by water—and that would follow from Morlock's talk about delaying tactics—then it was plain as day that the available shipping space could accommodate only a fraction of the troops stationed in the Crimea. Sooner or later the majority of those troops would suffer the same fate as the Sixth Army at Stalingrad.

During the past several years Kiesel had repeatedly considered where the division would run its last lap. He had thought of many possibilities. But that it would be in the Crimea was something he had never dreamed. As he stood looking out over the ravine, out up to the barren rims of the slope, beyond which the blue of the sky glowed like a chalice in eternity, his eyes misted over slightly and he felt a dull pressure in his breast. Between clenched teeth he exhaled against the window with a hissing sound.

'What's the trouble?' the commander asked. When Kiesel did not reply, the commander's mouth twisted in a weary smile. 'Don't worry about it,' he said quietly. 'We could scarcely expect anything else, and we have done our duty. You and I and all of us. But we undertook to do too much, and that is our misfortune.'

He lit a cigarette. Casually, he added: 'Incidentally, whatever happens in the Crimea need not cause you any personal concern. You will not be affected.'

'How do you mean that?'

The tired, superior smile flitted once more across Brandt's stern face. 'That I shall send you on leave before the end is reached.'

For a moment Kiesel imagined he had not heard right. Behind his back he dug his fingers into the wood of the window frame. Never, he thought. 'You aren't serious,' he said.

'Not serious?' Brandt repeated. He spoke with unfamiliar mildness. 'I am always more serious than you are inclined to think, Kiesel. I shall send you on leave before the noose is drawn and knotted, and I see no way for you to block me . . .'

'Do you think so?' Kiesel whispered.

Brandt nodded quietly. 'Your chances of fighting against leave are practically nil. Should you attempt to provide me with a show of heroism, you'll have a bitter disappointment. I am not a bit impressed by shows of heroism.' He leaned forward, smiling. 'You see, Kiesel,' he said serenely, 'you have misunderstood me so often in the past that one more misunderstanding wouldn't matter much. But since I am going to part with you, I want you to know why. You know the story of Noah.' His smile broadened. 'Noah built the ark and saved himself and his family from the Flood. He became the bridge between the old and the new humanity, and he took elements of both into the new world: the good and the evil. I am trying to do the same. I have given evil a chance, in the special case of Stransky, and I shall give the good a chance also, and no power in this world will prevent me.'

Kiesel still scarcely dared to breathe. After a long pause he said: 'You overlook one factor.'

'Which is that?'

'Noah saved himself in the ark.'

'Noah was not commander of a regiment,' Brandt retorted. 'Any more questions?' Kiesel shook his head silently. 'Then we can go back to our work. We still have a great deal to do before the Flood. Now let's see, Körner's battalion will . . .'

'One more thing, please,' Kiesel said.

Brandt looked up in surprise. 'What might that be?' he asked curtly.

'You've forgotten Steiner.'

'I haven't forgotten him. Steiner is a case all to himself. How late is it?'

Kiesel looked at his watch and gasped. 'Five to ten,' he said. 'The battalion commanders will be here any moment now.'

'Tell the sentry to show them the way,' Brandt ordered. 'They can wait in the next room till I call them. And one thing more. Telephone Killius and ask whether Steiner has reached the 2nd company. Hurry.' He bent over his work again and did not look up until Kiesel returned to the room. Something about his expression boded ill. 'What's the matter?' Brandt asked.

Kiesel hung back in the doorway. His voice thick, he reported: 'Captain Körner has already arrived.'

'And?'

Kiesel pulled himself together. 'Captain Killius informs me that one of his NCOs, Master Sergeant Steiner, was wounded by a Russian shell just ten minutes ago. He is already being taken back to the clearing station.'

'I see,' Brandt said. He kept his eyes on the desk before him as he continued. 'There you are, Steiner is a special case. I am glad I did not have to exceed my authority. Keep Captain Körner company for a while. When the rest of the officers are here, let me know. I'll finish this off alone. Go on now.'

He waited until Kiesel had left the room. Then he walked over to the window. Hands clasped behind his back, he held his face up to the sunlight which slanted down over the ravine. Star and flower, he thought. It was ten o'clock in the morning, and the hill opposite was bare as a board. The words went through his head in endless iteration: star and flower, star and flower. There was no colour in his face.

In the distance muted detonations rumbled out of the sky, to be swallowed up in the October stillness. But Brandt had not really heard them. There was a greater stillness in him than that which covered the horizons like a hood of glass. He felt unencumbered and content, like a man who has ordered his life and marked out his road. There no longer remained anything to do but wait.

Behind him the door was opened and he heard Kiesel saying: 'The commanders are here.' For a while the officers stood stiffly erect, looking at one another. Then Brandt walked slowly to his desk and tucked the assortment of papers under his arm. 'Well, gentlemen, here we are again.' he said.

XVIII

THE BATTALION HAD occupied its last position in the bridge-head. Second Company was posted at the exit of the tunnel, its front facing westward, and all the men except for the sentries had lain down to catch up on their sleep. Sergeant Schulz was in command of what remained of the company. He sat at the tunnel exit with Krüger and Faber. Their monosyllabic conversation had faded out entirely a few minutes before, and they were watching dully as Krüger, with ferocious care, inspected the miserable remnants of his socks. Suddenly he cursed and drive his fist through a huge hole where, a few hundred miles back, there had been a heel. 'Look at that thing!'

'Put your stinking socks away,' Schulz said in disgust. 'What can we do about it? Go see the paymaster.'

'Paymaster?' Krüger snorted. 'Maybe you can tell me where there's a paymaster on the whole eastern front? I tell you, either I'm going to get a new pair of socks or they can stick these up at both ends, the goddamned war profiteers.'

'I have only one pair myself,' Faber said, shrugging. 'You should have asked Fetscher.'

'Fetscher!' Krüger waved his hand grumpily. 'Did you see what a face he made when he saw Schnurrbart? Pretty near started to bawl. Though we had more reason to than him.'

'Where did you bury him?' Schulz said. He gazed out of the tunnel into the sunny October day.

Krüger's face hardened. 'There were a few trees around,' he said tersely. 'About two miles from the supply dump. Well . . .' He fell silent.

Schulz scratched in the dirt with his fingers. 'That was decent of Moninger, giving you the cart. You wouldn't have been able to carry him the two miles.'

Krüger nodded. After reaching the battalion he had gone to the commander of the first company and borrowed a horse-drawn, two-wheeled weapons wagon on which they had moved Schnurr-bart. Since Stransky had appointed Schulz temporary commander of Second Company until Steiner's return, Krüger and Faber had had no trouble leaving the company for two hours. They had come back a few minutes ago, and so far had not said a word about their brief expedition. Schulz asked no more questions. He began talking about the new battalion commander. The two listened to him in high astonishment.

'It's funny, changing commanders so sudden,' Krüger said suspiciously. 'Have you had a squint at the new one?'

'Not yet,' Schulz replied. 'He telephoned and said he would be coming up here this morning to look over the position. Stransky has just up and vanished. I wish I knew where.'

'Who cares?' Krüger grunted. He had already lost interest in the conversation and was gloomily studying his foot which lay, dirty and bare, beside the boot.

Schulz lit a cigarette. 'I wonder where the Russians are.' He looked up ahead where a heavy machine-gun was emplaced. The sentry stood motionless gazing across the railroad embankment toward the west, where there were no signs of life.

'They'll be along soon enough,' Krüger said. 'I'd be more interested to know what's happened to Steiner. It will be ten o'clock soon.'

'Me too,' Schulz said. He lowered his voice. 'I hope there's no stink about Triebig. If any of those fellows starts shooting his mouth off, there's going to be trouble.'

'How come?' Krüger said sharply. His apathy dropped away; all at once he was intensely alert. When Schulz shrugged and made no reply, Krüger leaned toward him. His voice sounded so menacing that Schulz edged away from him. 'Triebig had a Russian hand grenade blow up in his mug and that's all there was to it. If anybody says any different, I'll personally bash his skull in. Let's get that clear.'

'Don't shout about it,' Schulz said uncomfortably, looking around with a scared expression. But Krüger was not so easily subdued. His face flushed a deep red. 'I'll shout all I please, and if anybody has something against it he'd better come and see me with his steel helmet buckled on so he can pick up his bones later, the swine.'

He seemed on the point of continuing in the same tone. Faber laid a hand soothingly on his shoulder. 'Why work yourself up,' he said quietly. 'No one is shooting off his mouth, and if anyone does, we're still here. Till then we can hold our fire.'

Krüger slowly simmered down, He once more gave himself to the observation of his dirty feet, and thought that he simply had to get a chance to wash soon. Since this idea necessarily was connected with a bathtub, his reflections landed him back home in Königsberg. He sighed.

'What's the matter?' Schulz asked.

Krüger shrugged. 'I was thinking about something,' he said evasively. He turned to Faber. 'Why are you so quiet?'

'I'm not one for talking,' the woodsman said.

Krüger nodded. 'That's true.' It had never really struck him before, but now he realized how little Faber spoke. 'That has its points. I once knew a girl who was just as quiet as you.'

'She would be the wife for me,' Schulz put in. 'Why didn't you marry her?'

Krüger did not answer, and the other two felt it would be better not to press the matter. Schulz puffed away at his cigarette. Further back in the tunnel several men were vying with one another to snore the loudest. The sentry at the machine-gun stood with head drooping, half-asleep on his feet.

'Shit,' Schulz said. The other two looked inquiringly at him. He raised his shoulders and exclained: 'Everything.' A thought occurred to him. 'Is it true that your father was a Russian?' he asked.

'You mean me?' Krüger asked.

Schulz nodded. 'Yes, you. Someone told me that a while back —I don't remember who.'

Krüger drew on his boot. His face had darkened and his voice rumbled dangerously as he replied: 'Does Krüger sound Russian? If you want to know, he had Russian citizenship, that's all. Besides which he died five years ago.'

'Oh,' Schulz said. He dropped into an embarrassed silence. Krüger busied himself with the laces of his boot.

'What about your mother?' Faber asked.

'She's been dead a long time,' Krüger said, standing up.

He walked off, shoulders stooping. 'Shit,' Schulz said again. He tossed his cigarette butt between the rails, and yawned. For a few minutes he sat moping; then he picked up his tommy-gun and yawned again. 'I'm going to catch a few winks,' he said glumly to Faber. 'When the new Iron Cross hound comes by, wake me.' He walked a short distance back into the tunnel, where the others were sleeping, lay down beside the rails, shoved his pack under his head and closed his eyes. Faber watched him. Farther back the darkness was like viscous ink, while up ahead, no more than ten yards in front of Faber, the sunlight flooded into the tunnel entrance with such glare that Faber, as he turned his head again had to squint to see at all. He sat still for a while. Then he decided upon a short walk to see what the terrain looked like. He went past the machine-gunner and out into the open. The ridge through which the tunnel passed rose almost vertically above him, its muddy slope quite barren. Halfway up this slope several men were standing waist-deep in a foxhole, looking down at him. 'What are the Russians doing?' Faber called up to them.

One of the men laughed. 'Not a sign of them. I'll bet my arse they're still sitting in Novorosisk guzzling champagne. Where are you going? Reconnaissance?'

'Too dangerous,' Faber said. He was about to add a word or two, but was interrupted. From higher up came a loud call, and then a man said: 'Someone's coming.'

'A Russian?' Faber asked; from his position he could not see any great distance.

The man above shook his head. 'I doubt it; must be one of our men.'

Turning, Faber peered westward over the railroad embankment. The tracks glistened in the sunlight and merged in the distance into a single silvery ribbon that ran straight on into the blue sky. 'He's coming from the right,' the man above said.

Faber saw him hitch himself up out of the foxhole. With a sudden feeling of certainty that this was Steiner, Faber asked: 'From the highway?'

'Yes.'

Faber hesitated a moment longer. Then he said: 'I'll go see who it is.' He climbed down the embankment. To reach the highway he had to cross through a wide field of tall grape vines whose thick foliage cut off the view. Careful not to damage any of the vines, he squeezed his big body between wires and posts down to the road. At a glance he recognized Steiner trudging toward him, a cigarette drooping from the corner of his mouth. Steiner must surely have seen him, but he did not increase his pace, and his face remained a blank. He covered the rest of the way between them casually, as though he had been expecting this meeting.

A few feet away he stood still and took the cigarette from his mouth.

Faber looked back in the direction from which Steiner had come. 'The Russians might have been here by now,' he said reproachfully.

'I'd have seen them,' Steiner returned. 'I came back the same way because I didn't know where you were.'

'Didn't you find out at Regiment?' Faber asked.

'I forgot to ask. Besides, I didn't report that I was leaving. Have they asked for me yet?'

Troubled, Faber studied Steiner's face. It was somehow changed, although he could not have said what was different about it. 'Not yet,' he answered slowly. 'How did you come through the front line?'

'I have no idea,' Steiner replied, shrugging. 'What does front line mean here, anyway? Where's Krüger?'

'He went to lie down just five minutes ago.'

'I've got to talk with him right away,' Steiner said. 'I have to disappear. Take me to him.'

'You have to what?' Faber exclaimed.

'Don't waste time talking,' Steiner said impatiently. 'I have to leave, but fast. Has there been any fuss about me yet?' Seeing the blank expression on Faber's face, he added: 'I mean on account of Triebig.'

'I don't understand you,' Faber said. 'Why should there be any fuss?'

'Sometimes you get on my nerves,' Steiner snapped angrily. 'For Christ's sake, take me to Krüger.'

'All right,' Faber said. They turned off the road and made a path through the vines until they reached the railroad embankment. 'There's where we're stationed,' Faber said, pointing to the tunnel.

Steiner nodded. They still had about a hundred feet to go. They walked swiftly along the tracks, stepping from sleeper to sleeper.

Steiner just had time to hear the shell coming before an inconceivable force tossed him into the air. Wrapped in a cloud of black smoke, he was thrown to the side and crashed to the ground like a plank. He uttered one brief shriek. Then he remained lying motionless. Several men came dashing out of the tunnel, lifted him in their arms and ran back with him.

When he opened his eyes, he saw Krüger's face above him. 'So there you are,' he whispered.

'Yes,' Krüger said. He gulped. 'I was beginning to think you'd had it.'

What's the matter with him, Steiner thought. 'Why are you bawling?' he asked.

'I'm not bawling,' Krüger said, turning his head away.

'You are,' Steiner said. 'Where did I get it?' There were several other faces bending over him. These bothered him. 'Go away,' he said to them. Then he remembered that Krüger had not answered his question. He attempted a grin. 'Is my arse gone?'

'Not your arse,' Krüger said.

Steiner tried moving his arms, but could not. Because he felt no pain he became impatient and struggled to sit up. But Krüger held him fast. 'Don't make a fuss,' he said roughly. 'They'll come for you in a minute.'

'The gravediggers?' Steiner asked, and felt something moist run out of his mouth. He knew it was blood and thought: in the lung. Suddenly he also felt the pain. It was everywhere, in his back, in his chest, in his legs, in his brain—everywhere. He groaned and closed his eyes. What rotten luck, he thought.

'Don't be silly,' Krüger said. 'The medicos from the clearing station are coming for you.'

Steiner grinned. 'Comes to the same thing.'

'I wanted to go with you,' Krüger said dolefully. 'But Schulz won't let me go. I'm the last NCO here.' They were silent for a while. Then Krüger looked at his watch. 'Where the devil are they?' he murmured restively. 'It's more than twenty minutes already.'

'Since when?'

'Since you were hit. Took you ten minutes to come to and I was beginning to think you'd had it.'

The words sounded familiar to Steiner; when had he heard them before? But suddenly a noise reached his ears that drew his attention away. It was like a man screaming with his head wrapped in a thick blanket.

'Faber,' Krüger murmured.

'What's the matter with Faber?' Krüger did not answer. Steiner stared at his twitching face. 'What's the matter with Faber?' he demanded again.

'I think they're coming,' Krüger said. From the depths of the tunnel footsteps thumped over the sleepers, and a voice called: 'Where are the wounded?'

'Here,' Krüger called back. 'His eyes,' he said to Steiner.

'What about his eyes?'

'Gone,' Krüger said.

'Gone?'

'Both of them gone.'

Steiner let his head drop back. All he could see was the massive vault of the tunnel roof. He felt himself being lifted up and laid on a stretcher. Then Krüger's face reappeared above him, and Steiner said: 'Don't bawl.'

'I'm not bawling,' Krüger said while the tears rushed from his eyes.

'You're the last NCO,' Steiner said. 'You mustn't bawl.'

Krüger nodded.

'Are you ready?' a voice asked.

Steiner turned his head and said: 'Shut your damned trap.'

'You can take my tommy-gun,' he said to Kruger. 'I won't need it any longer.'

Krüger nodded. The men with the stretcher started forward, and Krüger walked alongside for a few paces. 'When you come back,' he said, 'you can bring me another bottle of perfume.' In this part of the tunnel there was light enough for him to see Steiner's face, and suddenly he stood stock still and shouted: 'You're bawling too.'

But Steiner no longer answered. He had turned his face to the side and was thinking: old fellow, good old fellow. With closed eyes he felt the darkness gather around him. Darkness and coolness. Suddenly he was shivering. He tried to draw his legs up closer to his body, and again felt the blood in his mouth. Damn, he thought. The blood trickled over his lips, and when he coughed a pain shot through his body that made him groan aloud. 'We'll be there soon,' a voice above him said soothingly. 'Clench your teeth.'

'All right,' Steiner murmured.

When he opened his eyes he saw how dark it was. Like a grave, he thought. Suddenly a terrible fear rose up in him, and he began to tremble. He had the feeling that it would always remain just as dark, as dark as it was for Faber who had lost both eyes. My God, he thought, it would be Faber, did it have to be Faber. The conception of Faber blind was so incredible that for seconds he forgot his own pain and stared, forcing his eyes as wide open as possible, at the place where the vault of the ceiling must be. The vault, and above it the blue sky. But for Faber there was no longer a sky; for Faber there were no stars and no trees, no green trees. Steiner felt a sob tugging at his throat. He opened his mouth and groaned. My God, he thought, my God. For a while he lay with closed eyes, listening to the nasty pounding in his chest and in his back. He felt the blanket under him growing wet from the blood that welled incessantly out of his torn flesh.

And it seemed to him that as the blood flowed out his body grew lighter. He felt like a feather sailing through the air towards a light. Towards a light? He opened his eyes and saw that it was getting lighter. At first there was only a grey gleam that crept across his face and slowly became transformed into a sparkling crystal that grew bigger and bigger, until at last its brightness was such that his eyes ached from looking at it. But he fixed his eyes upon it and moved his lips and whispered: 'Anne.' Then he saw her face distinctly, her mouth, her eyes looking at him, and he saw her smiling, and he smiled back and said: 'I'm coming, I'm coming, Anne.' So they carried him out of the tunnel into the light of day.